About the author

Campbell Armstrong was born in Glasgow and educated at Sussex University. After living in the USA for twenty years, he and his family now live in Ireland. He has been in the front rank of modern thriller writers for many years, and his bestselling novels include the acclaimed *Jig* series. His recent heartbreaking memoir, *All That Really Matters*, was also a remarkable success, particularly in Scotland and Ireland, where it was a No 1 bestseller.

By Campbell Armstrong

ASTERISK

BRAINFIRE

JIG

MAZURKA

MAMBO

AGENTS OF DARKNESS

CONCERT OF GHOSTS

JIGSAW

HEAT

SILENCER

THE TRADER'S WIFE

THE SURGEON'S DAUGHTER

BLACKOUT

DEADLINE

THE BAD FIRE

Non-Fiction

ALL THAT REALLY MATTERS

THE BAD FIRE

CAMPBELL ARMSTRONG

HarperCollins*Publishers*

This novel is entirely a work of fiction.
The names, characters and incidents portrayed in it are
the work of the author's imagination. Any resemblance to
actual persons, living or dead, events or localities is
entirely coincidental.

HarperCollins*Publishers*
77–85 Fulham Palace Road,
Hammersmith, London W6 8JB

www.**fire**and**water**.com

Published by HarperCollins*Publishers* 2001
1 3 5 7 9 8 6 4 2

A catalogue record for this book
is available from the British Library

ISBN 0 00 226201 0 (trade pbk)
ISBN 0 00 711756 6 (library hardback)

Typeset by Palimpsest Book Production Limited,
Polmont, Stirlingshire

Printed and bound in Great Britain by
Omnia Books, Glasgow

The people who bring Glasgow to life for me:
Annie Spiers, Erl and Ann Wilkie, Kevin and Susan
McCarra, Nigel Clark, Brenda Harris. Thanks.

1

On a hot Monday night in early summer Jackie Mallon went on a leisurely pub crawl. Dressed in a black suit and black shirt and a slim silver tie with a wide ostentatious knot, he allowed himself only one drink, Cutty Sark and water, in each bar he visited. A dandy at sixty-eight, thin hair held back with gel and dyed the colour of crow, his dentures vanilla-ice-cream white, he wore ruby cuff-links and his cuffs hung exactly half an inch from each sleeve. His movement was economical, his manner careful; he might have been walking barefoot on a surface of shaved glass.

He surveyed the customers in each pub, winking at the gilded girls who pierced their lips and eyebrows with safety pins and hooks, girls who knew nothing of his reputation as a ladies' man in the old days, a knight of nooky. He nodded at friends and acquaintances who waved and called out his name cordially and wanted to ply him with drinks or just be seen sharing a joke with him because of his rep, because it did no harm to say you knew Jackie Mallon, you even *drank* with him.

He was also conscious of the young turks who drifted in from the outlying housing schemes and were looking to make their mark. These neds sometimes caught his gaze directly, and he felt a hostile challenge in the way they stared at him. *Who the fuck does this old tosser think he is? High time he was put out to grass.*

Jackie thought: Snottery wee boys. Couldn't lick my black suede shoes. I'll be retired soon enough, lads. One last deal and I'm off into the big red yonder.

He rode from pub to pub in the back seat of his pale blue Mazda, chauffeured by Matty Bones, a former jockey with a pallbearer's face and a Smith & Wesson 4006 in the glove compartment. Bones drove him to the New Monaco Bar, where he bought everyone a drink. Next, they went to the Three Cheers and then the Clutha Vaults in Stockwell Street.

This was Jackie Mallon's terrain. This was where he'd been born and brought up, and where he felt secure. He had this part of Glasgow in his back pocket. He knew the tenements, the people, their feuds and marriages and divorces, their kids. His cocoon was an area bounded by the Duke Street abattoir, the Necropolis and the Gallowgate – a parish of tenements and tombstones and elaborate crosses that made eerie patterns on the Necropolis skyline. His territory encompassed Glasgow Cathedral and the spine of the Tolbooth tower where centuries before the heads of executed criminals were impaled on spikes for public enlightenment.

Jackie Mallon, who'd left school at the age of eleven, remembered Luftwaffe bombs falling on the shipyards, demobilized sailors and soldiers flooding the streets at the war's end, horny and high-spirited, government-issue orange juice that looked like neon chemical goo, old Granny Mallon's rabbit stews on Tuesday nights at the flat in Bathgate Street – but the city's true antiquity was a shuttered house to him.

He sat in the back seat of his car and surveyed the streets with proprietary affection. My town.

'Where to now, chief?' Bones asked.

Jackie Mallon wondered if he wanted another drink. He considered going back to his terraced house a few blocks north of Duke Street. He pictured Senga painting her nails flamingo or

2

scarlet, and drinking Crossbow in front of the TV. He heard her big merry laugh and saw her fleshy underarms tremble. If she'd drunk enough cider she might be listening to a CD of Eagles songs and looking melancholic, and she'd say: O do you still fancy me, Jackie? Say you do. I'm in the mood to feel wanted.

Eagles, he thought. 'Crying Eyes.' Electric cowboy shite. He was very fond of Senga, but her taste in music gave him the willies. He liked Sinatra. Elvis. 'All Shook Up' was an anthem to him.

He peered from the window. Bones was driving down Bell Street, close to the old Fruitmarket, now a venue for musical events. A lot of the old city had been stripped down and tarted up. Jackie Mallon preferred things the way they'd been before the developers came hurrying in with their big blueprints and their wrecking balls and their frantic greed.

It's changing, he thought, and I'm changing too. I don't look at crumpet the way I used to. And they don't look at me. The ashes in the grate grow cold.

For the first time in a long time, Jackie Mallon felt a touch of nervousness. He wasn't sure why. The last bit of business was going fine. The pieces fitted nicely, thank you. He'd go into the sunset with a small fortune. So. Was it the idea of retirement that upset him? What to do with his time? How to fill the days? Or was it because this job was a Big Score and he wasn't sure if he still had the goolies for that kind of action any more?

'Blackfriars next?' Bones asked.

'I don't know if I feel like another drink, Matty.'

'You usually finish off your night at Blackfriars . . .'

Jackie Mallon was quiet a moment before he said, 'Right, right, I'll have one last wee drink. You've twisted my arm.'

'Easy arm to twist, eh,' Matty Bones said, and smiled, showing a mouth filled with the stumps of old teeth. He parked, opened the back door for Jackie Mallon.

Mallon clapped the little man on the shoulder with affection.

'Righty-o. I'll drive down there and wait for you,' and Bones

3

gestured towards an area of wasteland about a hundred yards away.

'You'll not join me for one?' Mallon asked.

Matty Bones rubbed his stomach. 'Ulcer's playing up.'

'Milk of magnesia,' Jackie Mallon said.

'That stuff doesn't work for me,' Matty Bones said.

Jackie Mallon paused outside Blackfriars pub. He looked up. Starlings and swallows flew in the darkening blue sky over the city. Soon streetlamps would come on.

Blackfriars was dark and comfortable. He ordered a Cutty, added water from a jug, looked the place over – students arguing about an Italian film, and a couple of familiar faces from a local TV news show trying to look conspicuously incognito. He tossed back his drink, stood at the bar for a few minutes, eyed a flame-haired barmaid, then he went outside and walked towards the patch of wasteland where he could see the Mazda parked among other cars. The driver's door was open. A figure sat behind the wheel. Bones.

Cigarette smoke drifted out of the car towards a nearby streetlamp where thousands of moths created a frantic blizzard. Jackie opened the rear door. He got in and looked at the back of Bones's head.

'I thought you'd quit smoking, Matty. Had a relapse, eh?'

The man turned his thin face. He wasn't Matty Bones.

'What the fuck's this?' Jackie Mallon said. 'Where's Bones?'

The man had a smile that was a sneer, upper lip drawn way over the top teeth. The look was camel-like. He tossed his cigarette away. 'He had to leave.'

Jackie Mallon said, 'Bones wouldn't leave.'

The man had a thin moustache. His breath smelled of alcohol. He was twenty-five, maybe, and had a small silver stud in his right nostril, which was inflamed by a yellow cushion of pus. He wore a transparent plastic raincoat buttoned to the neck. Jackie Mallon knew him, and considered him scum.

'Are you ready to talk, Mallon?'

Mallon sighed. 'Take this back to your boss. I've got nothing

4

to tell. I've said it before, I'll say it again. And I'll keep saying it.'

'Oh my. That's going to depress him.'

'My heart aches.'

'Is that your last word, Mallon?'

'Aye.'

'The boss hates bad news.'

'Tough shite.'

The man's gloved hand rose to where Jackie Mallon had an unimpeded view of a gun, the barrel of which was pointed at his face. The gun was Bones's Smith & Wesson. This troubled Jackie, because Bones wouldn't let anybody – especially this scruff – touch his weapon.

Which meant.

Jackie Mallon didn't like to think what it meant. He didn't like to think what a plastic raincoat on a hot dry night meant either, although he knew.

I took my eye off the fucking ball. Complacency, the curse of old age. He stared directly into the gun, then the man's face. The man had a look in his eye Jackie Mallon had seen before, fear pretending to be bravado, terror masquerading as cool.

'That's a very dangerous weapon, sonny,' he said.

'I know.'

'Think. Think carefully.'

'Haggs doesn't pay me to think,' the young man said.

Mallon looked at the gun again. I'm an endangered species, he thought. Cold skin, hot night. He shivered. Mibbe I'm coming down with something. He heard moths buzz with the intensity of locusts under the streetlight and he had a sense of his life dwindling until he was no more than a fly-sized speck that might fit inside the barrel of the Smith & Wesson.

'Tell Haggs to go fuck himself,' he said.

5

2

The telephone rang and Eddie Mallon opened one eye: the bedside digital clock read 3:22 a.m. He was tempted to let the answering machine pick up and go back to sleep and see if he could reboard the train of his dream, which had been taking him on a pleasant ride through smooth green countryside that looked exactly like the land where the Jolly Green Giant lived, a place where peas were quick-frozen for freshness at the moment of picking. But he knew the locomotive would have gone from the station by now, and so he reached reluctantly for the handset and hauled himself into the real world.

The room was humid even with the window open; the dark was dead and heavy, the rasp of crickets somnolent and slow. He said his name into the mouthpiece, his voice thick.

'Eddie?' The woman sounded distant and nervous.

Mallon recognized his sister's voice at once. 'Weird time of day to be calling, Joyce. It's almost half past three here.'

'In the morning?'

'You got it,' he said. What was *wrong* with her? 'That makes it – what? About eight thirty a.m. where you are.'

'I'm not wearing a watch,' Joyce said.

Eddie's wife Claire woke and reached for the bedside lamp. The sudden pale light made Eddie blink.

'Who's calling?' Claire asked.

Eddie covered the mouthpiece. 'Joyce,' he said.

She looked surprised. 'Is she calling from Scotland?'

'I guess,' Eddie said. He spoke into the handset. 'Are you in Glasgow, Joyce?'

'Yes,' Joyce said.

'Something's wrong. I hear it in your voice. Talk to me.'

'I need you to come home, Eddie.'

'I *am* home. Queens is where I live, Joyce. Remember? Give me one good reason I should drop everything and come over there.'

'Because I bloody need you,' she said. 'Sometimes a sister needs her big brother.'

Joyce had never said such a thing before. She didn't even sound like herself, her voice was small and hurt, and she wasn't in the habit of calling him at this or any other time of day to ask him to go back to Glasgow.

A moment's silence on the line. He wondered if this call travelled through a cable on the dark Atlantic seabed, where no light had ever penetrated. He felt a touch of sorrow, thinking of the ocean's black width and the tourniquet of family and how tightly it was knotted even if you thought it had worked loose over the years.

He heard Joyce take a deep breath. 'It's Jackie, Eddie. Oh Christ, why is it so damn hard to say? He's dead. Jackie's dead.'

Something he couldn't identify turned over inside Eddie Mallon and dropped like a stone falling from a great height. A heartbeat skipped, an irregularity, a valve malfunctioning. He had a feeling of a screw being drilled through his chest. '*Dead*? How? How did it happen?'

'He didn't die in bed, Eddie. There was no gentle into that good night shite.'

'I don't understand what you're saying, Joyce.'

7

Joyce told him in a single spare ugly sentence.

He was surprised by the heft of loss. There was a weight inside him, an iron pendulum creaking back and forth. His eyes smarted. He had difficulty swallowing. He felt himself splinter. He walked with the phone to the window and pressed his forehead to the warm pane and looked down into the darkened back yard. He listened to the heavy silence of the house. A beam of light extended from the bedroom window into the yard, illuminating a narrow patch of grass. He looked beyond the light to a place where blackness concealed beech trees and he had the other-worldly sensation that the ghost of his father was out there beneath the thick limbs and silent leaves. *I'm leaving, Eddie. I wanted to say my last goodbye.*

'What is it?' Claire asked. 'What's going on?'

Joyce asked, 'Eddie? You still there? Hello hello?'

Eddie Mallon felt as if he'd floated from this room, transported back to a Glasgow street in the early 1960s, a little boy on a kerb with his small hand in his father's big palm, and tramcars clattering past on their iron tracks and sometimes in the rain an overhead wire sparking and the air smelling scorched.

Never cross until the way is clear, Eddie. Look left, look right, look left, make sure nothing's coming. Don't you forget that, Eddie.

Okay, Dad. Left, right, left again.

Good boy.

You're dead and I don't understand why, Dad. I loved you, yes, I did, no matter what.

He felt tiny and scared a moment, no longer an adult in an adult world.

Claire asked, 'Who's dead, Eddie? Who is it?'

Mallon didn't hear his wife. His head was racing. Questions crowded his mind. Professional habit. What kind of weapon had been used? Had he been alone at the time of his murder? Had a motive been established? He imagined the old man's pain, or maybe there was no pain, maybe it was all over in a fraction of time too tiny to calculate. 'Have you phoned mother?'

8

'That's your side of the world,' Joyce said.

Eddie pushed the thought of his mother from his mind; he'd return to it soon enough.

Joyce said, 'The funeral's Friday. The pathologist says he's finished with the body . . . I can't deal with this alone, Eddie.'

Claire was out of bed now, standing at Eddie's shoulder. 'It's Jackie, isn't it? It's Jackie who's dead . . .'

Eddie Mallon touched the side of his wife's face gently and nodded his head.

She said, 'Oh God, I'm sorry, Eddie,' and he held her against his shoulder, grateful for her comfort even as he was miles away in that place where he could still sense his hand wrapped in his father's spectral grasp. The past could ambush you. Like the way he smelled his dad at that moment, so *real*, so *close* – tobacco clinging to a woollen overcoat, damp socks drying in front of a coal fire, a whiff of Cutty Sark, these things bushwhacked you.

'I'm sorry, really I am,' Claire said. She had a genuine heart. In her world all setbacks were opportunities in disguise; deaths weren't doors that slammed shut. They were openings into other spaces, worlds we knew nothing about.

He spoke quietly into the handset. 'I'll call you back in a couple of hours, Joyce.'

'I'm feeling fragile, Eddie.'

'I'll arrange something. I promise you.'

'I'll be waiting right here by the phone,' Joyce said.

Eddie Mallon put the handset down.

'Sit beside me,' Claire said.

Eddie sat on the edge of the bed. Claire held his hand. He stroked her skin, which was damp. Eddie gazed at his wife's face. Once thin and delicate, a delightful skeletal construct, it had been made puffy by the mischief of time, the lines around the mouth deepening. But he still saw the beauty of a young woman in her. She was still the girl he'd fallen in love with more than twenty years ago. He wondered how much *he'd* changed from her perspective. His black hair, dense and curled, was streaked with grey, and he carried about fifteen pounds more than when they'd married, and some mornings he woke feeling the mass of forty-five years pressing down on him, and it was an effort to face another day.

The really *good* mornings, when you leapt out of bed, when you felt like a god who could overcome any crud the day threw in your face – a flat tyre, a cup of bad coffee, even a sniper in a tower with a scoped rifle and a bad attitude – were diminishing yearly. *I love you, Claire,* he thought. We're just not the people we used to be, those bright smiling kids in the old wedding photographs on the dressing table.

She said, 'You have to go.'

He heard her, but her words might have been filtered through muslin. He said, 'He was always talking about coming over here. Always wanted to see his grandson. When we spoke on the phone last New Year's Day he told me this was the year he'd finally make the trip. I don't know if he meant it. You might as well take a goldfish out of a bowl as the old man out of Glasgow.'

He thought of his son, Mark, fifteen years old, asleep in the bedroom down the hall. Mark had never seen Jackie Mallon. And now he never would.

Claire said, 'You could get a flight today. Joyce is going to need support.'

He hadn't seen his sister in five years, the time of her last American trip, when her marriage to the irredeemable Harry Haskell – a permanently unemployed freeloader – had just ended. She'd dressed in black clothes during her stay, jeans, T-shirts, sneakers, impenetrable sunglasses. She projected an attitude of mystery and cool. She looked as if she were wandering, in a distracted fashion, some Left Bank of her imagination.

But he couldn't bring to mind her features clearly, and this bothered him. He knew what it was: the world was out of focus all of a sudden, and his memory with it. 'There's a bit I haven't told you.'

10

'I'm listening,' Claire said.

He heard a pulse in his skull. It was the like the sound of a cork in water slapping time after time against the struts of a pier. 'I haven't told you how he died.'

3

At ten a.m. Charles McWhinnie drove his Rover south across Kingston Bridge. The heat haze had already burned out of the sky above Glasgow. It was going to be one of those days when light rose shimmeringly from pavements and tar surfaces melted. The headlines in the *Evening Times* would invariably read, TEMPERATURES SOAR, CITY SWELTERS.

McWhinnie, born and brought up north of the river, didn't like the Southside. The city seemed alien over there. Even the neighbourhood names struck him as strange. Crossmyloof. Strathbungo. Ibrox – which he thought sounded like a veterinary ointment for chafed cow udders. *A jar of Eyebrox lotion, please.*

He glanced at the narrow motionless river as he crossed the bridge. He saw the tall cranes that serviced the Govan Yard, and the George V Docks, but where these huge constructions had once crowded the skyline, they were few now – skeletal souvenirs of the shipbuilding that years before had been the city's most vibrant industry.

It had been a time, McWhinnie thought, when people took a pride in their work. What did you have nowadays? Social Security and welfare fraud and chancrous housing estates where kids

12

bought and sold drugs with brazen abandon and fried their brains on lethal concoctions; any stray traveller in such places might have thought himself in a suburb of Beirut.

Collar undone, tie loose, he parked his car in a narrow street of black tenements a quarter of a mile from the drabness of Govan Cross Shopping Centre. Govan had always been a shipyard burgh, a company town, vibrant and cocky. Now shops were barricaded behind steel shutters, and graffiti had been spray-painted everywhere, most of it cryptic save for the occasional sectarian slogan. *IRA Rules*. Bigotry had never truly died here, no matter what claims to the contrary certain civic leaders and flash media guys might make. It was still simmering in seg-regated schools and uneasy mixed marriages. Prods and Tims. McWhinnie despised this divide, this moronic anachronism in a city alleged to be surging into a glossy European future.

He took a big paper bag from his Rover, then locked the car. He entered one of the tenements, passing a group of very young kids who were smoking cigarettes. The kids glared at him with tribal hostility as he made his way into the building and walked the length of the close, which was dark and clammy, to the stairs.

He climbed. On the first landing he unlocked a door whose nameplate read: *A Factor*. He slipped inside quickly, nudging the door shut behind him.

'I want in and out of here as fast as humanly possible,' he said.

The little man who sat in the room and gazed at the TV said, 'Aye, I don't blame you. This place . . . I wasn't expecting the fucking Ritz, granted, but this is a bloody slum.'

'We'll deal with your accommodation at the appropriate time,' McWhinnie said. He tried very hard to be non-specific in his utterances. When you were precise, you often found yourself compromised.

He looked round the one-room flat; claustrophobic, faded daffodil paint, a window so grubby it was opaque, a rag of a curtain, a cracked porcelain sink. A single bed faced the window. On paper, the premises belonged to a certain Arthur Factor, who was non-existent.

13

McWhinnie put the bag on the table and watched the little man open it hurriedly. It contained a loaf of white bread, a packet of bacon, six small eggs, three apples, three oranges, a carton of milk, a box of tea bags, a paperback sci-fi saga entitled *Planet of Ice*, Tagamet capsules and a bottle of cheap blended whisky.

The little man looked at the label on the bottle with slight disgust, then surveyed the items on the table. 'How long am I staying here?'

'I can't say.'

'A rough idea.'

'A week,' McWhinnie said vaguely. He didn't have a clue.

'A week? Christ's sake. The telly's shite. You can't expect me to sit here and go blind looking at a picture as bad as that,' and the little man pointed at the TV, where a fat woman with big hair, blurred by snowy interference, wept in front of Jerry Springer. The caption on the screen read: *MaryLou Says Her Husband Made Love To Her Mother*.

Bones picked up the paperback. 'A science-fiction book. Beam me the fuck up, Scotty.' He looked at McWhinnie. 'This isn't my kind of thing, squire. I like anything by Dick Francis.'

'Your literary taste is noted. I'll send round a horsy selection,' McWhinnie said. 'And I'll find somebody to adjust the bloody TV. Do you have any more complaints? Or are we finished now?'

'You didn't bring a newspaper. I like the *Record*. I told you that. In a pinch, I'll read the *Sun*.'

'Tabloids tend to slip my mind. I'll arrange it.'

'White bread. I'm supposed to live on this?'

'Think of it as a starter kit. The duck à l'orange with potatoes au gratin and baby carrots comes later.'

'You're a card, son. People would pay to hear you. See, I've always watched my diet. I've sat hours in sweatboxes to lose a few pounds. And white bread is just not fucking *on*. As for bacon . . . fat clogs arteries fastern twenty rats stuck in a drainpipe.'

McWhinnie ran a hand over his straw-coloured hair. He had the look of a sprinter only a year or so past his prime. Women warmed to him instantly, but somehow prolonged relationships failed to happen. He was never sure why. Maybe women thought

14

he was too committed to the job, too anxious to be accepted into the bloodstream of the Force.

'Right, finished here,' he said. 'I'm offsky.'

'Just a minute, son. What school did you go to?'

'Beg pardon?'

'A toff's school, was it? A fee-paying school, eh? Your accent is posh Glasgow. Not like mine. 'Course, I only went to the local eedjit school with all the other toerags. I wasn't privileged, you understand. No silver spoon in my gub.'

'Get this straight. My name, my background – off limits to you. Think of them as protected by live high-voltage wires. Go near them, they barbecue you like a sausage on a hot grill. Is that clear?'

'You're a tough guy, eh? I'll tell you something, sahib. You don't have the stuff for this work. I can hear it in your voice.'

'I'll be sure to keep your opinion in mind,' McWhinnie said. 'One last thing. Don't even think about leaving here and wandering around. You understand me? It's in your own interests to stay indoors.'

The little man said, 'Your wish is my command,' and opened the bottle of scotch. 'You'll have one for the road?'

'On a cold day in hell,' said McWhinnie. It was insufferably hot in this room, and the trapped air irritated him, and he didn't like this little fart he had to deal with. In fact, this kind of thing wasn't in his job description. Nowhere. Buying bloody groceries for scum. How did he get into this? What did this have to do with law and order? He hadn't signed on as an errand boy.

Somewhat dejected, he stepped towards the door. *You don't have the stuff for this work.* The little man's observation rolled through his head.

'A wee minute, squire. Did you take care of that, ah, business matter?'

McWhinnie removed a plain brown envelope from his pocket and tossed it to the little man, who caught it.

'Twenty-six hundred all squared away,' McWhinnie said.

The little man looked inside the envelope. It was filled with slips of paper. Each was marked *Paid In Full*. Twenty-six hundred and ninety-seven quid of debts to bookies all taken care of in one swoop.

McWhinnie said, 'I'll leave you to your purgatory.'

'You might have put in a bloody phone,' the little man said.

'You don't get phones in purgatory, Bones. It's a place of solitude where you contemplate your sins.'

McWhinnie shut the door and went down the stairs two at a time, relieved to be making his exit. Outside, the smoking kids had gone, the front doors of the Rover lay open and where the expensive tape deck had been there was only a black slot, like an unsmiling mouth.

Those little fuckers, he thought.

Those bloody monsters. He clenched his fists and looked up. The bright sky over Govan turned angry black-red in his vision.

From the window of his dreich one-room cell, the little man looked down at the sight of the well-spoken prat in the bright white shirt striding in a spluttering rage around his shiny car, kicking at useless tyres, *fuming*.

Funny stuff. Ho ha.

He opened the scotch, poured a measure into a cup and sniffed it. Granted, nobody was obliged to provide him with liquor. But if they were going to, why did they have to donate sewage?

Bones took whisky into his mouth and swirled it for a time. *Purgatory*, he thought. So this is what good Catholics fear.

The waiting room. Where you find out if you're getting a ticket for the onward journey.

I know where I'm going, he thought.

He stared at the gloomy walls. The faded yellow. The crap TV. The single bed with what looked like an Army-issue blanket, rough as a bear's arse. It wouldn't take long before this place spooked the daylights out of him, and then the sheer force of the terrible thing he'd done would kick him, like the hoof of an angry horse, straight in the soft core of his heart.

4

Eddie Mallon arrived at his mother's house in Stony Brook on Long Island at dawn; a red sky, a frail arrangement of still clouds tinted by thin sunlight. He parked his Cherokee, then walked up on to the porch. He could hear the 24-hour radio station his mother favoured, big-band stuff of the 1940s, Glenn Miller, Artie Shaw. 'Stars Fell on Alabama.'

He opened the front door and called out, 'Hello?' and Flora appeared in the kitchen doorway. She rose every morning of her life at daybreak and set about pruning, clipping, planting. Her garden was no mild hobby. It was serious business, an escape to a fragrant world of petal, stamen, pollination.

She was a small white-haired woman with pale red cheeks and rounded features. She looked, Eddie sometimes thought, like the Universal Grandmother. She stood on tiptoe to kiss her son.

'Surprise surprise, a dawn visitor,' she said. 'Tea?'

Eddie shook his head. 'I'd prefer coffee.' Then he remembered she'd quit drinking caffeine. He wondered how to approach the matter of his father. Direct. Say what you have to, then deal with the consequences.

'I can do you a herbal tea,' she said.

17

'How about plain old water, Ma?' He followed her inside the kitchen.

'Just passing, did you say? You're so *transparent*, Eddie. I've been expecting you.' She flipped the switch of an electric kettle.

'You heard . . . ?' He wondered if Joyce had called after all.

'Rennie phoned from Glasgow to tell me.'

'Rennie?'

'A cousin of mine. She was married to Nick.'

Who the hell were Rennie and Nick? There were so many relatives in the old country, uncles, aunts, cousins, second cousins, people Eddie Mallon knew nothing about, strangers' faces in hefty photo-albums Flora dragged out whenever she'd had more than two glasses of vodka. *This is Sammy, my sister Sally's husband in Pollokshaws. Here's Willie and Anne at their silver wedding at the Grosvenor.*

'How are you taking it? How are you feeling?' he asked.

Flora said, 'It was like I'd been struck on the head . . . I'm not sure I believe he's dead yet.'

Eddie drank his water, then set his empty glass in the sink. The kettle boiled, switched itself off. Flora dumped a tea bag into a mug decorated with a toadstool. The tea smelled of raspberry.

Flora said, 'I turned the radio on a minute ago and the band was playing "Moonlight in Vermont", and I thought of your father, and I remembered we danced together at the Barrowlands Ballroom in Glasgow and that was one of the tunes they played. He loved to dance. He was so nimble.' She looked at Eddie. 'Did he ever tell you he wanted to be a soccer player?'

'No. I knew he enjoyed the game. He took me to a couple of matches, I remember.'

'When he was eighteen he had a trial for a team called Third Lanark. The coach wasn't impressed. Jackie was so *disappointed*. He wanted to be a football hero, get his face on a cigarette card, newspaper clippings. "Mallon scores winning goal in the last minute." His whole life might have gone in another direction if he'd played well that day.'

Eddie touched the back of his mother's hand and thought: she

18

seems to be taking it well. But why shouldn't she? She hadn't seen Jackie Mallon for thirty years, and so far as Eddie knew hadn't spoken to him in all that time. She'd loved him enough to marry him, but after so long a separation even the strongest of loves would surely deteriorate into a series of small regrets and smudged memories.

Eddie said, 'So he never became a football hero.'

'He didn't become any kind of hero.'

'We can't all be hotshots. Most of us make compromises with our ambitions, Ma. Dad made them. He quit dreaming and went into business.'

Flora looked at her son. *'Business?* Is that what you call it? Fireplaces and doors ripped out of old houses, fancy iron-work, lead guttering. He had that warehouse in Bluevale Street crammed with mountains of absolute junk piled up with no sense or order.'

Eddie Mallon remembered the warehouse, and how it smelled of rust and damp and paraffin. It was a wonderland of the used and discarded, busted statues and skewed sundials and rusted iron radiators, ancient Singer sewing machines and old Underwood typewriters and valve radios from the 1930s and '40s. Jackie always had a nightwatchman around in case of thieves, and warehousemen in grey coats who had pencils stuck behind their ears and smoked Woodbines all day long. At night guard dogs were left behind to roam the premises, fierce beasts with fangs.

Flora said, 'I always thought he could have done much better than become a glorified junk man.'

'Ma –' But Eddie wasn't sure how he wanted to continue. He was no junk collector, Ma. Let's give him some dignity: call him what he called himself, an architectural salvage dealer. When an old house was about to be demolished, he was there, studying, picking, assessing.

Flora smiled a little sadly. She spoke as if to herself. 'He was a beautiful man to look at. And charm? In *abundance.* He could talk the moon out of a cloudy sky. Sometimes we'd be walking along

19

Alexandra Parade and all the girls would turn their heads when we strolled past, and I was the one on his arm. I was so *proud*. Other women wanted him and they'd do anything underhand to get him. And your father was easily led, Eddie. He had the ego of a film star. He couldn't pass a shop window without glancing at himself.' *Couldnae pass* . . . She'd shed most of her native accent; but when she spoke of the past she sometimes slipped into Glasgow dialect. 'And then I think of that time in Largs and how sweet life was in the beginning.'

Whenever Flora spoke of Jackie Mallon, the coastal town of Largs invariably arose and her expression became glazed: she had a golden memory of Largs where she'd honeymooned with Jackie. Eddie wondered why she'd never found a new husband, or even a lover. She'd buried herself in teaching grade school and then when she retired she'd hit the horticultural books vigorously. And suddenly this little house in Stony Brook overflowed with plants; a greenhouse out back was crammed with growing things. Flora worked at her gardening with the zeal of a Victorian botanist.

She said, 'I confronted him a couple of times about his . . . amorous misadventures. He always looked so ashamed. It would never happen again, he'd say. But it did. Then after you were born my priorities shifted – I just wanted to keep a nice house and raise my family. Jackie could have had a harem for all I cared. I wanted respectability.'

She blew her nose into a tissue she plucked from a box on the table. '*Salvage*,' she said, as if the failure of the marriage could be crystallized in this one word she obviously found so distasteful that it seemed to stick, like some bitter tablet, at the back of her throat.

Eddie moved close to her, placing a hand on her shoulder. 'Joyce wants me to attend the funeral.'

'Jackie was your father, Eddie. If you want to see him buried, that's perfectly natural.'

Eddie Mallon was a little uncomfortable. He wondered if he was being disloyal to his mother. No, I'm not betraying her, I'm

20

going to help bury my father, it's what a son does, even if his parents have been estranged for years, even if he's lived with his mother in the United States and he hasn't seen his father since 1969 in Glasgow. Taking sides doesn't come into it.

Death negates the need for diplomacy.

He wondered if Flora knew about the letters and birthday cards that had started to arrive from Jackie seven or eight years ago or the phone calls Jackie made a couple of times a year, or the fact Eddie had phoned his father from Queens. Eddie could still remember how that first letter had begun: *Dear Eddie, It would be unnatural if you didn't think bad of me.* Christmas packages had begun to arrive later, gifts of Scottish origin, tartan scarves, fruit-cake, McCowan's toffee and Edinburgh rock for Mark.

During one of his phone calls Jackie had said, *What I did was a big mistake,* and there was the dolorous note in his voice of a man who'd drunk just enough to be honest. *Hacking the family apart like that was a bloody selfish cruelty, Eddie. Now I wish I'd told your mother to keep you and your sister together. But no, no, I knew better, I chose another way.*

If Flora knew about any of this, she never said so.

'Does anyone have any idea who killed him?' Flora asked.

'Joyce didn't say,' Eddie remarked.

'Killers always go to the Bad Fire,' she said.

He was surprised to hear her utter this phrase from childhood, and even more surprised by the fact she hadn't used it with any flippancy. She'd said it seriously. It was where sinners were sent in Glasgow. *You'll go to the Bad Fire if you steal, if you lie, if you cheat, if you swear . . .* Parents told kids that. Eddie would lie awake in Granny Mallon's third-floor flat in Bathgate Street and see flames created by streetlights in the folds of the blinds. He believed the Bad Fire lay in the street below and if he went to the window at night he'd see the pavement explode and people coming home from the pubs get sucked through a slit into the inferno.

'I stopped believing in the Bad Fire long ago,' he said.

'Not me,' she said. She stepped towards Eddie and held him a moment and he thought he detected a shiver run through her, as if she were suppressing an emotion. 'He must have had enemies, Eddie.'

Eddie shrugged. 'You don't know that. He might have been shot by somebody who didn't know him. A random slaying. A robbery. We don't have the facts.'

'That time he went to jail,' she said, then she paused.

Jail . . . Eddie remembered how he'd constructed a fiction in which Jackie hadn't been incarcerated for eight weeks in Barlinnie, that austere fortress in the far eastern reaches of Glasgow. No, Jackie was secretly working for the government in an unspecified country overseas, fighting in something called the Cold War, which Eddie always imagined took place in the Arctic, tanks camouflaged white, soldiers with frostbitten noses.

He wanted to be proud of his dad. He wanted to adore him.

Flora said, 'He was never quite the same after jail. He was harder under the surface.'

Eddie had to ransack his memory. What crime had Jackie allegedly committed anyway? It came back to him in a flash, a little nugget of recall. Possession of stolen goods.

Flora continued: 'He met men in jail who didn't think twice about violence. Hard men. And Jackie had never been a violent person. He never once raised a hand to me all the time I knew him. But after Barlinnie, nobody could ever convince me he was the same man. I don't mean he started beating us up or anything like that –'

'He was angry with the system, Ma. He was embittered. He always said he was innocent. He was adamant about that. I remember he kept saying he'd done nothing wrong.'

Flora wasn't listening to him. 'He became withdrawn and furtive and he'd vanish for days at a time. He had a look on his face that said, *Don't ask me where I've been, woman. Just don't ask.* So I never did. He came and he went . . . And then out of the blue we moved up in the world, from Granny Mallon's flat in Bathgate Street to a house in Onslow Drive, and I didn't know how Jackie could afford a place like that on the money he made selling junk out of that bloody warehouse.'

22

She sat down at the table. She was reflected in the polished wood like somebody drowning in brown water. Eddie Mallon remembered moving house. Less than a mile separated Bathgate Street from Onslow Drive, but the houses in Onslow Drive weren't decrepit tenements, they were smart terraced properties, your own garden front and back. People living there belonged to a class that enjoyed a certain genteel prosperity.

'Obviously he made some good business deals,' Eddie said.

'Is that what you really believe?'

'Why not? What are you trying to say – he sometimes walked on the wrong side of the street? He ran some scams, broke some laws? How can you be absolutely sure of that?' He thought of Jackie Mallon saying: *I was never a criminal, son. Remember that. If anybody says anything against me at your school, learn to ignore it. I was the victim of spiteful men. That's the truth.*

The victim of spiteful men.

You don't know anything about him, Eddie, do you? You don't know how the man lived his life. You remember him the way a small kid might remember the scent and texture of a long-lost security blanket or a favourite teddy bear. You wanted more than that. All through the years of separation you longed for reconciliation.

Flora patted the side of her son's face. 'Oh, Eddie. He's stone-cold dead, but he's still got you thinking good things about him. What a bloody great talent it is to get the benefit of the doubt – even after you're gone.'

Eddie Mallon said, 'I missed him when I was growing up, so okay – maybe I idealized him a little. A kid misses his dad.'

Flora said, 'If you go to Glasgow you'll get to meet the mysterious Senga.'

'Is she so mysterious?' Eddie asked.

'I don't know the first thing about her. Admittedly, I haven't inquired too closely. She's been with Jackie for what – twenty years? Just think. If he'd married her she'd be your stepmother. There's a thought for you, Eddie.'

Flora sagged suddenly; she hunched over the table.

23

'You okay, Ma?'

'Just a little breathless. It'll pass. My days are usually more humdrum. This is . . .'

'Are you sure that's all?'

'I'm sure.'

He stood over her. He noticed her hair was thinning, her pink scalp faintly visible on the crown of her head through a white lattice-work of strands. He imagined her growing infirm and still somehow managing to hobble out to the greenhouse, watering can trembling in her hand. He wondered if Senga looked the same age as Flora, and if she had that same grandmotherly vibe about her – then he remembered Joyce had described her as red-haired and tall and flamboyant, a vibrant character. My stepmother, he thought. But Jackie hadn't taken the conjugal route with Senga, who had the status of a common-law wife.

He said, 'I have to make some travel arrangements. You sure you're okay?'

'I'm fine, fine.' She walked with him to the door. She held his elbow tightly. Stepping on to the porch, Eddie saw distress on his mother's face. 'I missed him too,' she said.

5

Flora watched Eddie walk to his vehicle and thought: he looks the way his father used to. He moves the same way, that measured step, like a man afraid of standing on something unpleasant. He's taller than his father, and better built, but not as handsome as Jackie; he doesn't have that same flighty charm. But more dependable than his father.

He has more heart. Or maybe less camouflage around it.

She saw the Cherokee back out of the drive. The lights blinked on and off a couple of times, Eddie's goodbye signal. Then the vehicle swung out of sight.

He's going to Glasgow to bury Jackie, she thought. I'll never see Glasgow again. Bellahouston Park. The Botanic Gardens. A saunter down Buchanan Street, a left turn along busy Argyle Street. She wondered if there was still that awful smelly zoo in Oswald Street where they kept a couple of mangy lions caged.

It was all lost to her.

She went inside the kitchen and opened the refrigerator. She removed a bottle of Absolut from the freezer. The glass was cold and adhered to her hand. She poured a little, drank it down quickly, filled the glass again. What is happening to you, lady?

Two small shots at dawn. Strolling down Stumblebum Street. You shouldn't be doing this.

The radio was playing 'What A Little Moonlight Can Do'.

Oh aye. Oh yes. A little moonlight. Jackie's dead and there's a sharp stick in my heart and I remember what a little moonlight can do.

The honeymoon in Largs, the hotel room with the sea view, the big brass bed. Jackie was an energetic lover. He exhausted her. She loved that fatigue and the deep ache of it all. She recalled how it rained all week, but it didn't matter, because they never left their room. Jackie took the bedsheets and hung them between chairs, making them into a kind of tent, just for laughs. *I'm the sheikh*, he said. *Come inside my desert hide-away, Flower.* He often called her 'Flower'. Flora my flower, he used to say.

She picked up her glass and entered the greenhouse. She was a little out of breath: age, she thought, the system on the blink. She loved this glass room at dawn. The tranquillity, the quiet force of greenery, the subtle modifications of colour.

Flora my flower. What had replaced her? Senga my sunshine? Senga –

She remembered The Raid suddenly, the day she'd come home to the house in Onslow Drive from shopping and found it crowded with policemen, some uniformed, others in suits, and they'd yanked floorboards up, hauled drawers open, strewn clothing all over the place, dragged books from shelves and tossed them around, ripped open cushions and pillows – a mad intrusion, a crazy nightmare of vandalism.

This was when she'd first met a young policeman called Caskie. He had an easy manner. He'd taken her to one side and said, 'We have a warrant, Mrs Mallon,' and he flashed paper in front of her, but she pushed his hand away and raced from room to room, shouting at the policemen, throwing punches, and then Caskie had tried to calm her down, leading her gently into the back yard where he lit a cigarette for her and opened an umbrella to keep her dry from rain that had just begun to fall. She wanted to scratch Caskie's eyes out of his head.

But it wasn't Caskie's fault. He had a bloody warrant. He was doing his job.

Jackie was the cause of this. It was something Jackie had done.

She'd been expecting the sky to collapse ever since he'd come out of jail for possession of three 19th-century statues stolen from a country house in Ayrshire. He swore he'd bought them in all innocence from a dealer. She'd been dragging a sense of impending catastrophe around for more than a year.

And now this. Whatever this was.

She listened to the wreckage inside the house. Nails pulled out of wood, screeching. A closet ripped apart. 'What in God's name do you expect to find?' And she was shaking with rage, sucking smoke as deeply into her lungs as she could.

Caskie said, 'Read the warrant, Mrs Mallon.'

'Fuck the warrant,' she said. 'Just tell me.'

'We believe there are certain items in the house –'

'What items?'

Caskie, who wore a dark blue suit that was a little too baggy for him, looked like a young man who'd been promoted beyond his experience. This situation was obviously awkward for him. In other circumstances, she might have been touched by his immaturity.

He said, 'Specimens of counterfeit money.'

She laughed in disbelief. 'Counterfeit *money*?'

Caskie had pleasing blue eyes, a detail she remembered only later. And he had a hard time looking at her.

'And you have to tear my whole bloody house *apart* to search for this alleged counterfeit money?'

'Some of the men are a little . . .' and Caskie hesitated.

'They're brutes, Caskie. They're *enjoying* themselves, for God's sake!'

'I admit they're over-enthusiastic –'

27

'*Over-enthusiastic?* Who do I sue for damages if you don't find this alleged counterfeit money?'

'We try to leave things the way we found them.'

'And I sailed up the Clyde on a water biscuit. How do you put back broken vases and a broken mirror?'

'You'd be reimbursed for that kind of thing.'

'And my peace of mind – do I get reimbursed for that?'

Caskie touched her arm. 'We go through a rigorous process to get warrants like this, Mrs Caskie. They're not handed out lightly. Usually we get them only when we're sure.'

'And you're sure, are you?'

'I'm not enjoying this.'

'Somehow I believe you,' she said. She flicked her cigarette into the rain. 'At least my children are at school and don't have to see this demolition.'

A uniformed policeman stepped out into the yard and gestured to Caskie. Caskie placed the umbrella in Flora's hand and said, 'Excuse me,' and then he disappeared inside the house. She smoked another cigarette, listened to rain drum on the taut black skin of the umbrella. She cursed Jackie Mallon. She cursed him for bringing these men into her home.

Counterfeit money. No. Stolen goods maybe, just maybe; she didn't think he was beyond doing a dodgy deal concerning paintings, statues, antique jewels. But fake money was something else altogether, big-time crime against the financial structure of the country, against the bloody government. Serious business. Serious punishment.

Caskie came back. 'We found what we were looking for,' he said quietly.

Flora was dizzy, lost her balance, slipped against Caskie, who had to catch and hold her. She stood with her face pressed into his shoulder while he talked quietly and reassuringly about how his men were making the place tidy again, it wouldn't be one hundred per cent but it wouldn't look too bad.

She stopped listening to his individual words. She liked the soothing sound of his voice.

'Do you know where your husband is?' Caskie asked.

She said she didn't. It was true. He'd been gone for the last two days.

'Myself and another officer will wait for him,' Caskie said. 'And you can tell the children we're here to investigate the break-in.'

Jackie came home the evening of The Raid. He was arrested before he could enter the house. Cuffed on the street and tossed into the back of a car and driven away quickly; the kids didn't see it happen. No charges were ever brought against him. His lawyer argued that the counterfeit notes had been planted by police officers who had long-standing grudges against Mallon because they suspected him of crimes they could never prove. The only charge they'd ever been able to make stick was the business of the stolen statues – and that case, the lawyer contended, was so thin as to be downright transparent. Besides, the evidence of involvement in a counterfeit scheme was circumstantial at best.

Flora didn't believe Jackie was innocent. He'd brought illicit material into the house and he'd threatened the security of the only things she cared for, home and family. How could he have put everything at risk? She didn't doubt he loved her after his fashion, and she never questioned his love of the children. But the marriage had turned cold.

Flora. My flower. Flower of ice, she thought. Petals dipped in frost.

I gave you my heart, Jackie Mallon. And you dropped it.

Three weeks after The Raid, weeks of arguments followed by fragile truces and promises of future good behaviour, weeks of madness and acrimony, she and Eddie had flown to America.

Without Joyce.

Flora had made a deal with the devil and she'd never stopped regretting it. Not in all the years since she'd left Scotland.

She wandered through the greenhouse with the half-drunk shot of Absolut in her hand. She wondered what Christopher Caskie looked like now. They'd corresponded a dozen or more

29

times through the years. His letters were usually in response to her inquiries about Joyce: was she doing all right? In his last letter Caskie had written that his wife had died of cancer.

A blackbird flew over the greenhouse and was briefly reflected in sunlit glass. From inside the house the radio played Artie Shaw's rendition of 'There's A Small Hotel'.

6

Captain Zeke 'Marvel' Stock, Eddie's superior, was so big and wide that some of the men in his command referred to him as the Eclipse. He weighed an imposing three hundred pounds plus, much of it solid muscle. Eddie sometimes thought of the captain as an African tribal chief, a man you expected to arrive at a crime scene held aloft by a congregation of bearers.

Presently, Marvel was motionless under a traffic signal, and the red stop light gave the impression that his face was smeared with the bloody innards of a goat sacrificed in his honour moments before.

Eddie gazed at the dead man in an expensive overcoat who lay face-down in the middle of the street.

Marvel twisted his huge neck and scanned the grey edifice of a twelve-storey office building. 'A jumper,' he said.

'He's sidewalk salsa all right,' Bobby Figaro said. Figaro was Marvel's right-hand, yes-man and all-round gofer.

'Anyone got his name?' Marvel asked.

Figaro had it, of course. Figaro always had the scoop. 'John Boscoe Bentley, an address on East 32nd. According to what was in his wallet, he worked down on Wall Street for a brokerage firm called Something Somebody and Something Else Incorporated. I gather from a preliminary inquiry – to wit, a phone call to the company CEO – he was something of a player. How he came to be on the ledge of this particular building,' and Figaro shrugged.

'Coulda been pushed,' Marvel said.

'All possibilities will be explored, Captain,' said Figaro, with his ever-ready halogen-bright smile.

Detectives and uniforms were already inside the building, knocking on doors, asking questions; because it was only seven a.m., the building was largely unoccupied save for custodians and a cleaning crew, also a few lonesome workaholics, some of them demented guys who'd been in the place all night trying to balance ledgers or make sense out of spreadsheets.

Mallon stared at the corpse and wondered about a life terminated this way – whether he jumped or was pushed, it was a hell of a place for a guy to die; the hard pavement of a city street. He thought of his father and realized how few details he had about the old man's death. Was he gunned down in the street? At home? Were there witnesses? What calibre weapon? The questions buzzed him like gnats.

He watched Marvel yawn. It was an awesome sight; the mouth opened like a giant oyster about to yield a pearl. Gold fillings flashed in his mouth, which became one vast maw. 'I need coffee,' Marvel said. 'Somebody be good enough to get the captain a shot of strong java, huh?'

'There's a joint round the corner,' Figaro said. 'I'll go.'

Figaro disappeared. Brown-nose Figaro. Marvel looked at Eddie Mallon.

'Say, this ain't your shift, is it, Mallon?' Marvel said. 'Come to that, it ain't my shift either. So why have I dragged my sorry ass downtown at this time of day, you ask? Lemme tell you. Because I ain't been home, Eddie. I been struggling with paperwork. I been wrestling figures. Budgets. City Hall needs numbers to crunch.'

'Way over my head,' Eddie said.

'Way over mine too.' The captain lit a small brown-papered cigarette and stared at the corpse. 'My brain feels like a punchbag. I just stepped out for some air and take a look at this body we got here. What brings you out?'

'I need to talk with you,' Eddie said. 'I want some leave.'

'You got vacation time coming to you?'

'This would be leave of absence. Family reasons.'

'Somebody sick?'

Mallon saw lights go on in the upper floors of the building. He imagined the dead man, John Boscoe Bentley, falling through space, through darkness: what did you think as you dropped? You knew you were going to hit ground hard, and you'd break, so what went through your mind in those few seconds? Nothing? Everything? Or was it all just one blind deep-red searing panic? And at the end – what? A fraction of acceptance? A microsecond of tranquillity? Maybe you just blacked out, or your heart exploded out of fright halfway down.

'My father died.' Eddie turned to look at Marvel.

'Say. Sorry to hear that. Real sorry. How did it happen? Was he sick?'

Eddie said, 'He was shot.'

'*Shot*. Jesus Christ.'

'I don't know the circumstances.'

'Shot. Fuck. Fucking world we live in.' Marvel sucked on his cigarette and stared into the lit end a second. 'You got any heavy cases on your desk as of now?'

Eddie said, 'There's the dead girl we found in the empty brownstone . . .'

'That junkie kid nobody can ID?'

'Yeah,' Eddie said. He pondered the mystery of the missing teenage girl, a runaway from somewhere, and the fact her identity hadn't yet been established. Somebody must be missing her, waiting up for her, insomniac parents in a small backwater township in a faraway state.

'Tom Collins can deal with that,' Marvel said.

Tom Collins was Eddie's partner, a dark-jawed second-generation Irishman.

Eddie said, 'Apart from the girl, it's stuff that can wait.'

'Stuff that can wait, huh? I never heard of stuff like that before,' Marvel said, and smiled. 'Must be new on the market. I gotta grab myself some of that good shit. You take the time you need, Eddie. You want any help, you know where to turn.'

'I appreciate that,' Eddie said.

Marvel dismissed the gratitude with a quick motion of his hand and was already moving away, drawn towards the door of the building by the sight of Figaro, who was clutching a cardboard cup of coffee.

An ambulance appeared, lights whirling. Eddie Mallon watched the paramedics emerge. He saw them surround the body. And he felt weirdly lonely, out of touch with this world of his, as if he'd already left it, and was airborne, flying back to a place he barely remembered.

Glasgow, a city seen through a rainy mist, a fuzzy sketch in damp charcoal.

7

In the doorway of his parents' bedroom Mark Mallon asked, 'How long will you be gone, Dad?'

'A couple of days,' Eddie said. He marvelled at how tall his son had become; magically, he'd stretched from five feet to just under six in the space of a year. He was almost as tall as Eddie himself. Facially, he resembled his mother; he had a delicacy about him that gave him an androgynous look. Girls loved it. They worshipped the way his long hair lay against his shoulders. They telephoned him constantly. High-pitched little voices filled with squeaky hope: *Is Mark home?*

Claire was packing. She took special care with Eddie's best suit, a navy blue number for the funeral. It wasn't too late to change his mind, he thought. Cancel the airline ticket. But he'd already phoned Joyce and given her his arrival time, and she'd yelped with excitement at the idea of seeing him, and he felt good he'd been able to give her this much pleasure just by buying an airline ticket and rearranging his life for four days or so.

'Did somebody really shoot Gramps?' Mark asked.

'It seems that way.'

'Boy,' Mark said. 'You know why?'

'I don't know anything yet,' Eddie said. He flipped the pages of his passport, saw a picture of himself taken seven years earlier. Black hair, no grey. Face leaner. He thought he looked passably attractive in this picture, but gravity hadn't given him jowls back then.

'Was he, you know, like a crook?' Mark asked.

'A crook? What makes you ask that?'

'Something Granma once said. He was in jail for a while.'

'Sixty days. It was nothing, a mistake,' Eddie said.

'Why didn't he ever come visit?'

Eddie shrugged. 'He never got around to it, that's all. He was perfectly happy to stay home. He didn't like travel.'

'So why didn't *we* visit *him*?' Mark asked.

Good question, and Eddie Mallon had no easy answer; only excuses. He'd graduated high school, gone to the Police Academy, got married, bought a house in Queens, settled down, raised a kid, took his vacations in places as far away from any city as he could get, isolated cabins in Idaho or Montana, National Parks in Tennessee or Kentucky. A life went rushing past and it preoccupied you, and suddenly you realized you were never going to read *War and Peace* or sit drinking blood-orange juice at a sidewalk café in Florence or sail the Greek islands for a month. And all you could say to your son when he asked why the family had never visited Glasgow was, 'Somehow we just never found the time, Mark,' which wasn't a good explanation but close to the truth.

Thirty years of life. A bubble in the wind, drifting.

He touched his wife's hand. 'I wish you were coming with me.'

Claire zipped his case, smiled at him. 'It's only a few days. Anyhow, somebody's got to hold down the fort here.'

'Hey, I could do that,' Mark suggested. He was suddenly eager.

'Why does that offer make alarm bells ring in my head?' Claire asked.

'You think I'd throw all-nighters, big parties, invite hundreds of kids,' he said.

36

'Did I say that?' Claire asked.

'You don't have to,' Mark said. 'But it's what you think.'

Eddie stuck his passport in a hip pocket of his black jeans. He put his airline ticket in the inside pocket of his pale grey linen jacket, patted the place as if to reassure himself of something.

He looked at Claire. He was about to say it a second time: *you could still come with me*. Claire and Jackie Mallon had never met; the old man had always existed on the periphery of her life. Once or twice they'd talked on the phone and he'd made her laugh, but that was it. He was a dead stranger who'd spoken in a funny accent she sometimes didn't understand.

'If you're ready, I'd better get you to JFK.' She glanced at her watch, rattled car keys in her hand.

He gazed round the room in the manner of a man taking his leave of a place he'll never see again. Why did this departure from wife and son make him feel so goddam *melancholy*? He'd be back before they knew he'd even gone. They had lives of their own. Mark had friends, girls, serious hanging-out to do. Claire had a part-time job with Century 21 and every Wednesday and Friday she went to a health club where she rode an exercise bike and checked her pulse rate and blood pressure, then drank lo-cal fruit smoothies with her pals in a health-food bar.

'Ready,' he said.

8

Sun burned fiercely on the mouth of the Clyde. A launch, a thirty-footer, was anchored about a quarter of a mile from shore. Christopher Caskie stood unsteadily on deck and watched small boats sail towards Ardrossan, Ayr, the Isle of Arran. Sails dazzled yellow and white in the hard light.

Caskie was a card-carrying landlubber. The sea affected his stomach. The rise and fall of water was gentle but it made him queasy anyway, and he had to sit down. He closed his eyes, felt the sun on his eyelids. His short white beard was warm.

He heard footsteps on the stair that led from the lower deck. The man who appeared was six feet six inches tall. He had a tubercular appearance, circles the colour of grape juice under his eyes. His pear-shaped face was too small for the rest of his body. He wore a black silk shirt and white slacks. He farted quietly, sighed with pleasure, then sat down beside Caskie.

'There's nothing in the world as satisfying as a good healthy expulsion of gas,' the man said. His name was Roddy Haggs.

Caskie said, 'I suppose that depends on your priorities.'

'Ah. Are bodily functions off-putting to you? Note to self: do not discuss gases with Caskie.' Haggs studied other boats in the vicinity with his binoculars. 'Look at that. *Look* at that. Fuck me. I know what I'd like to do to her. Ooo.'

The object of Haggs's lust was a tanned blonde teenage girl in a neon lime bikini who dived from a small yacht about three hundred yards away. She vanished underwater, then surfaced laughing. She climbed back into the boat. She had a melodic laugh. Her water-flattened hair was pressed to her skull.

'Very nice,' Caskie said. He felt Haggs expected an appropriate response. They were members of the same club: men of the world. But different worlds.

'*Nice?* Show some enthusiasm, Caskie. She's completely shaggable. What they call a *babe*. Don't tell me you wouldn't fancy a poke at that crumpet.

A high-powered speedboat passed, sending waves towards the launch, which trembled a little. Caskie felt his stomach tighten.

'Beer?' Haggs asked.

'I'll pass.'

Haggs popped a lager and slurped it. 'I'm fascinated by the idea of squeezing out whatever deep secrets the former jockey knows about good old Jackie's mysterious enterprise. I'll pop him like a bloody flea. Talk to me about the daughter.'

Caskie shrugged. 'Divorced. Intelligent. She had a fondness for amphetamine a few years back but she kicked it. I seriously doubt she knows anything. She was close to her father. But I don't imagine for a moment he discussed his business with her.'

Haggs said, 'Which leaves Senga.'

'Senga's a good-hearted sort, but probably hard as bloody nails if you step on her toes the wrong way. I don't think she's privy to anything either . . . I'll tell you one thing, Haggs. Her heart may be good, but it's broken right now.'

Haggs was silent for a time, cracking his knuckles. Caskie wondered if the silence was some form of sympathy, then decided it was more likely that Roddy Haggs didn't have a clue what to say about grief. He just wasn't good with little sounds of commiseration, the *so sorrys* and the *oh dears* that were the basic currency of response to human tragedy.

'I bet she kept her ears open,' Haggs said eventually. 'I bet she knew Jackie's business.'

'Even if she did, which I doubt, it doesn't mean she'd be willing to repeat anything she heard,' Caskie said. He stroked his white beard. He thought it made him look almost nautical, like an admiral. How ironic.

'Sod it,' Haggs said. 'It doesn't matter who tells us what. We'll get it in the end anyway. There's just too much buzz vibrating along the grapevine for this to be a bag of hot air. That old tosspot Mallon was up to something, and it was big, and I'm not being left out in the fucking cold. Nothing passes me by.'

Loose talk in the criminal fraternity, Caskie thought; but enough to convince Haggs something profitable was in the wind. Caskie decided to risk standing up. He leaned carefully against the handrail and looked down into the water. Reflected light hit his sunglasses. His mouth filled with sticky saliva. He was going to throw up. His moment of courage passed and he made his way shakily back to his seat. I'll never be a seagoing man. No life on the ocean wave for me.

Haggs said, 'Jackie Mallon left Glasgow last Wednesday from Central Station. You any idea where he went?'

'It's news to me,' Caskie said.

'My man saw him enter the station, then he was gone in a flash.'

'Maybe he didn't go anywhere. Maybe he was playing games with your man.'

'He was seen buying a ticket,' Haggs said.

'And then your man lost him? Downright careless.'

'You know nothing about this jaunt?'

'Nothing. Anything else on the agenda, Haggs?'

Haggs gestured loosely. 'We're almost finished.' He ticked off the names on his fingertips. 'Matty Bones. Joyce. Senga Craig.

I'll deal with Matty when he's had a few more hours to sweat. You can cope amiably with Joyce. And Senga – do you want me to leave her to you?'

'Yes,' Caskie said.

'You're the expert on the Mallon family, after all. You're the authority. You're the historian.'

'Up to a point,' Caskie said.

'What you don't know about the family isn't worth knowing.' Haggs stretched his long arms until his elbow joints cracked. He smiled. The expression made him appear ugly and unwanted, like the solitary bruised Comice left in a greengrocer's display after all the others have been sold. 'It's a bloody shame Jackie was such a stubborn fucker –'

'I don't think he'd have told you anything in a million years,' Caskie said. 'He was never easily intimidated. If he didn't want to tell you something, that was the end of it. You could pull out his fingernails one by one, he still wouldn't tell you if he didn't want to.'

Caskie remembered Jackie Mallon the last time he'd seen him – Jackie's ruined looks, the glossy hair, the sunken cheeks that might have belonged to an old trumpeter. A chance encounter on Argyle Street on a busy Saturday afternoon last Christmas, the shops festooned with tinsel and light, an army of Santas everywhere, a kiddy choir singing 'O Little Town of Bethlehem', and Jackie walking one way, Caskie the other, and they'd collided. They shook hands vigorously, men who tolerated, perhaps even liked each other, despite the fact they worked different sides of the street.

What are you up to these days, you old rogue? Caskie asked.

All I do with my time is play dominoes in the senior citizens' centre. You didn't hear this from me, but we actually play for money. It's illegal, I know, I know. But where's the harm in gambling for a few quid, eh? Such are the innocent pleasures of sorry old men. I was never a reprobate. Jackie had smiled then, the easy-going smile that made you feel he was sharing an enormous confidence.

Caskie laughed. *And I believe in Santa.*

Aye, everybody should believe in Santa. Where's the spirit of Christmas if you don't believe in the gaffer?

They wished each other seasonal greetings. Jackie Mallon had patted Caskie's arm and walked away, bent forward a little against the wind that came rushing up from the Clyde and shook the decorations in the streets. Caskie thought he had a quality few rogues possess; he could make you believe he was incapable of the lawlessness attributed to him. He had about him an unsettling air of innocence. Charm, Caskie thought. All charm.

He blinked against savage sunlight. Unsteady as the launch shivered again, he wanted to tell Haggs – look, we didn't need to meet on this boat, we could have talked over a glass of wine somewhere nice and private outside the city; but no, you have to drag me out to this bloody vessel *because you know I don't have the stomach for water*. Haggs had a mean-bastard streak and enjoyed other people's discomfort.

'There's a son,' Caskie said.

'He lives overseas. So I hear.'

'In New York,' Caskie said. 'He may come back for the funeral. He's a cop, incidentally.'

Haggs did another stretching thing with his arms. He looked like a figure made out of pipe-cleaners twisted by a child. 'So what? Is this a cause for concern or something? An American cop, is that supposed to worry me?'

'I mention it in passing,' Caskie said. He thought of Flora Mallon. Had the years been good to her? When he first met her he'd been more than a little smitten by her beauty; she had the kind of presence that would turn heads at parties, the rich black hair and the square jawline that suggested pride and self-assurance and an element of ferocity, the mouth that defied you to kiss it, the dark chocolate eyes that saw straight through you. He'd felt clumsy and inadequate in her presence, he remembered. But he'd been kind to her at a time when she needed somebody.

How was she taking the news of Jackie's murder? Had she

ever stopped loving Mallon? Her notes never made any mention of him. The last time she'd written it was to say how very sad she was to hear of Caskie's wife Meg dying. Meg had been sick for a very long time, clinging to an existence that seemed worthless to Caskie. Slow death had been a lonely experience for her. And for him too. That pathetic solitude. You sit in a room and hold the sick woman's hand but you might be the only person on the planet. You want her to die. You pray for it.

Then you wonder if you want her to die for all the wrong reasons.

Haggs scrutinized Caskie for a moment. 'You don't like this, do you, Caskie? You and me involved in this. It makes you feel dirty. You think I'm a fucking lout, don't you? Beneath your station in life. You've always looked down your fucking nose at me. For years you've made me feel like a turd.'

'I'm cooperating with you,' Caskie said. 'Isn't that all you've ever needed? Feelings don't enter into it.'

'I could buy and sell you and it wouldn't make a fucking dent in my bank account,' Haggs said. 'In one month I probably go through more than your entire net worth. You know what this boat cost me? You any idea what I paid for my house in Rouken Glen? Did you know I have a villa in Lanzarote with a swimming pool?'

Caskie said, 'I'm deeply impressed, Haggs.'

'Fuck you. I have a real estate company that covers the entire city. I own six full-service garages and a car-rental firm with a fleet of forty. So don't turn your nose up at me, mister. Don't talk to me like I'm slime. What have *you* got, Caskie? Let me tell you. Qualms, right? You've got qualms.'

'I certainly don't have a fleet of damn taxis,' Caskie said.

'Qualms, for fuck's sake,' Haggs said. 'I never trust a word that doesn't sound the way it looks.'

'Can we go ashore now?' Caskie asked.

Roddy Haggs said, 'Why? Don't like the water?'

'I get seasick, Haggs.'

Haggs said, 'Note to self: Mr Caskie does not like sailing. Don't ask him again. It makes him want to vomit.'

Caskie stared at the shore. He thought: I have one year until retirement. I've never looked forward to it before now. One year and then I'm beyond Haggs's reach. Gone. All this will be a dream hurriedly dissolving: *you hope*. He couldn't wait a year. He didn't have that kind of patience. He sucked sea air into his lungs as if to cleanse them and thought, I need to get Haggs out of my life soon. Today. Tomorrow. The day after. First chance I get. He'd had dreams of killing Haggs. In one, he dropped Haggs from a great height into a vat of acid and Haggs, screaming, was skinned within seconds. In another he'd strangled Haggs with an old bicycle chain. These dreams always left him drained.

Roddy Haggs unlocked a small cabinet and took out a plastic Tesco bag which had been rolled over and wrapped with very thick rubber bands. He thrust the bag into Caskie's arms and said, 'Before I forget. Evidence for the prosecution.'

Caskie, whose heart thumped, and who felt gluey saliva rise again in his throat, took the bag with great reluctance. What have I done? he wondered. What in God's name?

9

Eddie Mallon sat in the sky, hunched forward in his seat while he waited for that moment when the wheels struck the runway and the aircraft with all its great weight roared to an unlikely halt. A time he always found tense and scary. All bets with gravity were off. You could die in an instant of fire.

When the cloud cover was blown away and he saw the city appear, he forgot his alarm. He found himself looking out at a mazy profusion of orange streetlamps burning in the night, the lights of cars on long ribbons of motorway, and in the west beyond the limits of Glasgow the outline of hills. He couldn't recollect the city having been so bright before. It didn't square with his boyhood memory. He recalled a grubby place, more shadow than streetlamp. A soot-cloaked city, darkness at noon, black buildings.

'Your table, sir.'

The young woman who wore the sombre blue uniform of the airline chided him for his failure to put his table in the regulation upright position. He did as he was told; only on planes was he so readily obedient. This high off the ground he had no control over anything, no choice but to defer to people cloistered in a cockpit, men and women who understood instrument panels, radar, all the rest of it.

His nervousness wasn't entirely founded in this lifelong dumb-ass fear of flying. He was also thinking of what he'd encounter when he landed. He was thinking of his sister and wondering how she'd handle her father's funeral. He was thinking about the old man's long-time live-in companion, Senga Craig. *What you see is what you get with Senga,* Joyce had said. *She's sentimental and she'll weep at the sight of a dead budgie in a cage, then out of the blue she'll hit you with a hard opinion or a tough insight you never saw coming. Under that pile of red hair there's a sharp brain.*

The prospect of finally meeting Senga made him a little uneasy; maybe it was the idea of seeing another woman in a house he'd only ever associated with his mother. Now somebody else slept in Jackie's bed. Somebody else controlled the household, chose the furniture, all the things Flora had done. *Jackie loves her,* Joyce had said. *And she's devoted to him. They're happy.*

He heard the thud of the undercarriage, a noise that always distressed him. The plane was four hundred feet, three, then two hundred, above the runway. And now, his nerves leaping like doomed kittens in a canvas sack on their way to a river, he watched the runway rush up to make contact. It was always easier when Claire flew with him; he had her hand to squeeze.

Landing. Touchdown. The wheels whined on the runway. Eddie clutched the handrest until he was certain everything was safe, then he sat back in his seat, relieved, as the craft taxied. Why the fuck was he scared in planes?

It had always been so, starting with the first flight he ever took, and that was the day he'd fled Glasgow with his mother, and he'd locked himself in the toilet and trembled, just stood there looking at himself in the mirror and *shaking*, not really knowing where he was flying to or why, except it was the end of the world as he understood it. Easy for a shrink to make something out of that, Eddie. You associate flying with upheaval. With change and

46

the fear of change. *You can get off the couch now, Mr Mallon. That'll be two hundred bucks.*

He unbuckled his seatbelt. He stepped into the aisle, opened the overhead compartment, hauled down the leather bag Claire had packed for him. This was the only luggage he had, which meant he didn't have to waste time at the baggage carousel.

He checked the inside pocket of his jacket, made sure his wallet was in place, then moved along the aisle towards the exit. In the terminal he stood in the Immigration line reserved for non-Europeans. He was a naturalized American. Stuck in this slow-motion throng, he wished he had dual citizenship, because people with European Community passports were streaming through other channels unimpeded. He shuffled in stages towards an official in a glass booth, a rotund individual with no neck and Coke-bottle glasses.

Eddie handed his passport to the official, whose name-tag identified him as Arthur Dudgeon. He checked Eddie's photograph against the real man, then said, 'Somebody wants to talk to you, Mr Mallon,' and he nodded in the direction of a man who was standing, hands in the pockets of a pin-striped suit, twenty yards away.

'Is there a problem?' Eddie asked.

Dudgeon said, 'It's a formality, I'm sure.'

You couldn't argue with passport-control officials. It was a waste of time the world over. These guys dreamed in their sleep of the Ultimate Rubber Stamp, the imprimatur of Total Authority. You possessed that, you had World Domination.

Eddie took his passport, picked up his bag, then walked towards the man in the suit, who shook Eddie's hand firmly; he was somewhere in his thirties and had thin ginger hair and a pleasantly bland face.

'Sorry to inconvenience you, Mr Mallon. I'm Detective-Inspector Scullion, Strathclyde Police. Will you follow me, please? We need just a wee minute of your time. Good flight?'

Eddie said, 'We didn't fall out of the sky or anything drastic.'

Scullion smiled. 'Ha. Indeed indeed.'

Eddie tracked Scullion along a narrow corridor to a room that was little more than a partitioned space with a desk and three chairs and a single metal filing cabinet and a neon strip in the ceiling.

'Sit down if you like,' Scullion said.

Eddie did so.

Two men entered the room. One, big and square-headed and business-like, had a build and complexion that reminded Eddie of cinderblock. He sat behind the desk. His suit was charcoal, his jacket buttoned tight across his midriff. The other man, who stood slouched, wore an unfashionable brown suit with a two-slash back flap, and thick-framed black glasses. He had a pale pink patch over his left eye and short silver hair cut in the fashion of a marine butchered by a half-blind barber. Hard to tell his age. Middle fifties, but he looked older.

'I'm Detective-Superintendent Tay,' the big man said. He shook Eddie's hand firmly and then gestured to the man with the eyepatch. 'This is Detective-Sergeant Perlman.'

Eddie nodded at Perlman who smiled and adjusted his glasses. Eddie wondered about the purpose of the patch under the lens. Perlman had the look of a man whose tailor had expired in the mid-1970s.

'You're here for your father's funeral, I suppose,' Tay said.

Eddie said, 'Your grapevine's working.'

'We like to keep our feelers out,' Tay said. He smiled now, but without enthusiasm. He had a small mouth and tiny teeth. His hands were granite things, enormous, like industrial sculptures. He had the watchful eyes of a prizefighter. 'I'm in charge of your father's murder investigation.'

Interested suddenly, Eddie leaned forward, elbows on knees. 'How far along are you? Have you identified the shooter –'

'So far,' Tay said, 'no, no shooter. All I can tell you is your father was killed by a person unknown using a forty-calibre handgun. He was sitting in the back seat of his car – a 1998 Mazda – when he was shot. We've ruled out robbery. Your father's wallet was in his pocket. He had a wad of money. Eight

48

hundred and twenty pounds, give or take. The man who was his driver, a longtime acquaintance by the name of Matthew Bones, AKA Matty, has vanished. Nobody knows where. He hasn't been seen.'

'Is he a suspect?' Eddie asked.

'He'd been in your father's company for several hours before the murder, and now he's disappeared, so let's just say we'd like to talk to him.' Tay spoke slowly. He appeared to weigh his sentences for possible ambiguities. His pauses were finely calibrated.

Perlman spoke now. His voice was gruff but sympathetic, although his accent was thick and hard for Eddie to follow. 'We're looking for him, Mr Mallon. You may be sure. We're checking all his usual haunts.' *Aw his yewshall hawntz.*

Matty Bones: Eddie Mallon searched his memory. He thought he saw a shadow more than thirty years old, that of a very small man with callused hands – had he encountered Bones in the company of his father a couple of times? But so many men had drifted into his father's orbit, men who drank bottled beer in the sitting room of the house in Onslow Drive and filled the room with laughter and cigarette smoke. Bones could have been one of those men.

Tay said, 'You're a policeman in Manhattan.'

Eddie said yes, he was.

Tay looked at Scullion. 'The Big Apple, Scullion. Kojak and such. I was there once. Didn't like the place. New Yorkers think they live at the centre of the universe. Everything else in the world is crude and unsophisticated. Including police activity. Let me say this. We don't get as much gun-play in this country as you do. So we do our policing a wee bit different here, Mallon.'

'I'm sure you do,' Eddie said. Three cops, he thought. Quite a welcoming committee.

Tay said, 'Some people in your situation – especially in your occupation – might fly into Glasgow gung-ho about finding their father's killer. That kind of stuff makes it hard for me to stay focused. And so I get cranky. Right, Sandy?'

Scullion, Tay's foil, said, 'Very. Worse than cranky.'

Tay said, 'So let's understand each other, shall we?'

'I don't intend to make a nuisance of myself,' Eddie said. 'All I ask is you keep me posted if anything develops.'

Tay said, 'No problem. We'll keep you up to date. A simple courtesy.'

Eddie said thanks, but he wasn't sure how deep the sincerity ran here. This could be the soft-shoe brush-off, the old we'll-call-you routine.

Tay asked, 'When are you leaving?'

'After the funeral.'

'And the funeral's . . . ?'

'Friday,' Eddie said. The subtext here was unspoken, but it wasn't subtle, he thought. Finding Jackie Mallon's killer isn't your concern, Eddie, old chap. It's the business of the Strathclyde Police. No outsiders need apply.

Tay consulted a typewritten paper on the desk. 'You're staying with your sister Joyce in Ingleby Drive, Dennistoun. So if I need you for anything, I know where to find you. Sandy will walk you out.'

Eddie moved to the door. 'I hope you find the killer.'

'I'm confident,' Tay said. 'I'm always confident . . .'

Perlman rubbed his hands briskly. 'Nice to meet you, Eddie. Sorry about your father. Really I am.'

'Thanks.' Eddie nodded at Perlman, then picked up his bag and walked with Scullion back the way they'd come.

Scullion said, 'Tay's an excellent policeman, Mr Mallon.'

'I'm sure.'

'Dealing with the public isn't his forte. He's brusque at times.' Scullion paused, smiled at Eddie in a forlorn way. 'I just wish you had a better reason for visiting our fair city, Mr Mallon.'

'So do I,' Eddie said.

'Anyhow,' Scullion said, spreading his hand in a gesture intended to suggest that the city might be surprisingly boun-teous just the same, 'welcome to Glasgow.'

10

Joyce was waiting for him in the Arrivals lounge.

She'd changed her appearance since he'd seen her last. She'd shed the black clothes and the aura of existentialist gloom in favour of faded old blue jeans, an oversized T-shirt with a camouflage pattern, tan sneakers with yellow-and-brown striped laces. She still wore shades, but the lenses were royal blue and tiny, not big and black. Her hair had been cropped short and dyed blonde. The style gave her oval face an undernourished quality. She threw herself at him energetically, clutching him hard.

'Eddie Eddie, oh Eddie.'

He held her tightly. He had a sense of love, like oxygen flowing to his head; it surprised him how easy it was to love her, because he often imagined absence and distance would eventually erode his feelings, and hers too, but that hadn't come about. And now all at once he was goddam tearful. It was what happened as you got older, he'd noticed. You sniffled more readily at things, choked up at reunions and soft-hearted movie sequences and farewells. One day you'd be a sentimental old fart in an armchair crying into a Kleenex during *It's A Wonderful Life*.

51

'I'm just so damned *glad* you came. Hold me and don't let go, Eddie.'

She felt thin, fragile. He wondered how her life had been lived in the five years since he'd seen her. They were neither of them letter writers. They spoke a couple of times a year by phone, and that was it. In New York he thought about her, missed her – but then, like everyone else, he got immersed in the currents of his own life and the promises he made to himself about calling Joyce more often were pushed to a backburner where they simmered. And that was sad, because the years were rolling inexorably away.

Then he was thinking of how far he'd drifted from Jackie Mallon too, and he wanted to say something to Joyce about him, but he was groping for words. Jackie floated before him, the thick eyebrows and the upright walk that was almost military at times, the cheeky dazzle of the smile and the habit the old man had of cupping a cigarette as he smoked, as if he were afraid of a wind blowing it away. It might have been a mannerism born in the drab post-war years, when cigarettes were precious.

I didn't have enough time with him, Eddie thought, I invented him from memories. And he was suddenly consumed by anger. Somebody had killed the old man, and that fucker, whoever he was, would goddam have to pay in the end –

He caught himself in mid-rage, breathed a couple of times deeply, sought calm. Don't go off the deep end. The police are looking for the killer. They'll find him.

Joyce said, 'I'm all cried out. Talk to me about the living, Eddie. Talk to me about Claire. Tell me about my gorgeous wee nephew.'

He spoke about Claire. He brought her up to date on Mark and the girls who chased him. She linked her arm in his and they walked across the terminal, which was new and shiny, a gilded palace that corresponded to nothing in his memory of how it had been years ago, a drab matchbox where you half-expected the only craft permitted to land would be 1940s Spitfires in need of fuel to continue the war against Jerry.

They went outside. It was dark and the night air warm, almost tropical. 'It feels like Miami,' Eddie said. Any subject but their father.

'We're having an extremely rare heatwave, Eddie. Enjoy it while it lasts. It'll probably be pishing rain again in a day or so. My car's over there,' and she pointed to her left.

The conversational transition from murder to the weather; it was wonderful comfort. How would people live their lives without a vocabulary of weather?

He said, 'You look . . . different. You were all dark last time. Your clothes, hair . . .'

'Oh, that was my black self. My tragic period. The troubled divorcee, et cetera. You think this haircut's too flashy for a woman almost forty? Too *gallus*?'

'Gallus?'

'Have you forgotten your Glasgow patois, Eddie?'

'Gallus,' he said, remembering. 'Wait. Brazen, swaggering.'

'See, it's like riding a bike. You never forget.' She led him across the car park. 'I love you, Eddie. We're too careless, the way we let ourselves drift.'

'I know, I know.'

She gripped his hand. He had a strange disorienting moment, as if he'd come to a city where he'd never been, and was talking with a woman he'd never met in his life – and then this web of illusion blew away and he was himself again, except for the fact that he had no idea of time, neither day nor date. Was it still Wednesday? Was it only this morning at 3.30 US Eastern time when Joyce had phoned him in New York? Time zones, loss of hours. He tried to calculate, but gave up.

Joyce unlocked a car, an old dark blue Mini. 'Just stick your bag in the back.'

He got inside. The space was small and his knees were jammed against the glove compartment. Joyce drove out of the lot to the freeway. *Motorway*: he corrected himself. He looked at the blue signs pointing to Glasgow. He couldn't recollect a motorway linking the airport to the city. It was new. So were

53

the bright tidy suburbs he saw from the window. And light. So much light.

'When did they do all this?' he asked, nodding at the housing estates.

'Who knows? Glasgow's a constant work in progress, Eddie.'

What had he expected? Everything the same, preserved in aspic? He thought: I don't recognize the city of my birth.

'We're right up there these days with the high-flyers,' Joyce said. 'Milan. Paris. We're dead cosmopolitan now, Eddie. No more soggy tomato sandwiches washed down with cups of nasty instant Nescafé. We've crossed into the promised land of croissants and cappuccino. We're Europe, Eddie.'

'And you – you're still educating the young?' he asked.

'What else would I do?'

Joyce, like Flora had done, taught school; she drummed Romantic poetry into the heads of fourteen-year-olds in a school in the Southside of the city. Once, Eddie remembered, she'd announced that the work was too exhausting for a mere human. These kids to whom she force-fed Wordsworth had enough problems understanding the lyrics of fucking *Boyzone*, for Christ's sake.

She drove in silence for a couple of miles.

'Did you know I identified him, Eddie? At least what was left of him. Did I tell you that?'

'I didn't know. I'm sorry.'

'Who needs more raw material for bad dreams? I've got some already.' She flicked her cigarette into the night and it was whipped away in a quick riot of sparks.

Eddie Mallon had seen the violent dead too many times, the faces of clerks shotgunned in robberies, the heads of people blown off for chump-change in filling stations. He touched his sister's hand and wondered why anyone had asked *her*, the stricken daughter, to ID the corpse. They might have been tactful and asked one of Jackie's friends, somebody hardened by the streets. But no. In their insensitivity or haste they'd turned to the daughter.

Is this your dad? Is this mess you see before you Jackie Mallon?

'Did the cops tell you anything?' he asked. 'Do you know if they have any ideas about who killed him, or why?'

'I just remember they asked me to look at the body. There were so many people drifting in and out, suits, uniforms, I was hysterical in a kind of slow-motion way. I remember a guy drove me home after I'd been to the morgue. He was nice. He asked me if I wanted to go for a drink with him any time I felt the need to talk.'

'He's a master of timing, this character,' Eddie said. 'What did you tell him?'

'I said call me in a month or two. But secretly I was flattered because he was drop-dead in a kind of little-boy-lost way. Any other time I would have said yes without thinking.'

'The last time you said yes without thinking you ended up marrying the guy,' Eddie said.

'Just as I'd forgotten all about Harry Haskell, you go and remind me. I wish you could do something about that American accent.'

'Am I supposed to sound like a guy who's been selling newspapers outside −' and he fumbled for a location '− St Enoch Station all his life?'

'Sorry to tell you this, Eddie, but there's no such station any more. Shut down long ago . . .'

A streetlight illuminated her face a second. She lit another cigarette. She looked, he thought, very young. A person too young to have her kind of history − a family hewn apart, a marriage that had been disastrous from the beginning, a murdered father.

'You wanna hear my American?' she asked.

Eddie Mallon said, 'I have a choice?'

'Hey, it's your loss, buddy.'

'That's bad, Joyce.'

'Bad as in good?'

'As in terrible.'

55

They'd slipped into banter, he thought. Steer clear of the real subject. Digress. He looked at his watch but the damn thing had stopped. 'I need to call Claire. She worries when I have to fly.'

'Phone from my place,' Joyce said. 'I just remembered the man's name.'

'What man?'

'The one that drove me home from the morgue. McWhinnie. Charles, I think. Detective-Sergeant. Posh Glasgow accent. He said yes instead of aye and didn't drop his gs at the end of -ing words. Classy, eh?'

'Very,' he said.

The car left the motorway and headed into the east end of the city, where Eddie had been born and raised; suddenly streets were darker, tenements overbearing and the occasional street-lamp was missing, presumed vandalized. Stores were shuttered, bars closed. The only place open was a fish and chip shop. Eddie saw a fat man behind the counter toss a chip in the air and, like a trained sea-lion, catch it in his mouth on the way down.

Joyce turned the car into Onslow Drive and parked outside the house that had been the Mallon family home in another lifetime.

Eddie said, 'I thought we were going to your flat. Why are we stopping here?'

'I want to see how Senga's bearing up,' Joyce said, and stepped out of the car.

Eddie didn't move.

He gazed at the garden, which was a tangle, a jungle of shrub. He stared at the windows, half-expecting to see a curtain drawn back and his mother's face appear there, or the shadow of his father pass in front of a pane. He imagined Flora calling, *You finished your homework, Eddie*? Or the sound of Joyce practising scales she could never master on the old upright piano in the living room. Doh ray me fah *clunk*, the lid slammed down in frustration and Joyce running upstairs to her room and Jackie shouting after her, *You won't learn to play the bloody piano by hiding in your room, young lady.*

I don't want to get out of the car and go inside the house, he thought. Jackie's *Daily Express* would be lying on the kitchen table and Flora might be peeling onions under running water and maybe some of Jackie's friends would be in the sitting room, laughing at a joke or talking in a low masculine rumble Eddie found impenetrable. And Flora would say, *If you're looking for your dad he's in the front room with his business associates, so-called.*

The dead walk this house.

Ghosts. Including the spectre of young Eddie Mallon.

'Come on, Eddie,' Joyce called. 'You'll like her. Don't look so worried.'

It wasn't the prospect of Senga that troubled him here. He stepped from the car. Joyce was inserting a key into the front-door lock and turning it; then she ushered him ahead of her into the hallway where the first thing he saw was the coat-rack where Flora had always told him to hang his blazer or raincoat after school. He looked down and yes, *Jesus*, it was *still* there after all these years – the same goddam doormat, he was sure of it, worn to nothing except a few flat bristles. *Wipe your feet, Eddie. That mat's not there for decoration, you know.* This house didn't exist in the present tense.

Joyce called out: 'Senga? Are you there?'

Music was playing very quietly from somewhere. The Eagles: 'Lying Eyes'.

11

Matty Bones, who'd finished his whisky a while ago, shut his left eye and surveyed Haggs through the bleary slit of his right. 'Did you bring me drink? Eh? I need more booze.'

Haggs turned away from Matty Bones and looked at the third man in the room. His name was John Twiddie. He wore a black leather jacket and gloves, and had a ring through one nostril and a wad of pus where metal punctured skin.

A plook, Matty Bones thought. That was the word for that kind of inflammation. A big fucking golden *plook*. If it grew any more it would be like an extra nose. This guy looked familiar but Matty Bones was lost in a boozy mist and all links with the world were tenuous.

There was also a young woman Bones had never seen before. Face like a dented medieval battle helmet, scar on her neck, tattooed knuckles, black hair combed upright and held in position by a complex arrangement of pins and metal clasps. She also wore gloves.

'You there,' Bones said.

'You pointing at me, jim?' she asked. A snarl.

'Aye, you. You bring me any drink, dear?'

58

'Don't point your bloody finger at me. I hate when anybody does that.'

'Oh, you're a toughie, eh? A hard case.' Bones laughed.

The girl turned one hand into a heavy fist and punched Bones in the face and he slipped and clattered into a chair before he fell. Anaesthetized by booze, he felt nothing. He lay on the floor and continued to laugh. He'd fallen from too many nags and no-hopers in his day to let this stumble worry him. He was known around the Scottish flat-racing circuit, Hamilton, Lanark, Ayr, as resilient. You fall off, you get back in the saddle.

Roddy Haggs said, 'Christ's sake, put a clamp on that temper, Rita.'

'Well, I'm sorry, but this fucking wee dwarf annoys me,' she said. She had an expression of permanent rage about her. Whenever Haggs was obliged to look at her, which wasn't often, he thought of somebody who dragged around her own private tempest in which all manner of wild emotions were tossed willy-nilly.

'Give me the booze, Twiddie,' Haggs said.

John Twiddie, who had a sorry thin moustache such as an adolescent might achieve, took a half-bottle of scotch from a pocket of his jacket. He passed it to Haggs, who opened it, then leaned down over Matty Bones and let some of the alcohol slide into the old jockey's open mouth. Haggs had a good view of the interior of Matty's gob; a dentist's nightmare. You could send down a hundred technicians with the latest in laser dento-technology and they'd pronounce this mouth condemned.

Matty Bones said, 'Aye, great, keep it coming, keep the stuff coming, Haggs.'

Haggs quit pouring. 'A question or two first, Matty.'

'Ask away. I'm your man.'

'Jackie Mallon,' Haggs said.

'Jackie and me. Best mates. Peas in a pod. You know that.' Bones felt a momentary sobriety. A shudder. He didn't like the world in clarity. Something bad had happened to Jackie.

Twiddie said, 'Fuck the talk. Just let me stick the boot in, Roddy.'

Haggs frowned at John Twiddie and his girlfriend Rita. They had hair-trigger brains. They were always on the edge, pissed off by the smallest inconvenience. Pierced like tailor's dummies, they were also embroidered with tattoos of flowers and guns. Roddy Haggs didn't want to be in the same room as them, but in this world you had to have your enforcers. And since Twiddie liked to work with Rita, they came as a pair. Lovebirds. Ugly ones.

Haggs grabbed the old guy's hand and squeezed hard. 'Listen, Matty. This is important. What was Jackie Mallon up to? What was he planning?'

'Up to? Oh, this and that. You could never keep track of Jackie. Too fast on his feet.' Matty reached for the bottle and Haggs drew it away with his free hand.

'Matty, you were his driver. You took him everywhere.'

'Pubs, here and there.'

'No, not just pubs, Matty. Other places you took him. Who did he see?'

'Now how the hell would I know, Haggs?'

Haggs crushed the little man's hand as if it were the dried carcass of a squab. Matty Bones moaned. The feel of bone crunching penetrated the armour of booze. He stared at his broken hand. It dangled strangely. Red and green lights jitter-bugged in his vision.

'Where did you take him and who did he see?' Haggs asked.

Bones had tears in his eyes. He shoved the broken hand into his mouth, thinking saliva might help ease the agony.

Haggs made a signal to Twiddie, who launched his metal-tipped boot into the little man's scrotum. Matty Bones went at once into a fetal position and his face lost all colour. Aw God, this is a bad fall, he thought. Right bad. He heard his horse gallop away. Hoofbeats on frosty earth. He was paralysed. Red Cross would be coming any minute. The morphine wagon.

He wanted scotch. He nodded his head at the bottle.

Haggs held the whisky high over Matty's face. 'Make it easy on yourself, Matty. Tell us what you know and you get to keep the booze, and we leave you in peace.'

Flat on his back, Matty Bones stared up at the ceiling. He had an image of Jackie Mallon stepping inside Blackfriars pub. It was clear as a photograph. Bones didn't like the picture at all. It brought stuff back he didn't want to look at. 'You said you wouldn't hurt him.'

'I say a lot of things,' Haggs remarked. 'Most of it unbelievable.'

'You fucking *snuffed* him. You said you just wanted to ask a couple of questions and you wouldn't hurt him but you bastards shot him.' Bones wept softly; a drunk man's black guilt. I loved you, Jackie. Really loved you. Honest to God I did.

Haggs said, 'Let's not sob like some wee lassie whose ballerina dreams have just been binned because she's got knock-knees. Let's keep on track here. Who did he see?'

'I drove him to Hyndland a couple of times to meet Billy McQueen.' Bones drew his cuff across his eyes.

'Wan-Fittit McQueen?'

'Right, the Stump –'

'And what were they scheming, Matty?'

'I sat outside in the car. I never joined in. I wasn't asked. Wait in the car, Bones. Take a walk, Bones. Here's a tenner for a fish supper and a pint, Bones.' Bones's voice was wheezy. His broken hand felt five times its usual size and still swelling.

Haggs asked again. 'What were they scheming, Matty?'

'Swear to God, I don't know. Jackie didn't tell me anything.'

'Right. Try this one. Where did Mallon go when he left Glasgow last week?'

'I never knew he left Glasgow,' Bones said.

'I'm to believe that?'

'It's the truth,' Bones said.

'His woman took him to the train station last Wednesday morning.'

'I never knew,' Bones said.

Haggs shrugged and looked at Twiddie. 'Do it,' he said. 'Just do it.'

Twiddie and the girl dragged Matty Bones across the floor and out of the flat and hauled him down the stairs by his ankles, and his head struck the edge of each stone step in a synchronized way. He was sobbing and pleading, *I've telt ye everything I know, I swear on my mother's grave, I swear to God,* but nobody was listening, God especially.

He was yanked out of the tenement and across the pavement and dumped in the back of an ancient Transit van. Haggs got behind the wheel and drove. Twiddie and his girl stayed in the back with Bones. They took turns kicking him, ribs, mouth, belly, skull, it didn't matter, anywhere they could land their boots. Bones curled up like a dying armadillo, and after a while he just stopped feeling anything. He drifted into a dreamy place where faces shimmered, visions of people he might or might not have known.

Jackie was there, hands folded behind his back like a stern schoolmaster. Let this be a lesson, Matthew Bones. Don't betray your pals, wee man.

Haggs drove along Edmiston Drive, heading west past the redbrick monolith of the Glasgow Rangers football stadium. For a couple of miles he listened to Bones whimper. In the back, the girl was smoking a cigarette. Haggs could hear her suck smoke deep into her lungs. Twiddie lit a cigarette too. Thugs on a tobacco break.

'He's a tough wee cunt,' Twiddie said.

'He's had enough,' Haggs said.

'I'm no finished with him.' Twiddie blew a long stream of smoke.

'Enough's enough,' Haggs said.

'He's still breathing,' the girl said.

'I want him out of the damn van,' Haggs said. 'I want the bugger dumped.'

He drove west until he came to a dim-lit street of houses which gave way after a half-mile or so to a path dense with trees and

62

weeds. Then he parked. A stretch of water called the White Cart flowed sluggishly nearby.

'Don't forget the shovel,' Haggs said.

Twiddie grabbed the tool, opened the door and pushed Bones out, then he jumped down and hauled the little man by the collar and dragged him between trees and through bushes and nettles to a slope in the land. Twiddie set the spade aside and took a spool of piano wire from the pocket of his jeans. He unravelled a length of it and wrapped it round Matty Bones's neck and pulled.

I'll fuckin' finish you here an' now, Bones, Twiddie thought.

Bones raised a hand to the place where the wire touched flesh. His eyes popped and he gasped, *No please no let me go, I'll say nothing to a single soul about what I know,* and Twiddie said, *You don't know fuck all anyway, you ignorant old git.* Blood fountained high from Matty Bones's throat when thin razor-edged steel sliced vein. Then Twiddie grunted and tugged harder, his knuckles sharp and almost luminously white, until Bones's head rolled to one side and blood was everywhere, over Bones's face and neck and clothing, as well as Twiddie's hands and shirt and face.

Bones slid over on his side and he thought he saw his dead ma at the finishing line at Ayr races in July 1967 when he brought home a high-strung no-hope gelding called Isaac's Lad at 33-1, and his ma waved, one pale hand raised in the air, and rain was falling on her flowery umbrella and the grass smelled good. He wanted to wave back but he had the reins in his hands, and then somehow they just slipped from his fingers and the horse quit and that was it, the book closed, and Twiddie rolled the body down the earthen incline to the place where, that morning, he'd dug a hole four feet deep.

One I prepared earlier, he thought.

With his foot he nudged Bones into the damp shallow pit, and the dead man's face was visible for a while. Then Twiddie took the shovel and heaped soft earth into the hole and after a few minutes he couldn't see Bones any more.

Breathing hard, he hurried back to the van. He climbed inside, and the girl pulled the door shut.

Haggs drove away quickly. He told himself: I don't need to be here, doing shite like this. I could pay somebody else to drive Weird Twiddie and the Deranged Bimbo back and forth. So why didn't he stick a driver on the payroll? Why was *he* behind the wheel of this clapped-out old van, running risks, instead of sipping aged brandy in the sunken living room of that expensive house in Rouken Glen with the marble Jacuzzi and the gold taps and the handprinted wallpaper and the murals?

Be honest, Roddy. You like the buzz of this, the action, how your blood races. You like the sport of it, rough company, dark alleys, doling out some pain now and then. Cracking the old jockey's frail hand. *Kerrunch.*

You like the wild side.

Girls. Gambling. Yachts. Deals. Making more and more dosh – all that was banal. But this, driving the night streets with murderous scum as your passengers – you can't go inside a fancy showroom and buy this. You can't get anything like this kick from the rat-a-tat-tat click of a steel ball rolling round a roulette wheel. You can't get it sitting in the Rogano or the Corinthian, sipping a Campari and smoking a fat Cuban. And you can't even get it between the velveteen thighs of some long-legged call-girl with big cow eyes who licks your ear and whispers, *Come for me, Roddy, oh oh shoot your wad, big man.*

This is the life.

You couldn't live in a world like Caskie's, say, a horrible wee cardboard box of law and order. Regulations and requisitions, screw all that shite. Hypocrite.

Haggs thought that Jackie Mallon, for all his cunning, his sly secrecy and stubborn ways, had been a more admirable human being than Caskie could ever be. In fact, in his own off-centre manner, he'd liked Jackie Mallon, and the decision to put him away hadn't been easy. But a time came when you had to make the move, establish your supremacy, plant your own flag on Mallon's moon.

And that's what he'd done. Or tried to.

What had he learned about Jackie's scheme?

Sweet Fanny Adams.

He thought of bloodstains inside the vehicle. 'We'll need to torch this bloody van, Twiddie.'

'I want to be the one to do it,' the girl said.

'Aye, Rita likes fires,' Twiddie said.

Haggs said, 'Why am I not astounded.'

Twiddie said, 'She likes playing with matches.'

'I was a Girl Guide once,' Rita said. 'Building bonfires was the only thing I liked. All the rest was crap. Crap games and stupid badges. Dykes running about giving you orders.'

'Make sure you do the job right.' Haggs glanced in the rearview mirror. Twiddie and his girl were kissing in the back. Twiddie covered in blood. *Kissing* his girl. Her T-shirt was up round her neck. Twiddie had one wet red glove on a bare tit. Haggs stared straight ahead. Note to self, he thought: love brings some very weird customers together.

12

Senga Craig, early fifties, a big tornado of a woman in a bright gold blouse and black slacks, somebody just a little larger than life, loomed in the open doorway to the sitting room. Her red hair was piled up and a long gold pin stuck through it. Her eyelids were swollen from crying. She seized and hugged Joyce and said, 'My darling, oh my wee darling,' and then she looked past Joyce at Eddie. Before he could speak, Eddie was clutched in an embrace so strong he felt almost faint, crushed like a man trapped in the forward surge of a mob. He smelled Senga's pungent scent and gin on her breath. Her arms were bare. She emitted raw energy; this wasn't a woman who'd waste away in grief for ever. She'd fight it and in time she'd win.

'Eddie,' she said. 'Oh, jeez, you're the spitting image. Isn't he the spitting image, Joyce? Oh my God.' She put a hand over her open mouth.

'There's a resemblance all right,' Joyce said.

'You're Jackie Mallon's boy,' Senga said. 'God in heaven, I can't get over it.'

She dragged Eddie inside the room. The music was issuing from a CD player, the Eagles singing 'Cheating Side of Town'.

Senga said, 'Jackie's favourite group, I was listening to them because I'm a silly old cow and I've had one gin too many and gin does funny things to me . . .' She somehow managed to get both Joyce and Eddie into a single hug now; three bodies pressed together, three heads in contact. 'If I can't have Jackie, then I can have his kids. Right? Right? I deserve some kind of consolation, don't I? I loved that man. Loved him.'

Eddie was vaguely conscious of the room beyond the tight limits of Senga's embrace. Years ago the walls had been covered with red and purple floral wallpaper. Now they were painted a flat grey colour and hung with black and white photographs of Scottish scenery in silver frames. The furniture was black leather. The effect was a little austere; Eddie couldn't imagine that Jackie, who liked clutter and wasn't the kind of man who'd give a damn about decor, had any say in decorating this room.

He tried to disentangle himself from Senga, but she was persistent and strong, and seized him harder, holding him in such a way that his cheek adhered to hers, which was fleshy and damp. Joyce, he noticed, had escaped from the communal squeeze, and was lighting a cigarette as she moved to a chair in the corner where a man with a white beard sat.

Eddie hadn't noticed the bearded man before. Joyce gripped the guy's hand, fingers locking for a moment. Then she embraced him, and he closed his eyes as she leaned down to press her face to his shoulder.

'Let me get you a drink, Eddie,' Senga said.

'A beer would be fine,' Eddie said. He observed a small tattoo on Senga's upper left arm, a half-inch below the oval mark of a smallpox inoculation. He thought the tattoo looked familiar, but it eluded him.

'I'm not sure we have beer.' Senga took a Kleenex from a pocket of her slacks and dabbed her damp eyes with it. 'I'm not sure what we've got in the kitchen . . .'

Joyce said, 'Senga, I'll look in the fridge; you stay where you are,' and she left the room.

67

The man with the white beard rose. He wore a blue double-breasted suit and a black tie. He shook Eddie's hand and said, 'Chris Caskie. We met before you went to America. You couldn't possibly remember me. You were about thirteen years of age and we saw each other two or three times at most.'

'You look vaguely familiar,' Eddie said. He wasn't sure if that was a truth or something he imagined. He felt weary, and sad. This house burdened him. Echoes of family and old songs.

'It would have to be a very *vague* memory,' Caskie said. He sipped from a glass of sherry. 'I was a friend of your mother.'

'She never mentioned you by name, as far as I can recall,' Eddie said.

Senga said, 'Chris has been close to this family for years. Haven't you, Chris?'

'Close enough.'

'Joyce has always been his favourite,' Senga said. 'After Flora, of course.'

'Senga, you know I don't play favourites,' Caskie said. 'I corresponded with Flora now and then over the years.' He turned to face Eddie again. 'How is she taking . . .'

'I'm not sure,' Eddie said. 'Shocked. But we're talking about thirty years of separation, so it's the kind of shock with a long slow fuse. It might burn out tamely.'

Senga filled a glass with gin and looked at Eddie, then linked an arm through his. 'I sympathize with Flora, I do, I really do, it's just, well, I'm trying not to think, just hold myself together, it's like I've misplaced something except I don't know what the hell it is, but if I keep looking I'll remember . . . I'm sorry, sorry, I'm just talking a pile of gibberish. Forgive me, the both of you. But I keep expecting Jackie'll walk through the door at any moment. Hello, my great big beautiful doll, he'll say. And I'll say, Tell me you love me, Mallon . . . Oh my heart's wrecked.'

She sniffed, tried to force out a little smile of fortitude, but it didn't work. She looked, Eddie Mallon thought, out of focus, a badly taken snapshot. The stark grief of this stranger his father

68

had apparently loved – it was odd to him, it lacked a framework into which he could place it. She and Jackie had built a life together. He needed to absorb this fact, and accept it.

Caskie said, 'You've lost somebody you loved, Senga. You're entitled to your sorrow.' He passed her a handkerchief, a neat square of folded linen he took from his jacket.

Senga blew her nose, then walked across the room. She sat down, balanced her gin on the arm of the sofa. She'd raised her spirits enough to welcome Eddie, she'd worked at seeming sober, but the effort had been too much, and now she'd lapsed into a place of silence and melancholy.

Alone in the corner of the room with Caskie, Eddie asked, 'How well did you know my father?'

'I tried to arrest him a couple of times,' Caskie said, and smiled.

'Arrest? You're a cop?'

'Just like you,' Caskie said. He looked a little amused. 'The truth is, I used to have a young man's crush on your mother – all totally innocent, I assure you – and when she left for America she asked me to keep an eye on your sister. You obviously didn't know about this, did you?'

Eddie Mallon shook his head. He was sure Flora had never mentioned Caskie. Or it had escaped him. It wasn't important. He could easily imagine somebody having what Caskie quaintly called a 'crush' on Flora, because once upon a time she'd been beautiful in a way men might find both haughty and challenging, as if her sexuality were a minefield you crossed at your own peril; and somewhere along the graph of time the colour had gone out of her rich black hair and she'd begun the decline into the little white-haired lady who spent most of her life stooped over potted plants.

Caskie said, 'I'd phone Joyce every three or four months. Sometimes we'd meet for a drink when she'd reached the legal age,' and he smiled here, raising one eyebrow as if the word 'legal' had a meaning only cops understood. 'Sometimes we had dinner. How are you doing, what's happening, anything new –

69

that kind of thing. I'd run into your father every so often too . . . but I could never pin a damn thing on him. Either he lived a life of total innocence or he was the most clever man I ever met.'

'Which do you think it was?' Eddie asked. He was remembering what his mother had said: *He's stone cold dead, but he's still got you thinking good things about him.* Yes, yes, I want to believe that. Apart from one godawful error in his life, he was basically a decent guy. What was so wrong in needing a little faith?

Caskie shrugged. 'I believe he kept some bad company. And maybe his business ledgers wouldn't have survived microscopic scrutiny.' He drank a little sherry. 'I don't think this is the time or the place, Eddie, to dissect your father's life.'

'I'd like to know more about him —'

'That's perfectly natural, but I'm not sure I'm the best person to help.'

Joyce came back into the room on the tail-end of the conversation. She handed Eddie a chilled bottle of Amstel and asked, 'Help with what, Chris?'

'Your brother's curiosity,' Caskie said. He moved back towards the sofa and sat down beside Senga, whose eyes were shut.

Joyce said, 'What are you curious about, bro?'

Eddie swallowed some beer. 'Just Jackie in general.'

'I knew him better than anyone, except maybe Senga. You have questions, Eddie, ask me.'

Before Eddie could respond, Senga got up from the sofa and approached him. For a tall big-chested woman she looked fragile; she weaved from side to side as she walked, like somebody trying to cross a tricky bridge in a fun-house. Caskie moved behind her in an attentive way, to catch her if she lost her balance.

'This has all the feel of a bloody dreeeeary wake,' Senga said. 'Och, Jackie would've hated this. He'd already be looking for the side door so he could sneak away. When I die, he used to say, play some happy music and drink yourself into a stupor. So I'm changing this . . .' She went to the stack of CDs — two steps to the side, one forward — and she found what she was looking for. She ejected the Eagles.

70

Suddenly the room was filled with Scottish dance music of a kind Eddie hadn't heard since they'd all lived in Granny Mallon's flat in Bathgate Street. Accordion and fiddle, diddley-dum-dee, jigs and reels, foot-tapping stuff.

Senga hooked an arm through his and said, 'Dance, Eddie. Come on. Dance the sadness away.'

'*Dance?*'

'You heard me, laddie. Dance!'

It was weird. Inappropriate. Maybe it was the deranged way grief made some people act. Eddie found himself spun in a reckless circle by the big-boned woman whose red hair had fallen down the sides of her face. Round and round. She whooped. The ceiling rotated. Eddie felt dizzy. Senga threw her head back and stamped her feet as she moved and the floor shook. This was her house, her stage, her performance. She dominated all the space around her.

'Dance dance *dance*, Eddie,' she roared, and tears slid down her face, and she placed an arm above her head in the curved manner of a Highland Fling, and held it aloft while she swung Eddie ever faster. She was strong, fired with the crude energy of grief. He saw the black-and-white photographs rush past like scenery glimpsed from the window of a high-speed train. He had a fixed smile on his face, but he wanted to stop this dance, put an end to this surreal interlude.

Senga said, 'Jackie loved to dance, he was so bloody light on his feet.' It was what Flora had also said about Jackie. He must have foxtrotted and waltzed into their hearts.

And then Senga was suddenly out of breath and had to quit, and she slumped into an armchair, head back, mouth open. Eddie looked at the long red hair and the gold blouse and the lipstick that had faded and the tears that continued to roll down towards the corners of her mouth. 'What I want to know is why some fucking bastard had to shoot him, for Christ's sake? Why, Eddie? Why? Why did they have to take his life?'

Caskie was quick to comfort her.

Joyce stood at Eddie's side. 'You're tired,' she whispered.

71

He shrugged and nodded towards Senga. 'I'm more worried about her.'

'I'll make sure she doesn't take any sleepers on top of what she's been drinking. I'll help her up to bed, then we'll leave.'

Joyce killed the music, and whispered in Senga's ear. Senga rose from the chair, leaning on Joyce's arm, and the two women walked together across the room.

At the door Senga looked at Caskie, then at Eddie.

'Joyce says I have to sleep, gentlemen. I have to drift away . . . Land of Nod for me.'

'Joyce is right,' Caskie said.

Senga said, 'Give me a kiss, Eddie.'

Eddie Mallon took a step forward and pressed his lips against Senga's cheek. She gazed into his eyes, not quite meeting them because drink had skewed her line of vision. 'We'll talk soon, you and I. We've got some catching up to do. Goodnight.' She blew a sad little kiss. 'The pair of you.'

The door closed.

'I think it's time for me to push off,' Caskie said.

Eddie said, 'He was shot in his car.'

'Yes.'

'And no witnesses.'

'Nobody's come forward,' Caskie said. 'But this isn't my case, Eddie. I'm not up to speed on it. If you want to know more about the investigation, Superintendent Tay's the man to ask.'

'I met him at the airport. He gives the impression he might not like questions.' Eddie gazed at Caskie's small white beard. It was tidy, well clipped. His eyebrows were perfect, no stray hairs. He had an easy smile. He was maybe fifty-four, -five, and in good shape.

'I'm sure he'll keep you posted if anything happens,' Caskie said. 'He's sympathetic. Don't let the veneer put you off.'

Eddie went on, his voice rising a little. He heard words echo in his head like gunshots in a tunnel. 'Tay told me Jackie hadn't been robbed. His wallet hadn't been taken and he had money in his possession. But who knows what else he might have had

72

in the car? Something in the glove compartment, say. Or in the trunk. Something Tay didn't know about. So how can he rule out robbery? And then there's the secondary mystery of the missing driver, Bones.'

'He'll show up, I'm sure. Probably he's scared and imagines he's going to be implicated, so he's lying low, who knows?' Caskie rolled his glass of sherry between the palms of his hands, then set it down unfinished. He checked his wristwatch. 'I'm tired. It's been a long one.'

Eddie wanted to quit talking, but he couldn't. It was like jogging and not wanting to stop even if you were breathless, because the adrenalin rush was addictive. 'Either Jackie was shot during an act of robbery, or he was killed for other reasons we don't know about. If I was running this investigation and it turned out nothing *obvious* was stolen from him, then I'd dig deeper and ask myself what the hell he'd done that made somebody want to kill –'

'But you're not running the investigation, Eddie,' Caskie said.

Eddie stopped, subsided, leaned against the wall. The hard truth of Caskie's statement silenced him. He'd been flying, buzzing in on questions that weren't his to ask. What the hell am I doing exactly? I've come all this way to bury my dad; his murder isn't my business. Whoever had fired a bullet into Jackie Mallon's face isn't my concern. Tay and his team were on the job. Justice would get done, but not by you. Take it easy, for Christ's sake. Slow down. But it was goddam hard to take the heat out of himself. *This ain't Manhattan, Eddie.* Remember that.

He said, 'I was getting carried away.'

Caskie said, 'It's understandable.'

Joyce came back into the room. 'She's out cold. I think we'll go, Eddie. If she needs me later, she can phone me. I don't think she'll wake for hours.'

All three left the sitting room and stood for a moment in the hallway at the foot of the stairs; the awkward etiquette of leave-taking. Who goes first? Who says what?

Caskie reached inside the breast pocket of his jacket and took out a business card. He handed it to Eddie. 'Here. If you need to get in touch while you're in Glasgow . . . It's been nice to see you again.'

'The same for me,' Eddie said. He tucked the card in a hip pocket of his jeans.

Caskie embraced Joyce. 'Call me if you need me.'

'I will, Chris.'

'Help with the funeral arrangements, anything at all . . .' Caskie raised a hand almost imperceptibly, and then he was gone, closing the front door with hardly a sound. Caskie had an undertaker's diplomacy, Eddie thought, listening to the quiet click of the latch. His body vibrated curiously to the aftermath of the spinning dance Senga had forced him through.

The dance of death.

He remembered he hadn't phoned Claire yet. He gazed up the stairway to the lamp lit on the landing. He touched the polished wood of the banister. He must have slid down that a thousand times when he thought Flora wasn't looking. He had a faded memory of Jackie coming down the stairs towards him, bright red braces and a white shirt with the collar open.

Jackie winked at him and said, *One day we'll hire a boat at Balloch and go fishing.*

That day had never come.

Joyce said, 'I don't suppose you want a quick tour of the old homestead, do you, Eddie?'

The prospect depressed him. 'But thanks for the offer,' he said.

'Another time.'

13

They drove the quarter of a mile from Onslow Drive to Joyce's place, a one-bedroom second-floor flat in a dark red sandstone tenement. Eddie took his bag from the car and followed his sister up the stone stairs.

'You can phone Claire from the living room,' Joyce said. 'I need a nightcap. You?'

'Maybe a soft drink,' Eddie said.

'Irn-Bru?'

'Irn-Bru, Jesus, I haven't had that in a lifetime,' Eddie said.

'You'll be happy to know it tastes the same as it always did. Dyed sugary water with loadsa bubbles.' She went into the kitchen.

Eddie looked at the bookshelves in the living room. They were stacked with paperbacks, many of them old orange-covered Penguins. Absently, he scanned the titles as he reached for the phone. Hugh MacDiarmid. Tom Leonard. A Scottish selection among European classics. *Kidnapped* beside *The Brothers Karamazov*. *Ivanhoe* leaning against *The Castle*. Joyce had always been buried in a book as kid. Granny Mallon, a sharp-eyed little woman with short silver hair and bulbous arthritic hands, used

75

to say, *Get her out in the fresh air with a skipping rope before she goes blind.*

Eddie picked up the phone, then realized he didn't know the dialling code for the USA. He decided he'd call collect – but what was the number for the international operator? He looked for a phone book among the general clutter of the room, magazines, ashtrays, empty glasses. Joyce's private chaos. The prints on the walls were arranged in no specific pattern. Lithographs and sketches of famous writers, musicians, prints that publicized gallery openings or museum events, a few San Francisco Filmore examples, Bob Dylan, Hendrix. There was also an assortment of half a dozen busts in classical style, faces carved out of old stone, one missing a nose, another an ear: they looked like Greek philosophers pondering facial surgery.

Joyce came into the room carrying two glasses. 'I hope you appreciate I tidied this place up for you,' she said.

'I'm grateful,' Eddie said. He indicated the busts. 'Quite a gallery.'

'I found them in Dad's warehouse over the years.'

She handed him a long glass filled with a fizzy red liquid. He sipped it; exactly as he remembered. So sweet he imagined sugar armies scaling the enamel battlements of his teeth.

'How do I get the operator?' he asked. 'I want to make a collect call to Claire.'

She told him, he dialled, got through to Queens in a matter of moments. Claire sounded close at hand, a voice in the next room. They talked inconsequentially of the flight, then Claire wanted to know how Joyce was. Eddie glanced at his sister and thought she looked exhausted.

'Hard to say,' he remarked.

'You can't talk right now,' Claire said.

'You got it.'

'You met Senga yet?'

'I did.'

'And?'

'She's . . . I guess she's what I expected.'

76

'You sound tired. Call me tomorrow.'

'I will. Love you.'

Claire said the same thing, then Eddie hung up. Cutting the connection caused him a little jolt of sadness: *I still love my wife after all this time.* He guessed that seventy-five per cent of his colleagues, maybe more, were divorced, separated or serially unfaithful. He couldn't imagine another woman in his bed.

Joyce closed her book, picked up her wine. 'Claire's okay?' she asked.

'Fine.' Eddie nodded. 'I like this room.'

'I'm glad, because you'll be sleeping in it. The sofa you're sitting on opens into a bed. It's comfortable.'

Eddie took a swallow of Irn-Bru. 'Tell me about Chris Caskie. I didn't know about his existence until tonight.'

'I suppose his name just didn't crop up,' Joyce said. 'How many times have we met since you left anyway? I've been to the States, let's see – three times in thirty years, Eddie.'

'It's not enough, I know,' Eddie said, and sighed. 'It's my fault. I should have made the effort to come over –'

'I'm not blaming you, Eddie. You have a whole life over there. Responsibilities.' Joyce placed a cigarette between her lips, but didn't light it.

Eddie watched her and thought, I could have made the trip on any one of my vacations, but I didn't, I was afraid, not of seeing the city again – but of coming face to face with Jackie and entering the maze of my own emotions.

What would he really feel about his father? That first contact, whether handshake or hug, how would that have been? Stiff and tentative, warm and welcoming? Uncertainty had kept him from Glasgow. He'd become accustomed to the phantom he'd constructed in his mind – an unreliable man, touched by a wild streak, but honest: a man who meant well most of the time, although circumstance and his own flaws sometimes conspired against him.

Joyce blew cigarette smoke. 'Chris Caskie was the kindly uncle nobody else in our family knew how to be. He had contacts in universities, he could get the low-down on what universities had the best teachers – the kind of stuff that was light-years away from Jackie's world. It's a funny situation when you think about it, the avuncular cop wondering how he can arrest the father of his adopted niece.'

'Did he want to nail Jackie?'

'I think it became a kind of standing joke,' Joyce said. 'But a serious one. They enjoyed each other, only they just couldn't relinquish their roles. In the blue corner, Detective-Inspector Caskie, career cop. In the red, Jackie Mallon . . .'

'Mallon the what?' Eddie asked.

'How can I put it? The alleged criminal?'

'No more than alleged?'

'I really don't think he did much more than chisel the Inland Revenue any chance he got. Sometimes I had the feeling Dad said stuff deliberately to get up Chris's nose. He'd make a reference to a crime he'd heard about, and how he might know the names of a few guys responsible. Chris always pretended he wasn't taking the bait, but you could tell he was storing it away to check later.'

I missed all this, Eddie thought. I missed Caskie's role in Joyce's life, the give-and-take between Jackie and the cop. He'd been robbed of something essential. Suddenly he wasn't the brother, he was a stranger staring through a window into a room he didn't know. His sister had made the transition from child to woman and whole areas of her life were blacked out to him. Her first lover, who was he? Her amphetamine infatuation, which she'd first mentioned five years ago, how had that come about? You could love her with all your heart, but you could never fill in the gaps.

He said, 'I want to know more about Jackie.'

'What exactly?'

'Anything.'

'Narrow it down, Eddie.'

'Start with his business. Tell me about that.'

'He mentioned retirement only a few weeks ago. He was saying how much he was looking forward to becoming one of the wrinkly leisure class. He was going to have a big sale of the inventory in the warehouse, then he planned to sell the building and the yard. I got the impression, right or wrong, that he may have had money worries.'

'If he sold his stock and his building, his cash concerns would have been over,' Eddie said. 'At least alleviated.'

Joyce said, 'Unless he had really big debts . . . but it doesn't matter any more, does it?'

'No, I guess not.'

'It's past, the business is history.' She stared into her wine. She ran a finger round the rim of her glass. 'You know, about a month ago he came here and his face was this boozy bright red colour, and he grabbed my hand and he said it had been a terrible mistake to hurt Flora, and it was something he'd regretted all his life. It was maudlin, but I believe he meant what he was saying. He hadn't been able to persuade Flora to stay with him, so he'd reacted with what he called "shameful cruelty". And then he just wept. I'd never seen him do that before. He buried his face in his hands and cried for a long time. It was the saddest thing.'

Eddie was quiet for a moment. 'Last time he phoned me, about six weeks ago, he said he wished he could go back and change the past. He'd been drinking then too.'

Joyce said, 'He couldn't express his feelings without a lubricant. It's all that macho Presbyterian stuff you get drummed into you when you're growing up in Glasgow. A real man never weeps, he just gets on with things.'

Eddie rose from the sofa and walked to the window and looked down into the street. The streetlamps were surrounded by so many small winged creatures the effect was of silvery liquid movement. His mind slipped back to the day of the departure from Glasgow, and he pictured Joyce as he'd stepped inside the taxi with his mother. He remembered Flora, weepy but trying to be all business, saying to the cabby, *Take us to the airport fast, we've got a plane to catch,* and the cabby, a man with a lazy eye that looked off into a wild blue yonder, coming back

79

with something sarcastic like, *Are ye sure ye don't want a bloody police escort, missus?*

Eddie had turned his face as the cab pulled away and he'd seen Joyce watching from the shadow of the house in Onslow Drive, skipping rope held limp in one hand, her black hair curled and a big bright blue ribbon on the crown of her head. Her look had been one of puzzlement and pain.

The image made him ache.

Eddie said flatly, 'He cut the family in two.'

'Like a madman with an axe,' Joyce said.

She walked to the window and stood behind her brother, and put her arms around him, clasping her hands against his chest. He covered one of her hands with his own and said nothing, just watched the streetlights. A car slid past slowly below.

'I can't imagine Flora's state of mind,' Joyce said. 'Your husband tells you he'll fight for custody of both kids, he'll drag you through the whole legal system even if takes years and he's got the cash to do exactly what he threatens. He issues an ultimatum – choose one kid, or risk losing both.'

This was the version Eddie had heard so many times from Flora. He looked at his sister. How frail she seemed in the soft light of the lamp; almost like a kid on the cusp of adolescence.

She said, 'Jackie always tried to do his best for me after Flora went. I couldn't bring myself to hate him for what he'd done. Oh, I tried. I really *wanted* to hate him. I used to get down on my knees and pray I could *learn* to hate him. God, teach me to hate . . . Daft. In the end, forgiveness takes less energy.' She smiled, sipped a little wine. 'Have you forgiven him?'

'I like to think so,' Eddie said. 'Or maybe I've just fudged what happened in the past. Discarded it. I'm not sure.'

'You know, I used to think Flora chose to take you to America because you were her favourite.'

'No. She thought I could cope with the upheaval better because I was older. She was obsessed for years with saving money and hiring a hotshot lawyer in the States to fight for custody of you, but time passed, and she could never get the cash together . . .'

80

Fatigued, Eddie moved to the sofa, lay down. He crossed his hands on his chest and stared at the ceiling where the lamp created an oval of weak light. Giving up a child, he thought. It would hurt like hell. It would be a pain you could never alleviate. Day after day you'd haul a sense of loss around with you, and people might detect it in your mannerisms, the far-off look that would come into your face. But it wasn't only Flora who'd given up a child. Jackie Mallon had deprived himself of his son by his own brute act of spite. He'd punished himself as well as Flora.

That one big mistake, Dad. That heartbreaking cruelty. That's where the halo is corroded.

He was beginning to drift now. Couldn't fight it much longer. After a while he heard Joyce stub her cigarette. He felt her kiss his forehead softly and say, 'We'll get through all this.'

'Sure we will,' he said. She switched the lamp off. The darkness was comforting. He heard her cross the floor and enter her bedroom. She closed the door quietly.

He lay, fully clothed, on an unfamiliar sofa he didn't have the strength to open into a bed.

He slipped into sleep, dreamed he was dancing, he and Senga waltzing on board a cruise ship. The orchestra played 'Moonlight in Vermont'. The conductor had Flora's face. In the dream he looked at the tattoo on Senga's arm and he knew what it was. It surprised him. He thought: I'm mistaken. He woke briefly, considered the tattoo, then everything floated away from him and he fell into a sleep that was deep and this time dreamless.

14

At six thirty a.m., Billy McQueen, AKA Billy the Stump or Billy Wan-Fittit, read the morning newspapers in his Merchant City penthouse. The building in which he lived had been a derelict warehouse before razor-brained developers realized that the city centre of Glasgow was a very desirable place to live, if you were of the cellphone, fast-buck, nightclubbing slick-car generation; and so Merchant City had been created out of shabby Victorian warehouses and banks and offices, its new apartments purchased by lawyers and glitzy media types.

Billy McQueen didn't come into these categories. He was a middleman, a fixer who brought people together to make deals, and he took a generous percentage of profits for his troubles. He insisted on receiving a portion of his fee upfront as a token of goodwill. Officially he was an accountant, the profession specified on his income-tax returns, which were invariably works of superlative invention. He had no training in accountancy; he lived and operated in cracks and shadows.

He was insomniac because he drank gallons of rich coffee every day. His internal clock was in a state of confusion. His complexion was the colour of cigarette ash. He had a pendant lower lip that gave him the look of a man trapped in a lifelong grudge. He Brylcreemed his hair lavishly; wherever he slept he left grease-pits on pillows.

Dressed in sky-blue silk pyjamas and matching robe, he flicked the pages of the papers quickly; he was interested only in information about the murder of Jackie. What he read was bland and unsatisfying. *The investigation is ongoing . . . yackety-yak.* He felt the journalists were keeping facts back. Or maybe it was the police. You could go a step further and think they were in collusion, a clique of scribblers and cops.

He got out of bed, leaving a trail of newspapers. He limped into the kitchen. Twenty years ago, at the age of eighteen, he'd lost his left leg below the knee when he'd been drunk and taking a short cut across a railway line in Cowcaddens, and a train had whacked into him. Since then he'd worn a series of prosthetic limbs, some better than others. His present attachment chafed his stump a little, but he'd learned to live with discomfort, although he'd never grown accustomed to his demeaning nicknames. The Stump was an insult. So was Wan-Fittit – or, more properly, One-Footed.

That bloody short cut turned out to be a longer cut than you ever expected, didn't it? his father had said to him after the accident.

Ho ho. Comedian.

The kitchen was a big white room with granite surfaces. The skinny girl at the table was smoking hashish and reading the magazine section of an old *Sunday Mail* which was mostly fluff about rockers and film stars. McQueen hated tabloids. He liked the broadsheets. He liked to think he was scuba-diving in the Sea of Information, not just floating on the surface.

The skinny girl, who had an urchin's white face, said, 'I just made coffee.'

'I'll partake,' said McQueen. He filled a mug from the per-colator. He sipped the coffee. His hands trembled. The girl's name was Leila, a regular supplied by a discreet escort agency he used. He liked to think of Leila as more than a call-girl. A friend. A lover.

Billy's life was separated into compartments. He lived with his manic depressive, ailing father in a four-bedroom flat in a respectable street in Hyndland. West End, red sandstone, classy. Larry McQueen didn't know about the penthouse in Merchant City. He thought his son travelled to distant cities on business trips.

Billy looked at the girl as he blew on the surface of his coffee. She wore a tight-fitting little sweater and black bikini underwear. He checked the time on his watch: 7:04. He knew his father would be awake. The old man slept only four hours a day, from midnight to four a.m. He was troubled by nightmares.

Billy picked up the phone, punched in a number and heard his father answer.

'How you doing?' McQueen said.

'Awright, awright.' Larry McQueen's voice was stressed. 'Where are you anyway?'

'Manchester,' McQueen said. 'Did you take your medication?'

'What are you – my bloody nurse? 'Course I took my medication, for all the bloody good it does me.'

McQueen held the phone away from his ear and let his father rant. He pictured the old guy sitting up in bed, moaning and whining. Billy tried to be a dutiful son. He did his best. He really did. It wasn't easy. Some days the old fellow would lie on the living-room sofa and stare at the ceiling and say nothing, lost in secret melancholic depths, or else he'd take out his dilapidated guitar and strum a few truly depressing Jacobite folk tunes, like 'Will you no' come back again?'

He wanted to put Larry into a nursing home, but he didn't have the heart to evict the old fellow. He'd even hired a part-time nurse to look in on his father a couple of times a week, but Larry was abusive to this scrawny old biddy who was called Thelma Rogan. Whenever he could, Billy escaped to Merchant City, fifteen minutes away from the West End by taxi. In the penthouse he could have Leila and a sense of privacy in a place where his father couldn't find him.

'What year can I expect you?' Larry asked.

Sarcasm, always the dead-weight sarcasm. 'A few hours. I'm not sure.'

'You're never precise, are you? It's a wonder to me that you ever made it as an accountant when you can't even tell the bloody time. Eh? How did you manage it? Did you bribe the examiners? You're a numpty, Billy.'

Drone drone. Insult insult. Billy held the handset away from his ear. His father's voice sounded like a gnat trapped in a bottle. Jesus Christ, Billy had spent his whole life listening to Larry carping at him. You're a useless waste of space, Billy, you'll amount to nothing.

Bitter old git. Never a kind word.

Billy said, 'I'll be back before the TV gets delivered.'

'What TV?'

'I told you about it yesterday and the day before that.' What was the point? The old man rarely remembered anything from one day to the next except to insult his son. His brain was a decaying sponge in a bowl of stale fluid. 'A new TV is coming, Dad. Digital.'

'Digiwhat?'

'*Christ*. We went through all this.' Billy killed the line before he lost his patience entirely.

Larry would assume that the sudden disconnection was a flaw in the cellphone, even though Billy wasn't using one. Sometimes Billy found the unpredictability of cellphones a useful ploy. Just went dead, Dad. Must have gone out of range. He often escaped Larry's abuse by severing the connection. Larry didn't understand cellphones anyway. In fact, he'd been so unhappy since the country had converted to decimal currency that he'd never used a public telephone after they stopped accepting the old-style pennies and the big black coin boxes had been removed.

When can I expect you? When indeed. Billy didn't want to leave this penthouse. He wanted to sit here with the slatted blinds drawn and never go anywhere again.

The girl came back and poured some coffee. 'Want any more, Billy?'

'Fill me up,' he said.

The girl poured into his cup. Then she sat down and stoked up her little hash pipe. She inhaled deeply before offering him the pipe, which he declined. She looked very stoned. Her eyes were two damp rubies. Billy studied her face, which was pretty in an emaciated way.

Leila had some story about how she was working her way flat on her back through university, and Billy believed it. He liked to believe most things, because all he ever wanted was an easy passage through life; no bloody traffic cones.

He wanted simplicity.

But now he was on a slip-road he didn't like at all, and he wasn't sure what lay ahead or even the direction he was meant to be taking. In the beginning it had been straightforward. A little tricky, but most deals had an element of risk. You expected that. What you didn't expect was a participant getting himself killed along the way –

Shot in the face. Awful.

And way out of Billy McQueen's league. This is what comes of consorting with hard criminal types.

A stern voice in his head said, *Cut your losses and run, Billy.*

Run where precisely?

The smell of hash was strong. He got up, opened a window. Very thin sunlight was rising over the city. He didn't like that. He wanted the dark to last a long time because it was comforting. Now Leila, doped to the deepest recesses of her brain, had begun to chatter. She spoke ramblingly of her affection for wire-haired terriers, her fear of death by suffocation and Ronald Reagan's role in *The Killers* – there seemed to be some political point in what she had to say about this movie that escaped Billy McQueen.

Billy couldn't just sit here and listen to a stoned girl rambling on about nothing. He didn't have time for that. He grabbed the handset of the telephone and jabbed the number pad with a fingertip.

The voice that answered was quiet, almost a whisper. 'Gurk.'

McQueen said, 'Look, I know events have taken, uh, an unexpected turn. But who could have foreseen anything like this?'

The man called Gurk was silent for a while. Something about Gurk troubled McQueen. Even the name. *Gurk*. Sounded like the noise made by an air bubble popping in a waste-disposal unit clogged with custard.

'I was meditating, man,' Gurk said. He was black with a London accent, East End or close to it. 'I don't like being interrupted when I meditate.'

McQueen imagined Gurk sitting bare-chested in a hotel room. He wondered if Gurk was running on all four wheels along the cerebral highway, or if he had a misaligned axle. All this meditation, his strange utterances, his talk of transcendence and harmony and the music of the spheres and what have you – it made McQueen, a lapsed Presbyterian, deeply uneasy.

'You got any news for me, Billy?'

'Emm, no, not yet.'

Gurk said, 'Too bad. Here's the bottom line, Billyboy. You and your friend Mallon got something that belongs to me and my associates, and we'll expect it returned unless the deal is done and dusted.'

'Well, naturally,' McQueen said. 'But Mallon –'

'Yeh. Well. That's tragic. Fella gets shot. But it's not my problem, Billy. The world turns. We go through cycles.'

Cycles? Billy wondered. 'I'll arrange to return my commission. No problems there. And I'll cooperate with you any way you like.'

'I know, I know. You're a man of honour.'

'My reputation's excellent.'

'A man who tells you his reputation is excellent is using himself as a character reference,' Gurk said. 'I'd be very careful of a man like that. We need to meet.'

'Where?'

'Call me back in an hour,' Gurk said. 'And don't think about buggering off, old son. Confucius say one-legged man never gets very far.'

McQueen heard the connection click.

Leila was chattering about Lee Marvin in *Point Blank* and whether the character he played, a guy called Walker, was actually dead or alive. In one sense, Leila remarked, the film might be construed as the tale of a vengeful ghost.

'It's a fucking *gangster* film,' Billy said.

'Ah, but only on one level, Billy. That movie has layers, man. Like strata.' She sucked her hash pipe and segued into a story she'd heard about a headless man alleged to be roaming the streets of Castlemilk, a housing scheme in the distant south of the city. Kids had reported sightings.

'Urban myth,' Billy said.

'Ah, but what gave birth to it? How did it get started?'

'I haven't a clue, Leila.'

'I have theories,' she said.

'Do you mind keeping them to yourself, hen?' Billy reached for her hand. 'See, I'm not clever like you, love. And who wants to be casting pearls before swine, eh?'

She gazed at him fondly. 'Am I too smart for you, Billy?'

'You're so far beyond me it's like I'm sunk in a trench and you're way up there in the bloody stratosphere.'

'I'm flying high,' she said.

'Bully for you. I'm up to my neck in shite and sinking.'

15

Eddie Mallon woke at first light. He was stiff from his spine-crunching sleep on the sofa. He rose slowly, rummaged inside his bag, finding toothbrush, toothpaste and comb. He left the room, guessed correctly that the frosted glass-panelled door across the hallway led to the toilet. He doused his face in warm water, brushed his teeth, ran the comb through hair that had always been too thick and springy to discipline.

He looked at himself in the mirror: sweet Christ, it was like seeing a younger Jackie Mallon just for a moment, a shade gazing back at him from the glass. It startled him, as if he'd stepped through the mirror into some other universe where the dead were resurrected.

Time zones and bad sleep, he thought.

He dried his face and went inside the kitchen. There was a note on the table with a Yale key placed on it. Joyce had scribbled: *Here's your key. If you wake before me, don't wake me. Appreciated. Love J.* He stuck the key in a pocket of his jeans, opened the refrigerator. He found a half-empty bottle of Chablis, a bunch of puckered black grapes, eggs, a can of Irn-Bru, a slab of cheese and a bruised orange. He plucked some grapes and opened the drink and sat at the table. Early light had begun to suffuse the backs of the sandstone tenements visible from the kitchen window. Brick changed from grey-black to red-brown as the sun rose. Pigeons flew among the tall chimney stacks.

He finished the drink and the last of the grapes. He left the flat and went down the stone staircase and out into the street where the colour of the sky awed him, because it wasn't a city sky thick with smoke and smog, it was limpid and sea-blue. Something unusual had happened to the weather here, a strange inversion, as if all the sun destined for the Mediterranean had gathered over Glasgow for a couple of days, creating this rarity.

He walked to the corner of Ingleby Drive and Whitehill Street then turned left and went south in the direction of Duke Street, a route that would take him past his old school. I must have come this way a thousand times, he thought. On either side of him the tenements were silent. Soon alarm clocks would rouse people and the day's outpouring of life begin, men and women rushing to their cars or hurrying to board crowded buses, children beginning another day of the long summer holidays.

Eddie could already sense heat building. He thought: All this was home once. These buildings, these streets and intersections, the school just ahead to his right.

He stopped suddenly. *Where was the damn school?*

That formidable 1890s dark red stone edifice, which had seemed so indestructible, had been demolished and now only the segregated entrance gates stood, one marked Boys, the other Girls; and where the school had been was a deep green forest of thistle and nettle and dock leaf and thorn. Shocked, Eddie stared into this density of foliage. You turn a corner, you expect a familiar landmark – but it's gone, the world has altered. This was the school he'd attended for almost two years before flight had been forced upon him. He remembered the narrow staircases, the classrooms, the toilets where everybody learned to smoke.

The disappearance of the school was one less thing to hook him to his boyhood. He wished he could blink his eyes and magic it back into existence if only for a minute, and see kids crossing the yard and the wind blowing scraps of paper into the bicycle shed. He wished he could see again the pretty brown-haired girl he'd fallen in love with at the age of thirteen: Dorothy, the name came back so easily. How miserable and how ecstatic that first love had been. This is how the heart works, young Eddie: welcome to the House of Paradox.

On a cold black winter afternoon in Alexandra Parade, she'd kissed him and he'd tasted sugar on her lips. He'd experienced his first real erection, and she must have felt it too, but it was a wonderful shared intimacy more than an embarrassment, and it added to the intensity of his love for her. Where was she now? in a middle-aged marriage? did she live in this city still? He had a sudden urge to see her, as if he might retrieve by looking at her the ferocious sensation of that kiss, that moment –

What the hell was he thinking? She was gone, a casualty of time. She'd drifted into the same slipstream that carried everything and everyone away. Eddie Mallon, 13, had been ferried off in the same spate as Dorothy McCallum. And drowned.

He continued to move, passed the corner of Roslea Drive. Nearby, in Hillfoot Street, there had been a snooker hall called Dan's that you reached by going along a dank narrow corridor, and he'd sneaked into it a few times to watch older kids stick coloured balls across green baize under lamps where cigarette smoke billowed. It was daring to enter this musty demi-monde. But the pool-hall would be gone by now, turned into something else. Bingo, he imagined. A video arcade. He didn't want to look to be certain.

He crossed Duke Street, the main thoroughfare that ran east–west in a long straggle of tenements and small shops. A few early buses blew foul smoke, a bakery van made a delivery of morning rolls to a store, newspapers lay stacked and twined outside a newsagent's door.

He stopped. He had a strange feeling, as if somebody had just touched his back lightly in a sensitive spot; it was shivery, and he couldn't attribute it to anyone because there was nobody within a hundred yards of him. Somebody walking on your grave,

Eddie. More buses passed, a couple of lorries, passenger cars; he caught a tick-ticking sound, a metallic tapping, maybe a car with a flaw in its engine.

He walked a couple of blocks then turned right into Bluevale Street. There was something new in the skyline, two tall concrete high-rise towers that resembled architecture he'd seen in photographs of old Communist countries, a suburb of Moscow or Minsk. The towers, drab and lifeless, had an oppressive quality.

He reached the warehouse at the foot of the street. The doors and windows were steel-shuttered and splattered with freaky Technicolor graffiti, and the enigmatic sign 'J MALLON, TRADER' needed a coat of paint. *Trader*: Jackie had chosen a description of his occupation that could mean almost anything. Eddie walked to the high wire fence that protected the open-air yard where the overflow from the warehouse was stored.

He saw a sign: BEWARE OF GUARD DOGS. He hooked his fingers into the wire and gazed at the stock: weathered bricks taken from dismantled chimneys, old sinks and cisterns, bird baths, rolls of chicken wire, rusted wheelbarrows, broken tools that had served no apparent purpose. He also saw a large white delivery van, a Mercedes with the name J MALLON on the side panel and the address of the warehouse.

He found himself wondering if Jackie's killer had ever come down Bluevale Street, on foot or in a car; if the killer had ever gazed through the wire fence and watched Jackie in the yard; if Jackie's murderer had tracked his victim and created a timetable of the old man's movements and knew where to locate him for the purpose of assassination – but that implied premeditation. That meant Jackie had been marked for death. I want to believe it was utterly random, Eddie thought. Jackie was killed in the course of a robbery that went wrong, an innocent party.

He imagined this. The killer says, I want your wallet.

And Jackie replies, Fuck off.

And then a struggle, hand to hand, a gunshot more accidental than intentional –

A dog barked from the yard, but there was no sign of the animal. I played here, Eddie thought. This was my kingdom. He gazed for a while, half-expecting Jackie to come out of the warehouse and cross the yard.

A man appeared and walked between the clutter towards the fence and stopped about twenty feet from Eddie. Sunlight made gold discs out of the man's glasses. He was in his early sixties and stooped and he wore a navy-blue warehouseman's coat with big breast pockets stuffed with pens.

I know this man, Eddie Mallon thought. What the hell was his name?

'You looking for something? You a reporter?'

'I'm Eddie Mallon.'

'Eddie Mallon? You? No way. You're kidding.' The man whipped off his glasses, came a few steps closer. '*Eddie Mallon*. In the name of Christ! So you are! Wee Eddie. Bloody hell. I wouldn't have recognized you in a hundred years. Look at the height of you! Jesus Christ almighty.'

The name came to Eddie. 'You're Joe Wilkie.'

'The very same Joe Wilkie that used to chase you out of here when we had a shipment coming in and we didn't want wee boys underfoot and getting squashed.'

Eddie lowered his hands from the fence. He realized he'd been gripping the wire tightly and it had left indentations on his fingers. He was tense without fully grasping why: this place so resonant with Jackie's life, so stuffed with reminders of his own boyhood, unsettled him.

Wilkie said, 'I'll unlock the doors and you can come inside and I'll make a cup of tea.'

He opened the gate in the fence and Eddie stepped through. Together, they entered the warehouse which smelled as it had always done, of rust and mildew and bird droppings. The ceiling was high and dark, pigeons infested the shadows, and shit covered whole areas like calcium deposits. In the poor light of the big metal building, Eddie saw Jackie's inventory in dim outline, the statues, stone columns, urns; it might have lain undisturbed for thirty years.

Suddenly a dog bounded out of the shadows, a massive Alsatian that circled Eddie and snarled, until Joe Wilkie said, 'Sit, Chet. Sit sit sit . . . Good boy,' and he thumped the dog's body with the flat of his hand a couple of times, and the pacified Alsatian slunk off to lie down a few yards away.

'He's all sound and fury,' Joe said. 'What are you, Chet? A right pussycat, eh? I always call my dogs after jazzers. Remember that? Chet Baker. The Alsatian before that was Lockjaw, after Eddie Lockjaw Davis. Then I had one I called Basie before Lockjaw. Oh, aye, and I had a Thelonious once too.'

'Wasn't there a Django?' Eddie asked.

'Django, aye, you're right. What a memory. He was a fierce bastard. I'd forgotten about him.'

Wilkie went inside the office, a small cubicle marked PRIVATE. Eddie followed, conscious of the dog's unbroken stare. Joe Wilkie plugged an electric kettle into the wall; the gas ring that had been used in the past was history. And so was the paraffin heater, replaced by an electric fire. The desk was the same – massive, strewn with invoices and phone messages on a long metal spike. The telephone was a clunky old black Bakelite job.

'No computer, I see,' Eddie said.

Joe Wilkie laughed. 'The idea of Jackie in the age of the Internet defies understanding, Eddie. I had to beg him to buy a bloody electronic calculator two years ago . . .' He opened a cupboard and took out a tin of tea bags and two china mugs.

Eddie found a chair and sat. 'It really hasn't changed much.'

'Not so many employees,' Wilkie said. 'There used to be four or five, now there's only me and my son Ray, and we run the place between us. Jacks of all trades. Nightwatchmen. Drivers. Stocktakers. We do it all.' Wilkie cleared phlegm from his throat and replaced his glasses. He sounded emotional. 'Your dad . . . You ask yourself: what's this bloody world

94

coming to – but you don't get any answers. Scum's taken over everything.'

'It's no different anywhere else in the world,' Eddie said, a feeble response to Wilkie's remarks, yet all he could come up with.

Joe Wilkie made tea, handed Eddie a mug. Eddie tasted the tea, which was hot and unsweetened.

'Your dad was awful proud of you, Eddie,' Wilkie said. 'My son's a cop in New York City, he'd say. He'd show a photo of you in uniform every chance he got. He kept it in his wallet. He never tired of it.'

Eddie had no idea that Jackie carried a picture in his wallet, and showed it to people. The notion touched him.

'I heard Dad was selling.'

'So he said.'

'Did he have a buyer for the place?'

'He never mentioned one,' Wilkie said. 'A guy came a couple of times, and they shut themselves away in your dad's office. I could hear them arguing sometimes. I got the impression he might have been interested in buying the business, but maybe he didn't want to pay Jackie's asking price, whatever that was . . . I couldn't say for sure, I just know they had violent shouting matches and Jackie always looked furious afterwards.'

'You know the man's name?'

'I know his name all right. Roddy Haggs. A lot of people know him and his reputation.'

'And what's his reputation?' A son's curiosity about his murdered father's life: that was justification enough for asking a couple of questions. He wasn't trespassing on anyone's jurisdiction.

'Bent and bad,' Wilkie said. He shuffled papers and looked tense. He didn't want the warehouse sold. This had been the only employment he'd ever known in his life. Without it, what was he supposed to do? His white face was a map of uncertainty and loss. 'I told the police Haggs was here,' he said. 'I told them about the arguments.'

'How did they react?'

'One of the cops – his name'll come back to me in a sec – wrote something in his notebook. That was that . . . Got it. Perlman. Detective-Sergeant Perlman.' Wilkie snapped thumb and middle finger together.

'When was Perlman here?'

'Yesterday afternoon. Nice enough fellow, a wee bit on the shabby side. But he has one of them faces that doesn't tell you what's going on in his brain.'

Eddie thought, The deadpan approach: give nothing away. He imagined Perlman, who looked as if he'd worked the streets for ever, would be adept at this.

'How's Senga?' Wilkie asked.

'It's a bad time for her. I don't know how she's handling it.'

'She loved Jackie. She used to come down here and help out now and again. I've often seen her roll up her sleeves and get stuck in. Never afraid of hard work. Some woman. Where are you staying?'

'At my sister's.'

Joe Wilkie said, 'How is Joyce?'

'Doing the best she can . . .'

'She's a good girl.'

Eddie, who realized he wanted to get out into the sunlight and away from the memories this place blitzed him with, finished his tea. 'Speaking of Joyce, I better get moving. She's probably wondering where I am.'

Wilkie walked with him into the yard and unlocked the gate in the fence. He held out his hand and Eddie shook it.

Eddie asked, 'You'll be at the funeral.'

'I'll be there,' Wilkie said. 'I knew your dad when we were growing up in the Gallowgate. That's a long time ago, Eddie. I wouldn't miss his send-off.'

Eddie clapped the old warehouseman's arm, then turned and walked slowly up Bluevale Street. And that was when it struck him again, the unsettling feeling he'd had before, the sense of something having brushed against him. The heat was sucked out of the day and he was cold for a moment as he gazed towards Duke Street where traffic was growing and bright red buses trawled along.

He stood still. He was conscious of the tenements looming over him, their dark secretive entranceways and the severe geometry of their windows, and suddenly he loved them as he'd loved them as a child because they were permanent, some part of himself would *always* belong here, but he had the feeling that these buildings, where people lived and bred and died, formed a protective shield around the mystery of his father's death, that if you could somehow penetrate to the hidden heart of the massive sandstone constructs you'd find the answer in the form of a man sitting at a table cleaning a gun, surrounded by oily rags and bottles of solvents, a cigarette crushed in an ashtray, pale lager going flat in a half-empty glass, and a cartridge clip lying alongside a lighter.

If you could find him. If you knew which stairs to climb, which door to knock.

16

'He's in Birmingham, is he?' Haggs asked.

'That's what he said on the phone. Birmingham. Or mibbe Liverpool.'

'Make up your mind.'

'He could be anywhere. How did he ever get to be an accountant? You need a brain for that, and Billy doesn't have one. His skull's empty. I mean, he lost a leg when a train ran into him. Hapless isn't the word. So, eh, where's the TV?'

'TV?' Haggs looked at the old fellow on the bed. He was thin and unshaven and had ketchup and egg stains down the front of his striped pyjamas. His face was thin as a hatchet-blade and his eyelids drooped. He looked as if he'd never smiled in his life. He had the expression of a man sitting on a thistle, but too self-willed to complain.

'Aye the didgie, whatever it's called. You're supposed to be delivering it, right?'

Didgie? Haggs wondered. He examined the army of little prescription bottles on the bedside table. The names of the drugs meant nothing to him. 'When's he coming back?'

The old fellow stared at Haggs in a vacant way. 'I want

to see the digital telly,' he said. He sounded like a spoiled kid.

Ah, digital. Haggs said, 'We'll get to that. Suppose you focus, McQueen, and tell me when Billy's coming back.'

'What's it to you? Just bring in the telly. Do you need his signature – is that it? Christ, man, I can sign for him.'

Haggs thought this was like talking to a brick edifice.

'Hey,' Larry McQueen said. 'How did you get in anyway?'

'You opened the door for me,' Haggs said. 'You don't remember?'

'My memory's . . .' With a look of irritation, Larry McQueen flapped his hand at the prescription bottles. 'I never remember when I'm supposed to take these bloody pills. They wreck my head and I get confused.'

Haggs walked around the room. He clenched and unclenched his hands, bones cracking. Note to self: be patient when there is no other strategy. The room smelled of pee and pot-pourri air-freshener. The area round the bed was littered with old newspapers, books about World War II, copies of *Watchtower*. 'What Christ's Resurrection Can Do In Today's World.' Not a fuck of a lot, Haggs thought.

A guitar with an ornate pick-guard was propped against the bedside table. A chamberpot of a blue floral design was visible just under the bed. It contained a little yellow pool of pish. The furniture in the room was good quality stuff.

'Larry,' he said. 'Would you happen to have a cellphone number for Billy?'

'He had a sky-blue marble when he was three,' Larry said. 'We lived in Kinning Park then.'

'Is that so?' Haggs said.

'Lost it, didn't he? Down a gutter. Plop and gone. Always losing stuff. A marble. A leg. Born a loser.'

Haggs walked to the bed. He grabbed the old fellow by the collar of his pyjama jacket and dragged his head up from the pillow. 'Where can I reach your son? Don't talk to me about digital TVs and marbles and such shite. Just give me a number for Billy.'

'Take your hands off me, Lew, I warned you.'

Lew? Who the hell was Lew? Some figure in McQueen's apparent dementia? Haggs said, 'I'm about to slap you in the mouth, Larry.'

'If I was a fifteen years younger, or even ten –'

'Aye aye aye. Let's not discuss the impossible.' Haggs raised a hand in the air. He wondered if a quick whack across the lips would do any good, if it would activate Larry McQueen's memory. Probably not.

Larry said, 'I don't remember any phone number, mister.'

'Think. *Think*.'

'Get your mitts off me,' and Larry McQueen made a funnel of his mouth and spat into Haggs's face, a wad of phlegm that struck Haggs in the eye.

'You disgusting old fucker,' Haggs said.

'Red card me for spitting then,' McQueen said.

Haggs punched McQueen half-heartedly in the nose, and the old man bled and cried out. Haggs had a mind to hit McQueen again but he knew it was pointless. Besides, there was no particular buzz to be had from bashing this defenceless old fart. The experience left him as flat as dead Alka-Seltzer. He'd crushed Matty Bones's hand, sure, but McQueen was a different matter.

Blood was flowing from the old fellow's nose. He appeared indifferent to it. As if the brief assault had never taken place, he glared at Haggs and said, 'Where's the telly then? In your van?'

Haggs stepped back from the bed. This encounter was like one of those weird nightmares where nobody ever answered your questions. You were inside a room and the walls sloped in a strange way, and people were staring at you as if the simple question 'Where am I?' was too difficult to answer.

He sighed and said, 'Okay. I'll bring up the telly. Where do you want it plugged in, Larry?'

'I don't want any sunlight shining on the picture,' McQueen said. Blood dripped from his lip to pyjama jacket, where it brightened the dull red-brown of old ketchup crust.

Haggs wrote his name and phone number on a scrap of paper and placed it on the bedside table, wedged between the medication bottles.

'What's that?' Larry McQueen asked.

'When Billy gets round to calling, tell him I need to see him. It's in his own best interest. Can you remember that?'

'Think I've got a problem remembering, do you?'

'You? Never.' Haggs plucked a fistful of Kleenex from a pop-up box on the bedside table and shoved them into McQueen's hand.

'Wipe your face,' he said.

'Right, treat me like a baby,' McQueen said. 'It'll be a dummy tit next, and nappies, and talc for my arse.'

'I'll get the TV,' Haggs said.

He paused in the doorway and looked back. McQueen had let the tissues drop to the floor. He was staring at Haggs and blinking in the brassy early sun that gatecrashed the room.

'You got any smokes, Lew?' McQueen asked.

'I'll find you some.' Haggs closed the door and left.

17

When Eddie Mallon reached the corner of Onslow Drive and Whitehill Street he saw Senga standing barefoot outside her house in a dark green robe with short sleeves. Her hair was in some disarray. Eddie walked towards her, thinking how she looked pale and depleted. She turned her face when she heard him.

'You're up bright and early,' he said.

'I woke at dawn and I couldn't go back to sleep again, so I stepped outside and lo and behold here I am.'

'You're not wearing anything on your feet.'

'I like the ground against my skin,' she said. 'As a wee girl I loved to go barefoot every chance I got.' She looked at Eddie sadly. 'I have this cringe-making memory of forcing you to dance last night. I'm sorry about that. It was lunatic behaviour.'

'There's nothing to apologize for.'

She took a packet of B&H from the pocket of her robe, removed a cigarette and lit it with a gold lighter. She squinted her eyes against the smoke and looked at Eddie carefully for a moment. 'So . . . do I measure up to Flora?'

The question surprised him. 'I never thought of comparing you and her.'

'Apples and pears, eh?'

'You made Jackie happy.'

'It was hard work at times.'

'He wasn't happy with Flora,' Eddie said. He wondered if this remark constituted a tiny betrayal of his mother.

'Oh, I know all about that old soap opera,' Senga said. 'How to use your weans as pawns in a stupid game. Jackie realized it was stupid and destructive, but he could be inflexible beyond belief at times. Breaking a family up – for what?' Senga hesitated a second. 'He used to agonize over what he'd done. One day I told him, look, Jackie, if it's eating your heart out as much as you say, why don't you write to Eddie? Why don't you tell him how you feel?'

'You were behind that? I didn't know. I'm glad you did it.'

'*Somebody* had to kick his arse. I helped him write that first letter. And when you replied, he was over the moon. You'd opened the door for him a little way. A belated chance at redemption. You hadn't condemned him. You should have seen how happy he was after he made the first phone call and heard your voice.'

'I always wanted him to meet my wife and son,' Eddie said.

'It just wasn't on the cards.' Senga rubbed her eyelids. 'You want my honest opinion? Your mother was as much to blame as Jackie. She should've scratched and clawed to keep her kids together, but no, off she went to America with her tail between her legs. And don't tell me it was because Jackie frightened her, because if it had been me I would've moved bloody heaven and earth to keep my kids.' She puffed her cigarette quickly. Her words were expelled in little spurts of smoke. 'Flora chickened out, no argument. Jackie behaved like a major prick. And you and your sister were the ones that paid the price.'

Eddie thought of Flora immersed in her world of plants and big-band music. Her lifelong loneliness. Senga was right. Flora hadn't fought for her kids. She'd talked and talked about saving

103

money for a lawyer, and how Joyce would be rescued and brought to America, but it was vapour, and it blew away. Maybe Joyce wouldn't have wanted to leave Scotland in any event. Had anyone ever asked her? Dysfunctional, Eddie thought. A family broken down and hissing steam like an old truck at the side of the road.

Senga folded her arms under her breasts. 'The neighbours probably think I'm completely daft standing out here like this. They think I'm eccentric as it is.' She looked down, wiggled her toes. 'Want some coffee?'

'Sure.' He found himself liking her, the way she shot from the hip, the apparent good sense she made when she talked about the Jackie – Flora saga. He glimpsed what Jackie must have seen in her, somebody straight, no hidden angles. *What you see is what you get.*

He followed her inside the house and walked behind her into the kitchen. This room had been redecorated since he'd last seen it – new stainless-steel appliances, recessed spotlights in the ceiling where a solitary bulb used to hang from a long flex.

'Pull up a chair, Eddie,' she said.

Senga was the kind of woman you found yourself obeying. She emitted, even in her grief, a sense of power and determination, as if heartbreak was something you could overcome if you worked hard at it. You got out of bed in the morning and kept on going, no matter what. She set cups and saucers on the table. He declined milk and sugar; he wanted his caffeine in an unadulterated rush.

He said, 'I walked down to the warehouse.'

'Was anyone there?'

'Joe Wilkie.'

'He's loyal,' she said. 'I like Joe. I like his boy Ray.'

'Joe hates the idea of the place being sold.'

'Jackie was always talking about selling,' she said. 'He blew hot and cold on the idea. But he couldn't have sold without my consent, because I own fifty per cent of the place.'

104

'I didn't know.'

'We'd been partners for more than ten years, Eddie. I invested a little cash of my own at one point when he was going through hard times, and in return I got half the company.' She stared at Eddie with a certain air of mock defiance. 'It's only a bloody scrapyard, Eddie, when you get right down to it. Okay, sometimes we get some decent stuff passing through, but not often. If I was a gold-digger, believe me, I wouldn't have taken up with your dad. In any case, I've got better business sense than Jackie ever had. I'm not just a pretty face.'

Eddie smiled. Partner in life, partner in business. What else didn't he know about the relationship between Jackie and Senga? For the first time since Jackie's murder, he considered the bureaucracy of death, a last will and testament, ledgers, files, bank accounts, unpaid taxes – all the stuff of life that the dead leave behind.

'Did Jackie make a will?' he asked.

'Damn right. I insisted on it. He left this house to me and his half of the business to your sister. I can't see Joyce wanting a half-share in the yard, so I'll cash her out if we can come to an agreement. We'll discuss it some time.'

Eddie was quiet a moment. 'Wilkie thought Jackie had found a potential buyer, a man called Haggs.'

'Skinnymalinky?'

'Who?'

'That's my name for Roddy Haggs. A long drip of a guy. His hands are always dead cold. He's like something dug up from the frost. It doesn't help that he looks a wee bit like Count Dracula on a bad day.'

'Tell me more about him.'

'He's one of those flash characters with his grubby fingers into everything going. A thug, but a rich one. Jackie pretended to like him, but he didn't trust him. I think maybe they did some business together a long time ago but they never got along. I met Haggs five or six times, usually if I was out having a drink with Jackie. He'd always shake my hand and hold it a wee bit longer

105

than necessary. It was like he wanted to flirt with me right under Jackie's nose.'

'He wanted to think he could upset Jackie,' Eddie suggested.

'Worth a try.' Senga was overwhelmed a moment by an apparently sad thought, and she frowned, plucked a tissue from a box on the table and blew her nose. 'I'll tell you something that's bothering me. Where the hell is Bones? He was never far away from Jackie. Why hasn't he come round to offer his condolences? It's not his style. He was Jackie's shadow.' She smoked a cigarette and stared into the lit end. Her eyes watered.

'Have you any idea why he might have vanished?'

'Chris Caskie asked me that same question last night. I don't know, maybe something bad has happened to him.'

'Don't jump to gloomy conclusions,' Eddie said. He thought of Caskie asking questions in his soft fashion. 'What else did Chris want to know?'

'You and him. You're a curious pair. Questions, questions.'

'Curious is a cross cops carry.'

She gazed at the kitchen window for a while. Eddie saw a certain earthy quality in her that must have appealed to Jackie. The large mouth, the powerful body, the long delicate fingers; she had a mature sexuality her air of grief didn't conceal. 'He asked why Jackie had left Glasgow last week, and where did he go.'

'And?'

Senga shook her head. 'And nothing. Jackie said he had some business to attend to. I didn't keep tabs on him. I trusted him, and he knew better than to disappoint me, believe me. I had the feeling he was going down the coast because he mentioned he was looking forward to getting some good sea air into his lungs . . . I drove him to Central Station, dropped him off, then picked him up the next day.'

Eddie saw a slight bafflement on her face now, the puzzlement that comes with the cold realization that everything's changed and your world will never be the same again. The structures have been blown away and you don't know what you're left with except the empty road that might be the rest of your life.

He finished his coffee. He found himself gazing at her tattoo, a tiny purple-blue figure etched into flesh; a man astride a horse. She caught the line of his eye and asked, 'Do you know who this is, Eddie? You remember your history?'

Old schoolbooks. Stories of violence and hatred. He said, 'It's William of Orange seated on a horse, and the date below it is July 1690. The Battle of the Boyne, if I remember correctly.'

'Right, when King Billy defeated James, and James ran away. A big day in the history of Protestantism.' She covered the tattoo with her hand.

Eddie asked, 'What did Jackie think of that?'

'He called it a disfigurement. He didn't have a sectarian bone in his body. I had this tattoo done when I was seventeen years old and I didn't know any better. I was brought up in a house of Loyalist maniacs who'd emigrated to Glasgow from Belfast and Derry, true blue do-or-die kill-the-Pope nutters. Catholics were beneath contempt. The Pope was the Antichrist. That was hammered into me. My dad, Willie Craig, was a high-up in the Orange Lodge and he believed the RCs were planning world domination. What chance did I have of an unbiased upbringing, eh? It's sick, all that stuff, and it takes a long time to break free of it.'

'But you're free now,' he said.

'I've been free a long time, Eddie.'

He got up from the table. 'I'll go see how Joyce is,' he said.

'Wake her up. She can be a terrible sleepy-head at times.'

Senga offered her cheek to be kissed and Eddie pressed his mouth against her skin and then let himself out of the house. He walked towards Ingleby Drive. His thoughts were like flashing detour signs directing him places he didn't want to go.

18

Charles McWhinnie spooned a touch of sugar into the foam of his cappuccino and surveyed the sunlit street from his table outside the café. Kelvinbridge, West End of town, McWhinnie's habitat of patisseries, food-of-the-moment bistros, upscale greengrocers where you could buy yams and Cape gooseberries; normally he would have been comfortable here, but this morning no, quite the opposite.

He sloshed some milky coffee down the side of his cup as he raised it to his mouth. A shadow fell across him and he raised his face and Chris Caskie was looking down at him through a pair of sunglasses.

Caskie sat, laid his folded copy of the *Scotsman* on the table and crossed his legs. He said, 'Glasgow's beautiful at times. The way stone changes colour in the sunlight. The varieties of sandstone. Pink. Red. Ginger. Blonde. Lovely place.'

'How is it all those marvellous colours look the same when it rains?' McWhinnie asked. 'How come they all look so damn *drab*?'

'Whoo. Tetchy, are we? Talk to me, Charles.'

'This whole thing isn't to my liking,' Charles McWhinnie said. 'I want that on record.'

'On record? Where? In a file? On a floppy disk? Hold your breath, Charles. You think this situation is a walk in the park for me?'

McWhinnie tried the coffee again. His hand trembled.

'The shakes, I see,' Caskie said.

'Sleepless nights.'

'I have a doctor who'll write you a prescription for Ro-Hypnol or something stronger, no questions asked.'

'Yesterday I had my Rover broken into in bloody Govan.'

'Dear old Govan,' Caskie said. 'Sometimes we go places we'd prefer to avoid.'

McWhinnie gazed at a double-decker bus roaring through a red light. His instinct was to note the number plate. 'I had honourable ambitions, Chris. Really. I saw my career in terms of nice little stages. I'd go from one case to another more important, then another more important still, a promotion every five or six years or so. Instead I'm sent to Govan with some sharp-faced little git with foul breath, and I get my damn car broken into and the sound system stolen. Now you've got me up at dawn and running around . . . I don't like these jobs. Even worse, I don't know why I'm doing them, and I don't know the reason behind them. What's this one all about?'

'You want advice, Charlie? You should have joined your dad's law firm. That way you might have kept your hands nice and clean. A little conveyancing. Drawing up a will every now and then. Being kind to nice old ladies in Bearsden.'

'I hated that prospect,' McWhinnie said. 'I would have been a partner within ten years. My father was *apoplectic* when I joined the force. Why are you so angry, I asked him. I'll still be on the side of the law . . . I remember exactly what he said to me in that stiff Victorian way of his. *I think you'll find the law has many branches, young man, and you're climbing out on the wrong one.*'

Caskie asked a passing waitress for mineral water then tilted his head back to receive the full blast of sun. He wasn't sympathetic to McWhinnie's situation. Nobody had forced Charlie into becoming a policeman. Nobody had twisted his arm.

'Don't go weak on me, Charles.'

'I'm not going weak,' McWhinnie said.

'I like fortitude and loyalty. Now tell me about your day.'

McWhinnie was quiet for a second. 'I think our man saw me. I can't be sure. He had a funny look on his face.'

'Funny?'

'You know the expression a piano tuner gets when he listens to a tuning fork vibrate? Similar to that. He appeared to be listening for something, but I got the impression he wasn't sure what.'

'Tell me his itinerary.'

'He left his sister's flat at five thirty,' McWhinnie said.

'An early bird,' Caskie said.

McWhinnie smiled. 'I must say Joyce Mallon is the one bright light in all this, Chris. I had the pleasure of her company after she identified her father. Easy on the eye. I drove her home.'

'She isn't your type, Charles. I can't imagine her sitting through a bloody rugby match. I'm prepared to bet she prefers a good book to camping in some sodden tent at the side of a freezing loch.'

'I could open new frontiers for her. She could recommend books for me to read –'

'The point, Charles. Where did our man go after he left his sister's?'

'To his father's warehouse. He talked to a fellow called . . .' McWhinnie referred to a little notebook. 'Joe Wilkie. He went inside, stayed perhaps twenty minutes, came out again. He walked back up Whitehill Street to Onslow Drive and encountered Senga Craig.'

'Encountered? Meaning what?'

'She was standing outside her house. Barefoot.'

'Poor dear,' Caskie said. He thought of Senga dancing last night. Sorrow and madness. He remembered how, after the death of his wife, he'd sat in the living room of his house in Broomhill and pictured the last holiday he'd ever taken with Meg, Bermuda, sun and sand, colourful rum cocktails, and how he'd been possessed by the need to mix some of these alcoholic

110

concoctions for himself in the kitchen, as if he might recapture an element of what had been lost years before . . . And then a few days after the funeral he'd listened to the rain fall miserably on the glass roof of the conservatory and drip from the waxen leaves of the laburnums, and he'd snapped out of the mood and stepped out of the gloomy room of his mind – wherever he'd been.

He'd felt a deep relief then. He was free of Meg, free of her dreadful sickness, liberated from his oaths and his responsibilities to a love that had died long before Meg's physical departure.

'Our man went inside the house with Senga,' McWhinnie said. 'Fifteen minutes later he emerged, walked back to his sister's place. I waited for a time. Then at eight o'clock I left.'

The waitress brought mineral water. Caskie sipped it.

McWhinnie said, 'It looked perfectly natural to me, Chris. A little nostalgic walk around the old neighbourhood. I'd probably do the same thing.'

Caskie looked at his watch. 'He phoned me half an hour ago. He wants to see the scene of the crime.'

'Morbid,' McWhinnie said.

'Probably,' Caskie remarked. I hope that's all it is, he thought. He drank half his water and stood up. He was wearing a blue and white striped shirt, sleeves rolled to just below the elbows. He carried his jacket slung over a shoulder. 'Take a break. I think you need one. I'll call you when it's time to move again.'

'Joyce was married once, wasn't she?' McWhinnie asked.

Caskie said, 'Briefly.'

'What happened to the union?'

'It fell apart.'

'His fault or hers?'

'It takes two to screw up, they say.'

McWhinnie watched traffic in the street. Cars and buses glowed in the sun, mirrors flashed.

He said, 'About my car.'

'Send me a bill for the cassette deck. I'll see what I can do.'

Feeling despondent, like a low-rent private detective in the pay of dodgy lawyers working squalid divorce cases, McWhinnie watched Caskie turn a corner and disappear. He suddenly remembered what the little man in Govan had said: *You don't have the stuff for this work.* Maybe I don't. He wondered if he should call Lou Perlman. Perlman, an odd bird in the aviary that was Force HQ, had taken him under his wing when he'd first joined the Strathclyde Police. Dear old Perlman, smart and big-hearted, that hair cut in tough-guy spikes, always had time for him.

Perlman, he thought. My rabbi.

He took out his cellphone and punched in Perlman's number, then killed the power before a connection was made. Work it out for yourself, Charles, he thought, don't go running to somebody else when you need rancid water pumped out of your system. Lou Perlman doesn't need your problems.

McWhinnie ordered another coffee, took a small diary from his pocket and made a note. He thought, I should be writing something like *Dear Diary, I am melancholy.* He closed the little book and wondered if he should tell Chris Caskie his white beard looked damned stupid.

19

'What a dump,' the detective-sergeant said. His name was Anthony Bothwell. He was a tall man with red hair and a wide nose that might have been broken at one time. He had the soft accent of a Highlander. In his spare time, he was a bagpiper.

'Be a sweetheart and open a window, Vicky. Place pongs.'

The uniformed officer, Constable Vicky Kyle, thought, *I'll be your sweetheart any time* – and did as she was instructed. Brittle flakes of old paint fell from the window frame. The window probably hadn't been opened in years. She watched Bothwell, a happily married man for whom she had a doomed infatuation, stroll round the room. PC Kyle wasn't altogether downhearted; she liked the idea of a secret longing. You needed some passion in your life, even if it was only dreamy make-believe stuff.

'Look in there,' Bothwell said. He pointed to a small bedroom that adjoined the kitchen. 'I'll have a shufty here,' and he began rummaging through drawers and opening cupboards.

Vicky Kyle stepped into the bedroom. A blind had been drawn down on the window. She tugged it and it rose quickly on its roller, *swoosh*, releasing a cloud of dust. The window was dirty.

Below, cars and buses slogged through the clogged thoroughfare that was Shettleston Road.

Discarded clothes covered the floor. Pyjamas, underwear, shirts, socks. The bed was unmade. A bedside table was littered with assorted cold medications and empty Nicorette boxes. Squeezed-out tubes and half-empty bottles and God knows what lay under a ceramic lamp which was crusted with dried gobs of gum.

Vicky Kyle opened the drawer of the table.

Old football pools coupons, three or four centrefolds, some of them obviously antique, a postcard from Skye signed by somebody called Tam. The message read: *Fishing's crap here and too many midges.* She looked inside a wardrobe; sports jackets hung crookedly, neckties dangled from hooks. There was a stink of camphor. A stack of old race programmes had been piled at the bottom of the wardrobe. She bent to examine them. A spider rambled across her knuckles.

She looked under the bed, saw dust compacted into balls and old newspapers and cast-off slippers and four empty scotch bottles, Haig's. She stood upright, straightened her skirt. The bedroom was airless and stale. She walked into the kitchen. Bothwell was checking under the sink.

'Nothing in the bedroom, Tony,' she said. 'This place is disgusting. I wonder when it was last cleaned. If ever.'

'The year dot,' said Bothwell, groping behind drainage pipes. 'BC or AD?'

Bothwell hummed 'Amazing Grace' and then 'The Black Bear'. Pipers' tunes. He loved getting kitted out in the full regalia, enjoyed the swinging weight of the kilt, the well-polished sporran, the *skean-dhu* tucked in the sock. He thrilled to parades and bagpipe competitions and Highland games.

He said, 'Ah hah. Now what have we here, I wonder.'

'You found something interesting?' Vicky Kyle asked.

Bothwell backed out from under the sink. The sleeves of his white shirt were covered in dark streaks. He held a plastic shopping bag in one hand.

114

He said, 'Let's see what secret the hidden bag holds, shall we?' He peered inside the bag. Then he looked at Vicky Kyle and winked. 'Well well,' he said. 'Well oh well.'

She thought his wink playful. She felt blood flush her cheeks. She wondered if it showed. If she was blushing. You're a big girl, Vicky, for the love of God, act your age.

'What have you got, Tony?'

'See for yourself.'

She looked inside the bag. 'Bloody hell,' she said.

20

The telephone rang at twenty minutes past ten. Alone in the flat, Joyce was still in bed; she answered on the third ring.

The caller was Flora.

'Ma?' Joyce said. Her voice was dry. Too much wine before bed.

'Surprised you, did I? Eddie have a good flight?'

'It was fine, Ma.'

'He has that daft phobia about flying.'

Joyce lit a cigarette – damned habit, why did she need it, especially when her throat was so dry? – and turned over on her back and looked up at the bedroom ceiling. She had a small unexpected flashback to her amphetamine days when the first thing she'd do on waking was drop a hit of speed and wait for it to fire her furnace just enough to get her out of bed and drive to school and babble at her pupils. *Wordsworth this and Keats that and here's what Coleridge wrote* . . . And the pupils, most of them dull-faced and sullen and listening for the bell that would free them, sometimes asked questions that turned out to be jokes so old they had beards . . . *Miss Mallon, what's a Grecian Urn? Five quid a week, ha ha ha.* By mid-afternoon she was always wilting; she'd go inside the staff bathroom and snap a tab in half and swallow it, saving the remainder for later. And so she got through her life, and her separation from Harry, riding the speed train through the hours of daylight and sometimes deep into the night too. She'd never loved Haskell, although she'd tried. She wept a lot back then, not because she missed Harry, but because she hadn't been able to get the marriage to work, she'd tried, oh Christ she'd tried, but she was never capable of sustaining the illusion of a healthy marriage. For his part, Harry couldn't come to terms with the fact that marriage wasn't always the beautiful dream he wanted it to be. You weren't always attractive and anxious to fuck. Your period was depressing, or you developed a cold sore at the corner of your lip, or you just drifted away into the private world of a book and you didn't want Harry to follow, dragging his hard-on.

All that. The mathematics of matrimony. The downs were troughs of low pressure. And suddenly there were just too many of them, and Harry had become a burden she couldn't carry and couldn't learn to love.

'Are you listening to me?' Flora asked.

'Of course I'm listening.'

'So how are you bearing up?' Flora asked.

'That's a tough one, Ma.'

'I know, dear. I know. I'd come to the funeral but . . .'

'It's okay. I understand.' Joyce thought, I dread the final goodbye. The ritual.

'I should have phoned before this . . .' Flora paused. 'Sometimes I just don't know what to say. Sometimes I feel so damn sorry for the way . . .'

'It's water under an old bridge, Ma.'

She tried to picture Flora in her tiny house on Long Island but all she could see were plants, a great forest of them. She remembered the afternoon five years ago when Flora had prepared a barbecue in her back yard and how the smell of burning meat had floated through the neighbourhood and dogs had begun barking everywhere. That was the day Joyce first realized her mother was shrinking with the passage of time. Becoming tiny, a little white-haired thing.

'I try to let it go,' Flora said. 'It's hard.'

Was she crying? Joyce wondered. Her voice sounded thin and quivery.

There was a long silence. 'It must be good to have Eddie with you,' Flora said eventually.

'It's great.'

'Is there any news?'

'No, Ma. Nothing.'

'Is Eddie there . . . can I talk to him?'

'You just missed him by about five minutes. He wanted to go into the city centre.' She was going to tell the truth, but held it back. 'He thought he'd buy some presents to take home with him. And I didn't want to keep him company. I hate shops, all the crowds –'

'You *love* shops. What are you *talking* about?'

'I've changed,' Joyce said.

'Last time you were over here, you couldn't wait for me to take you to Bloomingdale's. We did Macy's, and then all those funny little stores in the Village.'

'I remember,' Joyce said. 'I suppose that was my last shopping rush. Where do you go after Bloomingdale's anyway?' Why was Flora really calling? She telephoned maybe twice a year and it was always small talk, and now and again a family story that had assumed the status of folklore, a tale to be repeated and handed down.

'Joyce . . . he's not getting, well, involved, is he?'

'Involved, Ma? I'm not following you.'

'Interfering . . . in the investigation.'

'Is he acting the cop? Is that what you mean?'

'I guess so.'

'Ma, he's not a wee boy you have to worry over all the time. He talked to the police. But he's not out there trying to solve this crime, if that's what you're thinking.'

She thought: Of course Eddie's *involved*. He might not admit

118

it to himself just yet, but he's *definitely* involved. The moment he stepped off the plane, he was *involved*. Somebody murdered his father: was he supposed to sit back and accept? And now he was at the crime scene with Chris because he'd asked to see it, he thought he might learn something, whatever. Because he couldn't help himself.

She imagined that hideous slice of wasteland, Chris and Eddie studying the place, Eddie thinking he might unearth something the local gendarmes had missed, a spent shell, a discarded comb the criminal had dropped. *Not in the real world.*

'If you want reassurance, Ma,' she said, 'I'll get him to phone you.'

'No, it's okay . . . Have you seen Chris Caskie?'

'Last night.'

'How is he?'

Good question, Joyce thought. 'Normally he's his charming friendly self. Sometimes he broods.'

'Meg's been dead only six months.'

Joyce didn't want to talk about Chris or Meg. Meg's sickness. Sometimes she had the feeling that all human relationships ended in disaster.

Flora said, 'I love you, Joyce. You know that, don't you?'

'Yes,' Joyce said. 'And I love you too.'

'Keep in touch, sweetheart. And if you need me, I'm here.' Flora made a kissing sound and hung up.

Joyce rose, went inside the kitchen in her underwear, drank cold water. She found an old tartan dressing gown hanging on the back of the door, and she put it on, then she brewed coffee and drank it standing at the table, her robe open, her small breasts warmed by sunlight coming through the window. She felt a vague arousal she attributed to the heat; certainly there was nothing else nearby to cause it.

21

Billy McQueen sat in a black Ford Fiesta at the corner of Armadale Street and Ingleby Drive. Gurk, dreadlocked, was behind the wheel.

McQueen said, 'I'm not saying it's a waste of time, Tommy.'

'Spell it out. What the hell are you saying?'

'I'm saying mibbe it could be. *Mibbe.*'

Gurk looked at McQueen with eyes Billy thought just a little too intense to belong to a rational human being. There was a light in them that indicated either a form of madness or an extreme calm, Billy wasn't sure which. Gurk had an astonishing forehead, a brow that protruded prominently over his eyes like some abnormal outcropping of bone. His chin was almost a perfect square.

'I'm going up,' Gurk said. He prodded McQueen in the chest. 'And you, my old china, you sit right here until I get back.'

McQueen said, 'She may not be helpful.'

'It isn't experimental physics we're talking about, Billy. A, she knows something. B, she doesn't. No in-betweens. No fuzzy zones.' Gurk leaned close to Billy McQueen, eye to eye. 'You wear too much grease on your hair, mate. Grease is what you fry chips in. It's fucking unhealthy. Interferes with follicle development. Take my advice. Stop lathering your scalp in that shit.'

Gurk got out of the car and closed the door. Billy McQueen watched him in the rearview mirror as he walked along Ingleby Drive. Gurk moved with a confident kind of lope, lazy and loose. He obviously spent a lot of time in the gym, which showed in the rocklike musculature of shoulders under the red and yellow shirt he wore hanging outside his khaki slacks.

McQueen thought: This isn't a smart move. Coming here. I am unhappy. This has all gone wrong. He jumped when his cellphone rang, then calmed down enough to answer it.

Larry said, 'Where's that didgey TV?'

Billy wondered how Larry had found this cellphone number, then remembered he'd written it down months ago and the old man had stuffed it in the drawer of the bedside table. Okay, so he'd had one of his rare moments of clarity and remembered where he'd stashed the number and now the TV was worrying him.

'It isn't due to be delivered yet,' Billy said.

'Says you. The man was here. He said he was bringing it in from his van.'

'Are you sure?' Billy asked.

''Course I'm bloody sure.'

'He came into the flat?'

'No, he was shouting through a fucking loudspeaker from the pavement below,' Larry said.

Billy ignored the sarcasm. You had to. 'So, you let him in and he said he was bringing the TV –'

'Right. Then he went away and never came back. And here's the nice thing. Here's the lovely part. The bastard punched me in the nose.'

'He *what*?'

'Do you no' understand English? Hit me, Billy. He hit me. He stuck one on me.'

A delivery man who doesn't deliver. A delivery man who

punches a sick old guy in the face. Billy McQueen experienced an unexpected poke of dread. It was a brilliant sunny morning in dear old Glasgow, people were strolling in the city parks, it was picnic weather, ice creams were melting over cones and running sticky and white down people's fingers and crowds would be idling in their thousands through the Botanic Gardens: why was it so drab all of a fucking sudden?

Larry said, 'I mean, what the hell kind of delivery service is it when the man hits you right in the fizzog, eh? What kind of people are you *dealing* with, bawheid?'

I wish I knew, Billy thought. He slumped into depression. He wondered if it ran in families, this melancholy that increased as you got older. Would he eventually take to his bed like Larry and live in his own bleak little world?

'Here, I bet the telly was nicked,' Larry said. 'I bet it fell off the back of a lorry. Ask no questions and you'll hear no lies. Sometimes I think you and Lew are working together.'

Lew. Ah, good old Lew, the imaginary playmate who'd sprung fully grown from Larry's mind only last year. Larry and Lew had a relationship filled with contradictions, friends one moment, adversaries the next. A form of regression was going on in Larry's deteriorating brain: back to childhood and stamp-your-feet tantrums and people that didn't exist.

Billy glanced in the rearview mirror and saw Gurk vanish inside a tenement.

'By the way,' Larry said. 'This delivery man, he left a name and a phone number. Want me to read it to you?' Sounds of plastic bottles clicking, papers shuffling, the old man humming 'Charlie is my Darlin''.

Billy McQueen waited, tense as a rubber band in a cocked catapult.

'Haggs,' Larry McQueen said.

Billy switched his cellphone off at once and sat with his eyes shut. Haggs. Strike me down. Flatten me with a red-hot iron. Roddy Haggs. Jackie Mallon had once said that Haggs had been trying to find a way to muscle in. Gone to all kinds of trouble.

Questions. People in parked cars watching Jackie come and go.

If there was a single soul you didn't want within a hundred miles of you or your property, one human being you wouldn't want to travel with on the last interstellar ship carrying to safety the few remaining survivors of the Final Nuclear Holocaust on Earth, it was Roderick Haggs.

22

Caskie gestured at the crime-scene tape hung round the small area of wasteland. 'The night Jackie was shot, his car was parked here. He'd been having a drink in Blackfriars just along the street. He returned to the car, got inside and he was shot point-blank by somebody in the driver's seat.'

Eddie Mallon stared at the empty plot of land. There was space for a dozen cars, maybe more, but none was parked here today. Eddie thought: Jackie settles in the back seat of the car and the driver turns and shoots him. Like that. If the shooter was Bones, Jackie wouldn't have sensed danger. If the man with the gun was somebody else – wouldn't Jackie have recognized from the back of the guy's head that he wasn't Bones? Or maybe he wasn't paying attention, and he was feeling mellow from drink, and the light wasn't good anyway . . .

Eddie stepped closer to the tape. He looked at the ground, which was stained by drips of oil and car lubricants. He wondered what forensics had discovered, if there had been anything useful in the car, prints, fibres, anything, no matter how minuscule, that might indicate the identity of the killer. He put his hands in the pockets of his jeans and swayed a second on his heels, rocking slightly. This close to the place where Jackie had been killed, he was unnerved, even though there was nothing to see, but what you created in your mind could be more savage than the reality. He imagined the gunshot. The end of his father's life. The dying. The roar of the gun rolled and rolled through him. He felt a hollow in his heart.

A man appeared, a familiar figure who flicked the tip of his index finger against the crime-scene tape several times as he studied the ground. Then he nodded at Caskie.

'Chris,' he said.

Caskie didn't smile. 'Can't stay away, Lou?'

'Drawn back like an iron-filing to a magnet. You look at a place once, it strikes you one way. Look again, you get another impression. A third time, it's different. And so on to an infinity of mirrors and insanity. I lost my brains years ago.'

Caskie said, 'Eddie, this odd-looking reprobate is Detective-Sergeant Lou Perlman. He's one of the many dedicated souls working your dad's case, although I couldn't tell you what he actually does. He's a mystery.'

'We already met,' Eddie said. 'At the airport.'

Perlman reached under his glasses and fingered his eyepatch. 'How are you bearing up?'

'So-so,' Eddie said. He could still feel that hole inside. He wondered what it would take to plug it.

Perlman said, 'It's a bloody rotten end to a life, anyone's life.'

'What's the reason for the pirate impersonation, Lou?' Caskie asked.

'Minor infection of the eyelid,' Perlman said. 'Some say the patch suits me. I may keep it. Makes me feel like a pirate. A life of derring-do and keelhauling people you don't bloody like. I could go for that.'

'I expect you have a list of candidates,' Caskie said.

'I do, Chris, I do.'

Eddie asked, 'Did you know my father?'

'No, we never met,' Perlman said. A sly smile appeared on his lips. The sun shone on the silver scruff of his unshaved jaw and glinted against his glasses. For a second his face was an oval of pure light. 'You got a minute, Eddie?'

'Sure,' Eddie said.

'What is this? A private convention for two?' Chris Caskie asked.

'A word in Eddie's ear,' Perlman said. 'Nothing sinister.'

Caskie shrugged, hesitated, then wandered slowly about ten yards away and tapped one foot in an impatient huff. He whistled quietly to himself, a man excluded from a confidence.

'This must be bloody frustrating for you,' Perlman said quietly. 'Looking on from the outside.'

'Yeah,' Eddie said.

'You're a cop. You want involvement. A sense of participation.'

'Yeah. You got it.'

Perlman drew Eddie a few more yards from where Caskie stood and lowered his voice. 'Yon Caskie has a lean and hungry look.'

'Meaning?'

'I don't trust him.'

'Is this internal politics? Or personal?'

Perlman said, 'I'm not a political animal, son.'

Eddie hadn't been called 'son' in years. 'You've got something you don't want him to hear.'

Perlman said, 'I never want Caskie to hear *anything* I say. He's a great eavesdropper, our Christopher. He's got an ear like a fucking satellite receiver.'

'What's on your mind?' Eddie asked.

'I've been thinking about you since we met. You shouldn't be left out in the cold.'

'Tay would disagree.'

'Tay's territorial. He's sprayed his musk across this turf. I'm thinking about something else.'

'I'm listening,' Eddie said.

'I'm a great believer in using every resource available in any situation. Why waste a good man just because he's got a funny accent and he's out of his own patch and doesn't know the score, eh?' Perlman laid a hand on Eddie's shoulder. 'I suggest we cooperate. You and me. A private arrangement. Nobody else knows.'

'Explain.'

'I'm your man inside the Force. Your ally. You learn what I learn. You get the unexpurgated truth from me, and not some sanitized version of the investigation that Tay chooses to tell you.'

'And in return you get?'

'You become my connection to the Mallons. Your gleanings become my gleanings.'

'I don't think there's a hell of a lot to glean inside my family,' Eddie said. He thought about Joyce, and then Senga: what could they know that might help Perlman?

'Ballocks, son. In my long and often colourful experience of this fair city, I've found there's always some black secret in any family. Some faded old whisper. It might be repressed, or half-forgotten, but it's there. You just keep your eyes and ears open, and sometimes you notice the very thing you're looking for is staring you right in the face.'

Eddie smiled. 'You're saying some awful thing might be hidden in my family?'

'Don't go putting words into my mouth,' Perlman said. 'I'm not accusing anyone of wrongdoing. Maybe a friend of the family will be indiscreet. Or Senga will let some revelation slip without realizing what she's done. Maybe she knows somebody who had a murderous dislike of Jackie, only she's too upset to think about it. Or perhaps your sister knows something she doesn't even know she knows. The permutations are beautifully infinite. You'd be surprised how often families are sitting on a truth they don't even know about themselves. The trick for you is how well you pay attention.'

Eddie said, 'I think you're asking me to spy.'

'Boo hoo. Don't talk such shite. Spying, Christ. I'm asking you,

Eddie, to lend a wee helping hand in the matter of catching your dad's killer. I mean, you don't expect me to believe you came all the way here to bury your dad without some part of you positively *gagging* to help find the killer, do you? I'm not buying that, son. Unless I've seriously misjudged you . . . in which case I walk away and this chat never happened.'

Eddie cleared his throat. His mouth was dry. The heat pounded him. His hands were damp. Okay. Why deny it? Why go on keeping it tamped down? Perlman saw through him. Perlman, tack-sharp and shrewd, penetrated areas of Eddie he didn't want to explore himself. Right to the heart of it, Eddie: you wanted more than just a sense of Jackie Mallon's life and times, more than the history of your estranged dad. This was no quick overseas trip to say goodbye to your father and console your sister in the process. He hadn't come three thousand miles to be a goddam mourner. It wasn't his style to stand by in passive mode, the grief-driven son surrounded by his bereaved sister and his father's black-veiled common-law wife. He knew it now: it was about justice, sure, but it was also about playing a role in getting it.

'What you're asking me to do could amount to nothing.'

'Aye, it might. I'll take that chance.'

'Why are you doing this anyway?'

'Because I'm just a kind-hearted old Jew. Because I don't care for Tay, who's like some fucking cardinal with a ring you're expected to kiss. Because I don't have intimate access to your family environment, and I want you to be my eyes and ears. Take your pick. I always have a diversity of explanations just in case.'

'Plus you don't like the rule-book,' Eddie said.

'I do this job my way.' Perlman looked up at the sun. 'You can trust me one hundred per cent. Game?'

Eddie said, 'Game.'

Perlman sniffed the air in an exaggerated way in the manner of a man seeking signs of a change in the weather. 'I wish to fuck it would rain. This isn't right, this kind of heat in Glasgow, it's a travesty of nature, it's driving me up the bloody wall . . . I'm in the phone book, Eddie. Perlman, L. The one and only. Don't call me at work.'

'One thing,' Eddie said. 'I understand you went to the warehouse and interviewed Wilkie –'

Perlman dismissed this with a gesture of his hands. 'Who told me Jackie and Haggs had words. Big deal. I'm not breaking sweat. Don't get me wrong, I'll talk to Haggs. He's on my list. But an argument Haggs had with your father doesn't excite me, because I understand they had more than a few over the years, and none of them ever led to Jackie's demise.'

'Who else is on your list?'

Sighing, Perlman said, 'An alkie who says he saw the killer's face in dramatic close-up. A deaf old guy who claims he heard a gunshot. A retired priest who saw a man running away from the area. One or two others. It's not a promising gallery, Eddie . . . We'll talk.'

Perlman turned and walked away. Eddie watched him go around a corner, the flap of his jacket bouncing, the cuffs of the slightly flared trousers revealing yellow socks. Eddie thought: an ally in yellow socks and flared brown pants. It was something, a chink, a peephole. He might not be directly at the official heart of things, but an association with Perlman was better than a dose of leprosy. He felt an unexpected quickening of his nerves. Perlman had opened a door for him. A corridor stretched ahead. All he had to do was keep an ear open for a hint, a nuance of speech; an eye ready for some off-centre piece of behaviour, something out of alignment. *Families are often sitting on a truth they don't even know about themselves.* Maybe so. Or maybe it would turn out to be nothing. Neither secrets nor gossip nor webby skeletons. It was just Perlman covering his bases.

Caskie approached, still whistling. 'What was that old sod after?'

'This, that. He's gung-ho to catch the killer. Wanted to reassure me.'

'He always looks so damn conspiratorial to me. He's been a

cop since the year one. I've known him for about fifteen years and I couldn't tell you a thing about his personal life. If he has one.'

'Let's have a drink in this Blackfriars place,' Eddie said.

They walked along Bell Street. The sky was cloudless still, although the cross streets were in shadow. Building work was going on nearby, the transformation of a Victorian bank. Discarded chunks of concrete rumbled loudly as they clattered through a red plastic safety-tube into a skip.

'A new nightclub,' Caskie said. 'A restaurant maybe. The city grows and grows. You'll notice changes, Eddie.'

Eddie said, 'I keep expecting to see tramcars.'

'You'll only find them nowadays in the Transport Museum.'

The Transport Museum. Relics of old Glasgow displayed for public viewing. You could enter the lost city for the price of a ticket. His childhood was interred in demolished schools and motionless tramcars. That young Eddie had travelled a long way. *I grew up to spy on my own family. I'm staking out Senga and Joyce and whoever else comes into their orbit.* No matter how Perlman described it, it was still espionage, even of a small kind. But he couldn't hide from himself the fact he was uplifted by Perlman's proposal. A cop is a cop; and his dead father is his dead father. The one has to do something about the other, or else the world makes no sense, and everything's anarchy.

Blackfriars was just opening. A smell of food floated out of the big darkened room. Eddie stepped inside. *Jackie had come this way, crossed this threshold and he had maybe twenty minutes to live. Only he didn't know it.* What was in Jackie's head before he died? What thoughts and plans? Could Senga or Joyce know *anything*, even at the subliminal level Perlman had mentioned?

The dead left conundrums behind always. The living had the task of solving them. Or maybe it all vanished inside a mystery you can never penetrate.

Caskie asked, 'What can I get you?'

'Something ice cold. Lager.'

'Pint, half-pint?'

'A half's fine.'

Caskie attracted the barman's attention and ordered draught lager for Eddie, a shot of Macallan's for himself. He added a tiny measure of water from a jug to his glass.

'Your health, Eddie.'

'Cheers,' Eddie said. He tasted the lager, scanned the room. Maybe Jackie had stood exactly where he was standing now Maybe this was the very place where the old man had had his last drink on the planet. The dead man's spot: Jackie drinks in complete calm, looks round, perhaps he nods to somebody he knows. And the executioner is outside in the heat of the night. *I can't see the killer's face*, Eddie thought. *I can't imagine the features. They're clouded.*

He swallowed half his lager and studied Caskie in profile. He had fine symmetrical features and he drank with a slow controlled movement of his hand. Friend of the family, good old Chris, a gentleman.

Caskie finished his drink. 'Another?'

'I'd prefer some air.'

'Fine,' Caskie said.

Eddie set his glass down on the counter and strolled towards the door. Caskie followed and they walked for a while and then George Square opened out quite unexpectedly, a large sudden sunny space in the aorta of the city; it was if the shaded side streets were no more than tunnels that had been leading you all along to this great expanse of red tarmac which was dominated by the elaborate architecture of the City Chambers, a building of Italianate grandeur. Eddie approached the stone cenotaph located directly outside the Chambers and gazed up at the central tower, which rose with the all the pomp and self-assurance of the mercantile class of the 19th century: *Glasgow was an important hub of the Empire, and that would never change.* Or so they believed.

The city's motto was 'Let Glasgow Flourish'.

He turned away from the building. Nearby, a bald guy with

no eyebrows was selling copies of the *Big Issue,* and a deranged man, hollow-eyed and hair wild, sat on a bench and swatted the air with pale fluttering hands, as if to drive off imaginary flying insects. Lunchtime crowds sauntered in their hundreds, or sat eating sandwiches in the sunshine, ignoring the deprived and the demented.

The city flourished all right, Eddie thought, in the same way as cities did everywhere, vivid contrasts and screaming paradoxes, the gulch between rich and poor, sane and crazy. But today the sun shone and the sky was a sheet of pure cobalt and life was just fine and few people were thinking dark thoughts, except maybe himself.

He said, 'The place has changed a whole lot.'

'For the better,' Caskie said. 'It's cleaner. The air is breathable. It used to be a den of smoke and fog. There's more money around. You can see it in the amount of construction going on, and the way those wonderful old Victorian buildings have been cleaned up. Look about you, Eddie.'

Eddie stared back across the square. The busy buzzing pump of the city, Jackie's city. Where he'd lived and died.

And last week, for one night, Jackie had left Glasgow.

'Do you think there's a connection between Jackie's murder and his trip last week?'

Caskie frowned. 'Eddie, all I know is he caught a train at Glasgow Central.'

Eddie said, 'He got off somewhere.'

'He could have travelled to London and back. He might have gone anywhere in England or Scotland . . . I couldn't begin to guess.'

'And who did he meet?'

'You don't really expect me to know the answer to that.'

'It was rhetorical.' Eddie gazed at Caskie a moment, wondering why Perlman didn't trust him. Was it something Caskie had done? Something in his manner that Perlman didn't care for? They were opposites, sure, Caskie smooth and Perlman

132

rough around the edges, but that wasn't grounds for mistrust. What then?

Eddie said, 'I heard some guy might be interested in buying Jackie's business. Haggs.'

Caskie said, 'Haggs?'

'You know him?'

Caskie blinked, scratched at his beard and looked across the square. 'No . . . I'd remember a name like that.'

Eddie said, 'So you don't –'

Before Eddie could finish, the cellphone in Caskie's pocket rang and he took it out, answered it, listened, then flipped the cellphone shut. 'That was Tay,' he said. 'He wants to see you.'

23

Joyce heard her doorbell ring. Since she hadn't buzzed anyone up, it meant that somebody in the building had forgotten to shut the outside security door properly – probably old Mimms in the flat above. Sweet old guy, but he was forever forgetting to close the security door. She knotted the belt of her dressing gown and walked into the hallway. Through the stained-glass window of her front door she saw the outline of a man.

She hesitated halfway towards the door and called out, 'Who is it?'

The man said, 'We've never met, Miss Mallon . . . I was a friend of your dad. I heard about this terrible tragedy. And. Well. I thought I'd pay my respects, sweetheart.'

She stared at his outline and how it was bevelled by irregularities in the coloured glass. His voice was unfamiliar to her. An English accent, somewhere in the south, maybe London.

'What's your name?'

'Your Daddy knew me as Tommy G.'

'And you were close to him, you say?'

'Peas in a pod, love. We did a load of business over the years.'

134

'I never heard him mention you.'

'Come on, he must've talked about me once or twice.'

'No . . . I don't think he did. How are you spelling your name? G E E?'

'Just the letter G. Plain and simple, pet.'

'Just G? That a nickname?'

'Yeh, a nickname, love. Listen, I feel like a prat standing out here. I'm not the bogeyman, you know. I understand your concern about a stranger turning up outside your door because God only knows we live in times of dread – but you don't need to be suspicious of me, pet. I'll pay my respects and go.'

She took two steps towards the door, then stopped. She felt apprehension. She looked at the panes, which were orange and red and green and blue. She'd thought many times of replacing them with a more secure door, thick wood with a spyhole, but she'd been reluctant to remove the glass, an original feature of the flat. She was attached to the past. She liked a continuity with the endeavours of the dead.

She gazed at the shadow beyond the panes. You live alone in a tenement flat and there's only stained glass between you and someone on the other side of the door. A rapist. Anyone.

She said, 'I don't mean to be rude, but this is a bad time for me. Can you phone me, and we can meet some other day?'

'I'm leaving Scotland tonight,' he said.

'Okay. Next time you're in Glasgow.'

He didn't move. Why didn't he just go away?

She said, 'My number's in the book. Under my married name. Haskell. Okay?'

He moved a few steps back from the door and his shadow dimmed. She heard him say, 'Righty-o, sweetie. I'll give you a bell next time I'm here. Count on it. Ciao.'

She watched the shadow retreat from the stained glass. She went inside the living room. She'd sneak a peek from the window when he left the building, get an idea of what he looked like. Maybe she'd seen him before in Jackie's company and hadn't been introduced – people floated into Jackie's life and only a select few lingered for any length of time.

She stood to the side of the curtain and waited, clutching a wedge of dark brown velvet in her fist. He didn't appear. It took maybe thirty seconds, certainly less than a minute, to reach the street from the stairs, so if he hadn't emerged from the building, where was he?

She went back to the hallway. She opened the drawer of a small table and took out a can of mace and stuck it in the pocket of her robe. It was a Peppergard Pocket Model she'd bought on her last trip to America. She remembered it was advertised as having 'a finger-grip dispenser that fitted comfortably into a woman's hand'. It sprayed six to twelve feet. She had no idea if it worked, or if the chemical had lost its potency with the passage of years; she just knew she felt better with the cylinder in her robe.

She stared at the coloured glass for so long that the panes began to vibrate in her vision. This tension. He's gone. He was slow to leave the building, that was why you didn't see him from the window, perhaps he stopped on the stairs to tie a shoelace or roll himself a smoke, something, anything, you're getting worked up about nothing.

Perhaps he'd changed his mind and was coming back up the stairs to start all over again, wheedling, trying to get her to open the door. Why can't he just pay his respects through a closed door?

Tommy G. I've never heard of him.

She thought of picking up the phone and calling Chris Caskie and telling him about Tommy G and asking him if he could send a uniform round quick, but the Englishman hadn't done anything illegal, he'd just rung the doorbell and talked to her and that wasn't a crime. This is paranoia, she thought. This is what you used to feel on speed. The edge. People are watching you.

She saw a shadow fall outside the door and then coloured panes shattered and shards flew and the lead framework bent back as if dynamite had exploded, and Tommy G's hand came through the broken glass and grabbed the door handle and twisted it, and suddenly he was *inside her home, sweet Jesus,* and she was aware of his milk-chocolate skin and dreadlocks, and she found herself fumbling for the tiny canister of mace and she yanked it out and pointed it at him and pressed the button and the pressurized chemical mist struck him in the face but without any great force or density, and he covered his eyes with his hands and moaned, then he went down on his knees and made a choking sound. She wondered how long the effect of the chemical lasted. She stared at his colourful shirt and all the flecks of broken glass on the floor.

'I'm on fire,' he said. 'For the love of Christ, I can't see. Fucking hell.'

She thought, I'll spray the bastard again just to be sure.

He turned his face up towards her. His eyelids were shut. Tears ran over his cheeks. He was coughing harshly. She half-expected to see him spit out slivers of lung. She wanted to hit him, flatten him with something hard, an iron skillet. He crawled on all fours towards her then raised one hand blindly until his fingers touched the hem of her robe. He tugged at the garment.

'For fuck's sake, do something, get me some water,' he said, and he yanked harder on her robe and she felt herself being drawn down to the floor. He was strong and his hands were big. Even blind and gasping for air, he was capable of hurting her, and she knew it.

Use the spray again, she thought. Burn his eyes out.

She directed the canister at his face, pressed the button. Nothing happened. Panicked, she pressed it again, wondering if it was stuck through lack of use. The same result. Nothing. He reached up and his palm circled a naked leg. He tightened his grip at a place just behind her knee. He squeezed so hard she was forced to bend her leg. She lost her balance and the cylinder slid from her fingers and she fell against him and they rolled together on the floor. He smelled faintly of a long-ago scent. What was it? Some musk from hippie days. He kept coughing, like a man dying badly. Where the hell did his strength come from? Why wasn't he *screaming* with the pain of the mace? Why wasn't he on fire? Instead, he was on top of her, his eyes still shut. It seemed to her he had some weird way of seeing in the dark. He caught her hands and forcibly stretched her arms out on either side of her body and crushed her into the floorboards. Her robe fell open. The cylinder had rolled away, she wasn't sure where.

She could barely breathe under Tommy G's weight. She looked into his face. The red eyelids, the tears squeezed out between them, the white foam of spit at the corners of his open mouth. He coughed straight into her face. If I could get the canister, she thought. If I could reach for it. If it worked. Where is it?

He opened one eye. The white was scarlet. She couldn't bring herself to look into it.

Why hadn't her neighbours heard glass smash? Why hadn't the pathologically nosy-parker Mrs Curdy in the flat across the landing called the police? Why hadn't she seen Tommy G intrude?

'Listen . . . to me,' he said. His voice croaked. She thought of sandpaper on rough wood. She pushed against his grip and tried to raise herself from the floor, but he had brute strength.

'Listen hard, darling. I had a . . . business deal with your father. A big deal . . .'

'I don't know anything about my father's business,' she said.

'He has something that belongs to me, my lovely,' Tommy G said. *Somefink. Loverly.*

'I don't know shit about that. Let me up. Get off me.'

'Why? You're soft. A woman ought to be soft. I'm in pain . . . my eyes are killing me . . . I need something nice, something soft, where I can lay my head.'

She thought: the chemical had lost its force since she'd bought it. Just the same, she had only herself to blame for the way she'd surrendered the initiative. She ought to have clattered him across the skull when he'd been crawling around blindly. She ought to have hurried inside the kitchen and picked up a knife and cut him.

'What did Jackie tell you?'

'Nothing,' she said.

'Come on, sweetheart . . . What did he tell you?'

She said, 'I swear. Nothing.'

Tommy G slapped her, hand open. The blow stung her lip. She felt blood. It was the first time in her life she'd ever been struck by a man.

A morning of sunlight and broken glass. Her mouth ached.

He slipped a hand inside her robe and touched her breasts and she turned her face defiantly to the side. He whispered, *Nice tits, nice tits, oh yeh, warm.*

She pushed his hand away. He didn't resist. She felt strength go out of him, but she sensed he had the power to summon it whenever he liked. He rolled over on his back, coughed for a time.

Please just go, she thought. She listened to the hacking sound he made. She saw him draw the hem of his shirt up to his mouth. His brown body was muscular. He had long eyelashes. I could run, she thought. Get up and run. Out that door and gone.

He said, 'Pain is illusion. Pain's negative energy. Did you know that, love?'

'No,' she said.

She saw the canister. It was about a foot from Tommy G's right hand. She thought of reaching over him and getting it and maybe this time it would function.

'There's a portal through pain to the other side,' he said. His voice was a hoarse whisper. 'If you can reach it. If you know the way.'

Portal, she thought. Illusion. Had the spray affected his mind? He sat up. He turned his face towards her. His eyes were closed. His head was tilted to one side in the manner of a blind man listening. He had a menacing little smile on his face. He stood up with some effort, blinking madly as he peered through the slit of one eye. Broken glass crunched under his feet. He noticed the canister and kicked it and it rolled towards the door.

'You play rough, girl,' he said. 'Tell you what. Why don't you work on your memory, eh?' He tapped his skull with two fingers.

139

'I wouldn't like to come back . . . because the next time I'll really fucking hurt you.'

She watched him make his way to the door. He was unsteady. He stooped, picked up the canister, stuck it in his pocket. She heard him go down the stairs. Whistling. *Whistling.* She recognized the tune, couldn't name it, something cheerful out of Gilbert and Sullivan. 'My Object All Sublime' . . . was that it? She went inside the living room. She tried to light a cigarette but her hand was trembling. It took her four matches before she succeeded. She drew smoke deep as she could into her lungs. She sat down, still shaking, and she thought of Tommy G's eye, the colour of prime rib. *Christ, what is this legacy you've left us, Jackie?*

24

Detective-Superintendent Malcolm Tay's office was situated at Force HQ in Pitt Street, a few blocks south of Glasgow's most famous thoroughfare, Sauchiehall Street, which had had a certain bustling elegance at one time, but was now a yard or two downmarket, fast-food eateries and theme pubs and nightclubs, although a few department stores stood here and there. To the east of Pitt Street was Blythswood Square, formerly the red-light district, but genteel these days. South was the slab of the Hilton, close to the motorway that had been driven with civic disregard through the centre of the city.

Force HQ was a red-brick building attached to a glass office block that must have been constructed at an earlier time. The effect was of mismatched parts, botched architecture. The Strathclyde Police motto, Eddie Mallon had noticed in the brownish marble entranceway, was *'Semper Vigilo'*.

Tay's office was sparsely furnished. The walls were bare save for a cork bulletin board with a schedule pinned to it. Nothing personal here, no cosy family pictures, which didn't surprise Eddie. He imagined Tay's life as one of solitary self-containment. No encumbrances.

The superintendent, who sat behind a desk, was wearing the same charcoal suit he'd worn at the airport. Scullion was also present, standing with his back to the window. Chris Caskie leaned against the wall and looked up at the ceiling. Eddie Mallon felt he was a figure in a contemporary still life: *Hot Room with Policemen*.

Tay opened the middle drawer of his desk. 'I made you a promise last night, Mallon. I said I'd keep you posted.' He looked at Eddie, then reached into the drawer and produced a clear plastic bag with a cardboard tag. He laid the bag on the desk. 'And here we are.'

Eddie saw the gun under the kinks in the plastic.

'This is the weapon that killed your father,' Tay said. 'A Smith and Wesson 4006.'

Eddie felt blood hurry to his head and depth charges detonate in his heart. He was accustomed to guns every day of his working life, they were commonplace, but this one was different, this one was surrounded by static disturbances, as if an impression of the assassin's touch lingered upon the weapon. Eddie had an urge to pick up the bag, remove the gun and hold it in the palm of his hand and feel this instrument that had been used to slay Jackie. He looked at sunlight dulled in the folds of plastic.

'Whose gun is it?' he asked.

'Matty Bones's,' Tay replied.

'Bones?' Eddie asked.

'The only prints on the weapon are his. And there are any number of people who say they've seen Bones with this gun. It seems he liked flashing it when he was jarred. Something of the cowboy about our Matty.'

Scullion said, 'The weapon was discovered by DS Tony Bothwell and PC Vicky Kyle during a routine search of Bones's flat.'

'So you're saying – Matty Bones shot my father?' Eddie said.

Tay said, 'That's how it looks, Mallon.'

Eddie was incredulous. 'They'd known each other for more than thirty years. Long-time associate, intimate – then Bones

142

suddenly decides to shoot his old friend. Why? A brainstorm? A seizure? You got any ideas?'

Tay picked up a pencil and tapped it on the desk. 'Who knows? In my experience, money's usually involved somewhere down the line. Maybe Bones owed your father cash –'

'Which he couldn't pay back, so he shot Jackie?' Eddie said. 'That's too goddam drastic.'

'Is it? People get killed for all kinds of reasons, some of them seemingly very petty, even ludicrous, to you or me . . .' Tay picked up the plastic bag and appeared to weigh the gun. 'Maybe there was an argument we know nothing about. Or a long-standing grudge. Or maybe Bones was indebted to somebody who wanted Mallon struck down. Bones had the weapon and the opportunity –'

'Now you're looking at a weird-ass scenario in which Bones is a hired gun.'

'I'm throwing darts, Mallon. See what might stick to the board.'

This metaphor struck Eddie as inappropriate in the circumstances of a murder investigation, reducing the search for Jackie Mallon's killer to a game. He stared angrily at Tay and said, 'Fuck darts. Jesus Christ. Let's talk about your whole line of inquiry. Let's look at the big picture. Why are you so cheerfully embracing the half-assed conclusion that Bones was the killer? Because it's easy? Because you're too goddam lazy to go out there and shake the bushes?'

'Eddie, for God's sake, calm down,' Caskie said.

He ignored Caskie. 'Have you interviewed the people he did business with, Tay? Have you been talking to auctioneers and estate agents who might have worked with him when an estate was coming under the hammer and who might be able to point you in the direction of any deals he was trying to make? Have you talked to any of his competitors in the salvage business? Have you got people looking into where he went when he left Glasgow last week? God knows, that might be important. You're pecking at the goddam surface. You're just scratching around. And now you've got the murder weapon and Bones's prints are all over it and that's it, case closed, no loose ends.'

He was thirsty, and glanced round the room; no sign of a water-cooler. He watched a muscle work furiously in Tay's jaw.

'You've crossed the line, Mallon,' Tay said.

Eddie paid no attention. 'This gun that belonged to Bones. You're saying he used it to kill Jackie, then he took it back to his flat and hid it? Why didn't he toss the fucking thing in the river? Why run the risk of it being discovered –'

'Criminals aren't neurosurgeons,' Tay said.

'Some of them know about survival,' Eddie said. 'They know about covering their tracks. I'm getting the feeling you just want to shut the book on this and save yourselves a load of legwork. Chalk one up on the old blackboard –'

Tay stood up. His face was tense and when he spoke his lips barely moved. 'Shut up and listen. I'm satisfied we've got the murder weapon, and it's only a matter of time before we find Bones. And I'm damn sure he can be persuaded to tell us just why he shot Jackie Mallon.'

'Persuaded?' Eddie said. 'That has a nice sound.'

Tay beat a rhythm with the tip of his pencil, then he stepped out from behind his desk and unexpectedly clapped a hand on Eddie's shoulder. 'I'm not a sentimental man, Eddie. It's a well-known fact we Scots are only allowed that luxury on New Year's Eve. But I remember when my own father died I lost the plot for a while . . .' He appeared to run out of steam quickly, as if this moment of human contact was embarrassing to him. He sighed, raised then dropped his shoulders. 'I understand what you're going through. Grief. Pain. I understand all that. But trust me with this case, Eddie. I know what I'm doing. The Strathclyde Police knows what it's doing. Believe me. We'll find Bones . . .'

Eddie stood up. 'Thanks for the progress report.'

Tay said, 'You ought to get some medication to help you relax.'

I'll dope myself just for you, Tay. I'll be a zombie. I won't be a nuisance. Eddie went to the door, stepped out. Caskie followed him. In silence, they walked to the stairs.

Then Caskie said, 'That was bloody stupid.'

'Too upfront for you, Chris? Too open?'

'Bloody rude.'

'Oh, yeah, let's not forget rude. I'm the bad-mannered Yank. What do I know about fucking etiquette?'

Outside, in the shadow of the building, Eddie stuck his hands in his pockets and rattled some loose change. He watched uniformed cops enter and leave the hive that was Force HQ.

Caskie said, 'Even after you railed at him, Tay had the decency to open his heart to you. That doesn't happen often.'

'Was that his heart? I thought it was the hinge of a crypt creaking,' Eddie said.

'Give him some credit, Eddie. He was trying to be understanding.'

Eddie stepped out of shadow into sunlight. The blue sky was high and cloudless. The sun had no mercy. Why expect mercy anyhow? If Bones had killed Jackie, he'd shown no mercy to him.

If Bones had killed Jackie.

I'm not buying, Eddie thought. It doesn't make sense. Maybe to Tay it does. Cut. It's a wrap, guys. Go home.

A couple of black taxis were parked on the other side of the street. He wondered where Matty Bones, alleged murderer, was hiding.

'I think I'll grab a cab and head back to Joyce's place.' Eddie raised an arm, signalled, saw the taxi spin in a tight circle towards him.

Caskie's cellphone rang just as Eddie entered the taxi. Eddie watched him speak into the handset, saw his face change, that placid mask slip like flesh peeled from bone.

'Shit,' he said, and looked as if he'd just been struck by a club. He stuffed the phone clumsily in his pocket and climbed inside the taxi. His tone of voice was urgent. 'I'm coming with you, Eddie.'

145

25

Eddie's first impression was of broken glass everywhere, an explosion of bright colour, as if a rainbow of ice had fallen out of the sky and shattered. He saw Joyce standing at the end of the hallway holding a wet towel to her mouth. The cord of her robe was loose. He and Caskie hurried towards her. She fell into Eddie's arms, and he led her inside the living room and made her sit.

But it was Caskie who took her hand and stroked it with a slow gesture of concern. 'Eddie, there's some brandy in the kitchen. Would you mind fetching a glass for Joyce?'

Eddie thought, He's good with the women in Jackie's life. He's attendant physician, private nurse, counsellor, favourite uncle. Eddie wondered if he was envious of Caskie's role in Joyce's world. He looked at Caskie's neat little beard and the long fingers with the perfect nails, and he thought, yeah, I don't like the guy, and maybe it's connected to a mild jealousy or associated with Perlman's low opinion.

He went into the kitchen, found a bottle of cognac in a cupboard, returned with a half-filled glass.

Caskie was asking, 'Can you describe this character, Joyce?'

Joyce took the towel from her lip, which was only slightly swollen. Eddie handed her the brandy.

'Thanks.' She sipped, shuddered. 'He called himself Tommy G. G the letter, not G E E the name. He was black, wore his hair in dreadlocks. English accent. Sounded like London. Said he wanted to pay his respects to Jackie, but I wouldn't open the door. You see how expertly he overcame that trifling obstacle. I shot him with mace but it didn't work the way it was supposed to . . . He grabbed me, hit me. Right here.' She applied the damp towel to her lip again. She spoke through it, her words muffled. 'He was about five-eight. Muscular. Head sort of weird, square, I don't know what else . . . a line in oddball sayings.'

'Like what?' Eddie asked. He imagined somebody striking his sister. He saw a hand in the air, felt the contact of knuckle on lip. The picture angered him.

Joyce shrugged. 'Oh some crap about how you can overcome pain. How there was a doorway into a pain-free life, I don't know exactly. Ouch. I wish he'd left me the key to this magic doorway.' She lowered the towel. The collar of her robe was wet. She pointed to her lip. 'How does it look?'

'It's nothing, Joyce,' Caskie said.

'It feels about three feet wide,' she said.

'Did he hit you more than once?' Caskie asked. He sat down beside Joyce, still stroking her hand.

Joyce said no. One blow.

'And he told you he wanted to pay his respects,' Caskie said.

Joyce said. 'Yeah, but what he really wanted was to know if I had any information about a business deal he said he had going with Jackie . . . I told him no, which is the truth. Then he belted me.'

Caskie asked, 'What kind of deal? Did he say?'

'He just said Jackie had something that belonged to him.'

'But he didn't spell out what?' Caskie said.

Joyce shook her head.

'Tommy G,' Eddie said. 'Does that name mean anything to you, Chris?'

Caskie said, 'No, nothing.'

Eddie looked at Caskie. 'Can you run the guy's name through your crime computer?'

'I was just about to do that.' Caskie took his hand away from Joyce and rose. She drank her brandy, glanced at Eddie then lit a cigarette, which she smoked from the side of her mouth. Caskie stepped out of the room. Joyce patted the arm of the chair and Eddie sat, one arm hung loosely round his sister's shoulder. Caskie could be heard talking on the telephone in the kitchen.

'Did Tommy G say he was coming back?' Eddie asked.

'He said he wouldn't like it if he had to come back and hurt me.' She lowered her voice, as if she wanted to be sure Caskie couldn't hear. 'What in God's name was Jackie up to?'

'I don't know –'

'I mean, he mixed with some dodgy characters now and again, Eddie, but they were basically harmless. This is the first time I ever ran into anyone like Tommy G, and I didn't like it. This is one downright desperate bastard, and he scares me.'

Eddie looked into his sister's face. Jackie's deal, okay. But what kind of deal made a man smash through glass panes and attack Joyce? It was no ordinary transaction, no hundred-quid debt Jackie had left unpaid at his death. Jackie had something that belonged to the intruder and the guy wanted it back so badly it was worth physical violence to get it. One thing was sure: you didn't break and enter and cause havoc if you were walking the legal side of the street.

'I think Jackie was involved in something a tad more spooky than chiselling the Inland Revenue, Joyce,' he said. 'Unless they're sending out a whole new breed of tax collectors.'

'Definitely. So what was he doing, Eddie?'

Caskie came back into the room. 'We'll see what the computer spits out in due course.' He smiled at Joyce. 'I better make an official report.' He took a little notebook from his jacket. 'Let's run through it. He rang the doorbell and you went out into the hallway. Take it from there.'

148

Eddie only half-listened a second, drifted to the window, looked down into the street. He didn't need to hear this reconstruction. He thought about Jackie. He felt an ache that wasn't connected to Jackie's murder; it was the clouded insight into his father's world that disturbed him, that wherever Jackie lived was no place for the innocent. *Fuck it.* It was one thing to pull a few quiet strokes now and again, fiddle a ledger, massage the figures, buy merchandise that had quote unquote fallen off the back of a truck. That was part of the cash-and-carry business, and you winked at it and nobody got hurt. But when you were involved with a guy who behaved like Tommy G, it tethered you to something beyond crimes of funny accounting –

I was never a criminal, son. Remember that. That's the truth.

Yeah, Eddie thought: and I'm just loyal enough or dumb enough, or some weird filial combination of the two, to hold on to a sliver of hope that there's some reason behind Tommy G's actions that will absolve Jackie Mallon. But what?

Think.

Could Senga know anything about the intruder's identity? Could she throw a little light on Tommy G? He walked across the hall to the kitchen, drank a glass of water at the sink. He felt depressed, confused, he missed Claire, he wondered what she was doing in New York right at that moment. Three thirty p.m. Glasgow, ten thirty a.m. Queens. What day was it? Was it one of her working days when she dressed in her Century 21 blazer and showed prospective home-buyers property available in Queens? He wasn't sure. I'm lonely, I miss my life. I miss standing with Claire in the shower stall, holding her hard under the water jet, and the way water runs into her eyes and flattens her hair against her skull and how she looks beautiful against the tiles. Go home, Eddie. Ignore Jackie's business dealings, whatever they were. Ignore his life and death, attend the funeral, fly away. Do what Tay would dearly love you to do, and leave it alone.

But Perlman, goddam, was correct: I'm not made that way. I'm the son. The only son.

He skimmed the pages of the phone book, found Perlman's number, dialled it. He'd report the attack to Perlman because it fell within the parameters of their arrangement, if that's what it was.

All he got was an answering machine. He didn't leave a message.

He stepped lightly around the stars and chips of stained glass, opened the door and went down the stone stairs. Outside, he turned right along Ingleby Drive. The surface of the street shimmered in heat. Tenements blurred like buildings immersed in rippling water. A dead cat lay in the middle of Whitehill Street. Black fur and blood on the tarmac, paws crushed, head back and mouth wide. Flies. Three kids stood in a circle round the cat. A small red-haired boy poked the animal with a stick. *Telt ye it was deid.*

Beyond all doubt, Eddie thought, and kept moving. He was sweating by the time he reached the house in Onslow Drive. He went up the steps, rang the doorbell, Senga appeared. She was wearing a black silk blouse and smart black slacks.

'Eddie,' she said. She was pleased to see him.

He thought: Don't alarm her with the story of the assault on Joyce. She doesn't need to know.

'Come in, come away in,' she said.

He went inside the house, which was dark and cool, and he followed Senga into the living room. 'I was just about to go out,' she said.

He said, 'I can come back when it's more convenient, Senga.'

She looked at her watch. 'I ordered a taxi, which should be here in a couple of minutes . . .' The horn of a car sounded outside. Senga got up. 'There it is. I have an appointment at the funeral home.'

'I'll go with you,' Eddie said.

'You don't have –'

'I do,' Eddie said.

'I'm supposed to choose a coffin. A casket.' She tried a smile, but her face wouldn't make it. 'I don't want to do it, Eddie. It's so damn final. I put Jackie in a box and the bloody box goes into the flames and that's it. That's the end.'

'Cremation?'

'That's what Jackie wanted.'

Flames. Eddie had assumed a burial. He hadn't anticipated fire. What difference did it make anyway? Fire, earth. He wanted to say something credible about an afterlife, immortality, paradise. He didn't hold these beliefs. He wished he did, if only to comfort Senga. He walked with her into the street. The cab was waiting, engine running. Eddie opened the back door, helped Senga in. Her perfume was strong.

She leaned towards the driver and said, 'McGlashan's Funeral Home. Do you know it?'

'Riddrie?' the driver asked. He was a young man with a shaven head that looked as if it had been dipped in wax. 'That's the one on Smithycroft Road, is it?'

'That's the one,' Senga said. She sat back and was quiet a moment as the cab pulled away, then she turned to Eddie. 'I don't know what kind of box to pick.'

'We'll look,' Eddie said. 'We'll choose something.'

'He wouldn't have wanted anything fancy. He'd have said it was a waste of money paying out huge sums for something you're just going to burn.' Senga checked her face in a small compact mirror then snapped the lid shut. 'He never talked much about dying. He was full of life. So full of it, Eddie.'

Eddie gazed from the window. The taxi was travelling along Alexandra Parade. The cigarette factories, in which hundreds of young women had once run the machines that rolled the cigarettes, were empty now. The air used to smell of cured tobacco, as if a cloud of the pulverized weed hung over Dennistoun. Eddie remembered the girls at the end of their day's work, how they wore headscarves and linked arms as they walked along brazenly, gum-chewing and wolf-whistling any young man who passed. They had attitude, he thought, before attitude was invented. Street cred. *Gallus*.

151

Senga opened the window of the cab and the sleeve of her blouse rolled up and Eddie looked at the tattoo and he had a memory of how Jackie had once answered a question Eddie had asked about the difference between Catholics and Protestants.

Here's the difference, son. You cut a Catholic's throat and he bleeds to death. You slash a Protestant's throat and guess what?

What, Da?

He bleeds to death as well.

And, Da?

That's it, Eddie. There's nothing else, no difference between them.

Eddie could even place this conversation in the context of a pale blue summer twilight when he and Jackie had been walking along this very street from a cinema where they'd seen a Randolph Scott Western, *Ride the High Country*. Jackie loved cowboy stuff. Eddie didn't care what the movie was, he just liked going to the flicks with his dad. He liked how he felt secure in Jackie's presence. Besides, there was always vanilla ice cream afterwards at a café called the Bungalow a few blocks from the tobacco factories and a waitress named Serafina who gave him extra raspberry sauce.

Wait . . .

Something in the memory struck a wrong chord. He shut his eyes and imagined Jackie burning and the hideous intensity of heat, the coffin rolling towards incineration and Jackie reduced to ash. What was wrong with how Jackie had answered his childish question about religions?

He felt the warm breeze against his face and Senga's perfume wafted towards him and he remembered his dad saying, *No difference between them*, and Senga saying only this morning, *Jackie didn't have a sectarian bone in his body*. And then Eddie was spinning back, and the years fell away from him like so many discarded betting slips, and he was standing on the stairs of the Onslow Drive house and the living room was filled with Jackie and his friends, and Eddie could hear the clink of dark-brown beer bottles and rough grown-up masculine laughter, and he

152

could smell the heady reek of strong cigarettes. He paused the memory. Listened. The sound reverberated inside him. Jackie and his mates were singing 'The Sash My Father Wore', an Orange anthem, but that didn't make sense if what Jackie had said was true, and if Senga's claim was correct: why would Jackie be singing a Protestant song, an anti-Catholic song, why say one thing to your son and then act differently with your pals?

Eddie opened his eyes. Somebody had shouted: *Death to the Fenian cunts*. Then there was more laughter. A beer party, drunks, anything was possible. So Jackie and his mates sometimes sang Orange songs when they were inebriated, so fucking what? That didn't make Jackie a bigot. Eddie didn't doubt that when Jackie said there was no difference between Catholics and Protestants he was telling the truth. It was just that he felt obliged to act differently with his drinking pals and sing whatever they were singing, that was all. One of the gang. *O My Father Was An Orangeman, In the Good Old Days of Yore* . . . The words faded in Eddie's head. He'd never had any reason to memorize them. He hadn't been brought up in a sectarian environment. Flora never spoke of religion. But it jarred him now to be struck by this particular memory, which felt ugly and menacing –

'Something wrong, Eddie?'

He turned to Senga. 'I was miles away.'

'Let me guess. New York. You were thinking about your family.'

'You're clairvoyant,' Eddie said.

'You miss them.'

'Yeah.' Eddie experienced a flush of tenderness towards her and touched the back of her hand, feeling the big emerald ring on her wedding finger. The common-law wife's ring of respectability. He let his fingertips rest a moment against the stone. Senga's flesh was warm.

It wasn't a good time to ask her questions, but it was never going to be a good time. 'Tell me. Does the name Tommy G mean anything to you?'

'Who? Tommy G? No.'

'He's a black guy. English accent.' *He's vicious, Senga, he attacked Joyce:* but he didn't append this information. 'He was acquainted with Jackie.'

'People drifted in and out of Jackie's life,' Senga said. 'I couldn't keep track. Some he introduced me to. Some he didn't. Tommy G, no, I'd remember that name, I think. And I don't remember any black man.' She ignored the No-Smoking sign, lit a cigarette.

A dead end. A door clanging shut.

Eddie saw the massive structure of Barlinnie Prison loom up beyond the houses in the district of Riddrie, so dense and grey it swallowed the light of the afternoon sun. Row after row of narrow barred windows; men shut away in small cells. Jackie's *alma mater*, he thought. What was it Flora had said? *He was never quite the same after jail. He was harder under the surface.* The prison seemed impregnable, impossible to escape. Maybe when a man left this place he took some of it with him. Perhaps Flora had been right and Jackie had walked out of Barlinnie a different person, one inducted in the ways of crime and cruelty. But Flora's view was coloured by loss and bitterness: how could it be accurate?

The taxi stopped. Senga got out, pressed money into the cabby's hand. McGlashan's Funeral Home was a red-brick building; the name of the firm had been painted, in sombre gilt script, on the curtained window.

Senga said, 'I hate this.'

Eddie led her with gentle pressure towards the door. 'We'll be in and out in a couple of minutes, Senga. If you don't feel like talking, leave it to me.'

She dropped her half-smoked cigarette on the ground, crushed it with her foot. The cab pulled away, leaving a scent of diesel on the air. Eddie opened the door of McGlashan's and a bell rang, and Senga hesitated a second before she stepped inside. The place, air-conditioned and cool, was shadowy. People who deal in the disposal of the dead don't need bright

154

lights. They want shady corners, an easy sense of peace and eternity.

A man appeared in a doorway. He wore a three-piece black suit and a black tie with a large knot that had slipped slightly to one side. He had a drinker's red-tinted nose and he sniffed a lot.

'Robert Crichton?' Senga asked. 'We have an appointment.'

The man nodded. 'Mrs Craig?'

'Ms Craig actually.'

Crichton took her hand. He turned his face to Eddie. His breath smelled of gin.

'I'm the deceased's son,' Eddie said.

Crichton went directly into his spiel. 'This is always a sorry time. No matter what the circumstances are. You have my condolences. My most serious regrets. McGlashan's is totally at your service . . .' He led Eddie and Senga inside a room filled with coffins, dark glossy boxes in which muted overhead lights were reflected.

Crichton touched surfaces with a loving gesture, trailing his nail-bitten fingers across lacquered wood and brass handles and satin interiors. Senga stood very still, surveying the room with the look of a woman wishing herself elsewhere, because this, this damn *showroom*, was her idea of hell. All these bloody boxes and bolting Jackie down beneath a lid and turning the screws and into the fires with him. Bone-pale, she found a chair and sat down and gazed into her hands.

Crichton whispered to Eddie. 'She's not taking it well. It's hard. We'll do everything we possibly can. You're in good hands here . . . Shall we price some models?'

Eddie scanned the boxes. 'What difference does the price make?' he asked.

'It depends. The kind of send-off you want to give the departed. The matter of your budget, naturally.'

'You don't exactly budget for your father's murder,' Eddie said. 'It doesn't come into your general financial plans.' This room annoyed him. The boxes irritated him. Crichton's breath was offensive. They were supposed to be selling more than coffins here; factors like composure and calm came into the transaction. Eddie wasn't feeling calm. He hated the whole thing. Death was absurd, violent death more so. A gunshot in the night, a flash at twilight, snuffed out.

Crichton said, 'Well, murder, of course, you don't anticipate, you can't, I mean –'

'Damn right you don't anticipate,' Eddie said.

Crichton pinched his nose between thumb and forefinger as if he were about to plunge his face under water. Then he laid his hands on the edge of a shiny black casket whose interior was lined with off-white satin.

'This one is a bargain,' he said. 'And very handsome too.'

'And what do you call inexpensive?' Eddie asked.

Crichton mentioned a figure that Eddie tried to convert into dollars. He found himself gazing at Crichton's chewed nails and thinking it apt that a sordid little man with boozy breath and an off-centre necktie was the one to sell corpse containers, worm boxes.

Eddie touched the coffin. The wood was slick. Flames would peel the lacquer off in microseconds. 'It'll do,' he said. 'You take plastic?'

'Visa. Mastercard. We require, ah, a twenty per cent deposit.' Eddie gave him his Visa card and Crichton went off to swipe it through a machine.

Eddie walked to where Senga sat. 'Let's get out of here.'

'Did you choose that one, Eddie?' she asked. She pointed to the black casket.

'Yeah, that's the one.'

'It's nice. I'll repay you.'

'No.'

'I insist, Eddie.'

Crichton came back with the credit card and receipt. Eddie scrawled his name quickly on the slip, then escorted Senga in the direction of the front door. Outside, they stood together in Smithycroft Road, small shops behind them and square

156

grey suburban houses facing them; the leaves of dense trees floated sunlight back into their eyes. Eddie put a comforting arm round Senga's shoulders and she inclined her head towards him. Neither of them spoke for a long time: death laid a veneer of silence over them.

Then Eddie drew his arm away and said, 'Tell me a little more about Haggs. Is he well known in this city?'

'How do you mean well known?'

'Would he be well known in . . . oh, let's say, law-enforcement circles?'

'You mean would the *police* know him? Of course they would. He was tried four or five years ago for – what's the expression – tampering with a jury? It made a big splash in the papers at the time. He walked away without a blemish.'

Senga slipped an arm through Eddie's and they walked together in the direction of Cumbernauld Road, where they finally stopped outside the public library, an octagonal building with a view of Barlinnie, and waited for a passing taxi.

'Where does he live?' Eddie asked.

'Rouken Glen. I've got the address somewhere.'

'I'd like it,' he said.

She spotted a taxi and raised a hand and the cab braked. She climbed inside ahead of Eddie and asked, 'Why?'

26

'He calls me, orders me to find Billy McQueen. I don't care what it takes, he says, find him. Break a few skulls if you have to.' John Twiddie slurped up a good measure of McEwan's heavy into the funnel of his mouth. 'Haggs gets on my tits something serious. Go here. Do this. Do that. I'm like a dog on a leash, doll.'

Rita was busy rearranging her rings. She liked to move them around. It's true what people said, she thought; variety is the spice of life. She liked the reflections the little gems made. She finished her Bailey's and stuck the glass on the counter and tilted her head to catch the afternoon sun that came in at an angle through the window of the upstairs bar at the Ubiquitous Chip in the West End of the city.

'And where do I find Billy McQueen? Eh? Where do I start looking? I don't know the guy.' Twiddie drained his pint. His nose throbbed where the stud was situated. 'He's not at his house, Haggs says. So give that a body swerve. He might be in England, Haggs says.'

'England? Big place, England.'

'Needle in a fucking haystack, hen.'

Rita was finally satisfied with the arrangement of her rings.

158

'You have to respect Haggs. He's a self-made man. He's seen you all right with a few quid. You don't have to love him.'

Twiddie made a hawing sound, meaning mibbe, mibbe not. He was thinking of the way the van had caught fire last night. He was remembering flames filling the front, and black smoke drifting towards the wasteland, and the alkies waking up and pushing aside their sheets of newspaper and watching the van smoke and fizz for a time, then they crawled back under their papers or into their threadbare sleeping bags and wondered if they were having DTs.

Through the dull ache of hangover, Twiddie remembered the sound of the fire brigade in the distance, then him and Rita running away from the scene. Holding hands, laughing, collapsing near an old railway arch. And still laughing. They had fun together, and Twiddie liked that. He thought Rita was a knock-out in the looks division. She was sexy, firm tits, easy to arouse, keen to please.

Twiddie ordered two more drinks. Heavy for him, Bailey's for her. McQueen, one-legged man. How bloody hard could it be to track down Wan-Fittit?

He'd make some phone calls. He'd leave a few questions out there in the right places and mibbe get a few answers. He picked up his pint and winked at Rita. She leaned forward on her stool and adjusted the knot of his tie, which was an Armani knock-off, red with small pink dots. Twiddie thought it went well with his counterfeit Versace suit, a three-piece black number with very short lapels.

He set down his glass and spoke quietly. 'If that old fucker Mallon had talked, then we wouldn't have this shite to wade through –'

'*If* is a wee word with a big meaning,' Rita said. She adjusted the gold-plated paperclip that pierced her left earlobe then she poked Twiddie in the chest. 'Why don't you just make your phone calls, lover?'

'Will do.'

Twiddie looked round the bar. The clientele was mixed, some

159

shabbies hanging about in the hope of a free pint from passing acquaintances, a few low-class criminal types, a well-known author and a gaggle of his girlie acolytes, an undercover detective Twiddie made immediately, a drunken Australian woman who kept wanting to sing 'Waltzing Matilda' only to be shushed every time she uttered a few notes. It was a drab sort of place, but fashionably situated in a narrow lane close to Byres Road, where an assortment of students and trendies shopped and ate. Twiddie, who'd been born in the clapped-out Cranhill housing estate in the east of the city, the Drug Casbah, thought he'd come up in the world when he drank in The Ubi.

He found a quiet corner where he could use his cellphone. Reception wasn't terrific but at least he had a good view of Rita sitting up on her stool, long legs and red leather miniskirt and some spangled stuff in her hair that sparkled when the sun caught it. She looked a picture. A wanker's dream. He loved when they went to clubs and she danced her arse off for hours.

Twiddie punched in numbers. He talked to people in different parts of the city. Mad Cross-Eyed Logan, who ran betting shops in Shawlands and Govan, said he hadn't seen McQueen in months. Bobby McPherson, operator of a profitable ticket-forging enterprise and nicknamed Bobby Christ because of his intense religious beliefs, said he hadn't heard a dicky bird about Wan-Fittit in weeks. Patrick 'The Cowboy' O'Hare, who'd once borrowed heavily from McQueen to establish a chain of dry-cleaning establishments throughout the city, said he no longer did business with Billy, and his loans were all paid off. Teejay Guptah, owner of the Patna Palace Curry House in Bath Street, said he thought he'd seen McQueen the day before yesterday near George Square, but he wouldn't swear to it.

He made one last call, this time to Gio the Gasman, so-called on account of his occasional habit of wearing a World War II gas mask because he was allergic to petrol fumes and pollen. Most of the time the Gasman hung out on the corner of Sauchiehall Street and Dalhousie Street, chain-smoking cigarettes hand-rolled in dark brown paper. He spent hours watching the street, grooving to the sounds of his Walkman.

He answered Twiddie's call with his usual greeting. 'Hazzo.'

Twiddie asked, 'You know Wan-Fittit McQueen? You know his house?'

'Nope,' said Gio.

Twiddie mentioned the address in Novar Drive, Hyndland. 'I want you to go there. Keep an eye open for him.'

'How much is it worth?'

'I'll give you twenty.'

'Twenty-five and I'm scooting, Twiddie. Vrooom. Vrooom.'

'Right. But leave the mask at home, eh? Keep a low profile.'

Twiddie stuffed his phone into a pocket. He walked back to the bar, where Rita was finishing her Bailey's and was just about to set the glass down on the counter when a man approached her, and Twiddie thought, *Aw Christ, no.* The man, who wore a flesh-coloured eyepatch over his left eye, was Lou Perlman.

'Well I declare,' Perlman said. 'The Bobsy Twins, Rita and John. This is my lucky day.'

'Lemme guess,' said Twiddie. 'You played a horse and it won.'

'Only mugs gamble,' Perlman said. He moved close to Rita and Twiddie and extended his arms in such a way that he managed to draw them both into his embrace. 'My babies. My wee babies. And what have youse two been up to lately?'

Lou Perlman, in brown suit and a gold kipper tie that might just have been fashionable when Carnaby Street was new, had been born and brought up in old Gorbals, before city planners had demolished the place. Twiddie feared him: he was as hard as a bag of shaved steel.

'Up to nothing, Lou,' Rita said. 'Do you never shave?'

'Every third day.' Lou Perlman tightened his embrace. 'Your beauty takes my breath away, Rita. I gasp. I feel like Willie Wordsworth strolling through a field of daffodils when I look at you.'

161

'Pull the other one,' Rita said, and shook a leg at him. 'It plays "The Bluebells of Scotland".'

'So. Bring Lou up to date. Lou likes to be au courant with affairs.'

'Oh coo-rawn?' Twiddie asked.

'French, Tweedledum. Comprenez? I see your wee moustache is flourishing. Frankly I've seen more hair on a parrot's arse. You still running errands for Long Roddy, eh?'

'Who?'

Perlman laughed, a smoker's bark. Twiddie didn't like this proximity to the cop. Perlman smelled of police stations. Tobacco and sweaty shirts and something dusty and metallic, maybe rusty, like old radiator pipes, and a hint of cheap soap. These scents reminded Twiddie of hours he'd spent in custody.

Perlman released the pair. He looked at Twiddie, who couldn't hold the policeman's hard stare, then he turned to Rita, who was altogether more defiant.

'I wish you'd piss off and leave us alone,' she said. 'We've got a right to privacy, don't we? We've got a right to sit here in the Chip and have a quiet wee drink, don't we?'

'Rights,' Perlman said. 'People are always moaning and whining about rights. You know what rights do, Rita? They get in the way of *law and fucking order*.' He caught Rita by the wrist. Her assorted jewels jingled. She rang like a cash register. 'Where were you last night?'

'At home watching a video.'

'Boy Wonder here was with you, right?'

'Yeh, he's always with me,' she said. 'Aren't you, lover boy?'

'Aye,' said Twiddie. 'Never leave her side.'

'And what were you two scumbags watching? *The Towering Inferno*? *The Day the Earth Caught Fire*? Or something new from the Arsonist's Video Rental Emporium?'

Rita said, 'Just because I once set fire to an abandoned building you've got me down as a pyro.'

'You play with matches, dearie. Fire intrigues you. You're like the moth, Rita. Can't stay away from the candle.'

162

'That was years ago,' she said. 'You never let a person live anything down.'

'I'll try again,' Perlman said. 'Where were you pair last night?'

Twiddie asked, 'You deaf?'

Perlman caught Twiddie's nose firmly at the place where the stud had caused the bulb of inflammation, and he tugged Twiddie's head downward. 'What did you say, John?' Perlman asked.

'You're hurting me,' Twiddie said.

'Speak up!'

'I said you're fucking hurting me.'

'SPEAK UP, I'M LOSING MY HEARING.'

The suppuration on Twiddie's nostril erupted under the pressure of Perlman's fingers. Pus spurted into the policeman's hand. He gasped in disgust and grabbed tissues from the dispenser on the bar and wiped his fingers. 'Oh for fuck's sake, Twiddie. This is *scunnering*.'

'I got some on my suit,' Twiddie complained.

'It was *your* nose that exploded,' Perlman said. 'It was *your* conk that burst.'

Twiddie cleaned the lapels of his suit with tissues. 'This is pure Versace, Perlman. One hundred per cent. I'll sue. I'll take you to court.'

'Why don't you just shut your fucking face? If anybody's going to court, it's you.' Perlman crumpled the napkins and tossed them over the bar into a wastebasket. He had absolutely no desire to have Twiddie's body fluids on his skin; it was an intimacy he didn't need. He had better things to do than question the Weird Couple about their whereabouts. He had a murder on his mind. But he was the resident expert on Twid and the Fire Goddess.

He glared at Twiddie. 'You see? This is what happens when you don't deal with things, laddie. They fester. Sooner or later, oy, you've got a right bloody mess. One more time. Where were you last night?'

'Watching a fucking *video*,' Rita said wearily.

Perlman yawned. 'Name?'

'*Scream,*' Rita said.

'Engrossing.' Perlman turned to Twiddie. 'So you were nowhere near the vicinity of Orr Street last night?'

'I don't even know where Orr Street is,' Twiddie said.

Lou Perlman slid a finger under his eyepatch. 'Insect bit my eyelid, which is infected,' he said. 'This heat brings out some very strange flying things. As well as other oddities, such as a burning van near Orr Street in darkest Bridgeton, and a report – made by an alcoholic who was once an eye surgeon, if you like irony, if you know what irony *means* – that two people were seen running from the smouldering vehicle. This surgeon, a poor soul fallen on very hard times indeed, peered out of the cardboard box he calls home, and he saw a young man and woman flee the scene, positively *hooting* with merriment. It was the good doctor's impression that the couple was drunk and celebrating . . . And you two were watching a video called *Scream?*'

Rita raised a hand in solemn mode. 'Honest to God.'

Perlman sighed. 'You stand by this, Twiddie?'

'I do,' Twiddie said.

Rita said, 'Every time there's a fucking fire, I *swear,*' and she glared at Perlman, letting her sentence die.

Perlman looked round the bar. Then he said, 'The fire brigade did a damn good job, got the flames out quickly. It wasn't much of a fire, I'm told. An amateur job. Those fire-brigade guys, masters of their craft. I like to fish through debris. Get my fingers filthy.'

'Zatafact?' Twiddie said.

Rita shrugged and looked at her fingertips.

Perlman stared at the pair for a long time before he said, 'Hope and pray you don't see me again too soon. *Vaya con dios*, my wee pals.'

Twiddie and Rita watched him leave. Twiddie was sweating, and ran a finger between collar and neck. His nostril ached where the abscess had burst.

'You think he knows anything?' Rita asked.

'No. He's full of shite.'

'Will you mention this to Haggs?'

Twiddie said no, no, definitely no. The word *amateur* bothered him.

Rita asked, 'What does *vaya* – what did that old bampot mean?'

'Something to do with God,' John Twiddie said.

'Was that Spanish or Jewish he was talking?'

'They call it Yiddish,' Twiddie answered and frowned at the door through which Perlman had passed.

27

When he dropped Senga off, Eddie remained in the taxi and rode south. *What did he think he could prove by talking to Haggs?* she'd asked, but she'd dredged the address out of an old address book anyway. He opened the window and sat back and watched the city flicker past in the afternoon sun, shadow and light, fragmentary eclipses created by tenements and an occasional high-rise. *Trying to prove* . . . If Haggs had been the defendant in a prominent criminal trial five years ago, it was *impossible* that Chris Caskie didn't know his name unless he'd been vacationing outside the solar system at the time. Caskie, Caskie, confidante of the Mallon clan, friend to Senga, Joyce and Flora – for Christ's sake, *why* deny knowing Haggs's name?

Eddie had the feeling everything was connected in a way that was nebulous to him yet, a string of knots he couldn't unravel, Caskie's prevarication, the relationship between Haggs and Jackie, and the whereabouts of Bones, whose motive for the slaying of his old pal remained utterly obscure – unless you were Tay, who seemingly wanted quick closure.

Eddie felt the warm breeze in his hair as the cab headed down

166

Bellgrove Street. This trip to Rouken Glen, think about it: did he expect Haggs, even if the guy happened to have information about Jackie's life and times, and Caskie's dishonesty, to volunteer his knowledge freely?

Eddie Mallon, imbued with bright-eyed Yankee innocence, seeker after truth, pilgrim: Why did I never develop the deep cynicism of the long-serving cop? His partner, Tom Collins, once said, *You want to believe the best in everybody, Eddie, doncha?* The question concealed a criticism: Why doncha grow the fuck up, Eddie? The world is populated with sleaze. People will deny their wrongdoing until hell becomes a fucking health spa.

It's me, Tom. It's the way I am. Everybody deserves a chance to tell their side of a story, don't they? You don't rush to judgement.

Tom Collins said, *In fucking Walt Disney's head, sport.*

The taxi passed the expanse of open land that was Glasgow Green, and the former Templeton's Carpet Factory, built in the late 19th century to resemble the Doge's Palace in Venice. An extravaganza, exotic, *bold*, it should have been a wild incongruity, but somehow it managed to look as if it belonged here on the north bank of the Clyde.

The cab headed along Pollokshaws Road towards Shawlands, after which the tenements gave way to less cramped housing, some stout red sandstone villas whose tidy appearance suggested the inhabitants were prosperous and lace-curtain prim. God was in his heaven, and all was well in this corner of Glasgow.

The cab driver turned his face and glanced at Eddie. 'You said Langtree Avenue, jim?'

'Right,' Eddie said.

'Where money grows on trees. So they say.' The driver laughed.

Beyond Giffnock now, Fenwick Road, a big roundabout, a right turn followed by a left into Davieland Road which adjoined Rouken Glen Park, where Eddie saw sunbathers stretched on grass and dogs scampering and teenagers sitting in a huddle

167

that emitted a blue fuzz of smoke that might have been tobacco or something illicit. The cab swung left away from the park and entered Langtree Avenue. Eddie, a little tense and uncertain, leaned forward in his seat as the driver looked for the house, which turned out to be a big detached white-painted structure surrounded by a tall hedge.

Eddie paid the driver, then walked towards the gate, carved walnut with a white enamel plate screwed into the wood. The word Drumpellier was painted on the enamel in blue floral letters. A house with a name. He pushed the gate and entered the drive and his feet crunched on gravel the colour of a flamingo. The windows struck by sun were like long mirrors. A burgundy Jaguar was parked in a shaded space at the side of the house. The lawn was trim and a single monkey puzzle tree stood in the dead centre. The thick interlocking branches of the tree resembled a pine with advanced arthritis.

He walked to the front door, noticing a security camera about four feet above him to his right. He pressed the doorbell. He heard the camera whirr quietly as it shifted a couple of inches. He understood. You didn't get inside by ringing a bell. You gained entrance only if the person staring at a monitor inside granted you permission.

Eddie looked up into the eye of the camera.

A man's voice came out of a hidden speaker. 'Who are you?'

Eddie was startled, but tried not to show it. 'Eddie Mallon. I'm looking for Roddy Haggs.'

The voice said, 'Come in.' The door opened without human assistance.

Eddie went in, found himself in a big square entranceway with a marbled floor and a number of marble columns. The original rooms of the house had been demolished to make way for this one enormous space. From a hidden source came a muzak version of the soundtrack of *South Pacific*.

He crossed the floor a few yards, then paused at the edge of what people used to call conversation pits. Five steps down to a sunken square area furnished with casual chairs and huge pillows. 'Happy Talk' finished. Now it was 'Some Enchanted Evening'.

The man who approached Eddie was tall and cadaverous, and his head was too small for the body that supported it. But there was more to the man's unusual appearance than the size of head in relation to frame. It was his skinniness, the quality of near-transparency, that made it seem as if his height was artificial, as if he'd been stretched on a rack.

Eddie didn't need to be told that this was Roddy Haggs; he fitted Senga's description. And when Eddie accepted Haggs's handshake he wasn't surprised to discover that the man's skin was chilly. He sleeps in a box of his native soil, Eddie thought.

'Let's go down into the pit,' Haggs said.

The pit. How appropriate. Eddie descended, Haggs followed. 'Sit. Make yourself comfortable. Drink?'

Eddie refused the drink, then said, 'Quite a place.'

Haggs fixed himself a small tumbler of scotch from a decanter. 'Should be, considering the cash that went into it.'

A certain kind of person always wanted to tell you what they'd spent on their houses. They were usually self-made types. Eddie looked up; where the columns met the high ceiling assorted angels had been painted skilfully on plaster. He half-expected God to appear, staring down at him stern-eyed, a white beard in the clouds. Behave cautiously, Eddie.

Haggs said, 'You've come home for the funeral, I assume.'

Eddie nodded. 'Yeah.'

'Fucking *tragedy*.' Haggs sipped his drink. 'Me and Jackie had our differences. But I like to think we respected each other. I feel bad for Senga.'

If Haggs was an act, he was a pretty good one, Eddie thought. The sorrowful intonation in the voice, the expression of concern.

'You knew each other a long time,' Eddie said.

'Years and bloody years.'

Eddie hesitated before his next question. Haggs had a way of looking down the length of his nose at you, as if you were a specimen on a slide, something very small and hard to categorize. 'You ever do any business together?'

'I once gave him an opportunity to invest in a car-hire company, but he was a wee bit slow opening his chequebook, and the chance passed.'

'And that's all,' Eddie said.

'Aye. Did you expect more?'

Eddie shook his head. 'I'm not sure. I thought maybe you had some joint ventures in the past.'

Haggs shook his head. 'The big difference between Jackie and me is that he was interested in what he could pluck out of history, whereas I'm more intrigued by what I can make of the future. Show Jackie an old country mansion and he'd wonder what he could salvage. Show me that same house and I'd be thinking of pulling it down and putting up a block of flats. So, what brings you out into the wilds of Rouken Glen to see me?'

'I'm the executor of Jackie's will.' Sometimes the capacity to fabricate was so slick it frightened Eddie.

'And what does Jackie's will have to do with me? Unless he's left me something, a keepsake maybe.' Haggs laughed. It was a high-pitched sound, a hinge squeaking. 'Old bugger wouldn't leave me a cracked chanty.'

A *chanty*, Eddie thought. A chamberpot. 'About the warehouse.'

'That dump in Bluevale Street?'

Eddie nodded and went into his storyline. 'It's going on the market soon to satisfy some tax demands Jackie hadn't paid.'

'Jackie had a useless accountant, some fucking quill-pusher from the Victorian age. I told him a hundred times. Get up to date. Throw out every last abacus and plug into the new age . . . Did he listen? Did he fuck. And now the whole kit and caboodle is going up for sale, you say?'

'Probably at auction,' Eddie said.

'I still don't see any connection to me, Eddie.'

'No? I heard you were interested in the property.'

With an expression of amazement, Haggs laughed loudly. His

long body shook and he fine-sprayed the air with saliva. 'Me? *Me?* Do I look like a junk dealer? Do I look like a man who'd be interested in buying and selling rubbish?'

Eddie said, 'I heard you'd visited the warehouse and you and Jackie had arguments about the valuation of the business.'

'Jackie and me – we were oil and vinegar. We liked to argue. Christ, we thrived on it. Who remembers the reasons? When conflict's finished, I let it go.'

Eddie didn't buy that. He had the feeling Haggs was the kind of man who'd never forget a grudge or a slight or the name of anyone who'd walked on the wrong side of him. Okay. Realistically, what the hell *did* a rich man want with a rundown warehouse? Demolish the place and build a super-market or a bingo palace or a leisure complex? Wrong part of town, Eddie thought. Fine. Say it wasn't the warehouse or the space Haggs wanted, and Joe Wilkie guessed wrong. Say it was something else.

What did Jackie have that Haggs needed? What exactly?

He thought of Tommy G. Jackie *definitely* had something Tommy was looking for.

Had Jackie left troublesome loose ends all over Glasgow?

'I hear you're a cop in New York,' Haggs said.

'In Glasgow I'm just somebody's son trying to make sense of his father's affairs, and if I got the wrong end of the stick about you and the warehouse, let's drop it.'

'Gladly,' Haggs said.

The muzak played on. 'There is Nothing Like a Dame'. Sud-denly Haggs slapped his thigh and laughed again, and said, 'I'm trying to imagine myself sitting in Jackie's grubby wee office arguing about the price of such-and-such a sundial or an old HMV gramophone. Sorry, Eddie, I don't mean to mock what Jackie did for a living –'

'No big deal.' But it was, and Eddie felt a surge of irritation at the way Haggs belittled Jackie.

Haggs asked, 'You talked to the police about the murder?'

'Yeah, we've talked.'

'Is Glasgow's finest close to finding the killer?'

'They believe Bones did it,' Eddie answered.

'*Bones?*'

'Bones's gun was the murder weapon.'

Haggs asked, 'That wee man went around *armed*? Have they brought him in for questioning?'

'They can't find him.'

'Then he fucked off. Probably scared shitless. I can't believe he killed Jackie.'

'So who did?'

Haggs shrugged. 'I'm baffled.'

'Then we're all baffled – apart from the cops,' Eddie said.

'The cops won't change their minds. They're inflexible. And it wouldn't be the first time they've jumped to the wrong conclusion.'

'Am I hearing contempt for the Strathclyde Police?'

'You don't need to be a mind-reader. They're a right evil bunch of wankers.'

'I heard something about a trial you were involved in . . .'

'That was a bloody attempt to railroad me.'

'Why?'

'How many reasons do you want? They're jealous of my lifestyle. They don't like some of my business partners. They don't like to see somebody from my background get ahead. You read the sign on the gate when you came in? You see the word *Drumpellier* there?'

Eddie said, 'I saw it.'

'I was born in Drumpellier Street, in a district of this fair city called Blackhill. You're born and brought up in Blackhill, Eddie, you're not supposed to get out. It was crime and drugs and gangs, some of the hardest fuckers in Glasgow. The police didn't like to visit Blackhill, and they didn't like people spilling out of Blackhill into other places, especially people like me drifting into respectable areas like this . . . Are you getting the picture?'

'You've risen above your station.'

'And I stepped on a few toes climbing. And some people don't forget that. And some of these people have friends in the police . . .'

'So you have *Drumpellier* out there to remind you where you came from,' Eddie said.

'More than that. It's me giving them the finger, Eddie. It's me saying, fuck the lot of you, I walk where I bloody well please.' Haggs tossed his scotch back and drew a hand across his mouth. 'So the trumped-up trial, Eddie, was a scheme planned by morons who wanted to show me that even if I'd come up in the world, I could go down again as fast as *that*,' and he snapped his fingers. 'The police case against me was a load of ballocks. I walked out of that courtroom free as a bird.'

Eddie stood under the angels and the blue sky and the cloud clusters. Haggs carried deep black grudges against the social order. Did he have grudges against Jackie too?

'Who told you about that trial anyway?' Haggs asked.

Eddie plucked an easy lie out of nowhere and tossed it like a paper dart. 'Guy called Caskie. A cop.'

Haggs said, 'Caskie . . . Is he the one friendly with your family?'

'The same,' Eddie said.

'And how did my name happen to come up in conversation?'

'Because I told him you intended to buy the warehouse.' Eddie smiled.

'Now you can tell him you were wrong.'

'Consider it done,' Eddie said. 'Thanks for your time.'

Haggs walked with Eddie towards the door. On the right was a small wood-panelled room filled with glass display cases.

Eddie glanced at them. 'Quite a collection,' he said.

Haggs asked, 'You interested in guns? I've been collecting them for years.' He strode towards the display cases. There were almost fifty blackpowder pistols here, most of them genuine antiques, each gleaming and imbedded in dark brown wood.

Haggs took a keychain from his pocket and unlocked one of the cases and removed a long handgun with a walnut stock and held it out for Eddie's examination.

'Kentucky Flintlock,' he said. He handed the gun to Eddie, who was surprised by its weight, and then he carefully removed another weapon from the case. This one had a fancy curved handle and a barrel more than a foot long. 'This beauty is a Le Page Percussion Duelling Pistol. Lovely feel to it. I've also got a very fine original Colt 1860 Revolver and a mint-con Remington Percussion dating from 1858.' He gestured towards the display proudly. 'Been a hobby a long time. I always take my hobbies very seriously, Eddie.'

'This Kentucky is a very fine gun,' Eddie said, admiring the craftsmanship.

Haggs held out his hand and Eddie gave him back the flintlock and he returned it to the case, which he locked.

'Beautiful things make me forget my origins,' Haggs remarked. 'I'll walk you out.'

Outside, both men gazed at the monkey puzzle tree. To Eddie it seemed as if the tree had been tortured by sea storms, a thing you might find growing in godforsaken sand dunes.

He asked, 'You know Caskie, I assume?'

'You think I'd want a cop for an acquaintance?' Haggs laid a hand on Eddie's shoulder and massaged it a little too firmly. 'I'd rather use shite for toothpaste.'

Eddie smiled thinly. Sun reflected from the branches of the tree in a zigzagging pattern of light and a drab bird – probably a sparrow – popped out of the foliage and flew directly overhead.

28

The calamitous drumming in Caskie's head just wouldn't quit. Hot and flushed, he kept going over the same thing – his denial of ever having heard of Haggs. Reason, give me one good reason, he thought: I panicked. I slipped. I gave into a kind of idiot seizure of guilt. Moron. It was downright stupid, a magician dropping his cards during a sleight of hand, and Mallon – certainly no dummy – had picked up on it. Caskie was convinced of that.

What would it have cost me to say I knew Haggs by name? Nothing. He'd answered without thinking. *Haggs? Never heard of him. Nothing to do with me. Not part of my world.* He'd rushed into the denial too quickly.

The burden you've been carrying. You're on overload.

He watched Joyce, who stood at the window and looked down into the street. She smoked a cigarette. 'Where the hell did Eddie go? He just disappeared. He didn't say he was leaving. It's been more than an hour, hasn't it?'

'I don't know.' Caskie had lost track of time.

From the hallway came the sound of a man drilling screws into sheets of plywood. Caskie had telephoned him and he'd come at once to put the plywood in the place where the glass had been, a temporary solution, security for Joyce. She'd wondered how Caskie could find somebody so quickly. One phone call and *voilà*. The carpenter appeared within ten minutes. Probably an old favour. Caskie had hundreds of strings he could pull in this city. He'd already arranged for a patrol car to remain in the vicinity in the event that Tommy G returned. She had the feeling a single car wouldn't worry a man like Thomas G.

'It's the middle of the afternoon and I'm not dressed yet,' she said.

'School holidays,' Caskie said.

She looked at Caskie. He had a strange lifeless tone in his voice. 'I'd better put some clothes on,' she said.

She stepped into her bedroom, closed the door. She pulled on a T-shirt with the logo *McCools*, the name of a bar she sometimes visited when she was in a jazz mood. Then blue jeans tight at her hips. She stood in front of the long mirror of the wardrobe, thinking she looked undernourished. She remembered how the intruder had dragged her to the floor, the way his hand had parted her robe. She'd have bad dreams about him. He'd crash her head uninvited.

She sat in a green velvet chair, an item salvaged from Jackie's yard. She saw her image again, this time in the oval mirror of the Victorian dressing table that had once belonged to Granny Mallon, funny how bits and pieces of furniture and small items of jewellery are handed down through generations like genetic material passed from one person to another, and she thought of how often Granny Mallon must have gazed at herself in this very mirror, a young wife, barely more than a girl, brushing her hair stroke after stroke.

She touched her lip where Tommy G had struck her. It didn't hurt now. She'd pressed ice cubes to it for a while, and they'd helped. She heard a knock on the door. Caskie appeared. She looked at his reflection in the mirror.

'You all right?' he asked.

'I'll be fine. Just give me a minute to myself, Chris.'

'Checking,' he said. 'You want aspirin or anything else?'

176

'No. But thanks for asking.' She smiled at him in the mirror. He closed the door, retreated. She couldn't read his expression. Concern, certainly. Always. She wasn't sure what else. Something troubled him. Probably Tommy G. She heard the buzz of the carpenter's drill and a big delivery truck pass in the street and how it made the glass vibrate in the window frames. Flora popped into her mind and she thought, I want my mother, I want to lay my head in her lap, all the things lost to us in the crap of the years, all mother – daughter moments ripped away from us. Thank you for that, Jackie. Thank you. I loved you anyway.

Caskie fingered the spines of books. *A Scots Quair. Growing Up in the Gorbals. The USA Trilogy.* Motes of dust drifted in sunlight. He walked the room restlessly. He brought his face close to one of the busts Joyce kept on shelves. This one, smooth-eyed, blind, a Roman copy, seemed to be peering into a world outside the range of everyday senses.

'Counsel me, Senator,' he whispered to the bust. 'Look at the bloody awful state of things. Where do I go from here?'

'Are you talking to a statue?' Joyce asked.

Caskie turned quickly. He hadn't heard her enter, and he was a little embarrassed. 'I was conferring,' he said.

'Talk to statues often?'

'All the time,' Caskie said. 'They don't judge, you see.'

'You're afraid of judgement?' Joyce asked.

'Now and then.'

There was a noise in the hallway, and Eddie Mallon came into the room.

He looked weary, Joyce thought. His eyes were lightless. 'Where the hell have you been?' she asked.

'Choosing a coffin,' he said.

'Oh shit, *damn damn*, I was supposed to help Senga do that and it went out of my mind. I feel awful.'

'Under the circumstances,' Caskie said, 'you're allowed a little amnesia.'

Eddie flopped on the sofa and stretched his legs.

Joyce said, 'You've been gone a long time.'

'When you're buying a coffin you don't simply leap into the first one you see,' he said.

'Comical,' Joyce said.

'I need some light relief,' Eddie said.

'Don't we just? I think I'll walk round to Senga's. See how she's doing.'

Caskie looked at his watch. 'It's time I was going too.'

Eddie glanced at Chris Caskie, whose face was lightly tanned. It made his small beard seem whiter.

'Did you process Tommy G through your computer, Chris?'

'It's in,' Caskie said. 'Nothing's come back to me yet. We'll get something, I'm sure.'

'I'm sure,' Eddie agreed.

Joyce ruffled his hair. 'Back soon.'

Caskie said, 'See you later, Eddie.'

I know how to empty a room, Eddie thought. He heard the front door close. He thought of phoning Claire, but before he could lift the phone the motion of the day caught up with him – the taxi-rides that had zoomed him from one end of the city to the other – and he shut his eyes and dozed in a shallow way for twenty minutes, dreaming of Glasgow, a black-and-white Glasgow he'd never lived in, steamships on the Clyde, crinolined ladies stepping out of horse-drawn carriages, shoeless kids begging on street corners. The air stank of raw sewage and the dank river. Women in shawls sold fish from wheelbarrows, and men hauled on their shoulders sides of butchered animals.

He woke dry-throated, walked into the kitchen, drank some water at the sink. He felt a deep frustration. He didn't see how he could stay in Glasgow long enough to penetrate the reasons behind Jackie's murder, or identify the killer, as if the slaying and the people involved belonged in a Glasgow so secret it was out of his reach – like the monochromatic city he'd seen in his dream. He was due to leave the day after the funeral.

What could he achieve in so short a space of time? He couldn't drag out his visit, he had work at home, the case of the dead junkie girl in the abandoned brownstone, her identity and cause of death, and God knows what else might have happened in the meantime, what files dropped on his desk, what mysteries he was paid to solve –

Caskie and Haggs. Haggs the gun collector and Caskie the cop. What did they have going between them that required such facile fabrications? It was a fair assumption, he thought, that Haggs knew Caskie. He certainly knew *of* him. Say their paths had crossed. It was possible they'd met in orbit around Jackie. Assumptions, and Eddie wasn't enamoured of them, but sometimes they were the little building blocks that led to truth. He dipped his head under the cold water tap and let the stream run for a minute. Then he turned off the tap and stepped back from the sink and enjoyed water running over his scalp and down his face and thought: Caskie, lying sonofabitch.

You and Haggs are involved in something –

It was always *something*, this mystic *something*, this object that couldn't be defined. He dried his face and walked back to the living room and opened the phone directory.

29

The motorway roared half a block away. Petrol fumes hung brown in the still air like old muslin. Haggs, hands deep in pockets, gazed at the street through a high wire fence. This site, protected by the fence and an expensive electronic alarm system, was the location of a car-hire company called EasyGo, which Haggs owned. The lot was filled with Puntos and Ford Mondeos and VW Golfs. The Clyde was about five hundred yards to the south.

Haggs stared into the street, which had a derelict look. Across the way was an abandoned warehouse with broken windows. A gang of teenagers smoked crack and eyeballed the EasyGo lot as if they were thinking wads of drug money might be stashed inside.

Wasted fuckwits, Haggs thought. 'He comes to see me,' he said. 'On my fucking doorstep, bold as brass.'

Caskie, arms folded, leaned against the chassis of a Golf. 'I can't keep him chained, Haggs. He's not an easy customer.'

'Tells me he's the executor of the will and do I want to buy Jackie's warehouse.'

'He's not the executor of the will,' Caskie said. 'I happen to know Jackie's lawyer is the executor.'

'Okay, so he's lying. Then he asks me who do I think murdered his father and do I know a policeman called Caskie who, it seems, told him about that trial of mine years ago. I don't like this Yank cop turning up on my fucking doorstep.'

'I didn't tell him anything about you or your trial, Haggs.'

'So he's got a private agenda.' Haggs glared at the crackheads passing a pipe around.

'Private? His agenda's as bright as a lighthouse,' Caskie said. 'He's looking for the killer.'

'And that brings him to my doorstep.' Haggs cracked his knuckles a couple of times. 'He doesn't believe Bones did it.'

Caskie had the urge to ask *Where is Bones?*, except he didn't want the answer. Bones was to take the fall, and then he'd be smuggled out of Glasgow to safety. That was the understanding, the deal. But Caskie was having a hard time picturing Bones strolling down Regent Street to Piccadilly Circus or drinking ice-cold beer at a sidewalk café on the Boul St Mich, and clocking the passing crumpet. He felt cold inside.

Haggs said, 'I don't like the way Mallon stares at you when you're talking to him, because I get the feeling he's seeing right through your fucking head.'

'He sticks,' Caskie said.

'I wish he'd fuck off back to America. Is there a chance he knows anything about Jackie's business?'

'You think Jackie telephoned his son in Queens to tell him he had some furtive deal going on? Straws, Haggs. You're clutching.'

'I wonder.' Haggs made a V-sign at the scruffs across the street but they were too buzzed to be bothered by him. They had their crack and that was the limits of their universe and some tall skinny fucker gesticulating was an alien drop-in from another galactic system. 'Why's he so desperate to connect you and me?'

'Because he doesn't trust his local sheriff,' Caskie said. 'He doesn't believe anything you tell him unless he can verify it for himself.'

'I'd hate it if he became too much of a nuisance, Caskie. I'd hate to . . .' Haggs shrugged and looked serious.

Caskie saw a plane far to the south, rising out of Glasgow Airport. He wondered about its destination. Far away. Far far away.

Haggs said, 'The business we were discussing yesterday. Where are we with that?'

Caskie watched the plane vanish, a silver dot of light. 'Senga first,' he said. 'She knows nothing about Jackie's plans.'

'You're absolutely sure about that?'

'One hundred per cent. And the same with Joyce.'

'So what you're saying is Jackie confided his plans in nobody.'

'Nobody in the family anyway.'

'You're not just being gallant, are you, Caskie? The bold knight figure. The big man.'

'No, I'm not.' Caskie realized, not for the first time, how deep his hatred of Haggs had become; the emotion was hard and black like a stone dropped down a bottomless well. *I'll get you, Haggs.*

Haggs said, 'I've relied on you to suss out what these two women know, but if I find out you're lying and you're protecting either of them, you can forget all about your police pension and any perks you might be expecting. What you'll get instead, pal, is public humiliation so fucking shattering you'll need to slip out of Glasgow in the back of a turnip lorry –'

Caskie interrupted. 'I'm not lying, and I'm not protecting Senga or Joyce.' He looked up at the sun, blinked. 'It might interest you to know Joyce was attacked today.'

'Attacked?'

Caskie told him about the assault, and Tommy G. He was pleased to see that the story had a distressing effect on Haggs, who clamped his hands together and cracked his fingers quite rhythmically. 'Let me get this straight. This Tommy G said he had a *deal* going with Jackie?'

Caskie nodded. 'A *big* deal. His very words. Maybe it's even the same deal as the one you're so interested in, Haggs. Wouldn't that be a kick in the teeth? Competition for you.'

Annoyed, Haggs asked, 'Who the hell is Tommy G?'

'He's up from London.'

'That's really helpful. And what else?'

'Tommy G alias Tommy Gurk alias Thomas Gilfillan alias Tommy Zen. Any of these ringing your chimes, Haggs?'

'No.'

Caskie said, 'Jamaican Londoner. Did a short stint in the Scrubs for possession of hashish with intent to sell. A year, time off for good behaviour. Then he entered a monastery.'

'A monastery?'

'He became a Buddhist, Haggs. In Tibet.'

'So you're telling me that our dear wee Joyce was attacked by a pacifist vegetarian? What did he hit her with – a fucking bean-curd egg-roll? Note to self: always make sure you're armed with a sharpened parsnip when you're in conversation with a Buddhist.'

'Buddhist or not, he's connected,' Caskie said. 'He takes trips. Rotterdam sometimes. Also Zurich. He has associates in both places.'

'What kind of associates?'

'Business types.'

'Straight business or funny?'

'Funny, I'd say.'

'How funny?'

Caskie didn't answer. He loved to keep Haggs dangling. He looked at the dopeheads beyond the wire fence. The druggy underclass. Thin stoned faces blissed to the hilt. A wine bottle, label peeling off, was doing the rounds. One of the kids, a girl dressed in baggy jeans with a plaid shirt knotted round her waist, blew him a kiss and called out, *'Hey Santy Clause! Can I suck yer beard, eh?'* She tugged her khaki blouse open and flashed a small sad breast at him and then sat down with her back to the wall and rolled a cigarette.

'Nice wee tit,' Haggs said.

Caskie ignored the remark. 'As far as I can gather from the skimpy data I was able to access,' he said, 'Gurk is associated with a dubious character in Zurich called Josef or Joe Kaminsky. According to police surveillance reports, Gurk stays at Kaminsky's country house when he visits Switzerland.'

'And what's so special about Tommy Gurk that he merits surveillance? What business is he doing with this Kaminsky?'

'Anything that pays is my guess.'

Haggs said, 'Give me specific.'

'Kaminsky is wanted by the Israelis on charges of – I quote – currency irregularities. The Swiss have resisted extradition efforts.'

'Currency irregularities? Fuck does that mean?'

'It sounds like a catch-all phrase. Maybe he's evaded taxes, or traded illegally in securities . . . I don't know. There's also the chance it's a smokescreen to cover activities which have absolutely nothing to do with fiscal matters.'

'That's it?'

Caskie nodded. What he'd told Haggs wasn't the whole truth. But enough to rattle Haggs's cage. Haggs didn't need to know everything in the database. 'The Police National Computer has its limitations, Haggs.'

Haggs thought, *Jesus Christ*. Rotterdam. Zurich. Israel. A monastery in Tibet. It was getting out of hand, going international, spreading to places where he had no control and no affiliates, where he didn't know the bloody languages. He didn't like it when his ventures had connections beyond Glasgow or, at a pinch, the Scottish border, because it increased the chance of complexity, elaborate rip-offs, encounters with men whose ways of doing things might be alien to him. He couldn't make the link between Jackie Mallon and the Jamaican Buddhist called Tommy Gurk or G or Zen, between a terraced house in the east end of Glasgow and a country house in fucking Switzerland. He couldn't connect a junkyard near Duke Street with 'currency irregularities' in Israel. Weird planets were colliding. He felt as if the road he'd been travelling towards the hidden world of Jackie Mallon – badly signposted as it was – had suddenly reached a fork where the directions were posted in languages he couldn't translate.

'Get me more, Caskie. I need more.'

'Easier said than done. I could go through Interpol, but there are protocols.'

'Fuck protocols,' Haggs said.

A rock thrown from the old warehouse smacked the wire fence and made it vibrate. Haggs wished he had a rocket-launcher and he'd just blow those crack-smoking guttersnipes all to hell.

A young man with wild hair called out, *'How much is it to rent one of them fucken cars, eh?'*

Haggs turned his back on the crack crew and looked at Caskie. 'I suggest you dig a wee bit deeper, pal. If you know what's good for you.'

I'll dig your grave, Caskie thought. That's how far I'd like to dig.

A shadow moved at the back of his mind. Then it took definite form, brightening. He thought: Maybe. Why the hell not? He recalled what he'd experienced when he'd first run Tommy G through the computer – a dim awareness of possibilities, a disjointed sense of enlightenment – but it was expanding now, it was growing from seed to shoot.

Another rock struck the fence, then another, a third, eventually a fusillade. The restive crackheads drifted across the street. Ragged, white-faced, skinny, these kids looked like extras from a cocaine version of *Night of the Living Dead*. More rocks thudded the fence. Then faces were pressed to the wire and grubby fingers hooked the metal strands. The fence was kicked and rattled and shaken vigorously. A rock flew into the lot and struck the roof of a Ford Mondeo.

Haggs roared, 'Fuck off out of here, the whole bloody lot of you! You shower of shite! You bunch of arse-wipes! *Fuck off!* You hear me?'

Some of the kids laughed and hooted. A gaunt girl in yellow-tinted glasses and a mini-kilt and purple Doc Martens climbed a few feet up the fence before she fell back. A few of her friends cheered and helped her up and she began to climb again.

Haggs looked at Caskie. 'You're a cop. Do something about this scum, for God's sake.'

'They won't get over the barbed wire at the top,' Caskie said.

'I'm not counting on it,' Haggs said. 'Have I got to dial the police myself?'

'You know the number, Haggs?'

'Fuck you,' Haggs said. He took his cellphone from his jacket. The girl climbing reached the top of the fence and tried to seize the coiled strands of barbed wire. She cut her hand and fell, clattering against the pavement.

'You can never find a policeman when you need one,' Caskie said, enjoying his moment of supremacy – that and the fact the shadow was taking on ever more solid form, and he saw it clearly now. He felt a jolt, a thrill, of inspiration. *How to get Haggs out of my life* . . . How often had he asked himself that? And now he had a possible answer. But did he have the guts?

'Bloody joker,' Haggs said, punching buttons.

Caskie was miles away, thinking. Yes. One long-distance phone call.

30

Lou Perlman said, 'This pub's a kind of shrine for addicts like me.' He indicated old football photographs and posters that filled every available space on the wall. Glass display cases contained various editions of the green-and-white hooped jerseys of Glasgow Celtic Football Club. Medallions hung here and there, and scarves had been stapled to the ceiling beams.

Perlman went on, 'Traditionally, Celtic has had a predominantly Roman Catholic support – on account of the club's Irish origins – but not exclusively so. You remember your social history, Eddie?'

Eddie Mallon remembered. Jackie was usually disappointed when Celtic defeated their Southside rivals, Rangers. Eddie took the half-pint of lager Lou Perlman pushed along the bar towards him, and sipped. Perlman had a shandy, which he rapped cheerfully against Eddie's glass, and said, 'I'm a nut about Celtic, a passionate headcase – so what can I do? Some of these players on the walls are old heroes of mine. Charlie Tully, a right comedian on the wing, Willie Fernie, played like he had the ball attached to his boot with an invisible thread, Billy McNeill, tower of strength in defence . . . I'm

187

boring you, right? I always bore people when I go on about Celtic.'

Eddie said, 'I liked the game when I was a kid.'

'Ah, the game's only a small *part* of it,' Perlman said. 'It's the culture. It's Glasgow. It runs in the blood of the city. Of course, you'll find people who'll try to tell you they've got no interest in the two teams. View such individuals as suspect, son. They may be aliens from beyond the city limits. You'll find other people who take the game to extremes, and see it as a holy war. On one side is Ulster and the Union Flag and our beloved monarchy, on the other is the IRA. View these nutters with suspicion as well. They may be dangerous. And then some people will tell you we've moved on from all that shite, we're liberated from old hatred . . . take that with a pinch of salt, Eddie. We're impaled on the past like a pig on a spit.'

Perlman stared at the various posters in silence for a time. He smiled. He had a good smile. It changed his face the way sudden sunlight transforms a dark room. His lower teeth were slightly misaligned and discoloured by tobacco. 'So what's an old Jew like me doing supporting Glasgow Celtic, you wonder? They've been the immigrant underdogs, and Rangers the establishment. So who's a Jew with a liberal streak to support, eh?'

'Not the Presbyterian establishment,' Eddie said.

'Got it,' Perlman remarked.

They carried their drinks across the bar to a table hidden in a corner behind the jukebox. A few drinkers, wearing team colours, stood at the bar and argued about an arcane footballing matter. Perlman removed his glasses and wiped them on the sleeve of his jacket. The knot in his wide gold tie was undone and his collar unbuttoned. 'I'd rather talk football than crime any day of the week. Except crime pays my wages and football only fuels my passion . . . So crime it is. On the phone you said somebody attacked your sister.'

Eddie described the break-in, the assault.

'Your sister's never seen this character before?'

188

Eddie said, 'No. And Senga had never heard of him either. Slim gleanings for you, huh?'

Perlman held his glasses up to the light, then replaced them. The lenses were still smudged. 'The next question is – what's this situation between Tommy G and your late father? I assume you've asked yourself a few questions and come up with nothing.'

'Less than nothing.'

'No conclusions, no inspired guesses.'

'None. I thought Roddy Haggs might be able to throw a little light –'

'You talked to Haggs?'

'Was that a faux pas?'

'Didn't I tell you he was on my list?'

'I didn't think it could do any harm to see him. I hoped he might know what Jackie was up to, and maybe I could somehow hook that information to Tommy G –'

Perlman said, 'Let me tell you this. I'm the Force's numero uno Haggs Watcher. When it comes to Roddy, I'm like a fucking encyclopedia. The main thing to remember about Haggs is he's driven by a completely disgusting greed. He sees something he wants – slurp, out comes the tongue like a demented anteater, and the object of desire is digested. Roddy belches, and moves on to the next acquisition. If he believes your dad had something tasty, he'd want to suck that down too. Haggs is dangerous, Eddie. He's got some unpleasant cronies.'

'Are you saying I could be in trouble?'

'I'd be lying if I denied it.'

'I'll look out for myself,' Eddie said.

'See that you do. Seriously.' Perlman tore the filter off a cigarette. He lit the vandalized cigarette and regarded the filter with scorn. 'I hate these sorry attachments. So you say Caskie phoned Tommy G's name into Force HQ for a crime computer check?'

'Right,' Eddie said.

'I'll double-check, see what result came through.' He coughed and swallowed some shandy.

'Why? You think Caskie might just be going through the motions?'

'There's a whisper about good old Chris. I've been hearing it on the streets for donkey's. It's always been constant but quiet as a lullaby, and what it says is that Caskie's very friendly with Haggs. This isn't to accuse Caskie of anything illegal, don't get me wrong. Cops and criminals, they're in the same industry basically, so why shouldn't they know one other? But with Caskie the talk has always suggested something more, like he's maybe a wee bit *too* close to Haggs. People in Pitt Street have heard this gossip, but nobody's ever done anything about it. Most cops would put it down to criminal malice. Some wanker out there wants to spread a bad word about a cop, undermine him. But this particular whisper has been unusually long-lived.'

'Nobody ever looked into it?'

'Eddie, the world is bursting at the seams with criminals and assorted louts. Who's got time to probe a groundless rumour, eh?'

Caskie and Haggs, Eddie thought. Friends. What kind of friendship was it? What sort of benefits could they derive from such an alliance? He imagined Caskie and Haggs meeting in dark places, heads close together, whispers. An exchange of information, favours flowing back and forth between them. *Find out what Jackie Mallon is up to,* Haggs says. *You've got the inside track.*

Caskie, maggot in the apple, agrees.

A kid approached the jukebox, spread his hands against it, studied the playlist. He dropped in a coin and pressed a couple of buttons and then swaggered back to the bar. The music was an Irish tune played by a folk band.

'"Fields of Athenry,"' Perlman said, and laid a hand on his heart. 'My anthem.' He listened to the music a moment before he leaned across the table and said, 'Tay showed you the gun, I'm told.'

'I saw it.'

'Did he tell you where the gun was found?'

'Bones's flat.'

'Did he say where exactly?'

'Just the flat. That's all I was told.'

Perlman beckoned Eddie closer with his finger crooked. 'It was wrapped inside a Tesco grocery bag and stuffed under the kitchen sink. The *fucking* sink.'

'No way,' Eddie said.

Perlman said, 'Does the word transparent come to mind?'

Eddie said, 'See-through. A man has a gun that was used in a murder and he wraps it in a grocery bag and sticks it under his sink, which must be the most blatantly obvious place in the history of crime for stashing *anything*.'

Perlman said, 'Too fucking easy to find.' He blew smoke. 'You can bet your mortgage Bones didn't stash it there.'

'Then who did?'

'There's no other candidate *but* Bones, Eddie. That fact has come down from a very high place indeed. It's the gospel. Tay wants it signed and sealed.'

'What is it? Is Tay lazy? Is he too busy to dig any deeper?'

Perlman crushed out his smoke. The cigarette paper burst and flakes of tobacco stuck to his fingers. He blew them away. 'Laziness isn't a factor, Eddie. Tay is at his desk dawn till dusk some days. His assistant Sandy Scullion also works all the hours sent by God, although he's altogether a more pleasant human being than Cardinal Tay. But you know the shitty way it works. If the murder victim had been the Lord Mayor of Glasgow, you can bet your arse Tay would have been crawling all over the crime, witnesses and potential witnesses would have been hauled in on crowded charter buses.'

'And Jackie was a nobody,' Eddie said.

'Not quite,' Perlman said. 'Jackie Mallon wasn't the Marquis of Govan, right, but he had a criminal record, albeit small. Also he was suspected of various wrongdoings down the years. Theft of artworks. Masterminding a scheme to persuade some decrepit

191

aristo in his dotage to part with precious pre-Revolutionary Russian coins. Stuff like that. None of it ever stuck to your dad, but it occupied police man-hours, it produced paperwork and more paperwork, and so Jackie Mallon was something of a fucking nuisance if you worked in Pitt Street.'

'Now he's not a nuisance.'

'Score,' Perlman said.

'It sucks. It's −'

'Unacceptable? Unfair? Sure it is. It's like the fucking National Health Service, Eddie. If you're rich, and can go private, you'll get good service. If you're *Untermenschen*, you can wait a year or two for a hernia operation. Same with the law. If you're a star, you'll get star treatment. If you're a small-time fucking pain-in-the-arse like Jackie Mallon, and somebody shoots you − oy − you're off the books. It's the system, Eddie.'

'And that's what Jackie was, a small-time pain-in-the-arse?'

Perlman said, 'That's what they tell me.'

'Never big-time.'

'Unless he changed horses lately.' Perlman opened his cigarette packet and saw it was empty. He began to tear it in strips. 'You want him to have been sweetness and light, eh?'

'He'd never been that.'

'Okay. Let's say . . . worthy of love.'

Eddie finished his drink. 'That,' he said.

'Boys and their fathers,' Perlman said. 'Dear God, the complexity of it all. I'll walk out with you.'

They left the pub. Eddie looked at the darkening sky, then at Perlman who was smoking thoughtfully. 'You married?'

'Not any more.'

Eddie detected nothing in the response, no regret, no sadness: it was a dry fact dryly uttered. 'Any kids?'

'Never had the time. I'm going home. What about you?'

'I'll stroll for a while,' Eddie said.

'I'll be in touch. Mind how you go.'

'I will.'

Perlman turned and moved away.

Eddie walked to the end of the block, looking for a taxi, seeing none. *A small-time pain-in-the-arse*, he thought. It wasn't a bad judgement. He could live with that one.

But small-time didn't get you killed.

He paused on a street corner. The city was all noise, unfiltered and vibrant. He listened to the drone of the city. He picked one or two distinct sounds out of the auditory pile, a muted trumpet being played in a tenement, a vandalized version of 'I'll Be Seeing You' – bum note, stop, try again – a man tapping the sidewalk, the *pavement*, with a cane, and the sound of a dog-chain rattling quietly.

Another sound reached him, a constant ticking, and it occurred to him that there was a weird familiarity about this, he'd heard it before only he couldn't remember where, it had sunk into a deep pool of his awareness and lain there unexamined under the silt. For a second he was touched by mild apprehension, something that settled on him with the fleeting touch of a furry summer moth.

He gazed across the street. The car was dark green. The motor was idling. Something inside the engine was out of whack, a minor malfunction. *Tap tick*. The driver, face half-shadowed, was staring straight ahead, not looking at Eddie at all, not interested.

Go for it, Eddie thought.

He crossed the street quickly and caught the handle of the door on the driver's side and hauled it open and, reaching in, grabbed the man by the lapel of his dark blue blazer and dragged him out of his seat.

'Jesus Christ.' The driver slid to the ground, banging an elbow and rubbing it vigorously.

Eddie looked down at him. 'Funny bone?'

'Yes, but not remotely amusing, alas,' the driver said.

31

Larry McQueen woke, got out of bed and went in search of the TV deliveryman and wondered, as he padded in pyjamas and slippers from room to room, if he'd dreamed the fellow up, and all this TV delivery stuff was just a nonsense. But his nose ached and there was dry blood on his hands and he remembered the fellow punching him. He wondered how long he'd slept.

'Hallo? You there? Coooeeee.'

No answer. He looked in the kitchen. Checked out the bathroom in case the fellow was answering the call of nature. In the living room, where a bowl of wax fruit sat on a long coffee table, Larry looked from the window down into the street, which was clogged with parked cars.

He walked into the hall and stepped into his son's bedroom and gazed at the prints on the walls. Modern art. All lines and paint spillage, any moron could do that, what the hell did Billy pay for these bits of crap? Billy had more money than sense. And precious little sense anyway.

Back into the hall.

'Hello? TV man, where are you?'

The flat was silent.

Larry opened the front door and went out to the landing and stood looking down the flight of stairs that led to the street. Maybe the telly man was having trouble getting the box out of his van. Could be. Needs a hand. Larry descended a little shakily. He clutched the banister rail. At the bottom of the stairs he stopped and peered at the front door, a rectangle of dimming light. He stood motionless for a time.

Who was he fooling? He couldn't help the fellah lift the TV box if it was heavy. He wasn't young any more. He didn't have –

Then blank. He couldn't remember why he'd left the flat.

Bloody hell.

You get old. The brain. You don't. Things slip. Tilt. You used to play bingo every Wednesday night. You remember when the lamps in the street were lit by gas flame and coal was delivered in a horse-drawn cart and you needed a ration book for sugar and that time the Queen visited Glasgow after her Coronation and the population lined the streets and waved their little flags, that was when people had respect for royalty –

He was outside now and the royal-blue sky was very very high and he felt a wee bit dizzy between the tall red tenements and sun glancing off windows and he thought, if I sit down on a wall I'll be fine, and his heart was awful fast and when he reached for a wall he found it wasn't solid, it was shrubbery, and it parted under the weight of his hand and he fell through it and landed arse over elbow in somebody's garden where there was crusty dogshite and some old fast-food boxes containing onion rings from a prehistoric age and a burger covered with blue fuzz oh Christ and I can't get up.

'Billy,' he said quietly. 'Come and help me. Help your dad.'

His mouth was dry as cinders. He felt weak.

I am lying here because because . . .

He rolled on to his back and looked up. The sky had an inky quality. His left foot had become twisted in a tangle of shrubbery and the slipper was gone.

O Billy, help me.

Or that nurse Thelma, where was she, where was she?

Then somebody was speaking to him. 'Let me give you a hand up, mister.'

Larry had big spots in front of his eyes, like raindrops. The face that loomed down was young and friendly. Sideburns and short hair a funny orange colour and an unlit cigarette end between the lips.

'Come on, let me get you up. I'll just grab you under the shoulders and you hang on to me, right?'

'Aye right,' Larry said.

'I saw you come out of the close,' the young man said. 'I'll take you back inside.'

'Aye,' Larry said. 'I need my bed.'

'Where did you think you were going dressed only in your pyjamas, for God's sake?'

'I was . . .' Larry's head emptied like a cistern flushed.

'Never mind. Just hang on.'

Larry leaned against the young man. They went inside the tenement, then up the stairs. Ascending, Larry had a sense of having discarded his body.

Inside the flat the young man said, 'You live here on your own?'

'My son sometimes,' Larry said.

'Where is your son?'

Larry sat on the sofa and shook his head.

'You don't know where he is, eh?'

Larry said, 'He moves here and there. I need my nurse. That's who I need.'

'I'll give her a bell. What's her number?'

'In the kitchen by the phone, Thelma's her name.'

'Leave it to me,' the young man said.

Larry said, 'What's your name, sonny?'

'Giovanni. Gio.'

'That's a foreign name.'

'I was born right here in Glasgow. Nitshill to be exact.'

'I'm McQueen,' Larry said.

'Aye, I know, I saw the nameplate on the door.'

Larry listened to the young man go inside the kitchen, then the low rumble of his voice. Giovanni returned. 'Stale in here,' he said, and blew his nose into a big handkerchief. 'Your nurse is on her way.'

'You're a right Samaritan, lad,' Larry said.

'She also said she'd contact your son.' The young man looked round the room. 'I'll be off then.'

'Can you not stay?'

The living room was already empty. Open-mouthed, Larry wondered about dreams and that fuzzy borderline where what was real and what was not just melted into one incomprehensible experience. He wiped drool from the corner of his mouth.

32

The driver sat on the kerb and rubbed his elbow and made a moaning sound.

'How long have you been tracking me?' Eddie asked.

'Tracking you? What do I look like? A bloodhound? This is an outrage –'

Eddie said, 'First thing this morning I had the feeling somebody was scoping me out. I'm betting it was you. You were driving along Duke Street early this morning. I heard your car. That same goddam sound.'

'My blazer's filthy,' the man said. His car was still idling, still ticking.

'Nice jacket, too bad,' Eddie said. 'Who's paying you?'

The man rubbed dust streaks from his sleeve. '*Paying* me? Ah, yes, to keep you under observation, of course. I'm being reimbursed for that, I suppose.'

Why didn't the guy get up and launch a few punches? He was at least ten years younger than Eddie, and he looked fit and strong enough to retaliate instead of just sitting limply near his car and fingering his funny bone or dusting his blazer. Was he a coward? Gutless? It's not that, Eddie thought. The guy looked stressed; his indignation was only a front.

Eddie said, 'Unless I'm way off target, you've spent most of the goddam day hound-dogging me, and nobody works for nothing. So who's your paymaster? Simple question.'

'There's no such beast as the simple question.'

'It's been a long day. Talk straight.'

The guy stretched his arm out slowly, as if checking the integrity of his elbow joint. He held the arm level for twenty seconds, then lowered it. Eddie gazed at him impatiently. *Fuck this.* His mood had darkened. Reaching down, he gripped the lapels of the blazer and dragged the man to his feet and pushed him back against iron railings that surrounded a scrag of garden at the front of a tenement.

'Talk to me,' he said.

'I'm not tracking you. You're out of your skull –'

'Who's paying you?'

'I'm tired and my temper's frayed, friend –'

'My temper's not altogether unruffled either, *friend.*'

The man pulled himself free of Eddie's hold and took a step towards his car. 'If your fit of madness has passed, do you mind if I get in my car and bugger off?'

Eddie saw the man move purposefully to his vehicle, and he went after him at once, caught him by the shoulder, spun him round. Face to face. He smelled something sweet on the guy's breath.

'Show me some identification,' Eddie said. 'I want to know who the fuck you are –'

'I'm a motorist assailed by a deranged pedestrian,' the guy said.

Eddie shoved him against the body of the car. 'Your name, fucker. Your name, your *name.*' And he thrust his hand inside the guy's blazer and hauled out a slimline wallet of soft kidskin. The guy panicked and made a frantic effort to grab it back, but Eddie turned to one side and flipped the wallet open just as the man threw a punch that was partly blocked by Eddie's shoulder, but forceful just the same, sending a stab of serious pain like a corkscrew into the side of his neck. Bullseye. Starry nights and bright sunsets. Tenement buildings collapsing. The scream of motorways. Disoriented, he had an image of gridlocked traffic in the Holland Tunnel.

He went down on one knee, still holding the wallet, and he thought: I'm fucked. The guy made another swift lunge and Eddie held the wallet against his chest, covering it as if this were a game of football and he was shielding the ball. The guy launched a kick that hurt Eddie just under the ribs, but he didn't fumble the wallet in spite of the pain. Dear Christ, there had to have been a smarter way to control this from the first exchange, Eddie thought. I'm hurt and I'm really goddam *losing* it, down on one knee in a darkening Glasgow street, clutching the wallet of a man you've never seen before, one you think has been following you all day – is this squalid escapade why you came three thousand lousy miles through space and time in a *motherfucking aircraft*? Where's the dignity in this?

He made it on all fours to the railings, grasped one, hauled himself up. The guy grunted and stuck his knee sharply into the base of Eddie's spine and all air was expelled, and Eddie had the sense that his lungs were about as useful in the oxygen-processing function as two sun-dried apricots. He gasped and coughed and felt his stomach rise into his throat. But he still had the wallet, oh yeah, *the wallet is mine.* He collected his strength and, in the manner of an out-of-condition prizefighter, swung his arm round in a direct line, hard and fast, fist a ball of lead, and he made contact with the guy's face, and the guy went down like an empty set of clothes in a conjuror's illusion.

Eddie turned, leaning against the railings, and looked down at the man motionless on the pavement. He heard the rattle of his own hurried breathing. You used to be in great shape. American life has wasted all the muscle in you, endless bad coffee in waxy cardboard cups, donuts in sickly sugar-pink all-night joints, burgers dying in grease and hot dogs simmering in water that might have come unfiltered out of the Hudson, white bread and ketchup, the Beginner's Basic Cardiac Arrest

Kit. Claire kept telling him, *Wholemeal bread only, Eddie. Nothing fried. Fresh fruit. Chew on a raw carrot if you have the munchies.*

Carrots were terrific if you were Bugs Bunny, he told her.

He opened the wallet with a hand that shook from exertion. He saw the ID. *Detective-Sergeant McWhinnie, Charles. Strathclyde Police.*

He stared at it.

A cop.

He raised McWhinnie to a sitting position and propped him against the side of the car, which was still pumping out exhaust fumes, and ticking. Eddie reached into the car and switched off the engine and then went down on his knees beside the glazed McWhinnie. You never forget a name. The guy who'd driven Joyce home from the identification of Jackie's corpse had been called Charles McWhinnie. This had to be the same one. He was young and good-looking enough to cause Joyce a flutter.

'I think my jaw's broken,' McWhinnie said in the thickened voice of a novocained man.

'Let me get you inside the car.'

'Why? I'm comfortable here,' McWhinnie said.

Eddie said, 'We've attracted some attention. Just get in the car.'

A few faces in ground-floor windows. Lovers of street violence. Not so gory as telly, but more authentic. A pot-bellied man in a white undershirt stood at the mouth of a close. 'Feeble,' he said, and he slow handclapped. 'If you have to resort to fisticuffs, you might at least put on a proper show.'

Eddie said, 'Quit whining. It was free.'

'Free or not isn't the bloody point. That encounter was pure crap. You both need some time in the gym.'

'Fuck off, fatso.' Eddie raised McWhinnie and manoeuvred him into the passenger seat.

The man in the white T-shirt shouted, 'Pair of diddies. Big girl's blouses.' He turned and vanished inside the close.

Eddie got behind the wheel and slammed the door and drove

away. His ribcage throbbed. His neck was filled with forks of pain.

'We drive on the left in this country,' McWhinnie said. He rubbed the side of his face where Eddie had connected. 'By morning I'll look like the bloody Hindenburg. After the crash.'

'I'm not going to be bruise-free myself,' Eddie said. He aimed the car directly ahead, then somehow found himself on a motorway where the traffic that whizzed past him was disconcerting. He took an exit and steered carefully into the car park of the Hilton. He killed the engine and sighed and tried to ignore his aches and pains.

'It's a crime to assault a police officer,' McWhinnie said.

'So you'll report me.'

McWhinnie shrugged. He held one hand, palm flattened, to the side of his face. 'I don't know how much I feel like a police officer.' The tone in McWhinnie's voice was that of a man to whom promises made had been violated. Oaths had been empty words. He squeezed out a kind of smile. His face was already beginning to swell.

Eddie said, 'Talk to me some more.'

McWhinnie looked in the direction of the hotel. Taxis came and went. Porters hauled baggage. Beyond the glare of the hotel darkness was total. The sun was done with the day.

'I don't have to tell you a damn thing. I have no obligations to you. In fact, I should be cuffing you and asking you to accompany me to the station.'

'What's stopping you?' Eddie asked.

'Ha bloody ha, I don't have the strength for it,' he said. 'Damn, this fucking *jaw*! Christ, did you have a lead pipe hidden in your fist?'

'Pure bone,' Eddie said. 'You were saying?'

'Do you want to hear about the cop movie I saw at a Saturday afternoon matinée and it made me think I'd like to be a detective when I grew up?'

'You don't have to go that far back, Charlie,' Eddie said.

'You Americans always want to cut to the chase.'

You Americans, Eddie thought. He wanted to correct McWhinnie, *this is the city of my birth, my country*, but why bother? 'Hurry's our style. Rush rush. Go go.'

'You were right about one thing. I've been following you.' He touched his jaw again. Blood leaked from between his lips. 'You've dislodged one of my back teeth. Do I look like a balloon yet?'

'You're heading that way. Who gave the command?'

'Ah, the command. Follow the American.'

A tall man in a dinner jacket stepped out of a limo and, with an angelic gowned woman on his arm, entered the hotel. There was a sound of dance music as the doors opened, brassy stuff from the big-band era. 'Just One of Those Things.' Eddie was reminded of Flora. Flora in her greenhouse, thinking of Jackie, remembering the honeymoon in Largs, her long-lost love and his cruelty.

McWhinnie said, 'I don't want to go all philosophical on you, Mallon, but do you believe that in order to maintain the law we sometimes have to break it?'

'I think we walk very close to the edge at times,' Eddie said.

'But not over it?'

'It's debatable, Charlie. It's all grey areas and no maps. Why? Have you broken a law?'

'I'm an upstanding policeman,' McWhinnie said. 'I do what I'm told. If I have questions, I keep them to myself. If I have doubts, I choke them down.'

'And you're choking now,' Eddie said.

'I have . . . let's say, gristle lodged in my gullet.'

'I'm listening.'

'A small thing perhaps – but why the hell was I following you?'

'Yeah. Why?'

'The truth is, nobody told me and I didn't ask. I drove around. I watched. I made notes. But I'm not some bloody espionage agent, Mallon. I joined the Force because I had this notion of upholding the law, achieving something positive I could be proud of, if that doesn't sound Pollyanna and risible – not to waste my time and training running after a cop from New York who, as far as I could tell, wasn't armed and represented no threat to public order. Work like that . . . don't have a clue what its *purpose* is. And obviously I'm not even very good at it.'

Eddie thought, Charles McWhinnie in a nutshell: no sense of self-worth, needs to be valued, praised now and then. 'Somebody thought the job was important, Charlie. Who?'

McWhinnie swivelled his jaw from side to side. It made a clicking sound. 'I'm no Judas, Mallon.'

'I haven't heard the clink of thirty pieces of silver, Charlie.'

McWhinnie said, 'It's not only following you that depresses me, Mallon. It's not just that . . .'

Eddie waited. He understood he couldn't force McWhinnie to talk. He couldn't threaten him. He'd spent his violence. Anyway, what good would it do? McWhinnie would say what he had to in his own time.

More couples entered the hotel dressed for a formal dance. Women with crisp hairdos and long dresses, men in evening wear. It's too hot to dance, Eddie thought. Jackie and Flora in Largs, had it been too hot for them to dance, or had they held each other close and sashayed across the floor of their hotel? A fast foxtrot, a whirl, Jackie's delicate feet barely touching the floor and Flora desperately in love.

Why did he keep coming back to that honeymoon, like a man returning to the origin of a myth he'd never understood? An effect of pain, confused signals rushing this way and that through his head, messages coming in from unusual sources tapped out in a neural Morse he'd never heard before. He *hurt*. It was as if a ghostly figure, with no training in the healing arts of the Orient, was sticking acupuncture needles into his ribs in all the wrong places.

Oh boy. He needed painkillers, strong ones. Darvon. Percodan. Soon you can lie down and stretch out on the sofa in Joyce's flat. She's wondering where I am. The brother who goes missing. Sometimes for years in a faraway continent.

McWhinnie said, 'I'd like to step out of this car with the feeling that I haven't betrayed anyone, Mallon. I'd like to unload some of the dung I'm choking on, but at the same time I don't want to feel that I've regurgitated it in such a way that I'll have long sleepless nights bedevilled by questions of loyalty. Is that clear?'

'There's stuff you can't tell me, I understand that.'

'No. Stuff I *won't* tell you. I have a conscience like a sack of coal, Mallon. I'll set it down for a moment . . . Here's a shock to your system: Bones, alleged killer, was under police protection.'

Bones: the name fished out of the air. 'Protection? I don't follow that.'

'He was ensconced in a flat in Govan for his own safety after the killing.'

'Safety from what?'

'Don't interrupt me. This is hard enough. The flat, I assume, is used from time to time as a kind of secure house. It's a dump, a place people pass through. Witnesses, say. Informants. I bought groceries for Bones. I delivered them to the flat. I told him to stay there and I left. He was a reprehensible little shite with bad teeth. I didn't ask myself why we were being hospitable to him. Probably I just assumed it had something to do with the murder of your father, and maybe Bones needed protection in case the killer was looking for him too. I just did the job.'

'And?'

McWhinnie said, 'This job also involved paying off certain debts Bones had incurred with questionable bookmakers throughout the city. It was over two thousand pounds, it doesn't matter the exact sum. I gave the markers to Bones. I wasn't sure why we were buying him in such a *blatant* way – except perhaps to keep him cheerful while we interviewed him in connection with your father's murder. That's what went through my mind, I suppose. We were oiling a potential witness. We were bribing him, after a fashion . . .' McWhinnie tried another smile but the side of his face had swollen up, as if he had a crab-apple stuffed in his cheek. The smile looked like a gash. 'Some time

205

that day, Bones disappeared. I went in the evening to the flat to check on him, and he'd gone. Where and why? I don't know. Did he leave under his own steam or did somebody come for him? Again, I don't know. But that's only a part of the conundrum, Mallon . . . Answer this. Why was he stuck inside a safe house when he should have been taken to Force HQ for questioning immediately after the murder? Why were we being so cooperative to a man who's suddenly become the major suspect in the killing?'

'He wasn't a suspect immediately,' Eddie said.

McWhinnie said, 'He *should* have been, Mallon. That's my real point. Why wasn't he in your father's car when Jackie left Blackfriars pub? Where was he when somebody was shooting your dad? And then what – did he walk around for a while before he returned to the car and saw cops everywhere? You see, he should have been taken in and questioned hard as soon as he reappeared. Instead, he gets the soft-shoe treatment. Safe house. Gambling debts paid. Groceries. Scotch. He was given preferential treatment – why?'

'Where was he apprehended?' Eddie asked.

McWhinnie said, 'I don't know. I've talked enough. I draw a line here.'

'Did he go back to the car and somebody took him into custody? Did he walk into a local station and say here I am? Did he meet somebody by prearrangement? Who took him to the safe house in the first place? Whose idea was that? There must have been some short preliminary interview at the very least before he was given sanctuary. There has to be a written record somewhere.'

McWhinnie smiled. 'Oh really? A written record, you say? I used to be a big believer in written records. Now? Who knows? I've nothing else to say. I'm in pain and it's getting harder all the time to speak.' He opened the passenger door, and stepped out. 'Keep the car. Use it. I feel like drinking. Medicinal reasons. Sorry about the punch-up, it's not really my style, far too uncivilized, if you knew me better you'd realize that, and you'd know how

206

sick to my soul I've become,' and he turned and walked stiffly towards the hotel.

Eddie got out of the car and called to him. 'You haven't told me who issued the order to have me followed.'

'Right, I haven't,' McWhinnie answered, without turning to look.

'A name,' Eddie said.

McWhinnie kept moving. 'Not from these lips.'

'McWhinnie, wait,' Eddie shouted. 'Who gave you the cash to pay off the gambling debts?'

McWhinnie stopped and looked back. 'This is all I'll say. You know him.'

It had to be somebody inside the Force. Somebody who could pull strings, play power games. 'I know him . . . Is it Caskie?'

McWhinnie turned away, kept moving. He pushed the door and stepped inside the Hilton and Eddie saw the glass swing back in place in a quick little disturbance of distended light. He thought of going after McWhinnie, but he knew McWhinnie had nothing more he was prepared to say. Eddie didn't get back in the car. No way was he driving to his sister's place. Wrong side of the street, one-way systems, few recognizable landmarks. He was dragging ass now, and the night was closing down on him.

Outside the hotel he found a taxi to take him to Dennistoun. He sat in the back and he thought of what McWhinnie had said, and how he'd make sense of it.

33

On the phone, Billy McQueen told the nurse he couldn't come
to see his father. It was inconvenient, he had business meetings,
he plucked excuses out of the air. The call-girl, Leila, was dead
asleep on the floor. She'd passed out here a dozen times.

Thelma said, 'Look here. He's your father. Your dad. He was
wandering around in his pyjamas in the street. In the street,
mind you. That's serious. God knows what the neighbours
are thinking. I've given him something to help him relax,
but he's going on about a TV delivery and somebody called
Giovanni and I can't follow him. I strongly suggest you make
an appearance, because if you don't, well, I can't be responsible
if he decides to go walkabout again. I do have other patients,
Mr McQueen.'

Billy McQueen thought: I have had better days.

The deal is fucked.

Gurk gets maced.

And now Larry is wandering the streets in his pyjamas. Plus
this Giovanni – who the hell was he?

He said, 'It's difficult for me, Thelma. I'm up to my neck.'

'Neck? You'll be in over your head if you don't get here,

because I'll phone Social Services and tell them your father needs to be hospitalized for his own safety –'

'Thelma, I pay you to deal with all this –'

'I have other patients, Mr McQueen. I'm already late for a Parkinson's in Bearsden.'

'Right, right, I'll be there as soon as I can.'

'It better be quick,' she said.

Billy put down the handset. *Fuck you, Thelma*, he thought. He limped to the window and looked out. Darkness and orange lamps. I don't want to go out there. I don't fancy the streets tonight. Climbing in a taxi, take me to Hyndland, no way José. Bloody Larry in his pyjamas.

Leila turned over in her drugged sleep and muttered, *'On an ocean liner sure.'* Night trips, Billy thought. Sea-going escapes under cover of darkness. He wished he was inside Leila's dream and the big propellers of a ship were churning. Destination Tahiti, oh aye.

He picked up the cordless, punched in the number of Gurk's hotel room.

'Yeah?' Gurk said.

'I was wondering . . . are you all right?'

'Rinsed my eyes out a few times with Evian,' Gurk said. 'Sight has been restored. Lamps working, happy to say.'

'Glad to hear that . . . Look, I was curious to know if you wanted to step out, have a bite to eat, a drink, something? I know a nice place in the West End.'

'Kind of you. Have to decline, sorry.'

It's not your company I want, Billy thought. It's the safety of your presence. Be my bodyguard, please. 'It won't take long, Tommy. Half an hour mibbe. I'll send a car down for you.'

'No can do, me old son. I been talking with some of my people. Options are being discussed. People are openly worried. Money is out there, to say nothing of vanished articles. Makes me wonder about other dimensions, Billy. Can things disappear into alternative realities? Are there diversions along

209

the everyday continuum? Anyway, I'm stuck here waiting for the sodding dog to ring again.'

Billy said, 'But –'

'Tell you what. Gimme a bell later.' Gurk hung up.

Billy phoned the number in Hyndland. Thelma answered on the first ring. 'I hope to hear you say you're on your way, Mr McQueen.'

'Even as we speak,' Billy said.

'Your dad's ranting.'

'Fifteen minutes,' Billy said.

I should have stuck him in a home. He's dead weight, he's lumber I have to carry on my back, he's my cross. All I wanted was his affection. You've worked at that, and you're still not getting it, Billy. He put on an expensive black silk shirt, then black trousers and shoes. Camouflage. Creature of the night. He covered Leila with a cotton sheet then phoned his usual cab company for a taxi.

While he waited, he thought about Gurk's dark-red eyes. Beyond bloodshot. Like Halloween contact lenses, the colour of terror. He remembered how Gurk had come stumbling out of the tenement in Ingleby Drive after his visit to Joyce Mallon.

Why hadn't he tried harder to persuade Gurk to keep him company? The Dreadlocked One was obstinate. He made up his mind and that was that. Phone calls, associates, outstanding debts, a transaction gone all to hell: the pressures were stacking up. Gurk managed to escape into meditation and fanciful questions about diversions along some continuum.

Billy's questions were less esoteric but just as mysterious, such as: who shot Jackie Mallon and why did this sweet deal go all wrong? Sometimes the stars were light-years out of joint.

He sweated. His stump chafed against his prosthesis. He needed a splash of industrial-strength moisturizer. Go to Hyndland, appease Larry, stuff him with more medication. Why can't I just wash my hands of you, Larry, you bitter old sod?

His buzzer sounded. He pressed the button on the wall.

210

'Taxi, Mr McQueen.'

'Is that you, Alec?'

'Aye.'

'I'll be down in a flash.' Alec McGroaty. One of his regular drivers. He didn't want strangers. He turned the lights off, left his penthouse, descended in the lift where the mirrored interior reflected a multitude of Billy McQueens dwindling to infinity. I feel that tiny, he thought. A dot in a frozen eternity of silvered glass.

He entered the foyer, nodded at the night security man, Cutcheon, who'd once been a professional wrestler. He looked hard and bulky in his black suit. Alec McGroaty was standing at Cutcheon's desk. A small man in a fawn cardigan and baggy tartan trousers such as a golfer might wear, McGroaty had a deferential manner.

'Hot outside, Mr McQueen,' Cutcheon said.

'Aye it's like the Costa del Sol,' McGroaty remarked.

McQueen didn't feel like small talk. He followed McGroaty outside to the taxi. He climbed into the back.

'Novar Drive,' he said.

McGroaty said, 'On our way.'

McQueen observed the streets. He had the feeling he was travelling through the veins of the city. At Charing Cross he saw the lights of the Mansions Café & Bar. Fun. Life as average people live it. He had the urge to instruct McGroaty to drop him off at the café where he could lose himself in the throng, have a couple of drinks, loosen up. Then he thought of Larry in his pyjamas.

Out west now, over the River Kelvin and buzzing along Dumbarton Road and then up into the dark red sandstone maze of Hyndland where Billy eyed the well-maintained tenements, the ornate cornices and rosettes and high ceilings you could see in rooms where curtains hadn't been drawn. Comfortable lives. He longed to scratch his stump which had begun to itch seriously. He felt fevered.

Somebody will be watching the house. It's a dead certainty.

211

He leaned forward to the driver. 'Alec, go round the block.'

'Awright,' McGroaty said.

The cab completed a circle of the building. Billy McQueen glanced up at the windows of his flat. The light was on in his father's room. The other windows were dark.

'Go round again,' Billy McQueen said.

McGroaty drove round the block a second time. Then he parked outside the entrance to the tenement McQueen would have to enter sooner or later. Billy peered from the cab at the security door. No sign of anyone loitering. But how could you tell if it was safe beyond the security door? How could you know there wasn't an intruder waiting for you? And even if the close was empty, there were about a million cars parked along the street and a dark figure could be sitting in any of them, just biding his time until you got out of the cab.

Billy, Billy, this is no kind of life. He said, 'Alec. Do me a favour.'

'If I can, Mr McQueen.'

'See if it's all clear.'

McGroaty turned and looked back at his passenger. 'Eh, how do you mean all clear?'

'Go inside the building, see if there's anybody loitering.'

McGroaty said. 'Is there the possibility of danger here, Mr McQueen?'

'There's somebody I don't want to see.'

'Aye, but is there *danger*? Do I have a guarantee of my *personal* safety?'

'I'll make your tip excessive,' McQueen said.

'You're scared, right? And you want me to test the waters for you?'

'Scared? Not at all. Just a precaution, Alec.'

McGroaty appeared to consider this. 'How much of a tip are you talking?'

'Fifty.'

'Could you make it an even hundred? I've got a kid –'

'– at Eton, and the fees are high?'

McGroaty laughed. 'Aye, they're extortionate.'

McQueen said, 'A hundred then.'

'I'm to make sure nobody's loitering in the building, zat all?'

'Exactly. Here's the key to the outside door.' McQueen handed McGroaty a key-ring. 'The big brass one opens the security door. Just go inside, see if anybody's hanging around, then come back and tell me. Got it?'

McGroaty said, 'Got it.'

McGroaty left the engine running. McQueen watched him walk up the path to the security door. McGroaty unlocked it, entered the building. The door swung shut behind him. Billy thought, I'm having a bad moment. I'm cut off from my lines of communication.

A man materialized in the driver's seat. A black shape.

Billy banged a fist on the glass partition that separated him from the driver. 'Hey, you, what the fuck? This is McGroaty's taxi.'

The man said, 'Just a wee detour, Billyboy.'

The cab moved slowly forward.

His heart scampering like a hot greyhound sprung from a trap, Billy reached for the door handle. I'll step out, I'll get away, I can do it, gammy leg or not. The door to his right opened and a girl jumped in beside him. She was big and wore black gloves with spiked attachments on the knuckles, and under the muted glow of a streetlamp Billy saw that her face was battle-hard and unforgiving and that her mouth was set in an expression of vicious determination.

'*What the hell's this?*' Billy shouted.

'Shut your fucking gob.' The girl slammed him in the mouth with one of her spiked gloves.

Billy felt brutalized, his face lanced with buckshot.

'Not another word out of you,' the girl said. 'Unless I say so.'

'Right,' Billy mumbled.

'That was a word, diddy,' and she backhanded him hard, and he felt the taxi turn upside down like a carnival ride that was making him ill.

34

Eddie let himself into Joyce's darkened flat. He switched on lights, calling his sister's name. No answer. He remembered she said she was going to see Senga. She was probably still there. Inside the bathroom he rummaged through the medicine cabinet and found Solpadeine capsules. He read the ingredients on the side of the box. Codeine, *far out.* He swallowed a couple of caps then walked into the living room, sat down on the sofa and massaged his face. He was motionless for a long time, weary. He had to stay alert to call Claire.

He thought about time differences, then his mind wandered to sequences of time lost – such as the period between Bones's disappearance from Jackie's parked car and his sanctuary in the safe house. Okay, Lieutenant, what have we got?

One: by prior arrangement Bones had abandoned the car, leaving the way clear for Jackie's killer. So Bones was an accessory to the murder. At some point after leaving Jackie at Blackfriars, Bones was conveyed to a police safe house.

Two: the killing of Jackie Mallon had been sanctioned by at least one cop, who'd ordered McWhinnie to pay off Bones's gambling debts and then smuggled him to safety. But Bones, for reasons unknown, had vanished from the safe house. Why leave a secure place? Why take that chance?

Was he forced? Coerced?

Eddie felt the Solpadeine begin to kick in, the glaze of codeine, the way pain receded behind a barrier, and he lost track of his thoughts for a time. You could grow to love codeine, he thought. He suddenly wished he had Tom Collins with him and they could toss ideas back and forward, bounce notions off one another the way they usually did. Tom bites into his maple-glazed donut and takes a drag on his cigarette, smoke and sugared dough all mixed up in his mouth, and he mumbles, *This whole scenario involves a bad cop at the heart of it, Eddie. I don't like these things, when the good guys go off the track.*

They don't thrill me either.

And Caskie's your candidate. What's in it for him? Money? Power?

Eddie shut his eyes. What does friendly Chris stand to gain from any of his machinations?

Tom Collins said, *The next step is the real toughie, Eddie —*

I know, I know where you're going —

Unavoidable, man. If Uncle Chris smuggled Bones to safety, then he colluded in the murder of Jackie Mallon —

Yeah —

Even if he didn't pull the trigger himself, Eddie, even if he's a shoo-in for fucking sainthood in Senga and Joyce's eyes, he told Bones to take a hike because he was setting Jackie up. He promises Bones a safe haven where he can wait for things to die down.

Eddie felt a certain druggy slippage, a mind-slope he was slithering down. Scree.

Tom Collins says, *Hey, if Caskie's really and truly tight with Haggs, then you gotta consider Haggs is also involved. Maybe he's the shooter. Maybe he just provided the shooter.*

Caskie and Haggs. Laurel and Hardy. A team. Did they have secrets from each other, or were they joined at the hip? In a codeine haze, it was tough to concentrate. He shook his head, massaged his eyelids. He reached for the handset on the coffee

216

table, remembered the number of the international operator and asked to make a collect call to Claire.

'Hey, how are you?'

'I'm okay,' Eddie said. 'You and Mark?'

'We're great. You sound kind of . . . flat?'

'I'm just tired.'

'No, it's more than that,' she said.

How could she tell from a distance of three thousand miles? It was a gift she had. She knew from the first syllable of 'hello' if he was in a good mood or bad, if he'd had one beer too many, all kinds of things.

'I miss you,' he said. 'You're hearing a blue note.'

'By the way, Flora phoned,' she said. 'Wanted to know if I was doing okay. Like I'd founder in your absence. I love you with all my heart, Eddie, but I can still manage things here.'

'You told her so,' Eddie said.

'Gently.'

'Is Mark home?'

'He's at Chuckie Roth's house.'

'Tell him I called, would you? Give him my love. Tell him to look out for you.'

'I think you got that last sentence the wrong way round,' she said. 'Is Joyce hanging in?'

What was the point of mentioning the assault? He said, 'I think so. You know Joyce. She has different levels.'

'And you don't go there.'

'Nobody goes there, sweetie. Not even Joyce, I suspect . . .'

'Any news? Any developments?'

'Nothing special to report.'

'Are you being straight with me, Eddie?'

Fuck. She missed nothing. He pictured her in the kitchen, phone tucked between jaw and shoulder. He heard water running in the background. She might be cleaning salad leaves at the sink, or filling a kettle for tea.

'It's complex,' he said.

She said, 'Murder usually is.'

217

He covered a yawn. 'I'm beat, love. I'll say goodnight.'

'Stay out of trouble,' she said.

'I always do. I love you.'

'Likewise, Eddie.'

When he put the handset down he sat for a minute and let the codeine flow easy through his system. The pains diminished. He had a flash of the encounter with McWhinnie; he smelled the rust on the railings he'd stumbled against. He got up, walked the room, tried in vain to summons Tom Collins again.

Blanked, he walked to the kitchen, drew a glass of water, felt a slight swoon. He bent down under the tap and soaked his head, and tried to ignore the tweak in his spine, that ripple of nerve. Dripping, he went back inside the sitting room and then he stopped on the threshold of Joyce's bedroom.

He went in, flicked on the overhead light.

Double bed unmade, a big quilt of American Indian design, a pile of books on the floor by the bed, an ashtray filled to the max on the antique dressing table, books of matches from various bars and restaurants, *Groucho St Jude's*, *Trattoria Trevi*, *The Polo Club*, little mounds of clothing scattered here and there. It was a comfortable messy lived-in room. Eddie moved towards the fireplace which was made from carved walnut, little clusters of dark brown grapes and cherubs. The wood imparted warmth, like dark flesh under a hot sun.

There were photographs on the mantelpiece, some framed, others thumbtacked to the wall in a haphazard way. He saw Joyce on her graduation day, mortarboard and black gown and a smile on her face that suggested relief: I'm through with school. World, here I come. Jackie was alongside her, his hair not yet completely silver, sideburns a little unruly. He wore what looked like his best suit, the kind men always wear with an air of deferential discomfort, holding themselves as if the waistband's too tight and the pants starched. There was a wolfish quality to his smile. The light in the eye was sharp, but it was a middle-aged rake's light on the cusp of dimming. In this photograph Jackie had been – forty-nine? Fifty? He looked proud of what his daughter had achieved.

Next, photographed on the same day, Joyce and Caskie standing side by side. Joyce has the mortarboard held in front of her and her hair, long then, falls across her shoulders. Her smile in this shot dazzles. Caskie, beardless and strong-chinned, middle to late thirties, is as proud of Joyce as her own father. He's gazing into the camera with the straightforward honest look of a dad who's given wholehearted support to a daughter worth every drop of his sweat.

Fuck you, Chris, I want to scissor your goddam face out of the photo.

At the end of the mantelpiece there was a black-and-white picture Eddie had never seen before, and the sight of it disturbed him, although he couldn't say why precisely, except that the subject of this particular shot had been going through his mind like a hallucination only an hour or so earlier. Jackie holding Flora off the ground, cradling her as if she were as light as a baby, and Flora's black hair falls away from her face and she's smiling, she's happy, he's never seen that hot smile before, and Jackie – good-looking in a blazer and flannels, a genuine dude – has his head thrown back just a little, face frozen in mid-laugh. And just behind the stone steps where they're standing, just beyond wooden tubs of flowers, is the edge of a sign – 'IEW HOTE'. Eddie picked up the photograph and turned it over. Somebody had written, *Largs, June 1954, Seaview Hotel*. The honeymoon, Eddie thought. Young lovers. That blood fever, the crazed magnetism that binds husbands and wives together in a way that will never be quite the same again. It may stay strong, it may grow even stronger, but it will never be the same kind of bond as the first flourish, when even those simple words 'husband and wife' have an erotic charge.

Eddie fingered the picture as if he were trying to divine something that wasn't immediately apparent. He was suddenly depressed: the happy faces in the photograph couldn't know what thunderclouds were gathering ahead. You always saw old pictures with the privilege of hindsight. You knew the partings and the losses, the sorrows and the pains, that lay before the subjects. People were innocents when the shutter clicked. Frozen in a particular second, they had no futures.

He stepped away from the fireplace.

'Hello.'

He turned, saw Joyce. 'Caught me. I was snooping.'

'Feel free.'

'I'm sorry, Joyce.'

'No, seriously, I mean it, look around, take your time, I have nothing to hide from my own brother.'

'There are a couple of pictures here I hadn't seen before. Your graduation –'

'Lost youth,' she said. 'I look like I'm off to discover a new continent in those pictures. The intrepid explorer. Instead I teach secondary school in Shawlands.' She stepped closer to him. 'Have you been in a war? You're all wet and funny-looking and you've got a bruise like a map of Italy on the side of your neck. How did you get that?'

'I had an accident,' he said. 'I slipped.'

'Right, I noticed it's icy outside.'

He wondered if his ribs were purple too. The Solpadeine made these concerns remote.

'Tell the truth,' she said. She put a hand on her hip. He imagined her doing this in a class while she waited for one of her students to explain why he hadn't completed his homework.

'I was in a fight,' he said.

'A fight? You mean with fists? Who were you fighting?'

'I had a brief encounter with your acquaintance McWhinnie.'

'McWhinnie? You've taken to fighting with Glasgow policemen? Jesus Christ, Eddie.'

'We ended with a kinda truce,' he said.

'Dare I ask the reason behind the conflict?'

'He's been following me.'

'You're paranoid.'

'Bullshit.'

220

'Truth, paranoia, whatever. Are there any good reasons to get into a punch-up with a cop?'

'You sound like Flora when she was angry with me,' he said, and he looked at her small hand and how tightly it was clenched against her hip, which was thrust aggressively forward. Blue jeans, T-shirt, sneakers, even her clothes seemed combative. She wore no make-up, so no lipstick or face powder detracted from her eyes, which were burning on all cylinders.

'Well, fuck it, you deserve to be scolded,' she said. 'It's perfectly understandable that the Strathclyde Police don't like a cop from outside wandering round on their territory. You'd take kindly to some Glasgow policeman in Manhattan, I suppose –'

'Depends on what he was doing.'

'Tell me what it is *you're* doing exactly?'

'I have some questions about Jackie's death.'

'You and me both,' she said. 'We want the same thing, like what the hell he was up to at the end of his life, and what got him slaughtered in the back of his car, but fighting with the cops isn't going to help get answers.'

'You know what they're saying about Bones?'

'Chris told me.'

'Oh, right, Chris, good old Chris, he's practically family, after all,' Eddie said. The codeine forcefield short-circuited for a moment and he was a nest of pains, and suddenly furious. Restrain yourself. Chris was sacrosanct. He was a temple you couldn't enter unless you kicked off your shoes, then genuflected.

'I'm not a fan of easy sarcasm, Eddie. What have you got against Chris anyway?'

Eddie chewed the words in his mouth as if they were made from a substance he couldn't swallow. Pig's liver raw. *He's a goddam liar and crooked as a carnie game. You want the skinny on dear Chris, sister? He's bad to the bone. Let's ask Chris about Jackie's murder* . . . But he didn't get these words out. Instead, he took the merciful option. 'Look, the way I feel has probably got nothing

221

to do with Chris. My perceptions are skewed, it's the shock of Jackie –'

'Shock, I'm beyond shock,' she said. 'Right now all I want is to get through this funeral.'

'Right now, what I'd like best is to drive a goddam nine-inch spike into the skull of whoever triggered the old man.' The vehemence in his voice surprised him; it was his first direct encounter with a raw need for retribution, an ugly jagged emotion.

'Hard words,' she said. 'Maybe later I'll feel the same way as you. Maybe I'll develop a deep longing for revenge.' She stepped closer to him. Her smile was sad. 'We shouldn't argue, we need each other.'

He held her. She felt limp.

He saw them reflected in the oval mirror, brother and sister clinging together. He looked big and ponderous compared to the wispy appearance of Joyce. 'I guess I've missed too much of your life. I'm out of the loop.'

'Then get back in,' she said. 'The door's open.'

'I'm working on it.' He looked over her shoulder, drawn back to the photograph of Jackie and Flora, honeymooners in 1954 in the Seaview Hotel, Largs. But it was Christopher Caskie he was thinking about, and his eye drifted to Caskie and Joyce, graduation day at the University of Glasgow, a man and a young woman who might, to an untrained eye, have been father and daughter.

Eddie squeezed his sister, then let her go.

'I just want away from death,' she said, 'and back into the light, if you know what I mean.'

'I know what you mean.'

He looked at Joyce and saw her once again as that little girl staring at him as he vanished in the back of a black taxi, bright ribbon in her hair and skipping rope dangling from one hand, but now another form took shape to complete the mural of that day, a memory he'd misplaced or buried, a recollection of Jackie standing just behind Joyce, his hands resting possessively on her shoulders, his face shadowed a little by shrubbery, his expression that of a proudly stubborn man who thought it a sign of courage to conceal his feelings, a man above showing the pain of departures, one who wouldn't beg for another chance because begging was a weakness. He'd sooner let his family disintegrate than ask for a fresh start. He understood only the terrible logic of endings. And yet – there was something else, a look within a look, masked, and Eddie realized it was the first inkling of a sorrow that would take Jackie Mallon many years to discover and explore.

A sadness filled Eddie, and he turned his face away from his sister and gazed through the window at the moon climbing the warm night sky, and he wondered what the weather had been like on the day of his enforced leave-taking, but that was one memory lost in the dross of things.

35

'I think you've had enough, sir.'

Charlie McWhinnie, clutching a napkin filled with ice-cubes to the side of his face, looked at the fat-necked man behind the bar of the Hilton and asked, 'Have I been aggressive? Have I been insulting to your other customers? Can you honestly say –'

'No, sir,' said the barman, who had a bright red face and long sideburns. 'You've been generally well behaved. It's just that you keep falling off your stool –'

'Gravity is the drunk man's enemy,' McWhinnie said. He scooped a palmful of peanuts from a little silver dish and tossed them towards his mouth. Mostly they went shooting past his face. 'A question. Are you happy in your work?'

'Aye. It has its moments.'

McWhinnie belched. His perceptions were unreliable. The room was turning in a slow circle. He felt he was a passenger on a precarious carousel. He narrowed his eyes and looked at his little notebook, which lay open on the bar. The pages were wet with booze and his fountain pen lay in a puddle of spilled drink. *Dear Diary, life is shit. When I was six years of age I fancied playing rugby for Scotland, heroics in the Murrayfield mud.*

'I'm working on a story,' he said.

'You a writer then?'

'More a keeper of records,' said McWhinnie. 'This barkeeping lark, you think I'd be good at it?'

'Requires social skills,' the barman said.

'Those I have in abundance.'

A hand fell heavily over McWhinnie's shoulder. 'What are you doing to yourself, my young pal?'

McWhinnie turned, saw Lou Perlman. 'Lou? What brings you here?'

'You did. You phoned.'

'Fuck me. Did I?'

'And the Good Samaritan came running. You're pissed as a newt, son. What happened to your face?'

'My face is irrelevant, Lou. Listen. Listen to me. A question. Am I or am I not cut out to be a cop? Honest opinion, Lou. No fluff. Straight answer now.'

'You don't want any kind of answer in your present state of mind, Charlie. Why don't you let me just drive you home, eh? What do you say? Come on.'

McWhinnie felt his stool listing to one side. 'I don't wanna go home, Lou.'

Perlman said, 'You look like hell. You need to lie down. What are you drinking for anyway? You feeling sorry for yourself?'

'I'm questioning my purpose, Lou.'

'Usually better to ask the really deep questions when you're clear-headed, Charlie. Just lean against me and we'll get you out of here. Okay?'

McWhinnie stuffed notebook and pen into his pocket and stepped down from his stool. He lurched towards Lou Perlman, missed and fell over. Perlman and the barman hauled him to his feet, then Perlman moved him a few steps in the direction of the exit, but it was a struggle.

'I do not want to be a fucking solicitor, Lou. Uh-huh. Not on your life.'

'What's biting your arse, Charlie?'

'My hands are dirty.'

'Is that a metaphor?'

McWhinnie planted a slobber of a kiss on Perlman's cheek. 'You're my best pal, Lou. The very best. You're a great man.'

'Right, I'm a fucking hero,' Perlman said, and guided McWhinnie down a short flight of steps. 'So your hands are dirty, and you're feeling worthless and your life has no direction?'

'Spot on,' McWhinnie said.

'And you want to quit the Force, eh?'

'You see into my soul.'

'No, I'm only remembering what you told me on the phone. Let me tell you what I see, Charlie. One weary cop plastered to the gills. You need sleep.'

'And dreams.'

'Aye, good ones.'

'Fucking *Caskie*,' McWhinnie said. *Cashkey*. 'That fucking Caskie gives me shite jobs to do. He thinks he's God.' He stumbled into a wall. Cubes of ice spilled from the napkin and cascaded over his blazer.

'He *is* God, Charlie. He invented *your* world, didn't he?'

'Bastard,' McWhinnie said.

'Steady there, son.' Perlman steered McWhinnie towards the exit doors. 'Caskie's got no supernatural powers. He's just an ambitious turd with a black heart.'

'I want to be inside a murder investigation, Lou. I want to be right at the heart of a hurricane.'

'Don't let Caskie get you down. The time'll come when you won't be spinning in orbit around him. You'll have moved on. Patience, laddie. There's no fast-track to happiness, in love or work.' Lou Perlman nudged McWhinnie out of the hotel. The sky over Glasgow was clear, a great star-show. 'Me, I'm a lucky sod, I love my work. It's the only thing in my life, Charlie. Do you think it'll ever be that way for you?'

'Suffering Jesus,' McWhinnie said, and tripped. He sat on the ground and smiled and looked up at Perlman. 'Not if I can bloody help it.'

Lou Perlman helped McWhinnie to his feet. 'By tomorrow you'll think you dreamed all this, Charlie.'

36

A building site where, except for a couple of pale bulbs strung around the perimeter wire, there wasn't much illumination, and Billy McQueen stumbled, pushed from behind by the girl. Sometimes the guy with the little moustache and the nose ring elbowed him sharply in the ribs.

'There's some confusion here,' Billy said. 'I don't know either of you. You've got me mixed up –'

'Shut your face,' the man said.

'I have money, I mean, I think we can come to some kind of understanding,' Billy said.

'One more word out of you,' the girl said. 'Warning you.'

Billy glanced back at her. She was fearful, a frightener with the spikes on her knuckles and the black leather gear that creaked as she walked, and a face like Desperate Dan's sister – if Desperate Dan had a sister, Billy was in no frame of mind to remember the comics of childhood. Desperate Dan ate enormous cow-pies, he remembered that. The horns of the beast protruded from the fucking pastry.

Why were they forcing him across this building site? What part of Glasgow was this anyway? And what did they want with him? He had a flickering suspicion they were connected to Gurk, but he dismissed this because they were locals and he couldn't imagine Gurk using Glasgow heavies. He'd bring up muscle from London if he needed it.

The skeleton of a building loomed up in the dark, a structure in process, metal girders and framework and floors half-laid. It rose, solitary and sinister, to a height of about twelve storeys. Billy was aware of cement mixers and wheelbarrows and piles of brick around him, but these were marginal impressions because it was the incomplete building that seized his attention. What was it? A future block of flats? Offices? Another hotel? He thought: I was a moron to walk into this, to be lured from my beloved penthouse, to care enough for that bitter old sod Larry that I'd venture out into a night filled with danger – and for what?

This. A trap. I'll run. I'll run like the wind.

The Wan-Fittit Wind. You'll get nowhere, Billyboy.

He stared at the dim outline of the tower, saw here and there sheets of protective plastic.

'Here,' the man said.

'Here where?' Billy asked.

'You blind or something? Get on that.'

'On what?'

The girl shoved him forward. 'Move your arse.'

Billy McQueen shook his head. 'I'm not stepping on that,' he said.

The girl whacked his mouth with the spiked fist. Billy's head spun. Glasgow was going round and round.

'Just move,' she said.

She shoved him aboard the contraption, which was a wooden platform of the kind used by window cleaners. It was attached to the outside of the building by a couple of ropes – a pulley, a bloody pulley, and that meant only one thing: I'm going up, Billy thought. I'm going way way up. I don't have a head for heights.

The man and the girl stepped on to the platform beside him.

229

Billy shivered. His lips were numb. The night, although warm and wonderful if you were out on the town, felt arctic and spooky to him. He'd never been this cold. Well, maybe once, when the train in Cowcaddens went over his leg and he thought he felt the sub-zero chill of death settle on him as the ambulance-men raised him on to a stretcher.

'Up up and away,' the man said. He tugged on a rope and the platform began to rise.

'*On my beautiful balloon,*' the girl sang.

'Oh Jesus,' Billy said.

The platform swayed as it rose. It shoogled from side to side like an old Glasgow tramcar. Billy grabbed one of the ropes. There was nothing else to hang on to. No protective barrier, no handrail, just this sodding bloody rectangle of wood rising in the dark by means of ropes.

'Anything you want,' he said. 'Listen to me. I can give you each a hundred K cash. Just set me down on the ground and let me go.'

'*Would you like to fly, on my beautiful balloon,*' the young man croaked.

I am going to throw up, Billy thought. 'Two hundred each. Two hundred grand. Best I can do.'

The girl punched him in the stomach. The pain snatched his breath away. The platform continued to rise. Up and up, brushing close to metal girders, passing sheets of plastic, tendrils of unconnected electric wires that dangled and sometimes brushed the side of Billy's face. The air smelled of paint and fresh concrete and dry metal and epoxy.

The girl sang, '*On the roof where everything is free.*'

The young guy lit a cigarette. 'Great fucking view,' he said.

Billy looked, saw lights everywhere. The city was a triumph of the electric arts, yellow lamps, lights that shone on radio masts, traffic on motorways. Great view, completely terrifying.

Up and up, swaying, the creak of the pulley. He shut his eyes, but that was worse. How high was this tower? Height was an abstraction, the distillation of his fear. You couldn't measure it in feet or metres. You couldn't weigh it either. His body felt weird and buoyant.

'Must be great up here when there's a big wind blowing,' the young guy said.

I can only imagine, Billy thought. 'I can get you more money mibbe, if you give me a day or two.'

'Think you can buy anything you like, eh?' the young man asked. 'Sometimes that's not possible, McQueen.'

Suddenly the platform plunged six feet downward – and Billy thought, oh Jesus, this was the moment, this was when death came and took you. The grinning skull: *You're mine, sucker.* He was trapped in an airless space. The girl laughed, the platform swung away from the building, then the contraption levelled itself and the ascent continued as if nothing had happened, but Billy's heart was like that of a man wired to an electric chair and the clock is only seconds from the throw of the final switch. Oh sweet mother of Jesus, he thought. I'll do anything to get off this thing – and still it was rising, up and up for ever into a cosmic darkness.

Then the contraption stopped. The night was still and eerie.

'Step off,' the young guy said.

'Step off? Are you fucking mad? Step where?'

'Get off,' the girl said. 'End of the line.'

Billy saw only darkness stretch in front of him. The door of eternity. 'I'll fall, for Christ's sake.'

Suddenly a light went on inside the unfinished tower, a high-powered lamp at the end of a thick black cable. Billy blinked.

The figure who held the light said, 'Nice of you to come all this way, Billy.'

'Haggs,' Billy said. Oh Jesus.

'The very same, Billy. Now step off the platform and move towards me.'

'You're out of your mind, Haggs.'

The girl thumped him casually on the back of his skull. 'Do

231

as you're told.' She said to Haggs, 'I think he wet his nappy on the ride up.'

'He's challenged in the lower limb department,' Haggs said. 'You need patience and understanding sometimes. Generosity towards your fellow man.'

'Aye, right enough,' the girl said, and snorted.

'Come on, Billy,' Haggs said. 'There's a good strong wooden bridge between you and me. No funny spaces. No loose planks. The support girders are magnificent. The building isn't going to fall down. Come on now, get your arse over here to me. It's only ten feet and there's bags of room. Nothing to be afraid of. We'll have a nice little chat.'

'Oh, this is standard practice for you, is it, Haggs? Hauling people a thousand feet up in the air for a meeting?'

'Just move, Billy,' Haggs said.

Billy McQueen stepped on to the wooden bridge. He felt wood under his feet, but it didn't fill him with a sense of security. The planks shifted a quarter-inch or so under his weight, and creaked, and he sensed the long drop, the horror. He thought he felt the tower sway. He looked down at the wooden crosswalk, judged it to be six feet wide, so if he stayed in the dead centre away from the edges he'd be fine, just fine, yes indeed. He stared into Haggs's lamp. It blinded him.

'Well done, Billy,' Haggs said.

Billy stopped about two feet away from Haggs, aware of movement on the bridge behind him. The girl and the young man stood on the walkway.

The girl said, 'Wheeee, it's magic up here,' and she balanced on one leg.

Haggs put an arm round Billy's shoulder. 'You can see all the way across the city. The lights over there? That's Castlemilk. You can see Rutherglen and Pollokshaws and Cathcart and if you look just to your left you'll notice the lamps round the City Chambers –'

My turf, Billy thought. My penthouse. Where I belong. Not

232

out here on thin wood suspended between metal girders God only knows how high above the earth.

'There's Central Station and Buchanan Street – and look at all the bridges across the river and the way light reflects in the water. Can you see the Moat House Hotel, Billy?' Haggs had a certain proprietorial enthusiasm in his voice.

'I see it. Why am I here, Haggs?'

'Straight to business, eh? Don't like the spectacular panoramic view of our fair city?'

'I'm not fond of high buildings,' Billy said.

'Are you shivering, Billy? On a warm night like this?'

'I'm scared to fucking death,' Billy admitted.

Haggs clapped him on the shoulder. 'You've been hard to find. Why's that, I wonder? Troubles, Billy? Problems?'

'Oh, the usual business stuff. You know.'

'I think it's a wee bit different this time. Right? It's not your normal situation, is it? Speak to me about Gurk.'

McQueen shook his head. *There*. He was sure he felt the tower sway. It was one of those jerry-built affairs with cheapskate reinforced concrete, a corner-cutting operation, a fly-by-night cowboy piece of work. He wished he had something firm to hang on to. He wished he had a Velcro safety suit and could attach himself to a receptive surface.

'Gurk, Billy,' Haggs said. 'Talk. I am all ears.'

'Gurk. Right. Here's what I did. Mallon had some capital he wanted to invest. Sometimes I put people in touch with one another. One man has commodities, another man money. I get a commission.'

'Fuck's sake. Spare me your job description, Billy. So Mallon had money and Gurk had a commodity.'

'Right,' Billy said. He was morbidly drawn to peer over the edge of the walkway. He saw girders crisscrossing in the reach of Haggs's lamp; they were the colour of a battleship. Then you couldn't see the steel ribs, only dark, a big mouth waiting to be fed.

'What was Gurk's . . . commodity?'

'Don't ask me, Haggs. I only bring people together. I don't want to know what's passing from place to place. I only want my commission based on the total amount of the transaction, usually ten, sometimes fifteen, per cent –'

'I don't have the slightest interest in your fees, Billy. I'm asking you a simple question for the second time. What the fuck was the commodity Mallon wanted from Gurk?'

'I don't know. I didn't ask. The less I know the better. That's how I operate, Haggs. It also makes the principal parties feel better about doing business. Secrecy, confidentiality. They value that.'

'Twiddie.' Haggs nodded.

The planks of wood creaked. Billy was aware of movement from behind. His throat was seized in a fierce lock by the man Haggs had called Twiddie. Billy didn't have the strength to resist. Twiddie forced him to his knees then released him. Billy remained in this position, a supplicant before Roddy Haggs.

Haggs said, 'What you're telling me is you put Mallon in touch with Gurk, but you don't have a clue what was transacted between them?'

'Only in the fiscal sense.'

'Fuck fiscal! *Twiddie*.'

Twiddie's boot went into Billy McQueen's back. Billy felt a serious jolt of pain rush ruinously from spine to skull, and he fell forward on his face.

'I'll ask again, Billy. The commodity. The package. Whatever the fuck it was.'

'I told you, I don't ask questions like that.'

'Maybe you should. Maybe you should be more interested, Billy. *Twiddie*.'

Billy McQueen braced himself for more pain, but it didn't happen. Instead, Twiddie caught him by the shoulders and swung him round until his head dangled off the walkway and he was looking down into the void. How many storeys below, how far to fall? Billy shut his eyes, fought back a scream.

Haggs said, 'The leg, Rita.'

'The leg?' Billy asked.

'Remove the leg,' Haggs said.

'Will do,' said Rita.

'Hold on, wait a bloody minute,' McQueen said.

He heard a switchblade knife open and he tensed himself, expecting to be cut. But the girl didn't slash his flesh, only the material of his trousers, making a quick sharp slit to a point above the knee.

'Undo the thing,' Haggs said.

'Undo my fucking *leg*?' McQueen said. 'Wait, Haggs. Please.'

'Why? Have you got something to *tell* me?'

McQueen looked down into the black heart of the tower. He felt the girl's hand on his skin above the stump. 'It's the way I always do business, Haggs. I swear to God. I couple parties who may have mutual interests, and that's all I do.'

'Like a financial dating service, eh?' Haggs was quiet a moment. 'The leg, Rita. Yank the fucker off.'

'Please, Haggs,' McQueen said. 'If I knew anything more, do you not think I'd bloody well tell you?'

'The leg, Rita,' Haggs said.

The girl pulled on the exoskeletal prosthesis and said, 'It's hard. I never touched one of these before. What's it made of? Plastic? Wood?'

'It's a fucking peg leg and McQueen's Long John Silver,' Haggs said. 'Just tug the bloody thing, Rita.'

Rigid urethane foam, Billy McQueen thought. An inner foam core, outer lamination flesh-coloured, a solid ankle cushion heel foot – a SACH – attached with a bolt. *I am a trans-tibial amputee*, he thought. Clutching the edge of the wooden walkway and gazing down into the hollow spine of the building, he felt the girl remove the attachment roughly from his stump, and there was a jab of pain, and he shut his eyes.

'Toss it,' Haggs said.

'Toss it where?' Billy asked.

Rita let the prosthesis drop from her hand. It struck the walkway and bounced off the edge and fell into the dark and

Billy listened to it bounce against girders as it plunged and then there was a long silence and he knew what Haggs had planned for him and he didn't believe it.

Talk your way out of this, Billy. He had tears in his eyes. He turned his head, looked up at Haggs.

'Don't, Roddy. Don't. Oh God, don't even think about it.'

Haggs put his foot on Billy's spine. A little pressure. 'Here's the story, Billy. You only have to tell me what the transaction was about. That shouldn't be hard.'

'Haggs, listen to me, please, a guy called Kaminsky phoned me from Zurich, and asked me did I know somebody with cash to invest, and about the same time Mallon had been asking me if I knew how he could make a good quick profit, something for his retirement, and all I *fucking did*, Roddy, was plug the parties into one another. Kaminsky's man Tommy Gurk and Jackie Mallon. That's gospel . . . Maybe it was drugs.' Think hard think fast, Billy, think like you never thought before.

'Drugs? Jackie Mallon? Nope. He wouldn't touch narcotics. He considered them evil. Work of Satan.'

'Okay, how about stolen property, antiques and stuff?'

'He's got nothing but junk in that warehouse,' Haggs said. 'Floor to ceiling shite. I've seen better antiques at a dump.'

'He planked them somewhere else, a safe place.'

'You know where?'

Think harder Billy harder. 'Mibbe he rented an empty house and stored these antiques inside –'

'And you have the address, Billy?'

'No –'

'You're guessing, chuck. And I'm wasting my time.'

'Wait, Roddy –'

'Ah, fuck this,' Haggs said. 'Twiddie.'

Twiddie stepped towards Billy. Haggs said, 'Send him in search of his leg.'

You're sending me nowhere, you bastarts. Billy McQueen gripped the edge of the walkway as hard as he could. His fingers locked. His knuckles were like rivets. His body was bolted to the wood.

Nobody is moving me. Not so much as an inch. Then Twiddie stepped hard on his hand. Billy heard bone crack and pain fuse through him and he hauled his hand out from under Twiddie's boot. And before Billy could think of a response that might save him Twiddie smashed the boot down on the other hand, and Billy yelped and felt himself being pushed towards the edge, shoe-horned into the brink of a long dark descent. Rita and Twiddie dangled him from the walkway. Rita held the stump, Twiddie the ankle, and Billy hung lopsided in the air.

'Roddy oh no, for God's sake, have a heart.'

'It's not such a distance to fall, Billy,' Haggs remarked. 'Be brave. Be a soldier. Meet your maker with a brisk salute.'

'Noooo, Roddy, dear Jesus, no —'

Billy McQueen was released as casually as the wrapping of a toffee-bar and he plummeted, screaming for barely a few seconds, down the cylinder of the building. On the descent he had an illusory sense of flight, of angels feathering the air about him with their wings. We'll save you, William McQueen. He was dead before he hit the ground, his skull shattered against a girder.

Rita said, 'I bloody hate it when they scream.'

Haggs stared out across the city. He thought of his taxicab fleet going back and forth, ferrying passengers through the night. He thought of people driving hired cars from his company. Cash registers rang in his head. But he wasn't satisfied.

What he sought was out there somewhere, secreted in one of the many thousands of black pockets where no light fell. He thought: I'm missing something. And whatever it is I'm obsessed with it.

37

Was it Thursday, or had he mislaid a day somewhere?

Eddie woke at nine a.m., got up from the sofa. He pulled open the curtains: the sun was ruthless. He glanced into the street, saw a patrol-car parked diagonally across the street: Caskie's watchdog keeping Joyce safe. He showered quickly and dressed in a white SUNY T-shirt and black jeans. In the kitchen he found a carton of fresh orange juice. He poured some, drank quickly. He was dehydrated and his neck ached and his ribcage creaked like the hull of an old boat. There was a niggling friction in the small of his back and he pictured tiny vertebrae knocked a fraction out of alignment. He cut a chunk of cheddar from the block in the fridge, then filled his glass again.

Joyce stepped into the kitchen. She was smartly dressed in a green linen jacket and brown slacks. 'I overslept. I don't even have time for coffee.'

'What's the rush?'

'I have a meeting at school, some bloody boring committee business about the curriculum for next year.'

'You can't get out of it?'

'I could, but I feel I should keep busy, even if it's only

half-hearted.' She drank orange juice from the carton, then stuck it back in the refrigerator and looked thoughtfully at Eddie. 'Did you ever hear of a man called Billy McQueen?'

Eddie shook his head. 'Who's he?'

'I just caught an item on the news,' Joyce said. 'I wasn't concentrating on the details. A guy by the name of Billy McQueen was found dead last night . . . there are probably a dozen Billy McQueens in Glasgow, but one of Dad's old cronies was called by that name. I was just wondering if it was the same guy. Senga might know.'

'Dead in what circumstances?' he asked.

'Sorry. I wasn't paying close attention . . . the name just popped out at me.'

'I'll ask her,' he said. 'I was going to drop in on her anyway.'

She kissed Eddie's cheek, then she was gone in a flutter, before he could ask any more questions. He heard the front door close. Billy McQueen: the name meant nothing to him. How could it? He swallowed a Solpadeine. He rose from the table slowly; a mass of aches, bundled pains. He wondered how McWhinnie felt this morning. He walked back into the sitting room where the old busts regarded him balefully. He felt a kinship with their battered broken faces.

He left the flat. The morning was hot. The shadows between the tenements were warm and lifeless. He longed for a breeze, even one so weak it barely stirred shrubbery. He crossed Whitehill Street. He was sweating by the time he reached Onslow Drive.

Senga let him into the house, hugging him exuberantly in the doorway. How could she know the sensitive condition of his ribs? In pain, he bit his lower lip. He smelled gin on her breath; she kissed his cheek with her lipsticked mouth. She led him into the living room.

Two men sat side by side on the sofa.

'Joe Wilkie, Eddie,' she said. 'You already met at the yard.'

Wilkie wasn't wearing his glasses, and his pallid round face had the look of a full moon. 'Eddie,' he said. 'Nice to see you again.'

'Same here,' Eddie said.

Senga said, 'The good-looking one is Ray, Joe's son.'

Ray got up. Eddie shook hands with the young man. Ray Wilkie's grasp was slack and quick, as if he disliked the connection of flesh. Shy, Eddie thought. Or evasive. It depended on your point of view, on what you wanted to see. Ray Wilkie held himself in a slightly stooped manner – which he may have copied from the stance of Joe – and he had a tendency to avoid eye contact, looking down at the carpet much of the time. He wore a sharp black suit, lightweight, short lapels.

'Pleasure,' Ray said. His voice had the same pitch as his father's.

'You been in the wars, Eddie?' Senga asked.

Eddie smiled. 'I slipped, dumb of me,' and he wondered how many times he'd have to explain his bruises.

'We were just having a drink. Can I get you anything?' Senga asked.

'Water's fine,' he said. She went out of the room, patting Eddie's shoulder as she passed. He watched her go in big strides, her arms pale in her long-sleeved black blouse. A silvery thread ran through the material and glimmered.

Not ten a.m. yet. She'd started early, Eddie thought. He noticed a half-empty glass of beer in Joe Wilkie's hand, and Ray nursed a small shot of scotch. They'd all started early.

Joe Wilkie said, 'You must be thinking we're hard-core boozers, Eddie. Eh? When Senga forces a drink on you, you don't refuse it.'

'I can believe that,' Eddie said. He looked at Ray, who gazed into his drink. He had fair eyelashes.

Senga came back carrying a glass of water stuffed with ice cubes. Eddie took it. 'Cheers,' he said.

The Wilkies raised their glasses. Eddie held his iced water in the air. The atmosphere in the room struck him as a little awkward, as if he'd intruded on something of a private nature.

Senga said, 'We were talking about a man called McQueen.'

'McQueen? Is this the same man who was mentioned on the

radio?' Eddie asked. He felt a weird little flutter in his chest, a shudder of pulse: it was as if he'd had a premonition and it was coming true.

'Aye,' Senga said. 'You never knew him, did you? He was a friend of Jackie. They did some business together.'

'What happened to him exactly?'

'They found him on a building site in Maryhill,' Wilkie said. 'He fell off a high-rise tower some time last night. Work-men found him this morning early. Nobody knows what the hell he was doing up there to begin with. The place isn't even completed. A man with one leg . . . what's he climb-ing up there for? It's all scaffolds and ladders, for Christ's sake.'

Wilkie said, 'He lost the lower half of a leg in a subway accident years ago.'

'I heard it was a train,' Ray Wilkie said.

'Train, subway, what damn difference does it make?' Joe said to his son.

Ray shrugged and looked into his scotch, his expression one of deflation. It was obvious he never won arguments with his father.

Eddie said, 'You're telling me this guy McQueen climbed a building in the dark – an unfinished building – and *fell* to his death.'

'Aye, right,' Wilkie said. 'Fell . . . they say. On the other hand, mibbe he was shoved.'

'Shoved?'

'Well, I'm betting he didn't climb that fucking building just for the hell of it,' Wilkie remarked. 'I'm betting he had company *egging* him on.'

Senga shook her head, sighed in the manner of somebody retreating from the horror of the real world. Eddie glanced at her and wondered where she'd gone in her mind, what sanctuary behind those closed eyes, and then he thought of a man plunging from a high building through darkness. He remembered the jumper in downtown Manhattan the morning

241

of the day he caught a flight to Glasgow. Now a one-legged man, an occasional business associate of Jackie's, climbs a high-rise block in a place called Maryhill, then falls to his death. He was either a suicide or somebody had forced him to climb in the first place. You could menace the hell out of somebody if you were twenty storeys up and the building had no floors. You could get them to promise you anything, tell you anything.

An associate of Jackie's.

Coincidence? Was it a fluke that Jackie and McQueen had died within days of each other? Sometimes if you chipped away at coincidence you unearthed a message, if you knew how to decode it. At other times all you got was gobbledygook.

'What kind of business did he do with Jackie?' Eddie asked.

'He was sort of a financial adviser,' Senga remarked.

'Something like that,' and Joe Wilkie made a wobbly gesture with his hand, to suggest that 'financial adviser' was a term to be interpreted loosely in McQueen's case.

Senga said, 'Jackie liked him. Now he's dead. A couple of days after Jackie . . .' She reached for his empty glass. 'Refill?'

'Please.' He got up and followed her into the kitchen. He watched her fill his glass at the sink. He felt a heavy sadness: it was as if Jackie had fallen from that building and not McQueen, a complete stranger. They're connected, he thought. *They have to be.*

She handed him his glass. Eddie sipped. 'Tell me more about McQueen.'

'I didn't know him all that well. I saw him maybe half a dozen times in all. We exchanged a hello, how are you, but that was it. I seem to remember he lived with his father, who's an invalid.'

'Had he done business with Jackie recently? Did Jackie mention his name lately?'

'I'm racking my brain, Eddie. McQueen . . .' She drifted into silence, gazing at the kitchen window, the garden beyond, the entanglement of shrub and stalk that was dry in the sunlight. She looked at Eddie and snapped her thumb and middle finger. 'It seems to me Jackie said he saw Billy McQueen about two weeks ago. Maybe less than that. Jackie came in, sat at the kitchen table, opened his newspaper and then he said, quite casually, he'd seen Billy. It was an aside. Small talk.'

'Did he say why they met?'

Senga shrugged. 'He didn't say whether it was by arrangement, or if they'd run into one another on the street or in a pub. No details. I got the impression he *might* have talked to McQueen, but I didn't get the feeling it was for business reasons. Maybe they had a drink together, and passed the time of day and talked football. I don't know, Eddie.'

Senga reached out and held both his hands in a gesture he found strangely comforting. She emanated warmth. 'There's an expression on your face that puts me in mind of the look I used to see on my own mother when she was trying to stitch together a patchwork quilt. It's concentration with a dash of frustration. Is that what you're doing, Eddie? Trying to make your own patchwork quilt?'

'I didn't think of it that way,' he said.

'She pricked her finger with the needle sometimes,' Senga said. 'I remember that. When she bled, she always stuck her fingertip inside her mouth. Funny what we remember and what we forget.'

Eddie imagined the tip of a needle puncturing his skin: the moral of Senga's fable didn't elude him. He sipped water, played with a cube of ice on his tongue. McQueen meets Jackie. They talk. Both of them are dead within days of each other. What did it mean?

He looked into the back garden. Years ago, a wooden swing had hung from an old elm. The elm was no longer there. The swing was a phantom.

'You took Jackie to Central Station last week,' Eddie said. 'What time?'

'You're just like the tide, Eddie. You keep rolling in. Ten thirty-five a.m.'

'You sure about that?'

243

Senga said. 'That's a precise answer. Jackie was adamant about it. We had to get to the station no later than ten thirty-five. We got stuck in a traffic jam for about ten minutes and I thought he was going to blow a fuse.'

'But you made it,' Eddie said.

'We made it.'

Eddie touched the side of her face. He liked this woman. He imagined her looking after Jackie. Cooking his food, ironing his shirts, all the domestic support. Jackie was of a generation that didn't know how to do these things. He imagined Senga and Jackie Mallon fretting in gridlocked traffic, Jackie hunched forward and tense in his seat, Senga reassuring him. We'll get there. Don't worry. You'll make your appointment, whatever it is.

'He said he wanted sea air,' Eddie said.

Senga nodded. 'Aye.'

'Where could he go from Glasgow Central for sea air?'

Senga was quiet a moment. 'Ardrossan,' she said. 'Troon.'

'Largs?' Eddie asked.

'Largs, certainly.'

38

Tommy Gurk focused on his dish of passion-fruit ice cream so hard that the small pink confection appeared to glow. Staring at things to the exclusion of objects or happenings on the periphery of his vision – the other customers in the café, the clack of cutlery, the flutter of waitresses – produced an intensity of such purity he felt he melded in some way with the object of his attention. This ice cream was more than a concoction of fruit pulp and cream and sugar: it became an inherent part of Gurk's being. *The Oneness of Things.* Beyond appearance there was essence. Essence was eternal. Life was without end. You came back time and again. A human, a goat, a toad, whatever.

I want to be an eagle next time out, Tommy Gurk thought. His karma worried him, though. He had too much going in the debit column. He'd be a worm or woodlouse or tick, his bleeding luck.

His cellphone rang.

It was Joe Kaminsky, whose heavy accent Gurk sometimes couldn't penetrate. Polish, Russian, who could tell? Kaminsky, who'd feed you vodka until you were hallucinating, and force piles of wild boar and truffles and Beluga into you, who'd take the shoes off his feet and gift them to you if you happened to mention how handsome they looked, was an absolute skinflint when it came to his past. Like he was drawing a blackout curtain across his history. End of. Past is dead, man.

Gurk wondered, but never asked. Asking would be unhealthy. Perhaps fatal. He wasn't finished with this incarnation anyway. Things to do. Discoveries to make.

'I picked your message up,' Kaminsky said. 'McQueen has perished. This is bad.'

'Yeh,' Tommy Gurk said, remembering McQueen's invitation to dinner last night. If he'd accepted, then Billy might be alive today. You just never knew these things.

Kaminsky said, 'Murdered, of course.'

'He fell from a high place.'

'I know many people who have fallen from high places, friend. So now. What to do? What is next step?'

'I was hoping you'd have some wisdom to impart,' Gurk said.

'McQueen was the lemon. He might have been squeezed a little harder. Now we have no McQueen, and that means no lemon juice, correct?'

'As you say.' Gurk looked at his passion-fruit ice cream, which was melting. Buddha is in everything, he thought. In melting ice cream, McQueen's death, a canister of mace. All life was an encounter with the True Path.

Kaminsky said, 'I have always said this deal was stinking. Like a dead cod. It has never felt to me right. Find the ones who killed McQueen. Start there.'

'I can't just pluck names out of thin air, Joe.'

Kaminsky sucked on something. A slice of orange. Coffee. Maybe that tea with honey he liked. 'I will help you, of course. Information has been telephoned to me only in the last hour. It has come to me from a source in Glas-cow. Unexpectedly, but why look inside a gift horse's mouth, huh? I will give you this name. You memory it.'

'My ears are pricked.' Gurk pictured Kaminsky's small black

246

shades and the set of whiskers he sported. They made him look like an Eastern potentate.

'And no writing this on paper,' Kaminsky said.

'Gotcha.'

Kaminsky spelled out the name with exaggerated care, and then an address. He went on to add, 'To your hotel will be delivered a package. In a few hours from this time now. You will need what it contains. In Glas-cow, a car will be available to you. You will find details of the location in the package. Do this job. Do it fast and do it well.'

'Gotcha. Nod's as good as.'

'What is this, this nod?'

'Slang, Joe.'

'I never understand this English slang, never.'

'You need to be born into the environment, Joe.'

'Pah,' Kaminsky said, and cut the connection.

Gurk went out of the café and stood for a time watching seagulls in the morning sky and sun on bright water. He drew the smell of brine into his lungs: satisfying.

39

Eddie walked from the house in Onslow Drive towards Alexandra Parade, where he'd find a taxi for the city centre. On the corner of Craigpark and Golfhill Drive a wine-coloured Jag drew into the kerb directly in front him, braked hard and Roddy Haggs stuck his head from the window. Surprise surprise, Eddie thought. Haggs had been tracking him. How else to explain his sudden appearance in this part of the city?

Haggs said, 'Just the man I'm looking for. Get in the car.'

Eddie hesitated.

'A minute's all I need. Come on.' Haggs opened the passenger door without getting out. Eddie climbed in. The interior smelled of leather and cigar smoke. Haggs, dressed in an expensive pin-striped suit, smiled and cracked his knuckles. The car stereo was playing 'Rhapsody in Blue'.

'I like this,' Haggs said. 'Gershwin. Always like a bit of George and Ira. Funny name for a fella, Ira.'

'Yeah. What's on your mind?'

'You,' Haggs said.

'Any specific context?'

Haggs laughed: *chukka chukka chukka*. 'Always looking for the angles, eh? You've got a cop's brain.'

Eddie didn't like Haggs's laugh. He tapped his fingertips on his knees.

Haggs said, 'I won't delay you, wherever you're going. I have something for you. A wee present.' He reached behind, retrieved a white paper bag from the back seat and opened it. He removed a varnished pine box about eighteen inches long and six wide, with brass hinges. It was highly polished and Eddie saw his reflection in it. Haggs set the paper bag, which bore the name Emporio Armani, on his lap, and then laid the box on top of it.

'Here's the thing,' Haggs said. 'A man dies, and you realize maybe you should've been closer to him when he was alive, and a wee bit kinder. You following me?'

'You're talking about Jackie,' Eddie said.

'Right. I could've tried harder. We might've done business together if we'd been less stubborn. Allies. Know what I'm saying?'

Eddie looked at the box. 'Now you regret missed chances.'

'Aye. I was up late last night thinking about them and . . .' Haggs's voice faded away. 'Take this last deal he was into. We could've done something together . . .'

'What deal is that?'

'He never mentioned the specifics, Eddie. And I've been less than honest with you, I admit.'

'Really,' Eddie said.

'You heard we argued. I told you I'd forgotten the reason.'

'And that was a lie?'

Haggs looked contrite. I'm expected to buy the expression, Eddie thought.

Haggs said, 'This is the way it was. Jackie needed some extra cash to finance his deal. He asked me to participate. He didn't say what the biz was. I was supposed to trust him. I said, you're asking a hell of a lot, Jackie. He said, Haggs, you're too fucking cautious. And if I ever decided to put my faith in him I could come back with the green. Then I thought, what the fuck, I'll take a chance, a bit of a flyer, I'm not short of a few quid after all – but it was just too bloody late, and Jackie was . . .' Haggs shut his eyes a moment and looked sadly pious.

'He invited you into a deal,' Eddie said. 'Only you didn't know what it was.'

Haggs, eyes still shut, spoke softly. 'Aye.'

'You didn't tell me this yesterday.'

'I felt fucking awkward about it, Eddie. I didn't want you thinking I'd turned your dad away like that. Let him down.'

No way, Eddie thought, although he enjoyed Haggs's act, the flicker of shut eyelids, the dry solemn tone of contrition in the voice, the *mea culpa* of it all. He watched Haggs's eyes open and how they swivelled towards him without the man's face having to turn.

Haggs said, 'Maybe the deal still has legs. Maybe it's alive and kicking and just waiting to be financed. I'm thinking of Senga, Eddie. She might be hurting for money.'

'Ask her,' Eddie said. 'Maybe she'll be able to tell you something.'

'I have a sneaky feeling Senga doesn't like me,' Haggs said. 'Some past misunderstanding. I have every regard for her, Eddie. Believe me. But I think my best approach . . . well, it's through you.'

'You want me to ask Senga? You want me to tell her that Roddy Haggs would like to partner her in a business deal? Maybe even become her benefactor?'

Haggs smiled. 'You've picked me up wrong, Eddie. I'm not thinking along that road. I'm wondering if . . .' He hesitated, eyeballed the street as if he suspected that the scraggle of shrubbery might conceal an enemy.

'Wondering if *I* know anything?' Eddie asked.

'Right.'

'If Jackie confided in me?'

'Now you're talking.'

Eddie smiled, tilted his head back. From the corner of his eye he was aware of the glossy box in Haggs's lap. His gift. 'I hate to disappoint you, Roddy. Jackie phoned me a few times when I was in New York, but he never talked business.'

'Not once, eh?'

'Not once,' Eddie said.

'Ah well.' Haggs sighed and opened the box and took out the Kentucky Flintlock pistol and weighed it in the palm of his hand. 'I brought you this, Eddie. You seemed to admire it yesterday. I want you to have it.'

'I can't accept that,' Eddie said.

'Take it, for Christ's sake. I'll be annoyed if you refuse.'

'I can't take it, Roddy. It's too expensive.'

'Money, money's pish, there's always loadsa money,' Haggs said. He lifted the pistol and levelled it and, closing one eye, stared along the barrel at Eddie.

He held this position and the light in his eye was pure concentration, as if Eddie were a target. 'You could blow somebody's head clean off from this range,' he said.

'No problem,' Eddie remarked.

'You really could.'

'I'm convinced.' Eddie gazed into Haggs's face and the fierce brightness in his eyes and for one bad moment he wondered if the man had gone insane and planned to kill him. *American Cop Slain in Glasgow Suburb.* A random murder, inexplicable and irrational. He imagined Jackie looking down the barrel of a gun. Jackie's terror. Jackie's life came to this in the end, a hole, a bleak aperture.

'One shot,' Haggs said.

'That's all it would take for sure,' Eddie said.

He felt sweat form on his body and his T-shirt stick to his skin. Haggs wasn't going to shoot, this was some form of threat, a demonstration of what he could do if he took it into his mind. This was Haggs flexing muscle, pumping his own kind of iron. The gun was a Nautilus machine, an exercise bicycle. *I can shoot you the fuck into oblivion if I want, Eddie baby.*

Haggs said, 'Now if I had a beef against somebody. Boom.'

'Yeah,' Eddie said.

251

'Do I have a beef against you, Eddie?'

'I hope not.'

'I wouldn't like to have a beef against Jackie's son.'

'I wouldn't like to give you a reason,' Eddie said.

'Sometimes I wish duelling was still legal. Pistols at dawn. Name your seconds. One man facing another. Equality of chance. You'd tell me if you remembered Jackie mentioning anything.'

'Yeah, for sure.'

'I'm fucking serious, Eddie. I'd like to give Senga a helping hand. After all, she's a widow, give or take a legal document. So don't just put the matter out of your mind. Understand me?'

Haggs moved the gun an inch closer to Eddie. It was one of those moments when your life is a gyroscope turning on a wire. Eddie felt a drop of sweat slide down his nose and trickle to his upper lip.

'You have my word,' Eddie said.

'Your word, terrific. Wonderful.' And Haggs laughed, lowered the weapon. 'Note to self: Eddie Mallon doesn't like looking down the wrong end of a gun. Even when it's unloaded,' and he laughed again, delighted with Eddie's visible unease. 'Oh, Christ, I enjoy a wee bit of mischief. The secret lies in looking serious.'

'You looked pretty serious all right,' Eddie said. He felt strangely out of balance, as if sunstruck. He was thirsty.

Haggs boxed the weapon, shut the box and stuck it back in the Armani bag, then passed it to Eddie. 'She's all yours, Eddie. Look after her. Grease her from time to time.'

Eddie took the bag. 'I don't know what to say.'

'Just don't forget where you got the gun,' Haggs said.

'Count on it.'

Eddie pushed the passenger door open.

'Need a lift anywhere?' Haggs asked.

'No, really, I'm fine.' Eddie got out of the car.

Haggs laughed again and said, 'Hi-ho Silver,' and the big Jaguar screamed away, tyres burning, engine roaring. Motionless under the high hot cinder sun, Eddie clasped the Armani bag to his chest and thought, Yeah, Haggs looked pretty serious all right, goddam serious, like a man with more than a passing acquaintance with deadly violence.

40

Sometimes when Detective-Sergeant Lou Perlman listened to experts, forensic know-alls with their university ties and big brains, his attention wandered. After all, what did he *really* need to know about the temperature at which paper burned, or the amount of oxygen required to conduct flame through a narrow enclosed space. Cubic this and cubic that. It was all just so much slosh, like milky tea spilled into a saucer.

'Is there a point you're getting to, Sid?' he asked, sounding raspy and sullen. 'No hurry anyway. I've got all bloody day to waste.'

Sidney Linklater, a graduate of Edinburgh University, thirty-three years of age and a Force Support Officer – a *civilian* – blinked at Lou Perlman in surprise. It always astonished him that others could fail to be fascinated by his world of fibres and threads, of flames and melting points, of decomposition and putrefaction. He likened the non-scientific mind to an asteroid turning pointlessly in space.

'All right, I'll hurry along, Lou, if you're finding this a bit of a bore,' he said.

'Don't get your knickers in a twist, Sid. Some of us are cut out to be scientific. Others of us are just men with big feet and big bunions and wee brains. Like me. The dogged sort. We pound pavements. We're happy just chugging along. Clip clop. Fucking Clydesdales in human clothes.'

'I find false modesty indigestible,' Linklater said.

'So is all your fucking data, Sid. No offence intended.'

Linklater said, 'Sometimes I feel like a missionary preaching to savages.'

'I *am* a savage, Sid. Keep that in mind when you talk to me. Simple words. Short sentences. See Dick pish. See Spot shit. Remember, I was brought up in the Gorbals. Correction. I was *dragged* up. We'd only just got electricity installed the day before the demolition people moved in. I'm a child of the gaslight generation. We didn't have PCs and websites. Ours wasn't the Information Age. We knew fuck all.'

'And I was delivered by a stork.'

'Oy vey,' Perlman said. 'Those hankie deliveries can be tricky.'

Linklater shrugged and looked round his workroom. Assorted objects, seemingly unconnected to one another, sat on shelves. Two pairs of Wellington boots. A charred shotgun. A couple of hunting knives with shiny blades. Bottles of various chemicals. A bicycle bent out of shape. Spades, trowels, a big fishing net. A microscope, also a load of computer gear that Perlman, who was quite proud of being misaligned with the electronic age, couldn't identify – maybe they were scanners, or photograph enhancers, or some kind of UV equipment, who cared?

Not Lou Perlman.

Linklater, whose hobby was making charcoal rubbings from ancient tombstones, pushed his glasses up his long nose and gazed down at his work-table. He wore see-through plastic gloves. In his right hand he held a pair of tweezers. 'Let's go the number one route just for you, Lou. No frills. No fancy cocktails.'

'My boy,' Perlman said.

There was debris on the table, and Linklater poked at it. One plastic ashtray, a couple of misshapen cigarette filters. A small pile of wet ash and scraps of scorched paper. A square wallet of black leather lay to one side in a small dark puddle. There was a smell of petrol.

'These would-be arsonists splash a little petrol inside the van,' Linklater said. 'Strike a match, drop it in, buzz off. They leave the window on the passenger side open – a slit, no more than that. They overlook a basic principle of the firemaker's skill. Flame needs oxygen. This fire goes, but it isn't the spectacle it's supposed to be. Some of the spilled petrol burns, sure, but this isn't a movie, Lou. The tank isn't going to blow up. We get some flame, enough to destroy the fabric on the seats. More dramatic black smoke than flame. The fire suffers oxygen deprivation, so it's too slow for the light display the arsonists must've wanted. Anyway, there's bugger all in the back of the van to burn, no rags, no papers, nothing, just this wallet . . . then along comes the fire brigade, hoses blasting. The wallet was just beginning to ignite. There was blood on the floor of the van which the firemen, despite their zeal, didn't manage to hose entirely away. It's AB neg. No fingerprints on the steering wheel. Some in the interior. There's mud on the tires. Fresh.'

Linklater touched the wallet with a latexed fingertip. 'I emptied it carefully,' he said. 'I set the contents over here,' and he tweezered to the side a sheet of opaque plastic, under which lay banknotes that had been browned along the edges, scarred first by fire then doused with water. Linklater gently shoved the wilting money aside and concentrated on a sheet of lined paper.

'This appears to be a page out of a cheap notebook, Lou. The writing's felt-tip and the water's made it run. It seems to be some arrangement of numbers. An accounting, maybe. Somebody adding and subtracting.'

'Ah-hah. What else have you got?'

'It wasn't exactly *stuffed* with goodies,' Linklater said. 'But there's this.' He edged a piece of folded pink and green paper towards Perlman, who bent forward and looked at it through his one good eye. The other eye, lid still swollen from the insect bite, smarted beneath the patch.

'A driving licence,' Perlman said.

He bent until his face was only six inches from the table. There was no photograph in the licence, but the name of the owner was legible. Perlman heard birdsong in his head. He straightened up and smiled, and in a very bad voice cranked out an 80s song lyric. *'The tide is high, I'm moving on.'*

'What in God's name is that appalling noise?' Linklater asked, feigning great terror.

41

Eddie Mallon met Christopher Caskie in a café a couple of blocks from Force HQ. It was a fashionably relaxed place with ferns and high arches and pretty waitresses, unlike the mutton-pie and strong-tea brigade of grim aproned matrons Eddie remembered from Glasgow restaurants years ago. The girls who served you were good-looking, moussed hair, modishly pale complexions. Eddie ordered a bottle of mineral water, espresso and a chocolate croissant. Caskie, with a prim little nod of his head, asked for tea.

'Nice room,' Eddie said.

'I come here now and again,' Caskie remarked. 'Is that a bruise on the side of your neck?'

'I had an upset,' Eddie said. 'I lost my footing.'

'Sorry to hear that. I hope it's not too serious.'

'It's fine.' Did he know? Had McWhinnie told him? Eddie seriously doubted McWhinnie would make a report of their encounter.

'Been shopping?' Caskie nodded at the bag.

Eddie set it on the floor and said, 'Just something for Claire.'

'Nice thought,' Caskie said. 'You phoned, so am I forced to

258

assume you have more tricky questions for me? See if I can guess. It's about Tommy G.'

The waitress, a lovely trim girl in short black skirt, had a good-natured face. She set coffee, croissant, Strathmore water and tea on the table. 'If you need anything else, let me know,' and she was gone discreetly. Eddie swallowed the mineral water instantly, then tasted his coffee and bit into his croissant.

Caskie said, 'I ran the name, Eddie. The computer has no record of Tommy G.'

'I'm surprised,' Eddie said.

'I am too.'

'You'd expect –'

'I always try to avoid expectations,' Caskie said. He tasted his tea and made a face. 'I don't remember asking for herbal . . .'

Tommy G: a blind alley. Eddie swallowed the last of his croissant. 'Did you run it as Tommy G or Tommy G E E?'

'Both.'

'Are there other sources you can try?'

'They take time.'

I don't have time, Eddie thought. A funeral, then home. The end. Back to Queens. Back to a dead junkie in an abandoned house. 'You heard about Billy McQueen?'

Caskie said, 'On the radio.'

'You knew the guy?' Eddie asked.

'Barely.'

'Friend of Jackie, they tell me.'

'I believe there was a vague fiscal relationship over the years,' Caskie said.

'Why would anyone murder him?'

'Has it been confirmed that he was murdered?'

'Come on. You think he had some freaky thing about scaling unfinished buildings in the dead of night? Like a dangerous hobby that just got out of hand and he slipped? Maybe he dressed in some Spiderman get-up and went out across the scaffolding to look for handy dangling places.'

'A touch theatrical,' Caskie said. 'I can't begin to guess, Eddie.

If I knew the man better, maybe I could proffer an opinion.'

Caskie had a small half-smile on his face: Detective-Inspector Enigma. *This man might have been involved in the death of my father*, Eddie thought. He gripped the edge of the table and felt his hands tighten, and he saw the inside of his head change colour – as if emotions were tints – and the pattern of his thoughts went this way and that, and he suddenly wanted to reach out and grab Caskie by his striped necktie and drag his head down to the table and pound it and pound it. Then he let the feeling go, and he tried to relax, and he pushed his chair back from the table a few inches. *Complicity in a brutal murder*. What if you're wrong, Eddie? What if you've miscalculated? But your heart, sometimes reliable in the past, and occasionally impetuous too, says you're right. Believe in it now.

He leaned towards Caskie and said, 'Tell me about safe houses.'

'What houses?'

'Safe. Places where cops put witnesses for security reasons.'

'I've never had any use for such places personally, Eddie. I assume they exist. I may be wrong.'

'But you don't know for sure.'

'Why are you so interested in the subject?'

'It popped into my head, Chris.'

'Without reason?'

'All kinds of things pop into my head without reason.'

'You ought to control that tendency.'

'I try, Chris, I try. Here's another one. For example: Do you think it's possible for a cop – a senior officer, say – to run a kind of private fiefdom inside a force? Like his own little kingdom, I mean, where he could do what he liked, he could make his own personal use of manpower, use police property – like safe houses – any way he wanted, he could decide what was right and what was wrong without involving his fellow officers. This guy would be unaccountable. Up to a point.'

'The man who would be king, eh?' Caskie smiled. 'It's hard to imagine an officer abusing his power to such an extent.'

'Sure. But it could happen, right?'

'Is there some reason behind this little fantasy, Eddie? Or does it simply amuse you?'

'Is it a fantasy, Chris?'

'I imagine so.'

'Come on, Chris. Give me a better answer than that.'

Caskie pushed his cup aside and sighed, a long sound. 'When did you first decide you disliked me, Eddie?'

'You changed the subject, Chris. Didn't enjoy the last one?'

'I had a feeling it wasn't going anywhere. Now it's my turn to be curious.'

'Fine,' Eddie said. 'Dislike you? Funny, I can't decide if it's simple dislike or a more complicated contempt.'

'Contempt is strong. Where does it come from, Eddie? Do you despise me for being closer to your family than you? Is that the root of it? I knew your own father better than you ever did. Is that it, Eddie? I'm this stranger, this outsider who got to know your dad and your sister and you can't cope with that.'

'You wanted to sling Jackie's ass in jail, Caskie.'

'If I'd had the chance. Jackie knew that. He understood the rules. It didn't stop us being close.'

'The best of pals,' Eddie said. 'I doubt that. You didn't even trust each other.'

'We had a working arrangement. We were friends despite the obstacles. Which is more than you ever achieved.'

'And that was my fault? I was taken away, for fuck's sake. What chance did I have?' Eddie gazed past Caskie to the far side of the room where one of the waitresses was watching him in the glazed manner of the daydreamer. His eye travelled beyond her and into a shadowy place. He could have shown Jackie his home in Queens. Toured him around Manhattan. Empire State Building. Staten Island Ferry. The whole works. He could have taken him to a soccer game. Jackie might have

261

liked that, hotdogs, cold beer in waxy cups, the passion of the Hispanic fans. Lost ambitions. Such simple ones.

Eddie pushed his chair back from the table. Dislike. Contempt. He wished he had the kind of dignity that didn't allow him to yield so easily to these feelings. Claire would have said something like how we're only human after all and that means weakness as well as strength, vanity as well as humility, but right now Eddie could only think of the fact that his mind was smoking and the smoke smelled of sulphur. Claire had a world of her own, where charity and understanding reigned.

He got up from the table and looked down at Caskie. 'Tell me, Chris, how long have you known Haggs?'

'I believe I answered that question before,' he said.

'Why the fuck are you lying?'

Caskie asked. 'I don't remember lying to you, Eddie. You asked if I knew the man, I told you I didn't.'

Eddie smiled. 'You're cool, Chris. You're a fucking cucumber on ice.'

'I've been called worse. Don't forget your bag.'

Eddie picked up the paper bag. Outside he blinked in the unrelenting sun of this pink and blue city. Tarmac shimmered. Starlings flocked above rooftops, a glossy black swarm. He looked this way and that, thinking how clumsily he'd cut the ribbon of polite pretence between himself and Caskie, then decided his destination.

42

Although he was superior in rank to Perlman, Sandy Scullion felt like a trumped-up impostor in the older man's company. Lou Perlman, a legend in the Force, was a throwback to the old days, when DNA might have been the acronym for a savings bank, and electronic gizmos were primitive hand-held Asteroid games that came direct from Taiwan to the Barras market and lasted about forty-five seconds before going on the blink.

The car in which the two men travelled moved along Moss Road on the south side of the city. Scullion drove because Perlman hated cars. They always broke down on him. On the right was the dark-brown Victorian façade of the Southern General Hospital. A couple of young nurses walked across the lawn in front of the hospital; in sunlight their white uniforms had a fluorescent look.

Perlman watched the girls. He had a feeling he'd forgotten something he'd promised to do. It dogged him. 'Some days I feel my age,' he said.

'Don't we all?' Scullion eyed the rearview mirror. 'Where do I turn?'

'Left. Langlands Road.'

Perlman coughed into his hand. His lungs hurt. He wished he could kick the nicotine habit. 'Some mornings I get up and my throat's scratchy and I need to pee like my bladder's bursting and my bones ache and I think this is it, this is the day I'm writing the resignation note, and ballocks to it all.'

'Retirement,' Scullion said.

'Aye. Downhill Drive,' Perlman said. 'I could sit in the park and give crumbs to birds. I could buy a wee dog, take it walks, wait patiently while it poops.'

'You've got a couple of years in you,' Scullion said.

'Could you put a wee bit more enthusiasm into your voice when you say that, Sandy? I want to be convinced. What am I without my work? A hollow man. The walking dead. Take a left here.'

Scullion turned the car into Kennedar Drive, a street of shabby tenements. Kids played on the pavement. A van with a punctured tyre listed at the kerb.

'Number twelve,' Perlman said.

Scullion parked, pulled on the handbrake. 'You lead,' he said.

'I know these buggers,' Perlman said. 'They try my patience something fierce.'

'I'll be a silent presence, just along for the ride.'

They went inside the tenement. The close was dim and the air cool. They climbed to the second floor. Perlman held the banister rail, which was sticky – probably from some kid's ice cream or sweetie. At least he hoped it was something as innocent as that. The city rubbed off on you, he thought, in bad ways and good. Live in it all your life, you know its corners and its angles, you can rattle off bus numbers and routes, all fifteen names of the underground stations in any order, you remember the streets where the trams used to run, those clattery old bone-rattlers that travelled in seeming defiance of Newtonian physics, you recall buildings long ago demolished, even the names of people who lived in them. He remembered the old Jewish families. The Sakols. The Finemans. The Jesners. Others. Take a couple

264

of Jews and you've got a potential diaspora. Where had they gone? Where had all that piety gone? The respectable suburbs. Giffnock. Newton Mearns. Beyond.

You and the city, he thought, you're an old married couple conscious of each other's faults, and forgiving of them at least some of the time, but irritable the rest. He coughed again. The city was in his lungs, the spoor of the place. He wondered if a city could kill you. *Cause of death: Glasgow.*

He wiped his sticky hand on the side of his trousers. The brass plate on the door ahead of him read ELVIS PRESLEY & ANNIE LENNOX.

'Pair of wits,' Scullion said.

'You're half right.' Perlman rang the bell. It played the first few bars of 'Are You Lonesome Tonight?'

A man's voice came from the other side of the door. 'Who is it?'

'Perlman. Your friendly cop.'

'Aw, what the fuck is it now?'

The sound of a chain sliding, a key turning, the door opening half an inch. Twiddie's unsmiling face appeared in the slit.

'We're coming in,' Perlman said. 'Get the kettle on.'

Twiddie, in black T-shirt and yellow briefs, moved back from the door and Perlman stepped in, followed by Scullion. A Harley-Davidson motorcycle, big and malignant, was propped against a wall, dripping oil on newspapers. Perlman had long ago ceased to be surprised by anything he came across in the homes of people. A Pekinese in a microwave, a chopped hand in a food processor, and on one memorable occasion an entire car, a Vauxhall Astra built from stolen parts, inside a third-floor flat. How to get the vehicle downstairs hadn't been part of the scheme. *Er, what do we do with the car now? Ooops.*

'I see we've caught you with your trousers off, Twiddie.'

'I was sleeping,' Twiddie said. He touched his swollen red nostril in a self-conscious way.

Rita appeared in a doorway at the end of the hall. Her hair was

265

in blue plastic curlers. Without make-up, her face resembled a blanched potato. She was dressed the reverse of Twiddie. She wore black panties and a yellow T-shirt.

Perlman said, 'Look at this, Sandy, a match of clothes and a match of love. It's so adorable it just makes me want to take up embroidery. Little hearts on tiny cushions. Rita, you never looked more alluring.'

'Piss off,' Rita said.

Twiddie said, 'She's not at her best before she's had a cup of char.' He glared at Scullion. 'Friend of yours, Perlman?'

'This is Detective-Inspector Scullion, Twiddie. He's my boss. The way Haggs is your boss.'

'Haggs, Haggs, I wish you'd drop that. I haven't seen Haggs in a long time.'

Perlman said, 'I might look like a simpleton, Twiddie, but don't be deceived. You're never far away from Hot Rod. He snaps his fingers and you run. You're the messenger boy. Phone calls, quick meetings in out-of-the-way places, I know how it works.'

Twiddie waved a hand dismissively. 'That's shite.'

Rita retreated into the bedroom and slammed the door. Twiddie wandered into the kitchen and grabbed a pair of jeans from the back of a chair and pulled them on.

'How come you're still working anyway, Perlman? How come you've not retired?'

Perlman said, 'The Force needs me to keep an eye on the likes of you and the Bride of Frankenstein,' and he gestured with a thumb towards the bedroom door.

Twiddie muttered something that might have been *auld bastart*, then stuck the plug of an electric kettle into a wall socket. The kitchen was a mess. Sinkload of dishes. Pizza boxes and red sauce stains and dead cigarettes filling an old milk carton, and rolling papers spread around. No sign of dope.

Rita came into the kitchen now, wrapped in a red Chinese-style robe adorned with dragons. They breathed fire, Perlman noticed. Very appropriate. She was Arsonia, Goddess of Arson. She sat at the table and folded her arms and stared at him fiercely. 'Can you not leave us in peace?'

'That's not in my job description, love,' Perlman said.

Rita glanced at Scullion. 'Who's this prat?'

Twiddie said, 'He's Perlman's boss.'

Rita lit a cigarette, blew smoke at Perlman. 'So what is it this time, Perlman?'

'You know, Rita, I look at you and I wish I was thirty years younger,' Perlman said. 'Ah-har, shiver me timbers, Jim lad. My heart's tripping the light fantastic. Feel it. Give me your hand –'

'I don't want to touch any part of you, Perlman. Just get to the point.'

'That van,' Perlman said.

'Oh for fuck's sake, not *again*,' Rita said. 'The van this, the van that.'

'Something nags me about that van,' Perlman said. 'You want to hear it?'

'Not especially,' Rita said. 'But I'm going to anyway, I suppose.'

'Right, so you might as well pin your lugs back, my dear, and listen close, while the Swami, the Great Perlman, speaks. The van, the mysterious van. What is it that bothers the Swami?'

'Is there a point to this?' Twiddie said.

'You better fucking believe there's a point,' Perlman said. He moved quickly and stepped towards Twiddie and slammed him against the wall. Twiddie looked surprised, neck stiff and face held back by Perlman's forearm.

'Police brutality,' Rita said.

'No, police brutality would be if I was to give Twiddie a right brutal kicking,' Perlman said. 'If I was to whack him bloody hard in the ballocks, say, and when he dropped to the floor I'd kick the shite out of him. Now *that* would be police brutality. Right, Inspector?'

'Absolutely,' Scullion said, and smiled uneasily. He heard pages of a regulations book fly free from their binding.

Perlman continued, 'This is just to get your fucking attention, the pair of you. Just tell me who else was with you in the Transit the other night. That's all I want to know.' He stared at Twiddie through his one good eye. His unshaven face was set in belligerence; he had a street-fighter's jaw. Twiddie struggled to free himself from the strength of Perlman's forearm, but couldn't.

'Not bad, eh, Twiddie? Not bad for an old fart that should have been superannuated ten years ago. Who was with you in that fucking van?'

Twiddie's eyes popped. 'We told you, we were watching –'

Surreptitiously, Perlman kicked Twiddie hard on the shin. 'A video, I know, I heard that one. Tell me another.'

Twiddie groaned. Rita got up from the table. She appeared quite ready to launch herself at Perlman, but he had a way of glaring – even one-eyed – that made people hesitant about physical confrontation. It was the demonic look of a man who could promise you nightmares, and deliver them if you pushed him too hard.

'Understand this, my wee pals, I'm not pussy-footing,' he said. 'Who else was in the fucking van?'

'We don't *know* about any bloody van,' Rita said.

Perlman released Twiddie now. Twiddie rubbed his neck. Perlman paced the floor, hands in the pockets of his brown trousers. He had a grease stain on his wide gold tie; some of the older officers at Force HQ claimed to remember that same mark from the mid-80s.

'We've got brilliant new sciences these days,' Perlman said. 'We've got electron microscopes. We can test a single strand of hair and tell you the name, address and phone number of whose noodle it was attached to. Now this is *way* beyond my understanding, just as I'm sure it's way beyond yours. No matter, it's enough just to know that all this bright shiny new stuff actually works, which makes it harder for people to do things without leaving traces of themselves. A fleck of dandruff. Belly-button lint. These trifles are the gateways to whole new worlds . . . keeping all that in mind, if you can, I'll ask again. Who else was with you in the van?'

'I want my lawyer,' Twiddie said. 'I want Binks.'

'You think that babyfaced piss-artist can help you, John? You think Mr Henry Binks, solicitor and bullshitter and drunk, can help you out? He wouldn't know his arse from a hole in the ground, our Mr Binks. He's probably having a champagne cocktail in the Rogano even as we speak.'

'This is just bluff,' Rita said.

'Are you sure of that?' Perlman asked.

'Slurry I can smell a mile off. John, don't you listen to anything he says. And don't run to phone your bloody lawyer either. This old bastard,' and she pointed a finger sharply at Perlman, 'is blethering.'

Perlman pulled her towards him, clutching a fistful of her Chinese robe. She stared at him. The eye-lock, the contest. She wasn't yielding, nor was he. He saw in her eyes a lack of generosity and charity. Life was a sore struggle and she'd survived a loveless upbringing inside a decrepit rat-infested building in a world of cracked cups and broken porcelain sinks and outside toilets and all the hard crap a city conspired to throw in your path, and somewhere along the way she'd attached herself to Twiddie, minor thug, villain. It wasn't for love she'd barnacled her world to Twiddie. It was their mutual interest in the arcana of violence that bonded them.

Perlman felt a dip in his emotion, a leaking of energy, as if this brief insight into Rita's world forced him to confront an unfamiliar sensation: pity, or something like it. Getting softer as the years roll, Lou. My sand isn't packed quite so hard any more. It drifts through my fingers. I'll be a bleeding heart next. God forbid, a man with a social conscience.

He shook this mood off and zoomed back in on the ugly face that was so determined not to flinch from his look. But he'd lost eye contact. By the rules of this contest, he'd lost.

He recovered quickly. 'I forgot to mention. We've got blood samples from the back of the van.'

'And this is supposed to worry us?' Rita asked. She yawned, covered it loosely with a hand.

'To death,' he said.

Twiddie said, 'Perlman, for God's sake, we don't know anything about this Transit. I swear it.'

'Apart from the blood,' Perlman said, and paused, and held the silence a beat. 'We've got a wallet.'

'Wallet? What wallet?' Rita asked.

'You tell me,' Perlman said.

'I can't tell you a fucking thing,' Rita said. 'That's my last word on the subject.' She looked at Scullion. 'Unless you have some kind of warrant, Inspector, could you and your senile sidekick please see yourself off the premises?'

'Bones,' Perlman said. 'Matthew Bones. Name familiar to you?'

Rita shrugged. Twiddie turned away, picked up the kettle, made tea. 'Only from the newspaper,' Twiddie said.

Hand on chest, Perlman feigned cardiac arrest. 'A newspaper? You actually read, Twiddie? Quick somebody. Pass me the digitalis.'

'Excuse me if I don't laugh,' Twiddie said. 'This guy Bones is missing, right? Something to do with that shooting.'

Perlman said, 'Missing is correct. The jackpot of pennies rattles down Twiddie's chute.'

'So he's missing, who gives a fuck?' Rita asked.

'Why was he in the van you and Twiddie torched? I stand corrected: *tried* to torch.'

Rita spoke to Scullion again. 'Do you usually employ cops hard of hearing?'

Perlman said, 'Did I not mention it was Bones's blood we found in the back of the van? Did I not tell you that even as we speak men are going through the van looking for fingerprints – which they'll find. Yours and Twiddie's. And those of Matty Bones. So suppose you spare us all the time and trouble involved, and tell us exactly what happened that night, and where Matty Bones might be found? Eh? What do you say?'

270

'Go fuck yourself.' Rita picked up a magazine and thumbed the pages. Skinny girls in lingerie flickered past. Gaunt ghosts with druggy expressions.

Perlman thought: You don't break down a wall like Rita's with bluff and bluster. You don't make a dent with threats. Magic microscopes and forensics and blood samples and all the rest of it – it was a bag of cold chips as far as she was concerned. She had an in-built alarm-system manufactured on the streets and so far it hadn't issued a beep, and thus she felt secure. Somebody's wallet in an old Transit, so what? Blood? Gimme a break. And fingerprints . . . well, Rita and Twiddie would've been wearing gloves. They might possess stunted IQs, but they weren't suicidal. They weren't going to be linked to that van. Perlman had known that coming here. He'd known he couldn't con them into an incriminating statement, or menace them into giving up information loosely. No, this was something else, this was sifting the dross to see how it was constituted.

Rita buried herself in her magazine. Twiddie, clanking cups on a tray, said, 'Tea's up.'

'I'll skip the tea,' Perlman said.

Scullion looked at his watch. 'Me too.'

'Suit yourselves.' Twiddie set the tray on the table, edging aside an HP Sauce bottle to make space. It was, Perlman thought, a bleak little montage of a certain kind of tenement life: the brown sauce bottle with goo on the cap, the milky tea, the mismatched cups, one of which had no handle, cigarette burns on the surface of the table.

'When you two decide you have something to tell me, something to get off your chests, you know where to reach me,' Perlman said. 'I'll be expecting to hear from you. I'll be your Father Confessor . . . But don't try my patience. I'm waiting.'

He looked at Scullion, raised an eyebrow. They left the room. Twiddie, slurping tea, escorted them into the hall. 'Cheerio.' He closed the door.

Perlman and Scully went downstairs, out of the building and into the street. Scullion unlocked the car, got inside. Perlman slipped into the passenger seat, gazed through the windscreen. At the top of Kennedar Drive was a primary school and a row of terraced houses.

Scullion asked, 'You think they had Bones in the van?'

'Yes.'

'And you see Haggs's shadow fall across this.'

Perlman nodded. 'Twiddie and the Bride of Frankenstein are not what you'd call initiative-driven. The kind of ideas that occur to them wouldn't power a ten-watt bulb. Haggs tugs a string in Rouken Glen and Twiddie jumps in Govan.'

Scullion drove to the end of the street, turned right. He adjusted the sunshade. 'Let's say Haggs told them to take Bones for a drive. Why?'

'Maybe they were instructed to mess him up. A wee reminder of something. But it all got out of hand. Bones was Mallon's man, and we know there was no love lost between Jackie and Long Rodney. It gets tangled, Sandy. Maybe it's one of those fucking gangster sagas where somebody gets shot and it all boils down to nothing more than a matter of territory, or an insult blown out of proportion . . .' Perlman realized he didn't sound very convincing. It was more than territory, more than some inflated outrage.

'Tell me, Lou. How good is this witness of yours?'

'The alcoholic eye doctor? Bloody useless. For an eye-doc he's blind as a bat. Plus his head's scrambled permanently.'

'Oh,' Scullion said.

'But I believe he saw what he says he saw. Because I'm a fucking cockeyed optimist, Sandy.'

'And the blood?'

'Matty was AB negative, according to a report from the Victoria Infirmary where the wee jockey was taken in 1984 when he fell from a horse at Ayr races, and his face split like a pomegranate dropped from the Scott Monument. But AB neg is common as dirt. So common, Sandy, it's my blood type as well.'

'You're just an old-fashioned bullshit artist,' Scullion said, and smiled.

272

'Probably.' Perlman watched a big black mongrel strut in front of the car, pursued by a snot-nosed infant, in turn chased by his teenaged mother who wore her hair in curlers under a scarf. *Come back, ye wee bugger.* Perlman sighed, and his eyelid throbbed, and he remembered what it was he'd intended to do, and that was to see if Caskie had run Tommy G through the computer. Growing old, things slipping, fuck it.

Rita said, 'What do you think, doll?'

'I don't know what I think.'

Rita asked, 'Call Haggs?'

'No fucking way.'

'Haggs'll go mental, John, if it turns out Perlman's got something up his sleeve.'

'Haggs is already mental.'

Rita pouted and said, 'We can always shag this situation out of our minds.'

'I'm up for that,' Twiddie said.

'I notice.'

43

Eddie Mallon entered Central Station and walked under the high glass roof that allowed bright light to illuminate the huge interior. He stashed the Armani bag containing the pistol in a left-luggage locker. A smell of strong coffee floated in the air, and a vendor sold fruit and an assortment of nuts in the forecourt. Eddie bought a bag of cashews. He chewed on them while he walked to the location of the timetables, which were arranged on boards.

He found the schedule he was looking for.

A train left Central, destination Largs, at forty-five minutes past each hour. Jackie had been anxious to be dropped off at the station by 10.35 a.m. Why? Because he needed enough time to buy a ticket, he wanted to make sure he had a cushion of about ten minutes to spare him a crazy rush to catch the train.

Eddie looked at the station clock: 11:37. He went inside the ticket office and bought a day-return, then he walked quickly to the platform and took a seat on the train. The carriage was filled with women and little kids. A trip to the beach, a release from the dry streets of the city. He stared out, and wondered if McWhinnie had followed him to the station, if he was somewhere on the train. Or if McWhinnie had even bothered to go to work today.

The train moved. Eddie gazed at warehouses and factories, the unplanned outskirts of the city. Kids, some of them in swimsuits, scampered up and down the aisle. The Kiddy Express – except it wasn't an express, it stopped at a number of stations on the way. The first was a few miles from Glasgow: Paisley, Gilmour Street. More kids and mothers boarded here. Fugitives from Paisley. Eddie had an impression of bright sun-hats and pacifiers and baby-bottles containing orange juice. The women, pink-skinned for the most part, were dressed in lightweight shorts and summery blouses. They had the cheerfully relieved smiles of people jettisoning the drudgery of the city for a few hours at the beach.

He observed the landscape yield to deep green pasture. Out of the city's reach he felt a certain freedom. The sky had no limits here. The small towns and settlements the train zipped through were blinks of an eye. He imagined his father travelling this way a week before. He wondered if Jackie looked from the window, or if he read a newspaper, or if he sat with his eyes shut and dozed. Did he think of the honeymoon in Largs, the old days, first love? Had he chosen Largs as a meeting place because it had associations for him? Had somebody asked, *Where will we meet, Jackie?*

And had Jackie replied: *Largs, I know a hotel where we can talk in peace*?

Largs, Christ. All this could be a crazy construct of your own brain, Eddie, he thought. The conviction that Jackie had travelled this way for a meeting could be something you've cobbled together from the assorted odds and ends of your own imagination. The big hunch that turns out a total disaster. A misguided step in the dark. You just don't know.

Suddenly, startling as a great mirror of quicksilver, there was the sea, and in the distance through the haze of heat the awesome grey spine of an island – Arran, which looked like a man at rest. The train stopped at Saltcoats Station. The kids

275

yelled and laughed and pressed their faces to the windows as if they might smell the sea through glass.

Fifty minutes after it had left Glasgow Central, the train arrived at its destination. Eddie made his way on to the platform and walked to the main street. He smelled the sea air that stirred in a breeze so soft and slow you could barely feel it. He strolled past shops – the Baker's Oven, the Craft Shop, the Bagel Basket – until he arrived at the seafront, where a ferry of the Caledonian MacBrayne line was taking on passenger cars for the short trip to Cumbrae, a humpbacked island less than a mile off the coast.

The ferry was mobbed by screaming gulls. On the pebbled beach, gaggles of kids paddled in the shallows under the vigilant eyes of mothers. The kids consumed copious amounts of ice cream. Bold seabirds approached, scavenging for broken cones or any kind of appetizing spillage. The air smelled of salt and burned toffee.

Eddie turned right, away from the pier. Small, with well-kept gardens and neat bungalows in side streets, Largs lacked that tawdry quality he associated with resort towns. No high-roller casinos, no cheap eateries. Ahead, facing the sea, stood a couple of large structures that might have been hotels. The first one he reached was indeed a hotel, but it wasn't the Seaview. He continued to walk. *Am I getting warm, Jackie? Am I close?* He thought of Jackie and Flora, arm in arm, strolling this promenade. Young lovers who couldn't wait to be shut inside their room away from the world.

The board with the name 'THE SEAVIEW HOTEL' had been freshly painted in blue and gold. 'Bed & Breakfast. 70 Rooms En-Suite. Function Room. Bar & Restaurant.' The building was grey stone, flowerboxes on sills, a cheerful midsize hotel with an unimpeded view of Cumbrae.

Stay away, son, Jackie said.

Hey, you just don't go in here blind, unprepped, Tom Collins said.

Eddie climbed the steps, entered. The air was cool inside,

venetian blinds half-shut. For a second he couldn't see anything except the ghosts of things left in his eyes by the sunlight. Then he could make out the reception desk, a smiling girl in a floral dress, a wall-map of North Ayrshire, a sign with an arrow: BAR & RESTAURANT. He went inside the bar, a narrow room beyond which was a large fern-clogged dining room half-empty. He asked for a club soda with ice, then he sat down in a darkened corner of the bar and drank quickly. He ached. His head. His body. He wanted Solpadeine. He had none.

'Hot one,' said the barman.

'Pleasant,' Eddie said.

'I like it cooler.' The barman wiped the counter. 'There's a change coming. So I hear.'

Eddie finished his drink, set the glass down. Now. I get up, I go back to the reception desk, I ask them if Jackie Mallon was a guest here one day last week, did he have company, I show my NYPD identification and hope it pulls strings and opens door for me. *Jackie Mallon, you say? Did he stay here? I'm sorry, we can't give out information about guests, sir. And you're well out of your jurisdiction, I believe.*

Eddie paused in the doorway between the bar and the reception area. The girl at the desk, pretty, Nordic, smiled at him. She had wonderful straight teeth and a kindly look. Eddie took a step towards her, reaching in his hip-pocket for his ID, then he stopped, because a man in a bright floral shirt appeared at the desk and said something that made the receptionist laugh, and the man laughed too, then ran a hand over his dreadlocks and turned his face, scanning Eddie quickly before returning his attention to the girl.

Eddie couldn't move, affected by a sudden paralysis. He imagined this man breaking the stained glass of Joyce's door, charging inside her flat, attacking her.

The man made another joke and the girl smiled and said, 'I always forget jokes. Every time I hear one, in one ear and out the other.'

'Takes a special kinda brain, pet. An empty one.' The man laughed and then turned his face a second time to Eddie. Eddie felt he was being filed, stored for future reference. The eyes were sharp and calculating, no sign of mirth. The man moved from the reception desk and passed close to Eddie on his way to the bar.

Eddie stood still a moment. What now? What move to make now? You've come this far. You take the next step. He went back inside the bar and stood next to the guy, who was making banter with the barman.

'Biggest mistake the English ever made in Scotland was building a road that led south,' he said.

The barman said, 'Now that we've got our own Parliament, we'll throw all you English out.'

'Your own Parliament? That lot in Edinburgh are all gums, no teeth. They can't even fart unless they get the green light from Westminster.'

'At least we beat you at rugby last time,' the barman said.

'Once in a blue moon, mate.' The man turned to Eddie and said, 'What do you think, chief?'

'Think about what?' Eddie asked. This man *struck* Joyce, Eddie thought. Gurk's strength was evident from his muscularity. The powerful crag of brow suggested brute force. Joyce would have no chance with a man like this.

'Hallo? Is that American I hear?'

'Right,' Eddie said.

'Don't tell me. Lemme guess. Noo Yawk. The Great White Way. Times Square.'

'Cool,' Eddie said.

'There isn't an accent I can't get,' the man said. He held out a hand. 'Tommy Gurk.'

'Eddie.' The grip was very strong, combative, almost a challenge.

'Nice to meetcher, Eddie. You on holiday here?'

'Right. You?'

'Business. I sell novelty items to shops. You want suggestive

278

picture postcards or a yo-yo that whistles – I'm your man. Don't knock it, mate. It's a living.'

'I wouldn't think of knocking it. Been here long?'

'I'm in and out. Off and on. What's your game?'

'Retired,' Eddie said.

'At your age? Lucky sod. What was you before?'

'A cop.'

'Some of my best friends,' Tommy Gurk said. 'Drink?'

'Club soda. Thanks.'

Gurk ordered two club sodas. He clinked his glass against Eddie's. For a time Gurk was silent. He stabbed at an ice cube with a long brown finger.

'I didn't catch your last name, mate,' Gurk said.

'I don't think I mentioned it.'

'Travelling incog, are we?' Gurk nudged Eddie. 'I understand that. Bloke has his reasons for going around free as he likes using any name he likes. On the run from a wife, or more likely a wife's lawyers, hey, a geezer has the right to change his own sodding name . . . People looking for you, Eddie?'

Eddie shrugged, left the question unanswered. Let Gurk think what he liked.

'You play your cards close to your chest,' Gurk said.

'Force of habit, nothing personal,' Eddie said.

'No offence taken. None whatsoever.'

Gurk set his glass down. 'I'll be running along. Maybe we'll meet again.'

'Yeah,' Eddie said.

Gurk dropped a pound coin on the bar and inverted his glass over it. 'Your tip, Jack.'

The barman said thanks.

Gurk stepped out of the bar. Eddie heard him exchange some words with the receptionist. More laughter. This Gurk was a joker. He spread good cheer wherever he went.

'He's a character,' said the barman. 'Laugh a minute. He's been here more than a week and had us all in stitches.'

279

More than a week, Eddie thought.

The time-frame was right.

He felt the ghost of Jackie in the bar and imagined that if he turned his head he'd see the old man sitting at a corner table, inclined over a drink. The feeling of being haunted spooked him. He took a five-pound note from his pocket and slid it towards the barman.

'I've got a question,' he said.

The barman looked at the money, but said nothing.

'Has he had visitors?' Eddie asked.

The barman rubbed the side of his face. 'That wouldn't be for me to say, sir.'

Eddie dropped another note on the bar, a tenner. 'Now can you say?'

The barman leaned forward. He had a skinny face and his eyes were dark slits. 'Mr Gurk, our resident comedian, had two visitors last week. Dinner companions.'

'Describe them,' Eddie said.

'One was a guy in his late sixties about. Thin black hair. Looked dyed. The other was maybe fortyish. Walked with a pronounced limp. They had a few drinks, they stayed the night. That's all I know.'

Eddie looked at the ice melt in his glass. He smelled roasted meat waft from the direction of the kitchen, and strong vegetable matter boil, brussels sprouts, cabbage maybe. Gurk and Jackie and McQueen – all three of them had come to the Seaview to discuss business, but the deal had gone sour. Jackie and Billy McQueen had been murdered, and Gurk was left holding the bag, and probably under pressure from somewhere.

He was out in the cold.

And he wanted to come back in.

Tommy Gurk took the stairs up to his room. It had dark blue wallpaper. He sat on the centre of the bed, lotus position. He

280

had the slats of the blinds angled in such a way that the sun coming into the room was sliced. Light, dark, light, dark. He shut his eyes. He searched for the inner place, the garden, but it kept eluding him. He'd glimpse the path to the tranquil centre a moment, then he'd hear the niggling whisper of voices, the natter of all the monkeys in his brain, and his mood fell apart.

He walked the room. *I don't need any static*, he thought. He spaced the slats of a blind with his fingers and looked out at the water. A ferry was ploughing towards the island.

He thought about Kaminsky's missing property.

Then the American in the bar. That was bothering him. Ex-cop, or so he said. Listen, he's just a guy skipped out on his responsibilities, how do you know he's anything else? He's running away. He's got that fugitive look. Heavy alimony, can't hack it, takes a hike. That was one plausible scenario.

The American looked familiar, didn't he?

How could that be? You see a guy for the first time and he looks familiar, how so? He reminds you of somebody else, say?

He let the question go. He didn't have an answer for it.

He sat on the bed again. He took off his wristwatch and set it on the night-stand. He let his arms dangle loosely at his sides. Think of the garden. The garden. The garden. Think all the scents of the garden. Now let it go, let these pictures fall away, and step into the white zone beyond the garden, seek the peace where birds don't sing and nothing stirs because nothing exists in this zone except the thump of your heart and the thud of your pulses and soon you won't even hear these drumming reminders of life. You enter a place beyond nothing. You call it the Zone.

Here you are capable of anything because you are nothing, the embodiment of a paradox –

A wayward fly buzzed his face.

He opened his eyes, *damn*, pawed at it, missed. It flew

to a corner of the room and settled. A common housefly. The disturbances small things can create. He got up from the bed. He was out of the Zone because of a fly, but he still felt a measure of peacefulness, so much so that when he opened the padded envelope that lay on his pillow and let the stainless-steel pistol, a Ruger P90, slip into his palm he felt a glorious detachment from the violent capabilities of the weapon.

He studied the piece of paper stuck in the envelope. He memorized the information, looked at his watch. He had twenty minutes before the train.

He returned the gun to the envelope and he thought, The secret of doing violence well is self-knowledge.

Eddie waited in the Atlantis amusement arcade, surrounded by zap-technology, the roar of interstellar weaponry, lizard-monsters kids chased at high speed through mazes in space, the beeps and kapows and blasts of a form of entertainment whose attraction eluded him. Kids stuffed coins into slots and entered these strange worlds without having first of all to make any kind of mental adjustment, or so it seemed to Eddie; they passed effortlessly from the non-electronic dimension to its opposite.

He moved as far away from the machines as he could but the noise tracked and assaulted him. He watched the street. Across the way, tiny kids went round and round in miniature cars. Eddie thought, I can handle that. It's nice. Teensy cars that went in an undeviating circle lacked the evil complexity of electronic games where Space Wizards could take you to infinite dimensions –

Tommy Gurk appeared. He was carrying a black leather briefcase. He'd changed clothes. He wore a loose black linen jacket and blue jeans. Eddie drew back into shadow. Gurk strolled straight past. His expression was one of intense focus: *I'm going where I'm going, and nothing will stop me.* Eddie gave him thirty seconds, then left the arcade and walked about fifty yards behind him.

Gurk was heading for the railway station.

44

Christopher Caskie answered his telephone on the third ring.
He gazed through french doors into the back garden of his
house in Broomhill and remembered how Meg, when her
health had begun to decline, used to sit in the conservatory
with a book in her lap. Catherine Cookson sometimes. A P.D.
James mystery now and then. Invariably she fell asleep and
Caskie had to go out and fetch her and carry her inside.
This bloody house was like a prison, too big for one person,
he'd sell it, anyone with any sense would put it on the
market.

'Mr Caskie?'

'Speaking.' Caskie was conscious of his hand shaking slightly.
He fought to still it.

'Christopher Caskie?'

'Yes –'

'I have had you checked.'

Caskie said, 'Of course. I expected that.'

'A phone call from somebody in your position was unusual.
But you pass muster – is that the phrase?'

'That's the one.'

'I am wary. I check. Always. Check this. Check that. Check check. No mistakes.'

'Naturally.' Caskie shut his eyes. The room was too bright. It was like standing inside a tube of neon. Was it too late to take things back, to say no, *I've changed my mind, this isn't the way I want my personal affairs conducted?* I was a good cop once, an exemplary cop. I have awards, medals, citations. Now this. This rot I can't stop.

But I have to stop it.

He heard a sound at the other end of the line, a liquid falling, perhaps tea or coffee being poured. Say no to your conscience. Just say no to that interior sniper who shoots down all your bad thoughts. You never asked for him in the first place. It came with the way you were brought up. Here, swallow your daily spoonful of John Knox Juice. You'll feel bad if you don't take it. You'll feel a whole lot worse if you do.

'Now we will take the next step,' the caller said. 'My man will be prepared.'

'And the two women will not be involved.'

'My word. My hand is on my heart.'

The line was cut. Caskie put the handset down. He looked at his watch. Four p.m. exactly. He called McWhinnie's cellphone.

'Christopher, I'm sick,' McWhinnie said.

'How sick, Charles?'

'Flu type of feeling. Draggy.' McWhinnie's voice was thick, like a man speaking from inside a ski mask. 'Headache, upset stomach, the runs.'

'I know the symptoms. You've been in bed all day?'

'I went out for a time,' McWhinnie said. 'Our man visited Senga in Onslow Drive . . . then I felt sick in the car, so I came home and lay down. I don't know where he is.'

'You'll be right as rain tomorrow,' Caskie said. He thought of his conversation with Eddie Mallon, that stuff about a safe house. Out of the blue. It could only have come from McWhinnie. Ergo: they'd met, and McWhinnie, whipped by that conscience of his – so akin to Caskie's own – had talked. And Eddie Mallon had

285

dropped the subject into the conversation as if to say: *I'm ready to play any game you like, Chris.*

Caskie said, 'Stay warm, Charlie. Drink fluids, take aspirin. We'll talk in the morning.'

'Fine.'

Caskie hung up. Poor McWhinnie, saying he was sick. He lied badly. But it didn't matter. There was no hard evidence to link Christopher Caskie to any crime. McWhinnie might have broken the code of confidentiality in the presence of Eddie Mallon, and talked of safe houses – but it stopped there. How could McWhinnie verify his tale of carrying groceries to a safe house in Govan? Who at Force HQ would listen and believe? *Poor Charlie, nervous breakdown, terrible thing*. As for Mallon, well, he had no evidence either, and little credibility in Tay's eyes.

Caskie walked out to the patio and stood in shade. As if affected by heat, bees were cumbersome as they moved from flower to flower. This confounded weather. It couldn't last. Not in Glasgow. Global warming. This was more like global meltdown.

He walked back inside the house and poured himself a gin, which he packed with ice. He held the glass in the air and said 'Cheers' to himself, then he drank. He thought of the man saying, *My word. My hand is on my heart*, and he wondered if the same dry heat that held Glasgow in its grip also prevailed in Zurich.

His doorbell rang. He went down the hallway to answer it. He couldn't remember when he'd last felt this liberated, nor this awful. He had a war going on in his head and the heavy machine-guns were bombarding those trenches where the soldiers on the side of the angels flew white flags of surrender.

He opened the door. The sunlit street was harsh, the light like a lake of petrol burning.

45

Eddie Mallon stepped off the train at Central Station, walking about a hundred yards behind Tommy Gurk. It was a long time since he'd stalked anyone. He remembered the vigilance required, the almost unnatural sense of anticipation, the ability to detect any sudden alteration in the quarry's movements – such as that pause when the target turned and, as if struck by an inexplicable uneasiness, glanced back and thought: *Somebody is walking on my grave.*

Gurk moved along the crowded platform at a regular pace. He was in no hurry. Neither was he lagging. He held the briefcase close to his side. At one point he paused, scratched his head. But he didn't look back. If he turns, Eddie thought, if he sees me and raises a hand in greeting, it's no big deal, I'll say hey, we meet again, small world, whaddya know.

Gurk went through the ticket barrier. Eddie kept his distance. Gurk passed a couple of coffee shops and then, changing his mind, wheeled round abruptly and entered one of the cafés. He didn't look in Eddie's direction. Head down, Eddie kept moving, then turned after twenty yards and walked back. He glanced inside the café and saw Gurk pointing to a pastry in a glass case. A young girl slid the pastry on to a plate, handed it to Gurk, who said something to make her laugh – what a gift, the guy was a walking joker – and she put a hand up to her mouth as if laughter was against management policy. Tommy Gurk made another crack, the girl turned her face to one side and her shoulders shook. She poured him a coffee and he took it – coffee in left hand, pastry in right, briefcase clutched under is armpit – and he wobbled from side to side like a man who'd lost his balance, all part of the funny-man routine. He moved to a table, sat down, took a healthy bite from the pastry. He set the briefcase on the floor between his feet.

Eddie walked to a newsagent's that faced the café, bought a paper. Textbook. You bought a newspaper and pretended to read it and all the while you felt completely ridiculous, like somebody wearing a wide-brimmed hat in a hoaky black-and-white spy movie set in a foggy Balkan town before the outbreak of the Second World War.

Eddie opened the *Evening Times*. The front page depicted the skeleton of a half-finished high-rise surrounded by scaffolding. A photographic insert showed the plump face of a man with shiny black hair. The headline was lurid: *Mystery Death of Local Accountant*. The face was Billy McQueen's. Eddie read: *Police are baffled by the discovery of the corpse of William McQueen on a Maryhill building site early this morning. McQueen, who ran an accountancy business in Glasgow –*

Eddie moved, narrowing the angle of his view. Gurk was finishing his pastry, licking crumbs from his fingers. Where do you go from here, Tommy? Who do you hurt next? Senga? Is she on your list? Or do you have another shot at Joyce in your search for whatever it is that Jackie left behind? That fucking grail, that unholy treasure chest, whatever.

'Fancy meeting you here, Mallon.'

Startled, Eddie turned. Charles McWhinnie had materialized next to him.

'You almost stopped my goddam heart,' Eddie said.

'I can affect people that way.' One side of McWhinnie's face was discoloured, but there was little swelling.

'How the hell did you find me?'

'I saw you get on the train, which I managed to miss by the width of a pubic hair. So I waited. I knew you'd come back.'

'Terrific patience,' Eddie said.

'Now and again,' McWhinnie said.

'You don't look too bad,' Eddie said.

'Considering I sat up half the night rummaging through the nooks and crannies of my soul, while I sipped Macallan's with an ice pack pressed to my face. I concluded that I'm not a happy fellow. This job is a waste of my time. I have one life to live, why spend it on angst? So I called in sick, and I'll stay that way until I've decided what to do with the rest of my time on planet earth. I've decommissioned myself . . .'

Eddie scanned McWhinnie's face a moment. Changes were going on inside Charlie McWhinnie. You could see a darkness in his eyes that might have been tunnels going places Charlie had never been before.

Eddie said, 'Listen, that rough-house stuff last night, I apologize. That's not me, McWhinnie. Maybe twenty years ago, when I had a more aggressive streak, but last night I lost control. Put it down to frustration. Annoyance. A bunch of stuff, people giving me a hard time, being obstructive –'

'Let's forget it.'

Eddie laid a hand on McWhinnie's arm and positioned himself in such a way that if Gurk looked in this direction he'd see only Charles McWhinnie's back.

McWhinnie said, 'Why do I get the impression you're using me as a shield?'

'There's a guy in that café,' Eddie said.

'I'm not supposed to look, right? And he's not supposed to see you either. Is there a reason for this surveillance?'

'Here's the story, Charlie. The guy's called Tommy Gurk. He's looking for whatever the hell it was my father was doing before he got killed.'

'*Gurk*, you say? Caskie ran a PNC search on a fellow by that name yesterday.'

'He told me it came back negative.'

'Dear me, he lied,' McWhinnie said.

'No kidding.'

'Gurk, who has a bunch of aliases, is some kind of demented Buddhist who took a wrong turning down Satori Street and has been trapped in a cul-de-sac ever since. He's linked up with some characters on the Continent, in particular a guy called – let me think – Josef Kaminsky, who is reputed to be *seriously* dangerous, and involved in black-market activity.'

'What kind of black market?'

'Name it. He can get you anything.'

'Anything isn't very specific, Charlie.'

'Because, my friend, the computer says he dabbles in everything. You want American cigarettes from Norfolk, Virginia, delivered direct to anywhere in the world at one-fifth US retail price? Unused outboard motors in their original cartons or shock absorbers from Detroit as unsullied as the day they came off the assembly lines? No problem. Something less mundane perhaps? How about works of art pilfered from galleries? Perfectly valid credit cards stolen from the manufacturing companies? Easy for Kaminsky to acquire, if you have the scratch . . . Oh, yes, and if you step out of line, you might well disappear for ever. People who cross Kaminsky have a tendency to vanish. Nice, eh?'

'This is in his file –'

'I'm not making it up, Eddie. And the only reason he isn't behind bars is because he can walk on fucking water. I imagine he sits in Zurich and issues orders on his cellphones and his minions go out and do his bidding while the man himself sips Campari and nobody can point a finger at him. And Gurk is, quote, an *associate*. Which almost certainly means that Tommy is quite capable of anything.'

Eddie assimilated this, wondering what the deal was with

Jackie. Stolen artworks? Cigarettes? It was going to be a big score for you Jackie, right? Eddie looked at Gurk and his head clouded and he thought, The deeper I dig into Jackie's world, the less I like. ·

Where was the good father every kid wanted?

The good father I wanted.

And now there are two of them, Gurk thought. He didn't need this. He didn't need interference. He didn't want any fucking *aggro*. He couldn't afford wankers looking inside his fucking briefcase.

He'd wait, pick his moment, get up, walk out. They think, *He hasn't noticed us. He's just supping his brew and digesting his Danish.* He reached down and picked up his briefcase and laid it on his lap.

Then he got up. Immediately sat down again. Keep them on their fucking toes. Keep them dancing.

Any minute now, you go.

Eddie saw Gurk get up from the table, briefcase in hand. A train was disgorging its passengers and suddenly the area around Eddie was more crowded than it had been, a throng of red-faced people disembarking after hours at the beach.

McWhinnie said, 'He's on the move, Mallon.' Then he was swept aside by the tide of the crowd, but managed to push his way back to Eddie. Gurk stepped out of the café. It was confusing, this buzzing surge of people and the smell of their suntan lotion and sea-salt, men in baggy shorts, kids scurrying around, getting entangled in the legs of adults and playing games and making weird sounds like *zoop zoop zoop*, women carrying souvenirs of the outing, beachballs and baskets of seashells, and one little kid had a water pistol he fired into McWhinnie's face and said, *How's zat feel, eh?*

Gurk was moving quickly now, losing himself in the multitude that pressed towards the main entrance just as office workers and insurance agents and salespersons hurried inside to catch their regular commuter trains. McWhinnie rubbed water from his eyes and followed Eddie, who was shoving his way through the crowd and wondering if Gurk knew he was being dogged. So many goddam people pushing in opposing directions. Eddie felt like a man swimming against a mutinous current. McWhinnie was close, a few yards to the left. Gurk was maybe twenty or thirty yards ahead, barging forward to the main exit.

Then suddenly Gurk found some space for himself and jack-knifed right, hurrying towards the stall where a few hours before Eddie had bought cashews. Eddie kept after him, conscious of McWhinnie making a turn to stay in touch with Gurk's abrupt change of direction. A voice boomed on the tannoy system. *The train now standing at Platform Three is the 1800 hours for Ayr, stopping at Paisley Gilmour Street, Johnstone, Dalry . . .*

Gurk was moving in the direction of a side exit. We could lose him, Eddie thought, and ran into the swarm of commuters hurrying towards the Ayr train, elbowing his way through, ignoring the grunts of disapproval, the snide little remarks about his rudeness. *What happened to manners?* Eddie could see McWhinnie to his left still. He was making better progress than Eddie, he was closer to Gurk, fifteen yards behind the quarry.

Eddie was sweating. The air trapped inside the station was hot. Gurk knows, he thought. He has to know. Nobody moves like that unless he's being hunted. He's seen me. He's seen McWhinnie. He can't get bogged down in a goddam railroad station. He's got business ahead.

A beggar tried to thrust a tin cup into Eddie's face. *Please help.* Sorry. Another time. McWhinnie, somehow, had managed to shorten the distance between himself and Gurk to about ten yards. Maybe he had a better knack for sliding through crowds than Eddie. Gurk was already vanishing into the corridor of the side exit. Eddie found himself surrounded by a group of Germans with backpacks. Six or seven of them, poring over a big map. *I think Culzean Castle will be nice, yes?* Eddie swept the map aside and the Germans murmured in irritation, and one, a standard-issue Aryan, reached out for Eddie as if to drag him back and demand either an instant apology or rapiers at dawn, but Eddie was already beyond him.

Now he'd lost sight of both McWhinnie and Gurk.

He reached the exit passage. There were stairs he hadn't expected, and a metal barrier bisected the stairway. People obeyed no rules here, left side for those ascending, right for those in descent, some process of order. Instead, they went up and down as they pleased. There were collisions, dodges, confrontations narrowly avoided, the whole commuter lunacy, the urgent madness of the citizenry rushing to various destinations. So many people in flight. The city was burning. The doors of the asylums had been thrown open. Everyone was free to create chaos. Eddie was pressed to the rail in his descent. His back hurt. His arm was crushed to his side.

He saw McWhinnie at the bottom of the stairs, but no sign of Gurk. Maybe Gurk had been devoured by the city, disappeared, one of those posted missing in the mystery that was contemporary life. McWhinnie looked up, caught Eddie's eye, motioned towards the street with his hand. Did McWhinnie's gesture mean he still had Gurk in his sight? Eddie kept descending through the scrum until he reached the bottom of the stairs. He felt he'd been forced through a sieve. I'll have a portion of mashed Eddie, please.

A rectangle of sunlight ahead, a street, traffic, flocks of people entering the station or escaping it. Was there no end to the number of bodies? McWhinnie was outside now, and so was Gurk. From where Eddie stood it appeared McWhinnie had caught up with Gurk and grabbed his arm, and Gurk was arguing, trying to free himself. This altercation was observed by Eddie in an intermittent way, as if he were inside a cinema where the patrons in front of him kept getting to their feet and obscuring the view. Now you see McWhinnie, next second he's vanished. And Gurk was going in and out of the frame too –

Then there was one of those moments when your heart feels like glass that has suddenly developed a flaw, and you know something has gone badly wrong, something beyond normal commuting-hour activity has happened, something so extraordinary and unexpected that nobody knows how to react. There's a clearing in the crowd, a pocket of quite unnatural space, and people are hurrying back from the epicentre of the event, ground zero, and somebody shouts, somebody else screams, and Eddie finds himself rushing forward, stomach tumbling, knowing that whatever has taken place here isn't a happy occurrence, and before he realizes it he's reached the clearing and he sees McWhinnie lying on his side, his white shirt stained with blood, and more blood on the grey pavement, a bright pool reflecting the sun, so much blood you can't tell where it's coming from, and then Eddie is on his knees beside McWhinnie, who's dead, dead beyond dispute, dead as a body that might have fallen from a high ledge or a passing plane. Dead as McQueen, dead as the jumper in Manhattan.

McWhinnie's eyes are open. His mouth.

Eddie stands up, just as a woman with a pale shocked look points a finger without speaking, but Eddie knows she's indicating the direction the gunman took, and he turns and moves quickly and although his legs feel disconnected from his body he runs as if the woman's finger was a starter's pistol whose explosion he alone in all the world has heard. Renfield Street, through traffic, then crossing St Vincent Street against the lights, aware of buses and taxicabs and the sheen of sunstruck cars, but then he doesn't know where to go next – up St Vincent or down?

He stops moving, leans against the wall of a building, gasping, head down, a thin thread of saliva hanging from his open mouth, all his pulses raging. *I have one life to live,* McWhinnie had said.

Short life, Eddie thinks. Oh, you sad bastard, Charlie.

His back to the wall, he hunkered down, arms dangling uselessly over his knees. He didn't move from this position for a long time. He didn't know where he was. He didn't know how far he'd come from Central Station. A passer-by in a business suit said, 'Clean yourself up and find a job, for heaven's sake, have some pride in yourself, man,' and dropped a pound coin between Eddie's feet. Eddie said thanks but the man had already vanished round a corner.

Gone.

And Gurk had gone too. Into the ever more narrow arteries of the city, side streets, alleys, lanes, passageways too tight for any car to travel, places to which Eddie had no access.

46

Haggs had never liked the Jew, who brought to life a nascent anti-Semitism in him. Haggs rarely ran into Jews and generally had no feelings about them one way or another – but Perlman, this guy in need of a shave and a haircut and a complete sartorial overhaul, stirred up some deep resentments Haggs had acquired by chance on his way through life. Haggs believed, on the basis of no experience, that Jews were pushy, acquisitive, clannish, secretive, and loved to control great flows of cash.

This fucker Perlman clearly wasn't into the cash aspect, but he fell right into the pushy category. The way he blew cigarette smoke straight into Haggs's face, for instance, and the aggressive lock of his jaw, and how he flaunted his disgusting soiled tie, which anyone with any taste would have hidden *inside* the jacket – these things weren't designed to endear Perlman to you. What also troubled Haggs was the fact that Perlman had strutted into the members-only room in the clubhouse without a member's approval, and that was downright bad manners, like pishing on the floor.

Perlman said, 'Posh place. What does membership run you?'

'If you have to ask, you're not membership potential,' Haggs said.

'Relax, Haggs. I wouldn't join any club that accepted you,' Perlman said. 'So don't worry your arse about me filling in an application. Golf gets on my tits. There's something depressing about grown men hitting a wee ball for miles and chasing after it in clown-coloured clothes. I don't know about you, Haggs, but I sense retarded development and a Freudian thing.'

Haggs smiled and secretly longed to land a fist in the centre of Perlman's grizzled chops. 'You've got some gall to talk about clothes, Perlman.'

'I've got a lot of gall, Roddy, old son. Keeps me young and spry. As for my clothing, I don't give a shite. I'm a cop. I'm not on some bloody catwalk. In fact, I'm proud – in a contrary way – of my total lack of nous in the world of couture. I hope my appearance here is embarrassing the crap out of you.'

Haggs was uneasy. Of course he didn't want to be seen with Lou Perlman. He looked round the dark-panelled room, glanced at the roll of honour on which was gold-painted the achievements of past members, the windows that overlooked the first tee, a stand of pine, a stretch of glassy water in the distance. At polished circular tables members with prosperously ruddy faces and rings of chub under their polo shirts drank expensive single malts and smoked fat Cuban jobs and laughed at crude jokes they couldn't have shared with their wives.

'It's a man's world in here, right enough,' Perlman said. 'Dead butch. You can just smell the pong of rich leather polish and the Old Spice aftershave and a tiny wee hint of sweaty groin that's been talcumed. Very nice. You've come up in the world, eh? You're a star, Haggs.'

'I played my cards right,' Haggs said.

'Aye, but it was always your deck,' Perlman remarked.

'Control is power, Perlman.' Haggs lit a cigar which he poked at Perlman, who fingered his eyepatch. 'I come here for a quiet time and then you turn up looking like a lost dog, darkening my doorstep. What do you want anyway?'

'I like the way you carry all this off,' Perlman said. 'This swanky place. The clothes you're wearing. What do you call those trousers – plus fours?'

'Right.'

'And those fine red and blue diamond socks. Magic.'

'Get to the point, Perlman. What do you want?'

'Information.'

Haggs said, 'Information?

Perlman scanned the room. 'I wonder what the good people in here would think of your association with John Twiddie and Rita whatserface, both lowly denizens of Govan, both incurably violent sociopaths. What would they say if they knew you consorted with scumbags like that? Would you be blackballed, Roddy? Would they sling your arse out on to the street, eh? *Off you go, you fucking impostor, and no refunds.* Oh the shame, oh the scandal. Haggs expelled for fraternizing with nasty bastards.'

'Twiddie and Rita,' Haggs said and shrugged. 'I can't say I'm intimate with them, Perlman. They passed in and out of my world once or twice. It's not as if I'd have them at my house. I wouldn't sit down to dinner with them.'

'They wouldn't know what fork to use, would they,' Perlman said. 'They'd think the fish knife was for the butter. Rita would stub out her fags in the left-over mashed potato. Oh, it's a scary picture. When did you last see this awesome pair?'

'Who remembers?' Haggs said.

'Try, Roddy. Try for me.'

'I'm drawing blanks,' Haggs said.

Perlman said, 'What if I was to knock this table over and this nice Rennie Mackintosh lamp with it? What if I was to spill your drink in your lap? What if I pretended to vomit on these lovely waxy floorboards, I mean, give it the full boke choke right out of my gullet, you know what I mean? Wouldn't that be a humiliation for you, Roddy?'

'You can dance on the fucking table for all I care.'

'You wouldn't blink?'

Haggs shook his head. 'Neither eyelid would move.'

'And you wouldn't be embarrassed?'

'You can't pressure me, Perlman. You ought to know better.'

'You want to test me, Roddy? I'll go down on my knees and making puking sounds. Members will show grave alarm. Disgust will be evident. You're judged by the company you keep in the rarefied atmosphere of an expensive boys' club. It's no bloody skin off my back to be seen rolling on the floor. I don't give a fig, old son. Ready?' Perlman clutched his stomach and made a sound of discomfort. It was barely audible, but the threat was there. 'After I've rolled on the floor and made rude gurgling noises and farted, I'll throw this ashtray through the mirror behind the bar where all the single malts are lined up like smart wee soldiers. Glasgow Policeman Loses Control At Exclusive Golf Club. Sound good to you, Roddy?'

'Fuck you, Perlman.'

'I hear that refrain a lot.'

'Twiddie and Rita, when did I last see them – that's all you want to know?'

Perlman lit another cigarette. 'Tell me.'

'A week ago.'

'In what circumstances?'

'Passing on West Nile Street. We exchanged quick chat about the weather. I went my way. They went theirs. I wish I had more, Perlman. I wish I could bring sunshine into your life. But that's it.'

Perlman sucked smoke. Haggs was a good liar. He didn't have a giveaway of any kind. He lied barefaced. Probably because he believed what he was saying. He invented alternative realities and lived inside them. 'I was hoping for more, Roddy. Truly. Here's the thing. They set fire to a van, a Transit, but they're such rank fucking dildoes they didn't exactly light up the sky with their effort. I have a witness, a fellow that saw Twiddie and Rita run from the scene of their incendiary flop.'

'Stop right there,' Haggs said. 'You think this interests me? A pair of morons try to burn a van – come on, Perlman. Tell me a better story.'

'This one picks up,' Perlman said. 'In the back of the van is a wallet.'

Haggs had the sense of travelling in a small boat towards rough waters. 'A wallet?'

'Aye.'

'And?'

'The property of Matty Bones.'

Wallet, Haggs thought. *Bones*. The two words echoed in his brain like coconut shells struck together.

Oversight. Big time. The ship was drifting towards rocks and the lighthouse wasn't working. Haggs said, 'So what?'

'So how did Bones's wallet get in the back of this van, together with bloodstains that are precisely Matty Bones's type?'

I could kill, Haggs thought. 'I'm not exactly Twiddie's keeper, Perlman. How the hell would I know what he and that deranged crumpet of his get up to? I move in another world altogether.'

Perlman looked round the room and remarked, 'And very nice it is too.'

'I wish you luck, Perlman, I really do. But as for a burning van and Bones's wallet, listen, you've come to the wrong place if you're looking for alms.'

'I had my hand held out and I was expecting you to cross it with the silver of information,' Bones said. 'Daft of me. I live in great expectation, Roddy. I always believe that behind every closed door lies the dark truth. And in every burning Transit van is the clue you don't expect. Funny old world.'

'Funny's right,' Haggs said. Note to self, he thought: stay calm in adversity. Don't let it show.

'The van was stolen in Renfrew three nights ago, matter of interest. Were you in Renfrew by any chance?'

'Give me a break, Perlman. Do I look like I'd steal a Transit van?'

'Maybe you do,' Perlman said, and gazed in the direction of the trees, the lake, light from the sun spreading across still water.

A golf ball was flying through space, insignificant against the vast blue of the world. It came down like a shotgunned bird in the dead centre of the lake. Plop.

'People pay to play golf.' Perlman shook his head. 'Downright amazing.'

'Are you done with me?'

'Aye,' Perlman said. 'For the time being.'

'Call me first next time,' Haggs said. 'If there's a next time.'

'But you're such a hard man to reach, old son.'

'If at first you don't succeed.'

'How does the rest of that go, Roddy?'

Haggs clapped a hand against Perlman's shoulder. 'You're a smart arse, Lou. But I like you anyway.'

'The admiration is mutual, Roddy.'

'I never doubted it,' Haggs said.

'Remember, Roddy. I've got my eye on you. The good one. I'm this close to nailing you for *something*.'

Perlman walked towards the exit. As he pushed open the glass door and stepped outside, his cellphone rang in his pocket and he felt the closing door slap lightly against his back.

He spoke into the handset. The caller was Sandy Scullion, who said, 'Central Station, Lou. Now. It's bad.'

47

In his room at the dosshouse in Duke Street, Tommy Gurk stood
at the sink and plugged an electric razor into the wall-socket
and, concentrating on his reflection in the mirror, ran the razor
across his skull. His dreadlocks dropped like newborn minks
into the sink. He thought of the young geezer at the railway
station. *I want to have a word, you don't mind.* I was out of the
Zone, Gurk thought. I wasn't in a place of peace. I wasn't in
the garden. Where was calm? More locks fell into the sink.

Take your hand off me, chief.

A word, won't take a minute. You have some ID?

Never carry any. Don't need it. Free country, ennit? You a
copper?

Could I take a wee peek inside the briefcase?

What's in this briefcase is private, mate. For mine eyes
only.

I'd like to just check that, sir.

You're not listening to me, are you, copper?

Zzzzzz. Tommy Gurk switched off the razor and leaned
forward over the sink until his face touched the mirror. He
put his hands into the pile of dreadlocks that lay nestled in

302

old brown porcelain. Strip the identity down. Change. You can't go around this city looking the way you did. You can't do what you've come to do unless you alter your appearance. He pulled his lower eyelids down. Underneath, the pink tissue was pale and looked unhealthy.

He stepped back from the mirror. There. Bald now. Shaved to the skin. He gathered the thick lanks of cut hair and put them in a wastebasket, then ran water into the sink until all trace of stray hair was gone. The room smelled of old cigarettes and piss and disinfectant and the stale flesh of all those men and women who'd come and gone. A dosshouse. In the lobby downstairs he'd paid his money at the desk and the clerk in the cage hadn't even looked at him and the people who sat in beaten-up leather chairs paid him scant attention, they just shuffled newspapers or played draughts or snoozed and twitched in their wino dreams. He'd felt invisible. That was what he wanted.

He remembered, saw it clearly, how the gun came out of the briefcase.

Wait a minute, think, put away that weapon, sir.

All the faces in the crowd at the railway station had receded like people suddenly diminishing in size, the sky pressing down, the planet wobbling on its course through space, all topsy-turvy.

Just give it to me.

You want it, you got it, china.

The explosion jarred his hand but he didn't have time to feel the kick because he'd stuffed the gun back in the briefcase and then he'd run, he'd fled down side streets, this way and that, lost, not caring, needing to be beyond reach and recognition, then he'd found an underground station in Buchanan Street and gone down the escalator to the platform and boarded a train that carried him into the sweet anonymity of a black tunnel, and he'd come up into brassy sunlight in another part of the city and bought the razor in a second-hand shop and boarded a double-decker bus and after he disembarked he walked a few blocks until he found this dump, this great drab Victorian building where rooms were cheap and the clientele cheaper.

Catch your breath. Find the place. Enter the Zone.

He ran a hand over his hairless head. He felt bumps in his skull, and tiny crevices his dreadlocks had hidden. He couldn't find the calm. He was a long way off and his compass fucked. He was tuned to static. He thought, I'll phone Kaminsky, I'll tell him what happened, unforeseen circumstances – but Kaminsky never wanted to know about failure. The word wasn't in his vocabulary.

Down in the street an ambulance raced and screamed, an auditory explosion, how could you reach out for tranquillity in such a place? He had a flash of Tibet, the placid shadows of the monastery, monks in saffron robes, the gong that echoed in the arched passageway, wind-chimes, unflavoured cooked rice in his mouth. He'd go back to that if he could. Like a fucking shot.

He emptied the briefcase on the bed. The gun. The toothbrush and tube of tea-tree toothpaste he always carried in the event he couldn't get back to wherever home base might be. Healthy gums, very important. A disposable razor. A small phial of Total Shaving Solution. A bar of hemp soap in its original box. That was all.

The ambulance faded but now there were police cars and sirens and all hell. The city was a cauldron of jarring noises. He had to get the whole job done successfully and go back to Largs and collect his gear from the hotel – if that was possible, if the place was safe – and then head south, maybe by bus, he'd decide later. He walked to the window and pulled the net curtain back a little way and his fingers penetrated the dry moth-eaten material. He looked into the street and thought how a simple business deal – *let's shake hands on it, Mr Mallon, or can I call you Jackie?* – could go so easily to ruin.

He tossed his few belongings back into the briefcase and left the room. Punter's name on the paper, what was it, why was he panicked into forgetting simple things?

Too much chaos, too much swirl. Rise above it.

Begins with an 'H'. Higgs?

No, Haggs. Spot on. Got it.

48

Eddie Mallon sat in the back of a taxi with his head tilted back and the window down and warm air blowing at his face. Even with his eyes open he kept seeing McWhinnie, poor dead Charlie blown away – and for what? Some questions hung in the air like toxic gasses. You couldn't analyse them any more than you could disperse them. *What did McWhinnie die for?*

The driver said, 'They say it was a policeman.'

'Huh?'

'A policeman,' the driver said and glanced back to look at Eddie. 'The fella that was shot. You hear about it?'

'I heard,' Eddie said.

The driver's plump neck spilled over his shirt collar. His jaw was nicked from shaving cuts. 'The way this city's going,' he said, and he shook his head because he had no vocabulary for the horrors he saw.

'The whole world,' Eddie said.

'Aye, the whole world, right enough. I don't remember the last time a policeman was shot in Glasgow. It's bloody terrible, so it is. I blame Hollywood pictures and the general decline in Christian values. We used to look up to policemen when I was a wee boy. They told you what was right and what was wrong and gave you a good kick up the arse if you needed it. Nowadays that sort of thing would land them in court.'

Eddie wasn't listening. He was conscious of the number of police cars on the city streets. An officer was dead. Consequently, visible police presence everywhere. A communal sense of shock, grief, a dismal black mood dominant inside Force HQ. Subdued officers whispering together, sharing a single visceral truth: *one of our own has been murdered.*

Charlie McWhinnie should never have been involved, Eddie thought. If Caskie hadn't used him as his personal hound-dog and private gofer, McWhinnie would never have become entangled in the life and movements of Eddie Mallon, and maybe the disillusion spreading like bindweed through Charlie would have withered. But Caskie had forced Charlie into tasks he felt either demeaning or futile, and so he'd fallen asunder, baffled by the point of his life and the direction of his career.

Eddie stared at the passing buildings. To his right the turrets and spires of the Art Gallery, an extravaganza in red stone. The building seemed to float on air. He felt numb, then angry. His mood swung this way, that way. He shut his eyes tight, experienced the sway and vibration of the cab.

'Broomhill Drive you wanted?' the driver asked.

'Right,' Eddie said. He looked at Caskie's business card crumpled in his hand. 'Sixty-five.'

'Sixty-five. Here we are.'

Eddie stepped out, paid. He stared at the grey house, the stained-glass panes in the upstairs windows, the carved stonework above the front door. Grapevines and wheat sheaves, a rustic effect. What good does it do to come here? What can I possibly get out of this? A blind man and his fawn labrador guide dog went past and Eddie thought, That's what I need, something to lead me, show me the way. The man's white stick tapped on the pavement.

Eddie moved towards the front steps of the house. He'd tried twice to phone from the city centre to announce he was on his way, but the line had been busy both times, so he quit. He wasn't in the mood for politeness anyway, he was beyond niceties. He climbed the steps, rang the doorbell, waited. He gazed at the nameplate. I'll turn, walk away, leave. This is wrong. Confrontation isn't the approach. But the anger kept coming back in waves and he was powerless to stall the feeling. His skin was hot. His hands sweated. His scalp too. He rang the bell again and this time heard a sound from within, a click, a shuffle.

The door opened.

Caskie said, 'I'm surprised.'

'Invite me in,' Eddie said. He didn't wait to be asked, he stepped past Caskie into a hallway where a ceiling fan turned and there was awful wax fruit in a bowl and some cheesy watercolours of seascapes adorned the walls.

'Consider yourself invited,' Caskie said, closing the door.

Eddie entered a room to his right. A sitting room, some good solid furniture, glossy wood surfaces, shrubbery at the window, a leafy big garden beyond.

'You seem agitated,' Caskie said.

'Have I disturbed your siesta?' Eddie asked.

'I wasn't napping.'

'You go around in a robe usually?'

'When I'm unwinding, why not?'

Eddie looked at the navy blue robe and the pyjama trousers that matched and the marbled white feet tucked inside pale blue slippers. Hadn't Caskie heard? Hadn't this bastard heard about his boy McWhinnie?

Then Eddie noticed that the telephone handset was off the hook and dangled close to the floor. 'I tried to phone you,' he said.

'I was resting, Eddie. It's my day off. I hate being disturbed.'

'So you haven't heard?'

'Heard what? Clarify, Eddie.'

Eddie told him about Charlie McWhinnie.

Caskie stood slightly stooped, head forward, like a man

listening to a radio station he hasn't been able to tune. His expression didn't change. Sometimes he touched his beard. Eddie, throat dry, was light-headed. Memory bytes: *He was back at the station, looking at McWhinnie on the ground. He didn't want to see the dead man's blood again.* When he finished talking he watched Caskie step towards a chair and perch himself on the arm. Caskie drew his eyelids together, middle finger and thumb, and sighed, and shook his head. The material of his robe shimmered.

Eddie said, 'Probably your colleagues have been trying to contact you, Caskie. They want to tell you what's happened to Charlie.'

Caskie made no move to replace the handset. He stared at Eddie. 'You saw this murder happen?'

'I saw,' Eddie said.

'How did you know Charlie?'

'Oh, for Christ's sake, why don't we just strip the whole charade down? Why don't we pack up the fucking tents and admit the circus and all its illusions has left town? You had McWhinnie follow me from day one. He wasn't terrific at the job. So we met. We met, we talked, he was an okay guy.'

'Cosy,' Caskie said.

'He had problems,' Eddie said. 'You got him to work surveillance, Caskie, but you didn't say why. It's dog's work and long fucking hours, and he had these terrific cops-and-robbers dreams, but you didn't even stroke him a little, or lie and tell him what he was doing was of great importance to the Force. He desperately wanted to be good at his job. He was keen, Caskie. *Eager.* You remember what that was like, Caskie? When you were enthusiastic. You wanted to set the world on fire. But you – I know what it is, you're out of touch with people. You're arrogant. You don't know how ordinary people tick. You don't know what weighed on Charlie's conscience.'

'No? Let me clear it up for you,' Caskie said. 'It's standard operating procedure in our part of the world, Mallon, that subordinates do what their superiors tell them. We don't expect

309

misgivings and self-doubt and neurotic little twitches. And if any man has a problem with his conscience, we don't expect him to wallow in it. We expect only obedience. I'm deeply sorry about what happened to Charlie. Profoundly sorry. Shocked. You don't know how much I mean that. But he knew law enforcement work was not without its dangers.'

'What about *your* conscience, Caskie?'

'I don't have a problem with it,' Caskie said. 'I sleep at night. Deeply.'

Eddie heard a sound from the room overhead. A slight creak, then silence. An old house. Mice under floorboards. Whatever. He'd had mice in his house in Queens. He'd baited traps with cheese, and listened to them snapping murderously in the dark. Ah, Queens. I want to go home. I want Claire in my bed and the knowledge my kid is asleep in his room down the hallway and there's strong coffee in the morning and Danish fresh from Fiedler's Bakery on the corner. I want what I've left behind.

He gazed at Caskie. 'No problem, huh? Okay. Tell me how you square your conscience when it comes to my father. Did you arrange to meet Bones the night my father was shot? Did you ask him to leave the car at a certain time and meet you someplace nearby? Then what – did you drive him to a safe house in Govan while certain parties murdered my father?'

'I know you've been through a rough experience this after-noon, Eddie, you need something to relax you –'

'Don't even try to take me down that road, Caskie.'

'Too late. I think you're well and truly on that road already. Let me get you a drink. Scotch?'

'Fuck the drink. I don't want your booze. I want the truth, Caskie. You set my father up. You had to get Bones out of the way. You made promises to him. Just leave the car for a while. We'll look after you. Gambling debts? No problem, Bones. We'll take care of them too. So Charlie goes round squaring debts with bookies. And somebody shoots my father with Matty Bones's gun and then you stash the weapon in the old guy's flat under the sink – hidden in plain fucking sight – so a couple of hapless cops on a search can't possibly overlook it.'

'Surmise,' Caskie said. 'All of it.'

'Not according to McWhinnie.'

'Who isn't around to verify any of it, alas.'

'Sadly,' Eddie said.

'You're fucked,' Caskie said.

'I'll go to Tay. I'll tell him all this.'

'He'll listen? Ballocks.'

'I'll make the bastard listen.'

'How? Handcuff him to a radiator? You can't make Tay do anything he doesn't want to do. And he doesn't want to listen to you, Eddie. Believe me.'

Eddie slipped into silence. Exhaustion, weary to the marrow. A long brutal day. Shadows formed in corners.

'Just tell me. Is Haggs in this with you? Are you helping him in some way? I know he wanted a slice of whatever my father was getting into, and I guess Jackie wasn't sharing. So you decided to give Haggs a hand, you're well placed, you've got all kinds of connections –'

'That's a stretch, Eddie. You're overreaching. You're always trying too hard –'

Eddie held a hand up to silence Caskie. 'What can Haggs give you in return? Cash? Information? What can Haggs possibly do for you?'

'You're playing head games, Eddie.'

'Or it's something else,' Eddie said. 'Maybe he has a hold over you. Is that it? Behind the nice home and the respectable position in law enforcement, there's something festering in a closet, there's a grub inside the lovely red pippin, and Haggs knows about it, and it could ruin you – how about that? Am I getting warm?'

Caskie said, 'Ice floes. Polar bears.'

Eddie felt defeated. He moved this way, Caskie blocked him. He moved that way, Caskie blocked him again. He was weak suddenly, and hungry, but he knew he wouldn't keep food

311

down. His stomach was like that of a man sailing on a rough tide. He thought he'd drift off into sleep if he didn't get up and leave this house. He'd go back to his sister's and rest for a half-hour and he'd think of another approach, and maybe he'd go straight down to Force HQ and find a sympathetic ear for his story. Perlman's ear. But he had to get it clear first. He had to be sure of his direction. And suddenly he was woozy. The margins of his vision were fogged.

He moved into the hallway. Caskie stepped behind him.

'You also lied about Tommy Gurk,' Eddie said. One more deceit: what did it matter?

'I was protecting confidential police records,' Caskie said. 'Don't tell me you haven't done that once or twice in your life, Eddie.'

I can't remember, Eddie thought. Head blank. Whiteout. 'It's pointless to talk with you,' he said. 'I just don't have the energy for it, Caskie.'

He looked at the wax fruit and then raised his face to observe the slow-turning fan and the shadow it cast on the ceiling, and his eye was drawn beyond that to the stairway leading to the upper part of the house and he saw a figure in the dimming light at the top of the stairs, small and thin and wrapped in a robe six sizes too big for her, her short hair a mess, and he felt as if a hammer had been bludgeoned into the side of his head with such force that his brain emptied and his eyes failed.

She said, 'Eddie,' and her voice came out of the blackness.

49

The streets around Central Station had been cordoned off: a no-go zone. So many cops, more than a hundred certainly; Perlman couldn't remember when he'd last seen his colleagues out in such numbers except when they worked security at big football games.

He had to push his way through the crowd of spectators constrained by a phalanx of uniforms and a barricade of patrol cars and police vans. Mounted horses were present, big steady beasts seemingly unperturbed by the mass of people. There were cops making announcements through a loudspeaker system, telling the crowds to disperse, everything was under control – the usual pabulum for the public. But crowd control was no simple choreography in this situation; apart from the sightseers and sensationalists, there was the added complication of huge numbers of people trying to make their way out of the station, and others desperate to enter because they had trains to catch.

Madness, Perlman thought. Murder during rush hour. Commuter chaos. He was buffeted and elbowed as he pressed through to the Union Street exit where Scullion had told him to come. He wanted to say, Let's make it fun, let's turn it

313

all into a bloody big outdoor fair, a massive fête, hotdog stands and barbecues and brass bands, games the kiddies can play, helter-skelter and merry-go-rounds and three-legged races. Why not? Do away with all this morbid vigilance and bring on the dancing girls. If the crowd wanted entertainment, give it to them.

Bitterness, Perlman, he thought. Watch out for that. *En garde.* A young man dies – but not everyone in the crowd is a ghoul, there are those who want to get home to their families, and can you blame them for that? You solitary old fart. Been alone too long. You don't remember what a family was like.

He saw Sandy Scullion when he finally flashed his ID in front of a uniformed cop who ushered him through the throng. Scullion, in white shirt and red tie, raised a hand wearily. Perlman walked towards him. He was aware of Tay loitering in the background and a couple of other heavyweights from Force HQ – DCI Ralph Hannon, known as Ralph Cheeks because of his resemblance to a squirrel whose mouth was stuffed with crab apples, DCI Mary Gibson, a cheerful woman in her mid-forties who dressed like a woman in a Laura Ashley catalogue, and DCI Benjamin Bennet, sharp, a bachelor with a trim moustache and a ladykiller's rep. They were out in numbers, showing the flag.

The Force is with you, Perlman thought. Not always. Not for McWhinnie.

Scullion said, 'They tried to resuscitate him in the ambulance. But he wasn't coming back, Lou.'

'Who shot him?'

'We've got some witnesses,' Scullion said. 'The killer's a light-skinned black, five-eight or nine, muscular, wore a hat that was either brown or black, hair in dreadlocks.'

'Dreadlocks?'

'A hairstyle, Lou. Rastafarians, reggae bands. Don't tell me you don't know.'

'I know, dammit, it just slipped my mind a minute. You think I don't keep up with things?'

'You're snapping, Lou. Don't snap at me. I didn't ask for this situation.'

'You're right, Sandy. I apologize. Read my face.' Perlman felt his breath catch at the back of his throat. He didn't want to show emotion. Maybe later, when he was on his own. But not here, not now. You reserved a private table for your feelings and you said, Charlie, too bad it didn't work out for you. I'm sorry and I'm sad. You had a few things to fix in your life, but you didn't get your allotted span, son. You didn't get your biblical quota of years.

'What else have we got?' he asked.

Scullion said, 'The killer ran in the direction of St Vincent Street.'

'And then what.'

Scullion shrugged. 'I don't know. Jesus Christ, how damn difficult can it be to find a man with dreadlocks in Glasgow?'

'He won't have the fucking dreadlocks now,' Perlman said. He made scissors of his index and middle fingers. 'Snip snip.'

Tay came towards them. He appeared uncomfortable, like a man whose shoes are too tight, or whose cummerbund is pinching him after a heavy formal dinner. 'This has been a private nightmare for years. I keep arguing the police shouldn't carry guns, and then this happens and I wonder if I'm wrong, if my support of that policy's addle-headed, and we ought to be toting those bloody Magnums like they do in America.'

Irrelevant, Perlman thought. Whether you armed the Strathclyde police or you didn't, it was academic as far as Charlie's life was concerned. He ignored Tay and looked at Scullion. 'What else have we got, Sandy?'

'The killer had a briefcase – black or brown or tan, take your pick – and seemingly McWhinnie apprehended the man and demanded to see what was in the case.'

'Why?' Perlman asked.

'I don't know.'

Tay said, 'McWhinnie worked under Chris Caskie. Why isn't he here? He could tell us what McWhinnie's workload involved.'

'Caskie's not answering his phone,' Scullion said.

'Then I'll send some bloody uniforms to find him,' Tay said. He wandered off, clapping his hands for attention, roaring orders, stirring up the gendarmerie. The crowds all around seemed to simmer, like a human broth.

Perlman saw dry blood on the pavement. He looked again at Scullion. 'So Charlie hassles this black guy into opening his briefcase. And then what? The man whips out a gun and shoots Charlie dead?'

'That's the essence of it, Lou.' Scullion looked sad and placed a hand on Perlman's arm. 'I know you tried to guide him through the Pitt Street minefield, show him the ropes, I know you were a friend to him, Lou –'

'For Christ's sake, that doesn't have any bearing,' Perlman said. 'A fellow officer is dead and whether I liked him or despised him isn't even a consideration, Sandy. I know you want to be helpful and I appreciate it, but this is work. This is what we do for a living. Anything personal, drop it. Save it.'

'I was only . . .' Scullion didn't finish whatever he'd set out to say.

Perlman looked in the direction of St Vincent Street. So many people in the evening sun. Cops. Civilians. The buildings created warm pools of shade. 'What else do our witnesses tell us?'

Scullion said, 'I have three female witnesses who think there was another man in McWhinnie's company. This third party apparently went down on his knees beside McWhinnie, then he got up and took off in pursuit of the killer. According to one of our witnesses, he looked as if he'd seen a ghost.'

'And we don't know who this concerned citizen might have been?'

Scullion shook his head. 'We've got a description. Six feet or thereabouts. Thirteen stone rising to fourteen. Black jeans. Trainers, variously white or beige. White T-shirt with a logo. The guy had thick hair, curly, black going grey. One woman described it as "a mass" of curls. Another said he was handsome, kind of.'

'Anybody read the logo?'

Scullion looked skyward. 'The shirt said something like Sunny on it.'

'Sunny?'

'I'm only telling you what I've gleaned from hysterical people. Sunny, one woman said. But spelled with only one "N".'

'Suny. What's that? A Japanese fish treat?'

'Take it or leave it, Lou. Two of the witnesses were also certain that the T-shirt had the word Brook on it.'

'So we've got Suny and we've got Brook. We've got a funny T-shirt and a mass of curls and handsome kind of.' This was ringing a tiny bell in some remote steeple at the back of Perlman's brain. His memory often yielded details he had no idea he'd committed to it. Suny Brook. Mass of curls. Wait for it to come. Don't force it.

Always treat memory with courtesy and patience, Lou.

Scullion said, 'The man who went in pursuit never came back.'

'So he vanished into the mystifying air of dear old Glasgow,' Perlman said, and his eyes were drawn back to the blood on the pavement. One of the police horses whinnied. The crowds were beginning to thin in the manner of people who, having expected a spectacular of sorts, were shuffling off because the event had been cancelled and their tickets made null and void. The uniforms were allowing commuters to leave the station, pressing them into orderly lines. Those who awaited permission to enter, even if they knew they'd missed their regular trains, were being directed inside the station through the Hope Street entrance.

Perlman tried to imagine the man in the white T-shirt run towards St Vincent Street. But he couldn't see facial detail; his memory had stalled. Getting old, Lou. What is it they say? Memory is the second thing to go. But what's the first? Can't remember. That joke had blue mould growing on it.

He stuck his hands in his pockets and wondered why he'd been so careful of Charlie McWhinnie's welfare, his state of mind. *The son you never had*. Bullshit, Lou. It's something else inside you. It's that jellybaby heart of yours. You see unhappiness and you want to go to its rescue because you're the bloody schmuck who climbs trees to save stranded kittens or young kids clinging to limbs. You grit your teeth and you haul yourself up branch by branch.

Charlie McWhinnie had something of the quality of a kid dangling from a limb. And you wanted to help him down to safety.

Aye. You're a hard bastard, Perlman. A man to be feared, right enough.

Why was Charlie so unhappy with Caskie?

Fucksake. That wasn't a question. Everyone who'd ever worked for Caskie had been miserable. He treated his subordinates with all the affection of a 19th-century plantation owner for his indentured slaves. He cracked the whip. You worked for Caskie, you became a nonperson. He lorded it over you. Smug strutting bearded *pupik*.

This is not going to bring back McWhinnie.

'Somebody'll have to tell his parents,' Perlman said. 'His dad's a lawyer somewhere. Bearsden, I think.'

Scullion said, 'Tay's already assumed that role.'

'Somebody's also going to have to ask Caskie if he knows anything about the identity of the alleged killer and why Charlie confronted him.'

'You'll do that, I suppose.'

'Oh, aye,' Perlman said.

50

Haggs spoke into his cellphone: 'We need to meet, Twiddie.'

Twiddie asked, 'Something up?'

'I want a chat.' Haggs was aware of a happy bunch of golfers walking past, toting their bags. *A birdie at the twelfth,* somebody said. *When did you last see a birdie at the twelfth?* One of the players laughed and said, *It's not nice to toot your own horn, Archie.*

Haggs waited until the party had gone inside the clubhouse before he spoke again. 'Bring Rita.'

'Name a place,' Twiddie said.

'The usual,' Haggs said.

Twiddie powered off his cellphone and looked at his sausage sandwich. Brown sauce oozed out between the two pieces of bread and dripped on to the table. Rita, dressed only in a pair of pink panties that matched the glitter she'd applied to her nipples, smoked a cigarette and leafed the pages of one of the glossy magazines she so enjoyed. Other lives. Glamorous ones. Big houses with gardens, bright flowers and kids. Places where it never rained. You never saw rain in any of these glossy journals.

People fried in eternal sunshine. I want to go there, she thought. Out of here. Away from these streets.

'He wants to see us,' Twiddie said. He sucked brown sauce from the back of his hand.

'What for?'

'He sounded sharpish. Mibbe it's about that . . . van.'

Rita tossed the magazine to the floor. She dropped her cigarette inside a beer bottle and it sizzled briefly. 'The van, the van, I wish this bloody van would just go *away*.'

'You'd better get dressed. Haggs wants us. We've been ordered. Our Lord and Master has spoken.'

Rita stood up, stretched her muscular arms. 'And we obey.'

'I think I'm turning into one of them – what do you call them – an atheist.'

'An atheist?' Rita made a mocking *ooooeee* sound. 'Mother Philomena always told us atheists go to hell.'

'There's no such place.'

'If you're a dried-out old Mother Superior there is.'

'My nose still hurts,' Twiddie said, and touched his reddened nostril gently.

51

Shocked, angered, bewildered, Eddie walked into the sunlight in Broomhill Drive. *I didn't see it coming*, he thought. I didn't even get a sniff of it. He'd been preoccupied in a number of ways, sure, but just the same he felt he should have sensed *something*. He'd had a breakdown of his peripheral vision, of instinct. No, it was more, it underlined the distance between his world and his sister's, how far apart they'd been forced to grow. He stopped walking and thought of her as she stood on the staircase wrapped in what must have been one of Caskie's bathrobes, and the quiet way she'd uttered his name. A whisper. He didn't remember turning and marching out of the house, nor if she'd called after him. He had to get out, that was all he recollected, leaving her on the stairs, the big fan turning and Caskie's expressionless face in the hallway.

His throat was dry, and he had pain at the back of his eyes. He stopped at a traffic signal. He heard Joyce call his name and he turned, saw her half-walk, half-run, towards him. She wore a tan lightweight silk shirt that hadn't been tucked very well inside the waist of her dark brown slacks, and the strap of one shoe was undone, causing her foot to slip in and out, and the heel of the shoe to cluck against the pavement with each step she took. She looked as if she'd been glued together hastily and the parts were already coming undone.

She caught his arm and said, 'Eddie, I'm sorry.'

'It's your life, Joyce. I figured you might have better taste, that's all.'

'Fuck you,' she said, and her small face was pinched and pale and sharp. 'I'm trying to apologize for not telling you about this before, but if this is your attitude I'm wasting my time.'

'He's a shit,' Eddie said. 'Big-time.'

'You don't know him, Eddie.'

'I know enough. He lies. He manipulates. Where he should have a heart he's got a fucking icebox.' He fell silent, because the next sentence that came into his mind was one he wanted to withhold, to spare her, to leave her with something. Choke on it, Eddie. Tamp it down.

'You need to see it from his angle,' she said. 'He's been through a lot. His wife was ill for a long time.'

'And you were his solace, huh? You were his comfort.'

'Christ, you have a way of making things seem downright cheap.'

'Talk to your boyfriend. He knows about cheap.'

He turned away but she tightened her hold on his arm and swung him round to face her. 'I know how it might look to you. But he needed me. She was dying, and he hadn't loved her in years. Even so, he stayed with her until the end, Eddie. He went through her pain with her. He nursed her. He dispensed her medication. He bathed and fed her. He sat up with her for hours at a time, watching her pain. He's caring and he's good-hearted and maybe that eludes you, Eddie, because you don't know him –'

'Okay, the guy's a saint, a real sweetheart,' Eddie said. 'But he had you on the side to ease his burden, so that must have helped.'

She swung a fist suddenly. Eddie didn't see it coming. It stung

322

his ear and he heard a whining sound in his head. He caught her hand and held it against his chest.

'Don't make me hate you,' she said.

'Did Jackie know about you and your Romeo?'

'You can be so fucking childish, Eddie.'

'Did he *know*?'

'No.'

'Couldn't tell him? Ashamed to confess?'

'What was the point in telling him?'

'You were sparing his feelings?'

'Yeh, that's it. He and Chris were on different sides of the fence, Eddie.'

'Bullshit. When you come right down to it, they were on the same side of the fence. They were both crooked.'

'I don't believe that, Eddie.'

He touched the side of her face as softly as he could. He had to tell her now. He didn't have an escape route. 'Listen to me. Caskie knew Jackie was going to be murdered before it happened. Caskie, whose bed you've just come from, was involved in the mechanics of the killing – in conjunction with a man called Roddy Haggs.'

She put her hands on her hips and stepped back a pace. 'What kind of fucking person are you? How can you *possibly* say something like that, Eddie? How can you stoop so damned low? You really know how to get down into the gutter and come up with some pretty vile stuff, don't you? Why in God's name would Chris want my father killed? You want to hurt me because I lied to you, I omitted the truth, fine, I apologize, I am sorry to the bottom of my heart, but there's no bloody need for you to make up all this shite and throw it in my face, is there? We don't need this between us, Eddie. It's a wedge, and I don't want it.'

She doesn't want to believe, he thought. Who could blame her?

'I tried to kill off the relationship, I really did,' she said. 'When I married Haskell I thought, this is a way out of a bad situation.

323

But I couldn't get Chris out of my mind. The whole Haskell thing was doomed. I didn't want him. I wanted Chris. I'm not getting any younger, Eddie, and love is a substance that is bloody hard to find. What do you know? You've got Claire and a kid.'

Love, Eddie thought. Love was a thing you wanted so desperately you didn't always see things clearly. It was more than a life raft that kept you afloat in solitary waters, or the sound of another human voice in an apartment or the ruffle of somebody turning the pages of a newspaper while you read the magazine section on a Sunday afternoon. Love was a commitment of the heart, not a salve against solitary confinement. *I'm not getting any younger, Eddie.* 'How long has it been . . .' He left the question hanging.

'How long has it been going on?' she said.

He looked away. Butterflies flapped out of a hedge and flew close to his face, startling him. *Forget I ever asked, Joyce.*

'Buckle your seatbelt, Eddie,' she said. 'The first time was a few months before my thirteenth birthday.' She delivered this statement in a flat way, as if it were something she was reading from a prepared health bulletin. *The patient is comfortable and is off the critical list. We don't expect any further complications.*

Dear Christ. He didn't know what to say. Stunned. He'd assumed the affair was of more recent vintage – maybe the last six or seven years, on and off again. Now she was telling him something else, and he couldn't take it in. He couldn't find room for it. Couldn't get his mind round it.

'He'd always been so kind to me, Eddie, it just seemed that what we did was natural,' she said.

'Twelve,' he said.

'Almost thirteen.'

'What's the difference?' He thought, Twelve is only a word. Let it go. But no, he couldn't, twelve was a child, a kid, an innocent. Caskie had committed a crime.

'You consented to it,' he said.

'Yes.'

'Even if you gave your consent, it's still –'

'I know what you're going to say, and I know what you're thinking,' she said. 'How could he do it with a girl that young? He must be some kind of perve, a monster. Look at me, Eddie. Don't turn away. I *wanted* him to do it. It was all I had to give him in return because he'd been good to me. Here, my body, it's all yours, take it, I want you to have it –'

'I don't need to hear this,' Eddie said.

'But I damn well need to tell you. He was twenty-nine and married, and I was almost thirteen, and after that first time it became a regular occurrence. We'd meet, he'd find some place to take me, a hotel out of the city, he'd book us into different rooms just in case . . . So it went on.'

'And on, and on.'

'We tried to break it off a few times over the years.'

But true love conquers all, Eddie thought. It can vanquish any enemy. He couldn't picture Joyce, *twelve years of age*, spreading her legs for Caskie in a hotel room, Caskie entering her, man into child: did he speak of love, did he talk of a future? She'd fall for it. She was a kid, and optimistic. Yeah, she'd go for it. Eyes closed, a supplicant before her own future, she'd dream her romantic dreams even as Caskie thrust himself inside her and grunted, and the years rolled away and still he remained married, and her hopes diminished to the extent that she met and married Haskell just to escape – what? Her own disappointment? Some sense of shame? Twelve years of age, he thought. Jesus Christ. He felt unsettled, queasy. It wasn't his thing, schoolgirls and their little skirts and their blazers and their gymslips, their smoothly innocent faces and tiny breasts. For some guys, sure, it was a big twisted kick, they sat in the half-light of their computer screens and scoured the Internet for images to incite them, the Web pimped for them – but he'd never understood that kind of lust. He'd perceived it as sickness. He'd seen too many runaway schoolgirls raped by middle-aged men, sodomized and forced to participate in orgies and drugged and God knows what else. He'd seen them dumped inside derelict buildings or on abandoned railroad lines, alive, half-alive.

325

Joyce said, 'We couldn't stay away from each other, Eddie. It was a kind of insanity. It's always been like that.'

'It's an insanity, granted,' he said.

'Oh, you don't have to sound so damn smug. Who are you to judge?'

'I wasn't judging.'

'You prick. You can't help yourself.'

'Okay. I'm judging. I have a moral view. It's instinctive. I can't help it. Who else knows about you and your boyfriend?'

'Nobody.'

He placed his hands on his sister's shoulders and, lowering his head, looked directly into her eyes. What did he see in there? A tiny hint of sorrow because she'd kept her secret and the effort made her lonesome, or a touch of relief that she'd finally told somebody? He wasn't sure.

Twelve, he thought. 12. Two times six. Three times four. Work the figures any way you like, it still came out twelve.

He said, 'I think somebody knew.'

'I'm positive they didn't, Eddie.'

'Here's an educated guess. Roddy Haggs.'

She shook her head. 'No, not –'

'He found out. He had the knowledge. So he had the power. Do whatever I ask you to do, Chris old pal, or I'll blow the whistle and it's going to be heard all over the land. High-level cop fucks underage girl. Field day in the tabloids. They have a name for this crime, Chris. So cooperate with me, Inspector, or you're going to hell on a fast bus . . . It makes sense, Joyce.'

'We were careful, Eddie. Very careful.'

'You thought you were.'

'I *know* we were.'

'Secrets are the hardest things to keep. You're seen on the street by chance, or you're noticed stepping into a taxi or catching a train, or maybe in the parking lot of some rustic hotel you think is remote and nobody knows you, but it's a small world . . .' He dropped his hands from her shoulders. 'Do you really love him?'

'I don't know. I'm not sure what love is. When I was twelve I would have died for him. I thought he was damn adorable. He could've asked me to jump off a bridge and I would've done it without hesitation. When I was twenty I wanted to live with him, the whole domestic bit. Cook, clean, have kids by him. By the time I was thirty I realized I'd become accustomed to sex with him. There was still this spark, this passion. Now . . . now I think it's a pleasant habit, Eddie, one I can't imagine living without. Is that what love is in the end? A habit? I have an addictive personality anyway, for God's sake . . .'

'I hope to Christ you don't love him, Joyce. I think he's got all kinds of problems coming down on him sooner or later. I don't want to see you hurt. I don't want you drawn into something that can only end unpleasantly.'

'I don't believe he had any involvement in Dad's death,' she said. 'I'll never believe that. Not in a hundred years. No way.'

'In a hundred years we'll all be history,' Eddie said. 'And none of this will matter a damn.'

'You can't live your life from that perspective, Eddie.'

'When stuff gets unbearable, you can try.'

She suddenly wept then, pressing her fingertips against her eyebrows, inclining her face. He watched tears roll down her cheeks and he reached out and held her and he thought of the little girl with the ribbon in her hair who played *Chopsticks* on the piano with flamboyant movements of her hands, like a melodramatic concert pianist, and Jackie would say, 'Good Christ, girl, is there nothing *else* you can learn to play?'

Jackie's voice echoed in his head.

He was filled with a deep yearning to go home, and leave Joyce to the misadventures of her heart, and forget Jackie Mallon. What do you owe him anyway? Whatever illicit activity he was involved in was a link in a chain of lies and violence. You didn't do business with a killer like Gurk without making a statement about yourself: okay, so you didn't pull a trigger and kill somebody, Jackie, but you were prepared to associate with a man who was a shooter, so what did that make you? If you knew what Gurk was capable of, you were an accessory. And if you *didn't* know, then greed had made you blind. And if you were trying to recover any decency with your phone calls to Queens, and your regrets about how you'd driven a stake through the soul of the family, and how love had to be restored, goddammit, you let it all slip through your fingers, didn't you, Dad?

And yet he couldn't resist the thought: *Jackie wasn't responsible for his associates, was he?* You went into business with someone, and he turned out bad, it happened all the time to people . . . Screw it, Eddie, even now you're looking for an avenue leading towards forgiveness. Even after all that has happened, you still come back to the hope that you can find a cleft of light in your heart and a way to rescue Jackie from damnation. Why can't you just despise him, and let it go like that? You're a kid again, and he's telling you how he'll take you to Balloch and hire a boat and go fishing, except that day never came, *but you're still fucking waiting for it,* aren't you, Eddie, even when it's impossible . . .

The sun began its very slow summery descent. He listened to his sister crying, and he had the impression that the city all around him was built on foundations of deception and greed.

52

When she left Eddie, Joyce walked back to the house. Caskie was standing at the table in the conservatory and she pressed herself against his back and circled her arms round him and locked her hands upon his chest. She knew without looking that his eyes were closed. She knew him so well. She knew him better than anyone ever had.

'You told him,' Caskie said.

'I felt so bloody fraudulent, Chris. I don't want that feeling. Skulking, lying. I don't want that.'

'You went back to the beginning?'

She said yes, she'd gone back.

'How did he take it?' Caskie said. 'I don't have to ask, do I?'

'He looked unpleasantly surprised. Distressed. What do you expect?'

'And angry. He'd feel angry.'

She laid her cheek against his spine and smelled the cologne he wore and she wondered what it always reminded her of, she could never quite reach the heart of the scent. 'He said Haggs knew about us.'

'Did *you* tell him that?'

'He guessed Haggs had you in a bind. A stranglehold.'

'He's smart,' Caskie said. 'It's not always a good thing to be.'

Say it, she thought. Say the next bit. Spit it out. 'He thinks . . . He thinks you might have had something to do with Jackie's death. You and Haggs colluded. You conspired in some way.'

'That's what comes of being just a little *too* smart.' Caskie turned, caught her chin between his fingers. 'Look at me. Do you really think I had *anything* to do with your father's killing?'

'No, of course I don't.'

'You feel absolutely certain when you say that?'

'Yes,' she said.

He caressed her cheek. 'Haggs has had me in chains for years, you know that. I've done him some favours, things I shouldn't have done. Maybe I could have been strong enough to tell him no, turn him down, but that's water under the bridge. Killing, though, good Christ, no no, there's just no way – that's something else, Joyce.'

'I know that.'

'It's beyond consideration. I'd never agree to anything that brought you misery, never.'

She thought of their relationship, this little world they'd created, and how private it was. You could withdraw inside it and lock the doors and shutter the windows and light candles, and then it was only you and Chris and everything else could go to hell.

'It's going to change,' he said.

'What is?'

'This situation with Haggs. I'm going to change it.'

'How?'

'Just trust me. I have to get dressed and go into the office.'

'No, not yet.'

'I have to,' he said.

'No, don't hurry away.'

He hesitated, then lowered his face to hers, and she felt his warm breath upon the side of her neck and she enjoyed the soft touch of his beard, and she slid a hand down to the belt of his robe and she thought how easily he led her, how easily she wanted to *be* led, and how he'd had this same effect on her for years, even during the period of her miserable marriage to Haskell when she'd deliberately cut Caskie out of her life, but oh God she'd *longed* for him, Mrs Harry Haskell dreaming of her lover and how tender he was, and considerate, and remembering all the times they'd met in hotels, even when Meg was dying, yes, even then. He'd have a nurse come in to look after Meg and he'd slip away.

Sometimes she detected Meg's ghost in this house, like a quick shadow in a stairwell, or a brush of clothing against a wall. *I hadn't loved Meg in years*, he'd once told her. *Not in the man–woman sense. I don't feel guilt, Joyce, I never have about you.*

He slid her blouse off, and inclined his head to her shoulder and she felt his open mouth on her flesh and the touch of his teeth. She had her hand inside his robe, his cock in her palm, and she went down on her knees and pressed her face into him. She listened to the soft moan of pleasure he always made and it struck her that at the core of this sound there was something else, another tone, a kind of subdued lament. As if, like her, he regretted the years of subterfuge, and the voluminous lies. As if in some secret corner of himself he was sad, and this diminished his pleasure. She cupped his testicles in her palm and when she needed it least she heard an echo of Eddie's voice, *he helped arrange the mechanics of the killing*, and she dismissed the whisper, exploded it, sent the splinters flying out of her mind. One day, maybe, Eddie would know that the real Christopher Caskie was a sweet man, genuine, gentle and warm. One day.

'My girl,' Caskie said. 'Oh my dear girl. My love.'

331

53

Tommy Gurk took a taxi to Gorbals Street, south of the Clyde. The car was a bottle-green Fiat, parked close to the Citizens' Theatre. The keys were inside a magnetized steel box attached to the underside of the bumper. Gurk opened the box, got the keys. The heat inside the car made his hairless skull sweat. His head felt raw, like a rash was developing. He'd worn dreadlocks a long time now. It was bizarre having a scalp as naked as a baby's bum.

He glanced at the directions somebody had left on the passenger seat. Written on a sheet of blue-lined paper, they were easy and explicit. Gurk shook his head, amazed. See, this is where you had to hand it to Kaminsky, the way he had of doing things, he had minions all over the shop, geezers who did stuff without even knowing who they were working for, locating weapons, delivering envelopes, providing cars, no questions asked – there was a big intricate network of connections in different countries. People always owed Joe Kaminsky favours. And they always obliged. The consequences of failure, well, they didn't bear consideration.

Off we go, Tommy Gurk thought.

He drove along Pollokshaws Road, heading south. There were cop cars all over the place, and once or twice he felt he was being scrutinized, once or twice he had a little electric-prod of paranoia, but the trick was to look cool, and that meant you had to feel you had your shit together inside. You had the juice. Cool within, cool without. All the way, baby. You were just a guy driving along Kilmarnock Road, and the fact you had brown skin, tally-ho, that was no impediment. Just follow the directions, get into the rhythm of the road, put some miles behind you, drive into the sweet Zone. Then the directions got a little more complicated, but not much, he could handle it, he was beginning to feel more like himself.

Into the roundabout, zippedy-doo, no sweat. A few more blocks and here we are. And a jolly nice street it is too. Prosperous. Very much so. Go slow. This is white bread land and you stand out like Malcolm X at a Klan convention. He sang to lull himself. He did his Paul Robeson voice. *Old man ribber*. He was close to the house now, he checked the numbers, noticed how some of the homes had names because jokers who lived here thought that was posh. He sang Belafonte's 'Banana Boat Song' and stared at the name of the house and waited, slouched in the driver's seat, motor running.

54

Caskie usually made Lou Perlman feel that he was an inferior being, a dunderhead allowed five minutes of human conversation. Caskie's bearing was one of low-grade tolerance. They sat in Caskie's office in Force HQ and Caskie sipped coffee out of a plastic cup.

'It's tragic about Charlie,' Perlman said.

'It's a heartbreak.'

'He was a nice young guy. I'm sorry for his parents.' Perlman noticed how tidy Caskie's desk was. Pencils in containers. Pens lined up on the leather cover of a notebook. Caskie's fingernails were immaculate. He must have them manicured, Lou Perlman thought. Maybe at the hairdresser's he has the whole *schmear*, beard trim, manicure, hot towel shave.

'Tay's asked me to clarify a few things,' Perlman said. 'For the record.'

'Of course.'

'What was Charlie doing at Central Station, Chris?'

Caskie shrugged. 'I gave Charlie a broad remit, Lou. We'd have to look through his records, the logs he kept.'

'So you gave him his head, you let him run, is that what you're saying?'

'Exactly.'

And pigs have wings in that world, Perlman thought. You never gave Charlie an inch of breathing space. You kept Charlie in a black room of your own design. 'You're telling me you have no idea what he was working on that would've taken him to Central Station?'

'Come to think of it, he was quite excited about information he was gathering in a case involving the theft of a valuable coin collection from a house in Langside a month ago. We can examine his notes, Lou.' Caskie glanced at his watch.

A young man's dead and you're checking the time, Caskie. What does that tell me? You have another appointment, better things to do. 'So you have no idea about the identity of the killer?'

'I wish to God I did. Again, I can only say that we should look at McWhinnie's papers and maybe we'll find some kind of hint.'

I'm hearing a looped tape, Perlman thought. Check Charlie's notes. His log. Aye. Sure. Maybe Charlie had written, *I suspect a black called Winston Smith, 24 Garturk Street, Govanhill, of stealing a valuable coin collection and I intend to arrest him at Central Station during rush hour.* And that also belonged in the same world as jet-propelled pigs.

'He never mentioned a black guy to you?' Perlman asked.

'No, never.'

'All right. We'll look through his stuff. See what there is.'

Caskie was quiet a moment. 'I intend to take retirement, Lou.'

'Is that a fact?'

'I've written a letter I'll give to Superintendent Tay in the morning. You're the first to know.'

'Is this not a wee bit sudden?' Perlman was surprised that Caskie had confided in him. But it wasn't exactly an act of intimacy. There was no sense of sharing involved, no exposure

335

of self. Perlman felt Caskie simply needed an audience to make his announcement, and it didn't matter who was in the room with him. A tea-lady, a janitor, anybody.

'It's been coming a long time,' Caskie said. 'Maybe the death of McWhinnie's the last straw. I don't know.' He got up from his desk and walked to the window and stood with his hands tucked in the pockets of his double-breasted jacket. He stared down into Pitt Street where the falling sun had begun to create shadows and he wondered if he was being premature in announcing his retirement. What if things went wrong? What if the scheme he'd devised with Kaminsky became derailed? No, don't think that way. It'll work. Even as you stand here, it's in motion.

He thought of Eddie Mallon striding out of the house in Broomhill Drive, leaving the front door open behind him. And of Joyce, how tiny she looked inside the bathrobe, how quickly she dressed to catch up with Eddie Mallon. She wanted her brother to know she felt bad concealing the truth from him – all very fine and honourable, but Caskie wasn't so sure Eddie could take that truth calmly. He'd disapprove furiously. Adult men and pubescent girls – Eddie Mallon would see it as an immoral equation. He wouldn't understand that kind of love; it was socially unacceptable as well as criminal, and had to be carried out in hotel rooms and cars parked in lonely places. Caskie had never found delight in the illicit aspect of it. He'd feared the condemnation of men, and the disgrace of imprisonment.

And then there was Haggs.

Once, many years ago in a gloomy little motel outside Edinburgh, he and Joyce had been checking out at the reception desk when Joyce, in an ill-judged moment of impetuosity, a spark of affectionate mischief, had linked an arm through his, and laid her head against his shoulder, and run the tip of her shoe against the inside of his leg –

– and there in the lobby was bloody Haggs, registering this intimacy with a leer. Two days later Haggs had phoned. *I've been studying this situation, Chris. And you know what? I've got you by the family jewels. You're all mine, pal.*

And down the years Caskie did Haggs a favour here, a favour there. Overlook this, ignore that, help me out with this allegation of stolen property. Assist me with this, gimme a hand with that. You are my private cop, Caskie.

And then one day: I need help with the Mallons, Chris.

I need some assistance with Jackie.

When exactly had the final escalation begun? Caskie couldn't remember the date, there was a passage of time when everything accelerated, and he could recall only fragments. Haggs had become frantic because Jackie was up to something, and he couldn't find out what, and so he dreamed up a plan, and he needed Caskie to get Bones out of the way for a while, a few hours, take him someplace safe overnight, you can arrange that, Chris, dead easy for you, eh?

Caskie thought: Haggs didn't really need *me*. He could have used *anyone* to pressure Bones into taking a walk at the appropriate time. All he wanted was to drag me deeper into the mire of his life. Show me he had control. Remind me of all the years he had a hold on my world.

And make me a partner in murder.

Caskie tried to shut down his memory as a man might close a very old door, but the hinges were stiff with rust.

You want Jackie alone, Haggs?

Aye, for a wee while.

I'll see what I can do.

Try to deny it, but you knew in your heart that there was murder in the air. You could smell it as certainly as the stench of a long-dead carcass. You knew Jackie Mallon was being set up. Joyce's father. You wanted to stop it. Let Haggs blast his revelations all over the tabloid sheets. Live with the disgrace. You can go down in people's memories as that cop who molested a wee girl. Caskie, pervert.

But you couldn't. You turned your face, looked away.

You even took the murder weapon in a plastic grocery bag.

337

He felt deeply depressed. He thought, Soon I'll be free. 'It's time to draw the blinds and lock the door and hang a Gone Away sign.'

'You'll miss it,' Perlman said.

'Miss what? The hours? The flood of crime?'

The power, Perlman thought. That's what you'll miss. 'I take the point,' he said.

Caskie seemed suddenly expansive, but in his own detached way. It was as if he'd come down a rung or two on the ladder where he lived his life, and found it a risky descent. 'It's a liberation, Lou. I feel I've been carrying a backpack of bricks around for years. I've wanted to let go before now. But the time wasn't quite right . . .'

'And now it is.'

'Yes. I'm ready. It's time.'

You don't have the look of a man anticipating serenity, Perlman thought. There's no air of celebration about you. Where's the champagne spirit, Christopher? Where is that I-don't-give-a-shit good cheer?

Maybe McWhinnie's death has done you in after all.

Caskie released a smile, as if it were a lick-penny's offering dropped into a collection-box. He looked at his watch again. 'I have a few things to do, Lou.'

Perlman got up. 'Fine.'

'Feel free to ask me anything you like about McWhinnie. I'll be available.'

'Thanks,' and Perlman turned towards the door and that was when his brain kicked him. *Sunny. Brook. A mass of curls.*

55

Haggs drove his Jaguar along Nitshill Road for a mile before taking a right turn, which led him through narrow suburban streets. He marvelled at the tidiness of some lives. Blackhill, where he'd been born, was a squalid pit of tribal divisions and deprivation, of runny-nosed wee kids screaming in shite-soaked nappies that hadn't been changed in days, of men standing on street corners and bemoaning the failures of their lives and the general lack of justice, of petty thieves and burglaries and drunkenness and casual acts of violence, the swift arc of a razor, the violent flick of a sharpened steel comb. It was a million fucking miles in his wake and he was never going back that way again, and if Twiddie and his brain-dead crumpet menaced his pleasant little world in any little way, they were history.

Eventually the streets thinned out and he entered an industrial estate, one that was clearly not thriving. FOR RENT signs hung outside hangar-sized buildings. Companies long defunct had had their names whited out but sometimes you could discern a spectral impression in faded paint of these former tenants, THOMAS BAILEY & SON, WELDERS. Or half a name might

still survive in rust-coloured letters, like an enigma to be solved:
GR SON EXP S D S V CE.

Haggs parked outside a small brick building that he owned for various purposes. A car he was obliged to stash, a shipment of this or that passing through. A meeting he wanted to hold in total privacy. The building was functional, the roof metal. The sign outside said GLENLORA RENTALS, although there was no indication of whatever might be available for rent. Haggs unlocked the door and went inside. He turned on the light because there were no windows. A sink was situated in a corner. There was a rudimentary crapper behind a partition. The air smelled dead. The space was hot with the day's trapped warmth.

Haggs shut the door and walked to the middle of the room and stood with his hands in his pockets and thought of burning vans and amateur arsonists and diddies in general who endangered your way of life. And that fucking Jew was no dummy. You could practically hear him calculate. He couldn't have Perlman strutting inside his golf club. He couldn't live with that.

Haggs walked in circles. He jingled his car keys in his pocket. That bloody wallet. How could they have overlooked that? They hadn't checked the van before they tried to torch it. It was elementary shite.

He heard a sound from outside. The slam of a car door.

He heard John Twiddie's voice. Then Twiddie and the Bucket-Faced Girlfriend entered the building. Rita was all pins, jaggy protrusions, things like miniature knitting needles sticking out of her piled-up hair or dangling from her earlobes. There was some sharp object lanced through her lower lip and a shiny stud in an eyebrow. She wouldn't want to be outdoors in an electric storm, Haggs thought. He listened to the way her black leather trousers creaked as she moved. Twiddie, besuited in his counterfeit couture, wore a white slim-jim tie and a black shirt, what he considered gangster chic.

Haggs said, 'You're wondering why you're here.'

Rita said, 'Aye. It's a long way to come.'

'Oh, you're inconvenienced. I'm dead sorry. Note to self: do not inconvenience Rita in future.'

'So, eh,' Twiddie said. 'What's the score?'

Rita sniffed the air. 'Stinks a bit in here.'

'Only since you arrived,' Haggs said.

'Cheek,' Rita said.

Twiddie smiled. He understood the insult, and saw the need to defend Rita, but Haggs was the boss, and even if you despised Long Roddy his money kept you in cigarettes and clothes and food. He wasn't a man you crossed. So Twiddie's dilemma was resolved in a pallid smile.

'Fuck you grinning at, Twiddie?'

'I don't know,' Twiddie said.

'Fucking stupid grinning at nothing.' Haggs tugged Twiddie's tie out from his jacket and tossed the end of it over Twiddie's shoulder.

'Here,' Twiddie said.

Rita said, 'Leave him alone.'

'Don't you ever tell me what to do, bitch. Don't you open your mouth unless you're spoken to.'

'Fuck you,' Rita said.

Quickly, Haggs plucked a long needle from her hair and jabbed her face with it. He drew blood instantly. The girl yelped.

'I'm wounded. You've wounded me, Haggs.'

Twiddie said, 'You all right, love?'

Haggs said, 'She's not all right. You're not all right. You're both up shit creek. Pair of you. You couldn't burn that fucking van. Which would be bad enough. But you go one better. You overlook the old bastard's fucking wallet in the back of the fucking van.'

'Wallet? We didn't see the wallet,' Twiddie said.

'And your matches were damp as well, I suppose.'

'Some fires don't take,' Rita said.

Haggs's anger had the propulsion of a moon-shot. 'I've built myself a life. I like it. I like it an awful lot. I can't have it jeopardized by two completely worthless wankers like you pair. Do you understand that?'

'So, eh, what do you, ah, propose?' Twiddie said.

'I'd dearly like to torture you for a while, maybe a day or two, and then snuff you out.'

Twiddie laughed. Rita didn't. She said, 'Talk's cheap.'

Haggs cracked his knuckles. How in God's name had he ever become associated with this couple? There were moments of pleasure at times, sure, driving the dark streets, the sheer buzz of hands-on brutality, dancing with menace. But when you had Perlman in your own clubhouse right in your bloody face, when you smelled a bad tide swirling in your direction, then it was time for serious changes.

'You'll leave Glasgow,' he said.

'Is zat so?' Rita asked.

'You'll go to London. From London you'll catch a train to Holland, Germany, wherever, I don't give a fuck.'

'Wait a minute,' Rita said. 'I like Glasgow. I don't see why I should leave. My friends are here.'

Haggs said, 'You're not getting the picture, Rita. You don't have a choice. Either you leave the country . . . or some more permanent location is found for you.'

'You're talking about . . .' Twiddie paused.

'I'm talking about closing time, Twiddie. You know, when the barman says drink up and leave, and he flicks the lights, and you're out on the street? I'm talking about that kind of situation. Only there's no tomorrow, see. You don't go back to the pub next day because for you there is no next day.'

'You've arranged this?' Rita asked.

Haggs said, 'It only takes one phone call.'

'So we bugger off and live in poverty with a buncha krauts and you go on enjoying the good life. Fuck that for a lark.'

'You'll receive compensation,' Haggs said. 'Which is bloody generous of me, considering I have that other option I just mentioned.'

'I want fifty grand, Haggs,' Rita said.

Haggs said, 'I split my sides.'

'What's your figure?' she asked.

'Five K each max. No haggling.'

'Har,' Twiddie said.

'Take it, leave it.' Haggs shrugged. 'One way or another, you don't live in this city any more. I want you gone by tonight.'

'Tonight?' Rita asked.

Twiddie said, 'Can't be done.'

'No choice,' Haggs said. 'Life's like that. In the immortal words of a certain M. Jagger, Twid, you can't always get what you want. Remember that.'

56

Eddie let himself into Joyce's flat. He felt weak, liquid-headed. The sun was dying and twilight gathered slowly in the city. He slipped off his damp T-shirt, took a fresh white linen shirt from his bag. He buttoned the shirt then pulled his dark suit, the one he'd wear at the funeral, from the bottom of the bag. He laid it on a chair, smoothed it with his hands. It made little difference, but so what? A crumpled suit: small potatoes in the scheme of things.

The day came rushing back at him. The train to Largs. The great bright promise of the sea at Saltcoats and the happy faces of the kids at the carriage windows. Ice cream and candy floss and gulls and innocence.

How it changed.

McWhinnie dying. Charlie in blood. The day framed in blood.

And then Joyce. Hotel rooms with Caskie, the child and the man, crushed sheets and skewed pillows. Why did he imagine rain sweeping hard across a dreary car park and battering the window of a tiny hotel room where Caskie had drawn the curtains and Joyce was undressing by the light of the bedside lamp?

344

He heard the doorbell ring. He went down the hallway to answer. Lou Perlman, stooped, hands behind his back, stood in shadow.

Perlman said, 'Invite me in.'

Eddie stepped aside, Perlman entered. Eddie shut the door and led Perlman into the living room.

Perlman lit a cigarette and said, 'SUNY. State University of New York. Right?'

'Right –'

'And Stony Brook is a campus in the system. You had it on your T-shirt earlier today. And yesterday when we met.'

'You saw me today?' Eddie asked.

'Me, no. Some other people did. At Central Station with Charlie. So tell me this – why were you with Charlie and what did the pair of you have in common?'

Eddie looked at the brown suit and the soiled tie and the shirt with the collar tips slightly upturned. He wasn't sure why, but he'd always felt at ease with Perlman. Probably the man's lack of affectation, the fact he made no concessions to modify his accent for the untrained ear: this is me, Lou Perlman, and I don't come in any other wrapping.

Eddie said, 'McWhinnie was helping me chase Gurk.'

'AKA Tommy G. See, I remembered to check the computer.' He dragged on his cigarette so deeply his cheeks hollowed. 'You and Charlie were working together? He never said.'

'He didn't have time to say. It happened suddenly. He liked a taste of action, I guess. He was sick of working for Caskie.'

'He wasn't the happiest young man I ever met, I'll say that,' Perlman remarked. 'So you and Charlie were in hot pursuit of Gurk. Charlie caught up with Gurk in the crowd. A struggle, then . . .'

'I went after Gurk, but he'd gone. I walked the streets for a time. I don't remember which ones. Just streets.' He pictured McWhinnie, and felt as if he'd had all the air kicked out of him. There was that ache in his neck again, resurgent. His thoughts, darkening and gloomy, drifted back to Joyce, and how she'd appeared on the staircase in Caskie's house, and then he remembered his conversation with Caskie just before Joyce had materialized out of shadow. *You set my father up.*

Surmise, Caskie had said.

Eddie shut his eyes. Surmise, no. It wasn't surmise that had killed Charlie McWhinnie. Caskie's face formed in his head, that smug little beard, that look of self-assurance, and he was filled suddenly with an anger so deep that it depressed him he could feel such a disagreeable emotion with this *intensity*.

He looked at Perlman and said, 'What do you think of Caskie, Lou? What do you *really* think of him?'

'Really? Not much. He's a class-act shite. He's a *keech* in a good suit. Fortunately he's about to retire, so he won't be occupying my thoughts much longer.'

'He just walks off into the sunset,' Eddie said. And maybe Joyce walks with him, he thought. 'It's more than he fucking deserves, Lou.'

'And what precisely does he deserve, Eddie?'

'What usually happens when you're an accessory before and after the fact of a murder. Jail, right?'

'Hold on. Put your foot on the brake. *Murder*, you say?' Perlman turned his head sharply and his glasses slipped down his nose. He caught them before they slid from his face.

Eddie said, 'Murder. The killing of my father. Caskie pulled strings in the background.'

'Murder's very rich gravy,' Perlman said, and focused his good eye hard on Eddie. 'Can you make it stick to the wall, son?'

Eddie, gazing at the high ceiling, saw a spider's web in which a couple of dead flies hung. *Make it stick to the wall*. He heard himself talk about the safe house, and how McWhinnie had escorted Bones there, and how Caskie must have participated in the killing of Jackie Mallon in some way, and Haggs's role in the scheme of things, and the words tumbled out of him, and they kept coming, colliding one with another until his throat was dry and he was rambling, and he'd begun to repeat himself. He wondered how he sounded to Perlman. Deranged? The victim of delusion?

He fell silent.

Perlman ran a hand through his bristle of hair. 'It's great gravy, son, and my appetite is well and truly whetted, and if you think you see me drooling, you're dead fucking right – but it's still not sticking.'

Eddie said, 'Bones could have provided the glue, but God knows where he went. And McWhinnie knew some of Caskie's machinations, but that poor bastard isn't coming back to tell us. So . . .'

'So I hear you howling in the wind, Eddie. Unless . . .'

'Unless what?'

'Unless I can make Haggs talk. Problem is, he's a stone, and it's damned hard to squeeze blood out of something that has none.'

'You can try,' Eddie said.

'Oh, I'd love to try, I'd *love* it,' Perlman said. He plucked at his eyepatch and rubbed his hands together briskly as if he were pleased. 'Call a taxi, Eddie.'

They rode in a black cab through the south of the city. Eddie recognized a couple of landmarks when they were in the vicinity of Haggs's neighbourhood. The big roundabout. Rouken Glen. Langtree Avenue and the house called Drumpellier. Lou Perlman didn't get out of the cab at once. He gazed in the direction of the house.

'I'll go in alone, Eddie. Me and him, we talk the same talk.'

'You've thought how you'll approach this?'

'I wing shit all the time, son.' Perlman winked. 'Maybe I'll hint we've got some truly damning evidence, then see what happens. Or I'll say Caskie confessed to everything. Who knows? I'm a man of great invention when I need to be.'

'He'll call his lawyer immediately.'

Perlman said, 'We'll see.'

Eddie stayed in the cab. He watched Perlman push through the front gate. He moved with a quiet confidence, like an insurance salesman certain of a client's signature on a policy. Eddie waited. The driver listened to a talk show on the radio. Eddie gazed at the house. He heard a sound of breaking glass – a swift crack – then he saw Perlman come back. He'd been gone little more than a minute.

'Nobody's home,' Perlman said.

'What was that noise?'

'Noise?'

'Glass breaking.'

'Oh that.' Perlman looked slyly pleased. 'Those bloody security cameras depress me, Eddie. I mean, here's this thing on a fucking stalk peering into your face without permission. I'm a Luddite, son. So I took a fine stout branch to it. Whackety-whack.'

'You vandalized it,' Eddie said.

'I *pulverized* it.'

'Now what?'

Perlman settled in the back of the cab and looked thoughtful. 'Haggs could be almost anywhere. One of his favourite restaurants, say. His golf club maybe . . . Or.'

'Or what?'

'He's got this run-down place he sometimes goes when he needs privacy. He thinks it's his secret rendezvous, and nobody else knows about it. He hasn't got a bloody clue I've clocked the place more than a few times and I've seen him come and go. Great fun to watch somebody who doesn't know he's being watched. This is worth a try.'

Perlman leaned forward to instruct the cab driver.

57

'Wotcher, mates.'

Haggs turned towards the door. He hadn't heard it open.

The man who stepped in kicked the door shut behind him, and smiled a big white-toothed smile. His bald brown scalp shone under the electric light and he carried himself in an easy manner, as if he had the ability to slough off all life's problems.

'Who the *fuck* are you?' Haggs asked.

'Tommy Gurk.'

'Gurk?' Haggs asked.

'Got it in one. Pardon my bad manners, if you will, but I been eavesdropping your conversation. It seems to me I can save you all kinds of problems, providing you do everything my way.'

'And what way is that?' Haggs asked.

Gurk had a gun in his hand. Out of nowhere, conjured up like a magician's prop, there it was, steel enclosed in a firm brown hand.

Twiddie said, 'He's fucking armed.'

'Bright boy,' Gurk said.

'You're not going to use that,' Rita said.

'It all depends, my beauty,' Gurk said.

'Depends on what?' Haggs asked.

'What do you know about my business with Jackie Mallon?'

'Sweet fuck all,' Haggs said.

Without expression, Gurk turned away from Haggs and shot Twiddie in the head. It was done so quickly, so casually, it was seconds before Haggs or Rita registered the fact that a gun had been fired and Twiddie had buckled like a beast shot in a slaughterhouse and lay sideways on the floor, and blood was flowing in little streams around his skull. Rita slumped to her knees beside Twiddie and covered her open mouth with her hand. She was terrifyingly mute.

'Now,' Gurk said. 'Have I got your attention?'

Haggs had a falling sensation, as if his internal organs had slipped inches inside him. He wondered if Billy McQueen had felt like this on the high-rise when he looked down the dark shaft. 'Very definitely. What do you want to know?'

'I hear you're looking for a certain cargo that was the basis of a business agreement involving the late Jackie Mallon, the just as late Billy McQueen and my good self.'

'I expressed an interest,' Haggs said. 'Mallon wouldn't give me the time of day.'

'And so you had him snuffed. And then you had Billy the Stump snuffed as well because he couldn't tell you jack shit.'

'Let's say there was, ah, a breakdown in communication.'

'But you're still looking to get in, aintcha?' Gurk asked.

Haggs said, 'Aye, but I'm tired banging my head against a shithouse wall.' Was there a way out of this? he wondered. Could he ever walk away from this building and get in his car and go home? He was conscious of Rita bent over the dead Twiddie, and how she'd started to sob, and he imagined his life flushed down a toilet and swirling away, all the good things he'd accumulated sucked into sewers. He wanted to say *Spare me*. But he'd never begged in his life and he wasn't about to begin now. Note to self: Never ask for mercy. It lacks dignity.

Gurk looked at Rita and said, 'Here, love. Stifle that snivelling, eh? It's giving me the willies.'

Rita looked up at Gurk. Mascara ran down her face like ink spilled carelessly. Her hands were locked in upraised fists. 'You fucking *killed* him, you fucking pig, you fucking *cunt*.'

'Well, yeh. I did. I can hardly deny it, can I? So now you're lonely, is that it? Horrible being on your tod. Tell you what, love, I'll fix it for you. Cheerio, dear.' Gurk smiled and fired the gun and Haggs saw Rita's head split open like a squash that had dropped from the back of a vegetable lorry screaming down the motorway, and, sickened, he looked away from the sight.

Gurk said, 'You were saying, Haggsy.'

Haggs had a hard time regulating his voice. 'I was saying Mallon told me nothing.'

'He didn't mention the whereabouts or the nature of the cargo?'

'He never discussed any of that,' Haggs said. He might have had an old sock stuffed in his throat, so thick did his voice sound. He stared at Gurk's gun until it expanded and filled his vision entirely and then beyond even that. It was bigger than the world. His hearing had somehow been heightened – a tap dripped once every thirty seconds into the sink, a moth trapped and dying beat quietly at the metal roof, and something wet slid down the wall behind Rita but he didn't want to look.

'We weren't close, you know. We weren't friends.'

'Business involves trust, and me and my associates don't trust you, Haggsy. We don't like the idea of you looking under stones trying to find our property. We don't like you swanning around this dandy old city looking for something that isn't yours. I mean, what if you was to stumble over it, eh? You'd tell us, right? Yeh, sure, and I shit gold bricks. It would be gone in a flash, pal. And where would that leave me and my colleagues, eh? Out of pocket and no chance of recovering our goods.'

Haggs said, 'Look, I'd like to help, honest –'

'Oh, I'd like that too.' Gurk glanced at the gun in his hand. 'But my associates feel you've trespassed on their territory. You've been too fucking eager to muscle in on something that's got nothing to do with you. In short, you're out of fucking control, jack.'

'I can make inquiries on your behalf,' Haggs said. 'I know people, I can ask questions –'

'You been busy asking questions already, Haggsy. And it hasn't worked out very well. We're left with no cargo, and two dead associates. That's not kosher, is it? We can't have you giving us grief, squire.'

Haggs said, 'Maybe I can help. I know my way round this city, I know people who knew Jackie, the guys that worked for him in his warehouse in Bluevale Street, aye, you could ask them, or you could talk to the people he drank with, they might know something. Then there's his son Eddie –' *I'm begging*, he thought. *And I swore I never would.*

'Look at it this way,' Gurk said. 'This life is just a stage you're passing through. Shadows on walls, mate. Everything is appearance. You'll be back in some other form.'

'Once around the block is enough for me,' Haggs said. He couldn't think of anything else to say, any plea he might enter on his own behalf that would persuade this cold smiling brown man he was worth sparing. He took one step back and Gurk, who defined the past, present and future of Roddy Haggs, popped off a shot which Haggs heard only for as long as it takes an eye to blink.

'Fucking carnage,' Gurk said, and wondered how badly he'd dented the thin brass-plating of his karma. Very badly, he imagined. In his next incarnation he'd be a bleeding aphid with a lifespan of about forty-five minutes. He surveyed the bodies and stuffed the gun in his waistband and went outside just as a black cab came into the parking area.

A man got out of the taxi. That fucker from the hotel in Largs, Gurk thought. The one who'd chased him through the train station. Gurk moved quickly towards his car.

The man shouted, 'Gurk!'

Gurk fired off a single shot and it struck the door of the taxi and the man threw himself to the ground. Gurk opened the door of his green Fiat and got behind the wheel, aware of a second figure stepping out of the cab now, an older man who crouched low and was half-hidden by the cab door. The cabby had vanished, ducked down behind his wheel.

I finish them all off or I get the hell out of here, Gurk thought.

Did aphids fuck or did they procreate in some other way he knew nothing about? If he didn't jump out of the Fiat and shoot these people maybe he'd get a break on the karmic ladder, skipping the fruit-fly step and coming back a few levels up, a bee, say, buzzing from flower to flower, or a snail sliming along some damp basement.

Or a lawyer, he thought.

He drove quickly past the taxi. The guy from the train station was down on his knees, shouting something. Gurk couldn't hear what. The older fellow stood behind the open door, staring at the Fiat's plate, memorizing it. Fat lot of good that's going to do, Gurk thought. The registration was fake, no two ways, the car probably stolen. Gurk drove, tyres squealing, air dense with exhaust pall, through the streets of the industrial estate.

He didn't look back.

Perlman helped Eddie to his feet. The taxi driver, a chubby man with a liver-coloured birthmark on his neck, stumbled out of the cab.

'Fucking hell,' the cabby said. He examined the hole left by the bullet in the side door. 'Fucking hell,' and he said it several times in amazement.

Perlman showed him his police ID, as if this might mollify him. 'I'm sorry. That was unexpected.'

'Why the hell are you bastards riding about in taxis anyway? I thought you had souped-up squad cars,' the driver said. 'And don't even *think* about asking me to follow him, because I'm having none of that lark. Look at my hands, man. I'm shaking like a leaf. It's a Valium I need,' and he stepped back inside the cab and slumped chalk-faced behind the wheel. 'Fucking hell,' on and on, an incantation.

Perlman said, 'It's not worth chasing him. He'll dump the car first alley he comes to,' and he mentioned something vague and apologetic about reimbursement and repairs, then he walked towards the building. Eddie followed. He thought of the bullet that had slammed into the cab door, and Gurk's face which, with dreadlocks gone, looked intense and luminously determined.

It was hot in the building and the air smelled of blood. Flies buzzed.

Eddie stood over Haggs, who lay face down, one eye gone, the other wide and open and blind. In death he seemed a few inches shorter than in life, as if he were dwindling.

Perlman sighed. 'I wanted him. But not like this. No way.'

Eddie looked at the other two bodies. Violent death always unsettled him. He'd never quite developed the protective carapace he found so common among his colleagues.

Perlman said, 'Allow me to introduce you, Eddie. The woman is – *was* – Rita Wright. Rita Wrong would've been more accurate. The other's John Twiddie, something of an enforcer for our Roddy, and very very nasty. Rita was Twiddie's helper and lover. They were not nice people, Eddie.'

Eddie gazed at the girl, and had an impression of safety pins and metallic studs and steely clasps covered with blood. There was nothing left that resembled a face. He turned to look at Twiddie. Bare bone was visible where flesh had been blown from the side of the skull.

'Right piece of work, our Twiddie,' Perlman said.

Eddie was shocked to hear a slight expulsion of air from Twiddie's open mouth. He went down on his knees and listened. 'Jesus, he's still breathing, Lou.'

Perlman came closer. 'Only just.'

Twiddie suddenly raised a hand and with enormous effort clutched Eddie's arm. He whispered so quietly Eddie was obliged to bring his face level with the man's mouth.

'*You . . . eh, a priest . . . ?*'

A priest. Eddie said nothing. Twiddie was functioning at a level where it was doubtful he'd have understood a response. How he'd managed to survive the wound to his head was one of those freak occurrences that depend on such circumstances as the trajectory of bullet or hardness of bone, or even something as unquantifiable as the sheer will to linger in the world a little longer. Eddie had seen shotgun victims survive bullets to the brain and stabbing casualties whose cerebra had been pierced without fatal effect.

'I've done bad things, Father . . . I want to confess.'

Eddie looked into the man's eyes. The glazed blue light was dulling rapidly and the pupils were tiny. 'What bad things?'

Twiddie tried to focus on Eddie's face. His eyes lacked coordination and his body convulsed. His hand slid from Eddie's arm, leaving a streak of blood.

Twiddie spoke again, voice almost inaudible. *'Rita . . . where are you, doll . . . doll, you there . . .'* And then he was silent and his dead eyes stared directly into Eddie's face.

Perlman fingered Twiddie's pulse. 'He's gone. Christ knows where a soul like Twiddie's finds sanctuary. Look, get the cabby to drive you back to your sister's place, Eddie. I'm going to have to call Tay and I don't want you here when the heavy boys arrive. Tay'll ask too many questions, and you don't need to be involved.' He took his cellphone from his jacket.

Eddie walked outside. He heard Perlman talk on his phone. The cab driver was still slumped behind the wheel.

'Dennistoun,' Eddie said.

'You mind if we drive really slow?'

'Drive any way you like.'

Eddie climbed into the back seat and looked at John Twiddie's blood on his arm.

Twiddie, the enforcer. *I've done bad things . . .*

I want to confess . . .

Confess what? He wondered if it had been Twiddie who'd pulled the trigger on Jackie. If Haggs had ordered the slaying. Do the old man, Twiddie. Do it right.

He let the thought drift and stared out at the lamplit city and recognized nothing, street names, storefronts, bars. It was strange to him, and he had the feeling it always would be, a city he'd remember now and then, with diminishing clarity, when he was home in Queens.

58

In Joyce's flat Eddie sat on the sofa. Joyce wasn't home. He assumed she was with Caskie. He rang his home number, and heard Claire's melodic voice on the answering machine. *'We can't come to the phone right now. Please leave a message. Thanks.'* Fuck it, he felt lonely. He wandered through the small flat, drank tap water in the kitchen, looked out at the backs of the surrounding tenements. Laundry, lit by electric light from windows, hung motionless on lines below.

He ran cold water over his arm and rinsed Twiddie's blood off his skin, then he went back to the sofa and lay down, closing his eyes: a dark rolled across him and he dozed briefly. In his sleep he felt John Twiddie's hand circling his wrist. He woke, startled, trembling, half-expecting to see Twiddie stand above him, resurrected and murderous. He sat upright, clenched his hands together. I need alcohol, he thought, a shot for the nerves. He found a bottle of brandy in the kitchen and drank from it and he thought about Twiddie in the back of Jackie's car, waiting with gun in hand. Anticipating the moment. He thought of a twilight street and a half-acre of wasteland and Jackie getting into the Mazda and maybe he was humming a tune under his breath and Twiddie changed the whole picture into nightmare. He closed the brandy and set the bottle down and heard the sound of Perlman's voice in the hallway.

'Careless, Eddie. You didn't shut the door properly.'

Eddie couldn't remember getting out of the cab and climbing the stairs and returning to the flat. All blank. A kind of black-out. Going through motions. He went to the kitchen doorway. Perlman was smoking a cigarette in his avid manner.

'How did it go?' Eddie asked.

'Tay took total control. He likes to run his own show. He's excited, although you'd need an electron microscope to see any change in his expression. You'll be seeing Gurk's face, or a likeness thereof, on your TV screens before the night's out. Buzz buzz. The city's being turned over like a fucking pancake . . . You were never near the place, you understand. You never saw any corpses.'

'What about the cab driver?'

'I've spoken to him. He never saw you either. In fact, he saw nothing and he prefers it that way.'

Eddie was quiet a second before he came back to the inevitable and said, 'Caskie.'

'What can I say about him, Eddie? We've got nothing on him. The voices that might have spoken out – they're all silent. He just fades away into retirement, and that's the last of him.' He cleared his throat a few times. 'I need some night air. It's lovely out there. Crime to waste this kind of weather. You fancy keeping me company?'

'I'd like that.' The last of Caskie, Eddie thought. Not where Joyce was concerned. What did she see in the future? Herself and Chris yachting away on fresh tides? Love, albeit one constructed on lies and old subterfuges, prevailing? Why not. Maybe she deserved to believe in love.

Don't we all, he thought.

Perlman wandered towards the door. Eddie followed him down the stairs and outside. The air was curiously sweet; a hint of new-mown grass suffused the dark. They walked towards

358

Whitehill Street, then turned left to Duke Street. Perlman was a slow stroller, pausing now and again when he heard a strain of music from a tenement flat or the sound of a cat or somebody's voice upraised in domestic dispute. Along Duke Street the smell of deep-fried food hung in the air. Streetlamps glowed. A moon almost full sailed over the city. Perlman stopped outside a fish and chip shop. 'I need some grease to keep my strength up. Fancy anything?'

Eddie wasn't hungry, but he went inside the shop anyway with Perlman, who ordered fish and chips. The counterman dumped the food into a cardboard tray which he then tucked inside a paper bag. Perlman carried the bag outside.

'They used to wrap it in old newspapers,' he said. 'You could read the sports pages while you stuffed your face,' and he fingered a chunk of fish into his mouth as he strolled. He belched very slightly. Eddie looked up at the lights in tenements. A birdcage hung in a third-floor window. A woman reached up to drape a cover over the cage. From somewhere else in the city came the sound of cop cars, harsh and unrelenting.

Both men crossed Duke Street.

'The city feels different,' Perlman said. 'I like to think I'm tuned into the wavelength of Glasgow, and when there's inter-ference, I can hear it. Murder interferes with my reception. There's static.'

Eddie said nothing. He was seeing Charlie McWhinnie drop-ping to the ground and the crowd parting to create a space, and he was imagining Tommy Gurk, comedian, shooting Roddy Haggs; Gurk, wanted man, out there somewhere in the night.

They reached the corner of Bluevale Street, where Eddie said, 'I'd like to stroll down to the warehouse. I might never get another chance to look at it.'

'Planning to stay away for good? Don't like the city, eh?'

'Maybe I've been gone too long, and the drift's too wide.'

'Glasgow's an acquired taste,' Perlman said. He dumped the leftovers of his fish and chips in a dustbin.

They walked down Bluevale Street. When they reached the

high wire fence that surrounded the yard, a huge dog reared barking inside, a snarling flurry of fur and claws and bared teeth. Beyond, a subdued light was lit in the warehouse window, and it cast a rectangle of illumination across the yard. Inside the building somebody was playing 'Red River Valley' very softly on a harmonica. Eddie was reminded of old black-and-white prison movies, the condemned man shuffling along Death Row to the chair and some sad-eyed inmate playing a harmonica in the background.

The dog's eyes gleamed, and piles of old brick and sinks and cisterns became dim forms piled willy-nilly. The dog kept growling, throwing itself at the wire. The harmonica stopped.

'Shut up, Chet,' Eddie said. 'Cool it.'

The dog appeared puzzled hearing the sound of his own name and withdrew a moment and then, triggered by his training, he dashed himself again at the fence.

A door opened somewhere in the darkness and a voice called out, 'Who's there?'

'Eddie Mallon.'

Joe Wilkie appeared at the fence. 'This is a surprise, Eddie. I wasn't expecting company at this time of night.'

'Joe, you remember Detective-Sergeant Perlman?'

'Sure I do,' Joe Wilkie said. 'We talked already.'

'Indeed we did,' Perlman said.

Silence a moment. Chet backed off, walking in anxious circles. Joe Wilkie fingered the rims of his glasses and coughed.

Eddie said, 'I just wanted a last look at the old place. Can we come inside?'

'Now?'

'Is it inconvenient for you?'

'No, no problem,' Joe Wilkie said. He rubbed his jaw, a small gesture of uncertainty, then unlocked the door in the fence and allowed Eddie and Perlman to come through. He shut the door with one hand while he restrained the dog with the other. 'We were just doing some stocktaking.'

'At this hour?' Eddie asked.

360

'Jackie was never tidy. It always got on my wick the way he did things. I like to keep an accurate record of stock. You want to know what you've got, what's of any value and what's junk you can just toss. Jackie hoarded like an effing jackdaw.'

They went inside the warehouse. The door to Jackie's office was open a few inches. A light burned in there. Eddie surveyed the warehouse; here and there dim overhead lamps were lit. Stone columns and statues, piles of rusted scaffolding that looked like the bones of prototype robots that had failed, quarry slates in great haphazard stacks, chimneypots. It's weird, Eddie thought. Here was his childhood and suddenly he couldn't relate to it, not the way he'd done before in this place. The past was receding.

Joe Wilkie, cleaning his glasses against his sleeve, was emitting tension: was it because he didn't like being interrupted at work?

Perlman sniffed the air in the manner of a wine buff. 'You know, the smell in here reminds me a wee bit of the old subway system. That lovely underground damp and the scent of old oil.'

'Aye, I noticed that a few times.'

Ray Wilkie materialized from behind the stack of slates. He held a harmonica in one hand. He wore a warehouseman's grey coat, exactly like Joe's. He nodded and tapped the harmonica in his palm.

'So this is the musician,' Perlman said. 'Sweet stuff, son.'

'I just blow a few notes now and then,' Ray Wilkie said.

'He's modest as hell.' Joe Wilkie laughed. 'You should hear him when he really gets going. He's a wizard. Play some jazz, Ray. Play that Cole Porter thing. "Love for Sale."'

'Da, I don't feel like it.'

'Never hide your light under a bushel,' Joe Wilkie said. 'Make with the music, Ray.'

Ray Wilkie frowned at his father and then raised the harmonica reluctantly to his mouth and blew. Eddie recognized the tune at once, but Ray hurried through the melody and into an area of improvisation that rendered the piece unrecognizable.

'Boy's good,' Perlman said.

'He's as good as yon fella, Larry Adler,' Joe Wilkie said with pride.

Eddie listened as he walked around the warehouse. A rat scuttled out from below a heap of old tarps. Above, pigeons stirred on metal beams. He stopped beside a headless statue whose shoulders were thick with years of bird droppings, and he looked across the room. The big aluminium door leading to the yard lay open; directly outside, both rear doors of the Mercedes van were wide.

Eddie was conscious of Joe Wilkie watching him. 'Isn't he something, eh, Eddie? Isn't the boy a bloody marvel?'

Without turning, Eddie said yeah, Joe, Ray was really something all right.

'Come back and listen,' Joe Wilkie said.

'In a minute.'

What looked to Eddie like a stack of unwanted items had been piled inside the big Merc. Stocktaking. Discard the worthless. Busted lamps, formica-top tables and broken-legged chairs all in a tangle, stacked rolls of old linoleum. 'Love for Sale.' Ray Wilkie segued into another familiar old song, 'Dream A Little Dream', and Perlman laughed in a delighted way.

Eddie drifted to the open door and looked at the Mercedes. He stepped out into the yard and peered at the junk heaped inside the vehicle. The dog appeared and growled, standing between Eddie and the van. Eddie shushed it, calmed it, carefully ran a hand over the animal's great powerful head.

Joe Wilkie called out, 'You can't hear the music properly from there, Eddie. Come back inside.'

Eddie didn't answer. *Joe doesn't want me near the vehicle.* I wonder why. 'Dream A Little Dream' took off down musical highways Eddie had never travelled before. Ray's playing became frantic. The tune changed mood, darkening suddenly, its inherent tenderness altered.

362

Perlman clapped his hands and said, 'Oh, he's the goods, he's the goods all right.'

'He's got the juice,' Joe Wilkie said.

'God-given,' Perlman said.

Eddie was drawn to the jumble-sale items in the van. He stared at the rubbish, and realized that between the arrangement of unwanted goods and the front of the van was a space which seemingly contained nothing, nothing he could see, as if the broken-down furniture had been deliberately arranged to create an impediment to viewing the deep interior of the Mercedes, but that was a stray thought, a gatecrasher, and Eddie was about to let it drift out of his mind when something caught his eye and he peered through a tunnel in the clutter of crap and caught a certain smell, a whiff of lubricant familiar to him – and then he turned away, tense, a pulse in his throat, hoping he hadn't been noticed, sticking his hands in his pockets, 'Dream A Little Dream'.

He heard Perlman clap his hands and say, 'Brilliant, bloody brilliant,' and the kid stopped playing and Joe Wilkie came to the doorway and asked, 'Jazz not your thing, Eddie?'

'Sometimes. It depends.'

Joe moved past Eddie and shut the doors of the Mercedes.

It's too late, Joe. I've seen. I didn't want to. I wish to Christ I hadn't.

He stepped back inside the warehouse and Wilkie followed him. Perlman was lighting a cigarette and talking in a quiet voice to young Ray, who was showing the cop his harmonica. Two jazz freaks, they could probably talk for hours.

Eddie saw the door of Jackie's old office open and Senga appeared there in a pair of dark blue jeans and a pale blue sweater. Her hair, unpinned, hung to her shoulders.

'Well, *Eddie*,' she said. She came towards him, embraced him. 'Why did you not tell me Eddie was here, Joe?'

'You were busy with the books,' Wilkie said.

'I was bored to hell, so I was.' Senga linked her arm through Eddie's. That overwhelming warmth, that sense of inner strength:

363

Eddie thought some magnetic force flowed from the woman.

'I heard the music and I assumed Ray was just tooting for his own fun the way he sometimes does, I had no idea you were here . . . Who's your friend, Eddie?'

'Detective-Sergeant Lou Perlman. He's been involved in the murder investigation.'

'Oh.' She smiled and held her hand out and shook Lou Perlman's. 'Nice hands, Lou. You shouldn't bite your nails.'

'Bad habit,' Perlman said. 'I'm full of bad habits. You wouldn't believe.'

'I'd believe,' Senga said.

Eddie gestured round the warehouse. He felt he had to explain his presence. He cleared his throat. He was hoarse, dry. 'An exercise in nostalgia coming here.'

'It has a few good memories for Eddie,' Joe Wilkie said to Perlman. 'He was always in and out of here when he was a wee nipper. Right, Eddie?'

'Long before I knew him,' Senga said.

Eddie nodded. An awkward, fragile moment: something hung in the balance. *I saw what I wasn't supposed to see.* He was aware of Joe Wilkie running the back of his hand across his lips and Senga taking a cigarette out of a packet and Perlman, a gentleman, lighting it for her, and he was thinking of the van and the jumble of objects in back, and an old Scottish word came back to him that Granny Mallon had used to describe a mess, a *heelie-goleerie*, an expression he hadn't thought of in years. *This is a right heelie-goleerie*, she'd say when dirty dishes had been stacked in the sink or clothes lay about the bedroom floor.

'Let's call it a night,' Senga said. 'We can finish up the day after the funeral. I'm bone-tired.'

Eddie looked at her face. Without her usual make-up she appeared a little pale. Stocktaking on the night before the funeral service.

No, it's not that, not that at all.

Perlman said, 'I'm going back to the office. I've got some stuff to deal with.'

'The law never sleeps, eh?' Senga said.

'Only when criminals do.'

Eddie realized Perlman was flirting mildly with Senga. His body language was different, the stoop was gone, he was alert and smiling and his voice was less of a growl. They went out into the yard. Joe Wilkie locked the warehouse door. Ray made sure the van was secure, trying the back handles. The dog whined and whooped, knowing it was about to be abandoned for the night.

They walked into the street, all five of them, and Perlman said, 'I'll find a taxi.'

Joe Wilkie padlocked the gate. 'Taxi my arse. I've got my car right here,' and he indicated an old Honda. 'Not the most comfy ride in the world, but it'll take you anywhere you want to go and it won't cost you a penny.'

'I don't want to inconvenience you,' Perlman said.

'Come on, get in, I insist.' Wilkie unlocked the car. Ray climbed into the back seat, Perlman sat in front and looked cramped.

Joe Wilkie slid behind the wheel. 'What about you, Senga?'

'I'll walk home,' she said. 'I need the air and it's a nice night, and I've got Eddie for company. He and I can have a chat just between ourselves.'

Perlman said, 'I'll call you, Eddie.'

The Honda drew away in a stuttering burst of smoke, and Eddie stood without moving. Senga's arm was hooked through his. He was reluctant to move, as if by taking a step away from the warehouse he was abandoning his childhood for all time. When he moved, he didn't look back.

He walked up Bluevale Street to Duke Street, Senga attached to him. Neither spoke for a couple of blocks. When they'd crossed Duke Street and were heading up Whitehill, Eddie said, 'Tell me, Senga.'

'Don't ask.'

'Just tell me the truth.'

'The truth?'

'It would be a real nice change to hear it.'

365

Senga said, 'It's a rare commodity.'

'Practically extinct.'

'And you found it in the back of a big Mercedes van, didn't you?'

'It's a funny thing how hard you can look and how many people you can question,' Eddie said, 'but sometimes you find the truth by pure goddam chance.'

59

Gurk waited until the group had dispersed and the street was empty, then he crossed to the wire fence and looked at the sign: J MALLON, TRADER. This place was worth a look, he thought. Christ knows, he didn't have a whole lot of options. Earlier, while he'd been lurking in shadow, he'd heard the dog. A deep bark, trained guard dog probably, maybe a Doberman, maybe an Alsatian. It didn't matter. He had a way with animals. They sensed a oneness with him.

He took a run at the fence, which was twelve feet high. He caught the wire at around eight feet and hung there, gaining a toehold and raising his hands to the top. He'd haul himself up and over, one last effort, deep breath, easy-peasy.

The dog was going mental beneath him, snarling, barking, jumping at the fence.

Gurk said, 'Calm, boy, calm calm.'

The dog raged, curled, sprang. The stench of fur was strong. The teeth shone in what little light fell from a nearby streetlamp. Gurk caught the upper part of the fence: but in the poor light he hadn't seen the fucking barbed *wire*, compacted into wicked rolls and bolted along the top of the fence, that lacerated the palms of his hands. Jesus. *Ohhhh*. This world of pain. This world of mace and crucifixion on barbed wire.

He yelped, and dropped into the yard, and the dog streaked at his ankle and bit deep through cloth and flesh and muscle to the bone, and now blood flowed from Gurk's hands as well as his ankle. He kicked the dog hard and the creature squealed and came back at him, springing at his stomach, digging its teeth through the material of his shirt and locking on to his belly, and Gurk karate-chopped the beast with a vicious downward thrust, but the animal – enraged – continued to cling.

My gun, Gurk thought, I'll end this *now*.

The weapon was in the left-hand pocket of his jacket and it was his left hand that had been spiked by barbed wire and he couldn't grasp the gun. He twisted, tried to reach across himself and the snarling head of the dog to get the gun out of the pocket with his right hand, but the dog, sensing menace, dug fangs into the moving hand and burst the skin and veins and Gurk thought his right hand had been thrust inside an incinerator.

Right hand, left hand, stomach, he was bleeding from various punctures and wounds. How much fucking blood had he lost? He clubbed the dog with the side of his left hand – *aieee*, the pain of it – but the animal came at him again and this time Gurk got the gun out just before the beast launched itself in flight, but pain had slowed him and the dog bounded with such ferocity that the gun went spinning out of Gurk's hand and clanked to the ground somewhere close but dark.

He'd never find it.

He was leaking blood and he had no gun and no safe crawl space and the animal was *insatiably* violent. It circled, sprang again, battered his shoulder, and he lost balance and fell over into a pile of bricks, sharp-edged motherfuckers that pierced his skin. A bed of goddammed stone.

He crawled, hands soaked with blood, brick grinding into palms and knees, and the dog came after him and caught his cheek in its teeth and he imagined fangs penetrating flesh right to the teeth and through that to the soft roots inside the gum, and I am going to black out pretty fucking soon if I don't get this monster, this remorseless thing from hell, away from me –

Easy boy easy now –

His voice enraged the dog. It bolted up on to his spine and bit the back of his neck and held on and Gurk turned this way and that, locked in a struggle with the beast, smelling its vile breath and the stink of its fur and all the while aware that blood was flowing out of him at a rate he couldn't afford, because before long he'd be light-headed and pass out. He fumbled for a slab of brick and brought it down on the dog's head and the animal, perplexed, yapped and drew back, but Gurk knew it was a momentary relief, the dog was gathering forces, regrouping to come again, and this time Gurk didn't think he could beat the animal off. He crawled over brick and rubble and planks of wood.

The Zone. Enter the Zone. Fuck the Zone. There is no Zone.

He saw the white van a few yards away. If he could get inside the vehicle and slam the door.

The dog was barking, ready to fight again.

Gurk tried to open the back of the van. *Bastard was locked.* Sometimes fate doesn't have a kind word for you. You're fucked no matter what.

He slammed a lump of brick against the handles again and again, bang bang – yield, you bastard, open up, let me inside, gimme haven. The dog raced towards him and he swung, lashing out with the brick, catching the animal at the side of its head, and it fell over dazed, but Gurk knew it would come again and if he didn't find a hiding place he was mincemeat ready to be dropped on the sizzling hot coals, barbecued Gurk on a bun. Karmaburger.

The animal, vast in bad light, shook itself, recovered its senses, and soared at him, crossing space with a lethal grace that in other circumstances Gurk might have admired. Sleek flesh, density of muscle, defiance of gravity such as that possessed by a hawk on the wing, and those teeth, those precise surgical instruments. He stepped back, stumbled against the van. The dog came zooming in and caught him low on the thigh and the teeth went through his flesh and this time Gurk screamed because so much pain couldn't be contained in silence. Screamed, then grunted, then went down on all fours, face to face with the beast. They eyeballed one another, the dog's snout a few inches from Gurk's nose: in that cold canine eye Gurk saw no mercy. He crawled back, the dog watched him, waited, cocked a head to one side, growled softly. With his spine pressed to the rear doors of the van, Gurk wondered, could I make a run for it, a beeline for the fence, did I have the strength to get over that wire? He was lathered in his own blood. He was weak.

He watched the dog, listened to the throaty growl and wondered if maybe the beast was offering a truce –

But no. Dogs didn't do truces. They didn't understand the concept.

The animal came at him and knocked him down and he banged his skull against the van as he fell, and what he saw was the full moon in wayward flight across the sky and all the stars above the city opening like ripe silver flowers and he raised a hand wearily as if he might push the dog away, but the animal yanked off a finger between its teeth and Gurk felt the horrible tearing of his flesh. He'd never known a sensation like that before: a bit of his body just ripped off. Like that. Gone. In shock he struggled to his feet while the dog played with the finger. Shoulders slumped, he caught the handles of the van doors with his intact hand and suddenly metal snapped from the face of the door – luck *luck* – and Gurk eased the door open and a cascade of household furniture clattered down on him, tables and chairs and lamps, a crash of trash.

The leg of a chair poked him directly in the mouth and he heard a tooth break. He spat blood. He thought, I fall to pieces, and he hauled himself into the back of the van and lay among the disarray of formica tables and pleated lampshades. He drew the doors closed. He knew he couldn't get out. He was a prisoner. The upside of this was that the dog couldn't get in. He listened to it bark and bark and bark, and he heard it prowl round the

370

vehicle, and then there was silence. Or maybe he was faint and the world outside fading.

He crawled to the back of the van and his hands encountered objects he recognized at once and he thought, Jesus Christ in heaven, I know what these are, but before he had a chance to appreciate the dumb irony of his situation he went out like a meteor striking some lonely tundra, and his blood flowed and he didn't hear the dog sit in the dark growling every now and then as it waited.

60

The place where the school had once stood, that vacant lot of nettle and dock leaf, seemed hostile in the dark. Eddie ran a hand along the railings as he walked. Senga still held his arm.

'You shouldn't have looked,' she said. 'Very naughty of you, Eddie. Spying like that.'

Eddie thought the night had an emptiness about it, as if the pulses of the city had been stilled. The street was quiet.

'So, Eddie. What will you do?'

He hadn't thought. He hadn't had a chance to think.

Senga took her arm away from him and stopped, turning to face him. 'Your father did it for me, Eddie. I asked him. I told him what our people needed, and he found it.'

'Our people?'

Senga said, 'Our people, my people. It's in the blood, Eddie. You can't just squeeze it out of your system. Our people over there need the weapons.'

'There's never an end,' Eddie said. 'It goes on and on.'

'What do you imagine – that everybody buys all this disarmament shite? Come, we'll open our arms dumps and you can take a look and see how cooperative we really are. Fucking hell, Eddie, you can talk peace and coexistence until you've got steam coming out your ears, and the politicians can huff and puff about how bloody brilliant they are – oh, aren't we wonderful, we've brought peace – but at the end of the day you've got people who'll never trust each other, because there's been too much blood for forgiveness, and too much hate. There's no peace, Eddie. Only PR. Only the image. The shadow on the wall. No substance. Not where it counts,' and she laid a hand on his arm. 'We can never trust the other side. Understand that. We may fight among ourselves now and again, we may squabble furiously, but when it comes right down to it, we're united against the enemy.'

The enemy. Eddie stared into the haunted darkness of the schoolgrounds. He imagined cigarette smoke drifting from the boys' lavatory and the sound of kids playing football in the field beyond the bicycle shed, that space where annexe buildings, skimpy in their impermanence, had been erected to absorb an overflow of students. He grasped the railings and felt he was looking at the last resting place of innocence.

They strolled a few more yards. This time Senga walked a couple of feet away from him. She isn't touching me now, he thought. The intimacy has been abandoned.

'How did it work?' he asked.

'Jackie paid half the money upfront to Gurk in Largs, McQueen brokered the deal and got his share, and the cargo was duly collected by Joe Wilkie from a drop on the outskirts of a place called Port Glasgow. The other half of the money was due when Joe returned with the goods. But then that arsehole Haggs stepped into the picture and he brought disaster – so who pays up when Jackie is dead?'

'Somebody has to,' Eddie said.

'But who? I don't have the three hundred thousand plus, or whatever Jackie owed.'

'Jackie must have had it,' Eddie said. 'He intended to pay, didn't he?'

'Jackie always squared his debts, Eddie. I have no doubt he

had the cash somewhere. Finding where – that would be the real problem. Where did he stash it? There must be a thousand places, eh?'

She knows where Jackie hid his cash, Eddie thought. She knows.

He said, 'The cargo leaves Glasgow soon, I'd guess.'

Senga didn't answer this question. She said, 'Our people are waiting for it at the other end. They'll pay well for it. That's where Jackie made his profit.'

'But you won't use that money to settle the debt with the original supplier, will you?'

'Me? That was all Jackie's business. I don't know anything about these weapons or where they came from, do I? Look at me, Eddie, and you see a woman who just liked a few drinks and listening to the Eagles and keeping my man happy. An ordinary soul.'

'A nice façade,' Eddie said.

'And I played it well,' Senga said.

She's screwing with Kaminsky and his operation, Eddie thought. A dangerous line to walk. If Gurk couldn't get the cash or the return of the goods, somebody else would be despatched. And after that, if need be, somebody else. And on. Kaminsky would send his minions and emissaries into Ulster and Glasgow until he found out what had happened to his consignment. It was business, and he couldn't be perceived as soft.

Senga, locked inside an airtight old dream of Protestant ascendancy in Ulster, didn't seem to get this. People obsessed with ancient causes were blind to reality and change. Eddie thought of the van and the clapped-out furniture and the cargo that lay hidden in the space beyond the tables and chairs, and he realized that he and Perlman had interrupted work in progress, that Senga and Joe and Ray must have intended to conceal the cargo under tarps, inside boxes, whatever.

I shouldn't have looked but I did.

He said, 'Jackie wasn't a fucking bigot.'

374

'Bigot? Where did you dig that one up, Eddie? We're not talking about bigotry. I believe in what I'm doing. I was born believing in it. That hasn't changed. That doesn't make me a bigot.'

'Okay. What word do you prefer? Patriot? Jackie didn't support this decrepit cause of yours.'

'Did he ever tell you that?'

'When I was a kid, I remember –' He paused, bringing back to mind that night when Jackie and his cronies had sung Orange songs in the living room, and the air smelled of smoke and spilled beer, and he fell into a silence that was oppressive.

'Somebody should point out that it's years since you've been a kid, Eddie.'

'I remember he said there was no difference between people, no matter their religion.' No, those hadn't been his words exactly, he'd phrased it some other way, and Eddie, foundering in the shallows of memory, troubled by this whole situation, couldn't bring back the precise sentences. I've lost my way, he thought.

'He was kidding you, Eddie. He was always a great kidder.'

'No, you must have changed him, you must have influenced his way of thinking –'

'He liked to think for himself, Eddie. He knew where his sympathies lay. They weren't quite so strong as mine, but he knew.'

They'd reached the corner of Onslow Drive. Eddie saw a lamp go on and off in one of the terraced houses. In the brief illumination a middle-aged woman appeared in a window, then vanished, like a figure in the abrupt pop of a flashlight. He thought of Jackie Mallon disappearing in sudden darkness, slipping away, indefinable. *Dad*, he thought. *Just come back for a moment and defend yourself, make your position absolutely clear.*

'I'll report this to the cops,' he said.

She shrugged. 'I don't think you'll go to the police, Eddie.'

'What's stopping me?'

'Let me put it this way, Eddie. We have friends all over the world, Eddie. Sympathizers who see a way of life threatened, and they don't like it. They feel they're being forced into peace on terms they don't want. They see their traditions undermined and the tide's turning against them, and they're in no mood for going under. They don't want to share power with some people whose hands are very very bloody. These friends are serious people.'

He saw it immediately: Claire and Mark. A dark night. A morning at dawn. A new mailman delivering a package. A man pretending there was a fault on the phoneline or a gas leak, anything. Claire's car exploding as she turned the key. Mark struck by a hit-and-run driver while he cycled to school. He imagined empty rooms. Where a wife had been, or a kid, absences. His heart twisted in his chest.

He said, 'I don't believe what you're telling me.'

'I don't have to spell it out, Eddie. I like you. I'm fond of you. We're family, just about. Believe what I'm telling you, that's all I ask.'

'I fucking hate being threatened,' he said.

'Threatened? I was merely mentioning certain possibilities, love.'

He thought of the Mercedes. Automatic weapons in layers darkly shining at the front of the big van, some covered by tarp, a few visible. He had no idea how many. Hundreds of AK-47s or some similar automatic weapon, it was impossible to estimate the number of guns or the diversity of the consignment – there could have been thousands of rounds of ammunition, packs of plastic explosives, scores of grenades, and handguns. Without going back and checking the contents of the van, how could he know?

He gazed the length of Onslow Drive. *Our Orange friends need some hardware, what can you do for us, love?* And Jackie smelled the spoor of profit even as he heard the beating wings of the angels of Protestant righteousness. He'd buy the guns and sell them to Ulster connections at a hefty profit. Guns in oilskins, boxed and buried in fields, hidden in the outbuildings of lonely farmhouses, sunken in pits, concealed and ready for use when the time came.

He looked directly at Senga. *She'd threatened his family.* The full force of that struck him, and he was angry. 'Christ, you're such goddam neanderthals,' he said. 'You and all the people like you. Your marches and your tribal songs and your fucking banners. All right, Glasgow might be more superficially sophisticated these days and you might be better dressed and wear more fashionable clothes and maybe you visit your hairdresser once a week and get your fucking nails done, but the poison is the same as it always was. You're living in the past, and it's barbaric.'

'Believe me, I wish it was different, Eddie. I wish there was trust and peace and happy wee children from both sides of the divide holding hands and singing, believe me. But it's a barbaric world, and you're a part of it as well, so don't criticize me,' Senga said. 'Where the hell do you think the other side get their money and arms from? Smack in the heart of where you live your little bit of the American dream, Eddie Mallon. New York. Boston. Chicago. The money rolls in every time somebody sings "Danny Boy" in an Irish pub. Pass the coinbox. Let me make a contribution to the boyos. Well, we have to defend ourselves against all that cash rolling across the Atlantic into Ulster, Eddie, and there's not a damn thing you can do about it.'

'Now give me the speech about how the weapons are for defensive purposes only,' Eddie said.

'Of course they are, dear,' Senga replied. 'We're a peaceful people. But we're not weak.'

'You'll only shoot if you're shot at, right?'

'Naturally.'

Eddie shook his head: and I was born yesterday. 'What did you and Jackie see in one another, Senga?'

'We loved. We loved a lot.'

'And the Cause,' Eddie hated the sound of the word. 'Was that something you had in common, huh?'

'Oh we had more in common than that, pet. But love's a deep mystery. All kinds of people fall for one another and you never know why. Right?'

377

He looked at her face in lamplight. She was going somewhere with this, and he felt it, and he wanted to kill the conversation, but he waited, fascinated even as he sensed dread.

'Take . . .' She paused. She looked up at the streetlamp, concentrating on the torrent of moths, as if she were trying to count the numbers.

I know what she's going to say, he thought. I feel it coming.

'For instance, your sister,' Senga said. 'What does she see in Caskie? Makes you wonder.'

'You knew about that,' Eddie said.

Senga laughed. 'Oh, for years.'

Eddie sensed the light from the overhead lamp dwindle to little more than a faraway star. 'What about Jackie?' he said.

Don't tell me, he thought.

'Jackie knew from the beginning, Eddie. Jackie knew from the minute the stalls sprang open and Joyce was off and running into Caskie's bed.'

'She was *twelve*, for Christ's sake,' Eddie said.

'Mature for her years,' Senga remarked.

'I can't believe Jackie –'

'Oh, grow up, Eddie. He not only *knew*, he *encouraged* it.'

'I don't *believe*,' Eddie said.

'No skin off my nose,' she said. 'But Jackie wanted his own tame policeman. He thought Caskie might come in handy along the way somehow. So Joyce was deliciously sweet bait. Ripe and fresh, straight off the tree. And Caskie – poor love – he fell so hard it was almost comical. And seeing him try to hide his feelings around Jackie, God, it was farcical.'

Caskie had been handcuffed by Haggs; but Jackie was the one who'd been the original jailer.

Chris Caskie, tame house-broken policeman.

'You might say Jackie pimped his own daughter,' Senga said.

'*Might* say? Is there another expression?'

'I prefer to think of it as a strategic manoeuvre, Eddie. Nightcap?'

378

Eddie refused. He felt cold. Despite the warmth.

Senga said, 'Another time then. Goodnight.'

He watched her walk away, tall and loose in her movements, and he thought about going after her to dispute her version of events, then he decided no, why should he, he'd come to the end of the road. Like every other time he'd tried to exculpate his father, it would be energy wasted and another scar across his heart. There was a limit to the search for excuses: nothing about Jackie Mallon merited tolerance. He deserved to have been shot in the back seat of a car parked on a piece of wasteground on a Glasgow street at twilight, with a whiff of scotch on his breath and his face blown off.

He fucking deserved that kind of ending.

His life had been a bankrupt affair.

Eddie turned and moved slowly down the street in the direction of Joyce's flat. He let himself into the building and climbed the stairs. Bone-weary. Sweating. A man at the end of revelations too heavy to carry. He was dragging his body through time until the moment of departure. He thought about the guns. He thought about Jackie negotiating in Largs with Tommy Gurk. He thought about Caskie and Joyce, and how Jackie had brought them together in the event that he might gain something from that illicit relationship. The cunning and brute insensitivity of it.

Yes, Jackie, fuck you, you deserved your execution.

He unlocked the door of the flat and went inside.

Joyce sat on the sofa with a glass of wine in her hand.

'It's late,' she said.

'And I'm tired.' *You never knew you were used, did you, Joyce?*

She got up from the sofa. 'I heard about McWhinnie and those other killings . . . Chris says the police are turning the city upside down. It's awful to think . . .'

Everything was receding already, Eddie thought. The tenements, the streets, the names of the living and the dead. Joyce put her arms round him. *Yes, dear Joyce, it's awful to think.* He smoothed a strand of hair from her forehead with a gentle gesture. You love Caskie, he thought. You've made a settlement with your emotions.

And you never knew Jackie played the role of a dark cupid, a gargoyle. And Caskie didn't know either.

'I'm sorry I upset you before,' she said.

'I'm over it, Joyce.'

'Are you?'

He nodded. 'I hope it all works out for you. I hope it happens the way you want it to happen.'

'Is that your blessing, Eddie?'

'Bestowed,' he said.

'In a half-hearted way.'

'You expect more?'

'I don't know what I expect,' she said. 'I wish you liked him.'

Eddie said, 'Bad chemistry.'

'No. More than that. Those accusations you made.'

'Let them go, Joyce.' He lay down. The room seemed fuzzy. 'Early rise in the morning.'

She leaned over him, kissed his forehead, and he wanted to cry suddenly. He felt a sadness as black as night in the city. There was the ache of dead hopes inside him.

'Big day,' she said. 'Hard to believe he's gone.'

'Yes.' They held one another tightly for a long time and Eddie remembered the cab that had taken him and Flora away so many years ago, and all the wreckage since, lies, crimes, love misguided, love abused.

61

A hot stillness lay across the city. TV weather maps showed an infinity of clear skies. Forecast: brilliant. More of the same. Eddie sat in his dark suit in the back of a small limo. Joyce, subdued in a black suit, wore sunglasses. And Senga, a small black lace scarf covering her face, sat next to Joyce in silence. She reminded Eddie of a grieving dowager, imposing and dignified in her well-tailored clothes of grief.

The limo travelled east in the direction of Daldowie Crematorium; the car carrying Jackie's coffin was scheduled to arrive at the crematorium at the same time as the limo. The funeral service would begin at 10:30.

Eddie hadn't slept. He'd lain a long time in the dark, too fatigued to sleep. At one point he drank a glass of Joyce's wine but it hadn't helped him over the edge. He called Claire and spoke quietly to her, nothing words, just touching base – everything okay back there? Mark staying out of mischief? He loved the sound of her voice, her calm, the way she had of putting a favourable light on dark circumstances. *Yeah, but how would she deal, say, with letter bombs?* He imagined limbs blown off. His head was filled with images of destruction. He lay staring into the unlit sitting room, and the busts, outlined by a faint light from a streetlamp, seemed to be watching him like the members of a judiciary committee.

Do you really want to put your family in danger?

No, of course I don't.

Then will you say nothing about the armaments?

I can't stay silent. That would be –

What? Unprofessional? Dereliction of duty? Unethical?

All of the above –

And how do you find Jackie Mallon?

Guilty.

No mitigating circumstances?

I've looked hard.

None then?

None.

Bleary, he gazed from the limo into the sun and realized he was travelling deep into eastern regions of the city that were totally unfamiliar, ramshackle industrial buildings, used car lots, run-down housing. He had a sense that none of this was real, he was skirting the threadbare fringes of Glasgow, a man travelling inside a white-lit stereopticon. Something called Parkland. Then Carland. Then Zoo Park. McDonalds. St Peter's Cemetery. He wished he'd worn dark glasses.

He felt Joyce's hand on his own. He squeezed her fingers. He longed for sudden rain, more appropriate weather for funerals, mourners crowded under umbrellas, the miserable drip of water from trees, small puddles on the oiled wood surface of the coffin.

The limo entered the grounds of the crematorium and parked in front of the chapel. Eddie got out, helped Joyce from the car; she looked frail and unprepared for this. He glanced at Senga who raised her veil and smiled at him in a quiet way, and then dropped the veil back. *Remember, Eddie,* she was saying. *Keep in mind our talk.*

He scanned the place. Men in uniforms worked the memorial gardens, surrounded by rich-coloured roses. Here and there

382

people sat on benches in contemplation, remembering their dead. Eddie found himself gazing at the green metal dome of the furnace above the chapel building; heatwaves shimmered from the dome, and the air became liquid. At what temperature did the human body combust? Infernal.

The motorway beyond the memorial grounds droned and droned. There could never be any tranquillity here. Trucks passed day and night, cars, buses.

Joyce took off her glasses. She had that look of bewilderment, a mourner's disbelief: *This can't be happening. We'll wake from this any moment now.* Eddie held her by the elbow and took a few steps with her towards the chapel. He recognized the man from the funeral home, Crichton, dark jacket and pin-striped trousers and an expression of discreet sympathy. He nodded at Eddie very slightly just as Eddie entered the chapel.

Fluorescent lights, cream walls, a ceiling of deep red. Jackie Mallon's coffin sat on a plinth behind which were brass doors. The coffin would slide through those doors and down into the furnace, into that fiery kiln where wood and flesh and bone imploded in hot ash.

He sat beside Joyce. He was aware of Chris Caskie, dark-suited, sitting in the row behind. He felt an odd little flutter of pity for the man. Joe Wilkie sat alongside Senga: conspirators. There were others Eddie had never seen before, neighbours probably, some of Jackie's old friends. At the back, close to the door, was Lou Perlman. He raised a hand in Eddie's direction, a small gesture. Here we all are, Eddie thought, waiting for fire to begin its consummation.

Waiting for Jackie to burn.

A minister, dog-collared and pallid, stepped in front of the plinth. *We come to mourn our friend Jackie Mallon,* he said, and his voice was high-pitched and nasal, and Eddie, in a moment of irreverence, imagined him calling bingo numbers.

We come to remember him, and his kindnesses, and the goodness of his heart. We come to extend our condolences to his family members.

He was a man much loved by his friends and held in high esteem within his community. He was a man who loved life.

Eddie glanced at Caskie. But Caskie, with a distant depressed expression, was looking up at the ceiling, as if he wanted no connection of eyes.

We come today to pray for his soul.

Yes, Eddie thought. Pray hard. If you can find the man's soul. Jackie had lost it long ago in the streets of this city. *Caskie's shagging my daughter and he doesn't know I know. It's a bit of a laugh, intit? Have another glass of cider, Senga, eh?*

Was it only late in life you felt some shame, Jackie?

But it was way too late by then.

Eddie lowered his head, stared at the floor. Don't talk about the weapons. Say nothing, keep them secret. But that went against his grain. Such neglect would come back years later to haunt him, and he'd open a newspaper and read about a fresh atrocity in Ulster, or see a bomb-wrecked house smoulder in a TV film, and what would he feel then? I could have helped. I could have helped just a little. If I don't lift a finger, how will I live with myself? How will I teach my kid anything about truth? Okay, so I take extra security precautions, vigilance at all times, I live as if there's menace in everything, and if it comes right down to it we pick up and move and start all over: it was a lot to ask, a lot to expect. But what else could he demand of himself?

We come to pray that God takes Jackie into the heavenly masses.

Eddie held his sister's hand. She uttered a sob, raised a hand to cover her eyes. Caskie leaned forward and touched her shoulder to comfort her, and Senga, turning a little, observed these small movements from behind the mystery of her veil. Joe Wilkie blew his nose. Somebody else, situated at the back of the chapel, began to cry. Eddie expected he'd feel something, despite himself, maybe a reflex of grief, a spasm of sorrow, but no, he was beyond it now.

He remembered his hand in his father's and Jackie Mallon saying, *I was never a criminal, son. Remember that. If anybody says anything against me at school, learn to ignore it. I was the victim of spiteful men. That's the truth.*

You never knew what truth was, Dad.

Eddie realized music was playing through a sound system and that people around him were getting to their feet and singing 'What A Friend We Have in Jesus'.

I was never a criminal, son.

Eddie thought: You were worse than that.

Curtains closed in front of the coffin. Senga uttered a tiny cry and Joyce wept against Eddie's shoulder, and then he led her up the aisle and out of the chapel into the sun. He looked at the crematorium dome and the waves of heat rising from it, aware that Joyce had wandered away from him and was talking to Caskie, and that Senga, a cigarette in her hand, was surrounded by neighbours and acquaintances who wanted to offer a word of comfort, a hug, a kiss.

Perlman said, 'I like these things brief. Get to the point. I never believed in long-drawn-out funerals. I've been to some where I wished I'd brought a packed lunch and a bloody sleeping bag. Believe me.'

'It was good of you to come,' Eddie said.

'Everything I do has a concealed purpose, Eddie. I'm a cunning old bastard. I've been around the block more times than I can count. Never forget that. I've got my eye, and I mean that in the singular, on a certain person here.'

'Would he be a colleague of yours?'

Perlman said, 'Aye. A few wee problems have cropped up that I need to probe a little further.'

'Such as?'

'They concern poor Charlie McWhinnie and his relationship with Caskie.'

'Tell me.'

'It appears Charlie kept a small if somewhat cryptic personal notebook tucked away in his desk under paper clips and rubber bands,' Perlman said. 'A few entries are intriguing. Something about a safe house in Govan, and Matty Bones – which seem to

385

verify your own suggestions. Also, it seems there were certain irregular orders he took from Caskie beyond the call of duty. Of course, it might just be Charlie's imagination working overtime. He was unhappy with his lot, after all, and unhappy men are sometimes driven to flights of utter fancy.'

'Sometimes,' Eddie said.

'But not in this case,' Perlman said.

'Right.' Eddie looked in the direction of Caskie, who returned the look and smiled a little nervously. Lou Perlman lifted one hand, a lazy gesture of greeting at his colleague. Then Caskie stared away in the direction of men pruning roses.

Eddie watched his sister. Be strong, Joyce. And when things go wrong for you here, when the ground opens up and the plunge is a deep one, you know where I'll be, and you know I'll help. Then he gazed at Senga, tall and seemingly devastated by her grief, red hair tucked under her wide-brimmed black hat, holding court with friends and neighbours. She had a handkerchief in one hand and she stuck it under her veil to wipe her tears away. Eddie couldn't see her eyes, couldn't tell if she was looking at him.

He said, 'I don't see young Ray Wilkie anywhere.'

'Aye, right enough, he's missing,' Perlman said.

'I seem to remember I heard him say he had some overtime to do at the warehouse.'

'On the day of the funeral? Seems strange.' Perlman lit a cigarette and sucked smoke deep. 'There's an odd wee note in your voice, Eddie. Are you trying to tell me something?'

Eddie hesitated. But he knew where he was going and what he had to say. There wasn't a choice. There never had been. 'They had a load of quite fascinating crap inside that big Mercedes van, Lou. Maybe Ray's planning to dump it.'

'What crap?'

'Old tables and chairs, busted lamps, other stuff.'

'You sneaked a peek, did you?'

'I'm a nosy bastard.'

'And you think this van's worth me bothering about?'

Eddie said, 'Yeah. But you didn't hear it from me, Lou.'

386

'An anonymous tip.' Perlman sighed. 'We get a lot of them in this business.'

'Some good,' Eddie said.

'Others pure shite.'

'But you check them all anyway.'

'That's what we do,' Perlman said.

'No sign of Gurk?'

'Not yet. Ah, I daresay we'll find him soon enough.'

Eddie looked in the direction of the green dome and he thought, *You're burning, Jackie, you're ashes now*, and just for a moment he imagined his father hovering above this place, taking form in shifting patterns of light, a malign genie.

Burn, old man, float away, leave us. A father lost for all time.

But he'd always been lost. You only dreamed he might be found, Eddie.

There was a sudden breathless silence as if for a tiny fraction of time Jackie had taken all the sound of the world with him as he turned to flame, then Eddie heard people chattering on all sides of him, and someone crying, and the crinkle of plastic wrapped round a bunch of lilies held in somebody's arms, and Lou Perlman, activated by an anonymous tip, punching numbers into his cellphone.

Eddie felt sun hot on his face and heard the motorway buzzing like a machine fuelled to run for ever and he imagined the city spread out under a haze of heat, and light rise in shimmering films from the Clyde, and he thought: Welcome to Glasgow, and goodbye.

THE IMPERIAL WAR MUSEUM BOOK OF

THE WAR AT SEA 1914–1918

Julian Thompson joined the Royal Marines a month after his eighteenth birthday and served for thirty-four years, retiring as Major-General. His service, mainly in the Royal Marines Commandos, took him to seven continents. He commanded 3rd Commando Brigade, which carried out the initial landings to repossess the Falklands Islands in 1982 and fought most of the subsequent land battles.

He is now visiting professor in the department of War Studies, Kings College, London. He has presented a series of short Second World War commemorative films on BBC 1 and contributes to both newspapers and television documentaries on matters of defence. As well as writing books on military strategy, the Commandos and the Parachute Regiment, Julian Thompson has also written *The Imperial War Museum Book of Victory in Europe*, *The Imperial War Museum Book of War Behind the Enemy Lines*, *The Imperial War Museum Book of the War at Sea 1939–1945*, *The Imperial War Museum Book of the War in Burma 1942–1945* and *The Royal Marines*, and edited *The Imperial War Museum Book of Modern Warfare*.

Also by Julian Thompson

The Imperial War Museum Book of Victory in Europe

The Imperial War Museum Book of Modern Warfare *(editor)*

The Imperial War Museum Book of the War Behind Enemy Lines

The Imperial War Museum Book of the War at Sea 1939–1945

The Imperial War Museum Book of the War in Burma 1942–1945

The Royal Marines

THE IMPERIAL WAR MUSEUM BOOK OF

THE WAR AT SEA

1914–1918

Julian Thompson

PAN BOOKS

in association with

The Imperial War Museum

First published 2005 by Sidgwick & Jackson

This edition published 2006 by Pan Books
an imprint of Pan Macmillan Ltd
Pan Macmillan, 20 New Wharf Road, London N1 9RR
Basingstoke and Oxford
Associated companies throughout the world
www.panmacmillan.com

ISBN-13: 978-0-330-49172-3
ISBN-10: 0-330-49172-5

The publishers gratefully acknowledge The National Archives of the
United Kingdom (UK) for permission to reproduce Vice-Admiral Keyes'
plan of Zeebrugge mole (TNA:PRO ref.ADM 137/3894).

1 3 5 7 9 8 6 4 2

A CIP catalogue record for this book is available from
the British Library.

Typeset by SetSystems Ltd, Saffron Walden, Essex
Printed and bound in Great Britain by
Mackays of Chatham plc, Chatham, Kent

All Pan Macmillan titles are available from
www.panmacmillan.com
or from Bookpost by telephoning +44 (0)1624 677237

Preface

The remarkable unpublished material in the Imperial War Museum's Archives allows voices from ninety years ago to tell us what it was really like to be a sailor or an officer in the Royal Navy, not only in the major sea battles, but in the boredom and perils of the North Sea patrols and convoys in the Atlantic and Mediterranean; the cramped and hazardous conditions in submarines in the Baltic, the Dardanelles, or off the coast of Germany; flying unreliable aircraft over the sea and out of sight of land; young midshipmen and sailors towing boats in to the mayhem of the Gallipoli beaches; finding and fighting the U-boats that brought Britain closer to her knees in the First World War than in the Second. These and many other aspects of the Royal Navy's part in the First World War often get overlooked, perhaps because the controversial one-day Battle of Jutland overshadows them in the minds of so many people. My aim in this book is to ensure that a more complete picture is painted of the nature of the Royal Navy's service under, on, and above the sea.

The navy of nearly one hundred years ago was so different from the service today that I have devoted the first chapter to explaining what it was like to be an officer or rating in King George V's navy. This is also important, because it helps us to understand what made the sailors and officers in 1914 think the way they did, and influenced their approach to the life they led. The First World War navy would appear strange to today's navy, but how much more so to the vast majority of people who have no experience of the sea.

I have little doubt that there were many insufferably arrogant and autocratic captains or admirals in the Royal Navy before and during the First World War; and indeed for many years afterwards. This in no way diminishes my admiration for their achievements, their devotion to duty, and their steadfastness in the face of danger and uncertainty. The odds on them meeting a sudden and gruesome end were no less than those faced by the people they commanded.

As I make plain in my text, it is my conviction that had it not been for the efforts of the Royal Navy, Germany would have won the First World War. In the perception of many naval officers, especially the more senior ones, the Service, to use their terminology, in some respects had a disappointing war. But the navy never failed to provide the shield which enabled the British army to play an increasing, and in the end key, part on what modern soldiers call 'the main point of effort' – the Western Front. With admirable fortitude the officers and ratings manned the ships providing that shield through months and years of boredom often in appalling weather, with the ever-present prospect of being blown to pieces, or choking to death trapped in a compartment or turret as their ship plunged to the bottom.

People of my generation and older, the majority of whom served in, or knew someone in, one of the armed forces, need constant reminding that even middle-aged readers may be unfamiliar with service terminology, hardware, and attitudes. For this reason, I have paused in the narrative from time to time to explain these things; as well as including a glossary. To those who are well versed in such matters, I apologize.

Finally I make no claims for this book being a comprehensive history of the Royal Navy in the First World War.

Quotations   The text contains may direct quotations from written documentary material and interview tapes. These are reproduced verbatim wherever possible, but obvious errors have been corrected and minor confusions clarified. It has not been thought necessary to indicate where quotations have been abridged.

Photographs   All the illustrations in this book have come from the Imperial War Museum Photographic Archive, and have been listed with their accession number in the list of illustrations.

Acknowledgements

As with my previous books in association with the Imperial War Museum it would have been impossible to write this one without the diaries, letters, journals, and taped interviews of the people I have quoted. Their names are listed in the Index of Contributors, as are the names of copyright holders.

All copyright holders with whom I was able to make contact were helpful and kind, but I should like to make special mention of the following who went to considerable trouble on my behalf (the rank of the principals is as they appear in the book, although many of them subsequently achieved higher rank):

Mrs A. G. H. Bachrach, the granddaughter of Commodore C. E. Le Mesurier RN

Mrs P. Baillie-Hamilton. the daughter of Cadet, and later Midshipman, C. Wykeham-Musgrave RN

Mrs George Bower. daughter-in-law of Midshipman, and later Lieutenant, Bower RN

Lady Bowyer-Smyth, widow of Sub-Lieutenant, and later Lieutenant, Bowyer-Smith RN

Mrs Carlisle, daughter of Engineer Lieutenant-Commander R. C. Boddie RN, and his family

Mr D. B. Davies, the nephew of Midshipman F. H. Alderson RN

Mr Mowbray Jackson, the grandson, and Mrs Lynn Mallet Jackson, the daughter, of Midshipman H. A. A. Mallet RN

Colonel King-Harman, the son of Cadet, and later Midshipman, and Lieutenant, R. D. King-Harman RN

General Sir Frank Kitson, the son of Commander H. Kitson RN

Mrs O. R. Moore, the daughter of Commander the Hon. P. G. E. C. Acheson RN

Mr J. A. Spence, the grandson of Lieutenant-Commander F. H. H. Goodhart RN

Mr L. H. W. Williams, the nephew of Cadet, and later Midshipman, H. W. Williams RN, and his cousin Mr David S. W. Williams.

I must also thank Robert Crawford, the Director General, and the senior members of the Staff of the Imperial War Museum, and especially Roderick Suddaby, Keeper of the Department of Documents, who for several years has urged me to write a book about the Royal Navy in the First World War and thereby allow some of the many fascinating collections held in the Department from that period to be published for the first time. His help and advice were invaluable. Simon Robbins, Stephen Walton, Tony Richards and everyone in the Department of Documents were kind and helpful, not least allowing me to join their 'coffee boat'. Christopher Dowling, the Museum's Public Relations Advisor, encouraged me throughout the project. The Sound Archive was as ever a source of much help and new material, and to Margaret Brooks, Keeper of the Sound Archive, and her team, I say thank you. Hilary Roberts, David Parry and the staff of the Photograph Archive were unfailingly helpful and patient, as was the staff of the Department of Printed Books.

I am indebted to the Navy Records Society for allowing me to quote passages from their 2001 publication, *The Submarine Service: 1900–1918*.

William Armstrong of Pan Macmillan despite his long illness has been encouraging and supportive. I am also conscious that I am very lucky that Ingrid Connell is my Editor and Nicholas Blake is my Senior Desk Editor at Pan Macmillan. I value their advice and comment enormously. Wilf Dickie's design expertise is as always very much appreciated.

Jane Thompson has been a source of constant support and advice, as well as a tireless research assistant. Her editorial work has been invaluable, and without her the book would never have seen the light of day.

Contents

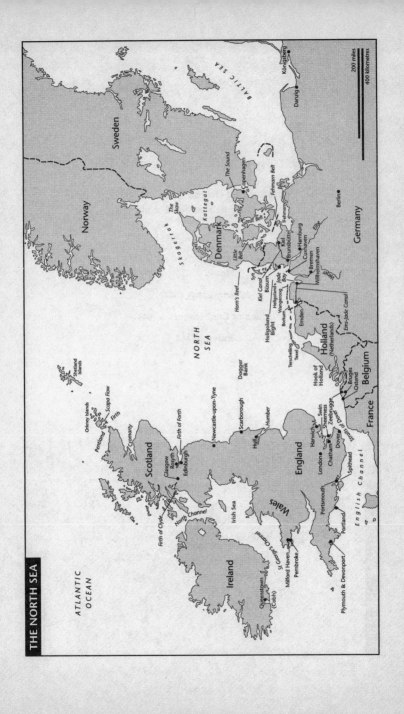

THE NORTH SEA

ATLANTIC
OCEAN

Ireland

Queenstown
(Cobh)

St George's Channel

Milford Haven
Pembroke

Plymouth & Devonport

Wales

Irish Sea

North Channel

Firth of Clyde

Scotland

Glasgow
Rosyth
Edinburgh

Firth of Forth

Cromarty

Pentland Firth

Orkney Islands

Scapa Flow

Shetland Islands

Newcastle-upon-Tyne

Scarborough

Hull

Humber

England

Portsmouth

Portland

Spithead

Chatham

Sheerness

London

Harwich

Swin

Dover

Straits of Dover

English Channel

France

Belgium

Ostend

Bruges

Zeebrugge

Hook of Holland

Texel

Terschelling

Holland
(Netherlands)

Emden

Borkum

Wangeroog

Ems-Jade Canal

Heligoland Bight

Heligoland

Horn's Reef

Sylt

Busum

Kiel Canal

Little Belt

Dogger Bank

NORTH
SEA

Norway

Skagerrak

The Skaw

Kattegat

Denmark

The Sound

Copenhagen

Great Belt

Fehmarn Belt

Fehmarn

Sweden

BALTIC SEA

Kiel

Brunsbüttel

Cuxhaven

Hamburg

Bremen

Wilhelmshaven

Jade Bay

Elbe

Berlin

Germany

Danzig

Königsberg

200 miles

400 kilometres

THE NORTH ATLANTIC OCEAN

Greenland

Iceland

Faroe Islands

Shetland Islands

Orkney Islands

Glasgow

British Isles

Liverpool

Ireland

Berehaven

Queenstown

Plymouth

Le Havre

Ushant

Brest

Bordeaux

Bay of Biscay

Lisbon

Cape St Vincent

Gibraltar

Madeira

Canary Islands

Dakar

Cape Verde Islands

Azores

Cape Race

Gulf of St Lawrence

Sydney

Halifax

Bermuda

Boston

New York

Hampton Roads

Philadelphia

Baltimore

Newport News

Norfolk

The Bahamas

Cuba

Jamaica

Caribbean Sea

Fort-de-France

Barbados

Trinidad

Colon

New Orleans

Gulf of Mexico

NORTH ATLANTIC OCEAN

500 miles

1000 kilometres

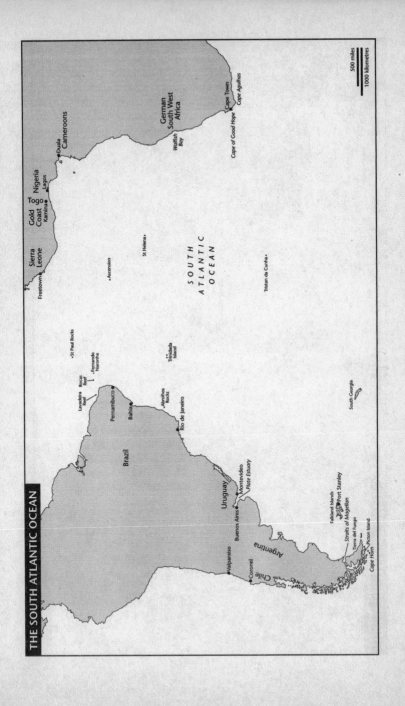

THE SOUTH ATLANTIC OCEAN

500 miles
1000 kilometres

Sierra Leone
Freetown
Gold Coast
Togo
Kamina
Nigeria
Lagos
Duala
Cameroons
German South West Africa
Walfish Bay
Cape Town
Cape Agulhas
Cape of Good Hope

St Helena
Ascension

SOUTH ATLANTIC OCEAN

Tristan da Cunha

St Paul Rocks
Fernando Naronha
Trinidad Island
Rocas Reef
Lavadeira Reef
Pernambuco
Bahia
Abrolhos Rocks
Rio de Janeiro

Brazil

South Georgia

Uruguay
Montevideo
Plate Estuary
Buenos Aires

Valparaiso
Coronel
Chile
Argentina

Falkland Islands
Port Stanley
Straits of Magellan
Tierra del Fuego
Picton Island
Cape Horn

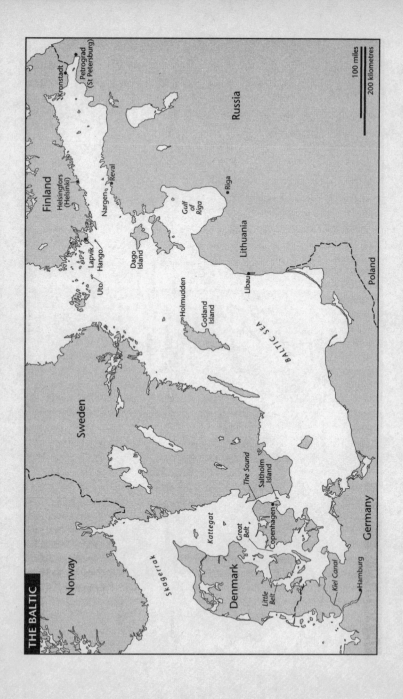

THE BALTIC

Norway

Sweden

Finland

Kronstadt
Petrograd
(St Petersburg)

Helsingfors
(Helsinki)

Lapvik
Uto Hango

Nargen Reval

Dago
Island

Gulf
of
Riga

Riga

Russia

Lithuania

Libau

Holmudden

Gotland
Island

BALTIC SEA

Poland

Skagerrak

Kattegat

The Sound

Saltholm
Island

Great
Belt

Copenhagen

Denmark

Little
Belt

Kiel Canal

Hamburg

Germany

100 miles

200 kilometres

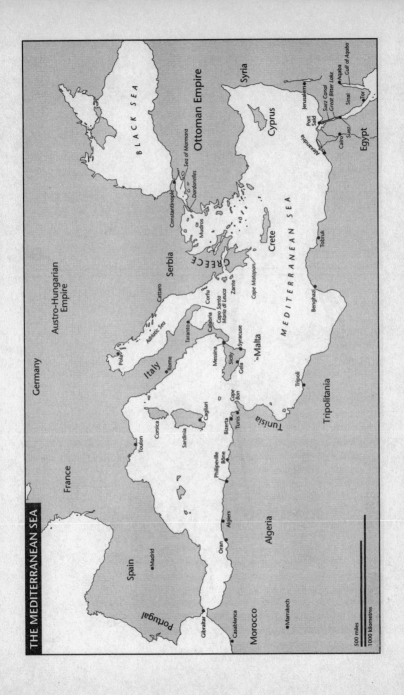

THE MEDITERRANEAN SEA

Germany

France

Spain

Madrid

Portugal

Gibraltar

Casablanca

Morocco

Marrakech

Algeria

Oran

Algiers

Toulon

Corsica

Sardinia

Cagliari

Philippeville

Bône

Bizerta

Tunis

Tunisia

Cape Bon

Tripolitania

Tripoli

Austro-Hungarian
Empire

Adriatic Sea

Pola

Italy

Rome

Taranto

Cattaro

Calabria

Capo Santa
Maria di Leuca

Corfu

Zante

Messina

Sicily

Gela

Syracuse

Malta

Serbia

GREECE

Cape Matapan

Benghazi

Crete

MEDITERRANEAN SEA

BLACK SEA

Sea of Marmara

Dardanelles

Constantinople

Mudros

Ottoman Empire

Syria

Cyprus

Jerusalem

Port Said

Alexandria

Cairo

Suez

Suez Canal

Great Bitter Lake

Aqaba

Gulf of Aqaba

Sinai

Tor

Egypt

Tobruk

500 miles

1000 kilometres

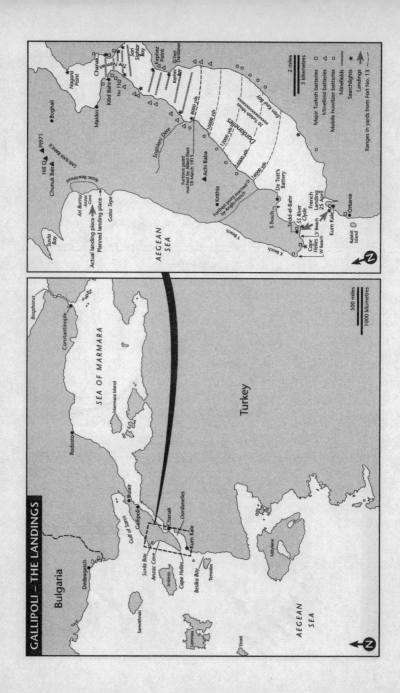

GALLIPOLI – THE LANDINGS

Bulgaria

Dedeagatch

Samothraki

Gulf of Saros

Bulair

Gallipoli

Rodosto

SEA OF MARMARA

Marmara Island

Constantinople

Bosphorus

Suvla Bay

Anzac Cove

Imbros

Cape Helles

Besika Bay

Tenedos

Chanak

Dardanelles

Kum Kale

Turkey

Lemnos

Strati

Mytilene

AEGEAN
SEA

N

500 miles

1000 kilometres

Suvla Bay

Chunuk Bair ▲

Hill Q ● ▲ P971

SARI BAIR RANGE ▲

Ari Burnu

Anzac Cove

Anzac Beachhead

Gaba Tepe

Sogbanli Dere

Furthest point
reached by Allied Fleet
18 March 1915

● Krithia

Furthest point reached
by Anglo-French

▲ Achi Baba

Maidos ●

Boghali ●

Kilid Bahr ●

No 13 □

Nagara Point

Chanak

Sari Sighlar
Bay

The Narrows

Kephez
Point

Kephez
Bay

Fort
Dardanos

1000 yds

8000 yds

10000 yds

20 Turkish mines

Kere Keui Bay

Dardanelles

12000 yds

14000 yds

16000 yds

18000 yds

Y Beach

X Beach

W Beach

Cape
Helles

S Beach

Sedd-el-Bahr

SS River
Clyde

De Tott's
Battery

French
Landing
25 April

Kum Kale

Rabbit
Island

Orkanie ●

AEGEAN SEA

Actual landing place

Planned landing place

Major Turkish batteries □

Mobile howitzer batteries △

Minefield batteries ○

Minefields xxx

Searchlights ★

Landings ↔

Ranges in yards from Fort No. 13

N

2 miles

3 kilometres

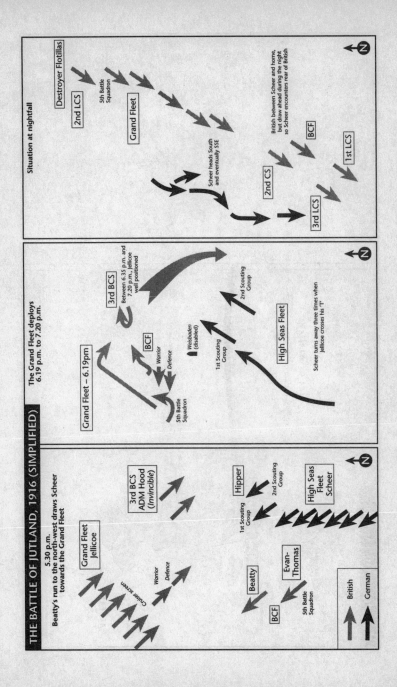

THE BATTLE OF JUTLAND, 1916 (SIMPLIFIED)

5.30 p.m.
Beatty's run to the north-west draws Scheer towards the Grand Fleet

Grand Fleet
Jellicoe

3rd BCS
ADM Hood
(*Invincible*)

Cruiser Screen

Warrior
Defence

Hipper

2nd Scouting Group

1st Scouting Group

High Seas Fleet
Scheer

Beatty

BCF

Evan-Thomas

5th Battle Squadron

British

German

N

The Grand Fleet deploys
6.19 p.m. to 7.20 p.m.

Grand Fleet – 6.19pm

3rd BCS

Between 6.35 p.m. and 7.20 p.m. Jellicoe is well positioned

BCF

Warrior
Defence

5th Battle Squadron

Weisbaden (disabled)

2nd Scouting Group

1st Scouting Group

High Seas Fleet

Scheer turns away three times when Jellicoe crosses his 'T'

N

Situation at nightfall

Destroyer Flotillas

2nd LCS

5th Battle Squadron

Grand Fleet

British between Scheer and home, but draw ahead during the night so Scheer encounters rear of British

Scheer heads South and eventually SSE

2nd CS

BCF

3rd LCS

1st LCS

N

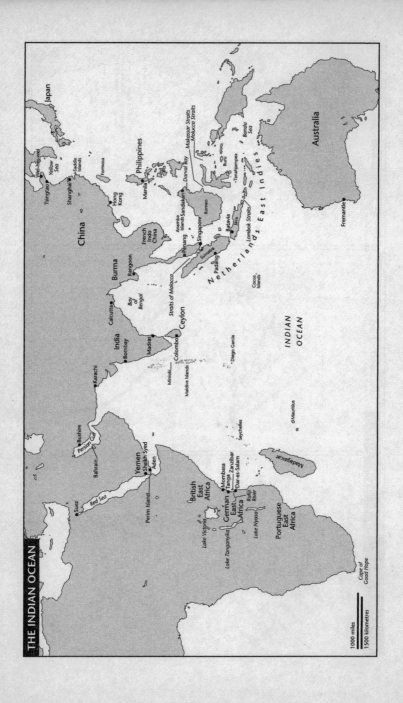

THE INDIAN OCEAN

Japan

China

Burma

India

Yemen

British
East
Africa

German
East
Africa

Portuguese
East
Africa

Philippines

French
Indo
China

Ceylon

Netherlands East Indies

Sumatra

Java

Australia

INDIAN
OCEAN

Wei-Hai-Wei
Tsingtao
Shanghai
Saddle
Islands
Yellow
Sea
Hong Kong
Formosa

Manila

Rangoon
Calcutta
Bay
of
Bengal
Bombay
Madras
Straits of Malacca
Penang
Singapore
Colombo
Minikoi
Maldive Islands
Diego Garcia
Cocos
Islands

Karachi
Bushire
Bahrain
Persian Gulf
Aden
Sheikh Syed
Perim Island
Suez
Red Sea

Mombasa
Tanga
Dar-es-Salam
Zanzibar
Lake Victoria
Lake Tanganyika
Lake Nyasa
Rufiji
River

Seychelles
Mauritius
Madagascar

Anamba
Islands
Sandakan
Borneo
Darvel Bay
Batavia
Lombok Straits
Makassar Straits
Molucca Straits
Banda
Sea
Buru
Tanahjampea

Fremantle

Cape of
Good Hope

1000 miles
1500 kilometres

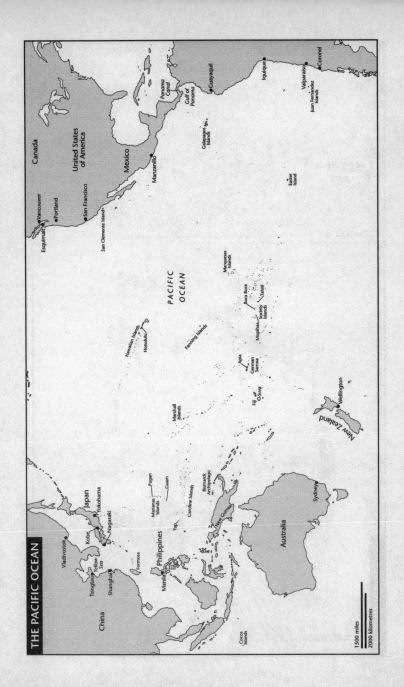

THE PACIFIC OCEAN

Canada

United States
of America

Mexico

Esquimalt
Vancouver
Portland
San Francisco
San Clemente Island

Manzanillo

Panama Canal
Gulf of Panama
Guayaquil
Iquique
Valparaiso
Coronel
Juan Fernandez Islands

Galapagos Islands

Easter Island

PACIFIC OCEAN

Marquesas Islands

Hawaiian Islands
Honolulu

Fanning Islands

Bora Bora
Tahiti
Society Islands
Mopiha

Apia
German Samoa

Suva
Fiji

Marshall Islands

New Zealand
Wellington

Vladivostok

Japan
Kobe
Yokohama
Nagasaki

Tsingtau
Yellow Sea
Shanghai

China

Formosa

Philippines
Manila

Marianas Islands
Pagan
Guam

Yap

Caroline Islands

Bismarck Archipelago

New Guinea

Australia

Sydney

Cocos Islands

1500 miles
2000 kilometres

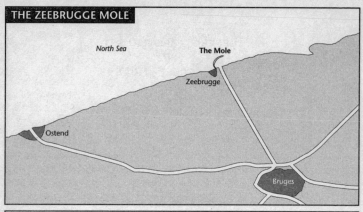

THE ZEEBRUGGE MOLE

North Sea

The Mole

Zeebrugge

Ostend

Bruges

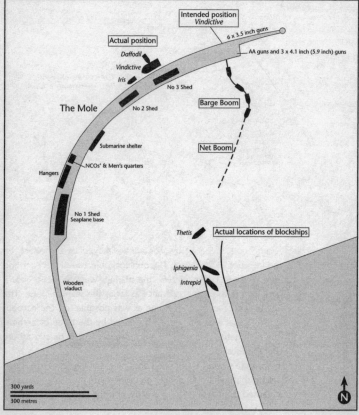

Intended position
Vindictive

6 x 3.5 inch guns

AA guns and 3 x 4.1 inch (5.9 inch) guns

Actual position

Daffodil

Vindictive

Iris

No 3 Shed

Barge Boom

No 2 Shed

The Mole

Submarine shelter

Net Boom

NCOs' & Men's quarters

Hangers

No 1 Shed
Seaplane base

Thetis

Actual locations of blockships

Iphigenia

Intrepid

Wooden
viaduct

300 yards

300 metres

N

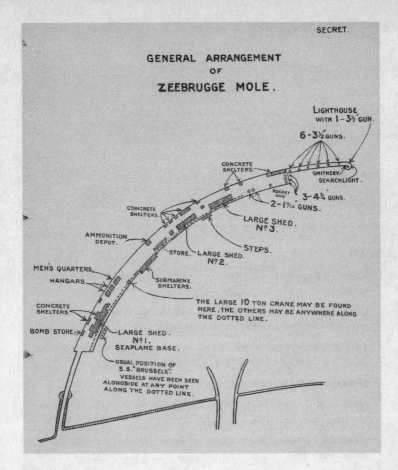

GENERAL ARRANGEMENT
OF
ZEEBRUGGE MOLE.

LIGHTHOUSE,
WITH 1 - 3½" GUN.

6 - 3½" GUNS.

CONCRETE
SHELTERS.

SMITHERY.
SEARCHLIGHT.

ROCKET
GUN

3 - 4¾" GUNS.

2 - 1⁵⁄₁₆" GUNS.

CONCRETE
SHELTERS.

LARGE SHED.
Nº 3.

AMMUNITION
DEPOT.

STEPS.

STORE. LARGE SHED.
Nº 2.

MEN'S QUARTERS.

HANGARS

SUBMARINE
SHELTERS.

CONCRETE
SHELTERS

THE LARGE 10 TON CRANE MAY BE FOUND
HERE, THE OTHERS MAY BE ANYWHERE ALONG
THE DOTTED LINE.

BOMB STORE.

LARGE SHED.
Nº I.
SEAPLANE BASE.

USUAL POSITION OF
S.S. "BRUSSELS".
VESSELS HAVE BEEN SEEN
ALONGSIDE AT ANY POINT
ALONG THE DOTTED LINE.

The plan of Zeebrugge mole prepared by Vice-Admiral Keyes for the attack on 22/23 April 1918 and included in his report. The principal objective of the storming party was the capture of the 4.1 inch battery; the marines were to secure No. 3 shed to prevent attack up the mole, then advance as far as the seaplane base. The demolition party was to 'inflict as much damage as was possible' on the harbour works and defences. The canal entrance was to be closed by the three blockships: *Thetis* would ram the lock gates, and *Intrepid* and *Iphigenia* would be run ashore at the southern end of the escalade.

The modern plan opposite shows the intended position of the *Vindictive*, the actual positions of the attacking ships while the landing parties were on the mole, the barge and net booms that caused the *Thetis* to ground early, and the final positions of the blockships.

Glossary

Albert Medal – An award for bravery for an action not in the face of the enemy. After the institution of the George Cross, living holders of the Albert Medal could, if they so wished, exchange it for the George Cross.

BE2a – A biplane with engine in front, of British manufacture.

BOATS

barge – A flag officer's or captain's boat. Usually had a hand-picked crew.

Carley float(s) – Rafts carried on the sides of a ship's upperworks that were released when a ship was about to sink.

cutter – A broad-beamed boat with a square stern. It could be rowed or sailed, and was used for carrying light stores or passengers.

Montagu whaler – The Royal Navy whaler. (See **whaler**.)

picket boat – A large steam-driven boat. It was too big to be carried by anything other than major warships as it had to be lowered by crane.

pinnace – A small eight-oared boat, or (steam pinnace) a small steam-driven boat.

sea boat – A boat ready for immediate lowering from the ship's davits at sea for such tasks as picking up a man overboard, or boarding other vessels. Usually a whaler. (See **whaler**.)

service boat – Any Royal Naval boat.

whaler – A boat pointed at both ends, and propelled by oars or sail, originally designed for whaling, and steered by an oar rather than a rudder. The naval version was a twenty-seven-foot-long yawl-rigged boat (two masts which could be unshipped when under oars) with five oars and steered by rudder fitted with a yoke whose ropes passed each side of the mizzen mast. It had a drop keel for sailing close-hauled. The sea boat was usually a whaler.

bridge dodger – A canvas screen erected to make bridge railing higher and provide some cover from driving spray.

brigantine – A sailing vessel with two masts, the foremast with square sails and the mainmast with square topsails but a fore-and-aft mainsail.

broadside mess – Broadside mess takes its name from warships whose guns were arranged to fire out of the ship's side through gunports in a broadside. In these ships, sailors lived on the gundecks, and at mealtimes tables were let down from the deckhead (ceiling to the landsman) between the guns. This arrangement can be seen in HMS *Victory* and *Warrior* in Portsmouth Dockyard. When guns were mounted in turrets and batteries, sailors ate on their messdecks, not among the guns, but these messes were referred to as broadside messes. This arrangement persisted until well after the Second World War.

This should not be confused with the term 'broadside messing', which with 'canteen messing' was one of the two systems of messing for ratings in the Royal Navy until well after the Second World War (see also canteen, and canteen messing). During that war general messing began to be introduced, with all ratings eating in a central dining room (or main galley, to give it its proper nautical name), and helping themselves cafeteria style.

In broadside messing the paymaster drew up a menu for all the lower deck members of the ship's company. The ship's cooks prepared the rations and cooked them in bulk, and each mess sent a 'cook' to collect the rations from the galley at meal times. If there were ten men in the mess, ten meals were supplied, or rather a portion for ten men. All messes were on the same menu, whether chief petty officers, petty officers or leading, able, and ordinary seamen in their broadside messes.

canteen – There were no canteens as understood today, selling a range of goods from razor blades to soft drinks ('goffers' to sailors of the late twentieth and early twenty-first centuries). Canteens merely stocked items to augment the basic ration.

canteen messing – Canteen messing is described by James Cox on p. 32. The meals so produced were also consumed in a broadside mess.

casing – The outer, top skin of a submarine, not part of the pressure hull. Water flows in and out when dived, and on the surface.

close blockade – A blockade of an enemy's coast by stationing ships within sight of that coast. In the Napoleonic Wars the Royal Navy maintained a continuous blockade of France and her Continental allies and defeated neighbours. This was possible because sailing ships could stay at sea for years. It would have been hazardous to maintain a close blockade against Germany in the First World War in the face of submarines, mines, and torpedo boats. But most dangerous, the High Seas Fleet, sitting safe in harbour, could have chosen its moment to bring overwhelming force to bear against the blockading force which because of the need to replenish with fuel and other stores could not have maintained itself at full strength for protracted periods. (See also **distant blockade**.)

commander – A rank and an appointment. In the latter sense, the executive officer or second-in-command of a major warship, cruiser or bigger.

conning tower – In a warship, an armoured compartment under the bridge, to which the captain could retire to take cover in action, and from which the ship was 'conned', i.e. commanded, and its course and speed directed. An early, if not the first example of a conning tower can be seen in HMS *Warrior* in Portsmouth. Fisher was the gunnery lieutenant in *Warrior*.

In a submarine, it is the tower on the top of the casing, which contains the bridge, and from which the boat is 'conned' when on the surface. A submarine conning tower is not part of the pressure hull, and water flows in to it to equalize the pressure to prevent it being crushed when the boat is dived.

coxswain – The senior chief petty officer or petty officer in a small war vessel, such as a destroyer or submarine. Usually took the helm in action.

dead ground – Ground into which observers cannot see because higher ground intervenes between them and target or enemy.

destroyer – See **torpedo-boat destroyer**.

dinner – The midday meal.

director firing – Firing the guns centrally from the gunnery director, a cabinet high up on the mast manned by the gunnery officer and his team. From this elevated position, above smoke and shell splashes, he was best placed to spot the fall of shot. Director firing was in the process of being introduced at the outbreak of the First World War. The guns in ships not fitted for director firing, or if fitted, when the director was knocked out, were controlled locally through a periscope in the back of the turret. (See **turret**.)

distant blockade – Blockading an enemy's coast from a distance, often several hundred miles, to preserve ships and crews. Because of geography, Britain controlled Germany's exits to the Atlantic and hence the world, and was able to maintain a distant blockade. (See also **close blockade**.)

division – Not to be confused with the army formation of that name. In the context of the Royal Navy the term had three meanings:

1. Part of a squadron or flotilla of warships.

2. The purely administrative sub-units into which a ship's company was, and is still divided. e.g. main top division, fore top division, etc. A lieutenant or lieutenant-commander was responsible for the welfare and day-to-day administration of the ratings in his division. Divisions did not fight as a body, and its ratings might be found in several different places in the ship both for day-to-day work and at action stations.

3. The port divisions, Devonport, Portsmouth, and Chatham, to which ratings belonged and returned when not at sea. A ship's company would all come from the same division.

DSC – Distinguished Service Cross, instituted in 1914, and awarded to officers of the Royal Navy (and Royal Marines when serving under naval command) for gallantry in action. Now all ranks are eligible.

DSM – Distinguished Service Medal. An award for gallantry for ratings. Now discontinued.

DSO – Distinguished Service Order, instituted in 1886, and until the awards system was changed in 1994, a dual-role decoration, recognizing gallantry at a level just below that qualifying for the VC by junior officers, and exceptional leadership in battle by senior officers. Officers of all three services were and are eligible. Since 1994, it is far less prestigious, and awarded for successful command and leadership in 'operational' circumstances. What constitutes 'operations' is open to question, since DSOs appear to 'come up with the rations' after so-called operations, such as Kosovo, when not a shot was fired in anger, whereas DSOs for tough fighting in Iraq were too sparsely awarded.

first lieutenant – The second-in-command of a small ship, vessel or submarine, which does not carry a commander. Sometimes known as the executive officer. In a large warship, there was, and is, a first lieutenant and a commander. In these circumstances the first lieutenant could be a lieutenant-commander.

fix – To 'fix' one's position on a chart by taking bearings from objects on land or by astral navigation.

flag captain – The captain of a flagship.

flaming onions – Forces' nickname for an anti-aircraft projectile consisting of about ten balls of fire fired upwards in succession, and looking like a string of onions on fire.

frightfulness – Slang expression used by the British in the First World War as a translation of the German *schrecklichkeit*, implying a deliberate policy of terrorizing the enemy, including civilians. By extension, when one was under bombardment one was being 'treated to frightfulness'.

flat – An open space below decks in a ship. Not an apartment.

group up, group down – Submarine terms for adding more batteries to increase electric power, or reducing number of batteries grouped together to decrease power, when submerged.

HE – High explosive.

hydrophones – Underwater listening device to detect a ship's or a submarine's propeller noise.

IS-WAS – A circular slide rule invented by the then Lieutenant-Commander Martin Nasmith VC Royal Navy in 1917. It was a simple device, and usually hung round the neck of the CO from a lanyard. The IS-WAS got its name from the problem faced by all COs in computing the director angle (DA), or where you had to point the submarine in order to obtain a hit. Because the submarine and target were both moving, computing the DA for where the target is now only identified where the target 'was' a second ago. But the target moved and so 'is' somewhere else a second later, so the DA had changed. The IS-WAS helped the CO compute where the target would be in future, assuming constant speed and course. I am indebted to the Trustees of the RN Submarine Museum for this information who sent me copies of archive material A1977/023 in support of my research.

libertymen – Sailors going ashore on leave, or on leave.

lighter – A large, flat-bottomed craft, without its own power, towed by steam picket boat, tugs, or occasionally a ship, used to transport heavy stores, coal, horses, and large numbers of men in an anchorage or harbour. Modified at Gallipoli especially as an ad hoc landing craft or pier, for lack of anything better.

lyddite – A high explosive with a picric acid content used in British shells. Named after Lydd in Kent, where it was first tested in 1888.

mess deck – Space in which ratings slept, ate and spent their time off. The size depended on the type of ship, the number of people in the mess deck, and the space available.

monitor – A shallow-draught warship with one or more large guns, designed to close the coast to bombard.

paravanes – Torpedo-shaped floats, deployed on wires one each side of the bows of the ship when underway. Each float was fitted with 'planes' or fins, like a miniature submarine. When water flowed over them, caused by the forward way of the ship, the 'planes' made the float dive to and maintain a set depth below the surface of the sea.

Paravanes had originally been invented to allow ships to survive if they unexpectedly found themselves in minefields. The wire caught the cable anchoring the mine to the bottom, and pushed the mine away from the ship, until the ship was clear. Paravane wires could be fitted with cutters to cut the mine cable and allow it to bob to the surface where it was destroyed by gunfire. This was the technique used in sweeping mines.

Paravanes would not justify manoeuvring in waters known to be mined, however, because at full speed and under full helm, the paravane on the outside of the turn came in much closer to the ship, and the stern swept quite a broad path of water, half sideways, which suited a mine perfectly.[1]

The explosive paravane was a device introduced to try to find and destroy a submerged submarine. It was not a successful weapon, accounting for a possible maximum of two U-boats throughout the war.

RANK (First World War)

Royal Navy – Army
Admiral of the Fleet – Field Marshal
Admiral – General
Vice-Admiral – Lieutenant General
Rear Admiral – Major General
Commodore First Class – Brigadier General
Commodore – No equivalent
Captain – Colonel
Commander – Lieutenant Colonel
Lieutenant-Commander[2] – Major
Lieutenant – Captain
Sub-Lieutenant – Lieutenant
No equivalent – 2nd Lieutenant
Midshipman – *No equivalent*
Warrant Officer – *No equivalent*

> *No equivalent* – Regimental Sergeant Major
> *No equivalent* – Company Sergeant Major
> Chief Petty Officer[3] – Colour Sergeant
> Petty Officer – Sergeant
> Leading Seaman – Corporal
> Able Seaman – Lance Corporal
> Ordinary Seaman – Private

rating(s) – All non-commissioned personnel, i.e. chief petty officers and below, were ratings.

sea and wind states – The Beaufort Scale, numerically 0 to 12, is used to describe wind velocity and sea state. So 4 on the Beaufort Scale indicates a wind speed of 11–16 knots: moderate breeze, sea small waves, becoming longer, fairly frequent horses. Force 11 indicates a wind speed of 56 to 63 knots: violent storm, exceptionally high waves; the sea is completely covered with long white patches of foam lying along the direction of the wind; everywhere the edges of wave crests are blown into froth. Visibility affected; possible maximum wave height is 16 metres (52.49 feet).

slip – To cast off a ship from a buoy or dockyard wall. To cast off from a buoy, a slip rope is rove from the ship, through the ring on the buoy, and back to the ship. The bridles, specially made-up wire hawsers, or chain cable, are then cast off. When ready to get under way, one end of the slip rope is let go, and the other end hauled aboard. To cast off from a dockyard wall, wires or ropes (warps) are singled up (reduced to a minimum) and at the right moment, dockyard hands cast the remaining warps off. The crew of a small vessel may rig slip ropes fore and aft and cast themselves off without assistance from dockyard mateys. (See also **weigh**.)

stokehold – The hold from which the coal is shovelled into the furnaces heating the boilers. It is replenished from adjacent coal bunkers.

torpedo boat (TB) – Small fast steam-driven vessels first commissioned into the Royal Navy in 1877. They had a swivelling torpedo tube to deliver the new Whitehead torpedo, which was propelled by compressed air. By the outbreak of the First World War, torpedo boats were relegated to harbour protection and coastal patrolling. See torpedo-boat destroyer.

torpedo-boat destroyer (TBD) – Introduced to counter the threat posed by torpedo boats, it was eventually equipped with torpedo tubes and took over the torpedo boat's role, and many others. The name was soon shortened to destroyer.

turret – Sometimes referred to as the gun house. Below is a diagram of X Turret in the *Queen Mary*, showing the typical layout of a battle cruiser or battleship turret.

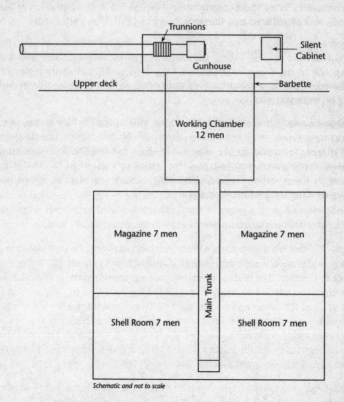

Schematic and not to scale

VC – Victoria Cross, the highest British award for bravery in the face of the enemy. To date, in the 149 years since its inception by Queen Victoria after the Crimean War of 1854–56, only 1,354 VCs have been awarded, including a handful of double VCs, and the one presented to the American Unknown Warrior at Arlington. This figure includes the many awarded to Imperial, Commonwealth, and Dominion servicemen.

Voisin – A 'pusher' aircraft, of French manufacture with engine and propeller behind the aircrew.

weigh – To hoist in the anchor. (See also **slip**.)

wireless – Wireless telegraphy (literally, sending telegrams without wires). The first demonstration was by Marconi, and witnessed on Isle of Wight in May 1898 by group of senior Royal Navy officers, including the then Commander Evan-Thomas (later Rear Admiral 5th Battle Squadron at Jutland), and introduced into the Royal Navy in 1898. Now called radio.

yeomanry – British volunteer cavalry force originally raised by Pitt the Younger's Act of 1794 calling for formations of volunteer cavalry troops in response to the threat of invasion by the French. All Yeomanry regiments were mobilized in 1914 and served either dismounted or mounted depending on the theatre of operations.

xebec – A small three-masted vessel, found only in the Mediterranean, often with square sails on foremast and lateen sails on the others. The rig could be altered depending on the direction of the wind and the desired point of sailing. Xebecs were very fast, and hence used by corsairs in the Mediterranean in the seventeenth and eighteenth centuries, a practice which had long died out by the First World War.

Prologue: They will come out

At 0900 on Thursday 21 November 1918, the British Grand Fleet came to action stations in accordance with the orders issued by their Commander-in-Chief, Admiral Sir David Beatty. The fleet, consisting of fourteen squadrons with accompanying destroyer flotillas led by the cruiser *Cardiff*, had weighed anchor at 0250 and steamed out of the Firth of Forth, the miles of ships at 18 knots taking nearly four hours to pass May Island at the mouth of the Firth. In ten minutes' time they were due to meet the German High Seas Fleet; not to do battle, but to escort it into internment.

As the High Seas Fleet approached, led by its flagship *Friedrich der Große*, the Grand Fleet in accordance with Beatty's orders turned so that the German ships in a single line were sandwiched between their escorts on course for the anchorage off Inchkeith.

Three days later, Beatty addressed the ship's companies of the 1st Battle Cruiser Squadron (1 BCS) assembled on the quarterdeck of HMS *Lion*, once his flagship. After thanking them for what they had done over the past four years, he told them: 'I have always said in the past that the High Seas Fleet would have to come out and meet the Grand Fleet. I was not a false prophet; they are out, and they are now in. They are in our pockets, and the 1st Battle Cruiser Squadron is going to look after them.' He went on to articulate the bitter disappointment he, and they, felt that it should have ended thus, in a tame surrender. For the internment of the High Seas Fleet was the direct result of the great victory won in France by the French, American, and above all the five British Armies under Field Marshal Sir Douglas Haig. The German High Seas Fleet had not been beaten in battle. A more accurate description of its state would be cowed into a state of sullen dejection, following its encounter with the Grand Fleet at Jutland in 1916. Wild plans by High Seas Fleet officers to sortie for a 'death ride' encounter with the Grand Fleet in November 1918 resulted in mutiny by crews infiltrated by Bolshevik agitators. Beatty alluded to what he called the military successes in one sentence in his address, but when he said that the war had been won by sea-power, he was speaking nothing less than the truth –

although understandably, given who he was addressing, he gave the impression that the Grand Fleet alone had been responsible for the triumph of sea-power, whereas the Grand Fleet was but one part of the maritime instrument that had enabled Britain to win the war at sea. For Britain nearly lost it, to the U-boat, and there was nothing the Grand Fleet could contribute directly to winning that contest.

The Grand Fleet's role was to be the shield behind which a multitude of other activities could be prosecuted. It was a role fulfilled: for example, major units of the German navy were unable to stop the smooth transportation of the British army to France or disrupt its cross-Channel line of communication for over four years. Germany was blockaded from the first day of the war, and the population was eventually reduced to a state of starvation and low morale, arguably achieved far more effectively by sea-power in the First World War than by the strategic-bomber offensive of the Second. British trade was allowed to flow; it was not without interference from surface raiders, but these were eventually sunk, because the cruisers that sought them out and brought them to battle could operate without fear of the battleships and battle cruisers of the High Seas Fleet, which, despite its name, was kept from the high seas by its jailer, the Grand Fleet.

So Germany resorted to unrestricted submarine warfare, which nearly brought Britain to its knees, mostly because of an incorrect initial response by the Admiralty. The pay-off, as far as the Entente Powers (France, Britain, and Russia) were concerned, was bringing America in to the war on their side, while, eventually, the application of correct tactics defeated the U-boats. Throughout the First World War, the Royal Navy exercised sea-power all over the globe in numerous ways, as it had done for over two centuries. As summarized by the naval historian Professor Marder, the purpose of British sea-power since well before the outbreak of the war was to maintain command of the sea in order to:

1. Defeat the enemy fleet
2. Deny the sea to enemy commerce
3. Support amphibious operations
4. Smash any attempt at an invasion of the United Kingdom
5. Ensure the uninterrupted maritime flow of supplies and food.

Readers can judge for themselves how well the Royal Navy fulfilled this five-fold aim.

1

The Royal Navy in 1914:
'the best navy in the world'

> The fact is that in 1914 the Royal Navy was almost totally unprepared for war and remained in that condition for most of the period 1914–18
>
> – Commander Stephen King-Hall[1]

If by a magical process an average early twenty-first-century man or woman was transported, without warning, back to Wednesday 29 July 1914, five days before Britain declared war on Germany, and positioned well out at sea off Weymouth Bay, he or she would see the Home Fleet steaming out of Portland Harbour. In the heat shimmer of that baking summer day the grey silhouettes would appear little different from those of today's ships, except perhaps to a naval 'buff'. Our hypothetical observer, unaware that most of the vessels were coal-burners, might have remarked that they appeared to be polluting the air with smoke, and muttered something about 'global warming' and complaining to the environmental agency. Had the same magic allowed our twenty-first-century observer to zoom in close enough to see the officers and ratings on the bridges of these ships, their uniforms would have seemed no different from the number-one dress worn today. The hundred years between the end of the Napoleonic Wars and the outbreak of the First World War had seen changes as rapid as those between 1914 and the present. Yet no one could possibly fail to notice the difference between the *Thunderer* of 1805 and her 1914 dreadnought namesake; and the officers' uniforms, or in the case of the ratings the lack of them, in the Royal Navy of Trafalgar would be unmistakable.

Because of superficial similarities between George V's navy and his granddaughter's, it is easy sometimes to fall into the trap of judging every aspect of the navy of nearly a century ago by the standards of today. But as L. P. Hartley remarked, 'The past is a foreign country: they do things differently there.' They did indeed do things very differently in 1914, and in the preceding years. The Victorian ethic of obedience with every man and woman in his or her place was taken for granted, and in the Royal Navy of 1914 every officer, midshipman, and rating on the active list had been born during the reign of Queen Victoria. The more senior officers had spent far the greater part of their service in her navy. Admiral Sir John 'Jacky' Fisher, brought out of retirement to serve a second term as First Sea Lord in October 1914, had been nominated for the Royal Navy in 1854 by the last of Nelson's captains still on the active list, Admiral Sir William Parker, Commander-in-Chief Plymouth.[2] At twenty-two, Fisher had been the gunnery lieutenant of Britain's first iron-clad warship, HMS *Warrior*, in 1863. Thirty years later, when Admiral Tryon's flagship HMS *Victoria* was accidentally rammed and sunk by HMS *Camperdown* off Tripoli, *Victoria*'s commander, or executive officer, John Jellicoe, was one of the survivors. Twenty-one years on, at the outbreak of war, he was appointed to command the Grand Fleet.

One distinguished author has referred to the period between 1815 and 1914 as 'The Long Calm Lee of Trafalgar'.[3] The Battle of Navarino in 1827 was the sole fleet action in those ninety-nine years. Britannia's rule over the waves was challenged not by battles but by attempts to build better ships, first by France and then by Germany. The French challenge was seen off most notably by the launch in 1860 of the ironclad *Warrior*, in her day the most powerful warship in the world. Subsequently Germany posed a more serious threat. That is not to say that there was no fighting involving the Royal Navy; but much of it was on land. All but four of the forty VCs awarded to the navy in the sixty years between the medal's inception in 1856 after the Crimean War and August 1914 had been won in actions by landing parties and so-called 'naval brigades'.[4] The navy lacked experience in sea fighting, and, until 1911, a staff to study how maritime operations might be conducted in future; it is hardly surprising that Captain Herbert Richmond, one of the cerebral senior officers in the Royal Navy of 1914, could say, 'There is no doubt that we are the most appalling amateurs who ever tried to conduct a war.'

Most naval officers and ratings would have hotly denied such an accusation. They were professional in the sense that they were supremely competent at their job: seamanship, navigation, the working of a gun turret, and the myriad skills that had to be mastered if they were to get the best out of the complex machinery crammed into a twentieth-century warship. They were brave and resourceful. 'We thought we were the best navy in the world, and it was invincible,' said Arthur Ford, who had joined as a boy seaman in 1910.

The British public in 1914 would have spiritedly endorsed Arthur Ford's view. Now, in the early twenty-first century, the Royal Navy is almost invisible, and comes to public notice only occasionally – at a time of crisis or after an unfortunate incident such as an accidental grounding or a titbit of salacious gossip in the tabloids. Today the Royal Navy is minuscule. In the First World War, Commodore Tyrwhitt routinely took more ships to sea from just the Harwich Force than all the frigates and destroyers in the Royal Navy today. The remark attributed to 'Jacky' Fisher, 'The navy is an impenetrable mystery surrounded by seasickness', is far more applicable today than when he uttered it nearly a hundred years ago. Every year from 1890 to the outbreak of the First World War, squadrons and individual ships visited the numerous seaside resorts around the coast that were packed with holidaymakers, especially during the August Bank Holiday (started in the 1870s). Here the public could visit the ships of 'their Navy', which was 'the object of deep, if ill-informed admiration by most of their countrymen'.[5] The navy was constantly in the public eye. The 1891 Royal Naval Exhibition attracted two and a half million visitors. The journal of midshipman Cyril Bower, then in the battleship *Hibernia*, records three Royal Reviews of the Fleet, between June 1911 and May 1912, at Spithead, Dublin, and Weymouth.

The sailors who basked in this esteem were volunteers, mostly from the industrial working class. Life at sea might have been tough, but was no worse than conditions in an Edwardian factory or coal mine, and the navy could afford to pick and choose who it took. By the outbreak of war, the average sailor was technically more efficient, and better educated and informed, than the bluejacket of the 1880s.

At the top of the navy's rank pyramid some captains and admirals were narrow-minded mediocrities who were unable to come to terms with the huge changes they had seen in their lifetimes. Churchill, the First Lord of the Admiralty, noticed 'a frightful dearth of first class-men in the Vice-Admirals' and Rear-Admirals' lists'.[6] He wrote to Fisher, 'We had competent administrators, brilliant experts of every description, unequalled navigators, good disciplinarians, fine sea-officers, brave and devoted hearts; but at the outset of the conflict we had more captains of ships than captains of war.'[7]

Commander Stephen King-Hall wrote, 'There were a number of shockingly bad admirals afloat in 1914. They were pleasant, bluff old sea dogs, with no scientific training; endowed with a certain amount of common sense, they had no conception of the practice and theory of strategy or tactics'.[8]

Most of the senior officers had been brought up in the days of sail. They had been promoted by a system that rewarded commanders (executive officers) of major warships for their skill in keeping their ships spick and span with gleaming paint and glittering brasswork – in a word, 'bullshit'. Every ambitious commander dug deep into his own pocket to buy paint to augment the stock issued by the dockyard. After the loss of HMS *Victoria*, a private fund was set up by Jellicoe's friends to reimburse him for the loss of paint that he had purchased before the ship sailed from Malta. The sum of £75 was raised; a fifth of a commander's annual pay in 1893, and the equivalent of £12,000 in today's money.[9]

James Cox, who served in the pre-1914 navy, described painting ship:

> The insides of the ship were normally painted by a special enamelling party, which was doing out mess decks and the like with enamel all the time. Although the Admiralty supplied paint it was very seldom used. Nearly all the poor officers had to buy enamel paint to curry favour, to make the ship look nice.* They didn't have to, but it was considered the thing. Of course a ship was judged by its smartness in those days – its brasswork and enamel. Some officers considered that efficiency. They curried favour by making their ships look smart, and hateful ships they were to be in.
>
> Painting the ship's sides and superstructure was an evolution that usually had to be done in a day. With one captain it would be every six or seven weeks, with another every six months – any time the Captain thought fit, or could afford the paint. All the sailors would be over the side on stages with brushes. Every brush you lost, you paid for. So you hung them round your neck. The painter made up barrels of paint, and the petty officers took the cans, filled them up and handed them to the men over the sides so they wouldn't have to come inboard and lose a minute.

Because the navy had expanded so rapidly, many senior officers were promoted above their ceiling. There was no naval staff until 1911, or staff college until 1912, when Churchill as First Sea Lord insisted on both being formed. Lacking the corporate brain provided by a staff to generate strategy, and what we would now call operational-level doctrine, most of the senior officers who were to be tasked with wielding the weapon system did not think through properly how they would deploy the skilfully worked ships and their gallant crews that formed that weapon. Those senior officers who did found themselves frustrated by superiors who lacked vision and subordinates who lacked initiative. Most senior officers, blinded by technology, were not interested in the higher aspects of warfighting. They neither held naval history in high regard, nor had any time for the study of the past as a guide to the

---

* Here he is expressing sympathy not commenting on the officers' financial state.

realities of war. As the American naval historian Marder remarks, 'It is fair to say that such defects or failings as British Admirals possessed were equally or more conspicuous in nearly all other navies'.[10] One should add, including the German navy.

Among the younger officers in both navies, there were notable exceptions. In the Royal Navy these included Beatty (the youngest flag officer since Nelson), Commodores Keyes, Goodenough, and Tyrwhitt, and captains such as Chatfield, 'Blinker' Hall, Phillimore, and Richmond. The German navy's brightest officers included Scheer, Hipper, von Spee, all the battle cruiser captains, and others. In the Royal Navy, submarine COs, destroyer-flotilla leaders and captains, many still lieutenants and of an independent cast of mind, were to show how different they were from their elders and supposed betters. Some of the Royal Navy's best destroyer captains and officers of the First World War would become the great fighting admirals of the Second.

The system of selection and training of officers in the Royal Navy tended to make them narrow, reactionary, inward-looking, and class-conscious.[11] The last trait would not have aroused much comment at the time, since the whole population was class-conscious. In the latter half of the nineteenth century, naval officers started their careers as cadets at around thirteen or fifteen (the age limit was wide). They spent a maximum of two years in the *Britannia*, an old hulk moored in the River Dart, followed by a spell in a training cruiser (until the 1890s often under sail), before being sent to the fleet as midshipmen at between fifteen and seventeen. Many boys attended crammers at an early age to enable them to pass the entrance exam for *Britannia*. To train the 270 cadets in seamanship there were four lieutenants, with warrant officers and petty officers. 'Steam' training was given by two engineer lieutenants, who had no workshops and whose tuition was confined to lectures. There were nine naval instructors, who taught navigation and mathematics. The general education of cadets was in the hands of six civilian instructors: one for natural science, two for drawing, two for French, and one for English literature and naval history. The poor standard of general education was a direct reflection of the small number of instructors in those subjects. Although sail was obsolete in the navy by the end of the century, the seamanship taught was that learned by the lieutenants, and other instructors who had been brought up in the era of masts and yards. Only towards the end of the *Britannia* era was an officer appointed to supervise each term (as each intake of cadets was known), called the Term Officer. The system never really took root. One officer who joined as a cadet in 1899 remembered that they never heard a Term lieutenant address his cadets on any subject but games. They were never given a lecture on how to be an officer, how to treat men, how to conduct themselves on or off duty. Harsh discipline, bullying, and poor food were what most remember of this period in their lives. Stephen Roskill wrote in his biography of Beatty that the system was 'based on forcing cadets into a preconceived and rigid mould by the application of harsh, even inhumane discipline ... Any signs of originality or independence were severely frowned on – if not actively suppressed.'[12]

All officers serving in the navy in 1914 in the rank of senior lieutenant and above were products of this system. It had been criticized by some senior officers as far back as the 1870s, who suggested that young naval officers would benefit from attending a public school before joining the navy at eighteen, but such a system, known as the Special Entry Scheme, was not introduced until just before the First World War.

Fisher, who became Second Sea Lord, responsible for personnel, in 1902, held similar views on the value of a public-school education, although he had never attended one himself – he was only thirteen when he was appointed a naval cadet in 1854. Preliminary enquiries revealed that public-school headmasters were loath to make special provision for naval candidates at sixteen, as they wanted to keep these boys as leaders in their own establishments. Fisher rejected the army's system, which took boys after they had completed their education at public schools into Sandhurst or Woolwich, before sending them to their regiments. He wanted to catch them young. He decided that the navy would have its own public school. Here there would be common training including engineering for all cadets irrespective of which branch they were to enter. The Admiralty had already made plans to build a college ashore at Dartmouth to replace *Britannia*, whose accommodation was now considered unhygienic, but because the college at Dartmouth would not be ready for another two years, and in any case was designed for the old two-year course, another site had to be found to accommodate the extra numbers. So the coach house and stables of Osborne House on the Isle of Wight were converted for this purpose.

Consequently, from 1903 on, cadets spent their first two years in the navy at Osborne, followed by two years at Britannia Royal Naval College, a red-brick establishment on the hills above the River Dart used to this day to train naval officers; it was described by a contemporary magazine as a combination of a workhouse and a stable. The curriculum at Osborne/Dartmouth was similar to that of public schools of the time, although with more time spent on professional subjects such as boat-work, navigation, and basic engineering, the breadth of scholastic subjects studied was narrower. The discipline was harsher – cadets moved everywhere at the double, and endured numerous inspections and 'hassle'. The standards of dress were more exacting, but the food was no worse, and in some cases better, than at the average public school. The modern reader may goggle disbelievingly at accounts of cadets starting their day with an obligatory cold bath, and being beaten for trivial misdemeanours, but such practices were still commonplace at many public schools in the early 1950s, and would not have seemed overly harsh to civilians in the 1900s. The regime at Osborne/Dartmouth was actually only a more extreme version of what the brothers and friends of naval cadets endured at their public schools, which in the first half of the twentieth century were tough and austere establishments.

Entry to Osborne was preceded by a written exam (which was qualifying rather than competitive), a medical, and an interview, Richard Young who joined in 1910 remembered:

> You went to your family doctor a year before going up [to Osborne], he removed your tonsils, your adenoids, did a re-vaccination, checked your eyesight and sent you to a dentist.
>
> At the beginning of your last term at Prep School you bought a number of little books from Gieve, Matthews and Seagrove [the naval outfitters – now Gieves & Hawkes], which contained past Naval Entrance examination papers. Having spent the whole term working through these papers ad nauseam, on entering the examination room, you were met by something only too familiar. What the examiners discovered about the candidates is not clear, unless it was that some had more retentive memories than others.

He recalled that at the interview:

> the Admirals were not in uniform and to my relief the whole atmosphere of that board room was one of friendliness; my only recollection of this ordeal is that I favoured the board with my views on the Union of South Africa, a subject that I had hastily mugged up because my far-sighted father had tipped it as a good bet for the year 1910.

Douglas King-Harman, who joined Osborne in January 1904 aged twelve and a half, wrote to his mother describing his first days there:

> I got a letter from Father with the inclosed [sic] cheque, which I took to the Chief of Staff, who told me to send it home. Please cash it and put £1–10–0 in the bank, but keep the remaining 10/-. We get up at 6.30, & have to take our dip in the plunge bath & dress by 7.0, when we begin work till 8.0. At 8.0 the bugle blows 'Cease Fire' & we are marched into the mess room. At 9.0 we have prayers and divisions (that is, fall in) & off we march to work, which varies as sometimes we have decent things like

Seamanship and Signals or Engineering, or do more prosaic studies, as Maths, French etc.

Yesterday when we were marched down to the workshops, the roads were simply filthy, & many chaps were coated with mud half way up their gaiters. Happily, I was the outside man. We get an awful lot of gymnasium and drill. I played footer yesterday, I got thoroughly stiff and tired, but I refreshed myself at the Canteen (otherwise the Grubs).

In the evenings we have about 1½ hours play in Nelson (that is the huge hall used for drill and assembly etc.) The play is terrifically rough, & you get hurled about like mad. All the same it is awfully fine fun, & you soon get used to it.

You can come down on any Wednesday or Saturday afternoon, as those are half holidays.

At Dinner [midday in the navy] today we had turkey with sausages, & plum pudding & mince pies. At 8.45 we have a glass of ripping milk & weevily dog biscuits, the only article of fare which is not splendid.

The letter is signed 'from Douglas K-H', and he has scribbled across the front page, 'Bring my fountain pen down when you come!'

Richard Young's first of many impressions on arriving at Osborne was 'the complete absence of women. A vast change from one's Prep School, where there were two mistresses for the lower forms, a Matron, dormitory maids, dining room maids, and a headmaster's wife'.

F. J. Chambers, who joined Osborne in 1912, remembered that:

Each term had a Lieutenant in charge of it, who disciplined us with tempered severity and looked after our games. We were taught practical seamanship by Petty Officers and Engine Room Artificers. Perhaps the first lesson we were taught was to respect these men, old enough to be our fathers, yet soon to be our subordinates.

Juniors were not allowed – except on Sundays – to walk anywhere; everything was at the double. The religious instruction might have been presided over by the Rev Charles Kingsley – God was firmly on the side of Great Britain and the Royal Navy. When confirmation classes started, the rumour went round that the whole object of the exercise was to discover whether we masturbated.

Slowly we climbed up the ladder of seniority until as 'sixth-termers' we could chase others about. There was no fagging, but sixth-termers could send juniors on errands for the purpose of 'shaking the first-termers up'. I don't think it harmed us but a lot of it was plain silly.

We were paid one shilling a week, and were allowed to draw another shilling from pocket-money provided by our parents. We were not allowed to possess any other money, and even tips from relations had to be paid into the bank. The notorious case of Archer-Shee (alias the Winslow Boy) had shaken the authorities a few years before, and they wanted no repetition.

As Commander Barry remembered, the punishments could, by today's standards, be severe:

> While I was there, two cadets ran away. They were brought back to the great hall where we all assembled. One after the other they were strapped down across a gymnasium horse, and given twelve of the best by a hefty marine in front of all the other cadets. They were dismissed the service.

Dartmouth was a tougher place, as Douglas King-Harman wrote to his mother in January 1906: 'The discipline is fearfully strict, and our ideas of smartness etc. have received a rude shock'.

Richard Young:

> At Osborne the senior terms were not much more grown up than the juniors, but at Dartmouth they had men's voices and shaved. One's two years at Osborne were no more than an interesting extension of one's prep school; Dartmouth offered manhood. The tone of Dartmouth was generally good, there was inevitably a certain amount of 'smut', and at least one cadet lost his virginity to the wife of the local pub-keeper, but his later life and happy marriage suggest that it did him no harm; and why should it? Virginity is a condition, not necessarily a virtue.

B. Dean had a slightly less happy recollection of Dartmouth:

> Having reached the eminence of Sixth Term at Osborne, one felt some-what deflated on joining RN College Dartmouth, as 'First Termers' again, far more of an ordeal than first term at Osborne. The Cadet Captains – great hulking chaps of nearly seventeen – were given almost a free hand in the ruling of their serfs. Every evening the 'gods' would sit in judgement on their raised dais at the end of the gunroom. The punishments for even the most trivial offences were severe. They frequently included a dozen strokes with a cane on the back of the hand. The time of day we dreaded most was going to bed. After evening prayers we would be marched off the quarter deck. On reaching the corridor we would break off; then ensued a wild stampede for the dormitories. In the few seconds it took to get there, everything undo-able was undone: jackets, ties, collars, shirts and even boot laces flying in the breeze. A Cadet Captain would have gone ahead and stationed himself by the door through which we had to pass to get to the wash house. Just inside this door was a large gong (one gong = brush your teeth; two gongs = say your prayers). Attached to the gong was a thick rope weighted with a solid glass globe. The time would be taken from the first cadet entering the dormitory to the last one leaving it – and this seldom exceeded fifteen seconds. But this was not quick

enough for the Cadet Captain. When ten seconds had elapsed, he would unhook the gong rope. As each cadet hurtled past him he would receive a resounding whack over the bare back with this formidable weapon.

Sailing and boat-pulling (rowing) were an important part of the curriculum at Dartmouth, preparing cadets for their life at sea. As cadets became more senior they were allowed to take boats away for picnics up the River Dart. The old *Britannia* was still moored off Sandquay, and as Cadet Ringrose-Wharton recorded in his diary:

In the morning we had sailing cutters, and as there was no breeze for sailing, we went along [to] the Ship [*Britannia*] and went over the mast, over the futtock shrouds and over the crosstrees; there [illegible] gave us some questions on the yards, then we pulled back to the bathing stage.

Sport played an important part in the cadets' lives. Douglas King-Harman wrote home about a rugby match against a local club first side:

Our team is quite good as one officer and a master are Internationals, and most of the others are county people. It speaks jolly well for the cadets that five of us were playing yesterday. I am jolly glad I have jacked [sic] soccer, as soccer is quite in the shade here.
    I am going in for the Racquets tournament which begins next week. I haven't been out with the Beagles this week so missed a couple of kills.

But despite the sailing, beagling, and plenty of sport, Douglas King-Harman wrote to his father in May 1907:

Here I am back again at this awful hole. I'm heartily sick of the place, and shall be most remarkably glad to get to sea, in spite of various sinister rumours that the new scheme Midshipmen are not to find life on their first ship a bed of roses.*

Life at Dartmouth was sufficiently repressive and set about with petty restrictions to cause some naval officers to look back on their time there with distaste. Stephen Roskill, the eminent naval historian, remembered that:

I was born on 1 August, which was the starting day for one of the three annual cadet entries. If I had been born a day earlier, I would have been automatically placed one 'term' earlier so four months senior; but the rigidity of the system was such that cadets could only choose their friends from among those belonging to the same four month age span as

---

* King-Harman as a member of the January 1904 Term was one of the early batches of cadets to participate in the new scheme for training referred to earlier, and which had started in 1903.

themselves, and in particular from those who slept (in alphabetical order of surnames) in the same dormitories . . . It was not surprising that, despite ameliorative efforts by some of the more humane and understanding masters, this system should have stifled any tendency to show originality. Perhaps the most revealing comment on the system was made by an officer of my own generation who had the misfortune to fall into Japanese hands after the Java Sea Battle of 27 February 1942, but later achieved Flag Rank. When asked about his experiences as a prisoner-of-war, he replied, doubtless partly in jest, 'After four years at Dartmouth a Japanese prison camp was quite a picnic'.[13]

To be fair, many an ex-public schoolboy might have given a similar answer. Dartmouth kept this reputation up to the Second World War.* For the privilege of attending Osborne and Dartmouth, the cadet's parent paid a fee equivalent to that charged by the average public school. So only those able to find an annual sum equivalent to the cost of a medium-priced family car (in 1903 the fees were £75 a year, in today's money about £16,000), could afford to send their offspring to the navy as an officer. There were reduced fees for the sons of officers of the Royal Navy, Royal Marines and army, and Admiralty civil servants.

From Dartmouth, cadets were sent to a training cruiser to introduce them to shipboard life. In King-Harman's case, this was the *Cumberland* (launched 1902 and completed in 1904). He wrote to his mother from Guernsey, where the ship was paying a visit, 'after two nights in a hammock, I have come to the conclusion that of all the uncomfortable places to sleep, a hammock takes first prize'.

On being sent to the fleet aged seventeen or so, as a midshipman, or 'snotty', life was even more demanding. The gunroom, where they lived, was ruled over by a sub-lieutenant, assisted by the senior midshipmen, who within certain limits were free to invent games to torment their juniors and keep them in their place. 'Snotties', so called because the buttons on the cuffs of their monkey jackets were allegedly to prevent them wiping their noses on their sleeves, had to endure ritualized bullying long after their civilian brothers and friends ashore had passed that stage. To us, the antics in the average early-twentieth-century gunroom appear at best immature, and at worst vicious.

The ventilation of some gunrooms was bad, and their scuttles [portholes, to the landsman] were too close to the waterline to be kept open in a

---

* Some would say until well after the Second World War. Cadets joining in the 1940s and 1950s after leaving their public schools at eighteen years old under the Special Entry Scheme envied their army officer cadet contemporaries at Sandhurst, where they were treated as adults, rather than as schoolboys.

seaway, so 'warts', as the junior midshipmen were called, were posted by the scuttles to open as the ship rolled up, and close as she buried her side. A senior midshipman with stick in hand sat on the table. If you let any water in, at the next roll you were not allowed to close the scuttle, but had to shove your head and shoulders out to try to block the flow. Your backside was then in a perfect position for the controlling stick.[14]

The sub-lieutenant (sub) of the gunroom decided whether the lives of the midshipmen, especially the junior ones, were tough but bearable, or sheer misery. He could act as a check on the senior midshipmen's torment of the juniors, or lead the pack. A ship's executive officer might rein in a sub who overcorrected; more often he would let it pass, as 'good for the snotties', adding a few punishments of his own for good measure. Between a 'hard-nosed' commander and a sub with a mean streak, a snotty's life was a hell at sea. Captain Walker, who served in the battleship *Resolution*, wrote:

> Gunrooms did vary to some extent according to the character of the senior sub, who would set the tone, but I think *Resolution*'s gunroom was typical of the era, and no one who has been through the mill ever forgets it. When [years later] I met a retired Admiral at a reunion dinner, his first remark to me was, 'Charles, how I hated those senior snotties in the RESO'.
>
> Here are two incidents which took place in my gunroom days, though not in the *Resolution*:
>
> 1. A junior midshipman in, I think the *Tiger*, was so driven to desperation that he stabbed his sub-lieutenant with a knife (though not to death).
>
> 2. Another midshipman (one of my own term) deserted from the fleet flagship for the same reason, but was caught and brought back. This was a very serious offence in wartime, but was hushed up (probably because he was the son of a well-known admiral). I never heard of it, until after I retired many years later, when my father who was a friend of the admiral's told me about it.
>
> You can thank your lucky stars that you were never a junior snotty in 'the good old days'.

Older sailors and petty officers would sometimes take pity on the wretched snotty. A story is told of a midshipman in charge of a boat who was being yelled at by the ship's commander from the quarterdeck as the boat drew away; a three-badge able-seaman said, 'Never you mind, sir. Just hold up your hand [to acknowledge the tirade of abuse], and when you gets tired, I'll hold up mine.'

But childish behaviour notwithstanding, midshipmen then had considerably more responsibility than their contemporaries ashore; and infinitely more than most sixteen-year-olds today. Most ships' boats, whether under sail, oars, or steam, were in charge of a midshipman. They were responsible for their boat's cleanliness and maintenance and for 'driving' it in all weathers by day and night. Thus they learned boat-handling and seamanship, which would stand them in good stead when they became the captains of warships, as well as command of men much older and more experienced than them.

Aged seventeen and a half, Douglas King-Harman was appointed as a midshipman in HMS *Lord Nelson*. He wrote to his father on 17 January 1909:

I am the Midshipman of the Picket Boat [steam driven], so that I don't get much time to myself. In fact I can't fit in a square meal edgeways. Just as I sit down simply ravening [sic], then it's 'Away Picket boat', and away I dash. It's very difficult steering, there being awfully strong tides and a perpetual gale, but I haven't had any serious bumps yet. We spent Wednesday and Thursday ammunitioning ship, and on Thursday night I was towing the empty lighters away till past 10.0 pm, simply soaked to the skin and in a howling gale.

Arbuthnot [the Captain] is a regular terror and no mistake and so is the commander, Whitehead, but as long as I keep clear of their wrath I shall be all right.

Any breach of gunroom etiquette is severely punished [by being beaten] with your own dirk scabbard. I append some of the immemorial customs of the Service.

If a commissioned officer (i.e. a sub[-lieutenant]) says 'Breadcrumbs' all midshipmen have to immediately stop their ears until further orders. If a sub says 'door!', every mid makes a dash for the door, and if not out in 5 secs the last one out does not sit comfortably afterwards. When a com-missioned officer is making himself objectionable at table, the President of the Mess shouts 'Dogs of War' and if the offender is not removed in a minute, the midshipmen sit down delicately for the next few days. We had a Dogs of War yesterday evening at dinner, when the Assistant Paymaster was making a row. He is a burly brute and the combined efforts of ten of us only just got him out in time, at the expense of a few plates, glasses etc. At first obedience had to be slowly and painfully instilled, but now we move as one man.

The admiral, Briggs, is a harmless looking person, who is completely overshadowed by our terror of a skipper. I am still in rather a blue funk as I never know when and what I ought to be doing, but in another week I shall have settled down into the routine of the ship.

Young King-Harman was not exaggerating when he described Captain Sir Robert Arbuthnot, Bt, as a terror. He was a martinet and physical-fitness fanatic, who made a practice of challenging his guests to boxing matches after dinner. On one occasion, he overheard two sailors to whom he had awarded a minor punishment threatening to 'do him in'. He ordered them to meet him on the quarterdeck, where each man was handed a pair of boxing gloves and invited to carry out his threat. They received such a thrashing that they would have done better to have kept quiet.[15] Lady Arbuthnot was one of the few people who could control Sir Robert, 'Bobby' to his midshipmen. Some months after joining *Lord Nelson*, King-Harman wrote about her:

> She has a notorious weakness for midshipmen, and has started by an offer of free teas whenever we go ashore. She is a most motherly dame who I fancy keeps the fierce Bobby in good order. There is rather an amusing yarn of her, that when a midshipman was steering a boat with her and the captain on board, the unfortunate youth made a hash of coming along-side. Bobby jumped up and said 'consider your leave stopped till further orders'. 'Nonsense' said Lady A, and the midshipman went his way rejoicing.

The Home Fleet summer cruise provided an opportunity for the officers and midshipmen to partake of hospitality offered by landown-ers. Midshipman Cyril Bower was serving in the brand-new battleship *Orion*, the flagship of Rear Admiral King-Hall, when she visited the Clyde in 1912, and noted in his journal:

> Saturday, Aug 17th Lamlash to Fairlie
> *Orion* and *Falmouth* weighed at 8.15 am and proceeded out of harbour, course being shaped for Fairlie where we arrived at 9.30 am in a heavy rainstorm. I played golf at Largs in the afternoon, and in the evening the officers of both ships went to a dance given by Lady Glasgow at Kelburn Castle

> Sunday, Aug 18th Fairlie
> A very fine day. Divisions and church were held on the upper deck. In the afternoon, Lady Glasgow invited all the midshipmen from this ship to tea etc. at Kelburn.

> Monday, Aug 19th Fairlie to Lamlash
> At 10.15 am, the Earl of Glasgow who is about 90 years old came on board; we weighed and proceeded off Largs.

What the lower deck found to do so far from the bright lights of Glasgow, Bower does not record.

Inevitably there were accidents involving boats. King-Harman:

Saturday morning, a service boat was being sailed close by us in a strong gale of wind, when a squall struck her and she capsized. Our picket boat was immediately called away – I dashed up on deck just as I was, without dirk or anything, and rushed to the scene of the action. Another ship's boat arrived just before us and they picked up everyone. The midshipman of the boat had a very near squeak as he was wearing an overcoat and seaboots, and was pinned underneath the mainsail for several seconds before being fished out by a seaman. It was freezing hard at the time with a heavy sea. While I was righting the capsized boat, another steam boat dashed up and ran right into us, so all I got out of the affair was a round cursing from the commander for bringing my boat back with a hole in her. I had gone away with no overcoat or seaboots and was soaked.

Punishment and strictures were the order of the day, and accepted without rancour; giving midshipmen a hard time was regarded as good for their souls. King-Harman:

Our officers are a very nice set indeed, and really the captain and commander are good sorts at bottom though very strenuous and strict service people. The seamen have nicknamed this ship the 'Lord 'Elp us'.

It is perhaps an indication of the attitudes of the time that when in 1910 Arbuthnot was dismissed his ship for criticizing the government of the day in public, King-Harman wrote:

There was naturally a fearful hullaballoo, and yesterday a new captain was appointed, Bobby being put on half pay. It is a beastly shame, and it has taken from the active service one of the best officers in the navy. His remarks were obviously tactless and could not have gone unreprimanded, but is abominable to put him on half pay. Bobby never did care tuppence for what anyone else thought or did, and I suppose he has run his head up against the powers that be once too often now. We are all very sorry to lose him, and so I think are the men, although not many of them would own it. Passing one or two fads he was the best skipper anyone could wish for.*

Arbuthnot did not languish on half-pay for long. He was soon appointed Commodore of the Harwich destroyer flotillas. He worked hard on improving the spick-and-span appearance and efficiency in seamanship of his flotillas, and included some night-fighting training. There was nothing wrong with the spirit and effectiveness of individual ship's companies, but little attention seems to have been paid to how

---

* Arbuthnot's fiery speech at a dinner of the Auto-Cycle Union attacking the Liberal government for its 'Little Navy' policy, and warning that the Germans were preparing for war, was reported in the *Daily Mail*. The Kaiser made a formal complaint.

the flotillas should operate as part of a fleet, and how they should be handled in a fleet action, especially at night. Despite the bravery of the men, these deficiencies in training were apparent when war broke out: for example, the British had not devised a system for using searchlights at night to anything like the degree achieved by the Germans. In the war, Arbuthnot, by now a rear admiral, was second in command of the 2nd Battle Squadron, and later commanded 1st Cruiser Squadron. Both commands were well above his ceiling, and he lived, and died, validating Churchill's judgement on flag officers that 'at the outset of the conflict we had more captains of ships than captains of war'.

The navy also raced boats on every possible occasion. Midshipman Cyril Bower, who had previously served in the battleship *Hibernia*, took part in six sailing races in twelve days between 23 January and 10 February 1911. His journal for Saturday 4 February in Arosa Bay reads:

> Midshipmen's sailing race for Lady May's prizes was held in the morning in a strong breeze. At the start the *Agamemnon*'s whaler capsized but the crew were picked up by *Hibernia*'s barge. Later on in the race, the *Glasgow*'s montagu whaler capsized, 4 men being drowned. The midshipman and 1 boy being picked up by the *Drake*'s sea boat.

Sixteen-year-old midshipmen also had to learn to deal with sailors far older then themselves who were the worse for drink. King-Harman gives an account of collecting libertymen from Deal pier:

> I towed the pinnace in to bring off 120 men at 10 pm. As I neared the pier there were loud cheers and yells, and when I came alongside, a heaving mass of men fell and rolled into the pinnace. About 20 or 30 of them were so drunk that they couldn't even sit up, while 80% of the rest were very far gone. I made the more sober ones come with me in the picket boat, and let the others stow themselves in the other boat. All the time there was a perfect pandemonium raging, and at last I shoved off in despair, leaving a few desolate figures on the pier linked arm in arm singing 'we won't go 'ome till mornin'' in maudlin voices. The row calmed down as we neared the ship, and more than half of them had collapsed into slumber as we arrived at the gangway. I brought the aforesaid few on board early this morning looking very sorry for themselves with the prospect of cells for breaking leave.

Pay in the navy at any rank was far from generous, and midshipmen were subsidized by their parents. King-Harman wrote to explain his finances:

> I get my pay of 1s 9d a day and also the £50 a year which Father pays to the Admiralty. The two combined which makes about £80 a year I get in

instalments every month – about £6 per month. I get 1/- a day pay for ordinary months, and the 9d is saved till the quarter, so that every quarter you get a double whack so to speak. Out of this [all per month], messing takes from 30/- to £2, extras such as tea in the afternoon, porridge etc. come to about 8/- or 10/-, if you have a glass of wine at dinner for 'the King', wine comes to about 7/6 to 8/-, then my servant gets 10/-, washing is up to 10/- or more. I think that for everything including an afternoon on shore once in a way for tea or games, I ought to be able to save about £2 a month for certain. As long as I remain mid of the picket boat though, my shore expenses won't be very great, as I can only get leave if someone consents to take my boat for me, and I have only been ashore twice so far in four weeks.

The £50 a year was an allowance that parents were 'called upon' to supplement a midshipman's pay,[16] and was only stopped in the early days of the First World War, when a father wrote to the Admiralty saying that while he understood that his son might be killed, he did not see why he should pay for the privilege.

King-Harman wrote to his father following up his earlier letter about finance:

I told you last mail about my money affairs, so that you see I shall not want any pocket money in future, if you will continue to get my clothes for me. I have had a very strenuous week with some unpleasant experience of the North Sea in winter. We were out all Monday doing firing exercises and anchored off Deal again on Tuesday morning in a howling gale. There was a funeral of one of our ABs on shore on Tuesday afternoon and I towed the funeral party and escort ashore. It was most appallingly rough, and as both the picket boat and the launch I was towing were very heavily loaded, I really thought sometimes we would never reach the shore. We were drenched every minute by waves and spray, and of course had to go dead slow for fear of swamping the launch. I managed to land everybody safely at last, and then lay off the pier, being thrown about like a pea in a pod for about 3 hours until the party returned. The return journey was accomplished in rain and sleet, and I eventually got on board after five hours in the boat in what was really very bad weather. The commander asked me to dine in the Ward Room next night and said it was very creditable to have landed the party and back without any accident, which made me feel quite bucked up as he is such a surly old bear, he never says you've done a thing well unless he can help it. It snowed the next day, which considerably added to my embarrassment as we were a good mile off shore, and by the time I had completed a trip, I was literally frozen to the ground [sic – deck?] and resembled a pillar of salt.

We have been having simply foul weather – a bitterly cold NE gale, with the temperature close on freezing. Last week I never had minute spare time from morning till night and rarely got to bed before 11.0. pm.

The midshipman of the motor picket boat ran into the ship on Friday and smashed a huge hole in her bows, and she was only just hoisted in before sinking. It was quite exciting. Our first lieutenant fell over board while getting in the remains of a target on Thursday, but was picked up almost immediately. It must have been a chilly proceeding.

I had a couple of doses of 'little Benjamin' (i.e. a stout walking stick) last week, and to my great joy the said Benjamin was broken over me (to the great grief of its owner).*

Again, in the Firth of Forth:

Saturday dawned the [most] poisonous day possible. Freezing hard, a strong easterly gale, and the sea running very high. I spent a frozen day in the boat with short spells for meals, and arrived back at 9.0 pm triumphant with no smashes. Today I was away from 8.30 am till noon and am going again in a few minutes. The sea is worse, and the wind if possible colder. It is really rather exciting. Of course we batten down all the hatches, so that it doesn't matter how much water we ship, but when we are going into the wind it is all one can do to prevent being washed overboard. The boat is in one smother of spray the whole time. Nothing can keep you dry, as the waves splash up round you under the oilskin and fill up your sea boots, while green seas find their way down your neck. Meanwhile your eyes are getting crusted with salt, and spray is freezing (literally) all over you as it falls. Gloves are useless as they get soaked through in a moment.

Midshipmen coaled ship along with everybody else, as King-Harman related to his father, Sir Charles King-Harman; he was the Governor of Cyprus, hence the allusion to Mount Troödos below:

The collier came alongside next morning early and we began coaling at 9.0 am. We wanted to get in the whole 1,800 tons in one day, and made strenuous efforts to do it. It was a most appalling day, and when the last hoist was inboard, at about 7.30 pm, I was absolutely cooked. Our average was 188 tons per hour, a splendid one for such a large amount of coal. We washed down decks the same night, and I turned in feeling as if I had removed Troodos single handed with a spade.

Midshipmen were also required to skipper sailing boats as competently as steam or motor picket boats:

---

*   He does not say who the owner is, probably the sub-lieutenant of the gunroom.

We anchored at 7.30 am this morning, and I was routed out at 7.50 am while sleeping the sleep of the just after the middle watch, and was informed that my boat, the 1st Cutter was going in for mails immediately on anchoring. We took up our billet at the proper time, and I had a long and chilly sail to the beach, in a howling gale and bitterly cold it was. However it was a soldier's wind both ways, and I made good work with it, with no reefs in and every one and everything piled up to windward.

Christmas 1909 found the *Lord Nelson* at Portland and was celebrated in naval style, starting with the procession of all officers round the mess decks just before dinner:

This last performance is a fearful ordeal. The decorations were really first class, the messes were a mass of flags and coloured paper. Each mess had a special scheme of its own. The men stand in two long lines, and at each mess there are men stationed with plates of plum pudding, cakes, ciga-rettes etc., and each officer as he passes is supposed to take something, and when you pass a mess with any of your division in it (my Division are Maintopmen) you will deeply offend should you fail to take a double whack of everything. As there are some 40 messes in the ship, you can imagine that the performance is equivalent to a good meal.

After this we left the men to their dinners, and adjourned to the wardroom, where toasts were drunk with immense enthusiasm. We then proceeded to the gunroom and commenced the serious business of eating turkey and plum pudding. We opened some of the champagne in honour of the occasion, and after a jovial meal, we spent the afternoon, both men and officers in a well earned sleep, from which I roused myself at 6 pm to dress for dinner as Mrs Millan had invited me to dine with them [ashore].

Bringing a battleship to a buoy involved taking a hawser in by boat, usually with a 'buoy jumper' who as his name implies jumped on to the mooring buoy to pass the hawser through the ring on the buoy to hold the ship while the ship's chain cable was paid out to secure the ship to the buoy using a shackle:

A cutter mid. has a great number of thankless jobs in the day's work, but the job that haunts the sleep of cutter midshipmen is bringing a ship to a buoy. Lately I have been at it two or three times a week, but each time it loses none of its thanklessness. You can *never* do anything right, and the only way to do the job successfully at all is to pay no attention to the array of captains, commanders, and lieutenants who will be bawling themselves hoarsely [sic] and incessantly through megaphones, but to console them with the occasional 'Aye, Aye Sir', and do the job your way.

The sailors also took a keen interest in pulling races and although it was illegal would bet on the outcome. King-Harman:

> Last week I saw the ancient custom of challenging a ship to a boat race for the first time since we commissioned. The *Dido*, a small cruiser had come in about ten days ago, and we heard that she had a very smart cutter's racing crew, which had a long string of victories to their name. She challenged and beat the *Superb*, and one day last week, she challenged us. I was on watch at the time, and about six o'clock, just before sunset we saw her cutter coming towards us. I never saw such a magnificent set of men as she had – fine big chaps they were, every one of the fourteen, and it was a fine sight as they pulled slowly round us. The whole ship's company crowded to the sides and followed them round in stony silence, evidently weighing the chances. The way to accept a challenge is to throw a boxing glove into the boat as it crosses the bows, but the *Dido*'s cutter swept by without a sign from our men.
>
> It was as good as a play to watch the faces of our men on the forecastle as the boat went by, and equally good to watch the expression of studied indifference on the fourteen faces of the *Dido*'s crew. As they got clear of the bows, there was a just perceptible exultation visible in the increased speed as they shot down the other side, but to the ordinary observer one would never have known that we had acknowledged the fact that they were too good for us. It was a still evening, but the whole time occupied by the rowing round, there was an almost unbroken silence, and the scene was very weird. The officers of the ships have nothing to do with racing crews, and it is an entirely ships company business, so I went forward after I had been relieved, and endeavoured by casual conversation with the quartermaster to find out the details of the tableau I had just seen. It seems that *Dido*'s cutter is making a bid for the championship of the Fleet, and has hitherto been unbeaten, and we being a Chatham crew and somewhat fainthearted, decided to accept the fact that they are the 'best men'. I don't think that if we had been a West Country crew we should have swallowed the insult, but Chatham crews are notoriously chicken-hearted. We have some very fine men in the ship, but I don't think we have anything that would beat the *Dido*.

*

Conditions for the lower deck in the Royal Navy had improved considerably between the end of the nineteenth century and the outbreak of the First World War, but there were some grievances that remained unresolved which surfaced in the latter stages of that war, and at intervals in the years leading up to the Second. Many of the reforms were the work of three men, Fisher, Lionel Yexley (an ex-petty officer), and later

Winston Churchill, the First Lord of the Admiralty. Yexley became the editor of a magazine, the *Bluejacket*, later *The Fleet*, and played a dominant role in the movement to reform conditions in the Royal Navy.

The class structure of Queen Victoria's navy was far more rigid than that of her predecessors. Promotion from the lower deck had produced a surprisingly large number of officers in the period up to the end of the Napoleonic Wars. This avenue was almost completely closed after that date. In the eighty-four years after 1818, only four men of lower-deck origin were promoted to lieutenant – for gallantry. In 1903, Fisher, then Second Sea Lord, introduced a scheme to promote chief warrant officers to lieutenant, but his system only benefited men nearing the age of retirement and they could not expect to be promoted further.

One indicator of unrest was the rate of desertion and frequency of cases of indiscipline. In the year 1906–1907 there were 1,896 deserters.[17] Between 1899 and 1914 there were twenty-four major incidents of collective indiscipline or mutinous behaviour in ships and establishments of the Royal Navy, often the result of excessive collective punishments such as stopping the whole ship's company's leave because of bad behaviour by a few men. One example will have to suffice. In March 1914, in the *Zealandia*, commanded by the fire-eating Captain Walter Cowan, a long period of unrest, mostly provoked by Cowan, ended in a large number of stokers refusing to obey orders. Some were arrested and placed in cells. A further demonstration ensued. Twelve men were chosen at random and tried by court martial, and eight were sent to prison with hard labour. In this case the Admiralty intervened, annulled the sentences on a technicality, and distributed the stokers around other ships.[18]

Discipline at sea was harsher and more arbitrary than in the army (and Royal Marines when ashore – at sea Royal Marines were subjected to the same system as the bluejackets). Officers were not taught to care for their men, and many naval officers looked upon and treated the sailors as children who could not be trusted to behave. Flogging in the navy was merely suspended in 1881, not abolished as in the army, though birching of boy seamen was abolished in 1906, and caning allowed only under orders from the captain. Punishments were often demeaning, and the powers given to captains of ships made them almost akin to God. There was a lack of consistency in the system of discipline. Sailors would ruefully remark, 'another ship, another navy'.[19]

The onset of war in 1914 did not necessarily bring with it a change in some of the more autocratic captains and a moderation in their harsh treatment of their men. A rating in the battleship *Canopus* wrote in his diary about the first Christmas of the war:

Christmas Day (at Sea). Signal from Admiralty to Admiral wishing us a very happy Christmas, which proved to be a very miserable one. Our officers had a very good one, best of food, drinking and singing all day. While the men were on corned beef and hard biscuits.

On 27 December he recorded:

Took 1,100 tons of coal from collier. Finished at 11 PM. This has been our hardest coaling as we were working in the sun and the temperature was 90 degrees. Quite a lot of men collapsed during the day and our Captain expressed his gratitude by telling us that the coal 'must damn well come in faster', if not he would walk around himself and we would know what that meant. Yes we all knew what it meant, he would get his suit dirty and could not drink so much whiskey.

On 31 December he noted:

we can hear our officers singing and dancing and ringing the old Year out, at 12 o'clock they all came on the Quarter Deck all the worst for drink doing the Turkey Trot etc. When the Captain came up and told the bugler to sound off Action. That meant that all hands had to go to their respective stations. One officer called a marine all the disgusting names he could think of, his only excuse was the following morning that he [said] he was a little worse for drink.

During the Dardanelles campaign, the *Canopus* called at Malta for repairs. Rooke observed in his diary:

Our Captain could only manage to give Canteen leave to 10 pm, a lot of discontent on board.* Took in 700 tons of coal, gave leave from 4 pm to 6 am the following morning, our first leave since the war started. There was no reason why everyone could not get 60 or 72 hours leave now, every other ship was doing so. Can see trouble ahead. If we can not get it by fair means, we will get it by foul.

When the first watch to be granted shore leave returned, sixty-nine men were absent, and when the second watch returned there were fifty-nine men adrift. The captain stopped everyone's leave. Rooke wrote in his diary:

Our captain is a good fighting man, but would be appreciated a lot more if he thought a little more of his ship's company. He could have prevented all this by giving leave the same as other ships. 7.30 pm, [he] thought

---

*   Leave to the canteen in the dockyard only.

better of things and served out rum.* I expect he is beginning to find out
that he has got men to deal with and not a lot of boys.

In 1914, the sailors of the Royal Navy were unique in being members
of the only service among the belligerents who paid for their own
uniforms (a system that was to last into the 1960s). In the decade up to
1914, it was estimated that some 500 men deserted from Chatham alone
each year because of petty harassment on matters concerning uniform.

By 1907, the quantity and quality of food had been improved thanks
to Fisher, by then First Sea Lord, and Yexley, whom Fisher used to
consult. A new system of centralized catering was introduced in HMS
Dreadnought, although decades were to pass before it became universal
in the Royal Navy. But even the free issue of cutlery was attended by the
'bullshit' so prevalent in the navy. In *Dreadnought* the cutlery had to be
burnished and set out in an elaborate standard pattern for Sunday
inspection. The men refused to use the cutlery and handed it back to
the paymaster.[20]

The training of sailors (ratings) was hard, and to us may seem brutal.
But they were fed better than many working-class children, and few of
them were strangers to a clip round the ear. The scholastic education
they received was of a higher standard than in the present-day British
'bog-standard comprehensive' (to use the words of a government minister in 2002). Most ratings joined young, at fifteen or sixteen. Many
began their life in the navy in the training ship HMS *Ganges*, an 1821-
vintage wooden ship-of-the-line at Shotley on the River Stour in Kent.
She was still rigged with masts and yards, as HMS *Victory* is today. The
sixteen-year-old William Broadway joined the *Ganges* as a boy signalman
in 1913. Only the most intelligent boys were selected for this training.

I had a very good reception really. They met me with 'put that cigarette
out'. The first evening they gave us a bath with plenty of disinfectant in it.
They gave us a good supper. A large lump of corned beef, a piece of
cheese and a basin of cocoa. The first thing we did was six weeks
seamanship: box the compass, knots and splices, boat pulling, physical
drill, mast climbing, and sea boat, a twelve-oared cutter.† We weren't as
big as the oars. The coxswain used to threaten us with the tiller. The

---

* Normally served with dinner, the midday meal.
† Boxing the compass = telling off the thirty-two points of the compass from north
clockwise all the way round to north by west. The original compass card was set out in
points – a point representing 11¼ degrees, which evolved in an age when it was considered
that a sailing ship could not be steered closer than a quarter of a point. Courses in the
navy in the First World War were still given in points, because although the gyro compass
marked in degrees (360 degrees to a circle) was in use in some ships, it was not universal.

treatment wasn't brutal but it was severe. If you were told to box the compass and if you stopped, you got a cut alongside the ear. We also had ordinary schooling, fractions, decimals, long-division and on the results of your schooling, you were 'classed up'. The first group were given the high gunnery class, the next signals, and so on.

William Ford, a farm boy, joined *Ganges* in 1910 aged sixteen years and nine months. After being woken,

you lashed your hammocks up, and fell-in on deck to have them inspected to see that they were lashed up properly. After stowing hammocks, you scrubbed decks, barefooted, you weren't allowed to wear shoes whatever the weather. After this we went over the rigging. If you lagged, there would be an instructor right behind you with a rope's end. There'd also be one on the fighting top to see you didn't go through the lubber's hole. You had to come up the futtock shroud, hanging backwards, toes hooked in and pulling yourself up by your hands. I did not know where I got the nerve from. I was frightened to get on a haystack. I knew I had to do it, or I would be ridiculed by the other boys for being a coward.

   If somebody wouldn't go, they would hoist them up in the bosun's chair. It was not done to be cruel, but to get them used to looking down. But no one was ever excused it. There were a lot of things that scared you at first. Like walking out on the boom to boats, with a lifeline to keep one's balance.*

   After going over the rigging, we would have breakfast, sausages, or kippers, bloaters, perhaps eggs – good food.

In 1906, James Cox joined the *Warspite*, a training ship on the River Thames run by the Marine Society for boys of good character to provide seamen mainly for the merchant service. There were four other training ships in the Thames then: *Arethusa* and *Exmouth*, for boys from orphanages and workhouses, *Worcester* to train officers for the merchant service, and *Cornwall* for boys who required corrective training. James Cox's father, who ran a greengrocery and coal-merchant business, at first refused to sign the papers to allow him to join *Warspite*, so he persuaded a retired sergeant of marines to sign it for him.

My father never objected. He said, 'oh well you've made your bed. Away you go'. And away I went. My mother didn't have much to say. She done what my father told her. All she done was breed and work. She worked in the shop from six in the morning, and worked until eleven or twelve at

---

* Boom: a rounded spar projecting from the ship's side at deck level, and to which boats were made fast. Boats' crews would run out along the spar and slide down a rope ladder into the boat.

night, looking after us kids, and doing a couple of hours washing every day. Terrible life for a woman.

The routine in *Warspite* was very similar to that in *Ganges*, and as always with boys food was important. He remembered that after washing down decks,

> We'd have breakfast of a basin of beautiful chocolate cocoa, big thick lumps they used to put in it, and it had about a quarter of an inch of fat on top, it used to go down very, very nice, hot boiling cocoa. With it you'd have a quarter of a loaf of bread, about half a pound in weight, because loaves those days weighed two pounds. And most mornings you'd have good pork crushed out like dripping on our bread. Other mornings we'd have treacle or jam.
>
> For dinner we'd have meat, mostly mutton, roasted or stewed, and potatoes with their skins on. On Thursdays and Saturdays we'd have boiled plum pudding, made in long lengths and cut off in slices. At supper we'd have bread, jam and tea.

Half of each day was spent at school:

> The education was on the three Rs of course – reading, writing and 'rithmetic. They always tried to instil in a boy the love of reading, because their principle was to say 'if we taught the boys the three Rs well, if he wanted to learn anything himself, he could always study it.'

Each night there would be a muster:

> We'd all be lined up on deck, the Captain would stand at the wheel at the half-deck. Every boy would go before him, report his name and number, turn left smartly and step off. This was to make sure every boy was aboard, and no one missing, or drowned. Then you went below, sling your hammock and turn in.
>
> In those days, even in school right from babies you were taught to obey. On *Warspite* it was no different. Provided you carried out orders, nobody interfered. But, my God, if you didn't the punishment was always half a dozen with the cane. It didn't happen very often. There was no cruelty. If a boy was to be caned, he was taken up to the quarterdeck, stretched across the gymnasium horse and given six.

On completion of training in *Warspite*, merchant shipping companies would seek boys for employment in their ships. Some, like James Cox, joined the Royal Navy, and went to the training ship HMS *Impregnable* at Devonport. Being already trained in the basics, boys from *Warspite* were given advanced education, such as algebra, and training in electrics, wireless, gunnery, and torpedoes. This enabled the navy to select men for the specializations demanded by an increasingly technological service. James Cox found the discipline in the navy more severe than in *Warspite*:

> The officers in *Warspite* were fathers to you. You could always go and talk to them. Of course you always gave them respect, they always insisted on that. But in the Navy, the officers were entirely apart. You very seldom addressed an officer unless he addressed you. All your contact with officers in the training ship was through petty officers. All the petty officers were severe. It's a kind of upstairs, downstairs. The cook doesn't go straight to the missus; she goes to the butler first. It was the same then in the Navy.
>
> Of course there's a lot to be said for discipline, because a well-disciplined ship is usually a happy ship, because everybody knows they've got a job to do. In a badly disciplined ship, everybody pleases themselves.

James Cox, while still a boy seaman, was disciplined for overstaying his leave by seven days. On his return he presented himself at Chatham Barracks, and was sent up to Scotland to rejoin his ship, the armoured cruiser HMS *Natal*.

> The Captain was Ogilvie, a little man, but a great man. I was taken before him, and I was a bit obstreperous. I turned and attempted to strike one of the ship's police. I was charged with attempting to strike a superior officer, a severe crime. If I had been a man I'd have got two years detention. I was let off light. I was sentenced to twelve with the cane and fourteen days cells. I was taken on to the quarterdeck in my white duck suit. All the boys were mustered, about forty of them. I was laid across a gymnasium horse, with a ship's policeman either side stretching you across it. I had twelve strokes laid on by the master-at-arms, a very big man. The tradition was that you never opened your mouth, if you screamed or cried out, you were a coward.
>
> In the cells I picked oakum. You take a foot-long piece of rope and work at it until it's like wool. It takes two days to produce a pound of oakum. It makes your fingers sore. I was still a growing boy, and after three days my God I was hungry. The Captain sent for me one evening. He said, 'Ha there you are my boy, I'm going to be lenient with you. First of all I want you to remember that we train lions in the Navy, and subdue them. I want you to remember that, but don't let it rest in your memory too much. You have spirit, but you've shown it in a very, very bad way. You're the sort of boy we want for our petty officers in the future. I'm going to release you from cells if you give me your word that you will never get yourself into trouble again.'
>
> I was ready to promise anything then. And I kept my word. I became a chief petty officer as the years passed. I always remember Captain Ogilvie and his words. He was great man; he understood boys.

Coaling ship was a filthy chore, and how frequently it was carried out depended on how often the ship went to sea, and how fast she steamed.* A battleship or cruiser might have to take in 2,500 to 3,000 tons of coal, and aim to load at a rate of 300 to 400 tons an hour. Coaling, like all other evolutions, was treated as an inter-ship competition. To prepare for coaling, stokers would fit bottle-shaped halves of iron between the coalbin holes on the upper deck and the coal bunkers in the ship's bottom, often through several decks, including mess decks, and bolted them together to produce a continuous chute, down which the coal was shot from deck level to the bunkers. As the coal rattled down the chutes, clouds of dust escaped, and the whole ship was covered in a film of it. Everybody except the captain and a few men on duty took part in coaling, and wore their oldest clothes – anything was acceptable. Most major warships had a Royal Marine band, and sometimes they played music to keep up morale. Usually the seamen were also stationed in the holds in the collier alongside, shovelling the coal into two-hundred-weight bags, which were hoisted to deck level by derrick, ten bags at a time (a ton of coal) and tipped out. Marines manning trolleys scooped it up, and emptied the coal down the chutes to the bunkers, where the stokers trimmed it. James Cox:

> And so it goes on all day long. The only refreshment you get is oatmeal or limejiuce depending on whether you're in the tropics or where you are. You keep going until you've finished, you might take eight to ten hours to coal, and then you've got to clean ship – wash everything down, all the paintwork. After that, you have a bath, and change back into your ordinary rig. You were exhausted.

On a coal-fired destroyer, like *TB 117*, Cox's next ship after the *Natal*, the task was even more arduous. James Cox:

> In a little destroyer, there would be four or five of us to take in fifty tons of coal. We used to run alongside every three or four days, because we were patrolling off the Nore.

The elite of the lower deck were the engine-room artificers (ERAs), whose skill was vital to maintain the machinery, engines, and hydraulic systems on which the ship depended to steam, float, and fight. Rather than recruit skilled men from industry who would bring trade-union practices with them, the navy decided to train its own boy artificers. But the navy realized unless ERAs were given special treatment, it would be

---

* For example, *Dreadnought* was very economical at full speed, burning 340 tons of coal a day. At slow speed consumption was heavy. Her maximum coal load was 2,900 tons.

impossible to recruit boys with sufficient intelligence and aptitude. Gilbert Adshead joined in 1909 aged fifteen, at the suggestion of his father, who foresaw a war with Germany and wanted his son to avoid being conscripted into the army. Although there was no conscription in Britain at the time, Adshead père must have been gifted with second sight, because it was introduced in 1916. For Adshead's intake, thirty-three boys were examined and interviewed, of which six eventually passed, and joined the old wooden battleship *Tenedos* at Chatham. Two old steel merchant ships served as workshops. An ERA's training took four years, and the end product was a highly skilled craftsman, capable of making almost every part of machinery in a ship in the workshop on board, then fitting it and maintaining it.

An ERA wore the same uniform as a chief petty officer, similar to an officer's, except with red badges instead of gold ones, with stiff white collar and black tie. For work he wore blue overalls. The routine in *Tenedos* was far more civilized than in the *Ganges* or the other training ships. ERAs under training were waited on at meals by pensioners. They slept in hammocks, but there were no physical punishments, merely stoppage of leave. For major infringements of discipline a trainee would be discharged from the navy, as happened to one boy, who had served for two years, and was caught painting a black eye on *Tenedos*'s figure-head just before Admiral's inspection. The young ERAs spent most of their day in the workshop learning their craft, and attended evening school after tea. Leave each week started at midday on a Saturday, according to Gilbert Adshead:

> and you had to be back on board at 8 o'clock on Monday morning. From Chatham Station they ran special trains to London and back. It was nothing for nine or ten thousand men to travel on the rows of trains that had been laid on.
>
> Halfway through my time, *Tenedos* was closed down, and we moved to HMS *Indus*, another wooden ship at Devonport on the Cornish side of the Hamoaze. Here there were four workshops, three in merchant ships and one in another wooden ship. There were playing fields ashore, we had boat pulling, boxing, gym and all kinds of sport. These were some of the happiest days of my life.

The increase in the size of the ERA training establishment was but one indication of the need for more technicians in an ever-growing Royal Navy. Gilbert Adshead's first ship, which he joined in 1913, was the battleship *Lord Nelson*, in which he was to serve for four and a half years. She was the last of the pre-dreadnought battleships, with recipro-cating engines rather than turbines. She was fired by a combination of coal and oil, and was one of the first ships in the Royal Navy to have watertight compartments. To get from one engine room, or stokehold, to another, one had to climb to a deck above the waterline, and descend again. She was also one of the first to be fitted with lifts down to the engine rooms. Adshead had a high regard for his officers:

They didn't join the Navy for a job, but as a profession. Many came from distinguished naval families. We had a fine Captain, McClintock, even he wouldn't be high and mighty, if he happened to walk along the upper deck, he would stop and speak to you. In the wardroom we had two lords, two sirs, and three honourables. One of the lords was a young lieutenant. They were gentlemen and they conducted themselves like gentlemen, and you couldn't help liking them.

The *Lord Nelson* was a flagship at the time, hence her blue-blooded wardroom; many admirals still made a practice of collecting their friends' sons and relations around them. Service in a flagship was sought after by the ambitious as a good leg-up in the promotion stakes. James Cox's views on officers were not necessarily shared by his fellow bluejackets:

in my opinion, the average naval officer, in that day anyway, came from a good family and were damn good fellows. Discipline was always good in the Navy. I've got nothing against discipline in the Navy because it was severe not tyranneous [sic].

ERAs lived in their own mess, and in this respect were accorded the privileges of petty officers.

There were twenty-three of us, including two chief ERAs, in a curtained off space about twelve by eight feet in the fo'c'sle. We used to have our meals in there, and perhaps a dozen of us would sling their hammocks in there, but the remainder would sling anywhere, perhaps in the torpedo flat, or further below, in the chest flat where sea chests were kept. In the daytime, hammocks were lashed up and stowed away. We sat on lockers, all the way round the table which ran the length of the room, each of us had one.

In our mess we had two stokers who looked after our creature comforts. They drew the food from stock, prepared it, took it to the galley to be cooked, and brought it down at meal times. They kept the mess clean and acted generally as servants.

The ERAs' mess was not large, but there was more privacy than on a messdeck where the sailors and marines lived. A ship's company was divided into stokers', seamen's, marines', and boys' messes. The seamen were further subdivided into four divisions, forecastlemen, quarterdeck-

men, maintopmen, and foretopmen, a hangover from sailing-ship days.
Each division had its own mess deck in which there were sufficient tables
to seat the men, at around sixteen to a table. Each table of sixteen constituted a mess. The table was hung from the deckhead (ceiling). James Cox:

> The tablecloths were rolls of lino, which we used to roll out at every meal.
> We had mess gear supplied to each mess, such as basins to drink from; we
> had no cups and saucers then. We had plates, knives and forks, which
> were replaced now and again. There was a leading seaman in charge of
> the mess, he was the mess caterer.
>
> Each mess was issued with a book of chits to be used in the canteen.
> The daily allowance per man from the Admiralty was half a pound of meat,
> including bone, a pound of potatoes, an ounce of milk, an ounce of tea,
> and small amounts of sugar, salt etc. Every man would take it in turn to be
> cook of the mess, two at a time. They would draw the rations each day.
> Anything extra they wanted, such as soup powders, or tomatoes, they
> would get from the canteen and charge it to the mess chit book. The cook
> of the mess would prepare the meal, for example: schooner on the rocks,
> which was a shin of beef on a dish of spuds; or a three-decker, which is a
> layer of meat, a layer of dough, another of meat, another of dough, up to
> three layers. He would then take it to the galley where it was cooked for
> him.
>
> We had breakfast at 8 o'clock, dinner at twelve. At four o'clock we used
> to come down and have a cup of tea. At seven o'clock you had supper,
> which was much the same as breakfast. Some cooks of the mess would
> make up something from dinner leftovers, or make fishcakes. You got
> tinned salmon in those days, it was a regular issue in the Navy. Tins of
> rabbit was another, it came in your ration. They accumulated in the mess
> shelves, because people didn't always want them. But they could be eaten
> for supper.

Rations could be augmented with food such as cheese, bloater paste,
and bacon using the allowance of fourpence a day credited to each mess
by the paymaster. Messes that 'overdrew' their account had to make it
up by going on short rations until sufficient credit had accumulated. No
money changed hands. This system of messing, canteen or broadside,
had hardly changed since Nelson's day, although the quality of the food
was better.* James Cox:

> There's no comfort in a broadside mess at all. All the average sailor's got
> to sit on is a form [bench] which takes eight men on either side, and a
> bare table with lino. If you want a nap during the dinner hour, you lie on

---

* For broadside mess and canteen, see the Glossary.

a nine-inch wide form, if you can find room. One form will take two people. Or he lays on the table with a ditty box for a pillow. If he has a short while before coming on watch at night and it is not worth slinging his hammock, he lays on the table, or under it.

Ships are built for battle. There are few portholes, only in the non-vulnerable parts. Over all the vulnerable parts is armour plate, its solid. That includes mess decks, so you've got no ventilation bar fans, bringing in fresh air from the ventilators on deck. In a mess deck at night, in a hammock, with eighteen inches between each hook, you're sleeping very close.

Life on board a destroyer was more to James Cox's liking:

Lovely. Men of my type who could stick the sea, always volunteered for destroyers. I never liked big ship life. There was more discipline in a big ship. In a destroyer you got no Naval Police, the only man aboard to discipline you is the coxswain. He's a busy man, he's a seaman, he's the purser, he takes the ship in and out of harbour, and looks after the navigation and charts. Everybody had his job to do. If he didn't do it, no one else did. We'd come in from sea, and the Captain would say, 'You can't go ashore for the weekend until the ship's cleaned up'. The ship would be spick and span before you left it. As soon as you'd done your job you were free to go.

Gilbert Adshead also preferred destroyer life:

When you went to a small ship, like the *Thisbe* the destroyer, with only seventy-eight people on board, you lived a different life, you counted for more as a person, than you did on a big ship, and the rules and regulations were not so strict. The man who's most responsible on a destroyer is the coxswain. He can make or mar the happiness of a ship. On the *Thisbe*, I went to after the *Lord Nelson*, we had a very fine coxswain.

In every ship rum was issued at eleven o'clock to petty officers and to the remainder of the ship's company when they went to dinner at noon. Petty officers had their rum neat, about one fifth of a bottle, and then everybody else had it with three parts water to one part rum. Life in destroyers could be more free and easy when it came to the matter of rum issue. James Cox:

In destroyers, of course I'm giving away secrets now, the coxswain and the Chief Torpedo Instructor, as I was, used to work as opposite numbers. If he was ashore, I did his job, so I used to issue the rum. We had a rum spirit stoppage book, to record the numbers of those who had gone ashore for the weekend, because when a man went ashore his rum was stopped. Suppose there was one hundred ashore, we would say, 'fifty stopped', and the other fifty tots would go down into our mess, and the warrant officers mess.

Rum was also used as currency for favours done, such as standing in for a duty. Gilbert Adshead drew his rum but did not drink it:

> Everyone was supposed to drink their rum at once, you weren't allowed to bottle it and stow it away. But I used to get a lot of things done for a tot of rum. I had a leading stoker who slung my hammock for me, and did all my washing. He was in charge of the hydraulic engine department which had steam pipes going through it. He was able to dry my washing on the steam pipes. I paid him ten shillings a month and my tot.

Sailors could make money by setting up 'firms' on board. James Cox:

> I took up haircutting. I invested in half a dozen razors and charged a shilling a month to a man who used my razors to do the shaving, while I did the haircutting for which I charged twopence.
>
> Another person would buy lemonade powder and a hundredweight of sugar off the pusser, and make a couple of buckets of lemonade every night, and sell it for a penny a glass. There were no canteens then like they've got now.
>
> Another person would make clothes. He would make a jumper and trousers, which are easily cut out. You'd get three yards of serge at one and threepence a yard, half a yard of jean [for the square collar], that used to be eighteenpence, so five bob, you've got your material. He'd have a little hand machine, and run you up a suit of clothes for a dollar [five shillings], and charge you ten shillings. We used to get one afternoon a week, called make and mend to make your own clothes. Instead of making, you used to pay this chap and he would make them for you.
>
> Someone else would do other people's washing. These were mostly married men because marriage wasn't recognised [by additional pay]. They'd wash your clothes for tuppence a piece, or for a blanket sixpence.
>
> Where money was involved you had to get the Captain's permission to set up a 'firm'. Usually they would grant permission for a barbering or a lemonade firm on each messdeck. If there was already one on your messdeck, you might go into partnership. Particularly two married men who wanted a few bob for their leave might go into partnership.

At the beginning of the last century, and well into it, Portsmouth, Chatham and Plymouth (and its satellite Devonport) were sailor's towns. There were soldiers and marines in them too, for each had a substantial military garrison, but sailors predominated. Each was a port division to which every rating belonged, and to which he returned between time at sea. On completion of training ratings were assigned to port divisions:

Devonport ('Guzz'), Chatham ('Chats'), and Portsmouth ('Pompey').
Ships were manned exclusively from one port division. Now Devonport
and Portsmouth are shadows of their former selves, with high unem-
ployment, existing on tourism and a modicum of light industry. Then
all three had thriving dockyards, capable of building and repairing any
kind of warship including battleships. When the fleet was in they
hummed with life. Even when it was out, there were enough sailors to
liven up the bars, and provide a living for the prostitutes. James Cox:

I loved Chatham. If you was inclined to run after women, you knew all the
places such as Mother Knott's and the Dover Castle, where you met the
women you wanted to see. In fact some of them had long standing
engagements with prostitutes, and were very friendly with them. On the
other hand, people who wanted to go up to London, could catch what
they called the theatre train. You could go for half a crown return [2s 6d],
go to a theatre, come back to Chatham on the milk train and be aboard
ship by seven in the morning.

I used to go to London mostly because I was a Londoner. Course I had
a girl in London, a regular one, that became my wife later on, that I
courted for a number of years. In Chatham one of the popular places for
sailors was the theatre, Barnett's, a popular music hall. Next door there
was a pub which the artistes used. We used to go in there with them.
Many of the chorus girls done a bit of 'sniping' on the quiet, because the
pay in those days was very bad for chorus girls. If she could earn five bob
off a sailor, well and good. And on top of that there was the homosexual
people you see.

The prostitutes were very good women too. We never picked them off
the streets, you knew the pubs where to look. They was all crowded with
women. But there was never, or seldom, a fight over women in pubs. You
see nearly all these girls knew somebody on the ships. They used to come
back to them time after time. I've found among prostitutes very, very
good women, irrespective of their lapses of propriety you might say. They
were good, friendly, honest and would always help you out if you was
drunk. The sailors used to treat them straight, and they used to treat us
straight.

In London once, I was in a pub drinking. Although I say it myself, I was
always clean looking, a tall, fair young man. I turned round and my glass
was filled up. I got talking to this girl. I said goodnight to her, and went
outside. I was standing getting my bearings, and she came out and took
hold of my arm, and said, 'you'd better come home with me. You're not
fit to walk.' She called a cab. In the morning I woke in a lovely room, with
a nice girl beside me.

I got up and looked through my pockets to see if my money was there,
it wasn't. I was going to go for her, and she said, 'You'd better look in

your boot, where you stuffed it last night'. Now that girl I knew for
months. I found out she was a young suffragette, from quite a good
family. I spent many weekends with her. She paid for it all the time. She
said, 'I've got an allowance from my parents'.

*

Like others before and since, Douglas King-Harman found life in a
destroyer a welcome change from a Home Fleet battleship. While still
a midshipman he served in the *River*-class destroyer *Teviot*. Here he
was able to observe what we would now call the 'laid-back' approach of
destroyer captains:

> We ran into thick fog, our skipper who is without exception the coolest
> person I ever saw, was not a bit down-hearted and boomed along at 12
> kts the whole way, occasionally running up to 15. I admired the skipper
> more than ever when he brought us alongside – he stood up on the
> bridge, looking bored to tears with everything, and without moving an
> eyelid, crashed full tilt into the basin, and we brought up with the wall six
> feet ahead, and a destroyer's nose almost touching our side. One thing is
> quite plain, even after a week in the flotilla – Panic as known in the fleet,
> Panic with a big P, is absolutely unknown in the destroyer service, possibly
> because there aren't any old foozles trying to take charge when they aren't
> wanted.

After service in destroyers, many officers found returning to a cruiser
or battleship tedious. Life in poorly ventilated steel ships in the tropics,
and especially on the East Indies station, which included the Persian
Gulf, Arabian Sea, Gulf of Aden, and Red Sea, before the days of air-
conditioning, was almost unbearable; sometimes tempers flared. In 1913
King-Harman, now a sub-lieutenant in the elderly light cruiser *Fox*,
wrote to his father about a row between the first lieutenant (No. 1) and
the captain:

> The situation between No 1 and the skipper came to a head a few days
> ago, when on receipt of a more than usually rude note from the skipper
> about some new orders for the officers, the First Lieut told him that he
> refused to serve under him any more, and also that since the end of last
> year, his (the Captain's) unreasonable orders, and inconsiderate conduct
> had turned the ship's company into a discontented and slovenly mob, and
> had undermined the loyalty of the officers – all of which is perfectly true.
>   He ended up by requesting to be court-martialled so that his action in
> applying to leave the ship might be vindicated. Now the skipper might be
> a perfect ass, but he knew jolly well that if many of the rows he has been
> the cause of come to light in a court martial, he would never be employed

again, so he simply forwarded the application for leave to the Admiral. It has been granted, & the Admiralty cabled out an offer to No 1 of the next new destroyer. It's just the job he wanted, as he is popularly supposed to be one of the smartest destroyer captains in the service.

A few months later he wrote:

The skipper is a little daunted by the heat – but not much. His greatest crime is his insisting on the officers and men wearing strict uniform, which is cruelty. All the other ships in the Gulf have always worn shorts and vests, not so Caulfield, who has given orders that officers on duty are always to be in uniform, and tunics buttoned up. Silly fool, I hope he gets invalided with prickly heat, which he's got already

Service in the Gulf involved a great deal of time spent on landing parties and boat cruises to search gun-running and slaving dhows. King-Harman wrote with reference to the previous crew of the *Fox*, who they relieved on station in 1911; his letter tells us something about contemporary attitudes to death:

It is rather a shame that they don't allow the Persian Gulf boat business to count as active service – as it seems to be accompanied with more than its [active service] discomforts with none of the honour and glory. The extraordinary thing is that it doesn't seem to be so unhealthy as one would think, they [*Fox*'s ship's company] only lost about a dozen men the whole time, including a few killed last year during a landing party, and none of the boats lost any men.

The *Fox* also landed parties on the coast of British Somaliland, where Mohammed bin Abdullah Hassan, known as the 'Mad Mullah', had been leading a religious revolt since 1899. It was finally quelled in 1920. At the time Somaliland was divided between the British and Italians. In July 1912 Douglas King-Harman

took the cutter into three places, and jolly ticklish work it was, as the landing was always on a sandy beach, with a heavy surf running. We used to run in as close as possible, and the interpreters would jump overboard and swim ashore. We brought over from Aden a certain Somali sheikh, the brother of the Sultan of a large Somali tribe. This gentleman is reputed to be a thoroughgoing rascal, ostensibly a friend of the English, but doing a roaring trade in gunrunning for the Mad Mullah at the same time. I had a most amusing time trying to land him and his retinue. His staff got through the surf all right, but the sheikh refused to risk his valuable life and begged to go in further. I went in as far as I dared, and was badly swamped by two colossal breakers in doing so, but still he wouldn't go overboard. I was getting fed up with plunging about in the surf, expecting every moment to be sunk, so without more ado I told him that if he didn't go, I would chuck him overboard – as he didn't believe me, I proceeded to do so – and his dignified protest as he was unceremoniously dumped overboard nearly made me burst out laughing. I expect he is gunrunning with more zest than ever.

At another village we were surprised to see a Union Jack flying over the mud fort outside, and discovered that the Mad Mullah had been there only two days before, killed 200 men, and carried off nearly all their goats and women. The unfortunate people are only armed with spears, while the Mullah has a plentiful supply of modern rifles which the French are pouring into Somaliland for him. One of the Somali boys came off grinning, saying that the Mullah had only succeeded in carrying off his sister, while his goats were safe! Altogether British 'protection' seems to be rather a farce. Berbera is the only place on the coast where we are allowed to land without an armed escort.

Unless appointed to a ship or shore establishment, officers existed on half-pay. King-Harman was appointed to the course at the Royal Naval College, Greenwich, and came home in the cruiser *Sirius* expecting some well-earned leave on arrival. He wrote to his father from Chatham:

Seeing that I shall be at Chatham on Saturday night, and have to be at Greenwich on Monday – I don't see where any leave comes in. I not only lose my leave, but thanks to both the 1st Lieut and the Navigator being married men, and Rogers being senior to me, I'm cooped up here in this beastly ship this evening and all tomorrow. Makes me a bit sick of life, especially as Miss Moffatt [his future wife] is staying with friends in Southsea, having come down from Scotland to see something of me.

Comes of joining a poisonous profession like the Navy – as much leave as a convict and the pay of a casual labourer. Still worse, apparently I was not re-appointed to *Fox* on promotion, & have therefore worked my passage home on half pay, a piece of meanness that I didn't think the Admiralty were capable of.

King-Harman, a gallant and competent officer, was to be awarded the DSC twice in the First World War and its immediate aftermath, and the DSO in the Second. But what of the state of the navy in 1914, despite King-Harman's very understandable disillusionment? Thanks to the drive of men like Admiral 'Jacky' Fisher and his disciples in the 'Fishpond', and notwithstanding what has been said earlier, startling advances had been made in a number of areas to bring the Service into the twentieth century.

The most astounding manifestations of new technology were the rapid development of two inventions that would enable the Royal Navy to fight below the sea and in the air, as well as on the surface. Only a handful of people (including Fisher and the gunnery enthusiast Admiral Sir Percy Scott) were sufficiently prescient to forecast that submarines and aircraft would eclipse the battleship as the principal means of striking the enemy both at sea and on the land, though eventually at distances and with a destructive power beyond Fisher's and Scott's wildest dreams. The ability to attack, and be attacked, in three dimensions was arguably a greater revolution than the change from sail to steam. Most naval officers and the public believed that in any future war, great battles would be fought with the big guns on which so much money had been lavished.

Contrary to popular myth, the Admiralty was not slow to see the value of the submarine, and had ordered five 'Holland-boats' by the end of 1900. To begin with the Admiralty was dismissive about the efficacy of submarines, as a ruse to discourage foreign powers from investigating the possibilities of this type of warfare.[21]

Twenty-year-old Sub-Lieutenant Cecil Talbot, having volunteered, was appointed to serve in submarines on 8 April 1905, some four years after the first crews had formed up. On 13 April, according to his diary, he went for his first trip in Number 4, one of the first Holland boats, or A-class as they were also designated,

> from 9 to 2.30, and was very pleased to hear afterwards that it was about a bad a day as it is possible to have. We went over to Sandown Bay & attacked TB [torpedo boat] 26; there was a nasty lop in the Solent, so we had the hatch shut down all the time and in consequence the atmosphere got a trifle thick; I was very nearly sick on the way over from the stink and kicking about. We dived several times; we once struck the bottom with a bump, through trying to rise by blowing the auxiliary ballast in 7 fathoms. On another occasion the boat started to sink when Hart, the captain of the boat, was on deck. By the time we got back to the *Thames* [depot ship], I had discovered where the 'hard line' [sic] money comes in.

Talbot meant 'hard lying' money or 'hard liers'. Submarine pay, as it was called officially, was paid to all officers and ratings in the submarine service from 1903. This almost doubled a rating's pay. Commanding officers were entitled to 'command pay', which, with submarine pay, doubled their salary too. The other officers found that they drew just over half as much again as their contemporaries in the rest of the navy.

Hard liers was well earned, not least for the hygienic arrangements. Telegraphist Halter:

> In E17 we did have a heads [lavatory] right aft. One of the exhaust pipes ran through it and you got boiled if you went in there. But because we'd

got so little food and drink you'd go days without wanting to go. In C18 and D4, we had no heads. Our Captain used to say 'everybody below', and they'd carry it out on the bridge, then come down, dive to twenty feet, wash it away, and come up again. But the conning towers were hollow, only casings. You could go down there in a bucket, and empty it through the holes in the side. If you were going to dive there was no worry about the mess. If it was only passing water, you did it over the lee side. Down below doing extended diving, you used a bucket quarter full of diesel oil. It wasn't offensive at all then.

In the early days there was no course to qualify officers for service in submarines, and within three weeks Talbot found

to my amazement I was put into B 1 as third officer, they having come to the conclusion that she wants three. Went out in her, ran trials in Stokes Bay, on the surface we got 11.9 [knots] with the engine and 8.2 [knots] with the motor; we also did a couple of submerged runs, but the TB with us took the times wrong. B 1 is a huge boat, 135 feet long.

The B-class boats, completed in 1905, were propelled on the surface by a petrol engine or battery-driven motor, and while submerged they relied on the battery motor. Submarines were inherently dangerous, and some of the trials were of the 'suck it and see' variety. For example Talbot records that 'Professor Haldane, the air expert, & the doctor & some others, 16 in all, went down in A 6 to be shut up for 24 hours, with the object of seeing what the air is like at the end of that time'. Talbot's diary:

Thursday June 8th [1905]
    A 8 has gone down with 14 hands; Candy (Capt) & Murdoch (Sub), her Coxswain, and one AB were saved, the only people who were on deck, but the remainder, including Fletcher of my term [in *Britannia*], went down.

Sunday June 11th
    The reason for the A 8 accident is now known. She had just risen after diving; Nos 1, 3, & 4 main ballast tanks were partly blown, No 2 was full; they went ahead with the gas [petrol] engine, and Candy noticing the boat was a bit down by the bows, ordered the diving rudder to be put hard up, instead of which it was put hard down, and she immediately dipped.

Tuesday June 20th
    The court-martial of the A 8 survivors was started today; it appears that the people inside were alive for 1¾ hours after they went down, when they were killed by the explosion from the chlorine gas; they must have

become unconscious in about 20 minutes after dipping, from the chlorine.*

The First Lord, Winston Churchill, took a keen interest in submarines, as he did in every aspect of the navy. In 1913 Talbot was in Barrow where the brand-new E6, of which he was CO, was being built. He was visited by Churchill, who often travelled in the Admiralty Board yacht *Enchantress*.

Monday, September 8th
Winston Churchill visited the works; the *Enchantress* anchored in Morecombe Bay and he came up in a tug, being expected at 10 and not arriving till 12. He went round E 6 first, making several thoroughly impracticable suggestions on small details, and being very rude to Vickers directors about their lateness in delivery of boats.

D and E boats had diesel engines for running on the surface and charging batteries, much safer than petrol. E boats were the most advanced submarines in the world at the outbreak of war the following year. An E boat weighed between 655 tons (E1 to E8) and 667 tons (E9 to E51) on the surface and over 100 tons more submerged. The earlier boats had four torpedo tubes (one bow, two beam, and one stern) and carried eight torpedoes. From E9 on, the class had five torpedo tubes (two bow, two beam, and one stern) and carried ten torpedoes. All E boats had two screws, diesel motors, two electric motors, a top speed of 15 knots on the surface and 9 knots dived, and a range of 3,000 nautical miles at 10 knots on the surface. Saddle tanks, first fitted in the D-class, increased internal space, and diesels eliminated the dangerous petrol vapour, responsible for explosions in the A- to C-class boats. An E boat could descend as far as 200 feet, and sit on the bottom for hours. They had a complement of thirty.

Oswald Hallifax, an early submariner, wrote:

There were no CO's training classes; a newly made captain when he got his first command learned how to attack by practice. If he was a good shot at partridges etc. he probably became a good attacker in a submarine. Enemy speeds were pure guesswork. The first attacks on a screened ship or squadron of battleships were made by the 8th Flotilla (D and E boats) at Torbay in the early summer of 1914. The first day the submarines had to keep on the surface for the attack and fly a red flag.
As 1st Lieut I was not allowed to carry out an attack, except on one occasion, as the 1st Lieut of an E Boat in Harwich in early 1915, nor could

---

* Chlorine gas was produced when salt water got into the submarine's batteries.

I get any information on how it was done. The only reply to questions on that point being that it was a matter of common sense. Of course as 1st Lieut of an A boat I never asked to do an attack, for the newly made captains had to take every opportunity to train themselves.

There were no attacking instruments until at the end of August 1917, Captain Nasmith produced the 'Iswas'. Before that all submarine captains attacked by eye alone. The pre-war targets for A boats were almost invariably a pick-up vessel of the Pygmy class. She had only one speed and steady courses were almost always steered. The submarine got into position about 4–6 points off the target's bow by eye – no estimation of the enemy's course was made by any of the captains I served under pre-war. As 1st Lieut of an A boat at Plymouth throughout 1913 (I was 1st Lieut of all three), I had several changes of captain. One of the main points in their turnover [when a CO handed over command to a successor] was the 'Magic Number', this being the deflection always used for the Pygmy.

We had a deflection table, but this was only referred to if the submarine happened to be badly out of position.

In submarines of that era the stench of human bodies, urine and excrement (the system of pumping out waste was rudimentary), and in the older boats, petrol, was enough to make the most hardened men gag at times. One should add to the physical discomfort the claustrophobic sensation of being enclosed in a metal cigar tube crammed with machinery, and the ever-present prospect of being trapped on the bottom with no escape.

*

The birth of naval aviation in the Royal Navy dates from spring 1911, when Sir Frank Mclean's offer of the loan of two aircraft and the use of a hangar and Eastchurch aerodrome for six months was accepted by the Admiralty. One of the first four officers to be taught to fly was Lieutenant Samson, who later wrote that

When the six months' course came to an end, the four of us were like fish out of water. The Admiralty had no ideas as regards our future. There was only one thing to do, to beard the lion in his den. A very fierce lion it was, Sir A K Wilson, First Sea Lord. With trepidation I entered the Admiralty. I had two little 'Queens' in my hand; one Admiral Briggs, one of the Sea Lords was an old captain of mine; the other, that I had once won the Middle-Weight boxing championship of the Navy, and had refereed the Channel Fleet Championships in the presence of the mighty 'Tug' [Wilson], and he had expressed appreciation of my work.

Samson was ushered into Wilson's office, to be greeted with, 'Hello, Samson, I suppose you want to go on flying; I don't see the use of it for the Navy for some years to come.' Samson:

> Feeling like a Serpentine bather on a cold Christmas morning, I plunged into a rapid explanation of my ideas, producing to amplify them a blue print of a weird and totally impractical flying boat. He listened to me and said, 'What do you want me to do?'
>
> 'Buy the two aeroplanes we have learned on; let us go on flying. Give me four engine room artificers, four shipwrights and four blue jackets, let me order a Hydro Aeroplane [seaplane] to be built by Shorts to see if it is possible to fly off the sea. I can however promise one thing, Sir; I will prove it possible to fly off a ship in six months.'
>
> I went back to Eastchurch without being able to impart much hope to my three comrades, but to our joy within a week everything I had asked for was granted.

Thus was born, in Samson's words, 'the incomparable Naval Air Service'. After much deliberation with Horace Short, Samson eventually decided that they would build an aeroplane that could 'use the water as an aerodrome', rather than a 'boat that flew'. The navy as a whole was not keen on aviation, regarding aircraft as toys of no practical use. Samson's problem was to convince his superiors that there was a great future for aviation if properly used.

An American, Ely, had flown an aircraft off a deck built on a United States Navy cruiser. In Samson's view this was too radical for his own service. He came up with the idea of a wooden trackway laid from the top of the fore 12-inch turret to the bows of the *King Edward* class battleship *Africa*. This gave him a 100-foot runway. Experiments with an aeroplane in still air showed that he needed 300 feet for takeoff. However, by sloping the trackway down towards the bows, and the fact that the end of the trackway was above the water, might, in his view, just allow him to get away with it when the ship was at a buoy.

Meanwhile Lieutenant Longmore, one of the four pioneers, and like Samson to transfer to the RAF in 1918, had been experimenting with air bags on the skids and tail of the aircraft, in the hope of being able to both take off and land on water – floats came a little later. Air bags were totally impractical for take-off, but Samson realized that if fitted they allowed an aircraft to take off from a ship using its wheels, and alight on water, whence it could be hoisted on board.

On 10 January 1912, the great day arrived for the fly-off. Samson had just seventy hours solo, 'not a great deal for the sort of work required', he remarked. Getting the aeroplane on board the *Africa* and hoisting it on to the trackway was a tricky business.

> I was in rather a bad state of nerves the whole time as I feared damage to the aeroplane. But once seated in the pilot's seat with the engine going and my hand on the quick release toggle, I felt quite normal. The trackway looked very short and I didn't feel at all confident that I would be able to get into the air. The mooring buoy looked 'grim' as if awaiting my impact. Unfortunately owing to the strength of the tide being more powerful than the wind, the ship was not lying head to wind and tugs were signalled for. I realised that the various high officials on the bridge wouldn't like to wait, so I said to the Commander, 'I won't wait for the tugs'.
>
> I pulled the quick release and started to toddle, and 'toddle' describes how it felt to me, towards the bows. I found a little difficulty keeping on the trackway, but fortunately no mishap occurred. As I neared the end I got my tail well up and I didn't attempt to get her nose up until I was at the very end of the run. To my delight, I found myself flying, but I missed the mooring buoy by only about three inches.

Samson's next experiment was with a 'Hydro' aeroplane, Short Number 10. The design of seaplanes was an unknown science at the time, including the optimum shape for floats, and their positioning and buoyancy. On 27 March 1912, Samson tested the first machine, but with wheels instead of floats, and she flew 'quite well'. He then carried out taxiing tests with floats fitted, and a number of adjustments were made. Number 10 was then embarked on board HMS *Hibernia*:

> and we all set off for the King's review of the fleet. On May 2nd [1912] I flew off the trackway erected on the *Hibernia* while she was steaming at 10½ knots. This was the first flight ever made from a ship steaming. I found no difficulty at all and left the trackway after a run of 60 feet. Next day, May 3rd, I took No 10 off the water and safely alighted after a 10 minute flight. This flight demonstrated the first practical seaplane. The results of the flights on January 10th, May 2nd, and May 3rd gave the Admiralty proof that there was a future in naval aviation, and from that time I got practical support.

Further innovations swiftly followed, including the Short brothers' brainchild of folding wings, allowing seaplanes to be carried on ships. Samson was the first to fire a machine gun from an aircraft, at Eastchurch on 10 February 1913. By the outbreak of the war eighteen months later, the Royal Navy had notched up several other 'firsts' for British aviation: flying across country by night; flying in formation; test-bomb dropping; and experimenting with wireless.

In the early days the naval aviators formed the Naval Wing of the

Royal Flying Corps (RFC), and its six pilots appeared as such in the 1912 Army List. The needs of the navy were different from the army, and the Admiralty was quite rightly not going to have policy matters for its aviation wing decided by the RFC. Actual control was split between the Admiralty (Naval Wing) and the War Office (Military Wing), and soon the Naval Wing was being referred to as the Royal Naval Air Service (RNAS). In 1913, the First Sea Lord produced a policy paper that set out the tasks and needs of the RNAS, whose aircraft would be a seaplane capable of operating from ship or shore, a scout to work with the fleet, and a home defence fighter.[22]

The RNAS experimented with all types of aircraft, refusing to confine its purchases to the Royal Aircraft Factory, or to ban monoplanes, which the RFC had done on grounds of safety. The Royal Navy was supported in this attitude by Churchill, who had been taught to fly at Eastchurch by Lieutenant John Seddon RN. By 1914, the Naval Wing was firmly the RNAS, and the modern Fleet Air Arm celebrates that as its birth year.

*

Fisher is perhaps best known for commissioning HMS *Dreadnought*, the all-big-gun warship, with ten 12-inch guns, which in 1906 made all other battleships in the world out of date.*

A massive building programme followed with nine more *Dreadnought*-class battleships with 12-inch guns, and another ten, starting with the *Orion* class, with ten 13.5-inch guns and secondary armament ranging from sixteen 4-inch up to fourteen 6-inch guns. Due to come into service were the first of the five magnificent *Queen Elizabeth* and five *Royal Sovereign* class battleships, each with eight giant 15-inch guns, two of which can be seen outside the Imperial War Museum in London. The *Queen Elizabeth*s and *Royal Sovereign*s all had oil-fired boilers, thus avoiding the back-breaking work of coaling and stoking. This in itself was a bold decision, for whereas there was plenty of coal in the British Isles, there was no North Sea oil on tap until the 1970s: Churchill, as First Lord of the Admiralty, persuaded parliament to buy a controlling interest in the Anglo-Iranian Oil Company to ensure the supply of oil. Ten battle cruisers had also been brought into service, the last, HMS *Tiger*, due to join the fleet in October 1914.

* The expression 'all-big-gun' means that her main armament was all of one calibre. This made spotting the fall of shot simpler, since one did not have to try to differentiate between splashes made by shells of different calibre. She had ten 12in guns, ten 12pdr guns, two 3pdrs, and four 18in torpedo tubes fitted below the waterline to fire broadside. Her successors all had secondary armament of various calibres.

The battle cruiser was another Fisher brainchild, his concept to have a ship as fast as a cruiser but with battleship-sized guns. These ships would be able to catch and crush the armoured cruisers that might threaten Britain's trade routes. To achieve the necessary speed, they were lightly armoured compared with battleships, which typically had an armoured belt of between ten and thirteen inches and turret armour of eleven to thirteen inches. But one should not imagine battle cruisers as eggshells armed with sledgehammers. Compared with modern warships they were well armoured, with six inches of belt and seven inches of turret armour, and the four magnificent 'cats' (*Lion*, *Princess Royal*, *Queen Mary* and *Tiger*) had nine inches of belt and turret armour.*

In Fisher's vision, as well as clearing the seas of cruisers threatening Britain's trade routes, the battle cruisers would scout ahead of the battle fleet, using their heavy guns to destroy the enemy cruiser screen, and their superior speed to escape the enemy battleships. All well and good, until the Germans built battle cruisers that were almost as fast, better armoured, and – perhaps most important – had more and better watertight compartments.

Fisher's concept relied on good gunnery. Gunnery ranges had increased dramatically in the period between 1901 and 1914, thanks to officers such as Percy Scott, Lord Charles Beresford (a hated rival of Fisher's), and Fisher himself and his 'fishpond'. At the end of the nineteenth century battle practices had been conducted at 2,000 yards. By 1911, ranges had increased to 10,000 yards, and the 1913 battle practices were fired at 14,000 to 15,000 yards, with battle cruisers shooting at 16,000 yards. The war found the navy in the process of introducing director firing, that is all main-armament guns controlled and fired by one man situated high up in the 'fighting top' or 'director'. Hitherto, the guns of each turret (usually two per turret in this war) were controlled by an officer sitting in the rear of the turret, looking out through a periscope.

As fighting ranges increased, good gunnery demanded accurate range-finding, and a means of correcting the fall of shot. There were two fire-control systems on offer: one invented by Dreyer, a naval officer, which was inferior to the one designed by a civilian, Arthur Pollen. Dreyer's system was based on trigonometry and only worked efficiently when firing and target ship maintained a steady course and speed, preferably on parallel courses. Pollen's system was in effect a manually operated analogue computer which could cope with the reality of fighting at sea, including changes of course and speed which produces an ever-changing

---

* These figures are maximum thickness.

rate of change of range. Pollen's Argo system incorporated a gyro mounting for rangefinding and target-bearing indication. The Admiralty bought forty-five of these in 1910 for trials. By 1914, six ships were fitted with the Argo Mark IV. One was fitted in the battle cruiser *Queen Mary*, and consequently her gunnery was always superior. But the Mark V, which produced constantly up to date range and deflection, was never tried or adopted by the Royal Navy before or during the First World War.[23]

The Admiralty chose the inferior system, possibly because they did not understand Pollen's, lacked the imagination and battle experience to see what advantages it offered, and Dreyer was a protégé of Jellicoe's with a reputation as a gunnery expert; it was also cheaper. Endowed with the benefit of hindsight, we should not be smug; the Ministry of Defence's procurement policy operates on similar lines to this day.

The British outnumbered the Germans in dreadnoughts and super-dreadnoughts; in battleships by 25 to 17 in 1914 (including two built for Turkey and one for Chile, which were requisitioned at the outbreak of war), and in battle cruisers by 10 to 7. The disparity would increase as the five *Queen Elizabeth*s, five *Royal Sovereign*s, and two *Renown* class battle cruisers were completed.

The Organization and Deployment of the Royal Navy

By 1914, the ships of the Royal Navy had been organized into three Fleets: the First consisting of the most modern ships; the Second of ships that normally spent most of the time in harbour with reduced crews; and the Third of the oldest warships. The First Fleet formed the Grand Fleet at the outbreak of war, and by itself was larger than the German navy.

In home waters at the outbreak of war, the Royal Navy had 275 surface ships, from battleships to torpedo boats, and 65 submarines. Guarding the northern outlets to the Atlantic, the Grand Fleet at the outbreak of war consisted of the 1st, 2nd, 3rd, and 4th Battle Squadrons (BS) based at Scapa Flow in the Orkneys, and the 1st Battle Cruiser Squadron (BCS), commanded by Vice-Admiral Sir David Beatty, which was soon detached from Scapa Flow; first to Cromarty Firth, then to the Firth of Forth. At this stage the Grand Fleet consisted of twenty-one dreadnoughts, and the eight *King Edward* class pre-dreadnoughts of the 3rd Battle Squadron. Beatty's command consisted of only four battle cruisers (three others were in the Mediterranean, one in the Pacific, and one in the western Atlantic). Under command of the Grand Fleet were the eight armoured cruisers (later redesignated just cruisers) of the 2nd and 3rd Cruiser Squadrons (each of four armoured or heavy cruisers) and four light cruisers of the 1st Light Cruiser Squadron, plus nine other cruisers and forty-two destroyers.

Blocking the southern exits to the Atlantic, the Channel Fleet based at Portland consisted of the 5th, 6th, 7th, and 8th Battle Squadrons, made up of the older pre-dreadnoughts. At Harwich, under Commodore Tyrwhitt, was a force of three light cruisers and thirty-five destroyers, whose task was to patrol the southern part of the North Sea, assist the sweeps by the Grand Fleet, and accompany the Channel Fleet if it steamed north. In modern terminology it was under operational control of the C-in-C Grand Fleet, but, as will become apparent, his instructions to the Harwich Force could be overridden by the Admiralty.

Patrol flotillas, consisting of the older destroyers in service, were based on Dover, the Humber, the Tyne, and Forth operated under the command of an Admiral of Patrols, later redesignated Rear Admiral Commanding the East Coast of England. His task was to attack any German vessels attempting to land troops on the east coast of Britain. Within two months of the outbreak of war, the Dover Patrol was detached, and put under command of Rear Admiral the Honourable Horace Hood (known to the sailors as 'the 'Onourable 'Orace), with the special task of denying the Straits of Dover to the Germans.

At the naval ports of the Nore (Sheerness), Portsmouth, Devonport, Pembroke and Queenstown in Ireland, local defence flotillas (LDFs) operated under their respective senior naval officers (SNOs). Their job was to support the defences of the dockyards against naval raids and patrol off the harbours. The LDFs were allocated the left-over ships and submarines: the oldest destroyers and torpedo boats, the latter a class of vessel which had been cut from the shipbuilding programme in 1907, and the old A, B, and C Class submarines, considered fit for coastal work only. The newer submarines, the D and E Classes, were based at Harwich under Commodore Roger Keyes (designated Commodore (S) for Submarines).

The western end of the Channel was patrolled by the 12th Cruiser Squadron; both it and the Channel Fleet were under direct command of the Admiralty. It should be borne in mind that the Admiralty, like its army counterpart, the War Office, was a department of state implementing government policy and providing assets (ships and men) with which to prosecute the war. But unlike the War Office, the Admiralty was also an operational headquarters. It could communicate directly with the fleets, squadrons, and individual ships by wireless, and thereby had the power to 'move the pieces about the board', even though it might not be in possession of the complete operational picture. If the Admiralty received information about enemy movements and intentions from wireless intercept, it could pass this on to the relevant fleet, squadron, or ship. As an operational headquarters, the Admiralty could, if so minded, interfere in the day-to-day actions of subordinate commanders, in present-day terminology 'back seat drive'; which it did from time to time, not always with the happiest of results.

The German Navy

Because of the disparity in battleship numbers, German naval strategy was based on the premiss that they were unlikely to defeat the British fleet if they encountered it when it was concentrated. For some years before 1913, the Germans had planned on the Royal Navy mounting a close blockade of the German coast. Accordingly, they would contrive to find detached units of the British fleet and crush them by superior numbers, or lure them onto their battle squadrons with the same outcome. In this way they hoped to whittle down the British until they could engage them on equal terms and defeat them. Following their 1913 wargame, the German naval staff came to the conclusion that the British would have difficulty maintaining a permanent close blockade, and would alternate between a close and distant blockade; but they would resort to a close blockade at the beginning of any war. Therefore they only made plans to cater for a British close blockade. This strategy is a good example of presuming your enemy will do what happens to suit you.

Whatever system of fire control one uses, accurate rangefinding is a prerequisite. The German pre-eminence in optical technology meant that they had better rangefinders and night-fighting equipment than the British. However, they did not have a director-firing system, and in other respects the German navy was not as wonderful as some authors have made out. They did not have a long-service enlistment for ratings; their sailors served for three years, unlike British seamen who signed on for a minimum of twelve. As a result the turnover of crews in the German navy was high. As so often in any service which has regular officers and conscripted ratings or soldiers, sailors in the German navy were even more remote from their officers than in the Royal Navy. The food was bad. Punishments were more ferocious, including flogging, which had been phased out of the Royal Navy in the previous century. German officers did not, as a matter of course, participate in coaling ship. In harbour, the officers remained aloof from their men, not troubling to see that sports facilities were provided; in short, the human factor was ignored.

The German Navy was even more class-conscious than the Royal Navy and German naval officers were acutely aware that they were the junior service to the army, which had far superior social status and prestige. The German army was the lineal descendent of the Prussian army, the instrument which had unified Germany after defeating, in turn, the Danes, the Austrians and the French in the previous century. The German navy had yet to prove itself.

The German navy was itself the product of a combination of pan-nationalist sentiment and envy of the Royal Navy by the neurotic Kaiser Wilhelm II, whose inferiority complex concerning almost anything English, his mother's nationality, was legendary. The German navy was also born of muddled strategic thinking which argued that provided it was large enough it would deter the British from standing in Germany's way of acquiring colonies and their propensity for riding roughshod over anyone who defied them. In fact it had the opposite effect, and was perceived, in the words of Edward Grey, the British Foreign Secretary, as the manifestation of 'Germany's itch to dominate'.[24] In Professor Marder's view, 'Naval rivalry did not cause the war, but it ensured that when it broke out, Great Britain would be on the side of Germany's enemies'.[25] Furthermore, as he points out, 'it [the German Navy] was not strong enough in time of war to protect German commerce or the German colonies, or meet its main rival in battle on the open sea.'[26]

Faced with a stronger opponent, the Germans were correct in adopting a 'fleet in being' strategy. The British were forced to remain concentrated and expend time and assets on dominating the North Sea, while the High Seas Fleet remained safely in port, as Napoleon had forced the Royal Navy to do between 1805 and 1814. Where the Germans made their biggest mistake was in building the fleet in the first place, for the reasons outlined above. But this was merely one example of the German penchant for taking leave of their senses, strategically speaking; which, repeated several times, was to lead to their defeat in two World Wars.

Finally Before the Fighting

Curiously, both Tirpitz, the architect of the German navy, and Fisher, his opposite number, shared a genius for organization and leadership, but neither was a strategist. Both Britain and Germany embarked on the First World War with weapons systems that they had not used in battle before, and had had little time on which to practise in peace. The dreadnought battleship had been in service for a mere eight years. Add to this mines, submarines, aircraft, and airships, and the learning curve for admirals, British and German alike, brought up in sailing ships, was steep. It is perhaps not surprising that the Royal Navy entered the war with the following deficiencies listed by Professor Marder:[27]

No minelayers

No purpose-built minesweepers

No system of night gunnery

No anti-airship gun

No anti-submarine tactics and equipment

No safe harbour

Inefficient torpedoes

Only eight ships fitted for director firing

He might have added, thanks to Fisher's strategic myopia, no equipment, training, or doctrine for amphibious operations.

British admirals and captains of cruisers and major warships at the outbreak of the Second World War had, without exception, taken part in the First. In 1939 they were no strangers to war fighting, were familiar, in general terms, with the equipment with which they went to war again just twenty years later, and had had the opportunity to absorb the lessons of the First World War, such as the need to practise night fighting. The admirals and captains in 1914 had no such experience to guide them.

2

Commence hostilities against Germany

'Mobilise!'

On 15 July 1914, a test mobilization of the Royal Navy's Third Fleet was carried out. This test had been planned since October the previous year, and it was mere chance that it coincided with the period of heightened tension in Europe following the assassination in Sarajevo on 28 June of Archduke Franz Ferdinand, the heir to the Habsburg Austro-Hungarian Empire, by a Bosnian terrorist (a member of the Serb 'Black Hand' organization). The Austrians, encouraged by the Kaiser, had presented fifteen deliberately humiliating demands to Serbia in an ultimatum which they hoped would give them the excuse to invade, when, as they hoped, Serbia would refuse to comply. If invaded, Serbia would be aided by Russia, who in turn would be supported by France. This would give the Germans the longed-for opportunity to smash first the French then the Russians. The unknown factor was Britain, who had no desire to become involved in a war in Europe, much to the irritation of the French, who had allowed themselves to believe that Franco-British staff talks in the years leading up to 1914 automatically guaranteed British assistance in the event of war with Germany. In July, the attention of most of the British government was focused across the Irish Sea, on the 'Ulster Crisis' brought about by the threat of Loyalist opposition to Irish Home Rule. The British Liberal establishment's opinion of the squabbles between Austria and Serbia at the time was articulated by the *Manchester Guardian*: 'if it were physically possible for Serbia to be towed out to sea and sunk there, the air of Europe would at once seem cleaner'.[1]

The Third Fleet, consisting of older warships, normally manned with small maintenance crews, was brought up to strength with reservists. James Cox:

> I was sent to *Goliath*, although actually I was on the books of *Vernon*, the torpedo school at the time. The ship was filled with a few regulars like us, but mostly Royal Fleet Reserve people who had finished their twelve years in the Navy. We brought these ships 'up to date', got all the telephones, gun control etc. working.

Cadet Lowry also took part:

In July 1914, I was in the junior term at Dartmouth, and should have stayed there for another two years. At the Test Mobilization, the College was cleared and I went to HMS *Prince of Wales*, an old pre-Dreadnought battleship with eleven others of my term for one week, before returning to Dartmouth.

On 18 July, a grand review of the whole fleet, First, Second, and Third Fleets, was held at Spithead. Eleven lines of ships, some over nine miles long, filled the Solent between Spithead and the Isle of Wight. The First Fleet alone consisted of twenty-eight battleships (nineteen dreadnoughts), four battle cruisers, seventeen cruisers, and seventy-six destroyers.

Cadet McEwan was a member of the first term of cadets to enter the Royal Navy under the Public Schools Special Entry Scheme:

On Saturday July 18th, 1914, HMS *Highflyer* moored off Spithead with other ships for the test mobilization. The *Highflyer* was the training ship for the Special Entry Public School Cadets and had 41 cadets on board. Just before noon the First Lord, Mr Winston Churchill came on board and inspected the cadets. During the afternoon two naval airships and numerous waterplanes [seaplanes] flew over the fleet.

The review itself was low-key by previous standards. Lieutenant-Commander Cecil Talbot, the CO of the Submarine E6, noted in his diary:[2]

Saturday July 18th
    left at 5.45 am for Spithead and took up our position close to Fort Monkton; the *Hazard*'s C boats, and the available D and E boats are all out here. The King was to have arrived about noon, but at 10 am we heard he was not arriving at Portsmouth till 5 pm, and would not come out to Spithead today; we afterwards heard it was due to the Ulster crisis.

Sunday July 19th
    Bathed from E6 before breakfast. The King came out in the [Royal Yacht] *Alexandra* about 11.30 am, went down some of the lines, and from 3 to 6.30 visited the *Iron Duke*, *King George V*, and *Collingwood*, then returning to harbour. As a review it was remarkably uninteresting; no guards and bands were paraded & ships were not manned, the ships' companies being merely called to attention as he passed.

On 19 July the combined fleets put to sea for exercises ending in a visit by all ships to Portland. On 23 July, the Third Fleet was ordered to sail to its home ports to demobilize, sending reservists home and regulars back to their establishments and instructional schools. Only minor vessels had dispersed when the news came through on 26 July that the Austrians were mobilizing against Serbia, having rejected the Serb reply to the ultimatum following the assassination of Archduke Franz Ferdinand.

In his private diary Midshipman Alderson of HMS *Lion* recorded:

> Sunday July 26th. The day begins quietly enough, many officers and men of our squadron (1st Battle Cruiser Squadron), confidently counting on going on leave tomorrow evening or at least Tuesday morning. But the evening is disturbed by many vague rumours regarding the European Crisis.

With war looming, and the possibility of a surprise attack by the German fleet real, now was not the time to lower the Royal Navy's readiness. So on his own initiative, the First Sea Lord, Prince Louis of Battenberg, cancelled the demobilization. Alderson:

> Monday July 27th. The rumours of yesterday prove to be only too well founded. Many ships in Portland including ourselves are hard at work coaling. The grabs on Portland coaling jetty are incessantly working to keep the lighters full. The *Southampton* (light cruiser) coaled alongside [the jetty not from a lighter or *Lion*], and left the jetty with heaps of coal piled on her upper deck.

Peace still reigned in Portsmouth dockyard. Talbot:

> Monday July 27th
>   Summer leave was to have started in the evening, but in the afternoon it was cancelled owing to the strained international situation. I tried to get torpedoes & warheads into the boats, but no one in authority seemed to think matters were serious. Went ashore at 4.
>
> Tuesday July 28th
>   At 1.30 am I was called by Lockhart, who came to say that *Maidstone* [depot ship] and submarines were sailing at 8 pm, and warheads and war stores were being got into the boats. Caught the 2 am boat from Asia Pontoon and spent the rest of the night hoisting in spare torpedoes, warheads, war stores etc. with quarter crews, the remainder being ashore. The remainder of the crews were on board by 8, and at 8.30 we proceeded to Spithead. Went alongside the *Maidstone* and filled up with fuel. I saw the Captain just before sailing, he said hostilities might commence any minute.

By 28 July, the navy had been placed on standby for operations by Churchill, who has often incorrectly been credited with halting the demobilization, but had immediately approved. Accidents took their toll as usual. Midshipman Burnett of the battleship *Colossus* noted in his diary:

> Tuesday July 28th 1914 at Portland
> We commenced coaling from lighters at 7 am. 1,000 tons were taken in. We finished at about 7 pm. Engineer Lieutenant Bury was killed at about 6.30 am by one of the main derrick guys. At about 11 am the man that was working the main derrick was killed.

Alderson:

> Early this morning [28 July] we took in beef and potatoes, and at midday we commenced filling up a lighter at Portland with stores of all kinds. We started unloading the lighter about 10 pm and worked through to the early hours of the morning. Austria-Hungary today declared war on Servia [sic].

The next day, the First Fleet sailed. Burnett (Wednesday 29 July 1914):

> Hands went to night defence at 8 pm. We steered a course to the westward so as to deceive anyone who might like to know where we were going. After about 2 hours we altered course and proceeded east, passing through the straits of Dover at midnight.

All ships were darkened and at night-defence stations in case of attacks by German torpedo boats. In the atmosphere of distrust of the Germans that prevailed at the time, combined with a total lack of war-fighting experience in the Royal Navy, this was thought highly possible. With hindsight, it is easy to scoff at such fears on the grounds that given the technology of the time (in particular, no radar), and without an accurate plot of the Grand Fleet's track, intercepting it at night would have been highly problematic. That is not to say that given the bellicose mood that had gripped the Germans, and if they had believed they could bring it off, they would not have grasped the opportunity of a mortal pre-emptive strike against the British battle fleet, effectively guaranteeing victory in the war at a stroke.

> Thursday July 30th 1914 at Sea
> Finished night defence at daylight. Ammunition was sent below. An order came to fuse all Lyddite and to load the 4 in guns with Lyddite. We exercised clear for action after divisions. Hoses were rigged & the 12 in guns loaded with common shell. War routine was carried out.

Alderson in the *Lion*:

Friday July 31st. Action stations during the forenoon. Curtains, tablecloths and other burnable luxuries are being stowed away. After divisions, the captain [Chatfield] spoke a few words bearing on the situation. He said that although the European situation is very grave, he considered the chances five-to-one against England going to war. He told us destination is Scapa Flow in the Orkneys, where we were going to coal.

We duly arrived at 5 pm, and immediately prepared the ship for coaling, taking in 920 tons, finishing at about midnight.

For the next four years and more, the back-breaking chore of coaling ship was the first task facing ships' companies on coming in from sea, however exhausted, and regardless of whether or not they had been in action, unless they were lucky enough to be in oil-fuelled ships.

By the evening of 31 July, the whole of the First Fleet, soon to be called the Grand Fleet, was at its war station in Scapa Flow. Others were also arriving at their war stations. Talbot in E6 anchored off Harwich at about midnight on 30 July, having carried out a dummy attack on the *Maidstone* after passing through the Straits of Dover:

Friday July 31st
Weighed at 5.30 am and proceeded into Harwich, securing alongside the *Maidstone* about 8.30. The Commodore [Keyes] sent for me in the forenoon, and told me that E 6 and E 8 are to proceed to the Heligoland Bight and see what we can do to draw blood. War seems certain.

At Dartmouth on 1 August, Cadet Lowry had

just mashed up a banana, covered it with Devonshire cream and sugar, when a Cadet Captain rushed into the canteen and said 'Mobilise'. I left it untasted and ran. I was still fourteen when I joined HMS *Lord Nelson* (I was fifteen on 18 August 1914) and except for 48 hours in February 1915, I did not have any leave for three years.

To start with we must have been a menace in the ship. The day after we joined, I was sent away in charge of the steam picket boat (56 feet long, 18 tons) and I had to stand on a wooden box to steer the boat. The Coxswain, a petty officer, kept a controlling hand on the wheel, but in a very few weeks, we found it was us who got into trouble when the boat was damaged and for other omissions, and not the Coxswain. We learned fast, and our best friends were the petty officers and three badge able seamen (men with over 13 years service) who in their own inimitable way taught us much and saved us from many foolish mistakes.

A letter written to his mother by the sixteen-year-old Cadet Herbert Williams (known to his family as 'Fat', although he was far from fat) on

1 August 1914, while still in the train bearing the cadets away from Dartmouth, conveys something of the atmosphere:

My darling Mum

Thanks very much for your letter. My leave had vanished into thin air also, for the present at all events. I am now on my way to Devonport to join the *Exmouth*.

Its all through this beastly war affair. Tuesday the Skipper got orders to stand by to mobilise and in the evening he gave us a jaw, and told us that we might have to join our ships at any moment etc.

Wednesday, we got a wire, 'War imminent, stand by to mobilise'. There was tremendous excitement of course. I was playing cricket in the afternoon, and we were all expecting to go at any moment. Sir Francis Drake playing bowls before the Armada wasn't in it. I made 19 and 22 not out; jolly good, and hit 3 balls running on to the roof of the stable. Wednesday evening there was another wire, and we had to pack our chests and get our sports gear together etc. It was thought we would have to go in the night, and messengers and people were stationed round the place all night to call us. However, nothing more happened and it was the same for the next two days and nights, but everyone had calmed down a bit. Tremendous excitement every night at 8, getting in the news from the Eiffel Tower by wireless. This morning the papers said it was very bad, but no one thought any more about it and train lists etc. were stuck up as usual for breaking up.

I was cricketing again this afternoon in a dense fog, one could hardly see the opposite wicket. We had been playing for two hours when at 4 o'clock we were startled by people charging through the fog and shouting orders to mobilise, whereupon everyone dropped their cricket gear and fled for the College, cheering like hell. I don't quite know what there was to cheer about but anyhow we all did. The 1st XI were playing Roehampton and they complained that for the first two hours they could not see the ball, and for the rest of the time they could not find the players. The Skipper had promised to have all the cadets and seamen away from the College in eight hours at the outside in the event of mobilisation, so we had to 'bustle some'. Eight hours sounds an awful lot, but the chests take such a time as they take three men to lift them. Most of the officers had already left the College during the week. We packed our chests and were then formed into working parties to get them all out. We greased the stairs and just let them rip down them, and then lugged them outside and loaded them into carts. All the carts from Dartmouth and the neighbouring farms had been commandeered, as each could only take about four chests. One third of the College went to Chatham, one third to Portsmouth and one third to Devonport, in that order. Thank goodness I was the last lot, so we had plenty of time, as it took years getting the chests across the

river. The passenger boat between Dartmouth and Kingswear was commandeered. The first contingent left after two hours; jolly smart work if
you think it over. By George! you should have seen those chests coming
out; all the masters and everyone helped. We cheered the various parties
off, and then the sixth term had a select sing song, at which we had
cheerful songs to pass the time. We left the College at 9 o'clock, and
marched down the town which had turned out en masse, and cheered us
in a very inebriated fashion, and I felt quite a hero. We took hours to get
over the river and into the train, as each luggage van only took about
eight chests. I saw Mr Reid and had a talk with him for some time. He is
going to write to you. All the masters are volunteering their services to the
Admiralty. It is much nicer to be doing something during a war; you don't
feel so useless.

It is now midnight and we ought to be arriving soon. I am very sleepy
and don't relish the idea of getting into a ship at all. We'll be useless for
the first week, but they won't expect anything of us just at first. We draw
war pay, 2/6 a day, and, I believe, are promoted to acting midshipmen,
so we get a good bit of seniority out of it with luck. I don't know if we join
our ships tonight, but I hope not. I shall be tired by tomorrow evening. I
don't know where we're going at all, Mediterranean most likely, or
perhaps, guarding places like Hull. The *Exmouth* is quite a decent ship,
Second Fleet, but there is some rumour that she has gone.

It is rather a curse having to go now, and I'm afraid the sports
committee at your party will be reduced to one, and Tip [his youngest
brother] will have to carry on the captaincy of the Bonvilston C.C.

Of course, all this may be merely a political move, but it seems as
though the real thing has come this time. Of course, Germany may get in
a funk and climb down. It seems rather rot that we should have to fight
because some ass shoots a tin pot archduke, but there you are.

Anyhow we'll never have such a favourable chance again. You can take
it from me that Germany are in for a devil of a hiding, as France and Russia
don't care a damn for Servia [sic], and have only gone in to get a whack
at the Germans, and so have we.

I must be stopping now; hope you will be able to decipher this, but the
train is jerky. Don't expect a letter regularly every week, as I may not be
able to. Will write again at the first opportunity and tell you my address
etc. It is a confounded bore, but now we are in it we'll give those damned
Germans such a devil of a time that they won't forget in a hurry. Look
after the dogs.

Best love to all of you,

Fat

Some ship's officers were not sure how to treat the newly joined
cadets. Fifteen-year-old Cadet John Brass, along with his fellows, spent

the first day in the old battleship *Russell*, flagship of the 8th Battle Squadron, being treated to a series of lectures from the sub-lieutenant, the first lieutenant, the commander, the captain and finally the admiral:

> From the Sub-Lieutenant, we learned that we were to keep our eyes skinned, ears open, bodies in perpetual motion, and make it our business to become useful members of society pdq, or he'd want to know the reason why, and by the more senior officers, we were told to conduct ourselves like little gentlemen, making every effort to learn our duties quickly and so become a credit to our King, country and the Service.
>
> Our ship, being commissioned for 'war only', carried no other gunroom officers besides ourselves. Our Sub-Lieutenant messed in the Wardroom, as it was considered beneath his dignity to live among company so very young and of such little account. A full-blown midshipman is almost the lowest form of naval life, and we were only cadets – referred to as 'War Babies'.

At the end of a week, to Brass's disappointment, and contrary to the treatment experienced by Dartmouth contemporaries in other ships,

> We were fallen in and told by the Captain that he would not permit us to wear midshipman's white patches at once instead of the button and twist of a Naval cadet; we were first to show him we were worth them, nor would he permit us to draw any pay until these magic patches were up; instead we were to be given a fixed sum monthly as pocket money.

The mother of fifteen-year-old Cadet Weld-Forester, drafted from Dartmouth to the *Goliath*, received a gushing letter from an unidentifiable correspondent, which is perhaps typical of the period:

> I <u>do</u> feel so deeply for all the mothers of cadets – they, the boys, have all gone to ships as officers – and if the Mothers could have seen the keenness and the cheerfulness of their sons when they left here they <u>would</u> have been proud – they were just as brave as little lions, though they are some of them very young – Forester being one of the youngest – they are all trained as officers. What they do or where their ships go no one knows yet though I believe the *Goliath* is at Sheerness. The *Goliath* is a battleship not in the 1st Fleet but in the 3rd Fleet.

The last sentence was intended to reassure the Hon. Mrs Weld-Forester, the implication being that the 3rd and 2nd Fleets were not nearly as likely as the 1st Fleet to see action. That was one of the reasons (a wrong one as we shall see) that the Dartmouth cadets had all been drafted to ships of the 2nd and 3rd Fleets; for despite the remarks above, not by any stretch of the imagination were they trained officers. The other reason was to fill midshipmen's billets in reserve ships that in peacetime

were manned by skeleton crews. Despite their youth and lack of training, the cadets plucked so swiftly from Dartmouth were to perform
magnificently, which says something both about them as people, and
the system, despite its faults. Young Weld-Forester wrote from the Royal
Naval Barracks Chatham on 3 August to reassure his mother on the
same point:

> My Darling Mother
>   I am at present at the above address, but am expecting to be moved
> any minute to HMS *Goliath*, which has sailed from here and is over at
> Devonport or somewhere. There is no cause for alarm about me. I shan't
> have to fight till all the first fleet is sunk. At present we are just coast
> defence.
>   I'm afraid I can't tell you much about what we've been doing and are
> going to do as we are liable under the official secrets act to get hard
> labour for disclosing any official news.

The following day he wrote asking, 'Please could you send me some
money as I haven't got any at all'. The Hon. Mrs Weld-Forester sent him
a cheque but had clearly been laying on the 'martyr act' in a letter
which no longer exists, because he wrote on 5 August saying, 'I quite
agree with you that you have the hard part especially as I can't tell you
anything'. Meanwhile events gathered pace.

On 2 August, the fifty-four-year-old Vice Admiral Sir John Jellicoe was
given the acting rank of admiral and ordered to take over as Commander-in-Chief (C-in-C) Grand Fleet in place of the sixty-two-year-old
Admiral Sir George Callaghan, whose tour of duty was due to expire on
1 October. Jellicoe protested strongly, sending no fewer than six telegrams to the Admiralty warning that this premature move would be bad
for morale. Churchill ordered him to effect the take-over on 4 August.

On 29 July 1914, the same day that the Grand Fleet had headed
for Scapa, Austria, abetted by Germany, declared war on Serbia. Russia
mobilized in support on the 30th. On the 1st, Germany mobilized
and declared war on Russia; on the 2nd she invaded Luxembourg and
demanded that Belgium allow German troops to cross her territory.
Britain had stood aside, but Belgium's neutrality was guaranteed by
treaty, and now she sent an ultimatum to Germany demanding that
Belgian neutrality be respected. On the 3rd Germany declared war on
France and that night invaded Belgium.

In HMS *Lion*, Beatty's flagship, Midshipman Alderson recorded on
3 August that 'Rear Admiral Beatty is now Vice Admiral Beatty'. The
next day he noted:

The Admiral made a speech to the Ship's Company this evening. He told us that an Ultimatum had been sent to Germany, which if it is refused (which it certainly would be) meant war with Germany at midnight (cheers). He spoke of his confidence in officers and men of *Lion* and rest of squadron, and he made it clear that War did not mean a 'blooming picnic'. We shall probably be at sea six months.

That evening, at midnight German time, the Admiralty signalled all ships and establishments, 'Commence hostilities against Germany'.

Douglas King-Harman, now a twenty-two-year-old sub-lieutenant in the pre-dreadnought battleship *Albemarle*, wrote to his father from Portland in a letter dated 4 August 1914, and annotated 'Tuesday Night':

In the middle of coaling ship this evening, the Admiral commanding the Second Fleet (our flagship is the *Lord Nelson*) made a general signal that 'Hostilities with Germany commence at midnight'. So we are in for it. The news was received with great enthusiasm by all hands. The whole fleet was cheering continuously. We are all ready for immediate action, and only hope that our First Fleet may leave a few of the enemy's ships for us to have a flap [sic] at. There is not much enthusiasm for the war itself, but there is a general feeling that it is now or never to polish off Germany, and the relief is immense. We are efficient and willing & I think the Second Fleet will give a very good account of itself if we have the good fortune to engage in a fleet action. We are sending a boat ashore with letters, so I suppose that means that will be the last opportunity. I want to square up a few things, I am not in the least pessimistic but we must face realities. I owe Gieve, Matthews and Seegrave about £16 or £17, of which a certain amount will be defrayed by pay now due to me. I owe nothing else, at any rate owe [sic] quite small sums which I am settling tonight. I am also going to announce my engagement to Christine, it is both my wish & hers that it should become known in event of war. I am asking her to choose a ring, I have about £10 in cash which I am keeping in the ship's safe, which will go a good way towards defraying the cost, and if I come to grief I hope you won't mind me asking you and Mother to make up the difference. I do hope you will not disapprove strongly of this step, but just now, when it is possible I may never see her again, I am going to do what she wishes.

She is a good girl, she has a thousand times more in her than anyone I have ever met, and I love her more than anything in the world.

I hope you will do what you can towards seeing something of her, her father has gone to America & she is alone, and she is naturally very anxious and troubled.

Home Waters and the North Sea, 1914–1915

Thanks to the Royal Navy, the British Expeditionary Force (BEF) was transported across the Channel without the loss of a single man or piece of equipment. This vital cross-Channel line of communication was kept open throughout the war, and the BEF never had to look over its shoulder and worry about enemy action cutting the ever-increasing flow of men and materiel from Britain to France and wounded and men on leave travelling in the other. Contrary to German expectations, the Grand Fleet did not, even as a temporary measure, impose a close blockade in the Heligoland Bight to cover the move of the BEF to France. Instead, Jellicoe blockaded the whole North Sea, and dominated the area with frequent sweeps. The Kaiser, fearful that his precious High Seas Fleet would be crushed by the numerically superior Grand Fleet, forbade it from interdicting the cross-Channel line of communication. A more aggressive policy might have paid dividends, especially if the Germans had exploited the unique air-reconnaissance assets they had in the Zeppelin, designed for just this purpose.* Until the advent of ship-borne wheeled aircraft in the latter years of the war, Zeppelins were a source of much concern to the Royal Navy in the North Sea. Probing attacks in strength by the High Seas Fleet towards the Channel ports would certainly have drawn out the Grand Fleet, and might have presented the Germans with opportunities to whittle down the British strength, especially as in the early days Jellicoe had to detach some of his ships on other tasks (of which more later). But despite British expectations that this is what the Germans would do, it was not to be.

The first encounter in the North Sea took place on 5 August, when the Harwich Force Third Flotilla met the German minelayer *Königen Luise*. She was a small holiday excursion vessel, painted to look like a Great Eastern Railway ferry, and sent to lay mines off Harwich. She was sighted by the Flotilla leader, the light cruiser *Amphion* (Captain Fox). Fox sent the destroyers *Lance* and *Landrail* to investigate, and although at first their quarry looked like another Harwich–Hook ferry, suddenly the *Laurel*, way out on the wing of the sweep, flashed by light that a trawler had seen the steamer 'dropping things overboard'. *Amphion* increased speed to catch up with the two destroyers, and with her bow 4-inch gun *Lance* fired the navy's first shot of the war. The shooting was

---

* At the outbreak of war they had one Zeppelin, with twenty-four seaplanes and aeroplanes. By the end of the year they had two, and soon many more. They were able to maintain patrols far out into the North Sea.

not effective at first, and it took several shells from *Amphion* and the two destroyers before *Königen Luise* sank. As her crew abandoned her, German officers fired revolvers at the men in the water. Five German officers and seventy sailors, many of whom had wounds from German bullets, were picked up by the three British ships. In *Amphion*, some of the prisoners were put in a compartment in the bows, the idea being that if the ship hit a mine, they would go up first.

The following day, while attempting to keep clear of the area mined by the *Königen Luise*, the *Amphion* made an error in her dead reckoning, ran into the minefield, and detonated a mine. The forepart of the ship was engulfed in flames, and all but one of the German prisoners was killed. Fox ordered his crew to abandon ship, just in time. The *Lark* stopped nearby and sent boats to help, and as her first lieutenant, Mead, wrote to his mother later: 'Suddenly there was a roar, and her fore magazine blew up with a tremendous explosion, the sky was black with smoke and fragments of the unfortunate vessel'.

Fox remembers seeing one of the 4-inch guns and a man turning head over heels about 150 feet up; this gun just missed falling on *Linnet*, much to the relief of her CO, who saw it coming and thought his number was up.[3]

Mead, whose ship was crowded with survivors including Germans:

One of *Amphion*'s shells came hurtling down, and burst on the deck not 20 yards from where I was standing. It was a nasty crash and smell of explosive, but the worst was the fate of two poor stokers who a moment before had been saved from burning in their ship. They both died, although one hung on for about an hour.

The wardroom and upper deck were a shambles; about half the miserable creatures were terribly burnt, and the next job was to get them patched up. Their heads were the worst, and two of them lost their sight. I can't think how they got on board. A German who had been shipwrecked twice in twenty-four hours soon died. They were shivering, and we gave them clothes; one German went off in my pyjama jacket, and another in a plain clothes suit of mine.

In the first few months of the war, the redoubtable Commodore Reginald Tyrwhitt commanded both the Harwich Force and the brand-new light cruiser *Arethusa*. The navigator of *Arethusa* and of the Harwich Force throughout the war was Lieutenant Watson. Although designed to be a thirty-knot light cruiser, she achieved only twenty-two in her early trials. Watson:

Tyrwhitt was naturally anxious about these failures in designed speed and on return to harbour reported them to the C-in-C Nore, Sir Richard Pore, whose reply, 'after all she was built to fight, not to run away', made Tyrwhitt very angry indeed. His complaint had been made with no thought of running away, but only of failure to catch and destroy an enemy.

But more disappointments arose when the gunnery trials were carried out with her powerful armament of two 6-inch guns, one forward and one aft, and six 4-inch guns of a special quick-firing design, three on each broadside. On trials, the 4-inch did nothing but jam.

The ship's paymaster (lieutenant equivalent) was Hugh Miller, whose action station was officer in charge of the transmitting station controlling the guns. Here he worked the Pollen-designed Argo clock. He wrote in his diary:

> The essential thing when in charge of a transmitting station is to keep cool as so many orders are received by the different voice pipes and so many orders passed on while at the same time the ranges and deflection have continuously be called to the transmitter numbers. When both sides of the ship are engaged, two Clocks have to be worked, one based on orders from the Fore Control, and the other on orders from After Control; the confusion becomes terrible unless everyone is most attentive to their duties. The Transmitting Station is forward below the water line, and the first mine we strike will kill us all. We have temporarily relieved *Amphion* which was blown up by a mine a few days ago. Her paymaster and all the people in the Transmitting Station were killed. I thought of this too much last night, and it has got a little on my nerves. I hope I am not going to be a coward. Tomorrow we go to Heligoland and there may well be a fight.

The Battle of Heligoland

Miller was right. The first clash between major units of the Grand Fleet and High Seas Fleet took place in the Heligoland Bight on 28 August 1914.

British submarines had been operating in the Bight from the outset of the war. At this stage the pre-war concept of operating submarines with the surface fleet was still thought by the British to be tactically sound, and they usually crossed the North Sea on the surface on their diesels, which was much faster than their underwater speed, and husbanded their batteries, which they used for propulsion when dived; sometimes, in the early days, they were towed part of the way by a destroyer. Commodore Keyes sortied in a destroyer, either *Lurcher* or *Firedrake*, providing surface reconnaissance and a wireless relay – British submarines, unlike German ones, then had poor wireless communications with limited range. He would give them notice of danger, and enable them to dive: in effect he was the huntsman working a pack of hounds, whose quarry was the German destroyers. It must be borne in mind that in 1914 there was no method of detecting a dived submarine from a surface ship, and even by the end of the war, detection methods were rudimentary. Detection from the air was sometimes possible, especially if the water was clear, conditions that rarely applied in the pea-soup-like North Sea. Until depth charges were introduced in 1916, the only methods of attacking a submarine were by shelling or ramming it when it was on the surface, or at periscope depth.

As a result of his forays, Keyes hatched a plan for Tyrwhitt's Harwich Force to attack the German destroyers his boats had reported in the Bight. This might lure out German cruisers in support of the destroyers, or with luck even bigger fry, which the British submarines could torpedo. Tyrwhitt would attack with two flotillas, a total of thirty-one destroyers with two light cruisers, the *Arethusa* and *Fearless*. Keyes would deploy his boats in two lines, the first to catch the German cruisers, the second to surface and lure the German destroyers out to sea. To the north Rear Admiral Sir Archibald Moore with the battle cruisers *New Zealand* and *Invincible* would provide the heavy back-up. Cruiser Force C, consisting of one *Topaze* class and five *Cressy* class cruisers, would be in reserve off Terschelling (*Amethyst, Aboukir, Bacchante, Cressy, Euryalus*, and *Hogue*).

At first the Admiralty, having approved the plan, omitted to tell Jellicoe of the impending operation, and then gave him a few snippets. To support Moore, Jellicoe eventually sent Beatty with the battle cruisers *Lion* (flag), *Queen Mary*, and *Princess Royal*, and Commodore William Goodenough's 1st Light Cruiser Squadron (*Birmingham, Falmouth, Liverpool, Lowestoft, Nottingham*, and *Southampton* (Commodore)). Neither Keyes nor Tyrwhitt received the signal that Beatty would be in their vicinity; it had been sent to Harwich and sat there until their return. Lieutenant-Commander Talbot's E6 was part of Keyes's force consisting of eight D and E class boats with *Lurcher* and *Firedrake*.

It was a confused battle fought in mist. Talbot's diary:

Thursday August 27th
    At 8.10 we left for the Heligoland Bight; we proceeded in two divisions in line abreast to port, boats 1 mile apart, 2nd division 2 miles astern of 1st division, *Lurcher* [Commodore] about 2 miles ahead of 1st division; I was No 1 of 1st division. We had a quiet trip across at 11 knots. At 5.50 the *Lurcher* ordered me to proceed to 12 miles N by W from Terschelling

Bar, which I reached at 6.30 pm. Had a short dive to check my trim, and lay on surface for about an hour.

At 8.15 proceeded at 11 knots for my position. It was a pitch dark night with no vestige of a moon, for which I was thankful. Met nothing.

Friday August 28th

Stopped at 3 am and dived at 50 ft for the remaining 3 miles to my position. I always dive from the start of dawn to daylight, as it is such a dangerous time for us due to the visibility changing so rapidly.

Rose at 4 am, and when I got to the bridge, sighted a German destroyer within a mile ahead of me, stopped. My role being to act as bait, I watched him from the surface for 15 minutes to attract his attention, then dived at him, when he disappeared to the NE. Rose at 4.45.

At 5 am a German destroyer appeared, stopped about 3 miles to the southard of me, and made, first a challenge, then a long signal, to me, who had remained on the surface; altogether we spent half an hour looking at each other. At the end of that time, as we were both stationary, I thought if he wanted to fire on me he had plenty of time to get an accurate range; so I dived at him, 5.30 am, when he cleared out pretty quickly to the southward.

Rose at 5.45

At 5.50 two German TBDs [torpedo-boat destroyers] came in sight, one to North and one to South. I dived out to the Westward with much fuss and splashing, to draw them after me, but after seeing me dive both turned away.

6.4 Rose. Nothing in sight. Proceeded to the westward on the gas engine [diesel] with much smoke, and charging batteries, for 6 miles, then turned to the eastward.

At 7.30, when on gas engine, sighted a destroyer steaming at me at full speed, about 4 miles distant. Dived and attempted to attack him; he was within 3,000 yards when I got under, and firing at me, so saw exactly where I was & saw my periscope each time it came up; he was going so fast, I should think a good 30 knots, that I could not get anywhere but right ahead of him. At the last moment I put my helm right over to give him the stern tube, when within 150 yards saw he had ported his helm to ram me, and I was forced to dive steeply to 60 feet; he passed over my bridge & must have missed the periscope standards by inches only. The whole show took about 8 minutes from the time we sighted him. Within about 2 minutes he passed over the boat a second time, and of course a tactful man in the forward compartment said he heard a chain dragging over us.

Remained at 80 feet and dived 2 miles out to the Westward.

8.30 Rose and sat on the surface. Misty.

9.25 Suddenly out the mist under the sun, in a cloud of smoke, loomed the hulls of two big cruisers beam on, 2 to 3 miles off steering south. Dived course South, to observe them. When I found them in the periscope a few minutes later, only misty [obscure?], they had altered course to about West by South and were so close that I had no room to do anything but go under them, which I did, passing under each of them. Nationality thought to be British, but not known.

After passing under them, rose to 20 feet, and observed two cruisers, or a flotilla leader and a large TBD, about 2 miles on the port beam of the previous pair and steering W by S.

10.40 Rose and lay on the surface.

11.45 Sighted to the SW, an action taking place between a German cruiser and some British destroyers, all approaching out of the mist.

Dived.

I could not see these through the periscope, but very slowly 2 lines of smoke appeared approaching me, and I heard a great deal of firing.

Although Talbot was unaware of it, at 0700 that day, *Laurel* of Tyrwhitt's force had spotted a German destroyer, *G 194*, and opened fire. *G 194* turned and disappeared into the mist. Tyrwhitt pressed on, encountering more German destroyers, who also fled into the mist. At this stage two German cruisers (*Stettin* and *Frauenlob*) joined the fray, followed by four more. A general melee ensued, in which *Arethusa* was badly damaged. Sub-Lieutenant Bower of the destroyer *Laforey*, in Tyrwhitt's 3rd Destroyer Flotilla, wrote to his mother:

at 7.30 am on Friday morning, after having been up all night, we sighted their destroyers, and chased them and soon opened fire. Shells started to drop all round us. Soon we sighted two of their cruisers, and later on we were within range of the Heligoland Forts, so you can just imagine the state of affairs then. It is an absolute mystery to me why we weren't hit, for there were shrapnel bursting in the air, and enormous white splashes all round us. One big splinter went through an iron ventilator about four feet from where I was standing. I sunk one German torpedo boat with my own gun. The poor little brute (she was only about 300 tons) was making a desperate attempt to reach Heligoland, but we got 3 or 4 shells right into her, one blew the entire bridge off, and another got the boilers. Having practically finished the two cruisers, the destroyers hauled off, & I thought that was the end of it, not a bit of it though. Back we went & soon saw a large 3 funnelled cruiser the *Mainz*, who put up a magnificent fight. Her shells were dropping, some of them just 20 yards short, and others 20 yards over us, I got drenched by the spray from one of them. Heaps of times we heard the buzzing of a shell just above our heads. It was most marvellous! I'm afraid she hit 3 of our boats [destroyers] & the *Arethusa*, a brand new ship was very nearly disabled.

Paymaster Miller in *Arethusa* described the day in his diary, beginning by saying, 'I have just lived through the horrible experience of an action at sea, and if there is anyone in the world who having once experienced such an event, says he desires to experience another, I should not believe him'. He continues, and we should remember that he saw only part of it,

Two, two-funnelled German cruisers appeared out of the mist, one went past, but the other tackled us with the help of some destroyers. The control on board broke down badly, and our firing was awful. I knew it must be bad from the frantic orders I got down the voice pipes. However we did our best. It is impossible to expect a newly commissioned ship to fire well. They picked up our range more quickly than we did theirs and gave us a very bad time. In the Transmitting Room I could hear and feel shell after shell strike home. We closed to 3,400 yards and eventually hit our cruiser foe badly with our 6-inch guns, and the Torpedo Gunner swears to having sent a torpedo into her. He was just congratulating the Leading Torpedoman on his shot, when the poor fellow had the top of his head blown off, and another member of the torpedo crew was disembowelled. Another shell went clean through our drying room, burst and made a big hole in the deck. It also struck the crew of the midships 4-inch gun, the gunlayer disappeared and another of the crew was blown to pieces, one of his flying legs struck a lieutenant. By now all our 4-inch guns were damaged, and only the after 6-inch gun was left in action. We were shot through our feed tanks. We were hit hard and had to withdraw.

When about 25 miles from Heligoland, and our speed had dropped to about 10 knots, we received an urgent message from the Commodore (S) [Keyes] in the *Lurcher*. So we turned back to their assistance and recalled the *Fearless* and her destroyer which had gone ahead. Soon we found ourselves in a hornet's nest. We engaged a three-funneller, which I believe was the *Mainz*, but may have been the *Köln*. The fighting was confused. Our firing was better, we had managed to repair all our workable guns and fill up the crews. We did not use the transmitting station, but controlled the guns direct. Another enemy, a four-funneller, which looked enormous, now appeared on our port quarter. Her first salvo fell just short of us, and some of our officers were convinced they were 8-inch shells. The Commodore ordered *Fearless* and her destroyers to attack her. They obeyed and at once flew straight at her from all directions. Evidently the sight of so many small craft making straight for her was too much for her nerves, for she turned tail and disappeared into the mist. A three-funnelled enemy now crossed ahead of us, and suffered badly. We got several 6-inch shot into her and put her on fire aft. She altered course to come down our port side and at the same time out of the mist to starboard appeared stab, stab, stab of flame, and our old four-funnelled friend once more appeared. The *Fearless* gallantly crossed over and charged her with destroyers, although many of them had little ammunition and no torpedoes left. Our case was becoming desperate, and I certainly thought it was all up. Suddenly I heard clapping and cheering and rushed on deck to see the light cruiser squadron and battle cruisers rushing to our help.

Watson, as navigator of *Arethusa*, could see more:

Tyrwhitt was standing on the port side of the upper bridge, looking towards the enemy and giving orders for the helm and for action. His flag Lieutenant and myself were next to him. Our particular enemy was the German cruiser the *Frauenlob*. Her fire was extremely accurate which we returned with little sucess, as our 4-inch guns jammed again.

Westmacott suddenly and silently fell over backwards seriously wounded by shrapnel and was carried to the far corner of the bridge where he lay obviously on the point of death. Our organisation being imperfect, no doctor arrived, but a very junior paymaster clerk, Crofton, keeping records on the bridge disappeared and returned with a glass of water and kept by him until he died. After the battle he suffered from shellshock, sitting staring into space.

The *Frauenlob* continued plastering us, which killed twelve of our crew, pierced the side and damaged the boilers which reduced our speed to 10 knots.

At 1129, Beatty, hearing from Tyrwhitt that he was in trouble, sent Goodenough racing to his assistance, and at 1135 followed with his battle cruisers. He arrived just at the right moment, at 1237. Sub-Lieutenant Bower:

Just at this time, when things were too hot for us, up came 4 light cruisers from the heavy mist these were followed shortly by 4 [sic] battle cruisers, so we hauled out of range & mustered round the *Arethusa*, who was only able to go 10 knots, & we had to go most of the way back with her at that speed. We were finally out of action at about 1245 pm, having been under very heavy fire for nearly 5 hours. We expected to be in action again that night; we never saw them again & it is just as well because we had precious little ammunition or oil left. I was on deck from midnight Thursday till 3.0 pm Saturday & only got 2 small sandwiches to eat the whole of Friday.

The Germans lost three light cruisers (*Mainz*, *Ariadne*, and *Köln* (flag)), and their force commander, Rear Admiral Leberecht Maas. By 1310, all contact with the enemy having been lost, Beatty ordered all British forces back to base. Miller in *Arethusa*:

The strain on our nerves in the Transmitting Station was very great. We could hear and feel the shot striking the ship, but could see nothing. We realised the control was not working properly, but it was not our fault – we had had no practice and the electric dials broke down because of a shot through the electric switchboard. I had to pass all orders by voice-pipe to the 6-inch guns, and spent ages shrieking to the forward 6-inch gun to fire, before I realised it had broken down. All the time the clock showed us how the range was decreasing. Electricians and others brought us harrowing news of the state of the upper deck, and we heard the engine reporting to the bridge through the lower conning tower that the boilers were priming. When after the first fight the guns were controlled direct, we had nothing to do which was the worst of all. I kept everyone down below in case the transmitting room might be wanted to pass orders by voice-pipe. Doing nothing and thinking are bad occupations in a the middle of a fight. One of my men, a ship's assistant steward, went off his head when the strain was over – happily he is better now.

I have a terrible headache and feel rather sick. We will all be very thankful to see old England again, and to have that terrible heap [of bodies] which is covered by the Union Jack removed from our quarter deck. I went aft to look at the Chubb's log to see what our speed was, and found myself stepping over streams of blood.

In the confusion, there had been at least two occasions when what we now call 'a Blue on Blue' was avoided by a narrow margin. During the battle, Talbot in E6 found himself

between the two lines, but nearer the northern line, which I found to consist of three 4-funnelled cruisers, which we at once decided were German, as according to programme, we were to have no ships of that description in this area. I attacked; on their original course I could not have got in [range], but they altered course about 5 points to port together, and I made what would have been a perfect attack on the last ship. At the last moments I had doubts as to their nationality, as shot were falling all round me from the cruiser I knew to be German and I could find nothing else these ships could be firing at. I approached so close that I could actually see the red in the ensign, well within 400 yards, and knew her to be British, one of the Southampton class [of Goodenough's 1st LCS]; we were closing so rapidly that I could only get clear by diving under her. It was a very severe trial of my self-restraint, and I was very thankful I delayed firing till there was no possibility of doubt; I was so close that I could not possibly have missed. The ships were chasing the *Mainz*.

1215 to 1230. British TBDs ahead of me chasing to southward.

1.45 Rose. Sighted the *Fearless* and some of the 3rd Flotilla SW, steaming out to Westward; and a large cruiser to the E approaching fast in a cloud of smoke. I turned round and attacked her, thinking she was chasing the 3rd Flotilla. I passed down her port side at 300 yards range, again waiting to see the colour of her ensign, and again finding her to be British and one of the Southampton class (the *Lowestoft*), which are the most German-looking ships we have. It will be a wonderful thing if I get two more such opportunities for a certain hit.

2.30 Rose 3 miles astern of above cruiser, and half an hour later the *Lysander* [3rd Destroyer Flotilla] closed and spoke me.

3 pm got under[way on] the gas engine, and shaped course for Harwich.

He still had to complete the dangerous passage back to base with an unreliable magnetic compass (gyro-electric compasses giving true bearings and unaffected by metal, were only beginning to be fitted in boats). Yachtsmen today, and indeed most naval officers, would regard the passages routinely undertaken by both British and German submariners throughout the First World War as little short of miraculous; partly dived and partly on the surface, often in fog, without the benefit of GPS, radar, weather faxes, radio beacons, mobile telephones, short-wave voice radio, night-vision equipment, weather forecasts, and echo-sounder – facilities that nowadays are available on all but the most down-market yachts.

6.30 Spoke to a British cruiser of the Cressy class patrolling NW from Terschelling Bar; I was glad I met them before dark.

9.20 sighted the loom of 3 destroyers in the pitch dark, & sheered off to avoid them; most probably British returning home, but at night just as dangerous as Germans.

Foggy night, doing 12 knots.

Had a good deal of fog between 1 and 2 am, with a few ships about, which I was careful to avoid for fear of being fired on; on one occasion the fog lifted & showed a ship within half a mile who had just switched on navigation lights; we both lay stopped, I watching her & she looking for me, I having foolishly blown my whistle in an especially dense patch. However I lay doggo for some time & then worked round her. Dived at 3 am to herald in the daylight, and continued down till 5 am, partly to allow me to get a little well-earned sleep.

Rose into a thick fog & continued our course for Smith's Knoll [off Harwich] at 9 knots.

At 6 am ran across the *Landrail* [3rd Destroyer Flotilla], who asked me her position; I gave her my view of it and the course we should steer, & took station astern of him. It is the greatest comfort to be in company with a destroyer, as it saves having to dive for our own ships.

> Made Smith's Knoll, in dense fog, about 8.30 am exactly where we expected to find it, though not where the *Landrail* did.

On arriving back at Harwich, Talbot learned that Commodore Keyes in the *Lurcher*

> did what I consider to be a splendid thing; he went alongside the *Mainz*, which was burning furiously and on the point of sinking, and took off 220 men from her, a great number of them wounded; the *Mainz* turned turtle and sank two or three minutes after the *Lurcher* got clear. The Germans seem brave men; two officers stood on the quarterdeck of the *Mainz* as the *Lurcher* was taking off the crew; they were beckoned to, but smiled, folded their arms, and went down with their ship. Another officer on the bridge of *Mainz* was very busy shooting anyone who jumped overboard.

Bower's letter to his mother describing the action continues:

> Poor old *Liberty* had everyone wiped out on the bridge, & *Laurel* & *Laertes* both had casualties. Re my personal feelings, I must say that on Thursday night the anticipation of the morning made me feel a bit nervous, but while actually under fire I felt perfectly quiet & happy, one's only idea being to hit the enemy, which I can assure you we did with much success.
>
> We have been congratulated from all branches of the service, and I think it is a case of offering great thanks to Almighty God for the great victory.
>
> Could you send me some Bovril or EM's food or something of that sort & some chocolate. It would be much easier to get down that sort of stuff when there is no chance of proper meals.

Amidst the gloomy news from France, with the Germans advancing and BEF still retreating, it was a welcome victory, if not a 'great' one. The British lost no ships, and only the light cruiser *Arethusa* and three destroyers suffered damage of any consequence. Thirty-five men were killed and forty wounded. Some were affected in a different way; Miller in *Arethusa* recorded that when they went to sea again:

> There is a marked difference in the feelings, both of officers and men to those shown when we set out on our first adventure. Then we were light-hearted and eager. We talked about hoping to see some 'fun'. Now it is very different. I do not believe there is one officer or man who was on board on the 28th who will light-heartedly enter a second fight. Fear is undoubtedly knocking on our hearts. We know too well the perils of the North Sea to a small light cruiser. We will all do our job – there assuredly will be no shrinking, but I at least can not help being terribly 'nervy'. I wonder if this is a terrible confession. I sincerely hope that I will become

callous very soon, as at present I am feeling the strain, though of course I can not show it.

The Germans lost three light cruisers, with three badly damaged, plus a destroyer, with some 1,200 dead, wounded, and taken prisoner. The effect on the Kaiser and the German navy was far-reaching. The daring foray right into German home waters served to deepen their fleet's respect for the Royal Navy. The Kaiser forbade his fleet to fight outside the Heligoland Bight or in the Skagerrak.

All had not gone smoothly in the battle cruisers, which is not surprising since this was their first taste of action. Midshipman Alderson in *Lion*:

> We fired about 138 rounds of 13.5 inch, which seems absurd as very few shots got home, whereas two good hits are quite enough to sink a light cruiser. It is to be hoped that this minor action has taught the men to keep cooler and not give way to excitement, which was the cause of the Argo jamming.

On arrival back at Scapa Flow, the battle cruisers were cheered by the battle fleet. This led to an embarrassing moment. Alderson:

> We arrived at our anchorage at 7.15 pm, but as our anchors refused to drop at the critical moment, we had to steam right round the fleet, with everybody cheering us as though we really had done something great. It was most embarrassing and the VA [Beatty] made a signal explaining what had happened, and apologizing for what looked like seeking praise entirely unearned.

Beatty wrote to Commodore Goodenough:

> My dear Commodore
>   I am very humiliated that an anchor should have jambed [sic] and refused to go with the signal.
>   It looked as if it was a Bombastic promenade thing to the Fleet the idea of which makes me shudder. Please apologise to your Captain or rather explain what appears to have been a piece of extremely bad taste.
>   Come and see me in the morning about Report etc.
>   Yours
>   David Beatty

Unjustly, this involuntary 'lap of honour', a prototype of the self-glorifying antics of present-day sports 'stars', was to be remembered by the Grand Fleet when the exploits of the battle cruisers hit the headlines on other occasions. The real reason for it was forgotten, while Beatty's reputation for cultivating the press was remembered.

Enter the U-boats

The Germans struck back. On 22 September 1914, Kapitänleutnant Otto Weddigen in U-9 torpedoed three old *Cressy* class cruisers, *Aboukir*, *Cressy*, and *Hogue*, patrolling the Broad Fourteens off the Dutch coast. The crews were mostly middle-aged reservists but included young cadets mobilized from Dartmouth. One of the latter in the *Aboukir*, Cadet 'Kit' Wykeham-Musgrave, aged fifteen, wrote to his grandmother on 25 September:

> Dear Grannie
>   Thank you so much for your kind letter and the sovereign you sent me. I had a most thrilling experience. We were steaming line ahead with a distance of three miles between of the ships. We were struck first. I was sleeping down under at the time. We were woken by a terrific crash and the whole ship shook and all the crockery in the pantry fell. Of course we thought it was a mine, and rushed up on deck, we had all the scuttles and watertight doors closed at once, and everything that would float brought up and thrown overboard, in as much time as we had. She then started to list heavily. By that time the *Cressy* and *Hogue* had arrived and had let down their boats. The *Aboukir* at last went down suddenly and we slid down her side into the water. Fortunately there was not a great deal of suction on the side we jumped off so with difficulty got clear. I swam to the *Hogue* and was just going on board when she was struck and sank in three minutes. I then swam to the *Cressy* where I was hauled up the side with a rope. I went down to the Sick Bay where I had a cup of cocoa, but directly I had finished she was struck also and we were forced to go up on deck again. We sat on the fo'c'sle and we saw a submarine come as close as 200 or 300 yards off, and we fire [sic] all the guns at her until we sank, I jumped off again and got clear and after swimming about for a long time found a plank to hang on to. I hung on to it until I was picked up having been 3 hrs in the water. I don't remember being picked up because I was unconscious. But I woke up in the trawler *Titan* which was Dutch. They had rescued about 300 survivors. They were awfully kind to us.

In a similar letter to his grandfather, he adds:

> at about 1 pm I was taken on board a destroyer which took us to Harwich. I am afraid there are very few saved, we only had about 50 I think of the 500 saved out of our ship. I am none the worse so far I am glad to say. I am wondering what ship I shall be appointed to next.
>   With best love from Kit.

The total number lost from the three cruisers was 1,459 officers and ratings. Cadet Hereward Hook, also fifteen years old and straight from Dartmouth, was aboard the *Hogue*, and wrote about the incident in 1919. After *Aboukir* had been hit:

> Our captain then did what appeared to be the right thing under those circumstances, and went full speed astern, stopping the ship about a quarter of a mile on the starboard beam of *Aboukir*. In about ten minutes *Aboukir* had taken a heavy list to port, and in about fifteen her condition was hopeless. It was my first sight of men struggling for their lives. The bilge keel and part of the ship's bottom were exposed to view, with hundreds of men's heads bobbing about in the water, while a continuous stream of very scantily clad men appeared from the upper deck and started tobogganing down the ship's side, stopping suddenly when they came to the bilge keel, climbing over it, and continuing their slide until they reached the water with a splash.
>
> Meanwhile we were doing all we could to save the crew of the sinking ship.
>
> At about 6.45 the *Hogue* was struck, nearly amidships on the starboard side by two torpedoes, the second explosion occurring within about a second of the first. The whole ship seemed to jump at least six inches out of the water, and an enormous column of water was sent up, some of which descended with considerable force upon my back and shoulders. The second torpedo must have gone through the hole made in the ship's side by the first, thereby nearly cutting the ship in halves, as No 3 funnel suddenly collapsed like a house of cards.
>
> The ship's company was made up almost entirely of Royal Fleet Reservists, and two or three badge Active service men, real seamen every one of them, practically the pick of the Navy, and I would never have believed it possible that there could be so little panic or excitement amongst them. I do not think I saw a single man running on the upper deck.

A few minutes after the explosion the upper deck was awash, and Hook took to the water and swam away:

> Shortly after I left the ship, she turned slowly on her side, having been on a perfectly even keel up to then, and within about six or seven minutes after the torpedoes struck, she was out of sight. I did not feel the slightest suction as she went down, but there were large fountains of water coming out of the scuttles, forced up by the air compressed within a compartment below.

Some boats had been launched:

> Our captain, after giving the order 'Abandon Ship', and shouting out 'every man for himself', walked over the side of the bridge as the ship

heeled over, down the ship's side and climbed up onto the bilge-keel, where a cutter came alongside and took him off, almost dry-shod.

Hook was picked up by a launch, and was pulling over to the *Cressy*. She was hove to about half a mile away, taking on board survivors, and with every boat away, as his boat was approaching:

> *Cressy* must have seen a torpedo coming, and suddenly went full speed ahead, washing us well astern with her propellor wash, and shortly afterwards the torpedo struck her on the starboard side. She listed over slowly to an angle of about 20 degrees where she checked herself and every one thought she would remain afloat. Apparently the German Captain thought so too, as he fired another torpedo which exploded her after 9.2 inch magazine and she sank soon afterwards.

Hook was rescued by a fishing boat and eventually taken by destroyer to Harwich.

> *Cressy* had the biggest percentage of men drowned, as when she went down all her boats were away picking up men from the other two ships. The Captain of the *Cressy* was drowned.

The cruisers were sitting ducks off Germany's front door, and in an area full of fishing boats, some of which were engaged in reporting naval movements to the Germans. The loss of these ships and so many men was the result of muddled thinking on the part of the Admiralty and in particular the Chief of the Admiralty War Staff, Vice-Admiral Sir Frederick Doveton Sturdee. When Keyes suggested that the cruiser patrol was unnecessary and highly dangerous, Sturdee argued that the Scheldt had to be kept open to traffic, and cited the precedent of the seventeenth-century Anglo-Dutch Wars as a reason for maintaining a patrol of the Broad Fourteens. Sturdee prided himself on his knowledge of naval history, but, in company with other senior naval officers, considered that tactics were not the concern of junior officers.

The British strategy of distant blockade has been mentioned earlier. The reasons for this decision were made clear to the officers of the *Lion* in a lecture, summarized in Midshipman Alderson's diary; and abridged below. It is interesting because it is a record of what was being said in the fleet at the time, without embellishment with the wisdom of hindsight:

> The first [British] plan was a relic of sailing ship days, when ships could remain at sea for months, and was to maintain a close blockade of German ports with small craft supported by larger ships. This plan was soon discarded because of the need for ships to return to base to coal. The ships

remaining to maintain the blockade, might be overwhelmed by a greater force. This plan also gave too much opportunity to enemy submarines, which were recognised as a formidable weapon.

The next plan involved a line across the North Sea to intercept enemy shipping. This was tested in the 1912 manoeuvres and proved a dismal failure. The attacking force could operate on any part of the line with superior force, and night attacks were made comparatively easy.

In the 1913 manoeuvres the plan was modified. Instead of single ships being spaced at intervals along the line, ships were placed in groups, but this plan failed as signally as the previous one.

The plan actually in use had had no test. Our ships patrol the seas in strong force, so that the enemy never knows their positions, and if they meet them, they either find them in superior force, or else able to fall back on a supporting force.

As regards the future, the enemy at present appear to be very quiet, but we must not fall into the error of supposing that they lie in harbour doing nothing. We know quite well that the High Seas Fleet is manoeuvring and practising firing in the Baltic just as we are in the North Sea. They will for the present carry on the campaign with mines and submarines. The latter are daily getting bolder and more efficient with practice. We must expect heavy blows. The final aim is the same as that of every campaign, namely a decisive battle. It is just possible that the High Seas Fleet may never come out, but may be used as a pawn when bargaining at peace. There is however a strong argument against this. Public opinion is sure to have an effect [on German naval strategy?]. When the [German] army is getting dead beat questions will be asked about what this great fleet is doing on which so much money has been spent. So we may confidently expect the High Seas Fleet to come out eventually, though they will probably delay as long as possible.

Paradoxically, the reactions of the German public in the event of perceived naval inaction forecast by the lecturer above were exactly those which would emerge in British public opinion as the war progressed, whereas in Germany, public opinion on naval matters, or anything connected with the war, was of no account; Germany's naval strategy was decided by the Kaiser.

Before the war, the radius of action of British submarines had been insufficient to complete passages equivalent to the distance from Scapa Flow to Heligoland and back, a round trip of some nine hundred miles. The Admiralty therefore believed that Scapa was invulnerable to German submarines (U-boats). They were proved wrong in the first week of the war, when a U-boat was sighted off the entrance. Until Scapa was made more or less submarine-proof with nets, blockships, and booms, which took until mid-1915, there were numerous submarine scares, causing Jellicoe to send his dreadnoughts to Loch Ewe, on the north-west coast of Scotland. The number of 'flaps' about submarines increased after the sinking of the three cruisers off the Dutch coast. Sightings of a periscope and reports of torpedo tracks in Scapa (probably seals) in mid-October led to Jellicoe ordering the dreadnoughts to Lough Swilly on the north coast of Ireland, where they remained until early November.

On 26 October, the battle cruisers were involved in what became known as the 'Battle of Jemimaville' at Cromarty Firth off Invergordon. Midshipman Alderson of *Lion*:

> Great excitement as we were sitting down to lunch at noon. A German submarine was reported to have entered the harbour and night defence stations were sounded off. Steam trawlers, picket boats, & destroyers patrolled everywhere. At 1230 on our port beam, we were lying bow up-stream the tide still ebbing, appeared close inshore a commotion in the water as if made by a periscope travelling at some 20 knots upstream.* At this we opened fire with great vim with our port 4 inch batteries, and hit the object, and also several houses in a small village having the appalling name of Jemimaville. A small fire was started at the eastern end of the village and in the wood to the eastward. Several ricochets appeared to have landed some distance inland.
>
> Everyone is undecided what the object was. Some swear it was a submarine and that they saw the conning tower. This is absurd, because I was looking through my glasses [binoculars] and I believe I saw a black shape being hit by a shell, but it might have been a whale or a torpedo. There is a great objection to believing it to have been a submarine. It was low tide and too close in to shore.

Alderson accompanied a party ashore and reassured the inhabitants of Jemimaville that the submarine had been sunk. There was only one casualty among the civilian population of the village, a small baby with a slightly injured leg. However, the 'flaps' continued, even more outrageously. Alderson:

> This evening, two submarines are rumoured to be lying at Allnes up the river. Later this proved to be false. A gamekeeper announced that he had spread the rumour for a joke! The man was arrested. The story was never given much credence owing to the small depth of water up there.

---

* This comment is an indication of the naivety and mystique about submarines widespread in the surface (= non-submarine) navy in those days. No submarine in the world at the time could make 20 knots on the surface, let alone dived. Not until the very end of the Second World War, with the invention of hydrogen-peroxide-fuelled U-boats, could dived submarines approach this speed.

The day after the 'Battle of Jemimaville', a far more serious event took place. One of the most modern battleships, *Audacious*, was at sea off the coast of Ireland, conducting battle practices with the 2nd Battle Squadron. Sub-Lieutenant Spragge was not involved in gunnery practice, and was in his bath. In his diary he recorded:

> 8.40 am. a heavy concussion was felt; thinking it was the first salvo [of their own gunfire], I went leisurely on deck to my torpedo control instruments. About five minutes later the port side of the waist was awash & Rhodes told me that we had stuck a mine. We were third ship in the line & turning to starboard to open fire at target, we had turned inside the wake of the next ahead & then we had struck on port side abreast of the wing engine room after bulkhead.
>
> All hands not employed below were ordered on deck & all boats and derricks were immediately cleared away. The *King George V*, *Ajax*, and *Centurion* immediately left us in case of submarines.
>
> We were still able to steam at about 10 knots with our centre shafts so we steamed towards Lough Swilly. After we had cleared away derricks & boats, rafts were made of all available wood.
>
> About 10 am the centre engine room was flooded to such an extent that the circulating air pumps would not work & we had to stop. By this time HMS *Liverpool* with the 2nd Flotilla destroyers and SS *Olympic* had closed in response to an SOS & other distress signals. We hoisted out all the boats except the steam boats, in the sea that was running, no easy matter, & sent away all stokers and marines. We also prepared to be taken in tow. As fires were out in all boilers, everything had to be manhandled.
>
> About this time Vice-Admiral Louis Bayly came on board.
>
> *Olympic* was first to take us in tow, but we were unable to steer & could not get any communication to the hand wheel flat owing to flooded compartments aft, so our bow swung about all over the place.

Towing wire and cables parted. The *Liverpool* got the next towing rope round her screw. Next to try was a collier, but the tow parted again. As the light began to fail, fifty volunteers were called for to remain with the ship, the remainder being taken to a destroyer. At about 1830 it was decided to abandon the *Audacious*; the quarterdeck was awash and she was rolling heavily. HMS *Liverpool* stood by for the night. At 2100 *Audacious* capsized and blew up. One man on the deck of the *Liverpool*, 800 yards away, was killed by a piece of flying armour plate; the only casualty.

The Admiralty, concerned that the loss of *Audacious* might have a serious effect on morale at home, suppressed the news of her sinking. Her crew was distributed round the fleet, the press was told that she was merely damaged, and her name was kept on the lists of ships' movements to the end of the war. This subterfuge was counter-productive, because American passengers in the *Olympic* could not be muzzled, and their stories were picked up by newspapers in the United States. Soon the news was out. The denials by the Admiralty merely persuaded the world, and people in Britain, that they were not being told the truth, and this had serious consequences after the Battle of Jutland.

The damage had been done by one of two hundred mines laid by a converted German liner, the *Berlin*, on the night of 22/23 October to the north-west of Lough Swilly. The captain had no idea the Grand Fleet was nearby; he chose the nearest convenient shipping lane. One mine sank a merchantman on 26 October, the day before the *Audacious*. It was fortunate that more of the Grand Fleet were not sunk at the same time. Mine warfare had been neglected before the war, and the Royal Navy had begun it with only ten old torpedo boats and thirteen trawlers fitted with sweeps. In modern vernacular, it was not 'career enhancing', and those in the minesweeping service were, in the words of one officer, 'looked on as no better than lavatory attendants'. With such poor anti-mine and anti-submarine measures available, it is not surprising that the fleet was becoming obsessed with the dangers lurking underwater.

Sub-Lieutenant Bowyer-Smyth in the Grand Fleet battleship *Superb*, 4th Battle Squadron, reflected in his diary the concern for the submarine threat and the 'spy' obsession that gripped so many people at the time:

Tuesday 3.xi.1914
    4.30 pm Weigh and proceed – apparently minesweepers and destroyers have reported 'all clear' also it is dark so we are safe from submarines. The gate of the boom defence is swung back – 4.45 proceeded at 19 kts – speed is our best defence against submarines. Everyone keeps on deck on way out [sic – except engine room and other watchkeepers presumably] – the idea seems to be that there is a sporting chance of being torpedoed – if one is on deck one has more chance.
    6.0 pm. It is dark – we are outside quite safely nothing happens after all. We are shaping course westward – goodness knows what for.
    The place is thick with spies – we probably have done all this so suddenly merely to avoid letting them know in time to have submarines waiting for us.

The Germans began basing U-boats at Ostend and Zeebrugge soon after they fell into their hands in late October 1914. Both were linked by canal inland to Bruges, where the Germans eventually built bomb-proof submarine shelters. The proximity of both ports to the sea lines of communication across the Channel was a source of concern to the Admiralty.

Both were well defended, so physically blocking them would be a costly and difficult operation. It was decided to try bombarding Zeebrugge from the sea to destroy the locks to the inner harbour to close off the U-boats' access to the outer harbour and thence to the sea. There was no question of the Grand Fleet dreadnoughts being exposed to the hazards of submarine and mines by closing the enemy coast, so Rear Admiral Stuart Nicholson was ordered to take two of the four *Duncan* class battleships which had formed part of his 3rd Battle Squadron, and were now based at Dover, to carry out the bombardment. The 1899-vintage HMS *Russell* had one forward twin 12-inch turret and one aft, and six 6-inch guns each side. She was not fitted for director control. Cadet Brass, with all the ship's officers, was summoned to the captain's cabin to be told that

he had received orders to carry out a bombardment of the Belgian coast. We were both delighted and excited at the thought of firing a shot in anger. There might of course be a few shore batteries to engage us, but we, in the gunroom, hadn't much of an opinion of shore batteries versus a moving battleship. A very busy day was spent filling up with ammunition, testing sights, and exercising fire and repair parties before setting out from Dover in the darkness so as to be in our firing position at dawn.

The object of our attention was Zeebrugge. As soon as it was light enough to pick out objects on shore, the points of aim were passed down and our two great 12 inch turrets and the light 6 inch guns slowly swung round into position. My action station was with the gunnery officer in the control position high up the foremast, so I got a magnificent view of the action. I could see what appeared to be a large hotel on the front, the railway station, and a high water tower as interesting landmarks. The former was alleged to be the German headquarters, and the latter our guide to the docks and canal locks.

The 12 inch turrets opened up on these two targets and very good shooting they made of it; our Lyddite shells throwing up huge columns of flame and smoke. The hotel was soon a mass of wreckage, but unfortunately we had no means of telling what damage we had done to the docks and locks.

The 6 inch guns had been instructed to deal with any opposition and I did see one or two flashes from enemy batteries close to the shore, but their shells fell a long way short of the ship. Our [6 inch] guns plastered the spot for a minute or two and, as there was no further reply, joined with the 12 inch in a concentration on the railway station. As far as I could see this was completely successful, and a train steaming out of the station and which I hoped was full of enemy troops was destroyed.

At this point we withdrew, having expended the time allotted to us for the operation – it was unsafe to stay too long for fear of attack by enemy submarines.

Despite Cadet Brass's enthusiastic account, the *Russell* and *Exmouth* fired over four hundred rounds with little effect on the massive installations.

So pervasive were submarine scares that when the 1899-vintage battleship *Bulwark* blew up at Sheerness on 26 November, there were initially some people who ascribed her demise to a U-boat: Midshipman 'Fat' Williams, now in the *Lord Nelson* class pre-dreadnought battleship *Agamemnon*, wrote to his mother:

> I'd had the morning watch and had just got out of a particularly luxurious bath at 7.55 and was going round to the gunroom flat to dress when I saw another distinguished officer going up on to the quarter deck in his shirt tails. I didn't think much of it, I don't know why, and proceeded to dress, but when I got half dressed a snotty came rushing down very breathless and on asking him what was on the go I heard that the *Bulwark* had been sunk. So I rushed up with my ever useful glasses and found that there was a gap where the *Bulwark* had been, filled with a mass of floating wreckage, a dense cloud of smoke drifting down to leeward and boats of all descriptions were dashing to the scene of the disaster.
>
> I asked one of the snotties who was on deck at the time what had happened and he said that at 7.53 there had been a violent explosion in the *Bulwark*. She was enveloped in an arc of flame, radius four or five hundred feet, all of a sudden and before the noise of the explosion reached us this flame had given place to a dense cloud of black smoke. In under a minute this drifted to leeward and there was a gap where one of His Majesty's ships had been. She must have gone down in 10 secs and there were no lumps of metal etc to be seen flying round that one usually associates with an explosion, just a pall of smoke over everything, enveloping not only the *Bulwark* but the next ship ahead and astern of her. The mighty roar heard in France that you read of in the papers is a lie; quite half of us didn't hear it at all. Of course everyone was stupefied and didn't know what was the cause of it. Luckily ships don't explode everyday and so everyone thought of submarines, floating mines drifting down the river etc.
>
> The Commander was very prompt and dashed up on deck at the noise of the explosion, saw what had happened and shouted out 'Away both lifeboat's crews, pull to the *Bulwark*, Port watch out port nets, Starboard watch out starboard nets.' Thank heavens I didn't have to go away in one of the cutters.
>
> We all watched thro' our glasses but could see no survivors swimming about. By the end of breakfast everyone had expounded their theory and we'd come to the conclusion that they must have dropped a Lyddite shell into one of the magazines. The Submarine theory was considered rot as everyone swore a Submarine couldn't have got into the river and that anyhow the *Bulwark* wouldn't have gone down as she did. Funnily nobody

seemed very perturbed about it and began talking rot about merciful deaths and what not. However it was brought home to us later.

An hour or so later our cutter returned in a state of wild excitement. They'd seen a submarine going up the river a foot of periscope visible, they gave chase but the submarine dived and poked her periscope up again further on before finally disappearing. This put everyone on the qui vive and our 12 pounder crews closed up etc, and we all stood with our eyes skinned. Somebody up on the bridge shouted out 'periscope on the starboard quarter' and sure enough there it was, going down stream at about five knots close inshore and well away from us. Both picket boats at once gave chase and we just stood waiting. It reminded me of those things that used to appear in the sketch 'Awkward situations I have been in'. Luckily as it turned out we couldn't fire as we'd have hit the oil tanks. The picket boats discovered that our periscope was only a bearing out spar floating down with the tide. It looked exactly like a periscope and everyone was had. We were rather annoyed and swore vengeance on that . . . submarine. The picket boats of the fleet and all the dockyard boats were armed with 3 pounders and sweeping gear and went away to sweep for the submarine and to search every barge etc. However, the Admiral had come to the conclusion that it couldn't have been a submarine and so we all packed up, rather annoyed in a way. Looking at it afterwards it could not have been a submarine.

They then began to arrive with the bodies which were rather gruesome. First a longshore boat came alongside with a couple of fellows, both dead. Then our cutter came back with some bits, one poor fellow blown clean in half at his waist, only just his chest and head, and a lot of other bits, legs etc all horribly cut about. All the officers were on the quarter deck looking sick as mud and I felt horribly ill, the doctors and the skipper were the only people who looked all right. It really was an awful sight, everything splashed with blood, just like a beef boat coming alongside, the whole bodies weren't so bad, but the bits were filthy and everyone was feeling rather rotten for the rest of the day, except the men who said 'they reckoned the explosion was the prettiest thing they'd ever seen'.

We picked up a lot of gear, amongst other things a till from a midshipman's chest, with a revolver and cartridges inside, absolutely dry, it must have floated up from below as the decks were blown away. A lot of extraordinary things like that happened, for instance a pair of pants stuck on the fore truck of the ship astern (ie. the top of the foremast) and some things were picked up absolutely untouched, chests of drawers and so on. We got a lot of gear and I had to make an Inventory of it all.

At first we were told that there was only one survivor but later we heard that there were twelve as you must have seen. The whole ship must have opened up as some people down below at the time were saved. The decks must have opened out like a sardine box.

It was an awful show and everyone was a bit jumpy for the rest of the day and at any sudden and unusual noise you could see everyone jump. But it's strange how quickly one forgets a thing like that, the next day it was a thing of the past and we all went our way as usual. It gave one an idea of what a fleet action will be like, but I don't think there'll be one.

There was an inquiry yesterday as to the cause of the explosion but nothing was divulged of course. They can never find out for certain of course but we know they'd been taking in ammunition the day before and were shifting it and striking it down below that morning. So it's as certain as can be found out that a Lyddite shell was dropped or sent up while being fused and that would have exploded the magazines. Lyddite is a nasty thing to play about with unless the proper precautions are taken. They are diving there now and a lot of bodies have been picked up.

Of course the submarine was rot and if one talked to the cutter's crew afterwards we found that none of them had actually seen it 'Well sir my mate 'e saw it and I saw the ripple myself, but blest if she 'adn't dived when I looked round'. It shows what fools people are. I suppose they got a bit jumpy and would have seen a Zeppelin if they'd thought about it.

Raids across the Channel

The next opportunity for a clash between major units of the Royal Navy and the Germans in the North Sea took place on 16 December 1914. The month before, German battle cruisers had bombarded Yarmouth as a cover for a minelaying operation. By December, minefields had been laid off the Suffolk coast, the Humber, and the Tyne as part of the German attempts to reduce the British battle fleet by mining and submarines. The news of the destruction of Admiral Graf von Spee's squadron off the Falklands, confirming rumours that the battle cruisers *Inflexible* and *Invincible* were in the South Atlantic (see Chapter 3), persuaded the C-in C High Seas Fleet, Admiral Frederich von Ingenohl, that the time might be ripe to mount a battle cruiser raid on Scarborough and Hartlepool. Luring the British battle fleet over a freshly laid minefield would avenge von Spee, and to this end the existing minefields would be extended by laying more off Filey (south of Scarborough). The raid would be carried out by five battle cruisers of Vice-Admiral Frans von Hipper's 1st Scouting Group. The High Seas Fleet would be in support, coming as far as the Dogger Bank, about halfway across the North Sea. Ingenohl did not tell the Kaiser this part of the plan, because it was in direct disobedience of his orders that the High Seas Fleet was not to be hazarded in this way.

Ingenohl was unaware that the Admiralty possessed the means to get wind of what he was up to – not the details, but sufficient to know some of what he intended in outline. Three windfalls had provided the British with the ability to read German wireless traffic. The first consisted of codebooks found when the light cruiser *Magdeburg* ran aground off the Estonian coast: Russian warships arrived in time to prevent the ship being destroyed, with effective disposal of the books. The second was a codebook for communicating between the German Admiralty and mer-chantmen as well as the High Seas Fleet, found by the Australians when they seized a German merchantman at the outbreak of war. The third was a code used by flag officers at sea, recovered in November, when a British trawler fishing off the Texel found a lead-lined chest in its nets which proved to have been ditched from a German torpedo boat sunk off the Dutch coast a month before.

A codebreaking organization was installed in Room 40 in the Admir-alty, where the cryptographers worked. To begin with there were teeth-ing troubles, not least because some of the more authoritarian senior naval officers in the Admiralty looked down on the cryptographers, who were mostly civilians. Room 40 took until 1917 to realize its full potential, but from the outset it was a priceless asset. The Germans never realized that the British were reading their codes. In this respect there is a superficial similarity between Room 40 in the First World War and the work done by Bletchley Park in the Second.

Although the existence of Room 40 was not known outside a small circle of officers and officials in the Admiralty, the security surrounding intercepts in the First World War was nothing like as tight as in the Second. Sub-Lieutenant Bowyer-Smyth in the *Superb* wrote in his diary while at sea on a 'sweep':

Tuesday 24.xi [1914]
    4.0 pm. Signal 'All German flotillas have been warned to be ready for service tonight'. This was a 'tapped' wireless message. We have their code – the Russians collared it some time ago from a ship that went ashore and of course gave it us.

From the outset, Captain Reginald 'Blinker' Hall, the Director of Naval Intelligence, was closely associated with Room 40, and in 1915 was responsible for setting up a chain of wireless direction-finding (DF) stations on the east coast. These DF stations could locate the positions of German warships when they transmitted, and were especially valu-able for pinpointing the C-in-C High Seas Fleet when he communicated with his subordinates.

Both the Germans and British came close to disaster on 16 December 1914. Forearmed with the Room 40 information, which did not include the fact that the High Seas Fleet was in support of Hipper, the Admiralty ordered Jellicoe to send Beatty's four battle cruisers (*Lion* (flag), *Queen Mary*, *New Zealand*, and *Princess Royal*), Rear Admiral William Pakenham's 3rd Cruiser Squadron, and Goodenough's 1st Light Cruiser Squadron to intercept Hipper when he withdrew. In addition Vice-Admiral Sir George Warrender's 2nd Battle Squadron (*King George V* (flag), *Ajax*, *Centurion*, *Orion*, *Monarch*, and *Conqueror*) and eight destroyers were to rendezvous with Beatty off Dogger Bank. Jellicoe wanted to take the whole Grand Fleet, but the Admiralty refused permission. Only luck prevented the Germans from achieving their aim of destroying part of the Grand Fleet and equalizing their strength.

In poor visibility, Warrender's destroyers bumped Ingenohl's screening cruisers and destroyers before dawn on 16 December. Ingenohl, thanks to squalls and fog, was unable to see what he was up against, although Warrender was only ten miles off. Thinking that he had encountered the whole Grand Fleet, and mindful of the Kaiser's strictures about not risking a general engagement, Ingenohl ordered a withdrawal, leaving Hipper exposed as he withdrew from Scarborough. Luck now swung in favour of the Germans. A series of mistakes, including poor signalling by Beatty's flag lieutenant and lack of initiative on the part of the British, allowed Hipper to escape by the skin of his teeth.

An opportunity was also lost to sink a German cruiser squadron consisting of the *Stralsund*, *Graudenz*, and *Strasburg*, accompanied by destroyers, whose withdrawal course after the bombardment of the coast passed within sight of Warrender's Battle Squadron. Sir Robert Arbuthnot, now rear admiral and in command of the Second Division of the Battle Squadron, reported that the enemy was in sight, but rigidly waited for orders rather than engaging the enemy. Warrender did not fire either, merely ordering three cruisers in pursuit and sending a sighting report which had the effect of sending Beatty off on a course which resulted in him missing Hipper.

Although not mentioned in other accounts, Jellicoe must have belatedly decided to reinforce Beatty and Warrender because he took the 1st and 4th Battle Squadrons to sea on the night of 15/16 December. Sub-Lieutenant Bowyer-Smyth in *Superb* at sea heading south-east from Scapa:

Wednesday 16.xii.14
    Hear BCS [Battle Cruiser Squadron – Beatty] are engaging their light cruisers – lucky devils – the BCs [battle cruisers] get everything. Still we seem to stand a better chance of a scrap this time than we have before – they really are out and we mustn't let them get back.
    No submarines or any excitement on way out.

5.0 Ship ready for action. Heading SE for rendezvous. In company: 1st BS [Battle Squadron], 4th BS [Battle Squadron], 3rd Cruisers [Squadron], Destroyer Flotilla & 4 armoured cruisers.

6 pm. There seems every possibility of action tomorrow or the next day. The High Seas Fleet are out – they were seen 150 miles off Heligoland at Noon. We have no news of their light cruisers. Signal received from Admiralty – 'do not go too far East', that is a bit hard on Jellicoe.

Thursday 17 December
'Action' sounded at 7.10, but this is to prepare ship and be ready by daylight, always a critical time. Everyone is full of apprehension, an action is really expected today; some of the married officers have long faces otherwise everyone on the top line [sic].

Hands remained at 'Action Stations' all day going to meals in shifts. 2nd BS [Warrender] and Battle Cruisers, also 3rd BS in company by 11. The former showed no signs of having been in action. Surely they can't have been given the slip by the enemy's BCs and light cruisers. Are we to be disappointed again? Heaven forbid – if the raiding squadrons get back untouched we will be dirt in the eyes of the public. We are already somewhat unpopular I believe & the man in the street can not or will not realise the size of the North Sea.

2 pm. Commenced to carry out tactics – this doesn't look very hopeful – everybody getting very sullen and disappointed. I suppose it means Scapa again – more cold, coal, and the disapproval of the people of England & derision of those of Germany to keep us going.

The events of 16 December are proof that good intelligence is not sufficient by itself to guarantee success. It may allow you to deploy to your advantage, but no plan survives contact with the enemy. Throw in Clausewitz's friction factor – the weather, human error, etc. – and commanders have to be faster on the 'draw' in a tactical sense to get the better of their opponents.

By now the seventy-three-year-old Admiral of the Fleet Sir John Fisher had been recalled to the post of First Sea Lord, sixty years after joining the navy. Admiral Prince Louis of Battenberg resigned on 28 October, writing to Churchill: 'I have lately been driven to the painful conclusion that at this juncture my birth and parentage have the effect of impairing in some respects my usefulness on the Board of Admiralty'.[4] Prince Louis of Battenburg was born in Germany, the second son of Grand Duke Louis IV of Hesse and the Rhine and Queen Victoria's second daughter, Alice. He had entered the Royal Navy as a boy of fourteen and served it faithfully thereafter. His nephew had been killed fighting in the British army in the Retreat from Mons, and his two sons were serving in the Royal Navy. Fisher, not one to suffer fools however highly placed, rated him 'far and away the best man inside the Admiralty building'. He became the victim of public hostility because of his German birth. His position was weakened because his wife's brother-in-law was Prince Henry, the Kaiser's brother and High Admiral of the German navy. All the reputable newspapers supported Prince Louis, only what we now call the tabloids howled for his resignation.

Fisher immediately made some changes at the Admiralty, including sending Sturdee to the South Atlantic where he was to make his name (see Chapter 3). Fisher's comment on the Scarborough fiasco was 'heads must roll', and a number of changes were made in the Grand Fleet. Fisher also authorized the move of Beatty's battle cruisers, and Goodenough's 1st Light Cruiser Squadron from Cromarty to join the 3rd Battle Squadron (now seven pre-dreadnoughts), and 3rd Cruiser Squadron at Rosyth, from where they would have a better chance of intercepting German raids on the east coast.

From the start of the war, Churchill had urged attacks on the Zeppelin bases at Düsseldorf and Cologne. In September 1914 these were still within range of Antwerp, where Samson and the RNAS were operating. Their exploits there with aircraft and armoured cars in support of the Royal Naval Division and the army, however, are outside the scope of this book.[5]

Two raids were launched from Belgium, the one on 22 September 1914, by four Sopwith Tabloids, being the first ever British long-range bombing raid. The two aircraft bound for Cologne turned back because of fog. Of the other two bound for Düsseldorf, one also turned back. One reached Düsseldorf but although two bombs hit the sheds, these failed to explode (the attack was too low, and the fuses on the bombs did not have time to arm), and one bomb dropped outside killed a few enemy ground crew. The second raid, on 6 October, with the Germans hammering on the gates of Antwerp, was more successful. A new Zeppelin at Düsseldorf was destroyed. Thick mist caused the raid on the sheds at Cologne to be aborted, but the railway station was bombed instead.

Once the Germans had taken Antwerp, the RNAS was denied the use of airfields from which it could reach Düsseldorf and Cologne. But the Zeppelin factory at Friedrichshaven on Lake Constance was just within range of Belfort near the Swiss border. The other possible target, Cuxhaven, was too far to reach from land bases in Allied hands. On 21 November, four Avro 504s took off, piloted by Squadron Commander Briggs, Flight Commander Babbington, Flight Lieutenant Sippe, and Flight Sub-Lieutenant Cannon, each carrying four 20lb bombs. Cannon's aircraft broke a skid on take-off and had to return. Carefully avoiding the Swiss border, the three remaining aircraft arrived at noon. Briggs, leading the raid, was shot down after dropping his bombs, and he was taken prisoner. Sippe hit some troops with one bomb, the Zeppelin shed with two, and the fourth 'hung-up', but he returned safely. Babbington hit the works manufacturing gas for the Zeppelins, and the resulting explosion nearly brought down his aircraft, but severely damaged a Zeppelin under construction. It was a splendid achievement, a bombing raid involving a 250-mile round trip, and another first notched up by the RNAS.

On Christmas Day 1914, Cuxhaven was the target for the first ever air raid launched from the sea. Three seaplane carriers, *Engadine*, *Riviera*, and *Empress*, carrying nine seaplanes, escorted by two destroyers and ten submarines, stopped twelve miles north of Heligoland and lowered their aircraft over the side. Seven seaplanes eventually took off, but surprise was lost and a running battle took place with Zeppelins and German seaplanes. The raid failed to find the Zeppelin sheds, thanks to thick mist and the fact that they were actually located at Nordholtz, some distance from Cuxhaven. Three of the aircraft returned to the ships, others landed on the sea and were picked up by submarines.

This Christmas Day raid was also remarkable for being the first occasion that surface ships were attacked from the air. The brand-new battle cruiser *Tiger* took part with her sisters providing distant protection for the seaplane carriers, should heavy units of the High Seas Fleet take a hand in the proceedings. She was a magnificent ship, the largest ship built for the Royal Navy until the *Hood*, and at 35,710 tons deep load heavier than any of the battle squadron dreadnoughts, including the *Queen Elizabeth*s. Armed with eight 13.5-inch guns, more heavily armoured than her sister the *Queen Mary*, and with 6-inch secondary armament in place of *Queen Mary*'s 4-inch, at full speed she could achieve 29 knots. Sixteen-year-old Boy Seaman Hayward described the scene waiting for the aircraft to return from the raid

> cruising around the aircraft carrier protecting her. We were thrilled when Jerry sent up one of these Zeppelins, the first we had ever seen. The great dirigible just cruised above us while we blazed away with our 3 inch high angle guns. The *Lion* fired shrapnel [sic – probably HE] shells from her A Turret, but the Zeppelin just disdainfully lifted up her nose and cruised away. We were firing short by at least a mile [sic].

The battle cruisers on the return from the raid experienced the North Sea weather at its worst. Even the mighty *Tiger* took a battering. Hayward:

It took us nearly four days to get back to Rosyth. Great waves tore at us and it seemed that the titanic fury would smash our massive bows in. At times the fore-part of the ship would be completely submerged up to the guns of B Turret, the lower bridge and superstructure being lost to view under water. Forward in the ship's company's heads below the forecastle, great steel supporting stanchions were bent and twisted like 'S' hooks. The waves tore at our upper deck fittings, and as we crawled up the sides of mountainous seas, we fell sixty feet down the green well with a sickening crash.

No one was allowed on deck and the second afternoon I had the watch on the bridge as a messenger. I went up through the main mast to get to the compass platform, but once there was speedily wet through to the skin with bitterly cold spray thrown up by the gigantic sea. The wind tore at us shrieking and wailing. Boats were swept over board, and guardrails bent like tin. Coming off watch, the Boys' mess deck was a scene of desolation. Heavy seas had come in through gun ports [of the 6-inch gun broadside battery?]. Mess tables and stools floated round in several feet of water, clothes lockers were wrenched off bulkheads. What food there was had been completely ruined.

During the storm, Hayward was ten minutes late closing up at his emergency station at his 6-inch gun, and once back in Rosyth, found himself in front of his captain, charged with being 'absent from his place of duty':

H B Pelly, our very good Captain, looked hard at me, 'According to King's Regulations and Admiralty Instructions, I could order this file of Marines to take you out on the quarterdeck and shoot you for desertion in the face of the enemy. However, the regulation states, "or such other punishment as hereinafter mentioned", so', and his kindly face broke into a smile, and my heart bounded with joy, 'I will forgive you. But do not be late again; six cuts with the cane', and aside to my divisional officer, 'Hmm, let him keep his trousers on'.

Ten minutes later in the midshipmen's flat I was tied hand and foot across a box horse and received six of the best. I stood the pain [without crying out].

The Battle of Dogger Bank

The next major action in the North Sea was a result of German suspicions that the unearthly ability of the British to forecast their actions must in part, at least, be because wireless-equipped trawlers on the fishing grounds of the shallow Dogger Bank were able to pass information of German fleet movements. In addition, Hipper believed that British light forces were almost permanently on patrol there, and planned a sortie to deal with them and the trawlers. The Kaiser forbade the High Seas Fleet from operating in support. On 23 January 1915, Ingenohl ordered Hipper to take out the 1st and 2nd Scouting Groups, consisting of the battle cruisers *Seydlitz* (flag), *Moltke*, and *Derfflinger*, and the armoured cruiser *Blücher*, with four light cruisers and eighteen destroyers. Although the *Blücher* had smaller guns than the German battle cruisers (8.2-inch compared with 11-inch), they could shoot further.

On Saturday 23 January 1915, the members of *Lion*'s gunroom were expecting Beatty and his staff for dinner that evening. Midshipman Alderson:

> The gunroom is being prepared with feverish energy. Black-list men scrubbed the deck this afternoon and Haines and I are working hard getting the mess polished and arranged. It looked ripping when we had finished; but we soon began raising steam for full speed, and later the Admiral cancelled his engagements. So all the preparations are wasted! There is a strong rumour that we have every chance of meeting the enemy tomorrow near the Dogger Bank. Passed under the [Forth] Bridge 8.0 pm. Steam for full speed. Outside 8.27 pm SE by E 20 knots.

The British, warned by Room 40 intercepts, set a trap for Hipper. Accordingly, Beatty sailed from Rosyth with 1st Battle Cruiser Squadron (*Lion* (flag), *Tiger*, and *Princess Royal*), Rear Admiral Sir Archibald Moore's 2nd Battle Cruiser Squadron (*New Zealand* (flag) and *Indomitable*), and Goodenough's 1st Light Cruiser Squadron. Tyrwhitt's Harwich force of three light cruisers and thirty-five destroyers was to rendezvous with him about thirty miles north of Dogger Bank at 0700 on 24 January. The gallant Keyes with *Lurcher* and *Firedrake* and his submarines were sent to position themselves near Borkum Riff (Friesian Islands). The 3rd Battle Squadron and 3rd Cruiser Squadron put to sea to provide cut-offs if Hipper came north, and the Grand Fleet left Scapa on the evening of 23 January to carry out a sweep in the southern part of the North Sea.

Midshipman Alderson in *Lion*:

> Jan 24th Sun I just had time for breakfast after the morning watch. Then we went to action stations, and I attended the navigator on Monkey's Island.* At 7.0 am there was only enough daylight to draw on the mooring board. We slowed to 14 knots to give time for scouting, but soon we saw gun flashes, and the *Aurora* reported four enemy battle cruisers.

---

* Strictly, the raised part of a ship's bridge round the compass binnacle. The whole area is known as the compass platform.

Surgeon Lieutenant Carey in *Southampton* copied into his diary the original draft of Commodore Goodenough's official despatch:

I have the honour to report that the 1st LCS consisting of *Southampton* wearing my broad pennant, *Nottingham*, *Birmingham* and *Lowestoft* arrived at the rendezvous ordered at 7 am Jan 24th.

At 7.15 am gun fire was observed ahead. Speed was increased to 25 knots and the squadron turned towards it.

At 7.30 *Aurora* reported enemy's cruisers ESE and battle cruisers SE At 7.40 am. enemy was sighted by *Southampton* and in a few minutes was made to consist of 4 battle cruisers with 5 or 6 light cruisers and destroyers.

The gunfire was the light cruiser *Aurora* of Tyrwhitt's Force shooting at the cruiser *Kolberg*. Paymaster Miller, whose action station in the *Arethusa* was now in the fore control, and thus in a better position to see what was happening than in the transmitting station:

At 7 am we went to Action Stations, and as I was taking up my position on the rangefinder, firing was reported on the starboard quarter. We could see huge flashes of rippling flame on the horizon and hear the dull boom of firing. It was evident to us that we had just missed the German fleet, but that *Aurora* and *Undaunted* and our destroyers had been sighted by them in the growing daylight. At 7.9 am we sighted the smoke of our own battle cruisers and light cruisers ahead. At 7.20 am we all turned to S 12 W [sic] and increased to full speed to chase the enemy who on sight of us made a beeline for Heligoland. It was the greatest pity that we were not on the other side of them. At 7.32 *Aurora* signalled that she was in action with the German Fleet.

Beatty and Hipper steered towards the gunflashes. Intercepted wireless messages and reports from the cruiser *Stralsund* of heavy smoke plumes sighted behind many enemy destroyers had warned Hipper that the British 'heavies' were out, and a trap was about to be sprung. He immediately headed for home. By 0750 Beatty could see Hipper's battle cruisers, and signalled for more speed.

Sub-Lieutenant Bower in the destroyer *Laforey* ahead of the battle cruisers:

we were booming along in the ordinary way & suddenly in the half light saw a row of flashes from the enemy ships. It was a tremendous shock to suddenly see the salvoes dropping all round. They were at extreme range & immediately they saw the battle cruisers turned & ran for their lives. Then we started the chase.

Surgeon Lieutenant Carey in Goodenough's light cruiser *Southampton*'s diary narrative: 'At 8.30 am one enterprising destroyer which had pushed on far ahead of the others was fired on by the *Blücher* and scuttled back. VA Beatty *Lion* then ordered all small craft to clear his front.'

Slowly the range came down, but the older battle cruisers *New Zealand* and *Indomitable* fell behind. Alderson in *Lion*:

> Just before 9 am we opened fire with A & B turrets at 22,000 yards. The guns are graduated up to 20,000, so the gunlayers aimed at the tops of their funnels. We were gradually closing the enemy. Our first salvo fell 400 yards to the right of the rear ship and short. Our second salvo went over. The enemy replied and their salvoes fell short. Half an hour of this, and then the enemy began to straddle, and I retired below to the lower conning tower, working [there] from 9.30 am.

New Zealand took a further 43 minutes to come into action, and *Indomitable*, the slowest of Beatty's battle cruisers, with obsolete shells for her main armament with less range than her sisters, did not open fire until 113 minutes after *Lion*.[6] Boy Seaman Hayward in the *Tiger*, at his action station in the starboard 6-inch battery:

> Our communications operator up in the starboard 6 inch gun control tower started to give us a running commentary on the action. The enemy were firing back at us and their shots were coming quite close. Through the gun ports we saw great pillars of water leaping up not far away; we all noticed that the spread of their salvoes was very wide.

By 0930 the battle cruisers were steaming with relative positions thus (not to scale):[7]

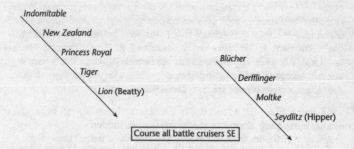

Carey in *Southampton*:

> By 9.55 the two fleets had closed appreciably and from our position between them and to one side of the big ships a magnificent view of the

action, which had now become brisk, could be had. On our starboard bow three German light cruisers could be seen almost hull down. A little further round came the 4 German BCs pouring out dense masses of black smoke from their funnels. From them balls of orange flame rolled out in the manner which is characteristic of big gun fire. The brown smoke of the discharge rose high in the air and hung over the funnel smoke in a distinct layer. At intervals huge splashes 300 ft high shot into the air and marked the arrival of our 13.5s. Further round the beam 3 columns of smoke and at an interval 2 more could be seen on the horizon. From the foremost three tongues of flame shot out as the *Lion*, *Tiger* and *Princess Royal* fired. The other two *Indomitable* and *New Zealand* could not keep up the tremendous pace and had dropped astern. With some difficulty we could see German shells bursting round our ships. On our quarter a huge cloud of smoke hung low on the horizon and showed where the flotillas were dashing along.

As Beatty and Hipper ran south-east firing at each other, *Seydlitz* was hit by a 13.5-inch shell, probably from *Lion*. It penetrated the barbette armour of the aftermost 11-inch turret, igniting charges in the working chamber, killing everyone in the turret, and spreading to the handling room of the adjacent superimposed turret, and up to this turret, incinerating the crew as they opened the hatch to escape. A total of 159 men were killed, and flames shot 200 feet into the air. The executive officer flooded both magazines, saving the ship. Boy Seaman Hayward in *Tiger* was still listening to a running commentary both from the 6-inch spotting tower and his own gun layer and trainer who apparently had gone outside the battery:

> Suddenly *Lion* found the range and nearly blew *Seydlitz* to Kingdom Come. Her after two turrets went up in a holocaust of flames and smoke. Our friend in the 6 inch gun control tower was very thrilled. You could hear the excitement in his voice as he described it. 'She's burning like a haystack'. We were very thrilled with our success, but our ship's gunnery was not too good. One of our destroyers, seeing that we were not finding the target, signalled to us spotting corrections.[8]

The *Blücher* was hit hard, and badly damaged, started to fall behind, but could still bite back. Carey in the *Southampton*:

> At 1015 am it became clear that the *Blücher* was lagging and she turned towards us and fired 3 or 4 shells at us, which went over. They fell unpleasantly close, one only about fifty yards away. We turned and increased our distance from her.
>
> At 1030 a Zeppelin looking like a silver sausage was sighted right ahead and stood over towards the nearest BC. The German BC appeared to

signal to her with star lights. We fired shrapnel at the Zeppelin without effect.

At 11.15 the *Blücher* appeared to stop and turn right round. Emboldened by this like jackals on a dying lion we closed to 14,000 yards, and hit him several times. But the dying *Blücher* was not so dead, and suddenly resumed course and speed at the same time dropping a number of 8.2s close to our ships from two of her turrets.

Although Beatty signalled his ships to fire on the corresponding ships in the enemy line, the captain of *Tiger* rather than taking on *Moltke* engaged *Seydlitz*, allowing *Moltke* unmolested to fire on *Lion*, who was also being engaged by *Seydlitz* and *Derfflinger*. Captain Chatfield of *Lion* wrote in a letter to a friend after the battle:

Ranges decreased to 15,600 <u>about</u>. But no ranges could be got. Their rate of fire at the end was very rapid, about 2 salvoes a minute. So it was like steaming through a waterfall & our fire was much affected as gunlayers could not see nor could the spotters even in Fore Top. We were quite alright [sic] however, although two shells pierced armour 5 inches at waterline & flooded engineers workshop, submerged flat, donkey room & several bunkers so we got a slight list to Port. All their shells fell on me (very accurate calibration) so either hit or missed & nearly all missed, but as a rule when *Derfflinger* hit it was always 2 shells within 10 feet of each other. Eventually 2 shells 1 fore and 1 aft struck us on the 9 inch armour just below the WL [water line] one forward and one aft. The plates defeated the shell but were driven in bodily like a gate about 3 feet. This let a lot of water in and the after one cracked the feed tank & filled boilers with sea water & stopped Port engine & we heeled to about 10° & dropped astern gradually. We were not seriously injured except for these two shell & the one in Body Room. All turrets except 1 gun in action. So we had bad luck. We had given much more than we got.*

Sub-Lieutenant Spragge, now in *Lion*, had been sent below the armoured deck with his 4-inch gun crews:

About 1030 some wounded came through our flat going to the dressing station & enemy hits became more frequent, shaking the whole ship. A shell burst close and one could hear the tinkle tinkle of splinters falling. A carpenter's party went aft to stop a shell hole. Altogether I was getting rather fed up with the action & hoping it would end soon. About 10.45 am we took a list to port of 10 degrees, & the mess deck we were on filled with smoke, so I went on to the main deck to look for a fire and put it out,

---

* Despite Chatfield's optimistic assessment, *Lion*'s side armour was shown to be less than effective.

but I could see no fire & nothing in the smoke left the hoses running & went below again.

Midshipman Alderson in the lower conning tower, as *Lion* listed to port:

a shell burst nearly above the hatch to the lower conning tower. The splinters pierced the armour deck, wounded some of the fire brigade, and sent a puff of filthy suffocating black powdery smoke all over the mess deck and down into the lower conning tower. This, together with the list and the cries of wounded men, seemed to us below, who could see nothing, very serious. And still we continued firing, but now we had to haul out of the line. I then came on deck to view the damage, which was not so extensive as I imagined, though that below is more extensive.

The *Lion* was hit seventeen times. At 1045, with her dynamos out of action, and port engine stopped, she dropped behind. At this juncture, Beatty thought he saw a submarine periscope and signalled a turn of eight points (90°) to port, which put his ships on a north-easterly course across Hipper's wake. This was a case of 'submarinitis', combined with lack of knowledge of what a submarine could be expected to do. Steaming at 26 to 27 knots, Beatty's battle cruisers were almost impossible to hit by the submarines of the period. There were no submarines in the area, although Beatty was not to know this.

Tiger had also been hit. The roof of Q Turret was peeled back by a heavy shell, killing or injuring several members of the left gun crew. The captain of the turret fetched men from below and got the guns back into action with the dead laid on one side and wounded evacuated. The worst hit on *Tiger* was on a large compartment below the signal bridge, where the tripod mast met the superstructure, called 'Rowton House' by her crew. An 11-inch shell tore through the starboard aerial deck to explode inside the compartment. Boy Seaman Hayward:

This was the station for the upper deck fire and repair party, under the leadership of an acting chief petty officer, the Canteen Manager. Having nothing to do, they were all sitting on the deck whiling away the time with a hand of cards.

After the action, I went up to see the damage, and found broken bodies, cards and money scattered everywhere. It seemed as if a cyclone had swept through the compartment, and all that was left of the Canteen Manager was a shattered arm and hand still clutching the ace of spades. Jerry had 'trumped his trick'.

Above 'Rowton House' on either extreme forward corner were mounted the port and starboard 6 inch gun control towers. The steel hatchway of the starboard one was closed, and all was well. But the port hatchway had been left open, and unfortunately the Engineer Captain of the Fleet had been standing by the open hatchway. He was responsible for the Engineering of the Battle Cruiser Squadron; he was acting as a spotting officer. He was killed instantly when a shell exploded. The Control Officer was also seriously wounded, but his life was saved by one of his crew, Boy 1st Class O'Brien, who carried the officer down the shattered ladder, although wounded himself. For this he was awarded the DCM.

As *Lion* dropped back, and Hipper looked like getting away because of the turn to avoid the 'submarine', Beatty tried to make clear to his captains that they were to press on after Hipper leaving *Indomitable*, who was trailing behind, and the light cruisers to deal with the dying *Blücher*. There were only two signal halyards left uncut by shell splinters in *Lion*, and no power for wireless or light signals. Beatty's flag lieutenant, Seymour, suggested hoisting Nelson's last signal at Trafalgar, 'engage the enemy more closely'. Beatty agreed, to be told that it no longer appeared in the signal book. Instead the signal 'engage the rear of the enemy', which was the best that Seymour could manage to suggest in the heat of the moment, was hoisted. Unfortunately the signal for 'course NE', for the previous submarine avoidance manoeuvre, was still flying on the other halyard. They were both pulled down together, so his captains read the signal as 'attack the rear of the enemy bearing NE' and the battle cruisers surrounded the *Blücher*. Carey in *Southampton*:

> The *Tiger* and *Princess Royal* now appeared astern of the *Blücher*, and at 1135 the last of the great drama which we had been watching since 7 am was performed. The *Blücher* came under fire from 4 BCs, with a few shells from us to help. She was a magnificent but dreadful sight as although burning furiously in many places and struck over and over again, she slowly fired her last remaining gun. At 1150 the *Tiger* dashed in at high speed.

Hayward in *Tiger*:

> When the range came down to 10,000 yards, we in the 6 inch batteries opened fire 'Rapid Independent'. It was a 'carve up', all the Squadron raining blow after blow on the enemy, an avalanche of steel and explosive, like a tired lame duck she absorbed this punishment, her speed slowly dropping away.
>
> At first firing common shell, we changed to the more deadly lyddite of greater explosive power. Soon our shots were exploding all over the cruiser. So short became the range, that we could see our projectiles exploding on the target. Ben Smyth, our trainer, at this dramatic moment stopped the gun following the target, saying, 'It's bloody murder, Bill',

shouting at the gunlayer who was firing, pressing the trigger by means of a hand grip on the handles. Billy Lowes promptly reminded everyone loudly 'what about the women and children those bastards have murdered', in his rich Liverpool Irish voice. The battle re-commenced without another protest.

We loading numbers were now having a bad time, the gun casemate being full of cordite smoke. We were firing on a forward bearing. As the gun fired and recoiled, the breech worker would open the breech to take another round, and the wind blew the cordite smoke and fumes back into the casemate, blinding and choking the loading numbers who began to drop out. We had no gas masks, but had been issued with black crepe bandages to wear across our mouths and nostrils. But this had to be soaked with water. We had no water and the captain of the gun refused to allow us to use the water in the rammer tub. He said, 'urinate on the bloody things'. Often I found myself having to load two projectiles one after the other, my opposite shell number being in a bad way. The 100 lb shells began to weigh heavy with continuous action.

Meanwhile, with *Lion* out of the chase, Admiral Beatty left his flagship.

Alderson: 'The destroyer *Attack* came alongside without delay while we still had way on and made fast – a very fine bit of seamanship.' The crew of *Lion* cheered their admiral as he stood on the *Attack*'s forecastle as she drew away. Beatty caught up his squadron, while they were finishing off the *Blücher*, and shifted his flag to *Princess Royal*.

Miller in *Arethusa* watched *Blücher*'s end:

She was stopped evidently disabled – shells from the 13.5-inch and 12-inch guns were exploding with terrific violence all over her and fires were raging on board. She was entirely obscured most of the time by smoke. We closed to within 2,000 yards of her and just before firing two torpedoes at her, she fired her last gun. We observed she had no flags flying, and signalled that she had apparently struck, but for another ten minutes until our signal was received, *New Zealand* continued firing. At 11.58 we were ordered to close the enemy, rescue the crew, and sink her as quickly as possible, as we were only 40 miles from Heligoland.

So at midday we closed our stricken enemy hardly believing our eyes when we saw some three or four hundred men on her upper deck. We thought that no one could have lived through that hell. As we came up with some destroyers those gallant survivors seeing us coming to rescue them gave us three cheers. It was evident that the ship was capsizing and we closed as near as we could – to 100 yards or so. Her upper deck was a shambles, the mast shot away, and fore funnel bent forward. Through great holes in her side one could see fires raging between decks. She gradually rolled over on to her side and as she did so, men fell or ran down her side into the water, a few of the wisest having jumped in before. Some I saw roll head over heels and catch up against the bilge keels, probably breaking their backs. Others were thrown over the opposite side and the ship rolled over and engulfed them. She then half righted herself, before sinking slowly back completely bottom up. Some men managed to keep on her and were washed off as she sank under them. There were no explosions and no apparent suction.

Then came a rush to rescue. We lowered boats and hung ropes ends over the side, while eight or nine destroyers did the same. Our men threw anything floatable they could lay their hands on overboard. But the water was terribly cold. Everyone worked with a smile, but in the midst of it a hostile aeroplane arrived and dropped two bombs, while the old Zepp was not far away. We hoisted our boats as quickly as possible, and ran to fire our anti-aerial [sic] guns, besides keeping a sharp lookout for submarines. The work of rescue went on, but I saw some men drown right alongside, while others further out were calling out 'save, save', without the strength to help themselves. It was a terrible sight. We rescued 120 officers and men, and I hope the destroyers rescued about 180 to 200 between them. I don't think a large percentage of those we saw on deck were drowned, but all the badly wounded must have gone down with the ship. Our captain (Arbuthnot) fell overboard himself trying to rescue a drowning German. Five minutes before we were trying to kill the very fellows we were now risking our lives to save.

Some curious remarks were made by the men as we pulled them on board. One said, 'So this is the saucy *Arethusa*'.

Another saw a Leading Stoker of ours named Clarke, and said, 'Hello Nobby, what are you doing here?' He had lived for years two doors down from him in Hull – he was only 17.

One officer half dead with shock and cold, gravely saluted and said, 'Good morning'.

Another officer was pulled in board by our painter and plumber in a collapsed condition. The painter gave him artificial respiration, and they carried him to the officers bath room and gave him a hot bath, saving his life. We took the officers aft and gave them brandy and hot tea or coffee, and turned them into our bunks, while the men looked after the men.

Blücher had taken at least seventy hits. Hipper escaped. Chatfield wrote, 'we thought that our 4 fresh ships would now finish off the crippled *Derfflinger* and *Seydlitz*, as *Blücher* had already been knocked out and was miles astern. However, Admiral Moore did not pursue them further, though why I am not quite clear. It was very disappointing.' Chatfield appeared to have forgotten the *Moltke* and *Seydlitz* were not crippled; both could still steam at high speed, although there is no doubt they were badly battered. *Derfflinger*, although on fire, did not suffer serious damage.

Rear Admiral Moore, Beatty's second-in-command, trained to unthinking obedience by the system, did not ignore Beatty's signal, though it made tactical nonsense, and did not press on after Hipper, as Nelson would have done. The navy revered Nelson, but in the intervening century had forgotten what made him operate the way he did. As Fisher said, referring to all the battle-cruiser captains, 'any fool can obey orders'.[9] Seymour, whose signalling blunders and slow thinking had cost Beatty success at the encounter following the Scarborough raid, had now fouled up this battle. Commanders should take responsibility for their subordinates' mistakes, but commanders should also sack subordinates when they have shown themselves to be below par. Seymour was to remain in post, with dire consequences the next time Beatty met Hipper, which was not for another sixteen months.

Meanwhile the *Lion* needed to get home. Bower in a letter to his mother:

> Then '*Indom*' took *Lion* in tow, a fine bit of seamanship & destroyers were round them the whole way back, 240 miles at 7 knots, and the Germans never had a shot at bagging those tow ships in that long & helpless trip. They will never get another chance like that. A sight I shall never forget was the '*Indom*' towing the damaged *Lion* slowly and majestically under the Forth Bridge with all the sailors crowded on her damaged decks & the whole harbour resounding with cheers. We were about 100 yards off & it quite gave me a cold shiver down the back, it was so fine.

Carey in *Southampton* remembered how during the battle

> It was almost impossible to keep the men at their stations below during these exciting events and nearly all the time the side of the ship was lined by a crowd that cheered wildly as each good shot was made – answering cheers came up from below from the various parties working there. No thought of danger entered anyone's head and everyone was in highest spirits throughout the action. The casualties were light, 11 wounded on *Lion*, five killed and 12 wounded on *Tiger*.*

Chatfield wrote to a naval officer friend:

> I have made a lot of recommendations which it is impossible to list here.
>
> Rapidity of fire and <u>Short Shots</u> is what we want in our Control officers minds. Whoever get the biggest Volume of fire that is hitting will gain the ascendancy & keep it as the other fellow can't see to reply. Range does

---

* British casualties were: *Lion*, 1 killed, 20 wounded, and *Tiger*, 10 killed and 11 wounded.

not matter as modern shell will knock an enemy out at any range you can reach. *Lion* fired too slowly hampered by all the orders and restrictions on the subject.

The enemy can fire very quickly and will do so [at] 15,000 [yards] and under we must get that into the heads of all gunnery Lieuts at once. The difficulty of controlling rapid fire is admitted but is nothing to the difficulty in controlling once the enemy's fire is more rapid than yours. *Lion* fired only 235 rounds! To match more than 1500 rounds fired at her. Nevertheless I think we hit the 3 ships we fired at more often than we were hit & if we had been bolder in firing we should have annihilated them alone. We were hit 14 times.

We now know that *Lion* hit three ships (*Blücher* once, *Derfflinger* once, and *Seydlitz* twice), but Chatfield's reasoning above seems open to question. If it took 1,500 enemy shells (according to him) to hit *Lion* fourteen times (actually seventeen), and if he thought he had done so much damage to three ships with only 235 shells, the argument that speed of firing was what mattered does not wash. The fact that he had not damaged the enemy as severely as he imagined is immaterial, the point is that this is what he believed. That his thinking was illogical, untypically for him, does not matter, what does is his obsession with speed of fire. As a gunnery expert and Beatty's trusted flag captain he had great influence in what was soon to become the Battle Cruiser Fleet (BCF), all three Battle Cruiser Squadrons all under Beatty. Speed of fire became all-important, with accuracy a long way second. The BCF, based at Rosyth, did not get the opportunity to practise as often as the Battle Fleet based at Scapa, and its gunnery accuracy was beginning to be the subject of criticism. Now here apparently was the answer, and one that appealed to the BCF's panache (perhaps 'cowboy' instincts is putting it too strongly); getting the maximum number of rounds off in the shortest possible time was the key to success. One way to achieve this was to circumvent the 'orders and restrictions on the subject' Chatfield referred to, by which he meant getting rid of the flash precautions that inhibited a fire in the turret from reaching the magazines, because these slowed down the passage of charges and shells from magazine and shell room to turret. If extra charges were stacked in turrets and the handling room below the turret this would further speed up loading. If the charges could have their flashproof covering taken off, loading would be faster still – ignore the fact that each cordite bag-charge had igniters at each end, which were no more sophisticated than a firework (which did not matter if the cover was taken off only at the last minute before it was rammed into the breech of the gun, and there were not several other 'exposed' charges littering the gunhouse).

The BCF began to adopt these highly dangerous ways, except in *Lion* herself, where the chief gunner, Warrant Officer Grant, bravely and successfully defied Chatfield and refused to allow such potentially lethal practices. At Jutland, Beatty, with the crew of his flagship, was to have good reason to be thankful for Grant's obstinacy. Three of his battle cruisers were not to be so lucky.

The Germans learned a very different lesson from *Seydlitz*'s escape from disaster at Dogger Bank, when her after handling rooms caught fire: the need to have even better anti-flash precautions between magazine, handling room, and turret. These were put in place in time for the next occasion Beatty and Hipper met.

3

Hunting the Raiders: Coronel, the Falklands, and the Rufiji River

At the outbreak of the First World War, Britain and her dominions owned 43 per cent of the world's merchant shipping. Germany, with 12 per cent, trailed well behind in second position. Third place was shared by France, the United States, Norway and Japan, with about 4 per cent each.

Britain existed on her imports. These included two-thirds of her food, and vast quantities of other essential commodities, such as iron ore, tin, rubber, manganese, oil, diesel, and petrol. Britain's many interests were spread round the globe. These with her merchant shipping, and her reliance on imports for survival, were vulnerabilities which Germany was determined to exploit. In the opening months of the war, the weapon they chose was the surface raider. The submarine would be used later.

Surface raiders came in two forms: warships and armed merchant cruisers. Because the Royal Navy closed Germany's exits from the North Sea, only those German warships stationed abroad at the outbreak of war were able to take part in commerce raiding. The most important of these were in Vice-Admiral Graf von Spee's East Asiatic Cruiser Squadron, based in Tsingtau, about a hundred miles north of Shanghai. The squadron consisted of two powerful armoured cruisers, *Scharnhorst* (flag) and *Gneisenau*, and three light cruisers, *Emden*, *Nürnberg*, and *Leipzig*. The two armoured cruisers, each with eight 8.2-inch and six 5.9-inch guns, winners of the Imperial Navy's gunnery prize, were capable of over 20 knots.

The light cruiser *Königsberg* was on the east coast of Africa, and the light cruisers *Dresden* and *Karlsruhe* were in the Caribbean. Germany had the world's third largest empire in 1914, but it was underdeveloped; the most serious deficit was a lack of overseas bases at which to coal ship. Under the terms of the 1907 Hague Convention, warships could take in only sufficient coal at a neutral port to allow them to reach their home base; and then could not coal in any port in that same neutral country for three months. Without the extensive chain of coaling bases round the world enjoyed by the British, the Germans would have to coal at sea or in remote anchorages, and from supply ships, prizes, or captured colliers. Coaling was a laborious evolution in harbour but infinitely more difficult in any sort of a seaway.

To provide an alternative for the lack of bases, the Germans selected areas of the world where cruiser operations were likely. Officials and commercial representatives were made responsible for coordinating the supply of coal, water, and provisions in each area. Stocks of these commodities were also pre-positioned in places known to German raider captains. A combination of strict application of the rules by neutral countries and the efforts of Allied warships ensured that within a few months the German system became unworkable.

The Germans had several fast merchant liners which were ideal for adaptation to commerce raiding as auxiliary cruisers. Other than the *Berlin*, whose mines had sunk the *Audacious*, the only other auxiliary to escape from a German port after the outbreak of war was the fast liner *Kaiser Wilhelm der Grosse*. She sank few ships and was caught in Spanish neutral waters off Africa by the *Highflyer*. The *Kaiser Wilhelm der Grosse* was so badly damaged in the ensuing encounter, her captain scuttled her. The liners *Kronprinz Wilhelm* and *Prinz Eitel Friedrich* were the most successful of these auxiliary raiders, but their careers were brought to a stop by their insatiable appetite for coal, and both were eventually interned in neutral ports.

When war was declared, Spee's squadron was spread over the Pacific. The *Emden* was in Tsingtau; Spee himself was in the Caroline Islands with *Scharnhorst* and *Gneisenau*; the *Leipzig* was off the Pacific coast of Mexico; and the *Nürnberg* was on passage to relieve her. *Leipzig*'s presence off Mexico paralysed shipping from Vancouver to Panama, but she sank only two ships. Spee recalled *Nürnberg*, and sailed for the Marianas. Captain Karl von Müller of the *Emden* slipped out of Tsingtau to avoid being trapped there, and joined Spee in the Marianas. Here a council of war was held, on 12 August. Spee decided to detach *Emden*, the newest and fastest light cruiser, to the Indian Ocean to disrupt trade. Spee headed east across the Pacific with the rest of his squadron, having ordered *Leipzig* to join him at Easter Island. His deployment was based on the premiss that Japan would come in to the war on the side of the Allies, and he wanted to put as much distance as possible between his ships and the Japanese Imperial Navy. He was proved right when Japan declared war on Germany on 23 August.

Müller in the *Emden* achieved total surprise when he appeared off the east coast of India, athwart the Colombo–Calcutta shipping route. In addition to Vice-Admiral Sir Martyn Jerram's China Squadron, the Japanese, French, and Russians joined in the hunt for *Emden*. But Müller proved to be a wily fox and before he was caught had sunk the Russian light cruiser *Zhemtchug* and the French destroyer *Mousquet*, as well as sixteen British merchantmen, behaving in a chivalrous manner towards the passengers and crews of the ships he sank. He destroyed oil-storage tanks at Madras, but perhaps his most daring exploit was his bombardment of Penang. He was eventually caught by the Australian light cruiser *Sydney* off the Cocos Islands. The *Sydney* with eight 6-inch guns outgunned *Emden*'s ten 4.1-inch. With his ship on fire, Müller ran her aground, and the crew surrendered.[1]

The *Karlsruhe* in the Caribbean, under command of Captain Köhler, was almost as troublesome as the *Emden* in the Indian Ocean. With the auxiliary the *Kronprinz Wilhelm*, the ships eluded the British armoured cruiser *Suffolk* by superior speed. Once out of sight, they parted company in different directions. The light cruiser *Bristol* was sent to intercept *Karlsruhe* but failed to catch her, and Köhler decided to shift his area of operations to the north-east coast of Brazil, which was less confined and more sparsely patrolled than the Caribbean. Here he sank sixteen ships. After a while he decided he had been in the area for long enough, and headed for the shipping lane between Barbados and Trinidad, but on passage the *Karlsruhe* was sunk by a mysterious internal explosion. Köhler was killed, but a few of the crew were rescued by a German supply ship, which evaded the blockade and arrived in Germany a month later. The searches for the *Karlsruhe* by the Allies had proved to be singularly ineffective, and had she not sunk by accident, she was set to give the British and French a great deal more trouble. The vast stretches of the South American coast provided a myriad hiding places, and by crossing the Atlantic to West Africa she would have found plenty of places to hole up there too.

After she was relieved on the Caribbean station by the *Karlsruhe*, the *Dresden* was on the way home when her orders were changed, and she was instructed to attack shipping off the River Plate. After sinking two merchantmen, she was ordered to the Pacific to work with the *Leipzig*. She was heading north up the coast of Chile when she heard that Spee was at Easter Island, and steamed to join him there. Meanwhile thanks to radio intercepts the Admiralty had discerned von Spee's intention to head for the western Pacific, but not his destination and plans.

Today we live in the world of satellite communications. With a tiny mobile telephone we can talk to someone on the far side of the world. But in 1914, although wireless telegraphy, or radio as we call it now, had been in service in the British and German navies for around ten years, it was subject to a number of limitations and neither side had used it in war. Direct communication between London and British ships in South American waters, and between Berlin and German ships in the Pacific, was not possible. Signals from the Admiralty to ships off the east coast of South America were sent by cable to Montevideo where the Uruguayan government allowed them to be transmitted by wireless to the Falklands. From here they were re-transmitted to ships at sea. Replies followed the reverse route. So signals could take several days to arrive and sometimes up to a week if atmospheric conditions were bad.

British ships in the Pacific could not communicate with the Falklands because of atmospheric conditions caused by the Andes. Chile was neutral and coded signals could not be transmitted to wireless stations there, so signals had to be sent to British consuls, and ships diverted to collect them. The German wireless station at Yap, which was in cable communication with Berlin, had been destroyed on 12 August 1914. However, the Germans were able to compensate for this once they were off South America. Here there were numerous German merchant ships in harbours along the coast, and some of the authorities in certain South American countries were not too fussy about enforcing the regulation which forbade the use of wireless in neutral ports by ships from belligerent nations. Berlin could cable one of their consuls, who would order a German merchant ship to relay the signal to Spee, if necessary putting to sea to do so.

Both sides quickly realized just how easily signals were intercepted and revealed the position of ships, so they took various measures to fool the enemy, such as getting one ship in the squadron to transmit all signals, so listeners would think that only one ship was in the area.

Surmising that Spee might operate off the west coast of South America or pass through the Straits of Magellan, the Admiralty ordered Rear Admiral Sir Christopher Cradock to concentrate a force to meet Spee. Cradock, who had been searching the eastern coast of South America for commerce raiders and intercepting German merchantmen, was told that his task was to search the Magellan Strait, followed by searching up the Chilean coast to Valparaiso, or returning to the east coast of South America. The Admiralty's signals to Cradock, which on average took about four days to reach him and in some cases contradicted each other, were a classic example of the old adage, 'order, counter-order, disorder', and were to show that 'back-seat driving' by a headquarters without access to all the facts could be dangerous; in this case fatal to two ship's companies. The poor staff work by the Admiralty makes nonsense of Churchill's 'yardarm clearing' statement, 'I cannot, therefore, accept for the Admiralty any share in the responsibility for what followed'.[2]

Although Cradock's cruisers were classified as armoured, neither the *Good Hope* (flag) nor *Monmouth*, both launched in 1901, were in the same league as the *Scharnhorst* and *Gneisenau*. They were outgunned by the Germans, and their effectiveness was further reduced because the guns in their lower casemates could not be operated in a heavy sea without flooding, whereas the guns in their opponents' were mounted further above the waterline. Cradock might have been able to go some way towards evening up the odds if he had taken the old battleship *Canopus* with him. But, like his armoured cruisers, she was crewed by elderly reservists and half-trained boys from the training ships. Her four 12-inch guns were obsolete and had less range than the German armoured cruisers' 8.2-inch guns, of which they each had eight. Her armour protection was marginally inferior to *Scharnhorst* and *Gneisenau*. None of Cradock's major units were worked up, and their gunnery was nothing like as good as the German crack gunnery squadron: for example, *Canopus*'s 12-inch guns had not been fired since she had been brought out of reserve at the outbreak of war. The only modern ship in Cradock's squadron was the steam-turbine-driven light cruiser *Glasgow*, with two 6-inch and ten 4-inch guns, and a designed speed of 25 knots.

Cradock had originally been told that the modern armoured cruiser *Defence*, with four 9.2-inch and ten 7.5-inch guns, would form part of his squadron.[3] When she did not put in an appearance, he asked for her three times. Each time his request was refused, and finally he was told that she would remain in Montevideo, and if he asked again, he would be replaced.

Instead of helping Cradock, the Admiralty wasted precious time second-guessing him. At one point they thought that he would take *Canopus*, which in Churchill's phrase would act as a 'citadel around which all our cruisers in these waters could find absolute security'.[4] This was a bizarre concept for a naval battle and indicative of Churchill's superficial knowledge of naval matters, and his itch to direct the war personally. Another guess was that Cradock would send *Glasgow* to shadow Spee, a correct use of a light cruiser, and wait until he was reinforced. Finally, the Admiralty instructed him to concentrate his squadron with *Canopus*, and wait for the *Defence*, which they had been holding back. But the signal was sent on 3 November, two days after the battle was fought.

Eventually, Cradock set off from the Falkland Islands, where he had coaled his squadron, to find and engage Spee. *Canopus* was not in company, as Cradock believed that because of the state of her machinery she could not steam at more than 12 knots. In fact she was able to make nearly 16 knots, but her engineer commander who was suffering from a bout of pre-battle nerves had exaggerated the extent of her defects. Instead, she was detailed to bring up the rear, escorting Cradock's colliers. The rest of his squadron consisted of *Good Hope*, *Monmouth*, the armed liner *Otranto*, and the *Glasgow*.

Cradock had sent *Monmouth* and *Glasgow* ahead through the Magellan Straits, as Engineer Lieutenant-Commander Shrubsole of the *Glasgow* wrote later to his father,

> to try and pick up news of the enemy. We cruised slowly north of Valparaiso without getting any news at all, but at Valparaiso we learned that considerable quantities of coal were leaving the Chilean ports in German ships. The quantity was so large that it amounted to a certainty that there was a concentration of German men of war taking place somewhere near. We acquainted the Admiral with this fact.

On 27 October, Cradock paused at the island of Auchilu Veshupi, landing Lieutenant Gould and a small party from the *Good Hope* to set up a wireless station there. As Cradock steamed north, he sent individual ships in among the islands to search for the enemy. The *Otranto* was one of these. She was fitted with two 4.7-inch guns, and known in the squadron as the 'floating haystack' or 'sardine tin'. Chief Petty Officer Spencer, the chief yeoman of signals in *Otranto*, was like many of Cradock's squadron a forty-one-year-old reservist recalled for war service. He was a survivor of the collision in 1893 between the *Victoria*, in which he had been a second signalman, and the *Camperdown*. As chief yeoman of the *Otranto*, he would have been on the bridge and aware of all the signals made by the squadron. He wrote to his wife on 9 November, using a signal pad for writing paper:

> we had been scouring through the various channels between the islands off the coast of Chili [sic] trying to get information, & pretty dangerous work for this big ship as most of them are badly charted, we had rejoined *Monmouth* and *Glasgow*, when we were ordered to Puerto Montt, a small German colony in Chili [sic] to get news. We could not obtain any, but I expect they telegraphed the enemy that we were there. Anyway we left on Saturday morning.

Meanwhile, as Shrubsole recalls, *Glasgow* was:

> sent on to Coronel to send and receive telegrams while the *Monmouth*, *Good Hope* and *Otranto* came slowly behind us. As we got into Coronel late on 31st October, we could hear wireless messages passing between German warships. We waited there for the night and left at daybreak to join the flagship.
>
> This was the 1st of November. There was a very heavy sea running &

we were rolling very heavily & when we met the flagship at about 4 pm, it was so bad that we could not lower a boat & had to put our telegrams in a cask & tow it across the bows of the *Good Hope*.

Spencer in *Otranto*:

The Admiral made a signal to say that he could hear German wireless very strong & expected that it was ahead, the squadron would therefore spread 15 miles apart & steer NW by N at 10 knots to find them.

At 4.30 pm we observed smoke off our starboard bow, & reported it to *Glasgow*. We both at once altered course towards it, as we got closer, we found it was two large armoured cruisers. We at once wirelessed *Good Hope* who was out of sight by this time.

Shrubsole in *Glasgow*:

They [the enemy] were steaming in a southerly direction & on catching sight of us, immediately gave chase. We turned and ran for the other ships, acquainting them with the state of affairs by our wireless. We all thought the Admiral would turn too & and run for the *Canopus*, whom we should have met about 9 am the next morning. He decided otherwise however & made a signal to turn and engage the enemy.

Spee had heard of *Glasgow*'s presence in Coronel through German diplomatic means, and had headed for the port. He had ordered all traffic passed on *Leipzig*'s wireless, to trick eavesdroppers into believing she was on her own, and when they met, both admirals still thought they were searching for a solitary cruiser. Cradock probably could have escaped, but closed without hesitation. At this stage, *Canopus* was 300 miles astern.

Spencer in the *Otranto*:

We were ordered to form in single line ahead as follows [sketch on signal pad]:

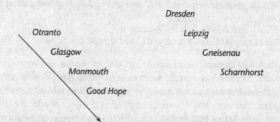

At this stage the *Nürnberg* was well astern of the rest of Spee's squadron. Shrubsole in the *Glasgow*:

> The light was very good, but the sea was so rough that the *Monmouth* and *Good Hope* could not fire their lower guns & our guns were almost awash. We tried to close the enemy but they avoided action & we began to think they did not intend to fight.
>
> However the German admiral was cleverer than we thought & all he was waiting for was the setting of the sun. As the sun set immediately behind us, we were silhouetted against the sky, while their ships were only black blurs in the failing light.
>
> The German ships now turned towards us & opened fire, their shots falling short. The remainder of my account is only what I have been told as I went below in the engine room and remained there until it was all over.

Cradock formed his ships into line of battle at about 5 p.m. He tried to close Spee to bring him to action immediately, so that the Germans would have the setting sun in their eyes. Spee backed off, using his superior speed to keep the range at about 18,000 yards. At this point, Cradock ordered *Otranto* to get away. At 7 p.m., when the sun dipped below the horizon, the Germans closed the range to 12,300 yards. Cradock, with only two 9.2-inch guns to Spee's sixteen 8.2-inch, closed to bring his 6-inch guns within range. Not only was the light advantage against the British silhouetted against the afterglow, and with the Germans lost in the gloom, but the heavy sea on Cradock's engaged bow interfered with many of *Good Hope*'s and *Monmouth*'s 6-inch guns. The Germans were able to use all their 8.2-inch and 6-inch. Soon their superior gunnery told.

Spencer in *Otranto*:

> the fire from our ships seemed to slacken. The *Good Hope* was down by the head, and apparently could not steam or fire, the *Monmouth* badly battered was on fire, the *Glasgow* hit twice. *Otranto* was not hit at all and in accordance with orders the *Otranto* shaped a course away from the fleet, as our guns would not bear, and being full of wood cabins would have been a sheet of flame if hit.

Leading Seaman Hawkes was a gunlayer in the *Glasgow*:

> in the first ten minutes the *Good Hope* and *Monmouth* were on fire. The *Monmouth* had her fore turret blown over the side. After a while there was a terrible explosion and we saw the whole of the midships part of the *Good Hope* blow up, the fire must have spread to her magazine. It was a shocking sight. After that her after 9.2 fired about twice, and that was the

last I saw of her. *Monmouth* was in flames, and she pulled out of the line. We carried on firing for about ten minutes.

At around 8 p.m., after about thirty-five hits from the *Scharnhorst*, the *Good Hope* was blown to bits by a magazine explosion, flames shooting 250 feet into the air. The *Monmouth*, with fires in several parts from numerous hits inflicted by the *Gneisenau*, had already pulled out at 7.30 p.m. The *Nürnberg*, having arrived, closed and opened up on her at 1,000 yards, with no reply from *Monmouth*, who sank at about 9 p.m. There were no survivors from either *Good Hope* or *Monmouth*.

Shrubsole in *Glasgow*, before the *Monmouth* sank:

We turned and ran. We reluctantly said goodbye to her as it was suicide to follow as all the enemy were concentrating their fire on us. They missed us in the dark, and the last we saw of them, was the flash of their guns as they fired on the luckless *Monmouth*. A single shot from one of their big guns might have sunk us and it was simply the mercy of God that we survived.

We were actually hit five times, but only by shots from the light cruisers. One shell passed through the Captain's pantry then into his cabin going clean through his kneehole table and bookcase. Another went through a bunker below the waterline without doing much damage. Another hit our funnel, and another got us below the waterline blowing a hole about 4 feet square in our side and bulged the armour deck. Four men were hit by splinters but were not seriously wounded. Some of the escapes were marvellous.

Glasgow fled south, with *Otranto*, to warn *Canopus*. (The Germans were jamming *Glasgow*'s wireless, so she could not broadcast a warning message.)

Hawkes:

It was a miserable night all round after we got away rushing at 24 knots against a head sea and leaking badly and shipping big seas. All we could do was to think about our Comrades we had left behind at the bottom of the sea and thank God he had brought us out of it.

Spencer unburdened himself in a letter to his wife:

My God it was awful on account of our helplessness in the face of a vastly superior force. It seems rough after chasing the enemy all round the coasts of South America for thousands of miles, we suddenly find him in company with the finest cruisers in the German Navy.

The *Glasgow*, *Canopus*, and *Otranto* bolted to the Falkland Islands. Spee did not follow for some time.

The loss of over 1,600 British sailors was a tragedy, but the destruction of two old cruisers was not going to make any difference in the cold accounting of war. The biggest blow was to morale. This was the Royal Navy's first defeat in a naval engagement in a hundred years. The Kaiser, overcome with joy, awarded three hundred Iron Crosses to the officers and sailors of Spee's squadron, which none would ever wear. His squadron put into Valparaiso for coal. He also needed ammunition, having expended 42 per cent of his 8.2-inch shells, but the nearest stocks were in Germany. When an admiring German lady in Valparaiso pressed a bunch of flowers on him, he is alleged to have said, 'They will do very nicely for my grave.'

A number of reasons have been advanced for Cradock's decision to fight Spee. Some officers believed it was his natural impetuosity; his close friend, Sir Robert Arbuthnot, said, 'he always hoped he would be killed in battle or break his neck in the hunting field'. Others believed that he did not want to be tried by court martial for failing to engage the enemy, like Rear Admiral Troubridge in the Mediterranean (see Chapter 6). Yet another theory, favoured by Churchill and other senior folk rationalizing their failure to support him, was that, although realizing that he was going to certain doom, he hoped to inflict damage on Spee that he would be unable to make good so far from any dockyard, while forcing him to expend ammunition that he could not replenish. At least Cradock achieved the second of his aims, if indeed that was one of them.

On their way past Auchilu Veshupi, *Canopus* had picked up Lieutenant Gould's wireless party, the only survivors of *Good Hope*'s ship's company. Gould had noted in his diary that when the squadron left the Falkland Islands, he had overheard Cradock telling his flag captain (the captain of *Good Hope*) that without *Defence* what they were being sent to do was suicide.[5] Gould as the ship's wireless officer would have been as well placed as most to overhear the conversation.

The news of Coronel arrived in the Admiralty on 4 November, mainly from exultant German sources. *Glasgow*'s signalled account arrived on 5 November. Within an hour of receiving the first reports, Churchill and Fisher made plans to deal with Spee. They assessed that he had four possible courses of action open to him. First, he might decide to interdict the food-supply routes from the east coast of South America to Britain. Second, he could steam north from Coronel, pass through the Panama Canal, defeat the West Indies Squadron, and allow the German armed merchant liners bottled up in New York to sail. Third, he might cross the Atlantic and interfere with General Smuts' and Botha's campaign in German South-West Africa (present-day Namibia). Fourth, he could steam to the German Cameroons, and destroy Allied shipping involved in the Anglo-French campaign there. Fisher and Churchill sent cruisers to meet the last two contingencies. The battle cruiser *Princess Royal* was sent to the West Indies to meet option two. Churchill proposed sending the battle cruiser *Invincible* to join *Defence* in Rear Admiral Archibald Stoddart's squadron on the east coast of South America. But Fisher wanted Spee annihilated, so within six hours of hearing the news of Coronel, and with Churchill's support, he ordered Jellicoe to send two battle cruisers, *Invincible* and *Inflexible*, to Devonport to prepare for overseas service. This was a bold move. The detachment of three battle cruisers from Beatty's squadron for an indefinite period was a strategic risk, since while they were away he would have only four battle cruisers against five in the High Seas Fleet. Jellicoe's margin of superiority over his opponents was whittled down to the lowest it would be in the whole war; an opportunity that the High Seas Fleet failed to exploit.

When the battle cruisers arrived at Devonport on 8 November, the dockyard officials examined *Invincible* and stated that necessary repairs would take until Friday 13 November. Fisher, in a fury, ordered that the ships sail on 11 November, if necessary taking the dockyard workers with them. Fisher also ordered that *Canopus* ground herself on the mud in Stanley harbour as a fort.

Fisher sent Vice-Admiral Sturdee south in *Invincible* as C-in-C South Atlantic and Pacific. He had just been relieved as Chief of Staff in the Admiralty, because Fisher blamed him for the Coronel debacle, and the disposition of ships that led up to it. He would now give the 'pedantic ass' a chance to make amends. He was told to join Stoddart off South America, steam to the Falklands, and using the islands as a coaling base, hunt down Spee.

Despite having been ordered to proceed south with all despatch, Sturdee's progress was surprisingly leisurely. He took twenty-six days. On at least two days, the battle cruisers towed targets for each other to practise gunnery; *Invincible* managed to foul one of her propellers with the towing wire, and had to stop for twelve hours to put divers over the side to clear it. Sturdee had to rendezvous with colliers and anchor off St Vincent Island to re-stock with coal; during the process, a boy telegraphist in *Inflexible* was killed, and having weighed anchor, both ships stopped while he was buried at sea. On 21 November, the crossing the line ceremony took place in the battle cruisers, lasting from 10 a.m. to 4 p.m. They were under way during this time, but contemporary accounts convey a lack of urgency about the whole passage south. On 26 November the battle cruisers met the *Glasgow*, nine colliers, and the rest of Stoddart's South Atlantic Squadron (*Bristol, Carnarvon, Cornwall,* and *Kent*), at the Abrolhos Rocks off the Brazilian coast. The *Glasgow* and *Bristol* were town-class light cruisers. The *Cornwall* and *Kent* were old armoured cruisers, sister ships of the *Monmouth* sunk by Spee at Coronel. The *Carnarvon*, another armoured cruiser, was about a year younger. A store ship was due on the 29th, and Sturdee announced that he would wait for her. On 27 November Captain Luce of *Glasgow*, aware that the Governor of the Falkland Islands was concerned that Spee might land there, persuaded Sturdee to sail before the stores ship arrived.

Sturdee's squadron arrived off Stanley on 7 December, at just the right moment. All except the battle cruisers started coaling, either in Port Stanley, or Port William, the large anchorage immediately north of Stanley, and the only access to the sea from Stanley. The following day, as Midshipman McEwan in *Invincible* wrote to his parents:

> we started coaling at 5.30 am. At 8.0 am a four-funnelled man-of-war was sighted on the horizon. We did not think anything of this, but ate a fair breakfast, and started coaling again. At 9.0 am two ships came close to Port William where we were coaling. The *Canopus* – the ship stationed at Port Stanley – fired on them. The ships made off at once.
>
> At 9.5 Action was sounded off, and coaling stopped immediately, and steam for main engines was ordered. At 9.15 the collier had proceeded, which was very smart work.
>
> 9.35 *Scharnhorst* [sic – *Gneisenau*] and *Nürnberg* had apparently stopped well out.
>
> 9.55 Enemy making off fast.
>
> At 10.0 am we had steam to proceed, and weighed anchor. We were third out of harbour followed by *Inflexible*.

Spee, totally unaware of Sturdee's presence in the Falklands, had sent *Gneisenau* and *Nürnberg* ahead to reconnoitre, preparatory to landing and destroying the wireless station and any stocks of coal he found there. He was one of the few people in the South Atlantic region who were unaware that the British had sent battle cruisers south. Security in Devonport had been appalling, and the two ships' destination was public knowledge, but enemy agents had difficulty getting the information back to Germany. The Germans signalled the news to their wireless stations in Chile, to be re-broadcast to Spee, but by this time he was south of the Horn, and out of range. His first intimation of what he faced was seeing their distinctive tripod masts over the promontory of Cape Pembroke. The two shells fired by *Canopus* caused the German ships to turn away, allowing Sturdee's ships to leave the anchorage. Had Spee concentrated his force, it might have been a different matter: he could have engaged the British in turn as they sortied from Port William

Engine Room Artificer Gilbert Adshead with his dog before the First World War. As a mark of their status, ERAs wore jackets and ties. [SR 27]

James Cox as a petty officer in 1916, as the coxswain of a destroyer. The chain round his neck is for his bosun's call (whistle). Petty officers, in common with all ratings, wore 'square rig'; now they wear double-breasted jackets like officers. [SR 85]

The broadside messdeck of a light cruiser, in which all the ratings in this picture lived, ate and slept. Tables are suspended from the deckhead. The scuttles are open, letting in light and air; in some ships messdecks were behind armour and without scuttles. Hammock bars are fitted just below the deckhead. Each kink in the bar marks a place to sling a hammock, which in this messdeck were slung fore and aft. [Q 18676]

Coaling the battle cruiser *Australia*. [Q 18753]

Right. The first Royal Navy aviators. [HU 67845]

Below. 1912, the first launch of an aircraft from a ship. Lieutenant Samson RN prepares to take off from a trackway laid from the fore turret to the forecastle of the battleship *Africa*. [HU 67846]

Our Naval Aviators.

1. Lieut. Samson, R.N.   2. Lieut. Gregory, R.N.
3. Lieut. Gerrard, R.M.L.I.   4. Lieut. Longmore, R.N.

Above, left. As a fifteen-year-old cadet straight from Dartmouth, Kit Wykeham-Musgrave, shown here as a midshipman, survived the sinking of three cruisers in one day. [Doc 172]

Above, right. Commodore First Class Sir Reginald Tyrwhitt, who commanded Harwich Force with distinction throughout the war. [Q 18288]

Left. Cyril Bower as a lieutenant with a DSC, taken when serving in HMS *Laforey*. [Doc 722]

Right. Admiral Sir John Jellicoe climbing a ladder up from the quarterdeck of his flagship, the *Iron Duke.* [Q 55499]

Below. The battle cruiser *Tiger.* [SP 1890]

Above. *Blücher* sinking after the Dogger Bank Battle, 1915, with members of her ship's company starting to slide down her side. [Q 22687]

Left. Sailors looking out of *Tiger's* Q Turret, pierced by an 11-inch shell at the Dogger Bank Battle. [HU 69071]

Below. Picking up German survivors, after the Falklands Battle, 1914. [Q 20896]

Admiral Sir Doveton Sturdee (*left*) with Rear Admiral Roger Keyes,
taken during the visit of King George V to the Grand Fleet in June 1917.
[Q 22960]

A Short Seaplane alongside a ship in the Rufiji River estuary,
about to be refuelled. [HU 66642]

Above. The monitor *Mersey* off the Rufiji estuary, East Africa. [HU 66650]

Left. The monitor *Severn*'s masthead camouflaged to blend in with the trees in the Rufiji River operation to sink the *Königsberg*. [SP 978]

Below. The *Königsberg* sunk in the Rufiji River: one funnel has collapsed. Taken by RNAS seaplane. [SP 989]

and caused considerable damage which might have allowed him to get clear. He now fled south-east. It is possible that since they would not have been able to see into the inner harbour at Port Stanley, the Germans thought the 12-inch shells fired by *Canopus* had come from one of the battle cruisers, and that therefore these ships were readier for battle than they in fact were. According to conversations with German officers after the battle, Captain Phillimore of the *Inflexible* gathered that the captain of the *Gneisenau* would not believe his first lieutenant's report that he could see 'two modern [battle] cruisers with tripod masts' and it was not until *Canopus* had fired twice that he was convinced. They imagined that the *Canopus* was ashore in the Magellan Straits and the *Defence* was the only big ship they were likely to meet. One of their officers after being brought on board of us asked 'Who is this ship?' and on being told, said, '*Inflexible*! You should be in the Mediterranean.'

Signalman Welch in the *Kent*, the only British ship at less than two hours' notice for steam, wrote in his journal:

> *Kent* proceeded to the mouth of the harbour at 8.20 am, & cleared for battle. Ship's company looking highly pleased. All wood work, ladders, timber etc. being thrown overboard. I went and stowed the wireless logs and signals down in the tiller flat & then with my note pad, pencil & watch got up on the upper bridge with the Captain & started taking notes. I could see the enemy steaming along parallel to the land towards the entrance to the harbour where we were stationed. We kept the flag ship informed of their movements. One was a four-funnelled cruiser [*Gneisenau*] and the other had 3 funnels [*Nürnberg*]. Things were now getting exciting & and I think all the men were jolly delighted at the chance of a scrap. The thoughts came crowding in – home, wife, child & all that a man has dear to him. The possibilities of the day occurred to me, but there was no time to think of the danger – all that seemed to trouble me was that the other ships in the harbour were taking so long to get under way.
>
> At 9.21 the *Canopus* fired 2 rounds with her 12-inch guns at extreme range, but they fell short. At 9.24 she tried two more with the same result. At 9.29 a little guard boat steamed into harbour & as she passed us made a signal that the two ships were the *Scharnhorst* [sic – *Gneisenau*] and *Nürnberg* steering south-easterly. The C-in-C made a signal to us to keep out of range. The *Scharnhorst* [*Gneisenau*] was only 16,500 yards. The two ships turned to seawards and started steaming away from us & at 9.39 were 17,500 yard from us. At 9.47 the range had increased to 20,000 yards & just then we sighted 3 more cruisers steaming up the coast & closing the others. These 3 were the *Gneisenau* [*Scharnhorst*], *Leipzig* and *Dresden*.

Frantic efforts had been made to get steam up in the British squadron. Engineer Lieutenant-Commander Shaw in *Invincible* was given the order to raise steam in all boilers. The *Invincible*, like many other coal-fired warships of the period, also burned oil, which was sprayed into the furnace to give a hotter fire, and higher steam pressure:

> I rushed away and passed the word to get the watch below and everything closed up and lit at once. As soon as the men heard news of the Germans they needed no hurrying to get below. We were just about as far from ready as could be: all the casing doors were off the boilers as the tubes were being cleaned; there was little coal in the boiler bunkers as we always fill up the upper bunkers first as they take the hardest work; so the 300 odd tons we had taken in did not help us much. The coal available was mostly small so we had to reach for knobs with which to light the fires. They came from all over the place, the upper bunkers mostly, and were carried down by hand. In the forward boiler room we had the ejector pump absolutely stripped, ready to remove the liner of the barrel; that had to go together again, and was ready before noon. In the engine room we had one air pump and two circulators adrift, they, of course had to go together before we could move at any speed. Anyhow the men smacked about [sic] splendidly and things fairly hummed. We got our oil fuel ready at once and as soon as any boiler was lit we smacked [sic] the oil fuel in at once. The result was that about 9.50 or 9.55 we started moving and by 10.10 were going 18 knots.

Torpedoman Pratt in *Invincible* had, like every other member of her ship's company, been coaling ship:

> My duty being repair party (electrical), I was able to get around the ship & now and then pop up on deck to see the enemy's ships steaming at full speed. I was kept busy all the time till quarter of an hour before we went into action repairing and seeing to electric lights. The guns crews went away half at a time and bathed so as to get as many as possible clean. I did not manage that luxury for 20 hours afterwards.

Lieutenant Danckwerts, the gunnery officer of the *Kent*:

> We were almost immediately followed by the *Glasgow*, who came out at full speed, having been told to follow and keep in touch as she is faster than us. We began to work up to full power, and were passed by *Glasgow*. The *Invincible* and *Inflexible* came out next [the former] flying the signal for general chase, followed by the *Carnarvon* and the *Cornwall*, and later by *Bristol* and *Macedonia* [armed merchant cruiser].
> The Germans were all steaming about SSE, having joined forces, and the last two of our ships were told off to destroy the enemy colliers. The five Germans were just above the horizon. We continued to chase slowly

gaining on the enemy, the old *Kent* [launched 1901] keeping well up but not giving absolutely all out just yet, for fear of bursting something. Presently the *Invincible* and *Inflexible* went on three knots more, and began to drop us. The *Glasgow* was a long way out to port.

We had a scrappy lunch, all cutting lumps off tongues and things, the wardroom by now deluged with water, in fact the whole ship was soaking as a protection against fire.*

I spent all the time on the bridge with the Captain and the Navigator, and we were all as happy as it is possible for a Naval officer to be. Everybody was photographing everybody else, and all hands, except the stokers on watch, were on the forecastle watching the chase.

Spee ordered his light cruisers to make a run for it, while he held off the British. Assistant Paymaster Duckworth, who curiously had no designated action station, took his camera up to *Invincible*'s main top:

The German light cruisers were observed to be parting company with their armoured cruisers and endeavouring to get away to the westward. The *Kent*, *Cornwall* and *Glasgow* were despatched to deal with this new development.

The *Invincible* and *Inflexible* now worked up to 27 knots. One could feel the unusual throb in the Main Top as we strained under the maximum speed ever got out of the ship. The *Inflexible* was on our starboard quarter. The signal was made to open fire by the Admiral, and *Inflexible* fired the opening salvo at *Leipzig* who was turning to join the others of her class who were escaping. However more pressing attention was required for the *Scharnhorst* and *Gneisenau*. The *Invincible* took on the former and *Inflexible* the latter. Our fire was not returned as we had the range of them for the first half hour. To me the battle looked a highly satisfactory affair – with a real Hun target at last. But suddenly the target retaliated! Then for the first time one realised that it was our turn to have a dose of shells and one appreciated the situation fully. The familiar sight of a ship firing her guns now appeared unpleasantly real. Whee-e-e-e-e-e umph! Five columns of water simultaneously shot into the air all round the ship. At the noise growing louder and louder, one involuntarily ducked one's head. It was a relief to find that the first salvo had not hit. But they had straddled. Our turrets replied instantly, which sounded most heartening. The row was deafening, enemy shots kept columns of water springing up just in the ship's wake or just short, everywhere it seemed and yet there appeared to be no hits. The *Scharnhorst* and *Gneisenau* both quickly closed us to do as

---

* In all ships, as part of the routine for action stations, fire hoses, fed by sea water, were unreeled, faked out (laid out) on deck, the water turned on and left running throughout the action.

much damage as their guns would allow them at the shorter range. This was at once countered on our part.

Danckwerts in the *Kent*:

About 1.15 pm the *Invincible* and *Inflexible* opened fire at the tremendous range of nearly 18,000 yards; every time they fired, the men cheered and clapped. Then there was a pause while the shot was on its way, and more cheering and clapping when it fell. They were getting pretty close to their object, when the Germans decided to have it in the neck! The *Scharnhorst* and *Gneisenau* turned sharp to port, and the three [enemy] light cruisers turned slightly to starboard and left them. The *Invincible* and *Inflexible* turned to port at once and opened fire with all guns, the *Scharnhorst* and *Gneisenau* doing the same.

Sturdee was trying to keep beyond the maximum range of Spee's 8.2-inch guns (13,500 yards), but within the range of his own 12-inch guns (16,400 yards). Spee on the other hand wanted to close to around 12,000 yards, a range at which he could use his 5.9-inch guns as well as his main armament, so he could throw the maximum number of shells at his adversary. The 4-inch guns of the two British battle cruisers' secondary armament were outranged by the German cruisers' 5.9s. After Spee succeeded in closing the range and landing several shells on the British battle cruisers, Sturdee used his superior speed to try to keep Spee at approximately 14,000 yards. He was also conscious that he was a very long way from any dockyard, and did all he could to avoid damage to his ships. Danckwerts:

We had the most magnificent view of the finest scrap I shall see for a long time. I have never seen any ship fire heavy guns (8.2-inch) so rapidly and continuously as the *Scharnhorst* and *Gneisenau*. They fought magnificently. The *Invincible* and *Inflexible* were loosing off as hard as they could, and we could see shots hitting the Germans. They appeared to be straddling our ships as well, but the latter were making so much smoke, that it was difficult to see the results of their shooting. They looked awfully pretty too, with their grey-blue sides shining in the sunlight. By the Grace of God it was a day in a thousand such as rarely occurs here, with no more than a gentle breeze, and bright sunlight.

Midshipman Montagu in *Invincible*'s A Turret:

In the turret everything worked well. We had great difficulty with the right gun, the breech having closed on the shot guide and jammed. The lock in the latter part of the action was causing misfires. The air-blast tube carried away, but these were patched up and we were hardly ever out of action. When one shell struck us, we got shaken up considerably, but that was all.

Shell dropping round us chucked up large quantities of water on the turret which poured down the hatch. I have no doubt that this was the most unpleasant.

Duckworth in *Invincible* decided to abandon the main top:

I had only one exposure [for the camera] that I wished to keep for the conclusion when one of the ships would be sinking. Things were getting distinctly warm now, and seeing no reason why I should expose myself needlessly to a stray shot passing through the Top, and being no mortal use to anyone as a spectator, coupled with a distinct desire for some armoured protection, I retreated down the interior of the vertical leg of the tripod mainmast. Gaining the main deck safely, expecting to be blown into the next world every minute, I groped my way in the darkness (for of course all lights had been switched off where not required), down to the After Medical Distribution Station. Here I found the Fleet Surgeon, Padre, and several Sick Berth Stewards in groups about the deck and sitting on stretchers.

I remained for about 20 minutes listening to the muffled roar of the after turrets (Q and X) firing above. One felt hits occasionally and the ship seemed to stagger and tremble. There was no loud noise of shots striking. There was now a short lull as far as we could tell. I went up into the after superstructure and saw the enemy still ahead of us, and this time trying to escape judging by appearances. The after conning tower was badly holed at its base.

I returned to the Distribution Station. The action was renewed, and we felt several hits. Suddenly without warning, the atmosphere became thick with smoke. The fan which was running hard keeping the compartment ventilated, was pouring in smoke. We quickly raised the hatch above to the mess decks, got out and were stumbling about in a thick fog of dust, steam and smoke. The hoses were running full on, and the mess was indescribable. The mess stools and tables and all the gear were lying in pools of water. With a loud report one of the upper deck bunker lids blew off, while a cold inrush of air from the blast of Q Turret momentarily knocked everyone flat. The fire was located in the sick bay but it was some time before it was got under control. About this time, the ship's canteen began blazing, but it could not be got at properly, and ultimately burned itself out.

Passing through what was left of the Wardroom, there was a heap of rubbish consisting of the long table and the meal that had been laid on it just before the fight began. I passed hurriedly through the Admiral's dining cabin, and the Midshipmen's flat. Here another gash in the deck above and sundry twisted pieces of metal marked the entrance of another shell. Down once more to the fore shell room. Once inside that cylindrical casing, one felt more or less secure. Here indeed there were signs of activity. Parties of men tending the loading trays, rolling the 'projies' into them and inscribing them with tender messages for the recipient. Here I remained for the rest of the action.

Lieutenant Hammill, watching the duel between the battle cruisers and the German armoured cruisers from the *Cornwall*, was less than complimentary about the standard of the battle cruisers' shooting:

Our ships' firing looked very wild and the conditions for their control officer must have been the reverse of easy owing to the dense clouds of funnel and cordite smoke they made. The Germans did not seem to be hit. The *Inflexible* appeared to be on fire very early on, but the fire was quickly got under control. I think all of us who watched the action turned to our own affairs decidedly crestfallen, not to say downhearted at the seeming lack of result of the BC's gunfire. The German fire had been in salvoes, fast and accurate.

The battle split into three separate actions. The *Glasgow*, and eventually the *Cornwall*, caught up the *Leipzig*, while *Kent* chased the *Nürnberg*. Hammill need not have been so gloomy. He is correct that the battle cruisers used a huge amount of ammunition – by the end of the battle, they had expended 1,174 rounds of 12-inch shell between them. But it is hard to fault Sturdee's tactics: frequent changes of course, endeavouring to keep at arms' length the constantly zigzagging wily Spee. But the consequence was that the thick clouds of funnel smoke of Sturdee's coal-fired battle cruisers obscured the spotting officers in the fighting tops, as Hammill observed.

Weight of shell began to tell, and by 3.30 p.m. *Scharnhorst* was on fire and listing heavily. She ignored Sturdee's signal to surrender, and sank with no survivors. Both battle cruisers, joined by the *Carnarvon*, turned their attention to the *Gneisenau*. Pounded at ever-decreasing range, she took at least fifty direct hits by 12-inch shells. Burning and listing, she still managed to get off the odd round from an undamaged gun. Her captain spurned a call to surrender, and blowing charges in her side, scuttled her. Nearly 200 of her 800-man crew were rescued.

As the *Kent* slowly closed the *Nürnberg*, she came under fire from the *Leipzig*, and Signalman Welch on *Kent*'s bridge recorded:

Things began to get warm & the shells from the *Leipzig* were whistling & scrunching all round us. It was very cheerful on the upper bridge for the shells were coming straight at us from ahead & dropping all round our bows, some passing between the bridge & the fore control. Captain, Navigator, Signal Boatswain & I stuck up there until 4.35 pm, then the

Captain turned to the Navigator and said, 'I think it's getting too warm up here, Harvey, we will get down in the conning tower.' So down we went under the bridge in the tower. We were all drenched by water thrown up by the exploding shells close by the ship, below water. One shell burst on the water's edge about 10 feet in front of our bow. Ye Gods! it was lovely – only a trifle further and there would have been a few gaps among us.

Danckwerts, in *Kent*'s control top:

The old *Kent* whipped along at 26.6 knots, exceeding the designed horse power by 3,000 [revolutions per minute]. Since she was built she never exceeded 22 knots. It was a pretty good performance by the engine room department. They did more to bag us that ship than anyone else. The *Glasgow* was soon in action with the *Leipzig* and for some reason abandoned the chase of the *Dresden*. We soon afterwards opened on the *Leipzig* followed by the *Cornwall*, but never got within range of her, as we were keeping to port in pursuit of the *Nürnberg*.

The *Leipzig* altered to starboard followed by the *Cornwall* and *Glasgow* and was soon out of sight. The *Dresden* had already got well away. The weather had been changing rapidly during the afternoon and it was now misty, with a stiff breeze astern. We only fired shots at the *Leipzig*, none of which reached her, although her shots were falling just short of us. None of them hit us, soon after, we began to pick up the *Nürnberg* more rapidly, and we learned from survivors that she burst two boilers and came down to 19 knots. She opened fire first (her guns all outranged the *Kent*'s) and her first shots went right over us. She quickly got the range, and kept it well, but her shots were nearly all missing for direction, though falling all round our bows, only one hit us and it smashed 4 WCs [in the officers' heads (lavatories)]. We were were firing at intervals from our foremost guns, until I thought we were getting up to her. It was exceedingly hard to see the fall of shot on account of the long range and the mist. We heard afterwards from survivors that we hit them twice during this chase. When the range had come down to about 8,000 yards, she turned to port, and we did likewise, and this started the real scrap, both of us were easing off [sic] our guns for all we were worth.

Welch in the conning tower:

The crash and din was simply terrific – first our broadside going off shaking our bodies, deafening, choking & nearly blinding us, then the shells from the enemy hitting us and bursting, throwing pieces of shell splinters and steel in all directions, & nearly poisoning us with the fumes. Shells were screeching all round us & and as they whizzed by the bridge & the deck, I could feel the rush of air. Some were going through the funnels. One hit the corner of the fore turret casing, glanced off & tore through the deck into the sick bay crumpling and tearing steel plating as if it were paper. One went through the chart house just over my head. Another burst outside the conning tower & sent a hail of pieces of shell in round us. I have since found that three pieces struck the armour & chipped it 6 inches on either side of my head, on a level with it. About two minutes later there were two fearful explosions very close to us in the fore part of the ship – one just under the conning tower in the Petty Officers' WCs. The other explosion was on the water line at the ERA's bathroom. Here a hole was blown out of the side of the ship as large as the door of a house & made everything inside into mincemeat. The explosion entirely swamped us up there in the conning tower. My clothes were saturated before, but now I had the additional luxury of standing ankle deep in water as well as being soaked to the skin. It was frightfully cold too. Possibly the need of food and a good hot drink made me feel the cold more. Luckily I had managed a couple of whiskeys & sodas during the day, which alleviated matters a little.

Danckwerts:

We closed in to 2,800 yards by which time she had 2 guns firing. Then she bound [sic – turned?] towards us as if to ram, and we crossed her bow at a slightly greater range, and turned ourselves and gave her the other side [of the broadside] for a bit. Then after turning again, I observed she had ceased firing, so I did the same, and informed the Captain. We waited a bit, but she did not surrender, so we gave her another 5 or 10 minutes of it and ceased fire again. She was burning pretty heavily all this time, but did not look like sinking, so we approached with the idea of sinking her by torpedo, as I expected her to go down with colours flying.

Welch:

She seemed badly holed below the water line & got a heavy list to starboard. Her upperworks were a picture – funnels all splintered & torn & jagged pieces sticking out. Nine of our guns were firing in salvoes at her & practically every shell found its mark & exploded throwing pieces of shell splinters in all directions. It must have been terrible slaughter aboard her. The *Nürnberg* was an awful sight – mast gone, ablaze, guns all disabled & falling from side to side with each lurch of the ship, the upperworks battered about and the ship sinking. I shall never efface the sight from my memory.

Danckwerts:

On coming close, we saw her colours still up and opened fire again, almost immediately she struck her colours, and we ceased firing for good. The entire action lasted slightly under 2 hours, and the real fight took about 50 minutes.

Welch:

The *Nürnberg* gave a sudden lurch to starboard, and sank smoothly down into the depths amid a mass of wreckage & dense clouds of smoke. The sight was one of fearful awe, and yet she turned over & sank with a graceful gliding motion as would a cup or tumbler pressed over in a bowl of water. Those who went down with her were game to the end for we saw a party of men standing on the quarter deck waving a German Ensign (tied to a pole) as she sank and so they went to their watery grave. They fought well and to a finish.

We did all in our power in the work of rescue – steamed right up to the spot where she sank – but could only get 10 of the poor beggars aboard. No doubt those who were not killed or wounded had little life left to struggle in the icy water & many must have been sucked down with the ship. We stayed there till after dark trying to find more of them, but with no success. All our boats were riddled with pieces of shell or splinters, but thanks to our Carpenter's staff in their smart work of patching up, the boats were away in 20 minutes.

After dark, the Captain dismissed me as there was nothing else to record. So I went down to the aft deck where the German survivors were being restored to vitality. I worked hard on one for more than an hour and a quarter with Dr Schafer's method, but could get no life into him. Only 7 of the 10 could we bring to after much hard work & hot stimulants.

Danckwerts:

Our losses were 1 killed, 5 died since the action, and 11 wounded. Nothing came very near me as far as I know. I was excessively cold, as I spent several hours on the fore top and the wind was icy. We were hit 36 times as far as we can see, but none of the damage is very serious. Our wireless was knocked out by a shell through the wireless room, and by the fore top gallant mast coming down, so we were unable to report the result to other ships. As we were out of sight of all the others, they did not know what had happened to us, till we got into harbour the next day. They were all very anxious, and we could hear them signalling for news of us and telling other ships to search for us.

Meanwhile the *Glasgow* and the *Cornwall* had been engaging the *Leipzig*. Lieutenant Hammill in the *Cornwall*:

We went to action at 3.0 pm and for an hour watched the *Glasgow* and *Leipzig* wasting ammunition at each other at an impossible range. The *Leipzig* however giving rather more than they got. At 4.17 the range from us dropped below 11,000 and we opened the ball with the fore turret [6-inch guns] and A Group [part of the secondary armament of 4-inch guns]. At the same time the *Kent* fired a few salvos, mostly short and then went after the *Nürnberg*. The Germans were replying to the *Kent* at first, but at about 4.23 shifted their fire to us and from that time we were the only target, the *Glasgow* not having another shot fired at her. She shortly afterwards turned and came under our stern taking up a position on our port quarter, where, although free from hostile gunfire, she must have been badly handicapped by our smoke from doing much damage.

Our first four salvoes were entirely occupied [sic] by finding the deflection which was decidedly hard to get correct, meanwhile the German shots got gradually nearer and we had our first experience of shell fire and the extraordinary whistle a close shot makes. A fair proportion of their shells burst on impact with the water, and there seems to have been a fair proportion of splinters forward. We then got a hit which brought down their fore topgallant mast and the latter in falling killed their spotting officer. Just after this hit we turned well away to starboard, partly to give her our broadside, partly to avoid the dangerous zone of her shell which we seemed to be just running into.

For the next hour and a half, the three ships manoeuvred and exchanged salvoes, with a few hits on both sides. Then at 6.15 *Cornwall* changed to firing Lyddite and began hitting more regularly, which affected *Leipzig*'s accuracy. After about half an hour *Cornwall* 'started to get the deflection' right, according to Hammill, partly because she was 'steering a steadier course than usual'. It says little for the standards of British gunnery that it took nearly three hours to establish the correct deflection. If *Cornwall* had been fitted with an efficient (Pollen) gunnery system she would have done this from the outset. Hammill:

By 6.55 she was well on fire, one in the eyes [forward] and one abaft the mainmast. These spread, and we ceased firing at 7.16, but the *Glasgow* was pumping into her for five minutes more. She was a pitiable sight, one funnel had gone and she was blazing from end to end, their guns were silent. I could not see her ensign, but understood she had one flying. We wasted some more ammunition from 7.55 to 8.11, the only result being to kill a large quantity of men they had left who could make no reply. They had only themselves to blame as any attempt at a signal to surrender would, I think, have been understood, but I think we were unreasonable as well. Finally about 8.15 or later they fired two verey's lights and we closed to rescue survivors. We stopped just off her at 9.0 and sent our port boats, but she turned over on her port side and sank at 8.23 [8.35 in some accounts].

Hawkes, a gunlayer in the *Glasgow*:

We could not get close to her because of the terrific heat, she was listing and we shouted to the Germans to jump. She went down without any explosion. Our four boats managed to save 14 of her crew (5 officers and 9 men). We then found out that we had been fighting the *Leipzig*. Those saved said there were only about 20 of them left alive when we finished firing. Near the end about 60 of them got on the forecastle and one of our 6-inch shell fell among them and almost killed the lot. They said they had finished fighting one hour before, but could not haul down their flag.

Extracts from a diary rewritten from memory by a warrant officer or equivalent stationed below the water-line in a torpedo flat almost directly below the foremast in the *Leipzig* give a German view of the same action:

When the armoured deck was struck it seemed as if the ship had received a blow from below. She seemed to leap up, and the propellers and rivet-heads quivered in the same manner. Twice the hits and concussion followed each other in rapid succession, and must have been quite near us, for the sound of the projectile striking and exploding was of a quite peculiar nature: a short, clear, singing note.

At about 6.20 I heard that we had only about 20 rounds left. I thought to myself that is the end. What were we to do without ammunition? During the last half hour we had to wear our smoke bandages in the torpedo flat, as terrific volumes of smoke came down from between decks.

Having fired three torpedoes, none of which hit the British ships,

As there was nothing more to be done, in order that our ship should not fall into the enemy's hands, the order came from the bridge, 'The ship is to be sunk, open sea-cocks, all hands abandon ship'. The torpedo flat was abandoned in a moment. I only kept back enough men to open the hatches, and then sent them away too, with the exception of the engine room PO and leading stoker. I gave orders for the sluice valves of both tubes to be opened quickly and we were immediately up to our thighs in water; then we too left the torpedo flat.

Then quickly up on deck. Under the forecastle on the starboard side there was wild disorder. Dead men lay near No 2 gun starboard and the ship's side was torn away. Everybody was busy searching for objects that would float, such as hammocks and balks of timber. I went aft to find something for myself. The poop was burning fiercely, and acrid smoke swept over the whole ship. The foremost hammock nettings were already empty. I held my nose and ran further aft. It was the work of a moment to seize a hammock and run forward again.* I went on the forecastle where every living being who could move had congregated. Many men were tying hammocks or other objects round their bodies or slinging them over their shoulders. I tied the lanyard of the hammock round me.

The top masts and rigging had been shot away; on the foremast nothing but the empty frame of the searchlight was left standing. The ensign was still flying at the main. The mainmast swayed ominously from side to side, and fell overboard with a crash. The foremost funnel had collapsed and the other funnels and superstructure were riddled with shell splinters. The upper deck was torn open in places, and on the starboard side there was a hole in the ship's side a carriage could have been driven through. Dead bodies and wounded and maimed men lay around every-where, and fragments of bodies were to be seen on all sides. I did not look too closely, it was such a dreadful sight. The dead bodies and everywhere else on the upper deck were covered with a thick film of yellow, due to the gasses generated by the enemy shells.†

When the mainmast fell, about 150 of us were assembled on the starboard side of the forecastle. Many of our number were severely wounded; one had lost his right leg up to the thigh, and the stump protruded from his torn trouser leg and was not even bound up. The left arm of another had been shattered and splinters of bone were sticking through his sleeve.

From the forecastle we could see the two enemy cruisers about 5,500 to 6,500 yards on our starboard bow. We all believed they would send boats to us, as our ship was now merely a drifting wreck on the point of sinking; however, we could see no signs of preparations to do so.

After giving three cheers for the Emperor followed by three cheers for their captain, the survivors sang the 'Flag Song'. After the second verse,

one of the British ships opened fire again. I saw the first shell burst and sparks fly up as it struck the surface of the water short of us, and heard the humming and whistling of the splinters. The second shell hit us. Round after round followed, most found their mark. The Captain gave the order 'all hands overboard'.

I went through the men's galley to the port side of the upper deck. The men were already leaping like frogs into the water. As the ship had a considerable list to port they had not far to jump.

---

*   Lifejackets were not issued in either the British or the German navies at this time.
†   This was not a gas in the sense of being a chemical weapon, but was given off by the Lyddite filling of British high-explosive shells.

The renewed shelling had killed and wounded many on the forecastle. After hesitating for a few minutes, while the shelling continued, and another man was killed beside him by a splinter,

I grasped my hammock, threw it into the water and jumped in after it. I now tried to swim clear of the ship, as I knew she would capsize to port. The hammock kept me afloat very well. I swam and swam and got a few yards from the ship, but as soon as I stopped for a moment, I was back alongside her once more. I tried again and again, but in vain. But I managed to keep clear of the mass of men who were struggling all round, for one of them might have easily clung on to me, and then we should both have been lost. The numbers became fewer and fewer, one or other disappearing every moment.

Continual explosions and crashes on the deck of *Leipzig* could be heard. I had tried to swim round her stern, but was unable to manage that either. When I first jumped in to the water I did not notice that it was cold, and only my fingers got stiff.

The reason why I could not get clear of the ship was because the wind had risen, the sea was getting rougher and was driving the ship towards me. That was luck, for otherwise I would not be alive today. The temperature of the water was 4° C (39°F). Towards the last I did not see many men in the water. The few who still survived were clinging to all kinds of objects, and they dropped off as their hands became numb.

The two remaining funnels fell overboard, more men in the water were killed by splinters, but finally the firing ceased:

The [subsequently] rescued Petty Officer Oexle, who had remained on board said the Captain had looked at his watch when the firing ceased and it was 7.45. From the water I saw our Ordnance Warrant Officer climbing up the port Jacob's ladder, which someone must have lowered over the side, and I thought I would follow suit. But this was not so easy. One of my men, Stoker Schramm, wanted to climb up too, but he did not succeed as with stiff fingers he could not untie the hammock soaked with water made fast round his waist. I tried to undo the knots with my frozen fingers, and after a great deal of trouble succeeded. The rough sea made things still more difficult. At my side a man was holding on to an iron ring and moaning 'help me. I have only one arm'. I tied my hammock to the dangling end of a W/T aerial and pushed it towards him; I could do nothing more. Meanwhile I held on to the jackstays of the 2nd cutter. When Schramm climbed up the ladder, I tried to follow. I gripped the ladder with my arms and crawled up step by step. The vessel had such a heavy list to port that only four or five steps remained above the water.

When I crawled on deck on all fours, a dreadful scene presented itself to my view. At least twenty corpses lay close around the gangway, many badly mutilated. The fire under the poop had subsided, there being nothing left to feed it; I went close up to it, I was freezing cold.

Attempts were made to launch the starboard cutter, to no avail as the list was too acute.

Meanwhile the enemy ships approached. One of them, *Glasgow*, signalled with her searchlight that boats were being sent. Our hopes rose again. At first we believed that the English would not rescue anyone. Two cutters arrived, but kept at a distance, they were probably afraid of being caught in the swirl of the sinking ship. Our men began jumping in the water to get to the cutters. By this time the deck was awash on the port side. I seized a baulk of timber lying nearby, threw it in, and jumped in after. When my head emerged above water, I could not find my plank, so swam towards a hammock to which a man was clinging. Holding with one hand, I looked round for *Leipzig* and just saw her as she lay over on her side with both propellers exposed. She lay for a moment, and plunged into the depths bow first with a bubbling hissing noise. I was about 60 yards away. Some fragments of wood shot up out of the water, and all was over. Our beautiful, proud *Leipzig* had ceased to exist.

The two boats now approached, and I saw men being pulled out of the water. We began to shout and wave our hands in the gathering darkness. I lost sight of one boat, and the other turned away. We each shouted in turn, but nobody seemed to notice us, then they came straight towards us. I was seized by the hands and dragged in. We would not have been able to hang on to the hammock much longer as our limbs were stiff. I lay down in the bows of the boat, and closed my eyes; nothing mattered now.[6]

Damage to both British cruisers was light. Shrubsole in the *Glasgow*:

We were very little damaged considering the number of shots we had fired at us. We lost one man killed and about five others seriously wounded. Some of the escapes were really miraculous. For instance a marine bugler got a fragment of shell in the centre of his cap badge which shaved the hair of his head and came out of the top of his cap without injuring him at all. A lieutenant, a paymaster, and a signalman were in the fore top, when a shell passed through their little box removing the signalman's hand without hurting the others.

We all chased the *Dresden* that night, but she got away in the darkness.

Lieutenant Hammill in *Cornwall*:

Finally it appeared we had been struck 18 times, but we had not a single casualty. The only serious damage was a bulge below the water line which had flooded two bunkers. In all 10 shells had burst. At the range at which the hits had been received, with a high angle of descent, most penetrated the deck. No fires were caused because nearly everything was kept wet. By the time the action was over we were very glad to pipe to cocoa at 9.20.

From the point of view of this class of ship [a heavy cruiser] fighting a German light cruiser, I doubt if this ship could have been better handled. Had I been controlling, I would have wished the *Glasgow* at the bottom of the sea. Under the extremely hard conditions of the latter part of the action, she served as an extra difficulty, not even taking advantage of her unfired at position to close to a short range when 4-inch would have been effective.

Miles to the north of the cruiser actions, the battle cruisers had been picking up survivors from the *Gneisenau*, and assessing damage. Assistant Paymaster Duckworth:

It was now 6.0 pm, a drizzling rain had set in with a biting cold southerly wind. The sea had a steady swell. Away ahead of us on the dull leaden sea appeared a small pale green patch of water containing a clustering mass of humanity, while the wind brought dismal cries to our ears from the only survivors of the sunken ship. Both the *Inflexible* and ourselves steamed slowly into the midst of this mass, lowering boats and ropes. Both ships stopped, heaving on the swell, funnels without a scrap of paint, and in many cases perforated through and through, no canvas round the fore-bridge, twisted guardrails in the superstructure, riddled bulkheads everywhere, and a four inch gun barrel rolling on the upper deck. This last had been blown clean off the mounting. Cutters were now loaded with survivors. All round the ships there were floating bodies, some on hammocks, some on spars. Some struggling, others drowning slowly before ones eyes before any boat could reach them. Most were so numbed they could not hold on to anything, and were helpless. Many were terribly wounded and mangled, others seemed very much alive in the circumstances. On all sides one saw all our men hauling half frozen bodies up the side and carrying them down to the Admiral's cabin. It was a truly terrible sight and one I hope never to see again.

Torpedoman Pratt in *Invincible* wrote in his diary:

We did not have a single hand killed or wounded, which I think was lucky considering the shells flew about a bit. The German prisoners told us that their ship's decks were blown away, and to jump overboard they had to climb out on the girders. They also fired a torpedo at us hoping to sink us at the last.

Still black with coal dust but happy. Revenge is sweet (*Good Hope* and *Monmouth*).

The damage described in a letter from Midshipman Montagu in *Invincible* shows the vulnerability of those of the ship outside the armoured belt to the effects of large shells, in this case the German 8.2-inch. *Invincible* was hit twenty-two times. The effect of battle-cruiser or battleship main armament would have been correspondingly greater:

A lyddite hit us on the starboard side, entered the Wardroom and exploded wrecking everything, reducing the tables, piano, chairs etc. to matchwood. It also stove a five foot hole in the deck. Splinters of shell and deck passed through all the bulkheads for yards around. I have one splinter that passed through five steel plates, so you can imagine the force of the explosion of these shells. The steel masts, decks etc. are twisted and torn like paper. Another shell passed through the poop deck and exploded in the Sick Bay, making a colossal mess and setting it on fire. A shell hit us below the water line abaft of the port turret filling the bunkers there with water. Another came through the side into the ship's canteen and exploding, making the funniest mess. Another wrecked the Wardroom Pantry and a cabin nearby. Splinters have made holes in every bulkhead on the main deck. None of the armour has suffered any damage, the electrical store caught fire, but it was put out pretty quickly.

Assistant Paymaster Duckworth:

There were now many things to be done before we could call the victory complete. Reports received by W/T [wireless transmission] told us the *Cornwall* and *Glasgow* had both satisfactorily dealt with the *Leipzig*, but not a word had been heard from the *Kent*. The Admiral fearing her loss at once set out for her last known whereabouts.

Our first telegram was now despatched to the Admiralty announcing our success. The Secretary, myself, Captain Beamish, the Flag Lieutenant and the W/T officer were all in the coding office wording the momentous message. Admiral Sturdee came in and having agreed on its phrasing, ordered it to be sent at once by W/T to Port Stanley, there to be sent 1,000 miles again by W/T to Monte Video, and from there direct by land wire to Their Lordships in Whitehall.

There was no mention of the sinking of the *Nürnberg* in this first telegram. Next day early we heard from Port Stanley that the *Kent* had arrived there with her W/T all smashed up and had reported her success visually. Whitehall was immediately informed.

With *Dresden* still unaccounted for, a sweep to Cape Horn was made by the two battle cruisers, but was soon abandoned when shortage of coal forced them to return to Stanley. After coaling, *Inflexible*, the least damaged of the battle cruisers, accompanied *Glasgow* in another search, but at this point the Admiralty ordered Sturdee to return with the two battle cruisers to home waters.

Fisher had still not forgiven Sturdee for his initial mistakes in deployment of ships, made while Chief of Staff at the Admiralty, and which had resulted in the destruction of the *Good Hope* and *Monmouth*. He was quick to criticize Sturdee for failing to catch *Dresden*, and the signal recalling the two battle cruisers reveals his impatience.

24 Dec '14 From Admiralty

Return home at once with two Battle Cruisers; replenish with ammunition at St Vincent. Leave to Admiral Stoddart the task of pursuing *Dresden*. Report fully reason for course of action you have followed since the action also number of German survivors.

An exchange of signals followed, with Sturdee explaining his actions and Fisher becoming increasingly irritable, asking him twice why he had not proceeded at once to Punta Arenas when the Admiralty told him that the *Dresden* had been spotted there. When Sturdee explained, referring to an earlier signal, number 30 in the series, the Admiralty snapped back 'your No. 30 does not answer the question'. Sturdee riposted by giving five perfectly good reasons and ended by saying:

Their Lordships selected me as Commander-in-Chief to destroy the two hostile Armoured Cruisers and I endeavoured to the best of my ability to carry out their orders. I submit that my being called upon in 3 separate telegrams to give reasons for my subsequent action was unexpected.

To which the Admiralty replied:

Last paragraph your telegram improper, and such observations should not be repeated. Their Lordships await your written report and despatches before coming to any conclusion.

On 12 December, at Port William in the Falklands, the sardonic Lieutenant Hammill, of the *Cornwall*, commented in his diary:

After lunch the captain read the congratulatory messages of which there were too many considering the marked superiority of our squadron and most of the thanks should have been devoted to the unlucky Germans who came to 'make look see', at the one moment when they should have hidden their heads anywhere else. However it was very encouraging to get congratulations from the King and at the end of the messages, the ship's company gave 3 cheers for the Captain, quite spontaneously too thank goodness, though I think they were a bit huffed at not having spliced the main brace.

The country, and the Royal Navy in particular, was overjoyed at the outcome of the action, which avenged Cradock, and quelled growing public criticism of the navy, based on a mistaken perception that it was not pulling its weight in the war. Sturdee was awarded a baronetcy, the first for a successful action at sea since 1814, but Fisher deleted many of Sturdee's recommendations for decorations and promotion from the list he submitted. When Sturdee called in at the Admiralty in February 1915, on his way north to take over command of the 4th Battle Squadron in the Grand Fleet, Fisher and Churchill saw him for about five minutes, during which time the battle was not mentioned. Sturdee received no official notification of Their Lordships' satisfaction, not even a personal letter from Fisher or Churchill.

Professor Hew Strachan assesses the Falklands battle as the most decisive naval engagement of the First World War, both tactically and strategically.[7] The annihilation of Spee expunged the shame of defeat at Coronel and raised British morale, but most important it removed the menace of the raiders from the sea. The *Königsberg*, the *Dresden*, and two armed merchant cruisers were now all that remained of the German surface raider threat, and the two merchant cruisers, the *Kronprinz Wilhelm* and *Prinz Eitel Friedrich*, were soon forced into internment by lack of coal.

The *Dresden* was run to earth at Cumberland Bay at Robinson Crusoe Island, in the Juan Fernandez group of islands six hundred miles off the coast of Chile.[8] Engineer Lieutenant-Commander Shrubsole in the *Glasgow* wrote to his sister:

> She [*Dresden*] had been violating Chilean neutrality for a very long time, nearly three months, by hiding in their territorial waters. One day the *Kent* caught sight of her, but had not enough speed to catch her. However she ran out of coal, and some time afterwards we found her off Juan Fernandez Island. She still had no coal and had been waiting there for nine days, although allowed to stay for only 24 hours. She hoisted her ensign when we approached.

Signalman Welch in the *Kent*:

> About 9 am we sighted *Glasgow* and *Orama* [armed merchant liner] coming up to the west. At 9.25 we spotted the *Dresden* at anchor in Cumberland Bay. Action Stations immediately & all ready for battle in time of one-two. She was empty of coal, & floated high up in the water. So our jamming of her wireless must have been the means of preventing her colliers locating her.

Hawkes, a gunlayer in the *Glasgow*:

We immediately opened fire at 6,000 yards range, the three of us. In two minutes she hoisted a signal. We ceased firing, she then opened fire on the *Kent*, so we opened fire again. We saw her hands jump over the side and swim for shore. We carried on firing for another couple of minutes, and she hoisted the white flag. She had caught fire aft. In the first couple of minutes firing we fired 36 rounds, *Kent* fired 30, and the *Orama* 12. It was a very short action.

Welch in the *Kent*:

A German officer came off to *Kent* in *Dresden*'s steamboat, but as the *Glasgow* was the senior officer, he was directed to her. At 10.40 am there was a fearful explosion in the fore part of the *Dresden*, and she started to sink slowly. The Germans had charged the magazine and fired it so we should not capture the ship.

Shrubsole:

We had our doctors ashore tending the wounded and the worst cases we took on board the *Orama* and sent to Valparaiso hospital. She lost about five killed and a few drowned so she got out of it pretty lightly.

We were all fishing about an hour afterwards and were hauling up huge fish hand over hand, when we saw something making a lot of fuss in the water. It turned out to be a pig from the *Dresden* which had managed to keep afloat. A couple of men dived in and brought it on board. It is as fit as anything and is a great pet. It is bathed every day, and on Sundays wears an Iron Cross round its neck.

By now, thanks to the Falklands victory, the Admiralty had recalled to home waters many of the ships hitherto engaged in clearing the seas and escorting troop convoys. German commerce warfare conducted by surface ships was a failure. The number of British-flagged ships sunk by raiders up to January 1915 represented no more than two per cent of British merchant tonnage. It would be very different when the U-boats started in earnest. Whereas German overseas trade halted on 4 August 1914, except in the Baltic, and was not resumed until after the Armistice in November 1918.

The *Königsberg*, last of the raiders, was the most elusive of all. She had established a base in the Rufiji River Delta in German East Africa (now Tanzania). Here the German survey ship *Möwe* had found eight useable channels – mostly unknown to the Royal Navy. Off the east coast of Africa, the *Königsberg*'s cruise began well; she eluded the slow, old cruisers of the British Cape Squadron. But her efforts were severely hampered by lack of coal. The British stopped her collier leaving Dar es Salaam, and purchased all the stocks of coal in Portuguese East Africa (now Mozambique). The *Königsberg* made furtive forays along the east African coast, obtaining coal at infrequent intervals from the few German colliers that had eluded the British. She sank only one merchant ship, but surprised and sank the elderly light cruiser *Pegasus* while she was repairing her machinery off Zanzibar. The threat was enough to delay the New Zealand ships from joining the great ANZAC convoy then assembling in Australian waters and bound for Egypt.

Eventually the British thought they had the *Königsberg* bottled up in the Rufiji River, as Midshipman Weld-Forester, serving in the pre-dreadnought battleship *Goliath*, explained in a letter to his mother, written in May 1915:

> I got a letter from Aunt Vi yesterday in which she is under the impression that we actually fought the *Königsberg* and actually states the number of times we were hit by shells. I don't know if you think the same, but the real truth of the matter is the *Königsberg* ran up a little creek called the Rufiji River and was discovered there. Our picket boat went up and tried to torpedo her and then sank a collier in the channel so that now she can't possibly get out.

The Rufiji Delta in which the *Königsberg* was hiding is far from a 'little creek', and covers an area of some 1,500 square miles, of islands, sandbanks, mangrove swamps, and channels. She was hampered by lack of coal and engine trouble, and at one point her boilers were transported overland to Dar es Salaam for repair. This episode and subsequent events were to form the basis of a blockbuster bestseller, *Shout at the Devil*, by Wilbur Smith, and a film. She was eventually located by the Royal Navy on 30 October 1914. She was well screened from seaward by mangroves, and mudbanks made access up the channels impossible except at high tide. Despite the assertion of young Weld-Forester that her exits had been blocked by the sunken collier, there were other channels she could use. The Germans even hatched a plan to get coal and ammunition to her overland from Portuguese East Africa, to enable her to break out. Spee was still on the loose; his whereabouts were still unknown to the Admiralty and the navy was hunting him. Bottling up the *Königsberg* tied up no less than twenty-five ships that could be ill spared from the hunt.[9]

By early 1915, the British campaign in German East Africa against the redoubtable General Paul von Lettow-Vorbeck was under way. The *Königsberg* blocked access up the Rufiji River, and the British decided to remove her. Some of her guns were landed to cover the approaches up the navigable channels, additional batteries were sited each side of the main channel, and she was withdrawn further up river under cover of trees. Attempts by the Royal Naval Air Service (RNAS) to bomb *Königsberg* failed.

Eventually two monitors were sent out from England, the *Mersey* and the *Severn*. These ships, under construction in British yards for the Brazilian navy for operations on the River Amazon, had been purchased by the Royal Navy at the outbreak of war. They each had two 6-inch guns and two 4.7-inch howitzers, and being designed for riverine warfare, had a very shallow draught. The howitzers were especially valuable as unlike naval guns they had a high trajectory and could lob shells over trees and intervening ground. The RNAS was to spot for the guns, not the first time this had been done, since it had already been practised in the Dardanelles earlier that year (see Chapter 6).

The two monitors arrived off the entrance to the Kikunja Mouth of the Rufiji Delta at 5.45 a.m., just as it was getting light, on 6 July 1915. The *Königsberg* was anchored behind Kikunja Island, about half an hour's steaming up river. Commander Wilson, captain of the *Mersey*, sent an account of the Rufiji operations to his friend Commander the Hon. P. G. E. C. Acheson, then executive officer in the *Inflexible*:

The Germans had two guns on the starboard side [on the river bank], one of which fired three blank charges, presumably as a signal of alarm; after that they fired first at the *Severn*, then at ourselves, going close, but never actually hitting. We passed through the entrance at about 6.0 am and opened fire with all guns at both banks.

The *Severn* sank a boat [armed] with a torpedo about half a mile up; we saw very little with the exception of a few men in trees, and bullets were pattering against the ship's sides most of the way up. 6.30 am *Severn* anchored [two islands away from and out of sight of *Königsberg*] and I followed a few minutes later. *Severn* commenced firing first, I followed very soon afterwards. At this time, *Königsberg* was ranging with one or two guns, but was always short, many shots falling in the woods. At 7.0 am she started to get closer, and shortly afterwards, straddled me with five guns. Up to this time we had received no signals from the aeroplane to tell us where our shots were falling. For about ten minutes shell fell very near but did not hit, then a salvo of four passed just over, with the exception of one round which pitched two feet short of the Quarter Deck.

The *Königsberg* was firing about five or six salvoes a minute, some thirty rounds a minute. The next salvo, a shell hit the Fore 6-inch gun, killing four of the men outright, severely wounding three others, and slightly wounding one man. The officer RNR Lieut did jolly well. When the shell exploded it set alight a charge which was just being loaded in the gun, this spread to another charge which had just come up from the magazine, and the flash of this went down the hoist into the magazine and slightly singed the petty officer in charge of [ammunition] supplies. Luckily there was not a charge here, or we should most certainly have been blown up.

The men were wearing swimming waistcoats, not for floating them in the water, but to protect against splinters. (When the 'K' [Königsberg] sank the 'Pegasus' last Sept, it was discovered her shell split into a million fragments, hence our reason for wearing the waistcoats.) These unfortunately caught fire, and severely burned two of the wounded men, and took a great deal of putting out. One man rushed up on to the boat deck, and a hose had to be put on him. I should not allow them to be worn again anywhere when there is a large charge of cordite used.

I slipped the stern anchor and pulled up the Bower Anchor, and went full speed ahead, just in time, for the next salvo all pitched just astern of me. We retired down river about 700 yards so see what damage was done, and found the Fore 6-inch gun was out of action.

By this time, Königsberg commenced to devote her attention to Severn and was straddling her. At about 8.0 am the aeroplane signalled a hit to Severn, and I anchored opposite side of river and commenced firing with stern gun, getting a hit very shortly afterwards. Severn was forced to move owing to her stern anchor dragging, and anchored close to me, and re-commenced firing. At this time Königsberg had only two guns firing and they were somewhat erratic. Four men were seen up a tree on an adjacent island, evidently spotting by telephone to Königsberg. These hastily descended when a 4.7-inch shrapnel burst over them and I have no doubt beat a hasty retreat or died a sudden death when three 6-inch high explosive shells fell amongst them. This undoubtedly spoilt the Königsberg's accurate shooting.

About 1.30 we shifted up closer to her and commenced firing again. The signalling [to the aeroplane] broke down completely so we could get no spotting or corrections. As it was all indirect firing over a wood, without spotting we could do no good. 'K' was firing one gun occasionally. At 3.30 pm we retired keeping up a steady fire on both banks of the river, but I think the tickling up they received on our way up was probably sufficient for them for we received no reply. At 4.0 pm we reached the entrance and received a 'welcome' from our friend on the Port side, who made very good shooting considering the big range he was firing at, actually hit our sounding beam with one shot and getting several shots very close to us.

At 8.0 pm we passed through the Fleet, and received a very warm welcome which was satisfying. Went alongside the Trent [Fleet Messenger ship], where I passed out [the] wounded – two of which I much regret have died since. After this I proceeded to sea to bury the killed, all of whom were most excellent men and can ill be spared. Severn was more lucky than myself in the way of casualties, for though straddled for some two hours, they didn't actually register a hit on her. The following morning we returned to our old friend Tirene Bay [7°49′S., 39°43′E], a near relation of Aden's, the last place on earth, though not perhaps as good.

July 11th at 8.0 pm we left this place and both of us had a tug to assist to pull us over to the Rufiji Delta. We reached the entrance at 11.20 am in exactly the same order as we went up before, having slipped the tug on getting near the bar. Our old friend on the starboard bank opened fire on *Severn*, and ultimately succeeded in getting a very good range on him, and then transferred attention to me, very successfully too, for he hit us twice, once on the after bulkhead of my cabin and exploded there, wounding three men belonging to the after 6-inch gun's crew, and knocking down Lieutenant Moncrieffe, Officer in charge of that gun. The other shell hit further aft on the Quarter Deck; this hurt no one and did no damage. Only one of the wounded was totally incapacitated, the other two continued to work at the gun after being dressed by the Doctor.

All the way up the river we fired heavily into both banks, which was nothing like as well guarded by the Germans as on our first visit. They still evidently had a few snipers, for the patter of bullets could be heard on the ship's side.

At 12.10 I turned broadside on to *Königsberg*, and opened fire on her, which she returned, but her salvoes passed a long way over then ultimately short of us. The *Severn* was at this time getting 1,000 yards closer to her, and I was to endeavour to draw *Königsberg*'s fire and thus allow *Severn* to anchor in peace; ready to open fire. As soon as she opened fire, I ceased so as not to interfere with the spotting arrangements, which undoubtedly was the cause of us not having completed the job on our first visit, two ships doing indirect firing with an aeroplane spotting is absolutely impossible.

Königsberg now commenced to fire on *Severn* and left me entirely alone. By this time *Severn* was just getting near the *Königsberg* but not actually hitting her. *Königsberg*'s salvoes were getting closer and closer splashing all round her but mostly just short; to show you how near they were, there were 47 pieces of shell picked up on her quarter deck afterwards, and no one hit.

About 12.35 or so, *Severn* got a hit followed by many more, which caused us all to cheer on board *Mersey*, and then at 12.50 I received a signal from aeroplane, 'I'm hit, send boat for us'. After which the observer made 'all hits are right forward on *Königsberg*'. This I should say was one of the most gallant episodes of the war. A small piece of shell pierced right through the water-jacket of the engine, which of course immediately commenced to fail. These two fellows went on flying over *Königsberg* getting lower and lower, and ultimately put *Severn* on to the target, vitally important. About two minutes after that, the engine seized up altogether and stopped. They then glided down towards us and made a perfect landing not very far from us, making spotting signals all the way down.

The machine was an aeroplane not a seaplane, so of course turned completely over when it hit the water, throwing the observer about twenty-five feet clear. Lt Cull, capital fellow, the pilot had not undone his belt so was left in the machine and was some little time under water, ultimately struggling clear of the many wires, but not before he had swallowed a great deal more than his share of the Rufiji River.

We picked them both up all right and they spent the remainder of the day watching the destruction of the *Königsberg* from a ship instead of from the air. About three minutes after these two fellows got on board, an enormous explosion took place in *Königsberg*. Her guns stopped firing altogether. I passed *Severn* and closed up to about 7,000 yards off *Königsberg*. Here I ran into an eight foot bank which appeared to go right across the River, and also hit something which dented the bow in. The chart we had was the most inaccurate thing one could ever want to use, nothing appeared to resemble anything on this river. We had had a pilot for the first trip up river, but we sent him ashore afterwards for he only got in the way and I could not get a word out of him once *Königsberg* opened fire on us. (this [indecipherable] got his head under an oil drum & pulled a sandbag round him, which caused No 1 to take a heavy toss as he was running aft. I believe the Pilot then got heavily biffed), so we were doing our navigation simply and solely by this inaccurate chart. When we got 8 feet in the chains [by sounding line] I thought it about time to anchor as the tide was about to ebb and I had no desire to spend a night up that river. We opened fire right away and got a hit third shot; another aeroplane was spotting for us by this time.

We continued to fire at *Königsberg* until about 2.45 by which time she was burning everywhere, one funnel fallen out of her, and eight separate explosions had taken place in her, so I should think there was precious little left of her. The poor wretches on board must have had a terrible time, but luckily for them, they had only to jump over the side and the shore was within twenty yards of her. Many probably did escape this way.

While high up the river, I came across what appeared to be a motor-boat, all ready under a bank with probably a torpedo, but the crew had bolted owing to the heavy fire put into the shore. We put a shot or two into this boat. There were some white flags hanging out on trees in places, I suppose put there by the natives, poor wretches; they had a pretty poisonous time of it. However, I expect after the first day they had all fled.

Nothing of importance took place going out of the river as *Pyramus* [old light cruiser] had followed us a bit of the way and fairly given both banks 'Tommy up the orchard'. Directly we got to the mouth, however our old and much esteemed friend fired at us again, but this time with no success. We certainly did not do him much harm, though we kept up a steady fire at him from every form of gun.

Between two ships in the two days we fired 943 rounds of 6-inch, 389 of 4.7-inch, 1860 3-pdrs, and 16,000 rounds of Maxim and machine guns; so you can imagine what our hearing was like at the end of each day.

We got into Tirene Bay at 8.30 pm that night and much enjoyed the best dinner they could put up, and all of us devoutly praying we would never see the inside of the Rufiji River again.

Some of *Königsberg*'s 10.5cm guns and other weapons, as well as a huge quantity of ordnance, including small-arms ammunition, was salvaged and made serviceable by her own artificers. Some of her crew also fought ashore. Thus she played a part in von Lettow-Vorbeck's brilliant campaign in East Africa right to the end. He was the last German officer to surrender, on 25 November 1918, fourteen days after the Armistice was signed in France.

4

Northern Waters: the Northern Patrol

From the first day of the war, the Royal Navy blockaded Germany and her allies. With passage through the English Channel denied to her, Germany's access to the world maritime trade routes lay through the North Sea and out to the North Atlantic. To begin with the 10th Cruiser Squadron was deployed in the northern North Sea with the principal aim of watching for the High Seas Fleet and other German warships. This squadron was soon tasked with stopping enemy ships escaping to the open Atlantic, and blocking the flow of raw materials and other supplies from reaching Germany.

Rear Admiral de Chair, flag officer, 10th Cruiser Squadron, wrote:

As early as July 31st, German ships at sea were recalled to neutral ports, and in the early days of August enemy vessels in the North Sea hurriedly put into Norwegian harbours, and laid up there till after the war. A most extraordinary action on the part of our Government, of allowing a free passage through the blockade to German Reservists, returning to their country after war had been declared, filled those of us who had the stopping of ships they happened to be in, with blank fury. Several neutral ships which my squadron chased and examined at sea, contained hundreds of these reservists returning to Germany to be enrolled in their army to fight against us. How the Germans must have laughed at this imbecile Foreign Office method of carrying on the war. One of the ships we released had the effrontery to allow a German band on board to play a German Victory March as she sailed away, I felt so angry that I would have liked to have fired into her.

It was not until August 8th that the full Tenth cruiser squadron was complete and on their station. An analysis of Lloyd's enemy vessels in Neutral Ports, after that date shows that no vessel got past them. The *Prinz Freiderich Wilhelm* of 17,000 tons and 17 knots, supposed to be a German armed merchant cruiser, had taken refuge in Bergen, and if it had not been a neutral port, I would have tried to cut her out.

Since 1801 Britain had treated all articles 'designed for and contributive to the advantage of the enemy' as contraband. The Declaration of

London formulated at an eight-power naval conference in 1909 had designated a 'free list' of articles not considered contraband, which included raw cotton, oil, rubber, and metallic ores. Britain did not ratify this Declaration, and it was hardly surprising that on the outbreak of war she announced that she would amend the contraband list. Space does not permit a full description of the convoluted rules regarding contraband, including changes made in the first year of the war, but in August and September 1915, virtually all goods destined for Germany were classified as contraband. The Foreign Office did not help. Their habits, which have remained unchanged into the twenty-first century, made Admiral de Chair wonder whose side they were on:

> A case in point occurred one day in August 1914, when the *Crescent* chased and captured a neutral ship laden with hides for Germany. I ordered a prize crew to be put on board, and the ship sent into an English port. Unfortunately I informed the C-in-C of my action by wireless, and the Admiralty, intercepting the signal, reported it to the Foreign Office, who immediately ordered the release of the ship. I protested, saying these hides would be turned into leather for soldiers' belts and boots. But the answer from the Foreign Office was, 'we are very sorry, but hides are not on the contraband list, and the ship must be released and allowed to proceed to Germany'. This sort of action from the Foreign Office made us the laughing stock of Europe.

The size of most merchant ships made a complete stem-to-stern search at sea impracticable, so the time-honoured procedure, of stopping a ship, sending a party on board to search for contraband, and either allowing her to go on her way if nothing was found or sending her into a British or Allied port under a prize crew, had to be modified. Instead, all ships whose cargo was considered doubtful by the boarding officer were sent in to a contraband-control base with an armed guard on board.

Neutral countries, and especially the USA, objected strongly to the delay caused to their ships by the blockade, despite the huge profits they were making thanks to increased sales of warlike material to Britain and her allies. American sensitivities had to be taken seriously by the British, since the principal cause of the War of 1812 between the USA and Britain was American merchants' anger at British blockade of their ports during the Napoleonic Wars.

Among the strategic miscalculations made by Germany which caused her to lose the First World War was the delusion that it would not last for more than three months. The German Chancellor, Theobald von Bethmann Hollweg, calculated that stocks of most materiel would be sufficient, and that any shortages would be allowed through under the terms of the Declaration of London. He gambled on Britain abiding by a Declaration which she had never ratified, although both Austria-Hungary and Germany had.

The British blockade was only made possible by the presence of the Grand Fleet, which inhibited the German High Seas Fleet from sweeping the blockaders out of the way. The 10th Cruiser Squadron originally consisted of eight old *Edgar* class cruisers built in the 1890s: *Crescent* (flag), *Grafton*, *Endymion*, *Theseus*, *Edgar*, *Royal Arthur*, *Gibraltar*, and *Hawke*. These cruisers, designed for service in the Mediterranean and Channel, were simply too frail to cope with the weather in the North Sea, the Faroes–Iceland gap, and the Denmark Strait north of Iceland.

Midshipman Adams served in the *Theseus*, which had been

a boy's training ship, and retained a high proportion of boys on mobiliza-tion. There was a nucleus of active service ratings and a balance of reservists of varying ages. We midshipmen were consigned to a very small mess aft on the lower deck, with just room for us to fit round the table. We slung our hammocks in the same flat, for which there was little effective ventilation when at sea. What with store room odours and defective bathroom drains, the atmosphere at sea was 'thick'. When one came down from watch at night, the rats scattered in all directions. I slept well enough not to notice any that ran over our hammocks, but others did.

Conditions on the mess decks could be bad in rough seas. There were two 6-inch casemates on each side of the mess decks on the main deck. Since these casemates were porous, they would fill and discharge their contents across the mess deck in alternate rolls. In a storm, not only were the messdecks under several inches of water washing from side to side, but sometimes a jammed scupper delivered a strong jet of water to hit the deck.

The normal patrol programme was 14 days at sea, followed by about 48 hours in harbour, commonly in Busta Voe (Shetland Islands). The first night in was spent coaling. These ships had no refrigerators, so our meat was mainly salt pork and canned beef.

The cruisers were eventually replaced by armed merchant cruisers, which had better sea-keeping qualities and longer endurance. The first to join the 10th Cruiser Squadron, on 28 August 1914, was the *Alsatian*, followed by the *Mantua* and *Oceanic*. Meanwhile the *Edgar*s remained on blockade until November 1914. Eventually some forty ships controlled the seaborne traffic north of the British Isles for three and a half years, the longest continuous service by any part of the Royal Navy in the First World War. Radar had not been invented, and although wireless intercepts, and other intelligence, might give warning of some ship movements, ultimately the final detection of any ship at sea was up to the Mark One eyeball.

From the outset, the greatest threat to the blockaders was the German submarines. Midshipman Alexander Scrimgeour was in the old cruiser *Crescent*. An acute observer of the scene, his diary provides a vivid record of life on blockade in what came to be called 'the Ragtime Squadron'. An early entry reveals the difficulties of finding and attacking a submerged submarine at this stage in the war, which remained true for most of it:

Sunday, 18th [October 1914]. – HMS *Crescent* was attacked by submarines. At 6.30 am the bridge lookouts reported an object in the water about five miles off. This was made out by glasses to be a submarine on the surface. The day had broken and light was getting strong, but the submarine had not sighted us. The Officer of the Watch woke the Captain and the Admiral, and we immediately notified the C.-in-C. and our adjacent ships fifteen miles distant either side, H.M ships *Edgar* and *Endymion*. It was decided to attack the submarine and we altered course towards it, ringing down for full speed, fourteen knots being almost immediately forthcoming. 'Repel torpedo attack' was sounded off (as night defence stations were considered more suitable for action with submarines even in daytime), and the guns' crews on watch closed up and loaded. About five minutes later, when about 8,000 yards away, we were discovered, and the submarine submerged. The order was given to fire, and the two fo'c'sle guns opened at 8,000 yards, the shot going over. By this time the Gunnery-Lieutenant [Guns] had arrived on the fo'c'sle with myself and his assistant, and he took over control from Lieut.-Commander Oxlade, R.N.R., who was on gun-watch at the time.

From the movement of the periscope of the submerged submarine through the water, she appeared to be moving towards us with the intention of attacking, but we were not caught napping, as the previous ships who have fallen victims to submarines have been. The guns now firing on her were the two fo'c'sle 6-inch (A 1 and B 1), also the two forward battery 6-inch (A 2 and B 2) and the two forward cable-deck six-pounders. The shot were falling about the periscope the necessary range having been attained (the rate of change was very high, approximately twenty knots), but none hit. Suddenly a white streak came at us broadside on, and passed fifty yards under our stern. It had been fired from another submarine, which had been lying submerged and had not been previously sighted by us. The port battery guns opened fire on the new enemy, whose periscope was visible, but the first salvo was badly short, showing that the torpedo must have been fired at long range. Our first submarine was now getting so close (for we were still steaming towards her at full speed) that the fo'c'sle guns could not be depressed enough to bear. Realising that we intended to ram her, she submerged completely, and only just in time. The port guns continued to fire, when suddenly the masthead lookout, who had gone aloft at daybreak, reported a third submarine on the starboard side. The starboard guns were slow in picking her up and never opened fire, as she soon submerged, and opinions differed as to whether she had ever fired a torpedo at us.

All three submarines had now disappeared, and we steered S.72°W. full speed (the engine room had now got us up to seventeen knots) to meet the *Edgar*. A wireless message was sent to Admiral [Sir Stanley] Colville, commanding officer in charge of the Shetland defences, and two of the Scapa seaplanes, which by luck were at Lerwick, came out about two hours later to search for the submarines, while we warned all our ships in the vicinity of their presence. At midday they were sighted submerged steering S.87°E., and a destroyer flotilla was sent from Scapa in chase, but they were not seen again. The time from our first seeing the submarine to when the last one disappeared was twenty minutes, perhaps the most exciting I have ever spent. The men behaved well, and any excitement shown was due to over-keenness. The fo'c'sle guns and port battery fired well, the laying and training being good, but efficient spotting was impossible, due to the semi-daylight with the rising sun in our eyes and the minute size of the periscopes, which were an extremely small object and at first could scarcely be distinguished with the naked eye. The starboard battery were so engrossed in watching the firing of the port side that they were unable to open fire when the third submarine appeared on their side.

And this, and the fact that the 'Klaxon' alarms did not work, were the only incidents that could be found fault with. Contrary to my expectations, the officers all went to their groups without any of the muddle which the obstinacy of J. Kiddle [executive officer] has so often caused in exercise actions. The Captain made a speech after quarters, congratulating the ship's company on their prompt answer of the bugle when turned in, and their general behaviour. It was the most exciting incident I have experienced. Some people think we sank the submarine on the port side, but I am convinced we did not actually hit her at all; if we had done so, it would have been entirely due to luck. In consequence of this attack, the line of blockade was changed from the north of the Shetlands (Muckle Flugga), north-westerly across to the Faroes, and then across to the Norwegian coast. Only one ship captured today, and that by the battleship *Russell*. Details of the loss of *Hawke* received; seventy-five officers and men saved.

German ships were still trying to evade the blockade:

Wednesday, 21st – Trafalgar Day anniversary. Very bad weather. *Endymion* captured grain-ship. At 4 p.m. we sighted a big petroleum ship with no colours, seventy-three miles N.N.W. of Foula, and altered course to examine her. Suddenly several shells whistled over the masts. The apparently unarmed merchant ship was armed with three new 4.1-inch guns, and was evidently a commerce marauder and also a submarine oiling-ship. We sounded off G.Q.s [General Quarters] at once, and 'Guns' decided to use the after-control, but before we were ready she had fired several rounds, but owing to the big swell her shooting was bad. One shot cut the port main shroud and passed through the maintop, and another cut the forestay. Then we opened fire at 7,000 yards, and more by good luck than good management hit her in the bows first time. This apparently set alight an oil-pipe for she burst into flames, and after we had fired another salvo, which went over and to the left, she hoisted a big white flag as a token of surrender. It was too rough to lower a boat, so we signalled to her in the international code to consider herself a prize. She managed to put out the fire in about twenty minutes, and then we convoyed her to five miles north of Muckle Flugga, where we told the *Dryad* [1894 vintage *Halcyon* class torpedo boat] to take her into Lerwick.

Thursday, 22nd. – The *Dryad* rejoined at 7 a.m. and reported the prize (now safe in Lerwick) to be a Norwegian steamer bought two months ago by Germany, to be used primarily as a long-distance submarine depot-ship, and has very likely been used by those in the west of Scotland. She has been badly holed in the bows, and it is unlikely that it will be considered worth while repairing her.

Meanwhile the weather had been worsening:

A very nasty gale got up during the night. and yesterday's bad weather is really far worse today. Made an attempt to get a sight [with sextant to fix position], but all efforts were absolutely futile. Two of the forward funnel guys carried away, and it is considered possible that the funnel may topple over, as the sea is so big, like those of the *Edgar* of this class did ten years ago in the Bay [of Biscay].

Friday, 23rd. – The sea got very big in the night, and when we altered course at 10.45 we heeled to about 45°. Everything got adrift; chairs, tables, chests, and boxes went careering all over the place. In all the offices everything was chaos. In the gunroom the table was smashed in half. Two anchors broke loose on the booms and swept about the upper deck. All the guns on the starboard side under water. Fifteen casualties on deck and twenty-one in the engine-room. Nine cases of concussion. All the gear in the gunroom smashed, including gramophone and records, and the majority of the crockery in the ship. The weather improved at daylight.

Sunday, 24th. – Boarded two steamers, but nothing of interest; one was Russian with rubber goods and stationery from Brindisi to Archangel, and the other Norwegian with fish from Newfoundland to Tromso.

Sunday, 25th – Left the squadron at midnight and entered Busta Voe at 7 a.m. Busta Voe is an inlet in the west of the mainland off the Shetlands, a deserted spot which is being used as a naval base now for our squadron. It has a post-office, a kirk, and four houses. It is twenty-two miles north-east of Lerwick, but thirty miles by road. Very pretty scenery with the sun rising over the hills. This is a very desolate corner of God's earth.

Friday, 30th. – Weighed and proceeded out of Busta Voe through Swarbacks Minn to the open sea at 1 p.m. Made for our patrol off Muckle Flugga. Saw several suspicious trawlers, but took no notice, as the *Endymion* was chasing a suspicious steamer at full speed, and we hoped to cut her off, as she was outsteaming the *Endymion*. We thought her probably to be that ship reported to have been minelaying off the Shetlands. We got up to eighteen knots, which was a feather in the cap of the engine-room. The *Endymion* came up with the ship at 1 a.m. on the morning of Friday, 30th, and shortly afterwards both we and the *Edgar* arrived. The ship proved to be the Norwegian liner *Bergensfjord*, which, by the way, we boarded some weeks ago. She had a cargo of contraband foodstuff on board for transference overland to Germany, so she was sent into Kirkwall as a prize under the convoy of the *Endymion*. A large number of German Reservists were found on board from the United States, and the German Consul-General of Seoul, the capital of Korea. The President of the Norwegian Parliament was also on board, and his detention may lead to trouble with Norway. Returned to the Muckle Flugga patrol at daybreak.

Ever the gossip, Scrimgeour noted:

Saturday, 31st. – At sea on our patrol all day. Very bad weather as usual. Big sea running, squally, and very cold. 'Guns' and Mr. Beasley added to the influenza sick list. In his absence had to do 'Guns' duties, and had a fearful row with Mr. Lowman, who tried to be too officious, also with Mr. Croughan. Wireless news reports that Lord Fisher has succeeded Prince Louis of Battenberg as First Lord of the Admiralty. Fisher is a strong man, though unpleasant and rather a cad; he won't be bossed by Winston as Prince Louis was.

On 2 November, Scrimgeour recorded in his diary:

The weather up here is so uniformly bad that in future I shall only remark in my diary when it is good, which I expect will be very seldom, as the only variation to the prevailing south-west gales with rain and big seas is a biting cold northerly wind coming straight down from the Arctic circle and Spitzbergen.

He soon broke his rule about the weather. Information was received that

minelaying cruisers will attempt to lay mines off Foula tonight, and we with the *Edgar* and *Theseus* are to attempt to destroy them Everyone on tenterhooks and very excited. Too rough to eat ordinary meals; everything a stand-up picnic.

Wednesday, 11th. – A sensational night. At twelve the Commander sounded the alarm by accident, and in two and a half minutes every gun was manned and everything ready for immediate action. Very disappointed that there was nothing doing, but the test was most satisfactory. Two hours later we heard that the minelayers had put back to Wilhelmshaven owing to the heavy gale. During the night the gale increased in intensity, accompanied by squalls of wind and hail. Big seas came in and swamped everything. At 4 a.m. a signal came from the C.-in-C. telling all ships to take shelter if possible, but by that time we were forty miles W.N.W. of Foula, and it was impossible. With the gale increasing, the temperature and glass steadily dropped.

The gale now blowing started about 2 a.m. on Monday, November 9th, increasing gradually for fifty hours in intensity until it became a regular storm at 4 a.m. on Wednesday, 11th. It raged with its maximum ferocity then for about eight hours till midday. During this period we waged a war against the elements of a most trying and arduous nature. For eight hours the wind was logged at 10–11, and the sea at 9–10 by the Beaufort standard. It was impossible to stand on deck against the raging wind, and huge seas swept over everything.

The storm came from the westward, and the seas were exceptionally steep and high, although uncommonly short for an Atlantic storm. This shortness made it most uncomfortable, as the ship had not time to rise to the seas, and consequently she took in tons of water, which swept over the decks.

The waves averaged, at the worst time, between 40 and 45 feet in height, and at times must have reached the phenomenal height of 50 feet; thus, considering the short length of the seas, it can be realised how steep the seas must have been. Squalls and gusts every ten minutes or so, accompanied by rain and hailstorms, increased the discomfort. The barometer dropped to about 28.1 inches, reaching its lowest at 7.30 a.m., and fluctuating rapidly, and the cold was very noticeable.

Everything below was swimming in water, about 4 inches on the maindeck, and regular streams through the hatchway cracks and gunport lids. All the flats and ammunition passages were also soaked. The Admiral's quarters were drenched through and through, and he had to move into the Captain's cabin. The wardroom was swamped. Everywhere a filthy smell prevailed. In the gunroom we got but little water, but being outboard the motion had its maximum effect. The ship rolled, tossed, and pitched tremendously, and everything was chucked about willy-nilly. Everything breakable like crockery was smashed, and chests, boxes, hammocks, etc., floated about from side to side, banging against everyone.

When the signal came from the C.-in-C. at 4 a.m. for all ships to run for shelter, we were head-on to the gale, and after consulting the Admiral and Navigator, the Captain decided that it would be impossible to turn and run before the gale for shelter, for fear of capsizing while broadside on, for even head-on we were rolling on an average 30°, sometimes going over as much as 40° either side. At 4.30 a.m. the starboard sea-boat (first cutter) was stove in, and half an hour later the port sea-boat (second cutter) was carried in and dumped on the booms, both davits carrying away. All the ready ammunition careered about the deck in most dangerous fashion. All the officers and ship's company were now roused, and the Commander wanted to pass an extra lifeline to prevent the starboard sea-boat being lost altogether, as one of the gripes had carried away. The chief bos'n's mate, the midshipman of the gun-watch, and myself, the midshipman of the watch (I had the morning watch), volunteered to get into the boat and pass the line. We managed to get into the boat after ten minutes' struggling with bowlines round us, but the Commander could not get the sea-boat's crew on to the booms, so we were unable to get the line after all, and had to come back.

Five minutes later the whole boat – davits and all – was washed away by an extra big sea. Lucky we had left it before! Then two of the foremost cowls carried away, and all the others went later, except two, making an absolute shambles of the upper deck; a mass of ropes, wooden spars, bits of iron, cowls and projectiles rolling about in all directions, making it impossible to get about.

Just before I went on watch at 6 a.m. the port sea-boat was smashed to atoms, and the fo'c'sle breakwater swept overboard. All such things as railings, etc. were swept away, and the quarter-deck and fo'c'sle were continually under the waves, and the batteries were knee-deep in water. I was thankful to get off watch, but rest or food were impossible, as all the galley-fires were put out, and we munched chocolate and ship's biscuit and then crowded into the decoding office and the after shelter deck except when required for duties, such as clearing away wreckage, by the Commander.

The wireless aerials came untied and streamed aft in the wind, thus cutting us off from communication. The dynamos were shut off and the ship lighted by candles below. Owing to an accidental short circuit, you got a nasty shock whenever touching the metal round the wireless office.

About nine a big sea took away the whaler, and it floated off most neatly into the sea, quite undamaged. The depression rails on the fo'c'sle were bent double, and then the biggest sea of all came. It smashed the fore bridge into smithereens, breaking all the glass and woodwork of the Wheelhouse and chartroom like paper. All the flags and signal books went by the board, but the signalman on watch escaped by a miracle. The Quartermaster and helmsman were badly cut about the face and neck, and the officer of the watch and the midshipman and yeoman of the watch and messenger were isolated on 'Monkey' Island. and it was three hours before they were able to get down by climbing down the foremost mast ropes. All the gear in the chart house was smashed or lost, although luckily the deck log was saved.

At the same time as this occurred the whole intelligence office was swept away from the fore shelter deck, with codebooks, signals, and everything. Captain Gillespie, R.M.L.I., who joined last Monday, was inside it at the time, and everyone thought he was lost, but by an extra ordinary piece of luck he clasped the starboard shrouds and did not go over the side.

The Navigator and Chief Quartermaster now conned and steered the ship from the conning-tower, as the officer of the watch was marooned on Monkey's Island, and the Quartermaster and helmsman of the watch were injured. All watches were kept in the conning tower for the next twelve hours.

Everyone thought the foretop would carry away, and the after funnel was very shaky, as two funnel guys snapped, but luckily both funnels and masts held, and except for the loss of the starboard fore range dial, nothing further was lost or destroyed of much importance.

During the worst of the storm we steamed eight knots (forty-two revolutions) in order to give steerage way, and could not go faster for fear of breaking the ship's back; even then we were making a leeway of about one knot.

De Chair rated it

the most appalling gale I ever experienced in all my years at sea, and we really did not think the old ship would weather it. The noise of the wind was like one continual peal of thunder, one could not hear what anyone said, however loud they shouted. The upper deck and ship sides began to give, and the seams of the decks to open letting water down into the boiler rooms. The fires in the foremost boiler rooms were put out as the water rose above the furnaces, but fortunately the after boiler rooms held, and we were able to steam sufficiently fast to keep the ship head to wind.

My sea cabin was swept overboard, carrying my gear and books with it far to leeward in the murky darkness, but happily no one was in it at the time. Water washed from side to side across the deck, and men had to swim and crawl along the lee scuppers.

A big gun broke loose and careered about in the after turret. It was only stopped by filling the turret with hammocks.

Scrimgeour:

About midday the glass began to rise, the squalls ceased, and the wind shifted to the north-west, we altering course accordingly. A watch of seamen was sent down to the stokehold to relieve the wretched stokers a little, as the wretched men were having a slave's time of it.

The storm began now to gradually blow itself out, the wind shifting towards the northward, and becoming colder than ever, although not nearly so strong. At midnight things were far better, and at 2 a.m. on Thursday, the 12th, the wind dropped completely, the gale having lasted altogether three days. The sea was nearly as big as ever, but the Captain decided to turn and run for port. There was one terrific roll when we turned, but once on our proper course we rattled off at fourteen knots for harbour and rest. A temporary wireless aerial was rigged up, and we learnt that the other ships in our squadron unable to shelter were the *Theseus* and *Edgar*, and both had been almost as badly treated as we had been, both losing several hands overboard, in which we were very lucky, as no one was lost, although several people were injured.

The only other warships out were the battleship *Marlborough* and light cruisers *Nottingham* and *Falmouth*, but these managed to find shelter, before the worst came, behind Westray. The centre of the storm passed to the northward of us, and eventually must have vented itself on the Norwegian coast, while the southern limit of the storm must have been about Cape Wrath. At daylight on the 12th we sighted land and entered St. Magnus Bay and steered for Swarbacks Minn, arriving at the entrance about 8.30 a.m.

Heard that even in harbour here they had a bad time, the *Alcinous*'s steamboat being sunk by the choppy sea. As we came to our anchor a heavy snowstorm broke out, and by nightfall all the surrounding country was white, being 2 or 3 inches deep in snow. Ronas Hill has been covered with snow for three days. Weighed and left for Scapa at 4 p.m. Big swell still running outside, and we had a most unpleasant time of it, as the ship rolled worse than ever, with the sea abeam from the N.N.W.

Friday, 13th. – Reached Scapa at 7 a.m. and anchored off Weddel Sound to the southward of Cava Island. The whole of the First Fleet [Grand Fleet] were at anchor off Flotta, and the Calf of Flotta, sheltering from the north-westerly wind. All the hills covered with snow. The Admiral visited the

C.-in-C. in the *Iron Duke*. A general signal from C.-in-C. congratulating the Tenth cruiser squadron on their successful patrol duties, which have been conducted in all weathers, and which he says are the most arduous being undertaken by any of our squadrons, but are none the less necessary, and their labours are fully appreciated by him although there may be no immediate recompense All the First Fleet is pleased with our work. Everyone very pleased as we thought the authorities might be apt to forget the poor old rag-time squadron away on its lonely northern patrol. We have been ordered to Greenock to overhaul after the storm. Snowing all day, very cold; all the hills several inches thick with snow.

Saturday, 14th. – Weighed and left Scapa Flow, going out through Hoxa Sound at 7.30 a.m. Steered a course for Cape Wrath encountered the usual bad weather, once outside the shelter of Hoy, big seas and frequent snowstorms. The Sutherlandshire mountains looked gorgeous, the snow glistening in the occasional glimpses of sunshine. Went only eight knots so as not to reach the Minch before dark, as hostile submarines have been sighted again in the Minch, and we are to go through by dark. Rounded Cape Wrath 4 p.m. and increased to fourteen knots after dark. Sighted three suspicious Swedish oilers off Stornoway; notified them to C.-in-C., but did not stop. Ran through the Minch narrows between seven and eight and shaped a course through the inner Hebrides for the Mull of Cantyre [Kintyre] Point.

Sunday, 15th. – Passed Oversay Light 2 a.m., and then went over to the Irish coast to communicate by flags with a signal station there, as the Belfast wireless station has broken down, and we have a message for the S.N.O. [Senior Naval Officer] Belfast. Then came across to the Mull of Cantyre [Kintyre], passed Sanda (where we saw Southend in the distance), then on past Ailsa Craig and up the Firth of Clyde to the east of Arran. Bute, and the districts round Rothesay, Dunoon, and Wemyss, looked very fine covered with snow. Ben Lomond, a great white mass lowering away to the north, lost in the dark mists. Fearfully cold with a stiff south-east breeze and a choppy sea in the Firth. Came past Gourock and anchored off Greenock for the night at 4 p.m. Found the *Royal Arthur* and *Grafton* also at anchor, as they have been sent to refit also, leaving four ships up in patrol with Captain Thorpe of the *Edgar* as S.N.O. I hope we shall get some leave while the ship is in dock for her refit, and the Sec [Captain's Secretary] seems fairly hopeful.

Monday, 16th. – The pilot and tugs came alongside at 7.30 a.m., and we proceeded up the Clyde. A lovely morning. Realised for the first time what a gigantic shipbuilding centre the long banks of the Clyde make. Just to mention a few of the biggest: London and Glasgow Ship Company at Govan, Beardmore's at Dalmuir, Fairfield Company, John Brown of Clydebank, Yarrow, and the numerous yards at Glasgow, Scotstoun, Port Glasgow, and Gourock. Passed several cruisers and destroyers building. Arrived off John Brown's yard at 8.45 and came alongside the basin jetty, preparatory to dry-docking later on.

The *Edgar*s were not destined to return to the 10th Cruiser Squadron. De Chair:

> The first three ships of the Tenth cruiser squadron were examined by Admiralty experts as to their future usefulness. The result showed the ships were in a very bad state, and that certainly they would in no wise be able to contend against the very heavy weather our ships in Northern waters were called on to face.
>
> So important did the Admiralty feel the Northern Patrol to be, that when they learned the condition of the old ships of the Tenth cruiser squadron, they determined to replace them by a large squadron of more suitable ships.

The *Edgar*s either became depot ships, like the *Crescent* and the *Gibraltar* (the latter for her old squadron), or went out to the Dardanelles, like the *Grafton*. By now more armed merchant cruisers were joining the 10th Cruiser Squadron.
De Chair:

> These vessels had all been taken up 17 November [1914], and soon the dockyards of the Clyde, Liverpool, Avonmouth, London, Hull and the Tyne, were busy fitting them out.
>
> During all this time I was not allowed to write or telegraph my wife as to our welfare. Enid, however, seems to have been fully aware of our circumstances.

De Chair also encountered the less than patriotic attitude of the trade unions, which the distinguished author Correlli Barnett has exposed in several books.[1] Rear Admiral de Chair:

> Some labour leaders took the opportunity to get the pay of workers in munition factories raised by using the power of their organisation to obstruct the supply and manufacture of munitions of war. The Army was dangerously short of shell, and we in the Navy also suffered at Liverpool, when I first came in contact with this go-slow practice, I threatened to imprison the leaders, which had a good effect. Factory workers were receiving high wages, while our soldiers and sailors doing the fighting were receiving much less pay.

On another occasion when confronted with a walk-out in Liverpool led by a union official, de Chair informed him that if the men working on board the ships of the Tenth cruiser squadron were not at work within one hour, he would be put in prison. This had the desired effect, and the work went on quickly. On December 29th, the following ships were on patrol:

A Patrol (North of the Faroes)	C Patrol (South of Sydero)	D Patrol (West of the Hebrides)
Teutonic	Otway	Hildebrand
Cedric	Orepesa	Calyx
Columbella	Hilary	Ambrose
Mantua	Bayano	Clan MacNaughton
Virginian	Digby	Patuca
Viknor		

Ships coaling at Liverpool were *Caribbean*, and *Changuinola*, with HMS *Alsatian* (my Flagship), to the eastward controlling all patrols by wireless.

The *Changuinola*, commanded by Commander Brocklebank, was almost new, having been built for the Hamburg Amerika Line by Swan Hunter, but bought by Elders & Fyffes for the banana trade. There were now twenty-four ships in the 10th Cruiser Squadron; all were armed merchant cruisers from various lines, including four others from Elders & Fyffes' banana fleet. The inclusion of these ships was the cause of the Squadron's nickname changing from 'the Ragtime Squadron' to 'the Banana Fleet', or 'Bananas' for short.

The *Changuinola*'s ship's company consisted of:

Rank/Rating	From	Numbers	Totals
Officers	Royal Navy	4	
	Royal Naval Reserve	14	
	Royal Naval Volunteer Reserve	1	19
POs & Men	Royal Navy	22	
	Royal Fleet Reserve	42	
	Royal Naval Reserve	35	
	Royal Naval Volunteer Reserve	15	114
Marines	Royal Marines	6	
	Royal Fleet Reserve Marines	16	
	Pensioners	3	25
Civilians		63	63
	Total	221	221

The marines were used for boarding parties as well as manning some of the guns. The civilians were cooks and stewards. The firemen (the merchant navy term for stokers and engine-room ratings) were Naval Reservists, and were sometimes a source of trouble, as they earned less money than their civilian counterparts.

Although the merchant cruisers were better sea boats than the *Edgars*, not all were suitable. The *Clan MacNaughton* foundered in a gale. It is possible that the cause was incorrect ballasting, which the Admiralty, not used to merchant ships, did not understand. Certainly, Brocklebank wrote home soon after taking command of the *Changuinola* that:

> Some days ago I wired Liverpool saying that I would want three hundred tons of ballast on arrival and last night comes a telegram from the Admiralty wanting a full report on the subject as they do not consider the stability of the ship necessitates any ballast; so I suppose it will be some months before I get my ballast. It is not the stability that is wrong but the trim. She is down by the stern and should be on an even keel and when very light of coal handling her in heavy weather may be awkward.

He reassured his family by adding: 'You need not be anxious about the ship's stability, she's not going to turn over'. Adding later, 'The ship is somewhat unmanageable as I told you, she is so light forward that her bows act like a headsail'.

Commander Francis Grenfell, the executive officer of the *Cedric* (Commodore R. E. R. Benson RN), a large White Star liner, had no doubt who was to blame, writing in his diary on 13 March 1915:

> The *Clan MacNaughton*'s officers were firmly convinced that nothing could save the ship from capsizing if she met really bad weather, and their fears were unfortunately all too well founded. The Constructor's Department at the Admiralty ought to render up some victims [sic] for hanging after the war; it is they who have passed the ships and allowed them to go to sea with empty holds and guns on deck and nobody with the least idea how these conditions would affect their stability.

Brocklebank commented in his diary about a new forward 6-inch gun fitted in December 1916: 'The new gun and great weight of structure make the ship dive heavily and take in big seas'. But weather conditions and Admiralty obtuseness did not prevent the armed merchant cruisers from carrying out their task. In doing so they steamed great distances. For example, in 1915 the *Changuinola* alone boarded a total of 159 ships, sending in 50 for checking. She steamed 69,991.5 miles, and spent a mere ninety-four nights in harbour.

German submarines also exacted a toll, as Commander Grenfell lamented in his diary on 12 March:

News this evening from C in C, regrets to inform us that the *Bayano*, a 'banana' was torpedoed by a submarine off Ailsa Craig as she was leaving the Clyde on the 11th. Casualties not yet known. This is the third of the 'Bananas' down. The *Ambrose* returning to Liverpool on Tuesday last was attacked three times by submarines off Rathlin Island but escaped.

On the whole the 'banana fleet' is having the full share of casualties – reduction by attrition must necessarily be more rapid than the rest of the fleet as we are always at sea and are constantly exposed there and entering ports, to the chances of weather, to subs and mines. That is all part of the fun, but still it is our job, though no doubt highly important, is not exactly militarily satisfying – even the chance of a little personal contact with the enemy in the shape of a submarine is a greatful [sic] change, and did us all good today. But who will sing of the 'bananas' when the epic of the war comes to be written? What chance have we of an honourable mention in history? Precious little!

Grenfell had actually had some excitement the night before, in the Fair Island Channel. The standards of small-boat seamanship, taken for granted at the time, were remarkable. Boats were propelled by oars, had no built-in buoyancy, and there were no short-wave walkie-talkie radios:

Just as I had turned in the Captain came into my cabin to say that there was a panic on – that we were ordered by the C-in-C to go to the aid of a Danish steamer, the *Canadia*, with prize crew on board stranded south end of Fair Island [between the Shetlands and the Orkneys]. Out I hopped. I turned the hands out to cocoa, and at 3.15 we turned all boats out in readiness for saving life on the wreck and our own skins if we were submarined, as the C-in-C had signalled to say that a sub was operating around Fair Island. I also stationed the hands at the guns. We finished this preparation at about 5.0 am, when the first glimmer of dawn appeared in the misty sky. We were then off the southern light house of Fair Island, about two miles off in a fairly lumpy sea and stiff breeze. We could see the faint lights of the stranded ship a little to the left of the lighthouse. At 5.15 we lowered two of the life boats. I took charge of one, Nelson of the other, and we pulled in to the shore. When within half a mile of the shore, the backwash off the cliffs and shoaling water knocked up a really big breaking sea, and it was difficult to see in the half light which were breaking waves in the open and which on the outlying reefs.

However, I got my boat into the cove or rocky recess in the cliffs in which the ship had stranded and to within half a dozen boats lengths of her, where I backed water and hailed through the megaphone. Her lights were burning but we saw no one on board, and no one answered my repeated hails. It was impossible to go alongside her as the seas were running along her sides, (she was lying bows to seaward, having been swung stern first on to the rocks by the waves) and breaking in great spouts of foam and spray over her fo'c'sle and bridge. She was grinding and working on the rocks, and obviously could not hold together much longer. Waves rolled into the cove and were piled up into big broken and confused masses that tossed the boat about in all directions; and shot lumps of water into our faces and down my back. There was strong current setting us down upon the ship and the outlying portions of the reef on which she was stranded, and over which the sea was breaking with considerable violence some 50 yards under our stern. It was no place to linger, though there was a weird beauty and grandeur about the scene. As we slowly hauled out, a signal light winked at us out of the blackness, 100 feet up in the cliffs in the farthest recess of the cove; it said 'go back'. It was clear that the crew had managed to get on shore, and this we found to be the case when we arrived on board. The Naval Officer in charge on the island had signalled that the crew had landed on an isolated rock, and that they were getting them to the shore by ropes through the surf.

Nelson in his boat got within a few hundred yards of the cove, but was carried by the current past its entrance. Seeing that further efforts were useless, we returned to the ship which had come within a mile of the coast. We reached her just in time, as the mist was driving down from seaward and soon obliterated the island. The Captain was not sorry to haul off such a dangerous coast of which he had no adequate chart.

Recovering prize crews demanded much thought, and once collected, they had to be distributed round their ships. Brocklebank wrote:

I have prize crews scattered all over the country; one is journeying from Lerwick in Shetlands to Aberdeen and thence here by train and motor lorry; two have been sent to Liverpool to wait our arrival, have been sent on leave from there and are lost. One of their officers arrived last night but knows nothing of his men, they hadn't returned when he left Liverpool.

His diary noted that he 'sent a marine to cells for five days for chasing a young woman at Kirkwall Hotel and not desisting when told by the corporal of his prize crew and for threatening the corporal'.

The boarding parties consisted of four to eight sailors or marines, armed with rifles, and commanded by a junior officer or petty officer carrying a sword as a sign of authority. The boarding officers, often midshipmen in their late teens, had to display diplomacy and firmness when dealing with masters who were perhaps old enough to be their fathers, and often not speaking English. Tactless behaviour on the part of the boarding officer might set off a ripple of consequences. The Foreign Office in particular were fearful of anything that might lead to an international incident, especially with the Americans, as the war progressed and they slowly edged towards joining the Allied side. Some of the experiences are typified by the report to de Chair by a young RNR sub-lieutenant from the *Virginian*:

> On boarding the blockade runner [an American ship], I found the Captain was pro-German, and as soon as the *Virginian* was out of sight, he informed me that he was not going to stand for any interference from me in regard to the navigation of the ship.
>
> At supper that night, the Captain said, 'Tell you what, there's too much Goddamn red tape about you Britishers. You think you can do as you like, but mark my words, you're in for a trimming, and I hope to God you get it good and plenty. I wonder what the hell they think I am? Do they think I'm going to stand for them sending a kid like you aboard my ship to tell me what to do? As far as I'm concerned, you don't exist. You hear that Master Mate, neither you nor any of my officers take orders from this kid. You understand'.
>
> This to the Master Mate who was at the table. The Mate looked mighty uncomfortable. My blood began to boil. Angry words came to the tip of my tongue. I stood up and spoke as calmly as I could, 'I'm sorry Captain that you should see fit to act as you have done. I must decline your hospitality. Please excuse me'.
>
> I left the table, went to my cabin, buckled on my revolver, and went to the bridge, checked the course for the Fair Island Channel. The ship was proceeding at slow speed. The Captain having finished his meal, climbed on the bridge. I took the initiative; 'Apart from your personal insults, do you intend to obey my instructions, or not?'
>
> 'You can go to hell, as far as I'm concerned', he replied ringing on full speed ahead on the telegraph.
>
> I told him to go back to his cabin and consider himself under arrest. I never saw a man so taken aback. He opened his mouth to speak, but no sound came. I expected open resistance, but when I took him by the arm, he came with me like a lamb. I locked him in his cabin, placed a sentry at the door, went up on the bridge and took charge. Next morning we were in Kirkwall.
>
> When I told the Senior [Naval] Officer at Kirkwall the trouble I had had with that captain, he had him brought to him and sent him to Edinburgh Castle to be interned. Three Germans were found among the crew masquerading as Dutchmen.

The boats used for boarding were usually oared; although the *Alsatian* had some outboards, these were useless in a seaway. To begin with, boats were lowered by davits with falls forward and aft, but a better method was evolved to cope with the huge seas encountered, using four ropes suspended from a hook on a line from a derrick which could swing further outboard than davits. On a signal, the boat could be lowered onto the peak of the wave, not into the trough, and at the critical point in the ship's roll. A ship hove to while lowering a boat, for boarding or transferring prize crews, was an easy target for submarines. Accidents still happened, as Brocklebank recounted in his diary:

> As we were closing a ship to board her, the boat was over the side with crew all ready for lowering and I was going astern [to take way off the ship] when the forecastle lookout reported an object in the water. My mind at once turned to submarines and periscopes. Wanting to know exactly what the object was so I could get the guns trained on, I hailed the forecastle 'were away' [an old-fashioned pronunciation of 'where'], an old sea term now falling into disuse. Shuter [first lieutenant], on the forecastle, understood me to say 'lower away', and without looking over the side, lowered the boat straight into the water. There was too much way on the ship, the boat could not get clear, was towed under and turned over. Clarke Inglis and the crew of six were struggling in the water, but we got them back safely, none the worse. The only damage being the loss of some pistols, minor stores, and Inglis's new sword, a presentation one from his father. Young Manby should have been in the boat, but was adrift [late] and thereby his life was saved as he can't swim.

Today's readers, wondering why life jackets were not standard rig for boats' crews, should know that well into the 1950s it was by no means unknown for the Royal Navy to dispense with them.

Midshipman Scrimgeour, with many of *Crescent*'s ship's company, was drafted to the *Alsatian*, the flagship of the 10th Cruiser Squadron, and found himself the senior snotty.

> Monday, 22nd. [February] – Gale went on like blue hell, but continuous snow supplanted the rain squalls we have had previously. Wind shifted to the northward. Very big sea running. Cold intense; the coldest weather I have yet experienced since I joined the ship; average height of thermometer 16° F., 16° below freezing-point, although at times it has dropped considerably lower. The spray flying over the bows froze before it reached the bridge, and cut your face with the force of the impact. All the decks not actually awash were as slippery as ice. Intercepted and examined the s.s. *F. Heredik* of Haugesund for the second time in a fortnight. She is bound from Goole to Reykjavik, and appears to be taking her time over it.

The Americans made a habit of protesting, as Scrimgeour noted in his diary:

MARCH, 1915.

Monday, 1st. – Weather as per routine, glass well below freezing again. An American ship refused to be boarded by the *Ambrose*, who thereupon applied to the *Patuca*, the senior officer of her patrol, for instructions. Shots were fired across the Yankee ship's bow (the *Navahoe* her name was), and she then hove to. A boarding party from the *Patuca*, who had come up, was sent under our old *Crescent* friend, Lieut.-Commander Bacon, R.N.R., and she was taken into Kirkwall as a prize for examination, in spite of the vehement protests of her captain and crew.

Changes in the contraband regulations resulting from an Order in Council of 11 March 1915 greatly increased the work of the 10th Cruiser Squadron, as de Chair recorded:

no vessel would be allowed to proceed to a German port; and all vessels which sailed from German Ports must hand over to the Allies all goods embarked in these ports; goods with an enemy destination, or which were enemy property, must be discharged in a British or Allied port; vessels which proceeded to an enemy port after being allowed to pass ostensibly for neutral destinations, would be liable to condemnation if captured on a subsequent voyage. This order aimed at the complete isolation of Germany through the operation of a Naval blockade.

It increased the amount of work until neutral traders with Germany found the game unprofitable. Many lives would have been spared and much danger to ships avoided, had this plan been in force at the beginning of the war. Although we were constantly urging the Foreign Office to do so, they were so undecided, and afraid of hurting the neutrals' supposed feelings, that it was left till nine months after the war was declared.

In the case of allied merchantmen which could be readily identified, an exchange of signals was sufficient. Neutral vessels were all chased and boarded, their papers examined, and a summary of them reported to the officer in charge of the patrol. As a rule, the vessels were sent in to Kirkwall with an armed guard for thorough examination by the Customs House Officials.

The War Trade Intelligence Department, established in January 1915, sifted and collated every scrap of intelligence about enemy trading activities, and was able to supply up-to-date information about every firm mentioned in a ship's papers. A valuable source of information was provided by intercepted correspondence, which often, though of an apparently disarming and domestic nature, proved, when decoded to contain important intelligence of contraband shipments. Contraband was carried in hollow masts, double decks and bulkheads, and even rubber onions. This last only discovered by an onion bouncing on the deck.

A permanent base for the 10th Cruiser Squadron at Swarbacks Minn was confirmed in 1915, by Rear Admiral de Chair:

In accordance with directions from the Admiralty, I proceeded in the *Alsatian* on April 15th to West Loch Roag, in the Island of Lewes (Hebrides), with a view to finding a coaling base for the Squadron. After examining the harbour, I came to the conclusion that Busta Voe and Olna Firth in Swarbacks Minn, on the west side of the Shetlands, were better suited all round as a coaling base and nearer our patrol ground. The supply of fresh water at the latter place was also more abundant and easier to obtain. For another reason, the Hebrides was likely to prove a more dangerous site. Early in April, U32 on the way to her cruising ground in the western approaches of the English Channel, became entangled in nets off Dover; she managed to free herself, but decided to return to Germany northabout. After this all U-boats were ordered to avoid the Dover Straits and use the Northern route. This increased submarine traffic soon became apparent, and we had many incidents of submarines attacking our ships and prizes. On one occasion an SOS from a ship brought one of my Squadron to the rescue, and steaming at full speed, she opened fire at long range on the attacking submarine, drove her off the neutral vessel, and escorted her out of range of the submarine.

At Swarbacks Minn there was room for seven of my Cruisers to lie at single anchor with splendid protection from the fierce gales which, in winter, were so continuous.

Sub-Lieutenant McKeag RNR, an ex-merchant navy officer, was appointed to the armed merchant cruiser HMS *India* in April 1915, 'a splendid two-funnelled ship of some 8,000 tons, and, although only a single-screw ship, she was capable of 18 knots, and even did 19½ on one occasion'. After evading some newly sown mines and a submarine, which dived when the *India* opened fire, she took up her station as part of the 10th Cruiser Squadron. The *India*'s patrol station

on the Norwegian coast off the mouth of Vestfjord [the fjord well north of the Arctic Circle leading into Narvik] was a very busy one, and we had the use of two armed trawlers to assist us by acting as scouts. Two German merchant ships were known to be in Narvik waiting their chance to make a dash and we were eagerly waiting for them. They made their dash and although one got through by running into territorial waters on the approach of our trawler the *Tenby Castle*. But it was at the expense of her [the German's] steering gear, which was smashed by a well directed shot from the trawler, before the German could cross into safety. The other German, the *Freiderich Arp*, was sunk by the *Tenby Castle*, and the prisoners, to the number of thirteen, who had been allowed to clear off the ship before the trawler opened fire were handed over to us for safe keeping.

There was also a Norwegian pilot aboard the German ship, and as we could not put him ashore, he was obliged to accompany us to Britain. We treated him in the best possible manner, and there is no doubt we reaped the benefit of it later, for when he returned to Norway after being landed at Glasgow and passing through Britain, he told the people of Narvik how well he had been treated, and the English went up in their estimation.

The *India* had a number of encounters with U-boats, but had no success in sinking any. On one occasion, a submarine fired a torpedo at the *India*, but McKeag relates, 'it happened to be exactly ten o'clock at night, and as we altered course to zigzag every ten minutes, we were on the swing when he fired, and the torpedo went harmlessly on a parallel course to us'. The *India*'s luck ran out on 8 August 1915, at 5.25 p.m., when she was off the Vestfjord keeping a look out for a Swedish steamer, possibly carrying iron ore from Narvik. In the summer, ore was shipped direct to Germany from Lulea at the head of the Gulf of Bothnia. In winter, the Gulf was iced over, so the ore came from Sweden overland by rail to Narvik, and thence by ship to Germany, often through the 'leads', the passage between the offshore islands and Norwegian mainland. However, by August 1915, the activities of British submarines in the Baltic (see Chapter 5) had severely disrupted the iron-ore trade. McKeag:

Suddenly we were all startled by a shout from the starboard look out, 'Submarine on the port bow'. Lt Clark ran to the starboard wing of the bridge, shouting 'submarine, submarine', followed by 'she's fired a torpedo at us'. I looked over the bridge dodger, and saw the wake of a torpedo. It seemed to be coming directly for our foremost magazine, and I braced myself for a terrible explosion. I froze, and looking over the dodger again, saw the torpedo apparently alter course and strike about ten yards abaft the after magazine. The ship shuddered terribly at the shock.

The commander gave the order for boats to be got away. I made my way to my boat, number 3. A number of men got into the boat, and Lt Nelson, the officer in charge, stayed to lower the after fall, while a seaman manned the forward one, and they started to lower away. As we reached the hurricane deck, a few men jumped in, but most waited for the boat to hit the water when they would slide down the falls into it. The ship had taken a list to port, so the boat caught on every projection on the ship's side, taking a long time to lower, and damaging the gunwale. Because there was still way on the ship, no sooner had our boat touched water, than it was carried half under the whaler behind us. We could not cast off or cut the falls, and one man was pinned under the whaler. He was eventually pulled out, but with a smashed arm and shoulder; he died subsequently in hospital.

The ship was sinking so quickly that by now the after well deck was awash and we found ourselves on a level with the boat deck, with tremendous volumes of water dashing over us. Men were being washed in and out of the boat, and seeing that it would be dragged down with the ship, I jumped.

I went down, and down, and still down, until it seemed to me that I would never stop. Then little by little I felt the grip of the water relaxing and I struck out upwards. I came to the surface, seized a breath, and went down again. This time it seemed as though I would never come up. All sorts of thoughts flashed through my mind. I remember feeling glad I had my best uniform on. Then my hands closed on a piece of wood in the water, and I thought I was saved. But it was only about nine inches long. Feeling as if I could not hold my breath an instant longer, I gave up hope for the first time. Wondering how my people would receive the news I was lost, I opened my mouth with the idea of getting it over quickly, and at that moment saw a faint glimmer of light through the water. Hope burned within me. Shutting my mouth, I struck upwards and reached the surface, to find a mast from one of the boats. Holding on, I looked in the direction of the *India*, to see the foremast quiver, and fall over the starboard side, followed by an explosion in or near the boiler room. I went under for the third time, but hanging on to the mast, I surfaced quickly. Looking round, the ship had gone, and all round me were men, some half naked, some fully clothed, hanging on to pieces of wreckage of which there seemed to be plenty.

Ahead of me was a waterlogged boat, with three men standing in it, and one hanging on to the bow. On one side of me was a man whose face was covered in blood. I swung myself up on the mast, and shouted to the men in the boat to bale it out. But that proved impossible, as the boat went gunwales under as the swell passed. Everyone around me was in the best of spirits. I heard the strains of 'Tipperary', and lighthearted bandinage [sic]. I secured a boat's water breaker which was floating past, under my arm to stop me rolling over.

The only person near me who showed signs of giving in was the Captain's writer. I shouted words of encouragement, and told him to swim to my mast. But he drifted away and was lost, poor fellow.

I drifted a good deal, and hearing my name called, saw the electrician, Mr Johnson, holding out a flask for me to drink from. Not wanting to leave my mast, I drifted past, and that was the last I saw of him alive. Looking round I saw a door floating near. Still keeping hold of my mast, I leaned my weight on the door. I drifted into a mass of wreckage, large pieces of wood banged on my back. I was feeling bitterly cold, and my boots were doing their best to take me to the bottom. A slight swell was running, and as I was borne up the sloping hills of water, I got my head dipped under. On the top of the swell, I saw the boat from the *Gotaland* [Swedish steamer] had been lowered, but whether I should be picked up in time or not I could not tell. I was fearfully cold and feeling sleepy. I rested my chin on the door, and knew no more.

When I came to I was in the bottom of a boat alongside the *Gotaland*.

McKeag was hauled up the ship's side by rope, stripped, had liquor poured down his throat, and was put to bed with one of *India*'s wireless operators. He was the last man to be picked up and had been in the water for three hours. Had he succeeded in reaching the man with the flask and drunk from it, he very likely would not have survived, for alcohol is deadly in the cold. They were well looked after by the crew of the *Gotaland*. She docked in Narvik, where they were visited by the British Vice-Consul. Some of the *India*'s survivors were brought in to Narvik by the armed trawler *Saxon*. She came alongside *Gotaland*, and the dead were lowered onto her deck, to be landed for burial. The living were transferred to the *Gotaland*, before the *Saxon* left to avoid being interned. The *India*'s survivors were well treated in Narvik. Under international law, because they had arrived in a neutral ship, they were eventually repatriated to Britain, instead of being interned for the duration of the war.

There were other instances of boarding parties being well treated, by Norwegians in particular. De Chair:

The Norwegian steamer, *Trondhjemsfjord*, which had been chased and boarded by the *Hildebrand*, and a prize crew put on board, was held up by a submarine and fired at. The Master altered course to bring the submarine astern, and proceeded at full speed, but the submarine easily overhauled her and fired again. The Norwegian ship stopped, and the submarine commander ordered the Master to come on board with his papers.

The little midshipman in charge of the prize crew on board asked the Captain not to say he had a prize crew on board, but the Captain said, 'I never tell a lie'. However, when he went alongside the submarine, and was asked if he had prize crew on board, he simply handed the list of his crew, saying, 'these are the men on board, all Norwegian names'. This apparently satisfied the German, but he said, 'I'm going to sink your ship with a torpedo'.

'But my wife is on board'

'Well', replied the German, 'hail them to abandon ship, and look sharp about it, I don't want to get caught by one of those 10th cruiser squadron ships'.

In the meantime the midshipman told his men to disguise themselves as best as possible, and the Captain's wife provided him with some of her husband's clothes, putting his uniform into a bundle of her own things which she carried over her shoulder.

The boats were lowered, and as soon as they were clear of the ship, the submarine fired a torpedo into her amidships, and she blew up with a loud explosion, spray flying over the masthead. The submarine towed the boats for about four miles, coming up alongside to examine the men in the boats, but did not identify any of the prize crew. The German U-boat captain noticed a red stripe on the trousers of one of the men in the boat [clearly a marine's blue trousers], and asked why he was wearing them. The Norwegian, nonplussed by the question, said 'why the hell shouldn't he'. This retort silenced the German.

The U-boat captain later held up the Norwegian barque Glance, and sent her to embark the Trondhjemsfjord's crew. He claimed to have sunk the Trondhjemsfjord because she had once been British owned.

Another case occurred on July 23rd, when the Mogua put a prize crew on the Norwegian steamer Fimreite, which was later held up by a German submarine. The Norwegian captain told the Germans that there was a prize crew on board, upon which the submarine captain said, 'I will sink the ship, and you are to let the prize crew sink with her'. But, the prize crew had disguised themselves, and were in the boats when the Fimreite was torpedoed. Smoke appearing on the horizon, turned out to be one of the Tenth cruiser squadron, the U-boat made off, and the crew was rescued.

In 1915, the 10th Cruiser Squadron was responsible for 220,000 square miles of sea, in all weathers, and infested with enemy submarines. During the year, 3,098 ships were chased and examined, of which 743 were carrying contraband, and were sent into port with prize crews on board. Two cruisers, the Bayano and India, were sunk by submarines, the Clan MacNaughton foundered in heavy weather, and the Viknor was lost with all hands. The squadron lost 64 officers and 814 men. The Alsatian (flag) had spent 262 days at sea out of 365, steamed 71,500 miles, and burned 40,287 tons of coal. Other ships could match these statistics.

McKeag joined the 6,000-ton armed merchant cruiser Octavia, equipped with five 6-inch guns and two 6pdrs. Her patrol station was near the Rockall Bank, out in the Atlantic west of the Hebrides. The weather in January 1916 went from bad to worse, and even coaling at Busta Voe became difficult, and

on some days impossible. The climax was reached on Friday 21 January. We were on patrol in the North Atlantic, hove to in the face of a hurricane that had raged for several days. About 4 pm a massive wave, bigger than any we had seen previously, swooped down on us, and, failing to rise, it broke over us. I was in the wardroom having tea, and such was the force of the wave, the whole iron front of the wardroom caved in. For a moment we thought the bulkhead would give, but it stood the strain. The bridge was wrecked, the wheelhouse smashed, and all the instruments in the charthouse broken. The officer of the watch was injured, and many others bruised and cut.

To make matters worse, the steering gear was smashed, and we were at the mercy of the waves until the hand steering gear could be brought into action. When it was ready, the ship was turned to run before the gale. This was very difficult, and many times we thought we were about to turn turtle as she rolled at amazing angles. Eventually we were able to set course for the Minch [the Minches, the sound between the Outer Hebrides and Skye]. We experienced great difficulty in making the Minch, for it was impossible to steer straight in, for doing so would expose our beam to the sea, running a grave risk of turning turtle. We zig-zagged our way in, and once behind the shelter of the Isle of Lewis, set a course for Glasgow.

On 1 March 1916, after leaving Glasgow, the *Octavia* intercepted the large American barque the *Dirigo*, which

ostensibly having a cargo of barley for Kalmar, Sweden, was carrying aeroplanes and armoured cars for the Germans. This was not discovered until she was fully examined in Lerwick, where she had been sent by us with an armed guard of one officer and four men.

That same day, McKeag along with his shipmates heard the news of the battle between the armed merchant cruiser *Alcantara* and the German raider the *Greif*. Rear Admiral de Chair had

warned my Squadron to be most careful when boarding ships (as they might be enemy raiders in disguise), they were to steam around, scrutinise all ships from a distance of not less than 4,000 yards, and then approach from astern, as cases had occurred of ships of the Grand Fleet being torpedoed by an unsuspected merchant ship. On February 28th, I had placed *Alcantara* and *Andes* in Lat 61.45N 0.58E and *Columbella* and *Patia* 48 miles to the westward, making two patrols steering north and south, and shortly after midnight directional bearings placed a German wireless signal from a transmitting ship about 180 miles south of these patrols. It might be a battle cruiser or a raider.

At 8.45 a.m., the *Alcantara* sighted smoke, increased to full speed to investigate, and went to general quarters. Midshipman Poole, in the *Alcantara* at his action station in the transmitting station (TS), received the order 'all guns load', followed by 'port side guns to be kept trained on the ship'. When within visual signalling range, the flag signal was hoisted 'Stop and give your name and destination'. She stopped, hoisted a Norwegian flag, and identified herself as the SS *Rena* bound for Tonsberg (Norway).

Having zigzagged round her, keeping her distance, and examining her through binoculars, the captain of the *Alcantara* was satisfied that the *Rena* was genuine. He ordered the ammunition supply parties to fall out, but guns to remain loaded and trained on the *Rena*, while a boarding party was sent across by boat to examine her.

From the TS, which was not, as in a conventional warship, well below the waterline, but just below the bridge, Poole was watching the *Rena* through a porthole:

There was a sudden swirl under her stern as her engines were put to full speed and hidden guns blazed away at us at practically point-blank range. Apparently, her captain seeing the boat being lowered realised his identity would be revealed, and decided to fight it out, surprise being in his favour.

The Norwegian flag and staff on her poop went over the side, and large German battle ensigns were hoisted at both mastheads. It was now ship against ship in the good old fashioned way with no holds barred between HMS *Alcantara* and HIMS *Greif* of the German Navy.

In no time we were throwing everything we could at her and she at us. A shell from her first salvo hit the boarding cutter when halfway to the water, killing and wounding several of her crew and badly damaging the boat.

The *Alcantara*, with a higher freeboard, was an excellent target, but had the advantage of speed. The unprotected voicepipes from the spotting position in the *Alcantara* to the TS and to the guns were soon cut, so the officer in charge of each gun went into local control, laying and firing independently. The *Greif* began by trying to put *Alcantara*'s bridge out of action, and several shells whistled through the TS. Fortunately these were armour-piercing shells, which passed straight through the light steel bulkheads of the TS without exploding. Poole, with nothing to do, now the guns were in local control, could hear the

thundering of the guns, the crack of exploding shells, the yells of the gun crews, and occasional cries of the wounded reaching us through the open porthole, intermingled with the staccato bark of the 3-pounder gun just outside the TS. The pace was too hot and range too short for the battle to last long. It was impossible to miss.

By this time the *Greif* had struck more grief than she bargained for. I saw one shell explode [the] ready use ammunition by her after gun. Suddenly there was a burst of yellow flame; exit gun and crew.

The 3-pounder outside the TS suddenly became silent. Shell splinters had smashed it, killing and wounding its four man crew. When communication was restored, two guns reported their training mechanism jammed. The guns crews from the disengaged side rushed across to help train them by hand. Brute force had to be used as we zig-zagged around at 18 knots. Each alteration of course causing the ship to list heavily, making it difficult to keep the guns trained on the enemy.

In the TS I was back again in business with my range clock, and at no time did it exceed 3,000 yards. Although the *Greif* twisted and turned to confuse our gunners, the range was too close for this to have much effect. This also applied to us. Suddenly a lucky shot from one of her torpedoes struck us dead amidships on our port side. A second one was reported passing close under our stern.

Eventually the gruelling punishment we were dishing out was taking effect on the *Greif*, as she began to lose speed. Yet she still kept up an incessant fire giving us as much as we gave her. Our port side was riddled like a colander by her armour-piercing shells. As the majority of them passed right through before exploding, it kept our casualties down.

After a few minutes she stopped and lay completely at our mercy. Although we poured salvo after salvo into her at close range, she remained upright and afloat.

Thirty minutes after the battle opened, her captain decided to call it quits. From what we heard later, her decks were a bloody shambles. To save further useless bloodshed, he decided to abandon ship with what remained of his badly reduced crew, and concede us victory. As his men left in the boats, their large battle ensigns were still flying. They had put up a good fight. As our captain saw the boats leaving, he ordered 'cease fire', she was then about 2,000 yards away.

Suddenly the silence was broken by a shell fired from the smoking and derelict *Greif*. Apparently the heat from the nearby fire had detonated a round left in one of the guns. Thinking the men leaving in boats was a ruse, our captain gave the order to fire. Although the *Greif* was definitely 'through', she still showed no sign of sinking.

By this time our ship was feeling the effects of that lucky torpedo hit and we slowly developed a list to starboard. It was apparent that the *Alcantara* had received her death blow, despite the efforts of the engine room staff, the list slowly and inexorably increased. When the list reached 15 degrees the captain ordered abandon ship.

We in the TS dropped everything and hurried to get our cork lifejackets. Lying across the door of my cabin was what was left of the body of our servant, with much of his blood splashed over my pictures. He had been one of a fire party in the alleyway when a shell exploded among them killing them all.

I hurried to the boat deck where the heavy list made footing difficult.

On reaching my boat station, port side forward, there was no boat; only a piece of wood about a foot long hanging from the forward davit. Of the fourteen lifeboats on the port side, seven ordinary and seven collapsible stowed beneath, not one remained. All had been blown to pieces.

I went to the starboard side to find all lifeboats gone, except one, still towing alongside, as if it was waiting specially for me. Astern, our moving ship had left a trail of lifeboats and bobbing heads in the water; some hanging on to wreckage. All the boats were full to overflowing, so that it was impossible to use the oars to go to anyone's aid.

Luckily the wind had fallen to a light breeze, if it had been the usual February weather I doubt if many of us would have survived. Our ship was still moving through the water at four or five knots, and for those of us left on the boat deck, the situation looked pretty grim, especially for the wounded.

We were a motley crowd, mainly from the engine room, boiler rooms and coal bunkers; being the last to get up on deck. Some were covered in coal dust, others with oil and grease, and others with dried blood and bandages over their wounds; some with yellow-stained faces from exploding shells. On the faces of the wounded was a despairing look of agony as they realised only too well that their chances of survival were worse than slim.

In a way it was tragically funny to see men crawl up to the high side of the boat deck, miss a hand hold, and slide back to the low side; some with helpless look of fear, others seeing the funny side of it; yet knowing in their hearts that the losing of a handhold, may mean all the difference between life and death.

Looking over the side, I saw that the one boat was still there, crammed to the gunwales, and being towed alongside, unable to cast off because the falls were so taut as the ship was still steaming ahead. Men searched frantically for an axe to cut the falls. The missing axe was my salvation. I climbed down the ship's side, via the porthole, which was easy thanks to the list of nearly 20 degrees, and managed to squeeze into the fore end of the boat, alongside one of our young officers, who had apparently fallen into the boat from the boat deck and broken his neck. He had no more worries.

I was no sooner in the boat, than the axe was found. In a matter of seconds the falls were cut, and the boat drifted astern. But we were out of the frying pan into the fire.

When the order abandon ship was received in the engine room, the engineers could not stop the starboard engine. As our boat drifted alongside the ship, the starboard propellor which was only partially submerged was slowly turning to the right. Because of the heavy load in the boat, it was impossible to force it away from the ship's side, consequently we drifted right into the jaws of that mercilessly revolving propellor. Down came the blades cutting right into the boat, capsizing it and flinging us into the water in a wildly struggling mass. Being right in the fore end, I was thrown clear, but not far enough and was caught in the swirling whirlpool of the wake, and dragged under.

As I went down, a man grabbed me, and we both went down kicking and struggling. After a few seconds I managed to kick myself free of him, and our lifejackets brought us to the surface. I had no sooner poked my nose above water and got a lungful of fresh air, when I was grabbed by another struggling man. He was not wearing a life jacket. He got a hard grip on me, and we both were dragged down by the swirling wake. Struggling desperately to free myself, at the same time hold my breath, our life and death struggle seemed to be stopping us from rising to the surface. Being twirled around it was difficult to tell in which direction the surface lay. A butt in the stomach released his hold on me, and we both shot to the surface. He managed to grasp a piece of floating debris large enough to support him.

My lungs, which had been on the point of bursting, were able to take a good lungful of air. I felt exhausted, but managed to cough up a lot of the sea water which I had swallowed. I could see our poor old ship moving slowly away into the distance, gradually losing headway as the steam in her boilers was used up; the list increasing.

The sea all round was littered with bobbing heads and lifeboats crammed to the gunwales. Even the lifelines on the outside of the boats were festooned with men. The majority of the boats had only a few inches of freeboard. Should the wind freshen and the sea get up, men would be drowned wholesale.

After floating and swimming around for what seemed an eternity, but was really not more than about 20 minutes, a boat drifted my way, packed and low in the water. By now the cold was working into my bones. As I swam towards it, I saw a vacant place on the lifelines, so I grabbed it. Alongside me was a marine in a bad way, in a coma and lashed to the boat. After a while I noticed something bobbing alongside me; it was part of his intestines. They had come out of his torn stomach, but had not been punctured. He had been left in the water for the cold to dull the pain and contain the bleeding.

A few minutes later there was a shout; 'the old ship is going'. Turning my head I saw her disappear beneath the waves; her two large battle ensigns bravely flying from her mastheads.

We drifted for what seemed an interminable time. Suddenly, a cry, 'smoke!' In the distance we could make out the outlines of two ships. Someone volunteered the information that the *Greif* had been shadowed by two destroyers until she was clear of the Norwegian coast, and this could probably be them. Our hearts sank as they bore down on us with a 'bone in their teeth'.

As we stared at them, there was a sudden yellow flash and a burst of smoke from the foremost one. Were they going to shell the boats? If so that would be the last straw. Suddenly one made an alteration of course to show the grand old white ensign flying from her gaff. As they approached, those who could howled themselves hoarse with joy. Leading was His Majesty's light cruiser *Comus*, followed by HM Torpedo Boat Destroyer *Munster*, one of the pairs hunting for the *Greif*.

The *Comus* and *Munster* picked up the survivors from the *Alcantara* and went on to finish off the *Greif*. The *Alcantara* lost two officers and 67 ratings. The German raider lost 98 out of a complement of 360. From prisoners it was learned that she had been built in 1914 as an ordinary trade vessel, and fitted out secretly at Hamburg with four 150mm guns and two torpedo tubes. She left Germany on 24 February and was steaming round the north of Iceland to raid commerce in the Atlantic, and if she could not get back, she was to make for German East Africa.

Just after the battle between the *Alcantara* and the *Greif*, Vice-Admiral R. G. O. Tupper took over command of the 10th Cruiser Squadron from de Chair, now Sir Dudley in recognition of his achievements. Rear Admiral Sir Dudley de Chair became naval adviser to the Minister of Blockade, where his experience and considerable talents were put to good use until he took command of the 3rd Battle Squadron in the Grand Fleet in late 1917.

In June 1916, with all *Octavia*'s officers away in prizes, McKeag, being the senior midshipman, was put aboard the SS *Nordnoes* with four men, and ordered to take her in to Kirkwall. His account of his subsequent movements reveal how complex the returning of prize crews to their own ship could be. The morning after arriving at Kirkwall, he

left at about 10 am and took a brake across the island to Scapa, where a drifter left at 11 o'clock, bound for Longhope, where I transferred with my guard to HMS *Imperieuse*, where I stayed the night, leaving her the next morning for the *Alouette*, an armed boarding steamer. The day following, I transferred to the *Duke of Cornwall*, which left Longhope in the evening, arriving at Busta Voe the next day. Here I was transferred to the *Gibraltar*, the guardship, and on to the *Columbella*, one of our squadron, who was leaving for patrol that night. I remained on *Columbella* until 16 June, when she rendezvoused with my own ship.

McKeag's experience was by no means remarkable: in August 1916, he was away from the *Octavia* after another prize crew trip for nine days, having passed through no less than six vessels before rejoining his own ship. The prolonged absence of officers and men on prizes threw a considerable strain on those left to work the ship while they were away.

Three days later he was off again, on a small Norwegian fishing ketch, the *Prima Donna*, ordered to take her into Lerwick. She was

bound from Iceland with fish. My armed guard consisted of one man. The ketch was very small, and had a combined forecastle galley, in the fore end of the ship where the men slept, had their meals cooked, and ate. Right aft was a tiny cabin whose furniture consisted of an absurdly small table, and a wooden form. Opening out from the cabin were four bunks, not quite long enough for a man to lie down in properly. One was littered with charts, packing cases, ship's stores, and odds and ends. The other three were occupied by the skipper, the boatswain and the cook. The deck was constantly wet, the whole ship was filthy, and everything was covered in slime and fish scales.

A spare bunk was discovered in the forecastle for my 'armed guard', but I was obliged to work 'watch and watch' with the skipper, using his bunk when he was on watch.

My first day was decidedly unpromising. Immediately the boarding boat had left me and my 'armed guard', the skipper and his men went below, saying if I wanted to go to Lerwick, I could take the ship myself. I was saved from this predicament, because the ketch was hove-to head to wind, and by remaining stationary, aroused the suspicion of HMS *Hilary*, who came up to investigate. The skipper of the ketch, deciding that resistance was useless, got under way.

The next morning we were closed by another cruiser of the 10th cruiser squadron, which asked if there was anything I wanted. I replied, 'no', but I was pleased she had appeared, because it demonstrated how well these waters were patrolled, and served to dispel any thoughts the skipper might have of running for it.

Two days later we were forced to heave-to because of a gale and heavy sea. On the third day, we were drifting a long way eastward, and I began to have my suspicions of the skipper. So I told him to get on with the voyage. After a long argument, I got my way, but had to bluff, as I did not want to use force unnecessarily. The ketch was riding perfectly well in the weather, and I decided to take no notice of the skipper.

The next day in place of too much wind, we lay becalmed, until the *Sweeper*, an armed trawler, arrived. According to the ketch skipper's reckoning we should have been twenty-five miles north of Muckle Flugga [the most northerly headland in the Shetlands], and actually we were fifty miles to the Nor-Nor-East [i.e. well past the Shetlands]. The *Sweeper* told off another trawler to tow us to Lerwick. The tow rope broke once, but we arrived at Bressay Sound that evening, too late to enter Lerwick harbour. We hung about all night, and entered in the morning.

McKeag's journey in a Norwegian schooner to rejoin his ship took seven days. He was under orders to take the schooner to Wick first. They found themselves passing through a prohibited area off Wick by night, where they were examined in the searchlight of a destroyer, who only sheered off when reassured by the sight of McKeag and his 'armed guard' in uniform. A train from Wick via Inverness completed the journey to Glasgow, where the *Octavia* was lying. McKeag requested, and was granted, twenty-four hours' leave before *Octavia* sailed on patrol.

As the war progressed, the 10th Cruiser Squadron was augmented by armed trawlers and the blockade became increasingly effective. Agreements with shipping companies and Scandinavian governments, along with other controls, ensured that ships did not carry cargoes helpful to the enemy. The German adoption of unrestricted submarine warfare on 1 February 1917, of which more in Chapter 10, resulted in increased attacks on the 10th Cruiser Squadron. Despite this the Northern Patrol kept its grip on the blockade. Once the United States entered the war in April 1917, the Northern Patrol was no longer needed, and its ships were transferred to convoy duties.

Space does not permit a full discussion of the part played by the blockade in the defeat of Germany. One school of thought holds the view that the blockade was *the* deciding factor in the Allied victory. More recent assessments consider that the blockade was not as decisive as this, arguing that the area being blockaded was the greater part of Europe; not just Germany and Austria-Hungary, but including the occupied parts of northern France, almost all of Belgium, Serbia, Romania, Bulgaria, Poland, and vast tracts of western Russia, as well as Turkey and much of the Ottoman Empire. The produce of Holland, Norway, Sweden, and Denmark, all neutral throughout the war, could be transported to Germany across the Baltic or overland. So the Central Powers were neither so reliant on sea lines of communication nor so short of key supplies as the pro-blockaders contend, although of course, commodities such as rubber, critical in modern war, were not available anywhere on the continent of Europe or its peripheries. The starvation conditions experienced in Germany towards the end of the war are explained away as the result of inefficiency in production and distribution on the part of the authorities. The case for the blockade rests on the answer to the question: What would have happened had there been no blockade? The German war effort would have been unimpeded. The Germans would not have had to resort to unrestricted submarine warfare, and it follows that the United States would have very likely not joined the Allied side. Germany would have continued to be able to raise loans on the American money market. So perhaps a balanced assessment is that while it was a war-winning weapon, the blockade was not as decisive as some of its proponents would like to believe.[2]

In recounting the story of the Northern Patrol, we have got far ahead of the narrative of the Royal Navy's activities at sea in the First World War in general, and of the war in Northern Waters in particular. It is time to wind the clock back to late 1914, and follow the story of the submarines in the North Sea and Baltic.

5

Northern Waters, 1914–1916:
submarines and Q-ships

British Submarines in the North Sea

As early as September 1914, it became clear to the Admiralty that submarine operations in the Heligoland Bight were not going to be as successful as had been hoped. The reasons for this included the large numbers of anti-submarine craft (including U-boats), ever-increasing minefields, the imaginative use of the German air arm, including Zeppelins, and the lack of targets. Of eleven attacks made by British boats, only one had been successful; Max Horton in E9 sank the light cruiser *Hela* on 13 September.

On 17 September, a conference at which Churchill was present was held on board the *Iron Duke*. It discussed, among other matters, the employment of the Royal Navy's longer-range submarines. Eventually, Keyes, Commodore (S), was ordered to send three boats into the Baltic, find the battleships of the German Fleet while they were on exercise, sink as many as possible, refuel at the Russian port of Libau, and return home.

Why the Baltic? The only entrance to the Baltic is through the confined waters of the Big or Little Belts (through the Danish islands), or the Sound between Denmark and Sweden. These passages were in neutral waters throughout the war, and could easily be blocked by mines, so the French and British were cut off from their major ally, Russia, except via the northern Russian ports, which had limited capacity to supply the theatre where the fighting was taking place. The Baltic being so far north has short summer nights and long winter ones. Large areas are frozen in the winter, especially the Gulfs of Finland, Bothnia and Riga. Naval operations in these areas were impossible in winter.

The Germans, however, enjoyed a great strategic advantage in that the Kiel Canal, linking the Baltic with the North Sea, allowed them to move ships from one to the other without making the passage through the Belts or Sound. Nor were they forced to pass through the maritime choke points of the Kattegat and Skagerrak round the tip of the Jutland Peninsula. In perfect safety and secrecy the Germans could switch from one sea to the other. They could be exercising in the Baltic without fear of interference one day, and appear in the North Sea the next.

Curiously, both the Russians and the Germans acted upon the assumption that the other's fleet was superior,[1] although when the Germans had the bulk of their fleet in the North Sea, the Russians had the advantage in numbers of ships, but not in quality. The Germans were preoccupied with the North Sea, and saw the Baltic as very much a secondary theatre.

Operations in the Baltic had not been entirely ruled out by the Royal Navy. Indeed Fisher had long favoured schemes for carrying out landings on the Baltic coast of Germany. Anyone with a rudimentary knowledge of amphibious operations, after about ten seconds' thought, could have told him his notions were preposterous, whereas the employment of submarines made eminent sense. Their appearance in the Baltic might give the Germans a very unpleasant surprise, forcing them to move anti-submarine assets there from the North Sea, and, as an added bonus, provide tangible evidence of Allied support for the Russians

Three boats, E1, E9, and E11, left for the Baltic on 15 October, aiming to pass through the Sound by night at two-hour intervals. E1 (Lieutenant-Commander Noel Lawrence) reached the Baltic on 17 October. But the presence of submarines had been reported to the Germans. This was confirmed when E1 carried out an unsuccessful attack on the old cruiser *Viktoria Luise*. The Germans increased their patrols, and withdrew their ships exercising in Kiel Bay, leaving no juicy targets. Max Horton's E9 entered the Baltic on 18 October, but could not carry out any operations because of a defective motor. E11 (Lieutenant-Commander Martin Nasmith) could not get past the patrols in the Sound, and returned to Harwich.

Both E1 and E9 eventually turned up at Libau, much to the Russians' surprise, as the Admiralty had not seen fit to warn them. However, they were greeted warmly, and eventually sent to Lapvik on the Finnish coast. Although the Germans now had attacks of 'submarinitis', similar to those being experienced by the Royal Navy, no successes were notched up by the British or Russian submarines before the onset of winter and ice brought operations to an end. Lawrence and Horton now settled down to wait for the spring thaw at Libau on the coast of Lithuania.

Meanwhile, despite the problems mentioned earlier, submarines of the 8th Flotilla continued to operate in the North Sea, but with orders to remain submerged in daylight when possible. On Boxing Day, submarines supported the RNAS raid on Cuxhaven. Nasmith in E11 picked up three aviators forced to ditch off Nordeney, although he was being attacked by a Zeppelin at the time, and two bombs exploded near him after he had dived.

In the New Year, the 8th Flotilla was depleted by sending boats to the Dardanelles, and later to the Baltic. In the North Sea, seaplanes and Zeppelins feature regularly in Commander Talbot's diary in E6. On 18 April 1915, while steering a course for Heligoland,

> a seaplane came down on us very rapidly from ahead; dived, she dropped two bombs near us, remained down for half an hour, and then rose and proceeded on my way. Arrived at my position 20 miles NW from Heligoland about 10 pm, lay on the surface, partly trimmed all night.
>
> Dived at 3.15 am as the day was breaking. Rose at 4.30 am; nothing in sight through the periscope, so came to the surface, to my disgust finding a seaplane about 800 feet almost vertically above us, so went down again.
>
> At 12.15, just after looking round through the periscope, heard a big explosion apparently in the vicinity of the boat, presumably from a seaplane, went down to 50 feet.
>
> At 12.55 heard another bomb. Went down to 70 feet. At 1.05 bumped the bottom, gauge showing 75 feet, and directly after got another bomb. We were evidently a few miles NE of our position, so I moved out to the westward to get into deeper water, crawling dead slow along the bottom so as to make as little wash as possible.
>
> 5.15, just after looking through the periscope, we had two more bombs, though the explosions were not so loud. Dived till 7.30, when it was practically dark. Went to the surface, nothing in sight, got under way with the engines and left for Harwich.
>
> I can hardly believe we could have been seen at 75 feet from a seaplane, although the sea was glassy calm. If it was a seaplane I should have expected to find crowds of destroyers round us when we rose.
>
> Came back at 13 knots. My battery was practically right down after 17 hours diving including going fairly fast once or twice to intercept smoke.

On 24 July, Talbot was ordered to cruise between the Western Ems and Nordeney south of 54° North: 'We took 6 carrier pigeons with us, the idea being to train them for long oversea flights so that in time they may learn to fly from the Bight. Released two pigeons at 5 pm, 120 miles from Yarmouth'.

The next morning:

> 6.20   Through the periscope, sighted a German submarine come to the surface about one and half miles to the westward of me.

Altered course to attack. The submarine appeared to be of a new type. Enemy started engine and proceeded westward. Her speed did not exceed 10 knots.

6.36   Rose to surface and chased at full speed. She fired a white light to which I replied with a white Verey's light, it immediately striking me a red or green one would have had more chances of success.

6.45   She dived when about 3 miles distant. Continued to the westward at full speed to get ahead of him, but at;

6.57   was forced to dive by the appearance of a seaplane

7.15   Zeppelin to southward. I worked out to northward.

8.30   (about) 5 TBDs appeared, steaming fast on various courses to 10 am

11.30   Rose to surface, but after 10 minutes forced under by Zeppelin.

Noon   55° 48′ N 6° 0′ E
posn

        While at 65 Feet bomb exploded in vicinity of boat. Went to bottom for one hour

1.27   Seaplane to SE

2.15   Position NW by N½N 3 miles from position of Borkum Riff light
pm   (removed).

        Diving at 22 ft, 2 knots, course 60°.

The boat must have snagged a mooring because:

        Boat suddenly became heavy by bow, and gradually sank with big and increasing inclination down.

        Tried to correct trim, but it needed a very large proportion blown from 1, 2, 3 and 4 Externals, before boat was buoyant.

        Two small bombs exploded near boat.

        Sank to bottom at 13 fathoms [78 feet]

        Went astern, the only effect being to lift stern up to a big inclination (more than 10° of gauge)

2.40   Blew 1, 2, 3 and 4 Externals and rose to surface, still with large inclination down; opened conning tower lid, to discover a Zeppelin a few hundred feet almost vertically over boat; saw nothing foul forward.

Opened the vents and sank to bottom with amazing rapidity, but when about 20 feet off bottom, the moorings which we had apparently lifted, touched bottom and the released weight allowed us to alight perfectly gently.

This gave me an idea. I blew enough water from 1, 2, 3 and 4 to raise the boat a few feet from the bottom, went astern and ahead for a few moments each, and then went astern, diving the boat horizontally.

3.15   Boat's nose suddenly flew up and boat rushed towards the surface. Checked it by vents, and found the boat apparently free of the obstruction and her more or less normal trim.

Dived out to the westward at 60 feet.

3.40   Rose to 22 feet, nothing in sight [through periscope]

4.   Bomb exploded close to boat. Returned to 60 feet, and remained diving until dark, fearing I might be towing a marker buoy.

While foul of the obstruction, the boat's position must have been very visible owing to the large amount of blowing, pumping, and venting of tanks.

8 pm   Rose to surface. Nothing in sight.

Talbot decided that he must warn the remainder of the flotilla alongside the depot ship *Maidstone*. He could not wait until he returned to Harwich, as he judged there was every probability that he would get caught in a similar way the next day, and might not get away. After midnight he tried using a kite to take his aerial up high enough to establish wireless contact, but neither of his two kites would fly, and eventually both were lost overboard. While struggling with the kites, he was passed by a German patrol trawler about five miles off, but was not seen. Then at

4 am   Released four pigeons (the remainder) with following message: 'To *Maidstone*. Sunday afternoon fouled NW X N 3 miles from Borkum Riff Light Vessel, submerged obstruction apparently consisting of heavily moored net, watched by enemy aircraft. I am now clear. Present position 53° 50N, 4K 20E. Am returning to station leaving minefield to southward.

8.45   dived for Zeppelin to SWards, which was in sight more or less continuously till 11.20

11.20   Sighted smoke and masts approaching from SEwards. Course as required to investigate. Three German TBDs appeared steaming independently at varying speeds on various courses.

* They appeared to be of G 197 Class, about 700 tons [sic].

12.36   fired port bow torpedo at TBD at 500 to 600 yards range. Allowed deflection for 15 knots speed. Hit about quarter or third of her length from aft.

* The TBD sunk was V 188, practically identified with above [sic].

The other two TBDs approached at full speed from different directions.

The vessel hit appearing certain to sink, her stern being practically blown off, attempted to torpedo the others, fired starboard bow torpedo at 12.55 at about 700 yards, and stern torpedo at about 800 yards, both missing; in first case enemy's telegraphs must have been rung to full astern the instant before I fired, in second case the torpedo was avoided. Damaged TBD had sunk by 1.5 pm, a large proportion of the crew were taken off by other TBDs, which apparently picked up boat in intervals between attempting to ram E6. One TBD then disappeared at full speed to the eastward, and the remaining one, with a new arrival, apparently commenced sweeping at about 20 knots.

Dived out to north east, was kept diving until 7 pm by a Zeppelin being almost continuously in sight until then.

After avoiding the Borkum Flat minefield, he went to his patrol station. The next morning he was forced down by a seaplane. In the afternoon, heavy rain allowed him to surface, and bad visibility kept aircraft away for the next four days. He returned to Harwich on 31 July:

We were fired on by our patrol trawler about 2.30 pm when 5 or 6 miles east of the Sunk [light vessel], though we had reported our arrival by W/T; stopped, let them come close, and made what I intended to be a very caustic signal.

Arrived at Harwich about 4.30 pm, being cheered up the harbour by the light cruisers who had intercepted my wireless signal reporting the sinking of the destroyer.

He was also a new father:

Had a wire from Fairfield to say Dilli and the baby are both doing splendidly. The Captain [8th Submarine Flotilla] sanctioned three days leave to half the crew.

On Monday 9 August, Talbot noted in his diary, 'An Admiralty letter came to say I am to select one of my crew, present on the last trip, for the DSM; I made the Coxswain, Senior Chief Torpedo Officer, and Chief ERA draw lots for it; the latter winning'.

In September 1915, some boats of the 8th Flotilla were based at Aberdeen and placed under what we would now call the operational command of Jellicoe, and tasked by him to sink U-boats threatening shipping in the Norwegian Sea. On 15 September, Talbot was on patrol off Norway, dived and steering north with the current, parallel with the coast.

At 12.32, I sighted through the periscope an enemy submarine. Of course the boat got negative buoyancy in blowing the torpedo tubes, and sank, so I had to manoeuvre for position in the dark [his periscope was below the surface], and only got my periscope up again about 20 seconds before firing. At 12.40 fired both bow tubes, torpedoes both set to diverge 2½° at about 500 yards range; one torpedo hit a few feet before the conning tower and the other presumably went ahead; I allowed 15 knots speed, but from the result she appears to have been going about 23. The submarine had disappeared before the smoke of the explosion had cleared away.

Rose to the surface and picked up 5 survivors, they being scattered over about 150 yards. One of them was nearly drowned and we had to pump him out. Then proceeded on the surface towards the southern side of the Fjord which I thought might be another submarine, but which turned out to be smoke ashore. At 1.20 pm shaped course for Aberdeen.

Our prisoners consisted of the 1st Lieut, the engineer, and three men. Her crew was 33, but they were four short, so 24 were killed. The boat was U6.

Uneventful passage back.

Thursday September 16th

Arrived at Aberdeen about 11.30 am. Went in a taxi to see the SNO about the prisoners, whose presence I had kept secret so as to prevent any demonstration or crowd. About 3 pm an enormous guard of soldiers came down and took them away in taxis to Edinburgh Castle, of course drawing a crowd.

Heard I have been given the DSO for sinking V 188.

Got a wire from Admiral Jellicoe sending his 'warm congratulations on our success'

On 29 September, Talbot was despatched to operate against a U-boat which was seen on the St Alban's Head–Naze trade route. 'It looks rather like finding a needle in a haystack', he commented in his diary. He also got a second wire from Jellicoe:

> Have much pleasure in conveying appreciation of Lords Commissioners of the Admiralty of your successful attack. Your name has been submitted to HM the King for appointment to the DSO [his second]. You are to submit the name of one of your crew for the DSM.

This time Talbot does not record how he chose the man to receive the medal.

On 17 October, he had another encounter with a U-boat:

> At 11.15, not having seen the sun or stars for days, and there being nothing in sight except a sail on the horizon, I came up with about 2 feet of conning tower out to take a noon sight; the sail turned out to be the conning tower of a large German submarine, 1½ to 2 miles off, half trimmed down and moving very slowly; we both saw each other and dived. Of course we did not see each other again; if only I had had one of the new magnifying periscopes, I should most certainly have got him.

British Submarines in the Baltic

The Soviet official history of the First World War claims that despite Russian requests for help during the attack on the Gulf of Riga, 'the British remained a passive observer throughout'.[2] The German maritime offensive into the Gulf of Riga was effectively the left flank of their land offensive on the Eastern Front. Libau fell to the Germans on 8 May 1915. The Gulf of Riga was the scene of much naval activity by both the Germans and the Russians for the next two years. It is hard to see what the Grand Fleet could have done, but no one can accuse the Royal Navy of not doing their best, because by sending submarines to cooperate with the Imperial Russian Navy, they were providing just what was needed in the Baltic. In June 1915, Commander Grenfell, the British Naval Attaché in Russia, recommended that more submarines should be sent into the Baltic, especially if the Germans, realizing that their operations in the North Sea were getting them nowhere, turned their attention to the Russians.

Two boats, E8 (Lieutenant-Commander Francis Goodhart) and E13 (Lieutenant-Commander Geoffrey Layton), sailed on 15 August to join E1 and E9 already out there. Two more were to follow when conditions were suitable.

E13 did not make it into the Baltic, running aground at 11 p.m. off

Saltholm Island thanks to a defective gyro-compass. Layton and his crew worked hard to free the boat, knowing that under international law he could remain in neutral territorial waters for a maximum of twenty-four hours. At 5 a.m., the Danish destroyer *Peder Skram* hove in sight and reminded Layton that unless he cleared Danish waters by 11 p.m., he and his crew would be interned. The Germans, hearing of the situation, sent two destroyers to the scene. With their customary arrogance, they brushed aside the protests of the Danish destroyer captain that they were in neutral waters, and one fired a torpedo at E13. It grounded in the mud, at which the Germans opened fire with their guns, setting E13 on fire. Layton ordered his crew to abandon the boat and swim for shore. The Germans continued to pound the flaming wreck, and lace the water with machine-gun fire. The whole of E13's crew would have died had it not been for the gallant captain of the *Peder Skram*, who interposed his ship between the Germans and E13, rescuing Layton and fifteen of his crew. Fifteen others lay dead or dying in the shallow water which had trapped their boat. Layton and his first lieutenant refused to give their parole, escaped, and returned to Britain to resume the war; and incidentally to report the war crime committed by the Germans, of which more later.

Goodhart in E8 reached Revel, and was followed by E18 (Lieutenant-Commander Robert Halahan) and E19 (Lieutenant-Commander Francis Cromie), bringing the total British submarines in the Baltic to five with a consignment of new torpedoes.

Lawrence in E1 struck the first blow, by hitting the battle cruiser *Moltke* with a torpedo. Little damage was done as it struck right forward, but it persuaded the German navy to withdraw support for the army's attack on Riga. In September, Cromie in E19 sank eight merchant ships in one patrol. In October, Horton (E9), Cromie, Halahan (E18), and Goodhart (E8) struck the German merchant fleet, halting the flow of Swedish iron ore to Germany. The most spectacular feat was Goodhart's sinking the heavy cruiser *Prinz Adalbert* on 23 October 1915. He kept a diary, describing this and other incidents in his Baltic tour. His racy style tells us how he viewed the Russians and his fellow submariners, and includes references to his wife Isa (sometimes 'Darling'). The entry for 23 October 1915, written the next morning, describes the events before, during, and after the attack on the *Prinz Adalbert*:

Saturday 23rd I'm writing this at 11.20 AM! I didn't feel like turning out a bit at 6.0, half an hour later than usual to make up for lateness last night. Greig [first lieutenant] had been working up to 2.30 AM. over the Starboard starting resistances. There had been various quaint results of earths. The ammeter of forrard Periscope Raising Motor had burnt itself out, but was rebushed by removing & shorting leads. Some idiot had closed off the cock to Diving pump, rather the limit when we were at 115 ft & orders given to watch carefully that we didn't get deeper! So when I blew we bounced out! Of course you never find who has done a thing like that but I informed everybody generally as to what I thought of the matter, & that the whole crew would be strafed some day if they did that sort of thing

Got on top & found all right, so charged for half an hour. Very cold but was able to see 'Auntie' [have a pee into the 'pig's ear' on the bridge] in comfort & have a cigarette. Dived at 6.55. Nearly broad daylight, but it had been bright moonlight on coming up so not much difference between the two. I steered 240° meaning to get back to trawler position & if still there wait with her, (but unseen).

However at 7.40. AM we saw the trawler returning to Libau [on the coast of Lithuania]. I felt very disappointed but decided against having a go at her & was glad I did so later on. Last night I was angry with her & said I should strafe her for leading us on a wild goose chase!! So I let her go & dived on west. Took a small snooze but didn't sleep. Had breakfast about 7.45. (Kippers Porridge) & felt better after that.

At 8.50. Pavlov [Russian naval liaison officer] looking out reported smoke on Starboard Quarter so I went to look at it there was plenty of it, so I watched & found its bearing was drawing forward (2°). So went on both motors & steered 340° then 350°. (about at right angles to his bearing). I decided at once that we should have to dig out to get in so went 700 on each (7 knots). Fine sunny & nice breeze from SSE a splendid day for an attack from our point of view.

By degrees we saw it was a 3 funnel ship 2 very tall masts with tops. Two destroyers were with her doing zig-zags on either bow, (one each side). I remarked to Greig that they need not worry us, as there were only (2) & the chances enormously against us fouling them! Smith was excellent with stop watch but I did not calculate speed by the after periscope method but just said I would allow 14 knots, but actually put on 22° Deflection.[3] (I changed to forrard Periscope from after one at about 9.15) I eased down as we closed but it was a really simple attack I never altered course a degree till well after firing! Fired bow Tube. It is hard to say what really happened. I wasn't (for a wonder) a bit worried till after firing. One destroyer crossed our bows about 200 yds off, & I kept our periscope up rather a long time (one min I expect) just as she was coming on to fire. I was a bit far off, didn't take masthead angle properly, but imagined afterwards it was about 3° (850 yds). But Torpedo HIT after 75 secs = just under 1,600 yds However probably she didn't pick up her speed at once so that is the maximum. I fired on fore bridge, 22°. I followed track of torpedo when I fired (for the first time) & saw it was running well. We came up to 18 ft on firing so I lowered the periscope a bit. Then up again to have a look again. Ship struck me as being a bit small, but later think she was either *Prinz Adalbert* or Pommern class.

I was looking right ahead when I suddenly saw a red line of flame along her waterline under the fore bridge. I thought they had fired fore turret at me!! & gave the order Port 20° & 50 ft at once. There was a terrific crash, I looked at the ship, & all that there was, was an immense cloud of thick smoke, she had gone off in one act!! A Mark VIII [torpedo] is some stuff, but it must have got her forward magazine. A marvellous sight & terrifically impressive, bits of the ship were splashing in the water fully 500 yds astern of her.

I called Greig to look as we turned away but he only just saw smoke before dipping. The crew were very bucked & clapped!! I hardly realized I had 'blown up' a ship. Poor devils in her, they can't have known anything about it. I think the flash knocked me back from the periscope, I thought at the time that a 12" shell had burst just in front of the periscope. I find that I really gave the order Port 20, 'Port beam stand by' before the explosion (all Tubes were ready) & so it shows that my brain had half realized I had missed!! & was preparing to make up for it.

I don't think the ship itself was zig zagging & if the fish ran hot as I think it did her speed must have been pretty exactly 15. They couldn't possibly have seen me but I was nearly outside range, however I'm glad we were not any closer as the bang was colossal! After getting to 50 ft I eased down & thought about things, closed sluice doors, everybody very happy & pleased, I not properly realizing the thing even then, it had somehow stunned my intellect but I could carry on with things O.K & really quite all right.

I decided to clear out of the billet right away, so after steering 30° I gradually altered round to NW for Ostergarn, Gotland [Island]. I came up to 20 ft after about 8 minutes. The two destroyers were stopped on the scene of the explosion & nothing of the ship to be seen anywhere. I am quite convinced that nothing was seen of her after that cloud had dispersed. 50 ft again after that for an hour. Then 4 destroyers on the spot 2 sweeping one leading & one circling ahead. They seem to expect a boat to stop on the same spot always! I came up every hour & they were getting fainter & fainter astern each time

Eventually at 1.0 we were going along as usual at 20 ft one motor, having been going grouped down both since our finally leaving the scene. I left those destroyers alone, firstly as I didn't feel it possible to interfere with them doing what they could to save any survivors & also (officially) because I did not want to disclose that I was there if they suspected a mine which is quite on the cards, as I don't think they can have seen me at all. We had our bottle of 'fizz' .

Feeling more & more pleased with life somehow, its awful to think of the personal loss of life, but looking at it from the proper war point of view its a good bit of work, & everybody in the boat deserves it at last. We carried on diving till 3. P.M. when nothing in sight I came up & continued on surface for Holmudden charging at 9 knots for two hours. Then 12 knots Passed the light about 10 PM & steered for North of Dago [Dagö Island in the Gulf of Riga]. The boats crew had a headache so Thomas told me & I had a slight one too. Could not sleep (too excited).

Sunday 24th. Pavlov's wording of report quite good: 'On 23rd attacked & destroyed ship of – class. Consider enemy T.B.D. escort may think it was a mine.' I added the last to keep the billet open if possible for others.

Got a congratulatory telegram from Pagouski (Capt S[ubmarines Russian flotilla]). We had no 'Fritz' incidents & arrived off Nagen [sic: Nargen] about 3.30. The shore was all snow covered & it was cold it finally started snowing as we entered harbour & continued all night very small snow. There was no pilot boat visible on our getting on the course in, so I headed in & the pilot boat met us about 1/3 of the way to the boom, as he appeared likely to ram us, I had to stop, & then they proceeded to cheer ship & finally the captain of her hailed us with megaphone congratulating us, so they knew all about it. Passing the boom the tug cheered too also another guard boat there. Then we continued by ourselves & reached harbour about 4.30. We had the black cat [flag] lashed to the wireless stanchion!

They gave us a great reception the Dvina (Russians) giving their Russian cheers with the Commander prominent on the gangway, then E18 & 19 alongside the Reinda gave us 4 good English ones, ably led by old Simpson on the bridge of 18. E1 is out!!! Her tubes a great success. They had got my Wireless early this morning, 5 stations trying their best to give us a reply which we couldn't take in. Great enthusiasm that a single Tube & Mark VIII should be so successful. I forgot to mention cheering by destroyers as we came in.

Went over to Dvina as I was, & had whiskey & soda with Simpson, Russian submarine officers there. The captain of Gepart [Gepard – Russian submarine] rather bottled having returned from unsuccessful tour where Cromie had been, having broken surface while attacking a cruiser & nearly rammed by destroyers as far as I could make out. He had fired 3 torpedoes at German TB's & naturally missed. Then to dinner at Consuls with Halahan, Cromie & Simpson. They were very nice & it was good getting among English people, & talking about other subjects. I was getting it rather 'on the brain' & it made things seem much more real & ordinary. We had fizz & the consul presented me with a bottle which I believe is his usual custom. Hear Horton has strafed 4 merchant ships so they are getting well hotted up. Alligator (Russian) is bringing German ship home as prize!

<u>Monday 25th</u> Captain of *Dvina* very nice & congratulatory. Gave me signal from C-in C which translated was as follows: – To Captain English Submarine *E8*. I congratulate the brave crew of English submarine *E8* on their glorious success – C-in C. Kannin.

Arranged interview with Pagouski in Europa for 10.0. Had whiskey & soda. Pagouski seemed much impressed at my patience in waiting for a big ship & not having gone for the merchant shipping off Libau which as a matter of fact would have been very hard to do.

Goodhart then called on the Coastguard Admiral:

He read us German reports re sinking of ship from escorting destroyers. 1st Report: 'explosion followed by detonation ship sunk all is calm' 2nd: 'have picked up 3 survivors no officers ask instructions'. Reply: 'Proceed South a few miles & return to Libau.' Ship apparently struck a mine & then they thought her magazine had gone off on its own. Submarine never thought of apparently. Russians have announced publicly that British Submarine did it! A mistake I think, however they know best.

Got back to lunch about 12.30 the skipper lunching late also, he is a good soul & we argued the matter of publishing he said it was done to increase morale of submarine fellows, which I don't think a very satisfactory reason. However very satisfying to know that we were absolutely unseen.

<u>Tuesday 26th</u> Horton got in, just as I was going to my bath. Had sunk 4 merchant vessels, very bucked at my show as I knew he would be. It is definitely fixed as the *Prinz Adalbert* now, possibly her reconstructed bow after bumping a mine being responsible for my thinking it might be a Deutschland. Halahan gone sick with blood poisoning from a Dentist who ought to be strafed. He went to hospital.

Coming in to harbour at night from his next patrol, Goodhart had a collision with the Russian submarine *Gepard* which was showing no lights, and crossed his bows. Both boats were damaged but not critically:

<u>Tuesday 9th</u> Cromie arrived thoroughly iced up having sunk small German cruiser, *Undine* 1st Mark VIII hot forward then V* aft, a very good egg & I am glad. He also strafed a German merchant steamer laden with wood & set her alight all in 35 mins saving a small puppy! as prisoner

Had an interview with Pagouski (Commodore S) & apologized for 'Gepart', the latter was stern lifted by large submarine salvage ship, 13 frames broken in after compartment making a good deal of water. My Starboard Hydroplane non est, & it will be at least 3 weeks before we are a running concern again. Very depressed in consequence down on my luck & very tired all day.

The Russian rigidity of thought was promising to put a stop to operations in the winter, as the next section of Goodhart's diary reveals:

Had a confab with Cromie & Horton after lunch re Helsingfors [in Gulf of Finland]. The whole business is that we ought not to give the Germans the rest entailed on our being iced in & going to Helsingfors means an additional month in that state. Of course the ideal condition would as Horton says be to get as near open sea as possible at Utö [an island outside Gulf of Finland] with 2 good icebreakers & go on running through winter. That place is apparently out of the question owing to difficulty of supplies &c. but there seems no reason for laying ourselves up when we need not. The Russian C-in C has given the orders re Helsingfors & I'm sorry to say that L. [Lawrence] is hardly likely to go against it. However we mean to have a dig at him on the subject. Of course 'personally' it would be more comfortable to stop running but we are not here for our comfort & it is up to us to stop anything of that sort ever being said against us. The Russians have been used to the idea of packing up for the winter, & cannot realize the possibility of overcoming the elements against them. That is their great failing they cannot 'try' & are very inclined to say 'well we have never thought of doing such a thing.'. it is impossible.

Russian attitudes are also revealed:

Pavlov during this last trip has been a bit of a disappointment, but he is very typical of them as a whole & of the best of them too. Of course he was ill but he was in a state of absolute panic coming in last night, & the trial dive I gave him on the trip shewed what a panicky nature he has. However I hope to teach him our methods & think he has it in him to learn. The Russian officers attached to these boats ought to learn a lot though it may sound conceited to say so. Their submariners are a rotten lot of officers, it was regarded as their 'bum' job before the war consequently they are not of the best, but times are changing very rapidly & their best officers realize the state of affairs. However there is a good feeling of jealousy of the 'British Submariners' evident at present & I do not think Pagouski is quite free of it.

The next day the Tsar visited to award decorations:

Wednesday 10th A Red Letter Day. The Czar inspected troops ashore first, who meanwhile made continuous cheering noise & then came on board followed by a very numerous staff.
   The Czar. started forward & walked aft shaking hands with us all, & saying something to everybody. He talks excellent English & is a much finer looking (though very like) man than our King. He looks you straight in the eyes & one must look straight into his. He said how elated they all

were when they heard of the P.A's defeat & I said we in the boat were enormously elated too!

He then gave Cromie & I St George's Cross saying he had much pleasure in presenting us with them. All I could think of was to say 'Thank you'. The Young Czarewitch [the heir to the throne] was with him a very lively looking young boy in grey overcoat & St George's medal Cross. All the staff congratulated us & Horton pinned the medals on for us as they were all ready made up. The Czarewitch's servant took our photos! The number of photographers knocking about was enormous! Cinema people as well! & they were funny when they tripped up over ring bolts &c.

The British submarine COs were invited to join the Tsar for dinner on the Imperial Train:

I had an excellent view of H M. all the time as he was in the centre on the opposite side. He has the pleasantest face of any Royalty I have ever seen, & does not make one feel the least bit shy at all, He looks at one as if he liked you & you were pals & slaves! of his right away. The dinner was short & wonderful, gold knives & forks & spoons for ice & dessert!

The most interesting evening I have had so far & the effect on ones feelings towards Czar enormous one now feels as if one knew him personally & receiving the St George's Cross from him too makes it all the more precious. (The St George's Cross 4th class is only awarded to you when you defeat a superior enemy) it was luck it all coming on so nicely so that he could give it to us himself.

Returned onboard where things were pretty lively. I retired early to write this up. Darling you will be pleased at all this I know & I'm thinking of you & have been doing so all through & it has made me happier than ever feeling that you will share it all too. Have quite got over downheartedness over our last trip & bump & so to bed! Great sickness of Russians because we did not cheer Emperor, even I thought it necessary but L [Lawrence] would not do it as he said he could not get men in position!

Thursday 11th Up in good time & had breakfast by 8.0 Admiral Phillimore [Rear Admiral Richard Phillimore, Naval Liaison Officer to Imperial HQ] arrived about 9.0. Went over to Dock with Simpson & found Gepard had left her hydroplanes stuck into anchor weight casting. It penetrated into No 2 Comp! No 1. External got 2 holes made by her propellor blades! At least a 6 weeks job I'm afraid. Fwd Firing Tank finished anyway. Returned to ship for sketches then back to Dock. I have decided to have casting taken out & welded together again. Very downhearted at the job.

Admiral P. blowing around with Horton all forenoon. In afternoon tackled Lawrence re a Court of Inquiry into my collision, thankful to say he rather jumped at the suggestion so it will come off in a day or two. The only trouble is that Russians have already decided to squash the whole business as it is wartime, but I want to get my end cleared in England if it is possible as it is awful two boats out of action for a job like that in wartime! when boats are precious. Horton & Cromie will be the court. Started writing to Isa in afternoon which cheered me up a lot

1915 was the most successful year for British submarines in the Baltic, as Russian operations in that theatre were bedevilled by jealousy and intrigue throughout 1916, and it was, according to Cromie, 'a wasted year'.[4]

In 1915 we had such an extraordinarily successful year (I never came back empty-handed from a trip) that the Russian submarine and other officers became jealous as women over our success and popularity, and, like women, spread every sort of scandal about us. In 1916 we were kept idle for months at a time.[5]

Maintenance of the British boats was difficult and the numbers available for operations fell sharply. In July 1916, the Admiralty decided to send more boats to the Baltic, but not risk the passage through the Sound and the Belts. Four old C-class boats (C26, C27, C32, and C35) were towed round North Cape to Archangel, to be loaded on barges for the thousand-mile voyage through the canals and rivers to Petrograd (St Petersburg) (E boats were too big to pass through) and thence into the Baltic through the Gulf of Finland. After an eventful journey the boats arrived at Petrograd on 9 September, but many of their batteries, shipped separately, were damaged. Eventually only two boats were able to carry out a patrol before winter and ice stopped operations.

During 1916, Lawrence and Horton were recalled. Goodhart, who was awarded the DSO for sinking the *Prinz Adalbert*, left in late 1916 to command the new submarine K14. By early 1917 the Russian navy started coming apart thanks to discipline and morale problems. Following the revolution, and seizure of power by the Bolsheviks in Petrograd on 7 November 1917, the Russians signed an armistice with Germany. The Germans immediately moved to seize the Russian Baltic Fleet. Lieutenant Downie, now commanding the surviving flotilla consisting of four E-class and three C-class boats, scuttled them – at first the Russians refused to supply icebreakers to allow the British to take their boats to sea before scuttling them, so Downie threatened to blow them up in harbour.

Cromie remained in command of the Baltic submarine flotilla until late 1917, when he became naval attaché in Petrograd. He was murdered by Bolsheviks in 1918. He never got the credit for all his excellent work in the Baltic, as the British press concentrated on Horton's exploits to the exclusion of all the other COs.

War against the U-boats, 1914–1916

What of Germany's submarines? While the British had failed to evolve any concepts or equipment for anti-submarine warfare before 1914, so had the Germans made no pre-war preparations for a submarine offensive on British trade. The British lack of planning was the consequence of their underestimating the potency of the submarine. The Germans believed that the war would not last for more than a few months, and would be won by their army, so the U-boat war got off to a slow start. Warships were of course fair game, and within the first five months of the war U-boats had sunk a battleship and four cruisers. But only ten British merchant ships were sunk up to the end of January 1915, numbers which the Admiralty did not regard as a threat to trade. To begin with, the campaign against merchant shipping was conducted under the rules of 'cruiser warfare': no sinking without warning. These regulations were not easy to adhere to; one of the requirements was that passengers and crews should be rescued and transported to a neutral port, but a submarine could not possibly accommodate the crew, let alone the passengers, of a ship it sank.

Admiralty complacency about the U-boat threat was not shared by the senior commanders in the Grand Fleet, and on 8 December 1914, Beatty commented: 'It would appear from the reports which come in daily that enemy submarines roam around our coasts absolutely undisturbed', adding, 'I would therefore submit that the whole coastal patrol and defence service requires organising and establishing on a different basis.' In June 1915, he wrote a long and angry letter to the Admiralty:

> I have the honour again to bring to their Lordships' notice certain points connected with the menace of enemy submarines. The gravity of this menace has now increased to such an extent that new measures and more drastic action are imperative. Six cruisers from Rosyth were vigorously attacked in various parts of that area, within a few hours steaming of one of our principal naval bases. We have in fact to realise that at present the German Navy indisputably commands the North Sea.

Meanwhile Rear Admiral Pakenham, now commanding the 2nd Battle Cruiser Squadron, had suggested to Beatty that a competition should be run with cash prizes for suggestions by officers for beating the submarine menace. Beatty agreed, and he notified all officers in the BCF that the prizes would be first, £15, second, £10, and third, £5. The proposed measures that emerged in this competition ranged from fantastic to practical: one concept involved an agent posing as a traitor on the Irish coast, supplying stores to U-boats, and eventually sinking a number of them while hove to. To win the Germans' confidence, to begin with, some U-boats should be allowed to proceed after being resupplied.

A net barrage watched by destroyers and trawlers, zigzagging, explosive sweeps, ramming submarines, and the use of small aircraft, were suggestions that were all put into effect in time, with varying results. Another idea involving torpedoes with time fuses that would explode even if they missed the submarine was simply beyond the state of technology of the time. This limitation also applied to the proposal involving a signalling bell positioned underwater, the theory being that any submarine coming between the bell and a ship fitted with receiving equipment would cut off the sound and reveal its position, a forerunner of modern underwater sonar sensor systems.

The possibility of ships flying kites made to resemble sea planes and towed from aft was also suggested as a means of deterring U-boats. Another idea involved ships towing a box kite fitted with bombs that could be released electrically to hit a submarine chasing on the surface. A more desperate measure called for a rowing boat to be fitted with torpedo suspended underneath. When a surfaced submarine stopped a ship and ordered a boat to be sent over, the crew would row towards the enemy, and at the right moment, jump into the water, having first started the torpedo's motor. The torpedo, now towing the boat, would strike the U-boat, blowing it up. This concept would re-emerge in the Second World War as the Italian explosive motor boat for attacking surface warships.

Altogether some sixty-four suggestions were submitted. One of them, signed with the nom de plume Endeavour, came up with the notion of merchant ships disguised as neutrals carrying hidden guns, to act as a decoy. Someone else had already thought of it, because the concept saw the light of day as the Q-ship in January 1915.

The competition was sparked by the Germans beginning to concentrate more effort towards cutting Britain's lifeline in earnest in early 1915. After the Dogger Bank battle of January 1915, units of the High Seas Fleet made six more sorties between February and May that year, but as they ventured no more than around 120 nautical miles from their base they did not encounter the Grand Fleet. This left the German navy frustrated and increasingly depressed at the lack of success of its strategy, and after much internal wrangling, the Germans decided to resort to a campaign of commerce-raiding using U-boats.

Following agitation in the German press, on 4 February 1915 it was declared that the waters round Great Britain and Ireland were declared a war zone: submarines would sink all merchant ships encountered without warning. The Germans quoted the British failure to ratify the London Declaration, and their ensuing illegal 'hunger blockade' against German women and children, as an excuse for this 'gloves off' approach to submarine warfare. The first unrestricted U-boat campaign began on 28 February, with a force of only thirty-seven boats, of which about one-third were available on patrol at any one time. From March to May 1915, U-boats sank 115 merchant ships for the loss of only five boats.

The British reaction was to arm merchant ships and order ship's masters to turn towards U-boats to force them to dive. Captain Fryatt, of the Great Eastern Railway ferry *Brussels*, did just that to U-33 on 28 March 1915. The German reaction was to send destroyers to intercept the *Brussels* in June 1916, and take the ship into Zeebrugge. Fryatt was tried by court martial as a *franc-tireur* – someone fighting in civilian clothes. He was shot. It did the German image no good. The neutral press was outraged, the *New York Times* calling the German act 'a deliberate murder'. As far as the British were concerned this was but one more example of 'Hun brutishness'.

On 7 May, the giant British liner *Lusitania*, a sister ship of the *Mauretania*, was on passage from New York to Liverpool when she was torpedoed off the Old Head of Kinsale in Ireland, by U-20. She sank in a few minutes, after being hit by a single torpedo, far more quickly than the *Titanic*, who three years previously had her side ripped out by an iceberg. *Lusitania* took with her 1,195 civilians, 140 of them Americans. The deaths included 94 children.

Soon after the loss of the liner, a Mrs Prichard and her son (neither of whom were passengers) wrote to as many survivors as they could find, seeking news of the fate of the other son, a passenger in the *Lusitania*. The replies, recently acquired by the Imperial War Museum, have never been published before. Notwithstanding the dignified and restrained language in the letters, so characteristic of the time, they allow us to see the tragic events after the torpedo struck through the eyes of the survivors.

Mrs Phoebe Amery wrote, 'after getting in our lifeboat and after it got filled [with people] it broke to pieces throwing me into the water and [I] was picked up by a boat by [using] a boat hook by my hair, and was clinging on the side for 2 hours'.

Mrs Margaret Beattie and her husband were below in their cabin when the torpedo hit:

While we were on our way to the deck, my husband remembered the lifebelts and went back to the cabin for them – when we reached the middle deck, we saw almost no one – all were up on the top deck where the boats were being launched. The ship by this time was very much over on her side. When we saw the sea breaking over the bows, my husband and I jumped into the water and swam for a little, and then we got hold of a plank to which we clung. After being in the water for about four hours, I was rescued by a trawler.

My dear husband was lost, but I had the great satisfaction of finding him on Saturday and seeing him laid to rest in the cemetary at Queenstown.

Some accounts talk of panic, while others say there was none. Many letters mention men giving up their lifebelts to women, again typical of the age. Mrs Beattie offers as a reason for Prichard's death:

Perhaps he was one of the brave men who gave his belt to a woman. While I was waiting for my husband to bring my belt, a man offered me his. In Queenstown two of the rescued women who were in the same room in the hotel where I was, told me that men had taken off their lifebelts and given them to them. There were many such cases.

This is confirmed by other accounts, which mention that as lifebelts were in cabins, passengers below deck when the torpedo struck had a greater chance of finding one than people who had to go below to retrieve theirs. The speed with which *Lusitania* sank caused many deaths, as boats were lowered while she listed. Mrs Amy Campbell wrote:

As far as I could see there was no panic, but hundreds jumped into the water, some had lifebelts on and others without, and the boat [ship] sank so quickly that hundreds must have been drowned by being sucked down with her. My husband and I got into a lifeboat on the high side of the boat [ship], the ropes jammed and had to be cut, we dropped 86 feet [sic] and were all thrown into the water, since when I have not seen or heard of my husband.

Mr Robert Gray was critical of the crew of the *Lusitania*, writing:

I am sorry to say there was certainly a lack of knowledge in the getting away of the lifeboats, in fact most of the boats went down with the ship, with the result that we had no altenative but to take to the water. You ask if there was panic. How could it be otherwise with helpless women and children. I shall never blot out the sight from my mind.

First Class Steward Heighway, in charge of a lifeboat, remembered:

All the 2nd cabin decks were a mass of people when the ship suddenly threw her stern up 200 feet in the air, throwing everyone headlong down among chairs, boats, seats, and all sorts of loose gear. Then the ship took a plunge and went to the bottom passing me with my boatload like an express train. I just got my boat two yards clear of the ship when this happened, and I am sure there were 600 to 700 people killed and taken down without a chance of saving themselves. Very near everyone had lifebelts, which there were plenty of. I saw hundreds of men and women dead with lifebelts on in the water after the ship had gone.

Miss Alice Middleton found that as *Lusitania* listed:

we had to cling to the side [rail] to keep us from rolling [about], then she exploded and down came a funnel, so over I jumped. I had a terrible time in the water; four and a half hours bashing about among the wreckage and dead bodies.

She was unconscious when picked up and landed at Queenstown:

In fact they piled me with a boat full of dead and it was only when they were carrying the dead bodies to the mortuary that they discovered that there was life in me, and ran [me] in a motor to the hospital, so with the good attention of the doctor and nurses they managed to get life into me.

Mrs Lillian Pye was travelling with her baby daughter:

When the ship went down it carried my darling baby girl and self with it and I held her in my arms under water until I became unconscious and she was dragged away from me, and I have never seen her since. Twice I went under the water, and the second time on coming to the surface I held on to a piece of wreckage and drifted around among the dead

Mr Tijon, a steward, was of the opinion that: 'A number [of people] were lost by the boats being lowered while the vessel was travelling at full speed, which smashed them to pieces when they touched the water and this threw the passengers violently against the vessel'. Although it is unlikely that the ship was still steaming at full speed, she clearly had forward way on her, which would have had the effect Tijon describes.

Mr Cyril Wallace remembered that many of the passengers were at lunch when *Lusitania* was hit:

there was fearful congestion among the above [those at lunch] in their frantic desire to all regain the boat deck at once. The stairs up were of average width but it is practically certain that some met their death in this wild scramble.

The *Lusitania* listed very heavily to starboard, sinking head first. I put

on a lifebelt and scrambled up on to the lifeboat deck. Hundreds of passengers were clustered around the boats and I was besieged by several
women with entreaties to save them. I gave mine to Mrs Fife of Glasgow,
who was luckily saved, and then helped to lower the boat for a few minutes, when the *Lusitania* suddenly quivered from stem to stern and began
settling very rapidly. I feared the vortex, so dove overboard swimming as
rapidly as I could away from the doomed liner. I had progressed some
thirty yards when the poor old 'Lucy' disappeared with a deafening roar.
I was swimming on my back at the time and could discern dozens of
people on the decks sliding out of sight as the ship disappeared. It was
heartrending.

Mrs Gertrude Adams wrote:

I lost a dear baby of two and a half years. Thank God I knew her end. She
died in my arms. Many mothers on board were separated from their
children at the time of the murder.

Murder was how the incident was seen in Britain and America. In
1915, the concept of total war was unknown. Today we are aware of
the horrors that have been perpetrated in the ninety years since the
sinking of the *Lusitania*, and some people may find difficulty fully com-
prehending the rage and incredulity which greeted the killing of so
many innocent civilians, especially women and children. The German
response was that *Lusitania* was carrying ammunition, which the Admiralty denied. We now know she was carrying shells and fuses, in the
exact spot hit by the torpedo, which accounts for the reports of a second
explosion, wrongly attributed to a second torpedo, and why she sank
so quickly. Furthermore the Admiralty failed to warn the *Lusitania* that
a U-boat was operating in the area, and that two ships had been sunk
in the vicinity of St George's Channel the previous day. Room 40 had
located U-20's patrol area by wireless intercept of her transmissions
to base, but the technology of the time did not allow the Admiralty to
pinpoint her position, and in fact she was miles from where they
anticipated she would be.

Conspiracy theories have flourished ever since, centred on a British
plot to allow the *Lusitania* to be torpedoed to bring America in to the
war. Like so many conspiracy theories based on a fantasy world of
ignorance and naivety, this one does not stand up. No one with a
knowledge of the odds involved would hatch a plot to sink *Lusitania*
that depended on the many thousands to one chance of a U-boat being
within a few hundred yards of her intended track, and in a good
attacking position. Far more likely, the failure was a cock-up by the
inefficient staff at the Admiralty, presided over by Vice-Admiral Henry

Oliver, Chief of War Staff. He was an arrogant officer who found it impossible to delegate, and did not fully trust the somewhat unconventional officers who staffed Room 40. This was neither the first nor the last such lapse by Oliver and the Admiralty.

Horrified though public opinion was, *Lusitania*'s sinking was not sufficient to bring the Americans into the war, although it brought them a step closer to the Allied side. Nor did it mark the end of unrestricted submarine warfare. That came about, temporarily, after the sinking of the British liner *Arabic*, by U-24 off Ireland on 19 August, with the loss of forty lives, including three Americans. This time the protests from Washington were enough to result in the German abandonment of unrestricted U-boat warfare on 30 August 1915. But August had been a good month for the U-boats, which had sunk forty-two merchant ships. The last act of the 1915 campaign was the torpedoing of the *Urbino* on 24 September.

In February 1916, unrestricted U-boat warfare flared up again after the leaders of the German army and navy had conferred and agreed 'that there are no military reasons against the resumption of the submarine campaign', and that 'a submarine campaign conducted without any restrictions will, by the end of 1916, injure Great Britain to such an extent that she will be inclined for peace'.[6] The campaign began in March 1916; in April thirty-seven British ships were sunk. Before this the Germans announced that any armed merchantmen would be treated as warships. However, American pressure was brought to bear again when on 24 March the unarmed French steamer *Sussex* was torpedoed between Dieppe and Folkestone. Although the ship stayed afloat many of her 380 passengers, including several Americans, were killed or injured. An ultimatum from Washington threatening an end to diplomatic relations unless the Germans abandoned their policy of unrestricted U-boat warfare was enough to bring about a temporary cessation until the Battle of Jutland, and its immediate aftermath, finally led Germany to opt for unrestricted submarine warfare regardless of its consequences.

Countermeasures to the U-boat were slow in coming. The deadliest weapon was the mine, but it had to be laid in the right place, and some U-boat kills were 'own goals'. Lines of heavy wire-mesh nets suspended from buoys and floats, strung out on likely U-boat routes, were tried, with some success, especially when combined with mines. Depth charges, when these appeared in 1916, were a long way second to mines, but effective in scaring off U-boats as well as killing them.[7]

Arming merchant ships certainly paid off, until the advent of unrestricted submarine warfare, as the table shows:

1 Jan 1916 to 25 Jan 1917

Defensively armed ships attacked	310
of which escaped	236
Sunk by torpedo without warning	62
Sunk by gun-fire from submarine	12
Unarmed ships attacked	302
of which escaped	67
Sunk by torpedo without warning	30
Sunk by gun-fire, bombs etc	205[8]

Convoys as a means of bringing home shipping with minimum loss continued to be rejected by the Admiralty and the civilian shipping companies as being in the 'too difficult' department. The Admiralty maintained that merchant ships should rely on speed and defensive armament, not escorts:

It is evident that the larger the number of ships forming the convoy, the greater is the chance of a submarine being enabled to attack successfully, the greater the difficulty of the escort in preventing such an attack. In the case of defensively armed merchant vessels, it is preferable that they should sail singly rather than in a convoy with several other vessels. A submarine could remain at a distance and fire her torpedo into the middle of a convoy with every chance of success. A defensively armed merchant vessel of good speed should rarely, if ever, be captured. If the submarine comes to the surface to overtake and attack with her gun, the merchant vessel's gun will nearly always make the submarine dive, in which case the preponderance of speed will allow of the merchant ship escaping.[9]

This claim defied the fact that troopships always sailed in convoy with escorts; but the modern destroyers that would form the merchant ships' escorts were in short supply as most were busy screening the Grand Fleet or operating in the Harwich Force. It is easy to be critical of the Admiralty, but as well as the shortage of escorts, all but a minority of senior naval officers were of the opinion that hunting submarines, not protective convoys, was the answer to the U-boat threat. The most serious omission in the armoury of countermeasures was a reliable means to detect, remain 'locked onto', and attack a dived submarine.

The most romanticized countermeasure was the Q-ship. Originally called Special Service vessels, they were usually small tramp steamers, manned by volunteers armed with concealed guns; the early ones had mostly 12- and 6pdrs, but later Q-ships had 4-inch and 4.7-inch guns, torpedo tubes, and depth charges. The concept relied for its success on the U-boat commander deeming the Q-ship too small to be worth a torpedo, and surfacing to close and sink her with guns, or by boarding and setting off charges: as the U-boat closed, screens and flaps on the Q-ship would be lowered, and fire would be poured into the enemy at point-blank range. The first Q-ship success was on 24 July 1915, when the *Prince Charles* sank U-36. This was followed by the *Baralong* sinking U-27 on 19 August and U-41 on 24 September.

Early successes led to more Q-ships being deployed, although by 1917 they were becoming ineffective. Before the Germans began unrestricted submarine warfare in earnest on 1 February 1917, Q-ships sank seven U-boats, while three Q-ships were sunk by U-boats, one was sunk by a mine, and one by collision. After February 1917, Q-ships sank seven U-boats, but twenty-six Q-ships were sunk by U-boats. In addition five Q-ships were sunk by other causes. The total score was fourteen U-boats for the price of twenty-nine Q-ships (thirty-six if the seven sunk by other causes are taken into account).

After a while some U-boat COs became quite good at identifying Q-ships, once it was known they were about. Franz Becker, who commanded three U-boats, albeit in the Mediterranean, remembered that he had

> an instinct for recognising Q-Ships, the captains were always Royal Navy officers [or RN/RNVR], they looked well prepared with new flags, taut ropes in the case of sailing ships, and the people on board moved like sailors of the Royal Navy.
>
> I met a ship once that didn't 'smell' right for me, and remained five kilometres distant, fired a shot across his bow, and signalled 'send a boat with your papers'. The boat came only a little way across, and stopped. They were trying to get me to come closer. I fired again, and at that the boat made a run for it, and the British had it back on board and were off. I fired on them but they got away.
>
> At the beginning of the war it was not easy for us to sink merchant ships, we preferred to attack warships. But, when we got home to Germany, could see how the country was blockaded, and how hungry our people were, it made us realise we needed to conduct war against merchant ships.
>
> In the beginning there were no strict orders on what we could and couldn't sink, and they kept on being changed by our Admiralty to ensure that America stayed out of the war. Only in 1917 did we have a free hand to do what was necessary.

George Hempenstall, a regular able seaman, served in Q-ships for nearly two years, joining in January 1915 the *Antwerp*, a Great Eastern Railway ferry on the Harwich–Hook of Holland run, which changed its name to *Vienna*. His captain, Lieutenant-Commander Godfrey Herbert

RN, had commanded the submarine D5. In December 1914, in the aftermath of the Scarborough raid (see Chapter 2), Herbert had been tailing part of the German force back to Heligoland, and had hit a floating mine dropped by the fleeing enemy. He and his coxswain were the only survivors. Hempenstall described the procedures, which would have applied in *general* terms across the Q-ship fleet:

> On joining we were briefed by Lieutenant Commander Herbert and told what we were expected to do, and if we objected to say that they didn't want to serve in the ship. No one objected. We were called decoy ships in those days, not Q ships. We were supplied with jerseys, with the letters GER, for Great Eastern Railway, embroidered on the chest. Later we were given 30 shillings to buy civilian clothes ashore.
>
> There were four active service ratings, and four reserve ratings in the ship's company as well as about eight seamen and eight firemen from the merchant navy crew, plus civilian cooks and stewards. There were two 12-pdr guns on the poop. We made dummy covers for the guns, looking like liferafts.
>
> In April 1915 all the Navy people were all transferred to the *Baralong* with Herbert as Captain. The *Baralong*'s master, officers, and merchant navy crew remained on board. Herbert's second-in-command was Lieutenant Steele, also a submariner. We had nine privates and lance-corporals of the RMLI commanded by Corporal Fred Collins, who was eventually made a sergeant.

Corporal Fred Collins RMLI was with the *Baralong* from January 1915 until she was handed back to her commercial company in Port Said in November 1916. The purpose in embarking marines was

> to have 10 specially picked marksmen, nine others and me the corporal. The submarine would be lured close, while I divided my men in three groups under the gunwale, when the alarm bell rang, my job with my Marines was to shoot down all the people in the conning tower straight away so they couldn't get any warning signals below, while another party of Marines shot at the forward gun crew and other parts. But later when this stunt became known to the Germans it was all long range work.

Hempenstall:

> We had two 12-pdr guns on each quarter, and later a stern chaser. The people fitting the stern chaser didn't know the other guns were aboard, they were so well hidden, and asked 'what's the use of this thing?' The guns were hidden by dummy lifebelt lockers with lifebelts painted on them, which came apart in two sections.
>
> We had name boards with various names painted on them, and national

flags, Greek, Spanish, etc. to suit the name of the ship and where we were operating. If we had the name board *Ulysses S Grant* up we would fly the American flag. Sometimes we would repaint the funnel at night with different shipping line colours.

Only Herbert knew where we were going. The other officers, including the Merchant Navy Master, didn't see the charts. They were treated as nonentities, and eventually left – they resented it. We didn't have anything to do with the Merchant Navy ratings, they were forrard we were aft. After a time, ERAs replaced the Merchant Navy engine room staff.

In port we kept quiet about what we were doing. We went ashore in civilian clothes [later this was changed]. We would be given white feathers and asked why we 'weren't in khaki'. To cope with this we were issued with badges inscribed 'On War Service', which I showed to a soldier who gave me a white feather on Liverpool landing stage one day.

To maintain security we never picked up a pilot going in and out of harbour. We were treated as special cases for coaling and stores – other ships in the queue for bunkering were elbowed aside. I didn't tell anyone what I did, even my Mother.

We heard from the wireless operators about ships being sunk by U-boats, that their crews had no consideration for survivors, and that they fired on women and children in lifeboats. We were anxious to get hold of U-boat crews – we had no compassion for Germans.

Herbert was a popular captain, according to Corporal Collins, and a 'real good man', in the sense of being a good fellow, telling Collins and his petty officer opposite number that he relied on them:

'I can't enforce naval discipline in this ship. You've got a good job, provided you do your job when the bell rings. I'm going to leave it all to you. If you want any help, just let me know'. But we never had any trouble.

He used to say to me, 'Good morning General, how are the troops this morning?' He was very efficient, no panic, deliberate and cool.

Baralong's crew, according to Corporal Collins, who kept a diary at the time, 'Had heard the signal from the *Lusitania* on the day she was sunk. We were about 50 or 60 miles away and couldn't get there in time. I saw the bodies of the women and children washed up from the *Lusitania* at Cork'. Lieutenant Steele, the first lieutenant and gunnery officer of the *Baralong*, recalled that his captain was sent for, possibly by someone on the staff of Vice-Admiral Sir Lewis Bayly (Vice-Admiral Queenstown – now Cobh in southern Ireland), according to him a Captain Richmond, who said: 'Well, Captain, this *Lusitania* is a shocking business. And our unofficial answer is – no prisoners from German submarines'.

They felt pretty angry about it. Hempenstall claims that Herbert never passed this on, saying, 'I never heard Herbert say "take no prisoners"'.

Nearly a century later, it may be hard for us to comprehend the hatred with which Germans in general, and U-boat crews in particular, were regarded by most British sailors and civilians. Some of it was deserved, but most of it was propaganda whipped up by newspapers. True or not, however, it was what people believed, in a far less sophisticated age than ours, and one in which the vast majority had little access to information; what there was consisted mostly of emotional articles in the newspapers. This mixture of hatred and propaganda was to influence the actions of those involved in what became known as the *Baralong* affair.

On 19 August 1915, while the *Baralong* was on patrol, U-24 torpedoed the liner *Arabic* without warning, about twenty miles away. The *Baralong* had intercepted wireless messages from the *Arabic* calling for help. Herbert and his crew were now well aware that the Germans had committed what, in their view, was yet another atrocity, when, according to Herbert's report:

> at 3.0 pm I was steering in hopes of falling in with enemy submarine reported in that area in the forenoon [i.e. the U-24]. My attention was called to a large steamer about 9 miles off bearing SW, making a large alteration of course. Almost immediately I received by WT, 'SOS, being chased by enemy submarine', and altered course accordingly, flying neutral colours. Within three miles of the submarine I hoisted VIC-QRA, meaning 'save life'

The *Baralong* was wearing American colours and the name board *Ulysses S Grant* was in position, and Herbert wanted the U-boat CO to think he was approaching to pick up survivors from the steamer, the *Nicosian*. Hempenstall:

> The alarm bell sounded, and we closed up to the guns, lying on deck out of sight. Because of the way the guns were positioned and couldn't be elevated, Herbert had to get within 600 yards. The crew of the *Nicosian* were in the lifeboats. The U-boat was firing at the *Nicosian*, while we crept up behind the steamer, keeping her between us and the U-boat, which was about 600 yards off. The order to clear away guns was given, the US flag came down, the name boards were dropped, and the White Ensign was hoisted. As we cleared the *Nicosian*, the submarine came in view. He fired a shot across our bows to stop us, and that was the last round he fired.

Our first 12-pdr Lyddite shell hit his conning tower, exploding. The Marines positioned round our ship where they could get the best shots opened fire with their rifles scattering the submarine gun's crew, who dived over the side. We fired until there was nothing to fire at. It didn't last long, the nose-fused Lyddite soon put a stop to them. That was that.

Herbert shouted 'cease fire' to Steele, the gunnery officer on the poop. There was nothing left of the submarine, just the *Nicosian*'s crew in lifeboats.

Herbert's report:

The *Nicosian*'s boats now pulled alongside, and whilst clearing the boats, I observed about a dozen Germans who had swum from their boat, swarming up rope's ends and the pilot ladder which had been left hanging down from the *Nicosian*. Fearing they might scuttle or set fire to the ship with her valuable cargo of mules and fodder, I ordered them to be shot away; the majority were prevented from getting on board, but six succeeded.

Herbert had adjusted his report to include the information about the mules, because at that stage in the action he did not know what cargo *Nicosian* was carrying.

Steele:

The Captain kept yelling at me, 'shoot at the waterline' [of the *Nicosian*, with the intention of sinking her]. The Captain of the *Nicosian* came on board and said, 'Look here, I've got 216 mules and munitions on board'. He also said there were about half a dozen rifles on board which they had left behind with ammunition.

My Captain said, 'Stop Number 1 [Steele]. We'll try to save her'. But there were Germans on board too, so he ordered the Marines to board. With masterly skill he brought his ship alongside, which wasn't easy in the big swell, and from the poop the Marines under the sergeant [corporal], dashed over.

Corporal Fred Collins:

When he [Herbert] ordered me to take men aboard the *Nicosian* to get the Germans out, his actual words were: 'Don't forget Collins, no prisoners aboard this ship. Get rid of them'. If I remember rightly he came down on the well deck on the boat deck as they were tying the *Baralong* to the *Nicosian*.

There were ten of us altogether. First we jumped on to the main deck. Under the rails of the *Nicosian* there were bundles of hay, it made a soft landing. I sent a couple of parties along to each hatchway, to start with, and took three men to search the upperworks. I didn't want to be caught with my trousers down. We searched the boat decks then the bridge;

while we were up there, I heard a scuffling down below and a shot. I never discovered who fired the shot. Then the Marines went down each hatchway to the next deck, which was a cabin deck. We didn't know who was what or how many of them there were. They found them; some of them on top of the [indecipherable], some in the passage, and the last in the bottom of the ship. Of course they just shot them. I wasn't down in the bottom of the ship. It was the lance-corporal and three others.

I turned to go aft on the after deck, when I saw somebody disappear through an alleyway. We knew that anybody alive on there was a Gerry. There was no question of asking who they were. I saw this bloke disappear, I looked along and saw a flush doorway – a radio cabin or something – I kicked this door open, this bloke shot out and I shot him. He was running, but I don't know where he could run; he toppled over the side. Godfrey Herbert was standing on the bridge with a revolver in his hand, and he saw him floating past. He threw the revolver at the man in the water, and he said, 'What about the *Lusitania*, you bastard'.

The man I shot was an officer – I don't know if he was the commander [of the U-boat]. He had no coat on, he had a waistcoat with lots of brass buttons. He made no attempt to surrender. We'd got our orders, and I know the Marines just shot first, anybody they saw.

Afterwards the commander [Herbert] ordered us back to the *Baralong* – it was about 3 o'clock. Some of the mules had been wounded by the shelling, and the vet was sent with two of my Marines and a couple of seamen, along with the Chief Bosun and the engineer. When it was dark they dumped the German bodies overboard.

Hempenstall is unequivocal about the Marines' action: 'the RN ratings supported them, and would have done the same if given the opportunity. We didn't think killing U-boat crews a big issue, it was perfectly reasonable.'

Steele stated in an interview that the captain of the U-boat (Wegener) was shot in the water, although how he knew it was the captain is uncertain. In this interview he claims that he boarded the *Nicosian*, but after the shooting was over. In a later interview, he said that he boarded the *Nicosian*, 'as things got out of hand', early enough to see that 'a couple of the Germans had rifles', and 'at first the Marines were firing shots to scare them'. He also claims that Wegener hid in the bathroom belonging to the master of the *Nicosian*, but the marines broke down the door with their rifle butts. Wegener, according to Steele, squeezed out of a scuttle, still wearing a lifejacket, and dropped into the sea, where he was shot by Corporal Collins.[10]

Neither of Steele's accounts squares with Collins's version, reiterated in a letter to Alexander Barrie, written twenty years before Steele's second interview quoted above, and it should be borne in mind that Collins kept a diary. Collins says in the letter:

> There was no other person at all aboard the *Nicosian* except my Marines and the Germans at the time, as Commander Herbert would allow no one aboard the *Nicosian* until I had reported back to him.

While there is no doubt that the marines shot all the Germans in the *Nicosian*, Steele's account is suspect. Collins is sure he was not there, and if he was there and saw what happened so clearly why did he not take charge? Steele was a gallant officer who later won the VC, but he was young and inexperienced at the time of the incident, which could explain his reluctance to step in – if he was there.

Other aspects of Steele's account make one wonder about it, such as his description of the U-boat CO's ability to squeeze out of the bathroom scuttle while wearing a lifejacket, his assertion that the Germans were armed with rifles, and that the marines were firing shots to scare them (no one in his right mind faced with an armed enemy fires a shot to scare him). Collins does not mention any of this, and surely if the Germans had been armed, much would have been made of such a key point in the subsequent British rebuttal of charges that a war crime had been committed. One can only conclude that the passage of time had affected Steele's memory.

Three months passed before the *Baralong* affair was brought to public notice as a result of some of the American muleteers from the *Nicosian* talking to the press in the United States. By this time, as recorded in *Baralong*'s log, Herbert, whose request to return to submarines having been granted, had handed over to Lieutenant-Commander Wilmot Smith on 3 September 1915, eleven days after the sinking of U-27.

Just over a month after the *Nicosian* incident, the *Baralong* was in action again. Collins's diary entry for Friday 24 September:

> Still steaming west. 9.15 am we saw a large steamer on our port bow, blowing off steam. We drew into [sic] her with the American flag flying as we saw she had a list to starboard. Then we saw a German submarine on top of the water about 1,000 yards off our starboard beam, making for us. The submarine hoisted a signal, 'Stop or we fire', and when she got to within 400 yards of us, we opened fire with rifles and two guns. She tried to get down on us so she could torpedo us, but she was too late. She sank in 3 minutes.

Two men survived from the U-boat, Oberleutnant Crompton and the helmsman, Godau. Later Crompton related under interrogation how their boat, the U-41 operating off the Scilly Isles, had sunk three merchant ships, before intercepting the cargo ship *Urbino*. The U-boat CO, Hansen, warned the captain of the *Urbino* that he was about to sink her. The crew took to the lifeboats and U-41 sank the steamer by shellfire. As she went down, the U-boat crew, standing on the casing, jeered at Captain Hicks of the *Urbino*, as he and forty-two of his crew, many of them wounded, pulled away. At that moment they spotted another ship (the *Baralong*) approaching. Having dived, Hansen brought U-41 to the surface, where she could make 14 knots, to intercept the newcomer. The ship stopped in accordance with Hansen's signal and appeared to be about to lower a boat, turning to make a lee. At that moment Collins's riflemen opened fire. Hansen tried to dive, but *Baralong*'s second shell blew him and six seamen to pieces. The submarine, with tanks beginning to flood and already starting to dive, headed down. Someone must have tried to correct her downward plunge, as her tanks were then blown. Crompton was caught in the conning tower with the helmsman. As the boat bobbed up, he and Godau were shot out and over the side, as U-41 slid towards the bottom of the sea.

Collins:

> We picked up the crew [of the *Urbino*]. These two Gerries were swimming about in the water. There was an empty lifeboat which had belonged to the *Urbino* floating about. The taller bloke got hold of the ropes on the side and swung himself in, and hauled the other bloke in.

Hempenstall: 'The man at the wheel must have been told to steer for the lifeboat and hit it. The Captain shouted to the Marines, "don't fire", and "no one speak to the survivors"'.

Collins:

> The Captain deliberately rammed the boat with the *Baralong*, chucked them back into the water. Eventually this bloke got back in and pulled his chum in again. Our Marines and seamen cheered the German for doing that. We pulled them aboard.

Crompton's account has the *Baralong* steaming off for up to an hour (possibly to collect the *Urbino* survivors), before returning to sweep past while he was still in the water, with the crew jeering at him, just as U-41's crew had jeered at the survivors of the *Urbino*. Only then did he and Godau climb into the lifeboat, to be rammed by the *Baralong*. Hempenstall:

> I thought the U-boat crews deserved some of their own medecine.
> I was at the top of the ladder when they came up, and the officer was the first up. I helped him on board. He said, 'thank you very much. I've only done my duty'. They were given dry clothing and boots, and put in a

sheep pen, which was quite clean and had not been used for years. He had a splinter in his head, which turned out to be a brass screw when he was operated on later. The other fellow, didn't have a scratch on him.

Collins provided hot Bovril for the U-boat survivors and a mattress for them to lie on. They were taken into Falmouth the following day, but not before the *Baralong* had been met by a trawler with two interrogators on board.

Because there were no neutral witnesses to this incident, and Crompton and Godau were prisoners of war, it was not mentioned when the news broke in America of the muleteers' accounts of the shooting of German submariners in the *Nicosian*. Some stories were exaggerated to the point of claiming that the marines had thrown the Germans alive into the stokehold furnaces. As the muleteers were not on board during the clearing operation, they could not possibly have known whether this was true. The story was picked up with relish by the German Embassy in Washington and exploited to its full in the battle for American public opinion by depicting the British as worse than the Germans.

The Germans demanded that the captain and crew of the *Baralong* be brought to trial by an international court. The British Foreign Secretary, Grey, riposted with a note in which he said that the British government might agree to the *Baralong*'s officers being brought before an impartial court composed of officers of the United States Navy, if German officers who had been involved in two massacres at sea were brought before the same court. The first incident Grey mentioned was the shooting of Layton's crew of E13 in neutral waters off Denmark, coincidentally on the same day as the *Baralong* shootings in the *Nicosian*. The second was the shooting of survivors of the steamer *Ruel*, by the captain and crew of a U-boat. The massacre was halted only by the timely arrival of the armed trawler *Dewsland* and drifter *Campania*, forcing the submarine to dive and leave the area.

Before Grey's note arrived, the German Chancellor, Bethmann Hollweg, made a speech to the Reichstag on 8 December, which included the pious passage, 'Where the hatred for Germany leads to we have seen with a shudder in the case of the *Baralong*'. He apparently had not paused to think why Germany, which had wilfully caused the war with its resulting bloodshed, might be hated. When Grey's note arrived, the Socialist deputy Noske foamed that it was 'the most horrible exhibition of cynicism in diplomacy which we have experienced in this war'.[11] To which, given Germany's record to date, and what was yet to come, one is tempted to say, 'You ain't seen nothing yet.'

All this diplomatic manoeuvring aside, armed with such facts as we have, which are by no means complete and never will be, we can conclude that the actions of *Baralong*'s marines in shooting unarmed Germans who were probably trying to surrender was illegal under the rules of war pertaining at the time and now. In the calm of book-lined studies, far removed from the scene of action both in time and place; not having just survived a cat and mouse game with a U-boat; remote from the fear, uncertainty, adrenalin rushes, hate, aggression, and the blood-lust of action, we can pronounce that the shooting of the submariners was totally reprehensible. Although it has to be said that this was by no means the first time in history that troops trying to surrender, or even after having their surrender accepted, have been shot, neither was it the last such incident in the First World War, nor in any war since, up to the present day. Which of course does not excuse it.

After the *Baralong* affair, U-boat commanders were increasingly inclined to torpedo merchantmen without warning; even if they did not they were infinitely warier, which made the use of Q-ships less and less effective as time went on. But it took some time to take effect, and perhaps one of the most successful Q-ship attacks was by the *Farnborough* (Lieutenant-Commander Gordon Campbell RN), who sank U-68 on 23 March 1916. He reported to Vice-Admiral Bayly:

> at 6.40 am a submarine was observed awash almost five miles distant on the port bow. It remained in view a few minutes and then dived. I maintained my course and speed. About 7.0 am a torpedo was fired at the ship from the starboard quarter and the bubbles rose under the forecastle, the torpedo evidently passing just ahead of the ship [this might have been intended as a shot across the bows, but was more likely a miss]. I maintained my course and a few minutes later the submarine broke surface about 1,000 yards astern of the ship, passing from starboard to port. When on the port quarter he fired a shot across our bows and partly submerged. I stopped blew off steam and ordered the stokers and spare men under Engineer Sub-Lieutenant Smith to 'panic'.* The submarine closed to about 800 yards and a few minutes later fired a shell which fell about 50 yards short. I ordered 'open fire' and hoisted the White Ensign. Twenty-one rounds were fired from the three 12-pdr guns. About 200 rounds from the maxim and rifles were also fired. The shooting was good, especially observing the range and bad light – several hits being observed before the submarine slowly disappeared. I steamed at full speed over the

---

* 'Panic parties' were part of the drill for Q-ships: sailors in civilian clothes launched the boats in the hope that this would induce the U-boat to surface, expecting to sink the ship with her guns, whereupon she would be sunk with the Q-ship's disguised guns.

spot and dropped a depth charge. The submarine came up about ten yards off the ship in a nearly perpendicular position, being out of the water from the bow to abaft the conning tower; no number was visible but there was a large rent in her bow, and one periscope had apparently been hit. I opened fire again with the after gun which put five rounds into the base of the conning tower at nearly point-blank range, when she sank. I again went over the spot and let go two more depth charges, a very great quantity of oil etc. and bits of wood coming to the surface and covering the sea for a considerable distance.

Campbell drew attention to certain officers and men in his crew, including his first lieutenant, Beswick, as well as 'Petty Officer Dowie of the after gun who did good shooting. CPO (Pensioner) Truscott gunlayer of the Maxim, AB Webb gunlayer of the 12-pdr, which fired 13 rounds and did good shooting, and AB Kaye RNR, the first to sight and report the submarine'.

Admiral Bayly forwarded the report to the Admiralty:

[1.] I wish to make the following remarks.

2. The operation was exceedingly well carried out. Had the officers and men of FARNBOROUGH not been thoroughly well trained, had one of them made a mistake, this success would have been a serious failure. And a more difficult operation it would be hard to conceive. After being fired at with a torpedo the ship had to steam on so as to appear she had seen nothing in order to attract the submarine nearer, but knowing that at any moment another torpedo might be fired and successfully.

3. During the whole winter the FARNBOROUGH has faced the gales and has stuck to it, and never for a moment has Lieut Commander Campbell wavered in the faith that he would get a chance. I have had a good deal to do with the ship and have found the same spirit throughout, being largely fostered by Lieut Commander Campbell and his first Lieutenant, Lieut W Beswick RNR who is an excellent officer.

4. I strongly recommend Lieut Commander Campbell, Lieut Beswick RNR, and one Engineer Officer (all did well) for some distinction as being most thoroughly deserving and encouraging for others. I would also like to rate up two or three ratings, and I suggest that every man be given two or three days [extra] pay.

5. The ships here go on from day to day in all weathers, always hoping, always trying, and such encouragement as I suggest above would help them and help me.

Within a week the Admiralty replied. Campbell was promoted to commander and awarded the DSO, and Lieutenant Beswick and Engineer Lieutenant Loveless the DSC. CPO Truscott, Morrison (an RNR ERA), and Andrews the wireless operator were awarded the DSM. Four ratings were given a gratuity (for example CPO Truscott received £36), and three of them were advanced, the Royal Navy's term for lower-deck promotion. Their Lordships also approved the sum of £1,000 to be distributed to the ship's company of the *Farnborough* except to commissioned officers of the Royal Navy. Some examples of how Campbell distributed the 'prize' money are as follows, with each share worth £1 18s 7d (the basic daily pay for ratings ranged from 2s 8d for a chief petty officer to 1s 7d for an able seaman):

Beswick	20 shares	£38 11s 8d
Lovelace	20 shares	£38 11s 8d
Truscott	10 plus 5	£28 18s 9d
Andrews	10 shares	£19 5s 10d
Dowie	8 plus 3	£21 4s 5d
Morrison	10 shares	£19 5s 10d
Webb	6 plus 1	£13 10s 1d
Kaye	6 plus 1	£13 10s 1d

– there were seventy-four in the crew altogether.

Less than a month later, Campbell struck again. On 15 April 1916 he was steaming at 5 knots on a windless day with a heavy swell hoping to intercept a submarine reported off Orkney two days previously. At 6.30 p.m., having passed the armed trawler *Ina William* about an hour previously, he was within two miles of a ship on his starboard quarter, but because of mist and calm he could not identify her colours, which drooped against the ensign staff. Then:

> A submarine broke surface between us; I took no notice until she hoisted a signal which I could not read. I then stopped and blew off steam, but kept jogging [sic] ahead to hedge in [sic] and avoid falling [broadside] into the trough of the heavy swell. At this time the submarine was lying full length on the surface with no one visible but two guns on deck.
>
> In addition to having my answering pendant at the dip [= I don't know what I am supposed to do], I hoisted 'cannot understand your signal'. She closed me and manned the foremost gun. In the meantime I turned out the bridge boat and gave my papers to Engineer Sub Lieutenant Smith RNR to take over to the submarine.

All these actions were intended to reassure the watching U-boat CO that Campbell was about to obey his instructions and to lure him in – Smith would not have boarded the U-boat. Campbell continues:

At this time, 6.40, he fired a shot which passed over the ship. Unfortunately one of my guns' crew, thinking she had fired [at us], opened fire. This forced my hand and I at once gave the general order to open fire, the range being about 900 to 1,000 yards. At the same time I proceeded full steam ahead to bring the after gun to bear. Altogether 20 rounds were fired from the 12 pounders, six from the 6 pounders, and 200 from the maxim and rifles. Of these I consider there were three good hits, four good shorts which might have ricocheted and only two shots missed over.

I think the submarine was damaged early in the action, as she lay with her bow submerged and stern upwards for a good five minutes. I judge that the last two shots hit either the conning tower or just forward of it – there appeared to be an explosion on board when she suddenly sank, making a great commotion on the water, and there was a cloud of dense steam and vapour on the surface for some minutes. Two of my gunlayers said they saw her heel over.

I proceeded at once to the spot and dropped two depth charges but saw no oil on the surface. As the depth of water was 81 fathoms [486 feet] and the submarine probably sank straight to the bottom this would not appear unnatural.

Campbell closed the steamer and found her to be the Dutch *Soerakarta* of Rotterdam. The *Ina William* had now closed the *Farnborough*, having heard her depth charges, and Campbell ordered to send a party to board the Dutchman.

Campbell was lucky, if we are to believe the report given to him by the master of the *Soerakarta*, and forwarded with his to Vice-Admiral Bayly:

At about 6.15 pm we met a German submarine which put up the signal TAF (bring your papers aboard). We lowered down the boat but at the same moment the submarine sent off a torpedo bound for the English ship which was in the neighbourhood, but missed her. The English ship began to fire and several on board, including me, saw the second shot strike the submarine in the midships which sank down immediately sinking stem upwards.

Another kill was approved, and again £1,000 was awarded for distribution round the ship's company of the *Farnborough*, as well as a DSC for one officer to be nominated, and three more DSMs.

The careers of two principal characters in this chapter touched on 29 January 1917. Herbert was appointed CO of K13, one of the huge K-class boats, which were three times as heavy as the E boats, and nearly twice as long. They were steam-driven on the surface, with an auxiliary diesel to drive a dynamo and provide power immediately after surfacing while the steam plant was being flashed up. They could achieve 24 knots on the surface, but only 9 knots dived (the same as the E-class). They were a remarkable technical achievement, unmatched by any other country at the time, but were also among the most dangerous to their crews. Like many dual-purpose weapon systems, in this case boats that were devised to operate with the fleet like destroyers on the surface, yet have the characteristics of submarines when dived, the design contained flaws, which gave them a reputation for bad luck. The K boats had funnels and watertight hatches that could be closed in thirty seconds, but small obstructions could jam these open.

When Herbert took K13 for a trial dive in the Gareloch, he had on board, in addition to his crew of fifty-five, eleven Admiralty officials, fourteen dockyard workers, and Goodhart, fresh from Russia, now the CO of K14. On this, her last practice dive, some hatches or inlets were not closed properly, and K13 hit the bottom at fifty-five feet, with her bows up. The rescue was slow and inefficient, and the forty-seven survivors in the remaining unflooded parts of the boat determined to try to get someone out to help direct the rescue. Herbert and Goodhart decided that the latter would exit through the hatch into the flooded conning tower and up to the surface, the pressure in the boat being greater than that outside at that depth. Goodhart shot up, but Herbert could not close the hatch behind him, and was sucked out too.

Herbert reached the surface, but not Goodhart. Herbert proceeded to take charge of the rescue, and thanks to his efforts, some fifty-five hours after her last dive, forty-six survivors climbed through a hole cut in the boat's bows which had been lifted clear of the water by a salvage vessel. There were thirty-three bodies in the hull, and Goodhart's in the bridge, having smashed his head on an obstruction. Goodhart was posthumously awarded the Albert Gold Medal.

During the period leading up to the Battle of Jutland, and for some months afterwards, the changing rules under which the U-boats operated militated against their being used to full effect, and really hurting the British. All this was to change in 1917.

6

War against Turkey, 1914–1915

On 5 November 1914, a court martial assembled on board the old battleship *Bulwark* at Portland to try Rear Admiral Ernest Troubridge, second-in-command of the Mediterranean Fleet. The charge: that Troubridge did 'from negligence or through other default, forbear to pursue the chase of His Imperial German Majesty's ship *Goeben*, being an enemy then flying'. If many of his naval contemporaries had had their way, he would have been arraigned on the far more serious charge of cowardice.

As Europe headed for war in late July and early August 1914 the maritime situation in the Mediterranean was uncertain. Britain had concentrated most of her naval strength in the North Sea, and planned on handing over responsibility for the Mediterranean to the French. The Austro-Hungarian Habsburg Empire seemed about to enter the war against Britain and France, but was not yet committed. Today both Austria and Hungary are landlocked countries, but in 1914 the Habsburg Empire could muster a fleet in the Adriatic consisting of three modern *Tegetthoff*-class dreadnoughts, each with twelve 12-inch and twelve 5.9-inch guns, and three *Radetzky*-class semi-dreadnoughts with four 12-inch and eight 9.4-inch guns, two heavy cruisers, and twelve destroyers, as well as around twenty-five torpedo boats, a couple of light cruisers, and five submarines.

For some years Germany had provided advisers to assist in modernizing the Turkish army, and had made concerted diplomatic efforts to woo the Turks. The Turks looked to the British for naval advice, and Rear Admiral Arthur Limpus headed the Royal Navy mission in Constantinople. Two battleships, the *Sultan Osman* and *Reshadieh*, were being built in British yards for Turkey. The crews to take them over had arrived in Britain. The funds to pay for them had been raised by public subscription in Turkey; women had even sold their hair in the cause of modernizing their navy. At the outbreak of war, Turkey's neutrality wobbled in the balance.

Italy, with some 165 vessels, including three dreadnoughts, seven pre-dreadnoughts, seven armoured cruisers, fourteen other cruisers, thirty-three destroyers, numerous torpedo boats, and twenty-one submarines, was a member of the Triple Alliance with Germany and Austria-Hungary. On 2 August Italy declared her neutrality, thus removing the threat of a Triple Alliance naval force superior to the combined French and British squadrons in the Mediterranean. However, her intentions cannot have been all that clear since on 3 August Troubridge signalled his C-in-C, saying, 'In view of uncertain attitude of Italy, I am not going with the heavy ships through the straits of Messina'.

The British Commander-in-Chief Mediterranean was Admiral Sir Archibald Berkeley Milne. 'Sir Archie Berkie' or 'the Great Arch Bark', as he was known in the navy, was a pompous officer, lacking intellect, who owed his appointment to court influence, and would not have seemed out of place in a Gilbert and Sullivan operetta. Six days before Anglo-German hostilities began, the Admiralty told Milne that his prime concern was to assist the French in shipping their African army from Algeria to France, by shadowing German warships in the Mediterranean and thus preventing them interdicting the French troop convoys. The Admiralty instruction mentioned the possibility of engaging individual German warships, but included the words 'do not at this stage be brought to action against superior forces, except in conjunction with the French as part of a general battle'. This Admiralty 'back-seat driving' might have been ignored by an officer with drive and initiative in his make-up, but not by one of the calibre of Berkeley Milne. It was to lead to a humiliating episode.

Milne had under command the 2nd Battle Cruiser Squadron, consisting of the *Inflexible* (flag), *Indefatigable*, and *Indomitable*; Rear Admiral Troubridge's 1st Cruiser Squadron of heavy armoured cruisers, *Defence* (flag), *Warrior*, *Black Prince*, and *Duke of Edinburgh*; and four light cruisers and sixteen destroyers available to be deployed independently or with either squadron as required.

The most serious threat to the French convoys was the modern battle cruiser *Goeben* and the light cruiser *Breslau*, under command of Rear Admiral Wilhelm Souchon. The *Goeben* was superior to any individual British battle cruiser in the Mediterranean, but Milne had a force that if concentrated vastly exceeded the Germans'.

The action can be followed in the wireless signal log of the *Defence*, Troubridge's flagship (timings are local Mediterranean). Of course this log does not include all signals exchanged between all British warships in the Mediterranean, or those between Milne and the Admiralty. The *Defence*'s wireless signal log also reveals the extent to which concerns about where to obtain coal was a constant theme even at the busiest moments (the subject is mentioned nineteen times in just four days). Compared with most navies today, who replenish underway, the endurance and hence radius of action of early twentieth-century warships was severely restricted by the need to restock with coal in harbours, or rendezvous with colliers in some sheltered spot.

On 3 August, Milne sent Troubridge to the south of the Adriatic to join destroyers already positioned there. The battle cruisers were sent west, and later that day *Indomitable* and *Indefatigable* were detached to make for Gibraltar to prevent *Goeben* leaving the Mediterranean.

That day, Churchill decided to requisition the two Turkish battleships, having learned the day before that the Turkish government, having signed a treaty of alliance with Germany against Russia, had offered to send the *Sultan Osman* to a German port. The fact that Churchill was probably right to take this step does nothing to ameliorate the fact that it was one of the critical steps towards war between Britain and Turkey. The ships became the *Agincourt* and the *Erin*.

At 9.50 a.m. on 4 August, Milne signalled Troubridge: 'The Germans bombarded Oran at 0600 today. Italy doubtful. Keep out of sight of Italian coast'. This was followed at 11.25 by *Indomitable* informing Milne and Troubridge 'enemy in sight position 37.44 N, 7.56 E. Enemy consists of *Goeben* and *Breslau*'. The Germans on their passage east after bombarding Bône and Philippeville on the Algerian coast had encountered the two battle cruisers heading west. Britain was not yet at war with Germany, and the British battle cruisers had to be content with wheeling around and following. Souchon drew ahead of them by dint of piling on speed, and headed for Messina to coal. British warships on overseas stations were still on peacetime manning; the *Indomitable*, for example, was short of ninety stokers, and had insufficient men in the stokehold to maintain full speed for protracted periods.[1]

Towards evening on 4 August there was still uncertainty about who was going to war with whom. Milne informed Troubridge that 'war will be declared 1.0 am' (midnight GMT); Troubridge asked 'Against what powers?' Back came Milne half an hour later with his orders including:

> Ultimatum to Germany expires at midnight GMT. Flagship will join battle cruisers to the Westward picking up *Chatham* & *Weymouth* on the way. 1st CS & *Gloucester* remain watching at the entrance Adriatic and are not to get seriously engaged with superior forces.

The signal continued by telling Troubridge:

> *Gloucester* or other vessel is to be sent to watch south entrance straits of Messina. *Goeben* [and] *Breslau* were 40 miles West of Martino [Marretimo, west of Sicily] at 5.0 pm steering to the eastward, have been followed at

full speed by *Indomitable* & *Indefatigable*. At present there is no declaration of war against Austria.

That day, Souchon was informed that Germany had concluded an alliance with Turkey, and was ordered to take his squadron to Constantinople (Istanbul), although the Allies were not to know this yet. At 6.12 a.m. on 5 August, Troubridge signalled his captains:

> In event *Goeben* coming through Messina and entering Adriatic the squadron will give him battle. But as the *Goeben*'s guns outrange our guns at least 4,000 yards, I shall endeavour to retreat at full speed to a position just inside Paxos Island [now Paxoi, south of Corfu] where I would endeavour to fight at a range that permits of our gun fire being effective. I do not know if *Goeben* has passed Messina but it is possible.

That same morning, Milne anxiously signalled Troubridge and the *Gloucester*, 'yesterday *Goeben* and *Breslau* steamed 26 knots. Warn *Gloucester*'. This was faster than *Gloucester*'s designed speed and that of Milne's battle cruisers. In fact this speed was exaggerated, but unfortunately the notion became fixed in Milne's mind that *Goeben* and *Breslau* could outrun and outmanoeuvre his ships. By mid-afternoon on 5 August it appeared from intercepted wireless traffic and other sources that Souchon's squadron was passing through the Straits of Messina. At about the same time, the Admiralty informed Milne by signal, 'Austria has not yet declared war on France and England. Continue watching Adriatic for double purpose of preventing Austrians from emerging & Germans entering'.

At 4.54 p.m., Troubridge told his squadron:

> There is a possibility of *Goeben* and *Breslau* being off Cape Calonna [Colonna, on the ball of Italy's foot] at about 11 o'clock making their way to the Adriatic. I have decided to try to cut off if information proves reliable fighting a night action with the aid of the moon.

At this stage Troubridge was about thirty miles off Capo Santa Maria di Leuca, on the heel of Italy, and had ordered any destroyers with enough coal to make the return trip to Malta to join him there by two o'clock the next morning. However, the next morning information was passed from the Admiralty and Consul-General Messina that *Goeben* and *Breslau* were still at Messina. That evening there was definite news. Troubridge told his destroyer leader in the *Wolverine*:

> *Goeben* left Messina 6 pm steering East probably *Breslau* also. Be under way concealed in Vasilico Bay [Zante, on the west coast of Greece] by midnight with steam for full speed.

A little later he told the remainder of his squadron 'ships are to be at night action stations tonight'.

When Souchon left Messina, Milne with the battle cruisers was well to the west, and Troubridge to the north-east. Milne, respecting Italian neutrality, did not follow Souchon through the straits with his battle cruisers, as a more thrusting admiral might have. Only the light cruiser *Gloucester* (Captain Howard Kelly) was close, and he kept both Milne and Troubridge informed of *Goeben*'s course and speed. Troubridge sent a general signal to Milne and his own squadron which included his proposed tactics:

> It would appear that *Goeben* & possibly *Breslau* are making for the Adriatic. I do not propose to engage him in the middle of the straits, my instructions being against it. If *Goeben* wishes to fight, I shall endeavour to use shoal water off [indecipherable] island to choose my own range.

Troubridge was patrolling off Cephalonia, south of Corfu, well positioned to intercept Souchon if, as the former confidently expected, he headed for the main Austrian naval base, Pola (Pula in Slovenia). At 10.08 p.m. and 10.25 p.m. *Gloucester* sent two signals to Troubridge and Milne telling them that *Goeben* had altered course to the southward and had increased speed, while *Breslau* had split away. This was confirmed when the light cruiser *Dublin* (Captain John Kelly), was on the way to join Troubridge with two destroyers, intercepted Souchon's wireless traffic.

From Messina, Souchon had feinted towards the Adriatic, before turning east, and then south. But Troubridge, thinking that Souchon's alteration to the southward was a feint, continued to steam north to engage him off Corfu. Howard Kelly in *Gloucester* clung to *Goeben*'s coattails, and was told to signal the enemy position to his brother in *Dublin*. It seemed that the *Dublin* might intercept *Goeben*, and John Kelly signalled 'expect to meet both enemy cruisers about 1.0 am at 37° 55'N 14° 18'E. [sic]' But in the darkness, *Goeben* slipped by. Troubridge continued north until just past midnight on 6/7 August, although Milne knew by 10.30 p.m. the night before that Souchon was going south.

Early the next morning *Dublin* re-established visual contact with the enemy, and she reported that *Breslau* had rejoined *Goeben*. The *Gloucester* joined *Dublin* and together they shadowed the enemy. At 2.10 a.m. Troubridge, now heading south to cut Souchon's track, signalled to his squadron:

> I am endeavouring to cross the bows of *Goeben* by 6.0 am & intend to engage her if possible. Be prepared to form on a line of bearing turning

into line ahead as required. If we have not cut him off I may retire behind Zante to avoid a long range action.

A few minutes later, Troubridge's destroyers told him they were on the way to rendezvous with him at about 4 a.m., and *Gloucester* told him that *Goeben* had reduced speed to 17 knots. At this stage, Troubridge's flag captain, the gunnery expert Fawcet Wray, twice suggested to him that he was taking an enormous risk. Deploying technical arguments he contrived to persuade Troubridge, no weapons expert, that his four cruisers with a total of twenty-two 9.2-inch, fourteen 7.5-inch, and sixteen 6-inch guns would be destroyed by *Goeben*'s ten 11-inch and ten 6-inch guns before they could get into range.

Against his instincts, Troubridge, a brave and respected leader, ignominiously abandoned his attempt to intercept Souchon while still 67 miles away. Fawcet Wray, an exemplar of the precept 'the definition of an expert is a drip under pressure', was fulsome in his praise for his admiral's decision. At 3.33 a.m., Troubridge signalled *Gloucester* and *Dublin*, 'Am obliged to give up the chase'. At 3.49 a.m. he told Milne:

> Being only able to meet *Goeben* outside the range of our guns & and inside his I have abandoned the chase with my squadron. Request instructions for light cruisers. *Goeben* evidently going to Eastern Mediterranean. I had hoped to meet her before daylight.

Milne, instead of sending the *Indomitable*, who had almost full bunkers, hot-foot in pursuit to the east, dallied at Malta while his whole squadron replenished with fuel. He then wasted precious time heading for the Adriatic, in response to a muddled signal from the Admiralty incorrectly stating that war with Austria had been declared, some six days before the event. The *Gloucester* and *Dublin* continued to shadow the Germans, and the former engaged *Breslau*, but had to break off the action because her bunkers were nearly empty. At 12.20 p.m. on 7 August, *Dublin* signalled Milne, '*Goeben* has passed to W/T station at Athens a coded message to Constantinople & signed *Goeben*'. This was perhaps the first intimation of Souchon's destination, but not heeded because for a while Milne continued to believe that Souchon might return if Austria declared war on Italy, or raid Alexandria or threaten the Suez Canal.

Souchon was allowed some sixty hours unmolested while he coaled in the Greek Aegean Islands. When the intensity of wireless traffic to his south indicated the approach of the British, he headed for the Dardanelles. *Goeben* and *Breslau* passed through the narrows in the Dardanelles at 5 p.m. on 10 August, while Milne and his battle cruisers were still vainly patrolling east of the Peloponnese, some 350 miles astern.

How different from a similar situation twenty-five years later, in the early months of the Second World War, when Commodore Harwood with one 8-inch gun cruiser and two light cruisers engaged the 11-inch gun pocket battleship *Graf Spee*, forcing her to run with her tail between her legs into the River Plate where she was scuttled by her captain.[2] But by then the Royal Navy had made much progress towards relearning the methods of initiative and the flexible tactics practised by Nelson and his captains, of whom Troubridge's ancestor, Thomas, had been one of the most brilliant.[3]

Fisher, at this stage still unemployed, but soon to be brought back as First Sea Lord, exploded in a letter dated 26 August 1914, addressed to 'My beloved Friend', whose identity remains a mystery:

> Had I been First Sea Lord I should have shot the British Admirals (shot a la Byng as I think a Court Martial is so tedious and dirty evasion of responsibility!). However that's a minor point so I forgive him for it.

Having fired a verbal salvo at Beresford, whom he loathed, Fisher continued in characteristic style with much underlining:

> German cruisers are fleeing for their lives & ought to be at the bottom of the sea but for two British Admirals who being Court sycophants get employed – D—m 'em! (I suppose the hereditary 'snob' in Winston over came him – a taint of Marlborough!)
>
> However bless you. We are going to come out on top! Buy the weekly 'Sketch' of Aug 12 – It's splendid on Jellicoe – do read it! It was sent by an American Beauty with £4,500 a year, she won't marry!
>
> Yours till the Angels smile on us.
>
> Fisher

Admiral Troubridge was acquitted at his court martial, but neither he nor Milne was ever employed at sea again. The episode revealed the low quality of staff work at the Admiralty, not helped by the dominant figure of Churchill, who relentlessly interfered, cajoled, and bullied. The Admiralty was the repository of nearly all intelligence on enemy movements, so quite properly passed on information to flag officers and private ships in order to bring them to action with the enemy. But as we have seen, the Admiralty too often followed up by meddling in what was strictly the tactical and operational business of the commander on the spot, compounding the error by sending contradictory and confusing supplementary signals.

The Turkish government fended off French and British protests that

Gallipoli, Anzac beach from seaward. [Q 13826]

The battleship *Albion* on 23 May 1915, aground off Gaba Tepe and under fire from Turkish guns. The recoil of her own guns and towing by the *Canopus* eventually freed her. [Q 13808]

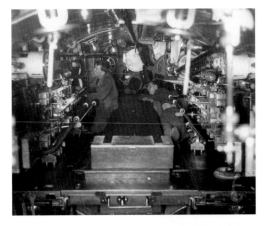

The motor controls in an E-class submarine. There are at least three men sleeping in this compartment, and one on watch on his knees because the deckhead is so low. [Q 18952]

Looking through the periscope in an E-class submarine. [Q 18651]

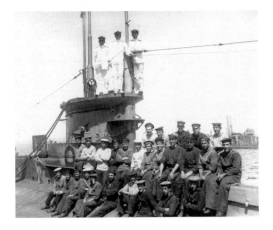

Lieutenant Commander Nasmith with his officers, and (below them) the crew of E11 alongside the depot ship at Mudros. [Q 13260]

Above. British submarine
E7, photographed off
Portsmouth. Lieutenant
Commander Archibald
Cochrane took this boat
through the Dardanelles in
1915. Her first lieutenant
was Oswald Hallifax.
[Q 22911]

Right. Vice Admiral
de Robeck. Taken
some time after the
Gallipoli campaign.
[Q 19511]

Above. Commander Samson in an Henri Farman in the Dardanelles. [HU 67870]

Left. Hoisting out a seaplane from a seaplane carrier. [HU 66635]

Below. Torpedo dropped from a seaplane. [Q 27453]

Above. Northern Patrol: the banana boat HMS *Changuinola* in dazzle paint. [SP 2036]

Right. Q-ship *Lothbury* with deck-house roof raised and sides collapsed ready to fire her after gun. [SP 2865]

Below. Lothbury dazzle-painted with a false deck house on her stern to conceal the gun. [SP 2861]

Above. Commodore First Class Goodenough, who commanded the 2nd Light Cruiser Squadron at Jutland. [Q 19511]

Right. Admiral Sir David Beatty, then C-in-C Grand Fleet, talks to King George V on the quarterdeck of the *Queen Elizabeth* at Scapa in June 1917. Beatty casually addresses his monarch: as well as hands in pockets, he is wearing a non-regulation six-buttoned jacket and cap askew. [Q 22944]

Below. The wreck of the *Invincible* at Jutland. [SP 2470]

HMS *Warspite* in dock after the Battle of Jutland, showing damage to one of her after turrets. The dockyard mateys lounging on deck give a good indication of the size of her 15-inch guns. [SP 3158]

Dropping depth charges. [Q 18853]

Left. An 'ace' Q-ship commander, Captain Campbell VC.
[Q 188803]

Right. An ERA (seated) and a seaman on a paravane.
[Q 83897]

Below. Airship over a convoy. [HU 67885]

in sheltering the *Goeben* and *Breslau* they were thereby breaching their neutrality, by claiming that these ships were substitutes for the two battleships, the *Sultan Osman* and *Reshadieh*. The Germans made a big play of 'selling' the *Goeben* and *Breslau* to the Turks, although the deal was fictitious. The ships were renamed the *Jawus Sultan Selim* and the *Midilli*. Souchon later became chief of the Turkish fleet with the gob-stopping title of Befelshaber der schwimmenden Türkischen Streitkräfte.

The arrival of *Goeben* and *Breslau* in Constantinople had two conse-quences. First it damaged morale in Britain and in the navy. The *Goeben* fiasco, together with other set-backs already covered in Chapters 2 and 3, brought about a growing and unpleasant realization throughout the country that 'the navy was not commanding the seas with the thoroughness that all Englishmen had been brought up to expect'.[4]

More serious, and with consequences that are still with us, the arrival of the German squadron was another major step in persuading Turkey to enter the war on the side of the Central Powers in November 1914. This led to the disastrous Dardanelles campaign. The closure of the Straits to shipping also led to the physical isolation of Russia from France and Britain. Russia's bitter defeat and withdrawal from the war was accompanied by revolution, attended by the gruesome Lenin, and the even worse Stalin. What followed affected not only Russia, but vast areas of the globe and still does today. This also holds true of events in the aftermath of the collapse of the Ottoman Empire and its post-war dismemberment. The resulting instability and incipient war and vio-lence in the Middle East has continued for nearly a century with no signs of abating. It is possible to argue that had *Goeben* been sunk or prevented from reaching Turkey, the world would now be a very different place.

For almost three months after the escape of the *Goeben* and *Breslau*, the British attempted to keep the Turks neutral. But at the end of October, Admiral Souchon took his ships with a Turkish squadron and bombarded Russian ports in the Black Sea. On 31 October, after the expiry of an Entente ultimatum, Churchill ordered the commander of the Dardanelles Squadron, Vice-Admiral Sackville Carden, to commence hostilities against Turkey. He bombarded the forts at the outer end of the Dardanelles, giving the Turks notice of future attacks at this very spot.

*

The war with Turkey forced the British to radically modify their pre-war policy of handing over responsibility for the Mediterranean to the French while they concentrated on the North Sea. Turkey's entry also resulted in four campaigns: in Egypt and Palestine, the Dardanelles, Mesopotamia (present-day Iraq), and Macedonia. Turkish naval power was negligible, but she had a powerful army which was able to threaten the Suez Canal and Britain's oil supplies in the Persian Gulf.

Eventually Turkish efforts to seize and block the Suez Canal, culminating in an attack from the Sinai Desert on 3 February 1915, failed. But until the Turks were pushed out of the Sinai at the end of 1916, the Royal Navy and troops from the British army and Indian Army were kept busy defending this vital waterway. Ships were also deployed in the southern approaches to the Suez Canal, in the Gulf of Suez, the Red Sea and the Gulf of Aqaba. The squadron deployed in these waters included the cruiser *Minerva* (nine 6-inch guns, plus secondary armament), whose gunnery officer was Lieutenant Bruce Fraser – thirty-one years later, Admiral of the Fleet Lord Fraser of North Cape. One of her midshipmen was the seventeen-year-old Maurice Parkes-Buchanan, who like all midshipmen was required to keep a journal, in which he recorded each day's events as well as signals sent and received by *Minerva*.

Just before the outbreak of hostilities with Turkey, the *Minerva* was ordered to Aqaba to join the coal-fired turbine-driven 27-knot *Beagle*-class destroyers *Savage* and *Scourge*. As soon as hostilities began, *Savage* signalled *Minerva*, 'Anchored off Akabar [sic]. Have destroyed Post Office and am negotiating for surrender of town', followed later by, 'Have landed a patrol to stop camels and stragglers to northward of town'. The destroyer *Foxhound*, south of Aqaba, chipped in with, 'There are three Bedouins driving a very large flock of sheep or goats along the road towards Akabar, also three or four men with camels'.

The opéra bouffe atmosphere continued well after the *Minerva*'s arrival, when it appeared that the town was not about to surrender, and even a few rounds of 6-inch did nothing to change the seeming indifference of the garrison to the arrival of the three warships. In fact, as the officer commanding the Royal Marines detachment in *Minerva* discovered much later, the Turkish garrison of about a hundred men had fled inland at the ships' arrival. *Minerva* operated with the destroyers off Aqaba until late January, returning to Suez from time to time to refuel and re-provision. Each time she departed, the garrison reoccupied the town, which Parkes-Buchanan describes as 'chiefly composed of mud hovels at the head of the Gulf of Akabar'. Although the Royal Navy continued to operate off Aqaba for the next two and a half years, the town was not cleared and held permanently until Lawrence and the Arabs captured it on 6 July 1917.

Extracts from Parkes-Buchanan's journal give a flavour of the operations by *Minerva*.

Monday Nov 2nd [1914]

At about 5.30 am the Commander went ashore under the White Flag to negotiate for surrender after yesterday's bombardment, but having seen nobody, returned to the ship. The hands were sent to breakfast, after which a landing party was prepared.

The landing party found two cases of rifles, and destroyed the empty barracks. The destroyers *Mosquito* and *Foxhound* relieved the *Savage* and *Scourge*, bringing with them a Captain Barlow of the Egyptian army. He suggested a sweep to a wadi north of the town, to which the Turkish garrison might have retired to establish telegraphic communications with their headquarters at Maan. The sweep operation was duly mounted the next day, and successfully located the enemy, but that was all. After a brisk exchange of fire, the landing party withdrew to the ship. Some desultory patrolling took place over the next few days, and time was spent blowing charges in the water to produce fish for the ship's company's supper.

On 9 December, on *Minerva*'s return from a trip to Suez, a seaplane reconnaissance of Aqaba was carried out. Parkes-Buchanan:

She 'taxied' [sic] along the surface for some distance and then attempted to rise, making a series of leaps. At last she made one last effort and flew about 15 yards just above the surface of the water; she then came down somewhat violently and broke one of the body stays. The whaler pulled away to her and towed her back, she was hoisted in, and the damage repaired. The pilot informed us that the reason why he could not rise was that he had too much petrol on board, also his rifle and ammunition made the machine too heavy.

Again at noon the plane was hoisted out and made another flight, which was more successful, though she was unable to climb the necessary height for clearing the hills. After reaching a height of over a thousand feet, the pilot brought her down and returned to the ship as he still had too much petrol. The seaplane was hoisted in and more petrol taken out, but by then it was too late to make another attempt.

On 24 December, after two more visits to Suez, and more abortive sorties by the seaplane, the *Minerva* was shelled from the shore by a 12pdr but to no effect. *Minerva*'s return fire was equally ineffectual. More desultory patrols and flights followed, until the marine detachment ran into a Turkish defensive position while on patrol in the vicinity of Aqaba. One private was killed and the captain of marines severely wounded. The seaplane made a forced landing, but the observer was recovered after dark, having walked several miles to the coast and evaded capture. The next day the pilot was picked up from the beach, exhausted but alive.

By 25 January 1915, after more visits to Aqaba and another landing at Tor, a small port in the Gulf of Suez near the southern extremity of the Sinai Peninsula, *Minerva* was recalled to Suez as the Turkish threat to the Canal intensified. It is hard to judge what effect the activities of *Minerva* and other warships, and their 'pinprick' landing operations, had on the operational situation in the Gulf of Aqaba and southern Sinai. Clearly, the Turks reinforced the Aqaba garrison, because Parkes-Buchanan's journal mentions the presence of cavalry and increased enemy activity, which might indicate Turkish fears that an invasion somewhere in the locality was a possibility, but in fact the British had no plans to capture and hold Aqaba until the Arab Revolt in mid-1916 was followed by a British advance east across the Sinai later that year.

The somewhat amateurish British operations ashore in the Gulf of Aqaba reveal the state of amphibious warfare in the Royal Navy by 1914; an art neglected since the successful opposed landing against the French at Aboukir in 1801, so all the lessons learned by the end of the Napoleonic Wars had been forgotten. This negligence was to be paid for with men's lives at Gallipoli.

Meanwhile the *Minerva* was ordered to take up station in the Great Bitter Lake at the southern end of the Suez Canal,

> ready to engage with our port battery. We eventually secured at 4.30 pm and the hands were there employed shifting sandbags and iron plating from the starboard to the port side. It was anticipated the Turks would attack tonight.

The Turkish attacks were to the north and south of the Bitter Lakes, which made tactical sense since these are the widest parts of the canal. *Minerva*'s only contribution to the battle was to fire on a patrol of Bengal Lancers. The Turkish columns were spotted by air reconnaissance and their attacks broken up by shell fire from British and French ships, and Egyptian army artillery. The remnants were repulsed by the stout defence put up mainly by Gurkhas and Indian troops. The Turks lost about 2,000 men to some 30 Allied casualties.

The *Minerva* took part in one more amphibious operation before leaving the Gulf of Suez. She landed four companies of the 2/7th Gurkha Rifles, who carried out a night march to surprise a Turkish force about to attack the garrison at Tor. For the loss of one dead and one wounded, the Gurkhas killed about 75 and took 109 prisoners, several of whom were wounded. On 25 February, the *Minerva* set out for Lemnos and the Dardanelles.

*

Space does not permit a detailed examination of the events leading to the decision to force the passage through the Dardanelles by naval attack alone. Suffice it to say that the moving force behind the decision was Winston Churchill, despite opposition by Fisher. However, moves were made to involve troops, if only to occupy the forts as the ships passed through. To this end a base was established at Lemnos around the large natural harbour of Mudros. The Royal Naval Division (which included a Royal Marine Brigade) was sent out to the Aegean. The Australian & New Zealand Army Corps (ANZAC), based in Egypt, was warned for a move to Lemnos. The British 29th Division, a superb regular formation based in England, was also alerted, and then stood down by Kitchener.

The Turkish defences against naval attack were formidable. Between the entrance to the straits and the Sea of Marmara were fourteen old forts, mounting large guns, some 9.4-inch, some 14-inch, and many 4-inch and 6-inch. Six of these forts dominated the Narrows, less than a mile wide. Although some of the guns were obsolescent, they were capable of inflicting severe damage on ships at short range, which because of navigational limitations would never be more than 5,000 yards. In between the forts batteries of howitzers had been dug in, but could be moved to prepared alternative positions. Most were sited so that they were in dead ground to warships in the straits. Although these howitzers could not sink battleships, they could cause considerable damage to upperworks, and kill and wound men in exposed positions. They were a major threat to the minesweepers required to clear the minefield laid from a point six miles short of the Narrows to the Narrows itself. A minefield is not an obstacle unless it is covered by fire, otherwise it can be cleared easily with little risk. Here the minefields were covered by heavy fire. Because of the mines, the battleships could not close the forts to destroy them, but until they had done so, the minesweepers could not clear the mines. Lacking minesweepers, the Royal Navy requisitioned fishing trawlers with their crews. With sweeps out, steaming against the constant strong current flowing south, the trawlers could make 3 knots if they were lucky, and were sitting targets for the howitzers. Eventually the civilian crews lost their nerve, turned tail, and fled. They were replaced by seamen from the fleet.

Carden's plan for forcing the Dardanelles was divided into phases: battleships would destroy the outer defences, if necessary by landing demolition parties; the minefields would be swept and the forts commanding the Narrows destroyed; then the fleet would enter the Sea of Marmara and head for Constantinople. On arrival, the Turks, overawed by the combined might of the Royal Navy and French Navy, would panic and sue for peace – that was the theory.

On 19 February 1915, Admiral Carden started his attack with a bombardment of Sedd-el-Bahr and Kum Kale, with the pre-dreadnought battleships *Agamemnon*, *Vengeance*, *Triumph*, and *Cornwallis*, the battle cruiser *Inflexible*, the cruiser *Amethyst*, destroyers, and three French battleships, *Bouvet*, *Gaulois*, and *Suffren*. The fire was not effective. The next attack, on 25 February, was more successful, partly because the following day parties of marines and seamen from the fleet landed to spike the surviving guns. There was little opposition, but this was to change.

Midshipman Williams in *Agamemnon* described the attack on the 25th in a letter to his mother:

It was not exactly a benefit this time and we had a very unpleasant ten minutes and at the time I would have given anything in the world to have been back at Portland. We were hit seven times in all, but were not badly damaged, and our casualties were quite light, 3 killed and 8 badly wounded. I was stationed in the conning tower and so had quite a good view. I found watching the enemy's guns fire and waiting fifteen seconds or so for the screech of the projectile coming over was a distinctly nerve-wracking experience, and I kept wondering if it would be the next one or the one after which would lay me out. I had to go for a stretcher party once and if any outsider had seen me streaking across the upper deck he might have mistaken me for a really good runner. I have come to the conclusion that only those who have been in action during the course of their lives know what real funk is. A little blood makes such an awful mess and I thanked heaven I was not a doctor, as a small fragment of a shell makes a ghastly wound.

The navy's obsession with paintwork had not abated, as Midshipman Denham, also in the *Agamemnon*, recorded:

Meanwhile, as our after [12-inch] turret was not closed up (only the starb 'nine-twos' being fired) I was strolling around recording enemy shots falling. The Commander was trying to get the disengaged side painted, but the men were not very willing and I cannot really blame them.[5]

On 26 February the howitzer batteries were shelled by ships from within the Straits, but they were well concealed in the hills, and moved when it became too hot to stay. An officer, probably the gunnery officer, from an unknown ship wrote to Lieutenant-Commander Acheson in the *Inflexible*:

These howitzer and field gun batteries of the enemy are the devil. You simply cannot see them & yesterday we were supposed to deal with them. The forenoon passed off very quietly but in the afternoon they started quite gently at first a few bricks at a time. I was sitting looking through my glasses – you know they are Zeiss spotting ones so my head is just below the level of the range finder hood – but I had the hood open; I had just seen a gun fire and was going to let fly at it & so called the range finder operator up to take a range, he had just got up when crack! and I picked myself up at the bottom & found myself alive also the operator!

A shell (about 4-inch) had landed bang on the hood to our right, it burst outside thank God but stove in the hood and smashed the range-finder & my glasses to pieces. It was a wonderful escape & except for the rangefinder operator being deaf (whether permanently or not I don't know) & for a few scratches on my face nobody was any the worse. But Gee! Patrick it was close enough.

Then we got annoyed and let fly 9.2 and 12-inch salvoes all over the country, this woke them up too & for about half an hour we had 100s all over us, none were hitting by the Grace of God, but the Aggie [Agamemnon] who of course must come and shove her nose into trouble got one, doing some damage I believe.

From 1 March, the batteries were bombarded most days. On 2 March, the battleships *Canopus*, *Swiftsure* (which had arrived the previous day), and *Cornwallis* bombarded Fort 8, which mounted seven guns, about eight miles from the entrance to the Dardanelles, on the Asiatic shore. Commander Kitson in the *Swiftsure*:

We never knew what damage we inflicted but tho we silenced this fort at the time – it was only for the time as there were certainly several guns firing from it a fortnight later when we were in its vicinity & from what we heard from other ships it was going strong again shortly afterwards.

We were hit on this day by a 6-inch howitzer shell which went thro the quarterdeck & burst in the wardroom – wrecking that place pretty severely – tho fortunately causing no casualties – everyone being at the time either below or behind armour. The *Canopus* had her main topmast shot away.

This was the beginning of a long series of similar experiences – which in the long run went to prove that it is almost impossible to knock out a fort from a ship – much less hit or put [it] out of action – at any rate without a large expenditure of ammunition & and the assistance of an aeroplane to locate the batteries or guns firstly & and then to assist by directing the fire of the attacking ships. We were a long time finding this out & paid for our experience.

On 4 March two companies of the RM Brigade (RN Division) were landed at Sedd-el-Bahr and Kum Kale to destroy the guns. Having achieved their aim at the cost of twenty-three dead, twenty-five wounded, and three missing, they withdrew. Provision had not been made to follow up these landings by the whole RM Brigade, and some five thousand Australians available on Lemnos, to establish a toehold. Consequently this sortie achieved nothing, except to alert the Turks to the prospect of more landings. By 25 March the one Turkish division on the whole Gallipoli peninsula had been reinforced by five more.

Day after day, ships bombarded the defences in the Narrows, but failed to neutralize the howitzers. Because the minefield prevented the warships from closing the forts, they had to engage them at ranges that were too great to do much damage to the forts. There was difficulty observing the fall of shot; overs sometimes fell in dead ground and out of sight of ships' spotters. Williams in the *Agamemnon* wrote in his journal:

6th March 1915
QE [*Queen Elizabeth*] firing from Gaba Tepe over land at forts around Chanak. *Ocean* and *Agamemnon* supporting her. We were fired on by concealed batteries but were not hit. Could not locate batteries but fired at observation parties.

7th March 1915
Weighed 11 am, followed by *Lord Nelson*. Went inside straits and bombarded forts 13 and 19, silencing both. Good show. Hit 5 or 6 times. Gun room wrecked no casualties.

He added in a letter to his mother:

It's very interesting out here but I'm pretty sure that the person who first talked about the glory of War hadn't done any fighting himself. It seems rather a poor game really, just killing each other. At present however I am longing for another scrap knowing perfectly well that when we do go into action again I shall wish myself back at Portland.
The illustrated papers are rather amusing and nothing like this place. I need hardly tell you that those mediaeval castles in the Illustrated London News are not at all like any self respecting fort.

Spotting from the air would eventually go a long way to assist bombarding ships. The first seaplane carrier, the converted merchant ship *Ark Royal*, had arrived at Tenedos in mid-February. But the six underpowered aircraft she carried were often unable to take off unless the weather and wind conditions were just right. On 19 February one of *Ark Royal*'s aircraft used wireless to adjust naval gunfire, but the wireless broke down. Subsequent attempts were unsuccessful because of the inexperience of both pilots and observers. All this was to change when Commander Samson arrived with his squadron in late March.

On 8 March, the brand-new 15-inch-gun super-dreadnought *Queen Elizabeth*, with *Vengeance* and *Irresistible* ahead and well out on each side and *Cornwallis* and *Canopus* astern and on either flank, attacked again. Midshipman Arthur Mallet, in the *Vengeance*, recorded in his private journal:

> The scheme was that QE [*Queen Elizabeth*] should bombard Chanak. The other four ships sit on [sic] any batteries which fired at QE. The scheme was not very successful on account of the mist hanging over Chanak.
>
> The *Irresistible* was the great scaremonger of the day. She was always reporting mines or submarines.
>
> 3.30   *Irresistible* hoisted 'Submarine' flag
> 3.35   *Irresistible* hauled down 'Submarine' flag.

Further attacks on 10 and 13 March resulted in the minesweepers reaching the edge of the minefield off Kephez Point. On both occasions they were forced back by heavy fire from howitzers. Morale in the fleet was sinking, and Carden, on the verge of a nervous breakdown, was ordered home. He was replaced by his second-in-command, Vice-Admiral John De Robeck, who on 18 March attacked, using the plan made by Carden. Midshipman Mallet explained how he saw the Scheme of Operations in his private journal:

> *Queen Elizabeth*, *Inflexible*, *Agamemnon* and *Lord Nelson*, these powerful ships were to take up position half a mile apart out of range of Chanak, and bombard forts 19, 20, 17, 13, 21 and 22.
>
> The four French ships and *Ocean*, *Irresistible*, *Albion* and *Vengeance* were to take four hour watches of going in fairly close and hammering certain forts should they find the fire too hot they were to circle round. *Triumph*, PG [*Prince George*], *Swiftsure* and *Majestic* were supporting ships.

The ships advanced in three lines. In the first line, *Queen Elizabeth* (flag), two pre-dreadnoughts, *Agamemnon* and *Lord Nelson*, and the battle cruiser *Inflexible* steamed in line abreast. In the second line, commanded by Admiral Guépratte, came the French pre-dreadnoughts *Charlemagne*, *Gaulois*, *Bouvet*, and *Suffren*. The third line consisted of four British pre-dreadnoughts, *Vengeance*, *Albion*, *Irresistible*, and *Ocean*. On the flanks of the force the British pre-dreadnoughts *Majestic* and *Prince George* followed the northern (European) shore, with *Triumph* and *Swiftsure* on the southern (Asiatic) shore. The force was accompanied by the light cruisers *Amethyst*, *Dublin*, and *Dartmouth*, as well as destroyers and trawler-minesweepers.

At first all went well. Mallet recorded in his journal: 'Seaplane report – [fort] 16 firing – 17 hit but firing. 19 hit, new battery at Kephez Point not manned'. Just after midday De Robeck signalled Guépratte to move up to engage the Narrows' forts at close range. The Turkish fire was fierce and accurate, holing the *Gaulois* below the waterline, and damaging the *Inflexible*, *Lord Nelson*, *Agamemnon*, and *Charlemagne*. Kitson in *Swiftsure* saw *Inflexible* hit': 'she had evidently been hit in the fore control position by a heavy shell & we could see them lowering the dead and wounded on deck. Clearly we were getting into hot water!'

Acheson in *Inflexible*:

We leading, opened fire at about 11.30 at No 16 [fort], and about 2 pm drew out of action to get wounded out of top & put fire out on fore bridge. Three dead & Verner and Blaker & two men badly wounded. After getting them down, closed up again & opened up on No 19 [fort].

The *Gaulois* was saved from sinking by being beached on Rabbit Island off Kum Kale. But at this stage less than a dozen men in the fleet had become casualties. The Turks were in a far worse condition. Some guns were jammed, others were running short of ammunition, some were masked by piles of earth and rubble thrown up by the explosions. In places communications were destroyed, and steadily the enemy fire slackened. At 2 p.m., De Robeck ordered the French to retire, as he wished to move up six of his ships to cover the move forward of his minesweepers. The French wheeled about, and steamed between the British and the Asiatic shore. Kitson in *Swiftsure*:

Suddenly I saw a terrific explosion apparently alongside the *Bouvet*. A great sheet of flame & then a cloud of black smoke. I remarked to the Captain who was then alongside me at the standard Compass that one of the French ships had been hit by a big shell & sure enough within a very few seconds this ill-fated ship was listing heavily to starboard.

She was steaming at high speed and I can see her bow-wave now gradually increasing as her list increased. Then she was on her beam ends & we could see plainly through a glass [telescope or binoculars] her unfortunate ship's company climbing over the ship's side. Then she was bottom up with her screws in the air & then nothing but a cloud of black smoke & great commotion in the water. It was all over in less than three minutes.

Only 35 of the *Bouvet*'s crew of 674 were saved. Either a 14-inch shell had penetrated her magazine, or she had struck a mine. The minesweepers were called for, but soon fled under heavy howitzer fire. The *Inflexible* struck a mine, and listing badly withdrew. Acheson:

At 4.10 PM a terrific explosion – ship shuddered and shook – men came up from magazine and said powers [sic] were dud. Went down with Giles (Sub Lt). Shell room and magazine flooding fairly quickly. Heard hands had gone to abandon ship stations. Had to get doors closed before going up. Giles nearly done in by fumes. Getting out of turret into fresh air was like a dream, what a relief. Ship had a bad list to starboard & we were making for Rabbit Island or Tenedos, depending on what we could do. We had been hit by a mine or a torpedo in submerged flat. Went down and assisted in shutting ventilation and anchored about 6 PM inshore off Tenedos.

Mallet noted in his journal: '4.15 *Irresistible* reported submarine – *Irresistible* listing heavily to starboard'. This time she had not been scaremongering, but had actually struck a mine. She was close to the shore and the Turkish gunners turned their full attention on her. De Robeck ordered the destroyer *Wear* to her assistance, and she returned with some 600 of *Irresistible*'s crew, including dead and wounded; the senior officers of *Irresistible* and ten volunteers remained on board to prepare their ship for towing.

The *Ocean* went to tow *Irresistible*. As she approached a 14-inch shell struck the fore turret 12-inch guns of *Irresistible* and they rolled over the side. A moment later the *Ocean* struck a mine and her engines were put out of action; the ship stopped and lay helpless with enemy shells pouring into her. The order to abandon ship was given, three or four destroyers came alongside and took off the whole crew except one stoker who was trapped below. One of the destroyers, the *Chelmer*, was hit while still alongside the *Ocean*, but managed to reach the *Lord Nelson* to offload the survivors. Midshipman Field in the *Ocean* wrote to his mother afterwards:

At about 4 PM the fire around us became rather hotter. One shot hit the foremast, shook us up a bit. Another, the waste steam pipe, clouds of steam, thought it was a fire at first. Wireless went. Bit of shell hit Mr Gibbons and just drew blood. Another hit my finger, but didn't even draw blood. We must have been hit by about 50 shots. An 11-inch smashed up the Gunroom. Then, about 5.30, we hit a mine and abandoned ship. Destroyers were quickly alongside, my destroyer was hit, but just got alongside the *Lord Nelson*, where, worse luck, I still am. Everyone, bar one scalded stoker was saved. I had a life-saving collar, which wouldn't blow up. I've got no clothes at all, bar what I stand in. I've got my wrist watch, and a knife and two pencils too. There's a chance we might go home.

As the battle had progressed, Kitson in *Swiftsure* was sent below to his action station in the main deck battery, while the captain moved to the conning tower.

My station was not a good one for seeing everything that was going on
outside the ship & what I did see I saw by looking out of the gun
embrasures or by going on the upper deck – which I did from time to time
to see that men were not straying away from their stations. This showed
to be a very necessary matter to pay attention to. It is a most difficult thing
in the world to impress upon people that they should not stray. Curiosity
is it seems the strongest of all impulses on these occasions and it is almost
impossible to prevent both officers and men from coming up to 'have a
look' no matter what the penalty or how dangerous. On one or two
occasions men have paid dearly for this.

Of course the news of the sinking of the *Bouvet* very quickly became
known below and later the same fate which overtook the *Irresistible* and
the *Ocean*. I do not remember observing that these events created much
concern – not outwardly. The general demeanour of the men who came
under my notice was admirable and there were no signs of nervousness or
depression.

Men at their guns on the disengaged side frequently dropped off
to sleep, others sat down and read books or chatted just as one has
been accustomed to see them do at target practice or other peace
manoeuvres.

Others such as gun layers or sight setters took advantage of their
telescopes to see all there was to see through their gun ports and
frequently would make facetious remarks on what they observed outside.

It was a very fine piece of work on the part of the small craft when they
rescued the crews of the *Irresistible* and the *Ocean*. The manner in which
the captains of those destroyers took their ships alongside under heavy
fire, and took off the ships' companies was splendid. If any officers can be
said to have acted up to the best traditions of the British Navy on that day
those officers in charge of small craft did.

The sun was now setting and darkness coming on and the signal was
made for all ships to retire. The *Irresistible* was slowly sinking and we were
heavily engaged with the batteries on the Asiatic shore endeavouring to
keep down their fire on *Ocean* and it was not until it was nearly dark that
we gradually turned round and came out towards the entrance, by which
time the flagship had repeated the signal to us twice and finally asked why
we did not obey and whether we were also in trouble.

I have a vivid picture in my mind's eye of the setting sun with the
Ocean listing heavily to starboard and two destroyers alongside rescuing
her crew with shells falling all round her from howitzers on the Asiatic
Shore. It was borne in on me then that the day had gone against us and it
seemed we had sustained a disaster. We did not know what damage we
had inflicted upon the forts – nor in fact do we know now, so there was
nothing to set against our losses.

De Robeck's signal marked the end of the attempts by the British and French navies to force a passage of the Dardanelles unaided by the army.

In a later note in his journal, Midshipman Mallet remarked, adding a diagram to make the point:

> It is fascinating to note how the ships on the right were hit. (Needless to say the left bank was considered the dangerous side and the right side the safe!)

Charlemagne (untouched)	Gaulois v. badly hit	Bouvet sunk	Suffren badly hit
Vengeance (untouched)	Albion hit	Irresistible sunk	Ocean sunk
			Inflexible struck

After dark the gallant and aggressive Commodore Keyes, who had been sent as chief of staff in the Dardanelles Squadron in February 1915, after leaving his post as Commodore (Submarines) in the North Sea, went in the destroyer *Jed* to see if the *Ocean* and *Irresistible* could be salvaged. He could find neither battleship, and concluded that both had sunk in the night. As he steamed towards the now silent Narrows, he gained the strong impression that the Turks were beaten, and one more strong heave would achieve a breakthrough. On his return to *Queen Elizabeth*, he pressed De Robeck to try again. But De Robeck refused – in hindsight, rightly. We now know that very little permanent damage had been sustained by the Turkish forts. Of 176 guns in fixed defences, just four had been destroyed. The fleet had lost almost seven hundred men, with three capital ships sunk and three more badly damaged. Only one line of mines out of about ten had been swept, and the prospects of sweeping more with the enemy howitzers still fully operational were nil.

Had the fleet, further battered and reduced in strength, managed by some stroke of luck to fight its way through the Dardanelles to Constantinople and cause panic among the population and government by bombarding the city, it is highly unlikely that any significant strategic results favourable to the Allies would have ensued. Without troops to immediately occupy both sides of the Narrows, any damage to the defences of the Straits could have quickly been restored. The fleet could have refuelled in a Russian Black Sea port, but short of ammunition would have been reduced to lurking in the Black Sea, or risking another passage of the Dardanelles. Even if the Turks had faltered at the sight of the Allied Fleet off the Golden Horn, once they realized it was bottled up their resolve to continue fighting would have been quickly restored. Keyes's assessment of the Turkish will to resist may have been based on the widely held contemporary opinion that, to use a modern term, they were a 'pushover'. They had already demonstrated that they were not, and were to do so again, time after time.

Kitson in *Swiftsure* wrote later:

> It is almost an impossibility for a ship to destroy a modern fort with a reasonable expenditure of ammunition. We who have seen bombardments and been bombarded ashore, can not fail to have been astonished at the small amount of damage caused by even the largest shells, and unless a shell makes a direct hit on a gun it will not destroy it or even do it any serious damage.
>
> It may tear up the ground, it may kill every man near its explosion, it may even capsize the gun and emplacement altogether, but the damage to the gun will not be irreparable.
>
> A position may be bombarded with hundreds of shells – but if the personnel have dug outs to retire to and ammunition stores are not arranged or stowed in very large heaps, it is quite possible that the materiel and personnel will suffer not at all.
>
> These observations which apply with such force to big gun emplacements as Forts, so called, apply with still greater force to moveable batteries of howitzers and it is this great disability [sic] of ships to knock out shore guns that has undoubtedly been the cause of our failures, both during the Naval bombardment and later.
>
> It is a thousand pities that we did not realise this before. Indeed I am doubtful that some of us realize it even now.

How right Kitson was.

7

Dardanelles – the landings

General Sir Ian Hamilton, the army commander, arrived off Gallipoli in time to witness the failure of the navy to force a passage on 18 March, which led to the decision to mount a joint operation. The scene was set for the next act in the Dardanelles drama. The landings would involve the ANZACs (Lieutenant General Sir W. Birdwood), the RN Division (Major General A. Paris), and the 29th Division (Major General A. G. Hunter-Weston), which Kitchener had finally agreed to release. A so-called French Expeditionary Corps (General d'Amade), actually the equivalent of two brigades with artillery, was added to what was now called the Mediterranean Expeditionary Force (MEF).

The landings did not take place until 25 April because there was no plan, and consequently no arrangements for logistic support. Furthermore, few units were loaded in the shipping from which an assault could be made, so most of the MEF concentrated in Egypt, while Hamilton and his staff worked up a landing plan and concept of operations ashore. Unfortunately De Robeck and his staff remained off the Dardanelles, which made joint planning difficult to say the least; and this was to bear fruit on 25 April and on subsequent days. This was but one of many examples of the abysmal standard of command and control on this operation.[1]

Surprise was totally compromised by the repeated appearances of ships off the Gallipoli peninsula. The *Agamemnon* alone made nine such excursions between 25 March and 25 April, as Midshipman Williams's journal records:

25th March 1915 Steamed up to Bulair, laid 3 buoys off Gaba Tepe

26th March 1915 Bulair, fired 44 rounds at house, supposed to be magazine.

27th March 1915 Steamed across to Suvla Bay. Fired several rounds at nothing in particular.

29th March 1915 Weighed 7 am, and proceeded to Bulair for usual day's frightfulness.

31st March 1915 Lowered boats and did sham landing at Bulair at dusk.

2nd April 1915 Good Friday: usual frightfulness off Gaba Tepe.

9th April 1915 Proceeded to Cape Helles to relieve *Lord Nelson*. Patrolled coast. Fired on some Turkish soldiers

10th April 1915 One of our special circular tours. Fired and wasted a great deal of ammunition. Bag three houses, 1 boiler, 20 cows, a dog, and village shelled. Great day.

12th April 1915 Met *Ark Royal* in Gulf of Xeros, and shelled village with indirect fire spotting by aeroplane.

The covert and clandestine specialized units employed to gather information about beaches, terrain, and enemy locations before amphibious operations in the Second World War, and ever since, did not exist in the First World War.[2] Hence there was no alternative to overt reconnaissance of beaches, which inevitably compromised security. When comparing what transpired at Gallipoli with the great amphibious operations of the Second World War, in Korea, and subsequently, we should bear in mind that no opposed amphibious landing against an enemy armed with modern weapons had occurred during the professional lives of Hamilton or any of his commanders, their staffs, or their naval opposite numbers. As an art it had atrophied.[3]

Commander Dix was to be in charge of the landing of the covering force at Gaba Tepe, and ultimately to be Assistant Beach Master there. Consequently he was involved in the planning process, during which the importance of surprise was continually emphasized. He, with the staff of 1st Australian Division, took part in the reconnaissance in the old battleship *Queen*:

> We arrived off the coast at early dawn and, steaming slowly along it from a point some ten miles above the landing place we were able to get some idea of the lie of the land and of its nature at first hand. There were signs of much digging and several gun emplacements all along the coast, but these were fewer where we proposed to make the attempt than at other points. Just south of Gaba Tepe great preparations had been made. On Gaba Tepe itself there was a great deal of wire and the foot hills to the north of it appeared to be trenched and wired for a distance of about 500 yards.

In addition to warships continually advertising British interest in the peninsula, an increasing number of aircraft had now arrived at Tenedos, and these, whenever the weather was favourable, conducted air reconnaissance over the likely beaches and enemy positions.

On 21 March, Commander Samson, whose squadron had been operating in France and Belgium, arrived at Lemnos with the advance party of his squadron aboard the French steamer *Abda*. 'I had altogether eleven aeroplanes; my own machine, two Maurice Farmans with 100 HP Renault motors, and eight Henri Farmans with 89 HP Gnome motors. These ten were all new machines purchased in Paris.' To begin with his arrival was ignored, but after reporting to De Robeck aboard the *Queen Elizabeth*, he was ordered to Tenedos, where the *Ark Royal* aviators had established an airfield. Two days later, while setting up ashore, Samson saw a German aircraft flying over the town. Samson wasted little time and on

1st April we gave the Turks our first bombs, which I dropped on a battery. I missed, but very close. On the next day we heard that the German was attacking the *Albion*. We started off at once, but saw no sign of him. On 3rd April we did our first flight spotting for a ship's fire with WT from the aeroplane. The ship was the *London*. In the afternoon Pearse and Collet spotted for *the Prince of Wales*. Most of the following days were the same spotting for ships twice a day.

The rest of his squadron soon arrived, bringing his strength up to eighteen aircraft. They were a heterogeneous collection of machines of British and French manufacture, and the pilots and observers were a mixture of Royal Navy, Royal Marines, RNVR, and two army officers. Samson was particularly enthusiastic about the Maurice Farmans – 'they can do about 75 miles an hour'. But his favourite was number 1241, a Maurice Farman Shorthorn, 'climbs like a rocket she can do about 67 miles an hour'. He worked his squadron hard, and from 28 March to 11 May it totted up 29,802 miles with an average of six aircraft available each day. The round trip to the entrance to the Dardanelles from Tenedos and back was thirty-two miles. The only diversion available was Rabbit Island. Samson:

On 17 April, we made an attack on Maidos to attempt to draw the Turks' attention so that E 15 submarine could pass up the Narrows. Unfortunately she ran ashore at Kephez Point. The attack on Maidos was successful three 100 lb bombs hit the town. We heard afterwards that one of these bombs had killed 23 soldiers. Later in the day 1241 with Maux and Batten carrying three 100 lb bombs and camera went up to the wreck of E 15 to take photographs and to attempt to destroy her. The bombs missed but scared away a cutter and a tug which were alongside the wreck. Anyway our bombs went closer than the ship's shells who tried to hit her.

On the 18th we got a visit from our friend the German who dropped four bombs on us. One was a very good shot and hit midway between our house and the camp. Davies went after him in 1241, but the German at 7,000 feet had a good start. Anyway we gave him [the German] some presents in return. Davies and Collet in 1241 made two trips and gave him six 100 lb bombs, which tore up his landing ground and got very close to his shed.

I got some luck on the 19th as I got one 100 lb bomb directly on top of a big howitzer, the result was one gun less for the Germans/Turks. I also got another hit on a battery of field guns and ignited some charges. I was very pleased with myself, especially the first gun it was the result of a careful sighting shot. The last one was rather a chance, as I was aiming at something else.

Attacks on Turkish positions were almost a daily occurrence.

Collet is a great bomb dropper, and is always producing bomb sights. Thomson and Major Hogg quite upset the equilibrium of a big camp with two 100 lb bombs, they hit a lot of tents and must have killed a lot of Turks.

We visited a big camp near Boghali twice and got some beauties into the middle of it at between 6.30 and 7 am, just as life was on the move in camp.

The amount of shells the Turks fire at aeroplanes nowadays must keep the guns hot. But the shooting is futile and after Ostend it is not worth paying any attention to. Of course they will get better with practice, and I'm afraid we give them plenty. So far the only hits on machines have been rifle bullets.

*

The Turks made good use of the sixty-five days between the first naval attack on 19 February and the assault on 25 April. Six divisions under the German General Liman von Sanders were deployed: two at Besika Bay, two at Bulair, and two in the Peninsula, held ready to counter any landing. Likely landing places were lightly held by companies and platoons. Trenches and gun emplacements were dug, beaches wired, and roads built to improve the mobility of units moving to threatened areas. On 25 April the Allies actually attacked at weakly held points, but the Turkish reaction was sufficiently swift to frustrate the Allies' inept attempts to stake out footholds well inland, and failure to exploit success when it occurred. We now know that there were about forty thousand Turks on the Peninsula, with some thirty thousand in reserve nearby. Since the objective was all too clearly Constantinople, the Turks could have brought in some of the thirty-six additional divisions they had available. Hamilton had about seventy thousand troops; he could and did achieve local superiority on the beaches, but it was important that he pushed inland fast, and in strength. He did not.

Thanks to their efficient spy network in Cairo, the Turks knew the exact order of battle of the MEF; Hamilton thought the Turks had only three divisions at Gallipoli, and knew very little about their deployment. His plan was as follows. A feint landing by the RN Division at Bulair was aimed at keeping the Turks there fixed. The Anzacs would be landed in the Gaba Tepe area, and the 29th Division at Cape Helles, where he expected the toughest opposition. Rear Admiral Cecil Thursby's 2nd Squadron would cover the landings at Gaba Tepe, and Vice Admiral Rosslyn Wemyss's 1st Squadron those at Cape Helles. The French would carry out a diversionary landing at Kum Kale on the Asiatic Shore, before transferring to Cape Helles after about forty-eight hours, where they would be joined by the RN Division, who would land at Cape Helles on completing their excursion to Bulair.

Upon landing, the Anzacs were to advance to seize the high ground at Chunuk Bair and Sari Bair overlooking the Narrows. The 29th Division was to push up the gentle slope of the 700-foot-high Achi Baba, and then on to link up with the Anzacs, where together the two divisions would dominate the eastern side of the Narrows, at which point the navy would pass through and steam into the Sea of Marmara. The beaches were designated as follows: at Cape Helles (clockwise from the south-east), S, V, W, X, and Y; at Gaba Tepe, Z (but soon just called Anzac). The French appear not to have used a letter system.

At each beach there was to be a beach party, commanded by a Royal Navy captain. Commander Dix described forming Anzac's in the days before the landings:

> The first two days were spent organising the beach party – one hundred men from eight different ships – arranging the manufacture of hauling-off buoys, indenting for Naval stores, arranging a beach communication chart. Looking back on it, some of our plans seemed rather funny. The brain storm concerning beach communications led to an elaborate chart being printed with green lines for telephones, red for visual [signalling], black for messengers, blue for megaphones, and so on. It was pretty, but in the event quite useless – we were expecting and planning for a beach [exit], not a second-rate goat track!

According to Dix, the planning considerations for Gaba Tepe were:

> (1). The landing of the covering force should be a surprise – which meant landing before daylight. (2) That the covering force, consisting of four thousand men, should be landed as nearly in one body as possible. (3) That there should be the least possible delay between landing the covering

force and beginning to land the main body. (4) That the landing must take place between Fisherman's Hut and Gaba Tepe.

There were no landing craft available for any of the beaches. Soldiers and marines would land in cutters, launches, pinnaces, and life-boats (borrowed from troopships) towed by steam picket boats. A few yards off the beach, steam picket boats would cast off their tows, and the final approach would be under oars. In the case of Anzac Beach, the first 1,500 troops of the Covering Force would be taken in by twelve steam picket boats, each towing three boats propelled by oars.

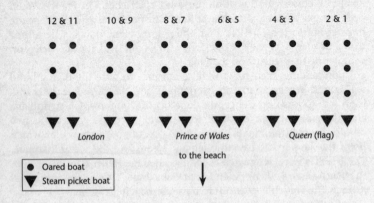

Troops would embark in boats at the rendezvous (in modern parlance the lowering position) some miles off the beach. The lines of tows, each 100 yards apart, would be led towards the beach by three battleships until signalled to 'go on', when they were to overtake the battleships, and still preserving their relative bearings and distances apart, push on to the shore, which was to be reached by 5 a.m. Follow-up waves would be similarly transported, and led in by destroyers, although some details differed. All landings were supported by naval gunfire bombardment, in some cases spotted for by aircraft.

When the MEF arrived at Mudros, rehearsals were carried out, mainly consisting of practising embarkation and disembarkation drills by day and night. No accounts mention practising command and control. At this time Dix wrote in a letter to his wife: 'I hope to find time to write one more letter before the stunt. Water and hospital ships present difficulties at present. I feel like Umslopogas* and smell blood'. Dix

---

* A Zulu warrior character in Rider Haggard's *King Solomon's Mines*.

elaborates in his memoirs on the administrative problems: 'The soldiers got anxious about the water supply, and those responsible for wounded woke up to the fact that they had accommodation for only about six hundred serious cases'.

Two days before the landings, Dix wrote again to his wife:

My Darling Maggs

This is the last chance of writing before the 'Great Adventure' as we call it, begins.

Tomorrow I spend onboard HMS *London* (one of our covering ships) and at a very early hour next day, I pilot the first tow in to their landing place.

The whole thing is a colossal undertaking – the text books say it is impossible, whatever that may mean; but although we know we are in for a devil of a 'doing' we are going to have a big push for it.

I am awfully pleased with life because General Birdwood has asked me to accompany him when he lands as a sort of naval staff officer! My khaki outfit would make a cat laugh. It consists of a pair of skin-tight khaki knickers [knickerbockers] and a Tommy's coat much too tight everywhere, with commanders stripes sewn on the shoulders, putties [sic], and my shooting boots and a Tommy's cap with my naval badge.

I have warned every fat colonel I have met that I shall follow him like a dog until he gets perforated and shall then strip him naked!!

Our bad time on the beach will be from about 3.30 am till 8 am by which time we ought to be reasonably safe except for howitzer fire.

He thought afterwards that being sent to the *London* was a mistake:

as officer in charge of the boat operation I should have been in the Senior Officer's ship, the *Queen*, the flagship of Rear-Admiral [Cecil] Thursby. But a much worse mistake had been made, the First Lieutenant of the TBD [destroyer] depot ship, Lieutenant Commander Waterlow, had been designated 'guide' of the operation and was sent to the *Queen*. This ludicrous muddle was not discovered until it was too late to change it, but was a Naval failure which had very marked results.

Everybody aboard the *London* was in high spirits, with the exception of Mr Ashmead Bartlett, the war correspondent. In conversation with me that evening he foretold the run of events with almost uncanny exactitude. He insisted that only in the event of having another division both at Helles and Anzac could speedy victory be obtained, and that long delayed success might, and probably would, mean eventual failure. However, that did not dampen the Australians' spirits, and it certainly did not affect ours.

The first of the main landings was planned to take place at Gaba Tepe, in darkness on 25 April, by the 3rd Australian Brigade, who were providing the covering force. Thanks to a strong north-flowing current and the fact that some of the pinnaces towing the boats were commanded by inexperienced midshipmen as young as fifteen years old, the Australians were landed north of the intended beach. Dix was woken at 1 a.m. and ate breakfast, then

On going on deck I found we were proceeding very slowly, and appeared to be in no hurry to arrive at the rendezvous. The reason for this was the brilliance of the moon. One could see for miles. In consequence we were a little late at the rendezvous, but very little, and the transfer of the boats took place without incident. Immediately prior to falling in, I suggested that men were given a 'tot' each to keep their cockles warm during their cramped and tedious passage in the boats. The embarkation took nearly forty minutes and it was some little time longer before the order 'go on' was given by megaphone. We were ordered to land with the right hand boat some five hundred yards to the north of Gaba Tepe and the left hand boat just south of the point since known as Hell Spit.

We gradually drew clear of the ships, and at first all seemed to be going well, but when three-quarters of the way ashore [to the beach] I saw the right wing steering across the bows of the centre, who were conforming to the movement, thus crowding the left wing away to port. By this time I was awake to the fact that we were already some way to port of our objective and in order to save as much ground as possible I took the left wing at full speed under the stern of the other column and hailed them to keep to starboard. I felt that as soon as the first boat got ashore, every other boat would at once put her helm over and do the same, and that the quicker we got there the less would be the error.

The approach of dawn was another reason for speed. Everything was absolutely quiet as we approached the shore, and there was nothing that would lead one to suppose that surprise had failed, but as the first boat touched the shore at 5.11 am, a single shot broke the stillness, almost immediately followed by others, and the firing became general.

The boats were ashore and the men out of them in wonderfully short time and, cheering lustily, parties immediately began to fight their way up the steep, scrub-covered hills. One of the picket boats fired a belt or so at the crest of the hill, and the flickering flame of a hostile Maxim gun was seen coming from a little lookout station half way up the ridge at Ari Burnu. This gun disappeared very quickly. Then the shells began to come from Gaba Tepe way, and turning to a 'bang' behind us, we saw our destroyers almost as far inshore as our picket boats and the soldiers already on their way to land.

The landing had taken place just about the frontage of the tows (5½

cables [1,100 yards]) to the north of where it had been intended.* This
was caused by an unexpected northerly set of considerable strength, and
because it was extremely difficult to make out any shore marks during the
approach. Had I not taken preventive action we must have landed at least
another half mile to the northward.

I think every boat got hit. Seven were shot through and were left on
the beach. The casualties among the Naval ratings – three per boat to
work the boats when empty – were slight, and the steam boats suffered
most in this respect. Two officers slightly wounded, one man killed, and
perhaps a dozen wounded came to my notice. The picket boat I was in
was hit five times, but the casualties amounted to one punctured Gieves
waistcoat and one bruised stomach. The situation at 6.30 am was that
everything was working at full speed and the organisation had so far
proved successful beyond our wildest dreams. A tremendous battle –
judging by the sound – was raging somewhere over the crest of the hills,
and it seemed as though our men were advancing.

Dix believes that as things turned out the landing was upon the only
stretch of beach where there was not much opposition, and therefore,
by luck rather than good judgement, in the best place. But he contends
that the cause of the subsequent inability to achieve the Anzac objective
was that

every soldier as soon as he was landed decided that he, and he alone, was
going to be the first man in to Constantinople. They were over the first
range of ridges like scalded cats, and some of them got half way across
the Peninsula before they met the steady and formed Turkish reserves
about half a division strong.

There is a widely held view that this headlong and uncoordinated
rush inland and landing in the wrong place were the reasons for failure.
There is evidence that this is overstated, and that a decision made by
Colonel Ewen Sinclair-McLagan, the Covering Force Commander *after*
landing, had a far more significant effect on subsequent events. Sinclair-
McLagan had been dubious about the task set for him by Birdwood,
thinking it too ambitious. When he landed, taking counsel of his fears,
he unilaterally changed his brigade's objectives, and did not cover the
full extent of the beachhead as ordered by Birdwood. He managed to
convince Colonel James M'Cay (2nd Australian Brigade), the follow-up
brigade commander, to change his objectives too. So instead of pressing

* The right-hand landing spot on the actual beach is 1,100 yards north of the left-hand
spot on the intended beach. But the centre of the actual landing place is 2,000 yards north
of the centre of the intended beach.

on to occupy the vital ground – Chunuk Bair, Hill Q, and Hill 971 – as ordered, M'Cay came in on Sinclair-McLagan's right where the latter feared a counter-attack. It is worth noting that the rate of build-up at Anzac was good (always a key factor in an amphibious operation). Five thousand men were ashore by 5 a.m., eight thousand by 8 a.m., and fifteen thousand by late afternoon. The Turks had only five hundred men in the vicinity by 9.30 a.m. and by dusk five thousand. But thanks to Sinclair-McLagan's changes, although isolated parties of men did reach the vital ground, in the words of the Australian soldier–historian Lieutenant General John Coates,

> the shaft did not follow the spearpoint. Some men found themselves alone with no one following. In consequence the bridgehead area remained confined and in full view of Turkish forces. Under the determined leadership of Colonel Mustafa Kemal the Turks wrested the initiative from the Anzacs, who never regained it.[4]

This, not landing about a mile in the wrong place and over-enthusiastic Australian soldiers, is the credible reason for failure.

Next to land was a composite force of 1st King's Own Scottish Borderers (KOSB) and the Plymouth Battalion Royal Marine Light Infantry (RMLI), on Y Beach. Astoundingly, no headquarters was placed in command of the two battalions, who were from different divisions; but to compound the muddle there was doubt about which CO was in overall command. The landing was unopposed, but neither CO was disposed to use his initiative and seize the opportunity of linking up with X Beach and threatening the rear of the Turkish positions at Cape Helles. Both battalions remained in the vicinity of the beach. Hamilton, who saw there was no resistance at Y Beach to begin with, did nothing. The Turks did not start attacking Y Beach until several hours after the landing. During the rest of the first day, and through the night, Turkish attacks on the beachhead continued. Finally, after running out of ammunition, with one CO dead, and lacking any orders or support, both battalions withdrew to the beach and were re-embarked on the battleship *Goliath*.

At X Beach, the 2nd Royal Fusiliers landed without difficulty thanks to Captain Lockyer of the battleship *Implacable*, who ignored instructions to fire on ridges behind the beach, and took his ship close in to engage the beaches at point-blank range. Lockyer relates that at the conference before the Cape Helles landings he said:

> 'As *Implacable* is the only one remaining under way during the landing, I propose disposing my tows on either beam, accompanying the tows as far

as possible and shelling the beach on the way in.' To which the Chief of Staff, a gunnery expert remarked in a very decisive manner, 'you will never be able to pick up the range quick enough'. I not being an expert remained silent. The Admiral [Wemyss] then said, 'you have all heard what has been stated, I leave the matter entirely in the hands of my captains, and I know you will all do your best for the success of the operations'.

On the same day the order for the other ships to anchor was cancelled – but I'm afraid the chief of staff's remark carried a great influence.

Unlike the other captains, Lockyer used his initiative and was as good as his word. After ranging shots while *Implacable* slowly nosed in towards the beach,

> The first rounds of 6-inch guns burst over the water about 10 yards from the beach. The sights were then raised and when the firing ceased, the boats proceeded in, followed by the ship using the Quick Firing guns [12pdrs and 3pdrs] along the ridges until the boats were disembarking troops. The ship brought up with 6½ fathoms under her stern about 500 to 600 yards from the shore.
>
> Having seen the disembarkation was going most satisfactorily, the ship then proceeded to its appointed anchorage off Cape Tekeh between X and W Beaches, and shortly after we saw the Fusiliers attack Hill 114 at the back of the Cape with great success, the enemy surrendering in great numbers.

Although the beach was defended by only twelve men, the Fusiliers found two four-barrelled 1-inch Nordenfeldt quick-firing guns, commanding the beach, loaded ready but disabled by gunfire. The beach had no barbed-wire defence, but was protected by a line of reefs invisible from seaward about sixty yards offshore; the boats grounded on this and the troops had to wade ashore: during the run-in of the boats, and especially as troops waded ashore, the Nordenfeldts would have inflicted terrible casualties on the soldiers had *Implacable* not already neutralized them. Small numbers of men with machine guns could massacre many times their number of assaulting infantry, as events on V and W Beach were to show.

Attempts by 2nd Royal Fusiliers to exploit south to W and V Beaches were frustrated by strong enemy opposition. Their commanding officer was wounded and wrote to Lockyer from the transport ship *Dongola* the next day:

> I had back luck yesterday & was hit about 1 o'clock & broke a foot. I am writing this on spec of its getting to you, to thank you and all your people for the real good time you gave us, we are all officers and men, very grateful to you indeed.

P.S. I am afraid we had 12 officers damaged in one way or another up to yesterday evening. [25 April]

The landings on S Beach, which was defended by one Turkish platoon, were also successful. Here the battleship *Cornwallis* (Captain A. P. Davidson) was supporting the 2nd South Wales Borderers (SWB), whose objective was De Tott's Battery. Davidson landed himself with some of his ship's company, having lent his marine detachment to 2 SWB, who were short of a company. The objective was taken, for the loss of sixteen dead and sixty wounded. Eventually the *Cornwallis* was ordered to V Beach to provide support there. Her intrepid captain, his marines, and the seamen landing party remained on S Beach for some hours. The CO of 2 SWB made no effort to exploit his gains, although the Turks had melted away. Again neither Hamilton nor Hunter-Weston saw fit to reinforce success, as Commodore Keyes wrote to Captain Lockyer after the war. At the stage Keyes is writing about, both Hamilton and De Robeck were aboard *Queen Elizabeth*, one of the few occasions during the amphibious phase of operations throughout the campaign when both senior commanders were in the right place; and together. Keyes, then De Robeck's Chief of Staff:

Neither [Hamilton nor De Robeck] would interfere – though I begged them both to do so on the evening of the 25th when we could see what was going on at de Totts and Y Beach – us British forces in unopposed occupation of the enemy's flanks – sitting still doing nothing – whereas Hunter-Weston and Wemyss were in complete ignorance of what was going on anywhere except at W and possibly X beach. Nothing would induce Hamilton or de Robeck to interfere.

The story on V and W Beaches was very different; although each was defended by only two platoons, the defensive works were formidable. Wire entanglements were laid below the waterline, and sowed with electrically detonated mines. Trenches were dug into the low cliffs overlooking the beaches, and protected with barbed wire. The beaches were covered by fire from machine guns sited to enfilade troops landing on them. The ground behind the beaches was also covered by fire from well-concealed positions.

At V Beach the only departure from the archaic landing methods employed elsewhere was the conversion of the collier *River Clyde* into a landing ship; the forerunner of many such vessels used in the Second World War, and up to the present day. The *River Clyde* was commanded by Commander Unwin, a retired Royal Navy officer recalled for war service; her first lieutenant was Midshipman Drewry, a twenty-year-old ex-P&O officer (both were detached from the *Hussar*); the rest of the company comprised nine seamen, nine stokers, one carpenter's mate, the captain's servant, and the original ship's steward.

The plan for V Beach involved the *River Clyde* carrying nearly two thousand men, of the 1st Royal Munster Fusiliers, some of 1st Royal Dublin Fusiliers, and 2nd Hampshires. She would be run aground under the walls of Sedd-el-Bahr fort. As she hit the beach, a steam hopper which she was towing alongside would be propelled forward by its own momentum and form a link with the beach (a highly problematic concept). Three lighters were also being towed alongside. Two of these would be positioned to form a bridge of boats to the steam hopper. The soldiers would run out of four doors cut in her side, along sloping gangways that ran down towards the bows on each side, leap onto the lighters, forward onto the hopper, and dash ashore. Meanwhile the Turks would be discouraged from engaging the disembarking soldiers by fire from Maxim gunners in sandbagged emplacements in the *River Clyde*'s bows, commanded by Lieutenant-Commander Josiah Wedgwood RNVR. Boats carrying the majority of the 1st Dublins would accompany *River Clyde* into the beach.

W Beach was to be assaulted by the 1st Lancashire Fusiliers in boats as at Anzac. It was not the fault of those who took part in the landings that such old-fashioned techniques were resorted to. Although Fisher had privately ordered flat-bottomed landing craft for his fantastic project of a landing in the Baltic, these were not available until the Suvla landings in August 1915. But the overarching deficiencies were a total lack of doctrine, training, or equipment for that most difficult phase of war, an amphibious operation.

Commander Samson was overhead as the boats carrying the 1st Lancashire Fusiliers approached W beach:

> When the boats were about 300 yards from the beach, the ships shifted [their fire] further inland. At about 200 yards from the beach, the Turks started firing, I could see bullets and shells hitting the water around the boats. It seemed certain they would all be killed, still they came on.

The hail of rifle and machine-gun fire on the packed craft killed or wounded many of the men at the oars. The Lancashires did the only thing they could, jump over the side. In many places they were out of their depth, and weighed down with rifle and equipment many drowned. The mines took a further toll, as did the underwater wire entanglement. Those that waded forward found that the beach was a death trap. In an outstanding act of courage and discipline the survivors of the first wave, having paused on the seaward side of the wire above the waterline, broke through onto the higher ground above the beach. In a bout of 'gutter fighting', with rifle butt and bayonet, they cleared enough elbow room to allow the next wave to land. For this the battalion was awarded six VCs.

At V Beach the assault was a shambles. Few of the Dublins landing in boats made the shoreline. A rating from the *Cornwallis*, who manned one of the boats, wrote to his sister from hospital afterwards:

> I am indeed a lucky chap to be here today writing this letter, as all of us here who have survived the Battle of the 25th are agreed in saying we went through the gates of hell.
>
> At 8.30 pm we got into our boats which were tied up astern [of *Cornwallis*] and she towed us all night. About half an hour before daybreak our steam boats took us in tow and we went to get our troops at daybreak. All the warships which joined us in the night started to bombard and you never heard such a noise in your life. All the boats advanced under cover of the ships' fire. Landing in six different places, our steam boats slipped us about two hundred yards from shore and we had to row the remainder. The Turks waited until we got close in and then opened a murderous fire. The troops started to fall like leaves. It was then I got hit in the right shoulder. Anyway we got the boat ashore, and those soldiers that could, got out. By this time all my boat's crew were either killed or wounded so we had to stop there under a hail of bullets from Maxims and rifles. This was 7 am and we remained there for about nine hours. Every time one of us got up to try to get the boat off we were met by a hail of bullets. The poor old Dublins.

When the *River Clyde* grounded, the hopper, commanded by Midshipman Drewry, shot forward but veered off to port and beached in the wrong place, to one side and not in a position to form a bridge to the shore. Unwin decided to use two of the lighters to connect the ship to a spit that ran out about forty yards from the beach, off the *River Clyde*'s starboard bow. He and Able Seaman Williams set about this assisted by Midshipman Drewry, who had waded ashore:

> meeting a soldier wounded in the water, with another soldier from a boat, we tried to carry him ashore, but he was again shot in our arms, his neck [cut through] in two pieces nearly. So we left him, and I ran along the beach towards the spit. I threw away my revolver, coat and hat and waded out to the Captain. He was in the water with Williams wading and towing the lighters towards the spit. I pulled for a few minutes and then climbed aboard the lighters and got the bows lowered.

There was nothing on the spit to which the lighters could be fastened, so Unwin, standing waist deep, wrapped the rope from the lighter's bows round himself to provide an anchor. Williams grasped the rope to assist, and Unwin shouted to *River Clyde* for the landing to begin.

The troops landing from the *River Clyde* were mown down as they ran out of the doors in the ship's side. Williams was hit. Unwin, in trying to save him, dropped the rope, and the lighters drifted off away from the spit. Drewry:

> The Captain was wading towards us carrying Williams. I pulled him on to the lighter and [another man called] Ellard carried Williams on board the ship on his shoulders. Williams was dead however. Then with difficulty hauled the Captain on to the lighter, he was nearly done, he went inboard, and I was alone.
>
> I stayed on the lighter and tried to keep the men going ashore. It was murder and soon the first lighter was covered with dead and wounded, and the sea round the spit was red. When they got ashore they were little better off, they were picked off before they could dig themselves in. They stopped coming, and I ran on board into No 1 [hold] and saw an awful sight dead and dying lay round the ports.
>
> I went up to the saloon and saw the Captain being rubbed down, he murmured something about the third lighter. I went down again and a picket boat came along [with Lieutenant John Morse RN and Midshipman Wilfred Malleson in the second wave]. It gave the reserve lighter a push that sent it as far as the hopper. Just as we hit the hopper, a piece of shrapnel hit me on the head knocking me down for a second or two and covering me with blood. However we made fast to the hopper, and I went below and a Tommy put my scarf round my head and I went up again.
>
> Now we wanted a connection to the other lighters, so I took a rope and swam towards the other lighters, but the rope was not long enough and I was stuck in the middle.

All the while a few men huddled under the walls of Sedd-el-Bahr, where they were in dead ground. Boats drifted offshore packed with dead and dying. Samson arrived over V Beach in time to see

> the water simply whipped into foam by the shells and bullets. We could see the lighters full of dead and the sea stained red with blood all along the beach. It was hardly believable that any Turks could stand the heavy fire poured in by the ships against Sedd el Bahr. Salvo after salvo from close range.
>
> The corpses on the beaches and the blood in the water [on both beaches] were sights that made you feel rather rotten, sitting up there doing nothing except spotting the ships' fire.

Drewry:

I sang out to Malleson to throw me a line, but he had no line except the one that had originally kept the lighters on the spit. He stood up and hauled in some, and then as I had drifted away, he swam towards the lighter I had left and made it fast.

This brief connection to the beach did not last long, and Drewry now made for home, but had quite a job climbing up the lighters for I was rather played out. When I got on board, the Doctor dressed my head, I was awfully cold. He would not let me get up and I had to lay down and listen to the din.

Then I went to sleep and woke at 3 pm to find the hopper's bow had swung round and there was no connection with the shore. I got up and found that nothing was going to be done until dark. At dark the firing seemed to cease, and the connection was made to the spit again.

The Captain and one or two volunteers had taken seven loads of wounded from the lighters to No 4 hold by the starboard side. A great feat which everyone is talking about. About 8 pm the troops began to land again.

While the troops were going out, I had a party getting wounded from the hopper and lighters and putting them on board a trawler. An awful job, they had not been dressed at all and some of the poor devils were in an awful state. I never knew blood smelled so strong.

The *Queen Elizabeth* with Hamilton and De Robeck on board was one of the bombarding ships for V Beach. Her selection as a headquarters ship is an indication of the total ignorance about the requirements of two commanders in a joint operation, which include the need to go to the place where command can best be exercised, and not be tied down to a supporting task – in this case naval gunfire support of landing operations. The ear-splitting crashes of her guns must have made it difficult for the army staff confined below to contribute anything worthwhile – although for all the influence Hamilton exerted on the battle, it was immaterial where he was located. Lieutenant Claris, a watch-keeping officer, wrote in his diary:

When the QE arrived it was of course broad daylight and a more dreadful sight cannot be imagined. Boats upside down floating past, dead and wounded, also what looked like thousands of men dead on the sand in front of V Beach. Not a Turk was visible, but every time one of the men moved either from the wooden horse [the *River Clyde* was given this nickname by some witnesses], or from the slight cover afforded by a small sand bank in front of the trench, maxims rang out [sic] and pom-poms and it was impossible to see where from. Three battleships shelled these trenches, buildings, No 1 Fort, and the cliffs until it was dark that night, about 7 pm and yet our troops were unable to advance. You could see them being shot again & again and yet could not help. Any boat sent in was at once wiped out, and so there wasn't a chance of a rescue.

Unwin, Drewry, Malleson, and Williams were among the six VCs awarded to the Royal Navy for that day. The *River Clyde*, although a brave attempt to make up for a total lack of purpose-built landing ships, was a death trap. Its design meant that two thousand men were funnelled two abreast through the most dangerous place in a seaborne landing, the waterline. It might have been a different story had there been several such landing ships, touching down on the beach simultaneously, on a broad front.

There is also little doubt that the effect of naval gunfire was overestimated, and the targeting was faulty – especially as the beach defences were easily discernible from seaward. Captain Thomson, commander of one of the 29th Division's artillery batteries, was detailed for duty for the landing at V Beach as the artillery adviser to the Gunnery Commander in the battleship *Albion*. He wrote:

A preliminary reconnaissance of the Peninsula was carried out by the *Swiftsure* a few days before the landing, I and the RA officers allotted to other battleships being in the foretop. The *Swiftsure* took us first to Suvla and then steamed around the tail of the Peninsula to Sedd el Bahr, keeping within 1,000 yards of the shore. The trenches and barbed wire were clearly visible, but no shot was fired at us and we saw no sign of life. If any troops were there, the orders as to concealment were meticulously obeyed.

Thomson was not able to pass on what he had seen, interpret events ashore with a *soldier's* eye, and possibly influence the battle, because, thanks to poor naval staff work, he could not be transferred to *Albion* during the night of 24/25 April as planned. Late on the evening of 25 April, after many vicissitudes, he joined *Albion* off Sedd el Bahr, where he saw the huddle of survivors on shore behind a low bank a few yards from the waterline. Further landings from the *River Clyde* had been stopped. The next morning he was in *Albion*'s foretop:

Somewhere about 11 am I saw four men suddenly climb the bank from the beach. As they straightened themselves out on top, all four were shot down. They had obviously been machine-gunned. The *Albion* moved closer and yet closer in, and I finally spotted through my field glasses a couple of machine-guns firing through an embrasure in the centre bastion of the south-western face of Sedd el Bahr fort. From the foretop the officer in charge of the port 6-inch group [of guns] was asked if he could see the machine guns and if he could lay a gun direct on to them. After a pause, he announced excitedly he could do both. The range was taken and reported to the foretop as 600 yards. I gave the order to fire that gun myself. It was a real bullseye; a great bite was cut off the bastion where the machine-guns had been firing from, and as the smoke cleared away, a body of men rose and advance unharmed up the slope. That was the beginning of the assault, which ended successfully about 2 pm in the capture of the whole of the high ground dominating the V Beach 'amphi-theatre'. During the assault, the 6-inch guns of the *Albion* fired direct on to Turks who could be clearly seen moving about in the trenches of the old fort on the crest of the high ground.

The gunfire support of the landing was a sorry tale of naval failure to appreciate the military problem. The lessons took some time to sink in. Lieutenant-Commander Adrian Keyes RN, a beach master and brother of Commodore Keyes, was of the opinion that naval gunfire support in most places was highly overrated for much of the early months of the campaign, and especially so on 25 April. Major General Archibald Paris, the Royal Marine Artillery officer commanding the RN Division, echoed this view, writing on 5 May 1915: 'One of the disappointments has been the results of the enormous expenditure of ship ammunition.'[5]

Lieutenant Claris's diary entry for 30 April 1915 also has something to say on the subject of fire control and command. Having commented that enemy aircraft coming to bomb the ships offshore treated the *Queen Elizabeth* with respect because of her 'high-angle' gun (which was then a new-fangled invention), he continued:

> Our own aeroplanes have done very good work from an observation and bombing point of view, but are useless for spotting for ship's guns. It is either inexperience or a bad method of signalling. The arrangement between the Army and the Navy for signalling has been shocking. Navy never knows where Army is when advancing or retiring, where the end of the line is etc.
>
> Except for the Captain of the *Queen Elizabeth*, the Vice Admiral has a very poor staff. At present the position in the Dardanelles is in my opinion very unsafe. We are pecking at the whole thing. It will cost thousands of men, but if done in force, instead of small attacks, waits of a week or so etc. it would cost fewer men in the end.

Claris is being hypercritical of the RNAS spotting efforts. Samson was caustic about some bombarding ships that in the early days did not pay sufficient heed to corrections being given by spotters, either because of lack of practice or overexcitement on the part of gunnery officers and their staffs. But most important, Samson, along with most others, grossly overestimated the effect that bombardment, both aerial and by guns, would have on enemy gun emplacements and defensive positions. The extent of the damage to guns and crews came nowhere near what was hoped for, and indeed reported and believed. This is hardly surprising. Even as late as 1944, when the techniques for naval gunfire and air bombardment in support of amphibious operations had vastly improved, and aircraft and bombs powerful beyond the wildest dreams of the First World War aviators were used, it was commonplace for even open-topped gun positions to survive to fight, let alone those with overhead cover.[6]

The small gains by devoted men on V and W Beaches were eventually expanded, the former after dark, and over the following days they carved out more elbow room. But to the very end, the Cape Helles beachhead was never more than four miles deep, and two miles short of Achi Baba, an objective for the first day. At Anzac two days of bitter fighting and over five thousand casualties failed to expand the toehold carved out by the gallant Australians and New Zealanders.

Meanwhile the Royal Navy played an indispensable part in the campaign, and to the troops ashore the grey shapes offshore were visible proof of their support. On 26 April, the *Lord Nelson* was off V Beach providing supporting fire. Boy Telegraphist Blamey noted in his private journal:

> We had aeroplanes and seaplanes up all day giving us directions by wireless where to fire. As yesterday we packed up at 9 pm, but remained where we were all night just off V Beach. Every now and then Asiatic Bill [nickname for a heavy mobile Turkish gun on the Asiatic shore – possibly more than one – more usually referred to as Asiatic Annie] would send a huge shell whistling in our direction, and more often than not it fell on the beach among stores, provisions and the Red Cross place. Fire as we would it was impossible to hit this fellow, as he had a way of disappearing as soon as he fired.

As a telegraphist, Blamey was involved in receiving wireless messages from spotting aircraft to his ship. He does not comment on their efficiency or lack of it. Messages correcting the guns for range and line were transmitted by the spotter in the aircraft by Morse key, and received in the 'short distance wireless office' below the waterline in the ship. Corrections would be passed on to the gunnery officer or transmitting station by the telegraphist, presumably by voicepipe or more likely in a cylindrical container in a pneumatic tube. On 27 April, Blamey noted:

> Aeroplanes are up spotting again to day & here on *Lord Nelson* these spotting signals from the aeroplanes are received by Dyer and myself, two boy tels, and we are down below near the fore 12-inch magazine, with all the watertight doors closed on us, so if the ship went down we may as

well say our prayers. The office is only about 4 feet 6 inches by 3 feet 6 inches, so with all doors closed on us and hot water pipes running all over the office and below it the heat can well be imagined. We have to keep our flannel, jersey, shirt, cap, boots & socks all off & then we sweat as if we were in a furnace, being only in our trowsers [sic] & sometimes its got that hot we've took our trowsers off and kept watch naked. Our watch was an hour, it was impossible to stay on longer, & so we worked an hour and hour about. We only man it during the day, as we do no firing by night for fear of hitting our own troops.

Day after day, ships closed the shore and bombarded the enemy. It was therefore a blow to morale when first the *Goliath* and then the *Triumph* were sunk. The *Goliath* was sunk while off Morto Bay in a daring attack by the Turkish (ex-German *S 165* class) destroyer *Muavenet-i-Millet*. Midshipman Weld-Forester wrote to his mother:

My Darling Mother

I hope you got my telegram saying I was safe. The old *Goliath* was struck by 3 torpedoes in quick succession on Wednesday morning at 1.28 am. I was woken up by the explosions. The ship heeled at once to an angle of 5° to starboard. There was no panic as it was all too sudden for any one to realise what had happened. I went up to the quarterdeck in my pyjamas. The ship was heeling over fast. When the starboard side of the deck was level with the sea, she stopped for about 30 seconds. Then she heeled rapidly up again. I dived from the port side. I struck the side of the ship with my face. It was horrid feeling my nose slithering over the wet side. I suppose I dived about 30 feet as I saw a good many constellations when I struck the water.

I swam about 200 yds away and then turned round to see her sink. She had heeled back to almost an even keel and was going down bows first with her stem about 40 feet in the air. You could plainly hear all the crockery and furniture tumbling about and breaking up inside her. Then she heeled completely over till her bottom was uppermost and she slid right under. You could hear the cries of drowning men all round. I swam down with the current to the *Cornwallis* which I could dimly see in the dark about 2 miles away. There was a five knot tide helping me.

When I was about a mile from the scene of the disaster, I came across a big spar about 30 feet long. I hung onto it for a few minutes to get my breath, and then abandoned it as I could get on quicker without it. I was eventually picked up by the *Lord Nelson*'s cutter and taken to a trawler. In the morning I was turned over to the *Lord Nelson*.

I am now on a torpedo boat which promises to be exciting work.

Best love from

        Wolston.

Of *Goliath's* ship's company of 750, only 183 survived.

By now the Germans had sent U-boats to the eastern Mediterranean, and on 25 May, U-21 torpedoed the *Triumph* off Anzac Beach in full view of both sides – the Turks cheered and the Anzacs groaned. Dix on Anzac:

> At about noon on May 25th, while we were busy sending a surplus of army carts back to the ships, I saw an explosion alongside the *Triumph* who had been strafing the Turks from a position off Gaba Tepe. She turned over and sank completely seven minutes later.

The submarine had been sighted earlier. Leading Seaman Hemenway in the destroyer *Grasshopper*, after a submarine had been reported seen off Cape Helles:

> Closed on *Swiftsure* at full speed. When we got to her, we was all told off for our patrolling stations. At the same time looking for periscopes. We had not been on our course for more than 5 minutes when we saw the *Triumph* torpedoed and heaps of black smoke over her. At once there was a race for life by all destroyers. The *Triumph* and a TBD fired a few rounds at submarine [periscope] but she dived. The sinking ship had her [anti-torpedo] nets out which prevented her from getting her boats out. We could see her gradually listing over to starboard and then we saw her keel.
>
> The Turkish field guns fired on rescuing parties with shrapnel but luckily no one was hit. About 10 minutes she remained keel up, and slowly began to sink. There was not much of a swirl when she took her final dip. No one had found the submarine.

U-21's torpedo had been fitted with a net-cutting device. The loss of *Triumph* led to De Robeck withdrawing most of the battleships to Imbros. But each day two battleships were sent to provide naval gunfire support, mainly to reassure the soldiers that they were not being abandoned. The *Majestic* was torpedoed the next day off W Beach. General Paris expressed amazement that the she had remained at anchor, and wrote: 'Even naval officers expected she would be sunk & one Captain RN told an officer on board that he better get up early and come ashore.'[7]

Only 43 of her crew were lost. After this the U-boat successes in the Dardanelles tailed off. Because of the large number of small warships in the vicinity of the Dardanelles, any time spent by a U-boat surfaced was dangerous. But the small UB-class boats had a weak battery capacity and could spend only a limited time dived. They carried few torpedoes, which restricted their time on station. In September, newer, larger boats arrived, and eventually they had some forty boats, mainly in the western

Mediterranean, where they continued to attack the long lines of communication up to the end of the war. The RNAS struck back at the Turkish navy on 29 May. Samson:

> Osmond in a Voisin and myself in old No 50 [his favourite BE2a] went off to attack the *Barbarossa* [the *Heireddin Barbarossa* ex-*Kurfürst Friedrich Wilhelm*] an old Turkish battleship that used to cause annoyance to Anzac with her 11-inch guns. She lay close to the Asiatic shore about 6 miles above Nagara.
>
> I had to turn back owing to my engine starting to miss very badly. Osmond reached the *Barbarossa* which got underway as soon as it saw him. He let go one 100 lb and two 20 lb bombs at it and said he hit with the big one. This was confirmed afterwards by an American at Constantinople who reported that she had arrived with one turret damaged and ten men killed.

This was the first attack in history by an aircraft on a battleship, albeit an obsolete one. The *Heireddin Barbarossa* was eventually ambushed and sunk off Constantinople by Nasmith in E11 on 8 August 1915.

Every day the RNAS spotted for naval guns, employing up to six aircraft a day. Samson:

> We all loved the *Prince George* as she used to do implicitly what we told her. She used to waste no time at all. One day with her, the shells were getting too close to the Turks to stay any more, and we could see them running away in a big body to the rear. We signalled, 'Salvoes. 100 yards more range', and to our delight, within 20 seconds two beautiful bursts were right among them.
>
> The Monitor M 15 [one 9.2-inch gun with maximum range of 22,000 yards] in latter days used to shoot wonderfully well. Firing at a range of 20,000 yards [nearly twelve miles] she used to place shell after shell directly where we told her. One day there were two steamers about 150 feet long lying alongside each other. We put her on to them, and after three shells, she hit one of the steamers. We signalled, 'hit'. The next shell hit the second steamer. Another day with her we spotted a steamer alongside Ali Bashi pier. She hit the steamer with the fifth shell.
>
> Spotting for the *Abercrombie*, a 14-inch monster [two 14-inch guns, range 19,900 yards], the target was a gunboat and two destroyers lying in Chanak Bay. The first shell landed only 100 yards short and about 50 yards left of the gunboat. It was wonderful how quickly they got underway and steamed through the Narrows. We chased them the whole way with 14-inch shells.

By June it seemed that the stalemate on the Gallipoli peninsula would never be broken. Commander Dix, usually the most upbeat of people, and who cheerfully returned to duty after being wounded twice, wrote to his wife from Anzac Beach on the 6th:

> Six weeks today! And we are no further!! The time has come to say quite clearly that the military tactics & strategy are too B childish (and have been all along) for words. Why anyone out of an asylum should start to reduce a peninsula 41 miles long at its carefully prepared tip could only be explained by a soldier!!!
>
> Our position here has always been the kernel of the nut & if the BF of a C-in-C could send us a division here, we could do the trick for him & the whole position would be cleared up. But this must be done soon. The Turks are working like busy beavers on our flanks & every day will make it harder.
>
> The guns which shell the beach are getting most bestial. Instead of bombarding at regular hours, they suddenly drop one in without any warning and then a burst of fire for 10 minutes. Then they'll lull one into a false sense of security before starting again. It so often happens that one is out in the lighters when the swine start and that is the risk.
>
> I go for long walks round our trenches and visit our lookout stations when I'm not wanted on the beach – it is so much safer, as well as cooler, and less fly-ridden!
>
> There was hard fighting down south [at Cape Helles] last week. I fear the results were not wholly satisfactory. Nothing doing but bombing up here with some shells and constant rifle fire. We are all right and only need 15,000 men HERE to win a big victory.

In fact plans were afoot to reinforce Anzac and mount another amphibious assault in an attempt to break the deadlock, but Dix was not to see it. He had been discussing the plans to take in another eighteen thousand men to Anzac with General Birdwood and his staff and was on his way back to his headquarters when he was wounded, for the third time, by shrapnel from a bursting shell. He wrote to his wife on 2 August 1915:

> Bummish sort of stunt isn't it? What it is exactly is a shrapnel bullet which went in by the achilles tendon and lodged in the middle of all that long stuff which I call the ankle joint. Anyhow, an operation merely sufficed to prove that if it was taken out I should have a stiff ankle for the rest of my 'natch'. Whereas if it is left in I may not have. As far as I can gather that is the fair way of expressing it. We may both thank God it is no worse because your Cabe got badly mixed up in a 4-inch shrapnel burst. It went straight through my thick shooting boot & perhaps might have gone through altogether, but if 'ifs and ands' – etc.
>
> There is another way to consider it, & that is that anyone told off to live for 14 weeks on that beach might just as well sign his will and yet I have

come thro' it with what after all are two minor injuries. Where I do feel it is that my one big chance has escaped me and by a matter of a week! There was I in a big position for a junior officer doing big things and ready for a very big thing – keenly enjoying it and quite able to cope with it, when it all suddenly goes 'phut'! I don't mind in the least confessing that I had hopes of snatching some little kudos in the shape of a DSO, but now I feel others will reap where Cabe sowed and ploughed too.

In his memoirs he remarks that General Birdwood came to bid him goodbye:

one of those little things that made him so beloved – and I was carried down to a picket boat through a crowd of appreciative Anzacs, and so left a beach which I found that I loved for I was crying. I expect I was touched by the very unexpectedly friendly demonstration. I had great admiration for those Australians and New Zealanders, but I had been compelled to keep a stricter discipline on the Beach than they had been used to, and I know that made them think me a bit old-fashioned. They called me 'that fucking old bastard Neptune' and that I was a 'bloody hard-hearted old fucker', but they had great respect for my range of language, having only one word – starting with F– themselves which they greatly overused as noun, adjective and verb, and they realised I suppose that I took some interest in their welfare.

Dix was awarded the DSO, but missed by a few days the moves he had been working on and hoping for. The plan was for a major offensive by the Anzacs to take Chunuk Bair, Hill Q, and Hill 971, which dominated not only the bridgehead but also the Narrows on the other side of the Peninsula. Troops were landed on three successive nights to reinforce Anzac for this assault. There were to be two other attacks: a minor one at Cape Helles by the British 29th Division aimed at drawing Turkish reinforcements to the south, and a major one at Suvla, timed to coincide with the Anzac offensive. The amphibious assault at Suvla by Lieutenant General Sir Frederick Stopford's newly arrived British IX Corps (the 10th, 11th, and 13th New Army Divisions, and 53rd and 54th Territorial Divisions) was aimed at drawing Turkish reserves away from the Anzac sector and capturing high ground about five thousand yards inland to link up with the new Anzac bridgehead. Thus, at last the Allies would cut the Peninsula and be in a position to seize one side of the Narrows, and the fleet could go through, the aim for which so much blood had been expended – at least that was the hope.

Much new equipment had arrived in the theatre, including more monitors for bombardment, and, at last, fourteen specialized landing craft. These craft, Fisher's progeny, were motorized, armoured, capable of carrying five hundred men each, and had bow ramps; the direct ancestors of today's landing craft. They were painted black and were dubbed 'beetles' because the long projecting ramps in the raised position looked like antennae. Now there would be no wretched plodding progress ashore under fire in rowing boats. The air arm had been reinforced, allowing raids of up to fifteen aircraft to strike targets on the Peninsula and the Narrows.

The actual landing at Suvla was a great improvement on its predecessors in the campaign. Midshipman Drewry persuaded Unwin, who commanded the 'beetles', to take him with him (Unwin's and Drewry's VCs for Cape Helles were not gazetted until 15 August). Drewry wrote to his father:

> He [Unwin] worked it all right, and on the 2nd or 3rd of August, I put a shirt or two in a pillow case and joined up on K14, that being Unwin's flagship. K14 was similar to the other lighters except that it was fitted for a 4.7-inch gun which however was at the bottom of some supply ship's hold and could not be got at. 10 am on the 6th and we were told today's the day; we arranged ourselves in order brow down on the quay and waited.

After embarking troops and taking them out to the towing vessels:

> At dark we sailed, surely the strangest fleet that has ever sailed. First came the towing ship full of troops, then the lighter with 500 [men], and astern of her was the picket boat attached (each lighter had one). Unwin had a picket boat to himself, run by Midshipman Price DSC RN. I was simply a passenger. Soon after we started, Helles opened up a good fire and so did the flanking ships making a jolly fine display. As we approached Anzac a searchlight opened up on the Anzac hills as immense fire opened. It was a remarkable sight from the sea. One large space of hillside lit up brilliantly by destroyer searchlights and exploding shells [the start of the Anzac attack]. At sea nothing to be seen except the numerous hospital ships anchored off Anzac with their band of red and green lights and yet the sea teemed with life.
>
> About 11.30 pm we stopped and all cast off tows, being then very close inshore although we could only see just the outline of the beach. Of course silence and [no] lights was the order, but the motors seemed to make a terrible row and I think every one cursed them under his breath.
>
> It was not a happy sensation for we all remembered the last landing and what we met. What was going to happen if they expected us. They would mow us down for our decks were thick with soldiers.
>
> It was a beautiful beach with a good stretch of clear white sand and then a ridge with scrub over which we could not see without going up to

it. The lighters were able to beach just as wanted and when the brow was
lowered the men were able to walk ashore with dry feet. This was C Beach
between a mile and a mile and a half south of Nibrunesi Point. Immediately
north of us was B Beach [in fact B and C Beaches were the other way
round, C Beach being immediately south-east of Nibrunesi Point]. A Beach
was in Suvla Bay and unfortunately not a great success as the water was
very shallow there. The men had to wade ashore some distance up to their
waists, most casualties were here, they met a party of about 50 [enemy]
almost at once but a short fight soon dispersed them.

They landed a little earlier there than us at C & B and the firing started
just as we landed. Here and there along the coast a rifle would go off and
a few bullets flew around, but I saw nobody hit.

When we [in Unwin's picket boat] cast off from our tow, we stopped
for a few minutes, long enough for the first lighter to reach the beach,
and then ran in and saw she was all right. We visited them all as they ran
ashore and saw things were going well.

Within thirty minutes four battalions were ashore, and heading for
their objectives. Unwin left Drewry in charge, while he went to sort out
a broken-down lighter. Drewry could hardly believe what he was seeing:

I stayed on various motor lighters until ashore and had a run on the
beach, but it was uncanny. The troops got ashore in record time and
then came batteries, mules, and munition. I could not understand it, I
stood on the beach and saw guns being landed, and horses, and behind
us a few yards away was the dark containing what?

There was little firing, now and then a sharp rattle close and then
silence. I thought of Helles and wondered if we had landed by mistake at
Lemnos or if we were ambushed and the Maxims were going to clear the
beach of living in one sweep.

Midshipman Williams of the *Agamemnon*, by now seventeen and a
half, was also among those involved in the landings; having landed troops,
his task was casualty evacuation. Some years later he added a note to his
journal entries:

I had a picket boat. We joined the assembled armada of small craft at
Imbros with no knowledge of the impending operation except that it was
imminent.

The afternoon preceding the night of the attack a staff officer came,
told me we would be sailing for Suvla as soon as it was dark and that I was
to follow two trawlers each towing four lifeboats to a point just south of
Nibrunesi point. There the trawlers would stop, transfer troops to the
lifeboats, and I was to take over the tow of four boats and land the troops
at a spot on the beach he marked on my chart. Then, if all went well,

return for a second tow of the four other boats. The beach was thought sandy and steep-to [i.e. a steep beach gradient and ideal for landing troops dry shod]. He gave me two lines of morphia tablets (not encouraging) and wished us luck.

That was all I knew of the operation at zero hours.

In a letter written to his mother on 11 August 1915, he recounted his part in the landing:

A tremendous procession of ships left Mudros at dusk, destroyers and motor lighters full of troops, trawlers, picket boats, hospital ships. Even then we did not know where the landing was to come off. It was a dark night and pretty cold. We started across slowly, no lights or noise, and I was told off as a kind of messenger boat keeping the trawlers together. It was choppy and wet in the picket boat. I arrived at Nibrunesi with a crowd of other ships at about 1 am. It was jolly dark and all the swells on God's earth seemed to have collected in that blooming bay. The first troops had been landed already and we could hear intermittent rifle fire from the beach and gathered the Turks were not ready. Still it is unpleasant being fired at in the dark from goodness knows where, and 2 am is not a very good hour for feeling full of beans and ready to do or die.

I lay off until 4 am when I took a tow of boats for wounded. The evacuating of wounded in small boats is a very slow job, but we loaded up several boats at last. Just as I was loading my last boat the Turks started searching the beach up and down and all round with shrapnel. It's nasty stuff on a flat beach with no cover. All one can do is to pray for luck and hope it will not touch you.

All had not gone well the first night at Suvla. The vicissitudes of the troops evacuated by Williams were typical of many from the 11th Division, the leading formation of IX Corps. They had been heading for a low hill called Lala Baba less than a mile from where they had landed. These, the first men of Kitchener's New Army to go into battle, were inexperienced and totally without training for a night advance in strange terrain with no opposition, let alone against a formidable enemy such as the Turks, even in small numbers. To add to the confusion, there were insufficient maps and compasses. Although, to their credit, they found their objective, they suffered heavy casualties, and eventually collapsed shocked and exhausted into the enemy trenches. Their orders were to move on and seize Chocolate and W Hills before daylight. But at dawn the two leading brigades of 11th Division were still on Lala Baba, and the beach. In the first twenty-four hours IX Corps achieved none of the first night's objectives, and suffered 1,700 casualties at the

hands of a Turkish force that numbered around 1,500 soldiers commanded by a German, Major Willmer.

Although by 9 August Stopford had three divisions ashore, he did not
push his troops resolutely; instead he dallied on the beach, personally
supervising the construction of a shell-proof headquarters. Willmer's
resolute deployment of his 1,500 men against Stopford's 20,000 was
decisive, and by 10 August, Liman von Sanders had moved two Turkish
divisions up onto the key ridge before Stopford could get there.

The Anzacs, having taken their initial objectives against desperate
opposition, pushed out patrols but found no troops from IX Corps, with
whom they should have joined up and advanced. The Anzacs eventually
succeeded in linking their beachhead to that of IX Corps, but thanks to
Stopford, seizing Hill 971 and Chunuk Bair was beyond them. It was not
for lack of trying; eight Victoria Crosses were awarded to Australians
alone for the August fighting. The hopes of a successful conclusion to
the campaign began to wither.

On a more cheerful note, 12 August saw another 'first' by the RNAS.
A seaplane from the carrier *Ben-My-Chree*, flown by Flight Commander
Charles Edmonds, attacked a 5,000 ton Turkish supply ship by torpedo.
Edmonds reported:

> I glided down and fired my torpedo at the steamer from a height of about
> 14 feet and at a range of 300 yards, with the sun astern of me. I noticed
> some flashes from the tug [in the vicinity], so presumed she was firing at
> me, and therefore kept on a westerly course, climbing rapidly. Looking
> back, I observed the track of the torpedo, which struck the ship abreast
> the mainmast, the starboard side. The explosion sent a column of water
> and large fragments of the ship almost as high as her masthead.[8]

It was the world's first successful torpedo attack by an aircraft, and
was followed on 17 August by another. Edmonds sank three tugs. Flight
Lieutenant D'Acre in a Short seaplane had engine trouble and landed on
the water at False Bay. He pressed on, taxiing towards a large steam tug,
and fired his torpedo, hitting the target, which blew up and sank. Now
lighter without the torpedo, with bullets lashing the sea around him,
D'Acre managed to get airborne and returned to the *Ben-My-Chree*.

Launching and recovering an aircraft from a seaplane carrier was
a rather different evolution from taking off and landing on a true aircraft carrier with a flush deck, the first of which did not come into
service until 1919. The seaplane was started while on the small afterdeck,
and the crane hooked into a sling on the top wing. Lieutenant Donald
RNAS:

The crane hove you a few feet clear of the deck, swung you over the side on the quarter – depending on how the ship was lying and the weather – and lowered you into the water. As soon as your floats touched the water, you got rid of that hook as quick as you could, and the chaps aloft who knew their stuff hoisted the hook out of the way in case it fouled your propeller. Then the wind took you clear of the ship's side, and it was like any other seaplane takeoff. Get her head to wind, and take off.

Getting back was more tricky. You had to taxi right up to the ship's side on her quarter, judging it pretty carefully, and stop your engine as close to the ship's side as possible, but not too close or the propeller would hit the side, or any projections. You had to take care not to get under her stern, because if you came up there you got crushed. Your observer had to leap up and grab the swinging hook as it hung from the crane. If he missed, too bad because you drifted away very rapidly with your engines stopped, and you had to re-start which was not all that easy.

If he grabbed the hook all right, and hooked it into the sling on the top plane, the chaps on the crane had to know their stuff. They had to take in the slack very quickly and lift her just as she rose on the wave, hold it as the wave dropped away, and hoist as soon as you were properly clear of the water. She came up swinging a bit, and chaps on deck with long bamboo poles with padded ends made sure the wing tips didn't foul the shed or other projections. The chaps with poles would steer her round as the crane lifted her and swung her inboard, and dropped her on to a trolley.

A few days after the Suvla landing, Midshipman Williams was temporarily based ashore for casualty evacuation duties. He wrote to his mother on 15 August 1915:

I'm writing this in my dugout. It's most damnably hot and thank heavens things are pretty quiet so far as we are concerned. About two miles away inland the Turks and our people are doing their level best to kill one another and judging by the noise and amount of ammunition expended must be succeeding fairly well. The wounded will begin to come down this afternoon and I expect that we shall have the usual harrowing tales of defeat etc. over again. We are getting used to that now: the badly wounded always have awful yarns, however much we advance. Poor devils I don't wonder that their nerves give way under the strain. Even here, a couple of miles behind the firing line we hear very little of how things are going. We have spent one or two very anxious nights, when the wounded come in in crowds, and people imagine that the rifle fire is getting nearer every minute.

We are in the middle of a big curving beach, like the beach between Porthcawl and the mouth of the Ogmore: a pier has been built and is used only for the evacuation of the wounded, and the casualty station is up at the back of the beach under a small bank so is fairly safe from direct shell fire. The day before yesterday we three dug a splendid funk hole in this bank, a place we could hide in if they shelled us; but today it is being taken over by the field ambulance people as they want all the available space there. We are right out in the open and have red cross flags up in a commanding position. The Turks play the game fairly well and don't shell us much now. If they see a mule or stores of any description being landed they make known their objection in a very practical manner. So we are learning things by degrees, and keep stores, mules, wagons etc. well out of sight.

Last Thursday we put up a large mast and a red cross flag at the end of the pier as the Turks had dropped several large shells on the beach. I think the Turks must have used this mast for ranging on, as next morning at 7 am, just as we were getting a crowd of wounded off, and as I was halfway thro' breakfast, they started to shell us, or rather the pier, starting with big 8-inch high explosive. We had to dash down to the pier to get the wounded off, but thank God the Turks didn't get a direct hit on the pier, altho' shells seemed to be blooming well all round and we all got soaked by the columns of water they sent up. Of course I was in the most horrid funk as usual. I am quite sure I shall never get used to shell fire. The only difference after weeks of it is that one gets in a collected sort of funk and doesn't duck or dash round cursing. Anyhow on this occasion the wounded got so active that one could hardly tell who were wounded and who weren't and we got the boats loaded and pushed off in record time. Just as the boats pushed off they started shrapnelling us but there were not many casualties and for the next five minutes we sat under a high bank and finished our breakfasts while the Turks shelled an empty beach. Shell fire does make people shift. One or two shells bursting over clear the beach quicker than anyone would imagine.

By now Stopford had been replaced as GOC IX Corps at Suvla by Major General Beauvoir de Lisle. A new offensive was ordered for 21 August. Fortunately in view of what transpired, Hamilton reined in de Lisle's over-enthusiastic plan to seize the high ground which had been the ultimate objectives for the Suvla landing. Instead he was ordered to take W and Scimitar Hills, and Hill 60 which threatened the left flank of Anzac.

As usual, ships were in support, in this case the battleships *Venerable* and *Swiftsure*, the heavy cruiser *Euryalus*, and the light cruiser *Talbot*. By now the techniques of spotting by aircraft had greatly improved, but at this stage in the war much had still to be learned about a well-entrenched enemy's ability to sustain heavy bombardment and emerge to fight when it lifted; and not only at Gallipoli, it was a military fact of life that had yet to be mastered on the Western Front. Midshipman Baldwin in the old battleship *Venerable*:

Sat 21st. At 2.30 the commence was sounded, and all four opened fire with 6-inch or 7.5-inch. The idea was to capture a certain low hill which was well trenched and defended and to advance a good bit to the right of this. Each ship used about two guns and the land batteries were firing as hard as they could go. On the right flank of the attack the *Endymion* and *Grafton* [heavy cruisers], two Monitors and the Australian artillery and some of the batteries on Lalabala [sic] were keeping up a heavy fire. The ground over which the advance was to be made could hardly be seen for bursting shells and soon a large part of it was on fire and the smoke added to the already dense clouds. The noise was deafening. The Turks were not idle, covering our front and reserve trenches and all our known communications with shrapnel.

At 4 pm all ships ceased fire and the advance began. Despite the bombardment the resistance was stubborn. Only a glimpse was caught of the attack from the ships, but our men were seen to top the rise of the hill known as Hill 70 [he means Hill 60].

Despite Midshipman Baldwin's description of fire raining down on the enemy, shortage of artillery ammunition had restricted the fire plan for Hill 60 in particular. Viewed from a ship it might have looked impressive. But it was not enough to win the day. Despite the gallantry of the New Zealanders, Australians, the 5th Connaught Rangers, the 10th Hampshires, and the remnants of two Gurkha battalions, Hill 60 was never taken. Scimitar Hill resisted all the efforts to take it by the 29th Division, brought round from Cape Helles especially for the purpose. The 11th Division failed to capture W Hill, and the 2nd Mounted Division, a yeomanry formation fighting dismounted, was massacred attempting to reinforce failure.

The lack of success at Suvla signalled the end of the Gallipoli campaign. In mid-October Hamilton was ordered home and replaced by General Sir Charles Monro. At the same time Keyes suggested that there should be one more attempt to force the Narrows, by a headlong rush at dawn in conjunction with a push by the army on the Peninsula. His plan, which had the support of De Robeck's second-in-command, Rear Admiral Wemyss, was imaginative, including smokescreens, and old merchant ships filled with flotation drums to set off the mines. Keyes was sent to London to argue his case, where he was maddened by what he considered the cowardice of the Admiralty. Meanwhile Kitchener was out in Gallipoli, where the generals told him that a further offensive was out of the question. Consideration was given to evacuating Suvla and Anzac, but retaining a toehold at Cape Helles. After much agonizing, on 23 December the War Cabinet decided on a complete evacuation.

Meanwhile the Royal Navy continued to bombard and support the army ashore. Flying too near the bombarding ship could be risky, as Sub-Lieutenant Bremner discovered:

> I used to fly circles round the target, followed by an extended sweep over the ship, to see if she had laid out any signalling panels on deck to indicate that she had finished and you could go home, and then go back over the target. On occasions I did a figure of eight and crossed the line of fire, being very careful not to do this until I could see the top of the gun barrel, when I knew I was under the trajectory. Once just as I was crossing her; I wasn't high enough above because a 15-inch shell passing underneath me created such a disturbance that my machine went down like a stone.

Much of the later bombardments were by monitors such as the *Earl of Peterborough* (two 12-inch guns, two 12pdr and two 3-inch anti-aircraft guns, and one 2pdr gun). Lieutenant Dusting of the *Earl of Peterborough* kept the flying report of the spotting aircraft (Pilot: Flight Commander Busk, Observer: Captain Jopp). After spotting for a shoot on Galata aerodrome on 2 December 1915, the report states:

> Hostile aircraft bombing monitor – A Taube was sighted after the 3rd round at aerodrome and it appeared to drop bombs on the monitor, one of which fell directly under her port bow and one astern.

> Hostile aircraft attack – we proceeded to attack and owing to our height (9,000 feet) got over the Taube at Karabili as it was making for home. We dived reaching its level (6,000 feet) when about 40 or 50 yards astern of it. We opened fire with our machine guns. The Taube also dived, turned broadside and opened fire with a machine gun on us. We pursued to a height of 1,000 feet, maintaining the same range slightly below it in height. After firing 70 or so rounds our gun jambed [sic] and was unable to return his fire. He continued to fire and we abandoned pursuit. Machine gun fire was opened on us from the ground at Karabili.

Samson commented:

> This combat was a very fine performance as it was carried out miles inside the Turkish lines and there were plenty of Turks helping the German by firing machine guns and rifles at our machine. It is no joke flying at 1,000 feet over country black with soldiers.

To the very end the RNAS kept up their offensive spirit, and the attacks covered in this chapter are a sample only. In early December, Samson noted that 'we are at present making fittings to carry a 500 lb bomb. If we hit anything with this, it will suffer'.

The evacuation of Suvla and Anzac was carried out concurrently; one could not be relinquished without exposing the other. The *Earl of Peterborough* was one of the monitors covering the withdrawal. She drew only 9 feet 7 inches, about a third of a battleship's and heavy cruiser's draught. Even the largest monitors drew only 11 foot 8 inches, so could go in close. Dusting:

Dec 19 1915 Sunday

At dusk we weighed and proceeded to our position to cover the right flank of Suvla & anchored about 1,000 yards from the beach. Being told we were in the *Grafton*'s way [a heavy cruiser], we shifted billet to about 750 yards off the beach. We could see the troops embarking quite plainly on the lighters, these taking them to the transports, and returning for more. This was all carried out splendidly due (as we afterwards heard) to the Turks thinking that the large fleet in the bay was a fresh landing start to a general push by us, accompanied by a bombardment from our fleet. The Turks promptly dug themselves further than before and put up massive entanglements. At daylight we proceeded to Kephalo [Cape Kephalo, Imbros]. During the whole show last night there were only four wounded and two killed, although 21,000 men got off. Early in the night a staff officer came on board to direct our firing if we were required. We were to look after Suvla's right flank to Anzac's left.

Thanks to a brilliant deception plan and immaculate organization and discipline, both Suvla and Anzac were evacuated without the Turks detecting what was up. Unwin was last off the Suvla beach in his picket boat. At Anzac Captain Stavely RN, the beach master, departed last, only just preceded by Birdwood. As the New Zealanders filed down to the boats, one soldier said to his battalion commander, 'I hope, Sir, that those fellows who lie buried along the Dere will be soundly sleeping and not hear us as we march away.'

Sub-Lieutenant Bremner had a brush with a German Fokker the day before the evacuation at Helles.

I was flying an old Voisin, a queer old machine built of bicycle tubing, with a four-wheel undercarriage. If you made a bad landing, it galloped across the aerodrome and you had to get off again. Once you got it off it went on galloping in the air till you could get control of it; its maximum speed was about 50 knots. I'd been spotting and my Observer wanted to see something further up the Peninsula, and suddenly I found a Fokker behind me. I had only a Lewis gun which my Observer could fire forwards and downwards. The Fokker fired several bursts at me and made off. I found my engine revs dropping, it was a 14 cylinder Canton Unét situated behind me, and he'd put bullets through my cylinders. I couldn't get home and landed on the emergency aerodrome on the Peninsula.

I cleared the front line trenches by about six feet and popped down on the aerodrome. They'd got a dugout there, a slot in the side of the hill, which would just take an aeroplane and prevent direct hits. The mechanics rushed out, pushed me in, and I tried to get hold of a demolition squad to destroy the machine. But they wouldn't let me set fire to it, because they were evacuating that night and didn't want any fires that might indicate they were destroying stores. As we had already evacuated Suvla, the Turks were expecting us to go any time, and any little thing might have given them a clue when the withdrawal from Helles might take place.

I was sent to W Beach and went on to a lighter, and sat from about six o'clock in the evening to about one o'clock the following morning. Lighters were tied up against a pier on W Beach; the pier took four lighters each side, and the width of the pier was such that men could march eight abreast. When they got a few yards up the pier, the rank divided into fours, and each column streamed into the four lighters. When they were full, they were towed away, and four more were brought, and so on until one o'clock in the morning. All the time the gun Asiatic Annie fired from the other side of the straits. It never made a direct hit; luckily they were using high explosive not shrapnel. Everything went like clockwork. There wasn't a sound. At one o'clock I embarked on the SS *Partridge*, the second last ship to leave the Peninsula.

A bugler had been posted on the ramparts at Sedd el Bahr, who blew a long 'G' every time he saw the flash of Asiatic Annie firing, so men could move off the track into the ditch alongside. The evacuation on Helles had been brought forward at the last moment by a day. Lieutenant Spragge in the destroyer *Fury*:

Jan 8. the evacuation which was to have taken place the evening of Jan 9 has been changed to tonight.

Jan 9. Arrived off C Helles at 1 am, & loafed about. At 2 pm the last soldiers were arriving at W Beach & they lighted the stores and tents that had to be left behind. One ammunition lighter made a great popping as .303 inch [rifle ammunition] went off in the flames & finally blew up. Shortly afterwards half the peninsula seemed to go into the air & as I was on the forecastle about 3 cables away, I retired under my gun shield & prayed lustily for the space of 30 seconds while rocks fell round. They had blown up about 100 tons of ammunition. Shortly after this at 4.30 pm we managed to get alongside the pier and embarked the Naval beach party. These gentlemen being the last British to leave the peninsula.

After we had shoved off, we tried to take a pinnace in tow but after several attempts we gave it up & she proceeded at slow speed for Kephalo where we arrived with her at 8 am. We went alongside *Lord Nelson* & embarked some 200 troops and 5 officers for passage to Mudros.

From the account of the soldiers, the Turks had taken a trench and nearly broken through our lines on Jan 7 in the afternoon, but on the night of the evacuation they had shown hardly any activity at all; certainly on W Beach there were very few shells falling, till after we left, when about quarter of an hour after we shoved off a lot of shrapnel started falling, and our ships replied with very heavy fire at the gun flashes on Achi Baba. The last we saw was Achi Baba covered with smoke and spurts of flame and three of the Talbot class [he means *Eclipse*-class cruisers, of which HMS *Talbot* was one] & three monitors firing as if their sole object was to get rid of ammunition as quick as possible. I do not think the Turks had any knowledge that the evacuation was taking place that night.

Again a well-conceived deception plan and sound organization had ensured a successful evacuation. King George V sent a signal to the Mediterranean Fleet:

I heartily congratulate you and all concerned on the well conceived and successfully carried out plans by which the troops have been withdrawn from Gallipoli without loss.

The combined Naval and Military operations within this theatre will always rank among the finest achievements of this war.

However, as Churchill remarked about Dunkirk in 1940, 'Wars are not won by evacuations'.[9] One might add that they are not won by defeats either, and Gallipoli was just that, costing around 265,000 British, Dominion, and French casualties for no gain whatsoever.

8

Dardanelles – submarine operations

Among the brightest episodes of the whole Dardanelles campaign were the exploits of the British submarines, which began well before any other major activity in the theatre of operations. Once the land campaign started, British submarines were sent in to the Sea of Marmara to cut the Turkish maritime supply line to the Gallipoli peninsula. Taking a submarine through the Narrows was a hazardous endeavour, especially when one remembers that the techniques of subsurface operations were still in their infancy. A three-to-four-knot current flows from the Sea of Marmara to the Dardanelles, in which layers of fresh and salt water provide an unwelcome challenge to a submariner attempting to maintain a steady trim and depth. In fresh water a submarine is less buoyant, and may suddenly plunge down (a 'depth excursion' in modern submarine jargon); if when trimmed for fresh water it encounters water with greater density, it will tend to bob to the surface.

Ten lines of mines off Kephez Point were a further hazard. Once past these lay the Narrows, less than a mile wide, constantly patrolled by gunboats and covered by numerous guns and searchlights. On 13 December 1914, Lieutenant Holbrook had taken B11 from Tenedos through the minefields guarding the Narrows. The B8–11-class boats built in 1906 were obsolete. Their top speed dived was 6 knots, which they could maintain for only three hours before their batteries became flat. They could make 4.5 knots for eight hours dived, a speed which allowed little headway against the current, so Holbrook delayed diving until the last moment. He had been briefed about the lines of mines at the entrance to the Narrows. In daylight, and dived, as he approached the first known line of mines, he saw through his periscope the elderly Turkish battleship *Messudieh* anchored in Sari Sighlar Bay. To get into a firing position, he had to pass five rows of mines, and as he closed his target, he was spotted. The boat kept 'porpoising' as it passed through water of differing density. In a letter to Keyes, he wrote:

Often she came up as far as forty feet then went down again without altering speed or helm. When I wished to bring her up I had to give her full helm and speed for up to 500 [rpm] on two [motors] and even then sometimes remained at twenty feet for quarter of an hour or more, before she would come up the remaining twenty-five feet to see. When I sighted the *Messudiyeh* [sic] I altered eight points to starboard to attack her, and the boat immediately sank to eighty feet and remained there, and nothing would bring her up till I blew two auxiliaries for five minutes. I think the cause of this was the sudden change of tide [current] from ahead to the beam. At the time of firing the diving was very erratic, the depth varying from fifteen to forty feet. On firing the boat sank to forty feet (I made men run forward) and took some time on three [motors] before she came up, then she refused to dive till I flooded the auxiliaries I had previously blown.[1]

As he fired two torpedoes, he was under fire himself from every gun that could bear, from shore batteries to the *Messudieh*'s secondary armament. Both torpedoes hit, and the *Messudieh* turned turtle in a few minutes.

He was fired at several times on his return trip; on the course he took with only thirty feet of water under his keel, his conning tower was above the surface for much of the time. He grounded at one point, but got clear. When he arrived at Tenedos, he had been submerged for nine hours with almost dead batteries, and only the fact that he had the current with him allowed him to make it. He was awarded the Victoria Cross, the first naval VC of the war to be gazetted, and first ever to a submariner. The Turks sowed more mines in the Dardanelles, and withdrew their larger warships to Constantinople, well out of range of the B-class boats.

The four E-class boats that arrived in the theatre on 5 April 1915 were a considerable improvement on the B-class. Many of the E boat COs had 'cut their teeth' under Keyes in the North Sea, and were straining at the leash to show what the young submarine service could do.

Two attempts in April 1915, by E15 and the Australian AE2 respectively, were unsuccessful. The fate of E15 was covered in the previous chapter. On 27 April, Lieutenant-Commander Boyle in E14 reached the Sea of Marmara, where he sank a Turkish gunboat and damaged a transport. On his return he was awarded the Victoria Cross.

On 19 May, E11 under command of Lieutenant-Commander Nasmith joined E14 in the Sea of Marmara. After dinner aboard the *Queen Elizabeth* with De Robeck, Keyes and Boyle, Nasmith left Imbros at 1.10 a.m. on 20 May, and by sun up was dived off Nagara Point where he saw the Turkish battleships *Torgud Reis* and *Heireddin Barbarossa* accompanied by several destroyers. The two battleships fled up the Straits and were lost to view in clouds of smoke. The destroyers attacked whenever

Nasmith put up the periscope, which at speed created a large ripple, easily seen in the low morning light. Nasmith followed the two battleships but could not get near them thanks to the destroyers.

By 21 May, and well inside the Sea of Marmara, he sent his first lieutenant, D'Oyly-Hughes, to board a small coaster, where he 'stole four chickens, offering in payment the enormous sum of a 1/-. The same being refused by a much frightened and extremely polite Turkish skipper.'[2]

On 23 May, while approaching Constantinople, E11 sank a gunboat, but not before it had put a 6pdr shell through the foremost periscope, putting it out of action. The next day, E11 intercepted a small steamer, which was boarded. Having spotted a 6-inch gun lying on deck, and that the holds contained ammunition, she was sunk using a demolition charge. Another steamer was sighted, and Nasmith followed her to Rodosto, where she made fast to a pier. Nasmith approached but grounded about 2,000 yards away. He fired one torpedo which struck the steamer midships, and slowly backed off. Turkish soldiers on the pier fired at him with rifles, hitting but not damaging his remaining periscope.

No sooner was E11 clear and still dived than Nasmith saw a small paddle-steamer, which he approached on the surface. She stopped when fired at by rifles, but realizing that E11 had no gun she made for the shore, gamely turning to ram when E11 closed. Because Nasmith could see horses and barbed wire on board, she was a legitimate target, and he pursued, keeping up a fusillade of rifle fire, until she ran ashore and her crew jumped overboard and swam to shore. Nasmith edged in to the shallow water, intending to place demolition charges on the steamer, when two Turkish mounted soldiers were seen galloping towards the shore, followed by nearly a hundred more. They dismounted and engaged the E11 with a fusillade of small-arms fire. Nasmith, wisely, withdrew. In this, one of the few, perhaps only, battles between a submarine and cavalry, the latter decidedly won. Nasmith tried to destroy the steamer with a torpedo but the shallowness of the water forced him to fire at long range, and as the vessel was stern-on, and presented a small target, he missed.

The next day, Nasmith took E11 into Constantinople harbour. He took two photographs of the Blue Mosque through his periscope to prove he had been there, before firing both bow tubes at two ships lying alongside the Arsenal Wharf. He was very lucky. The port torpedo circled back, just missing his boat. The starboard torpedo missed its intended target and hit a larger ship nearby. Nasmith was unable to observe the strike because he was fully engaged trying to prevent his boat being swept ashore by a strong tide, and trying to evade what he thought was an enemy wire-guided, shore-launched Brennan torpedo but was actually his rogue from the port tube. The boat kept being bumped to the surface in the strong tidal flow, only countered by going full speed astern and flooding all internal ballast tanks. He then felt his way out along the bottom, until with sighs of relief all round he was clear and could set a course for the Sea of Marmara.

He was doubly lucky, because, unknown to him, the ship the starboard torpedo was intended for was the USS *Scorpion*. The Americans had sighted E11's periscope and saw the torpedo running about thirty yards away, hitting lighters alongside the steamer *Stamboul*, and blowing a hole in the side of the *Stamboul*. The *Scorpion's* captain hastily ordered the American ensign hoisted at the main mast.

The next day, Nasmith sent hands to bathe, and ordered a make and mend, 'it being necessary for everyone to have a rest'.[3] Early on the 27th he spotted a large battleship in the moonlight, but was chased off by escorting destroyers as he closed for the kill. Well out in the middle of the Sea of Marmara he declared an official washing day, and 'certainly not before they needed it, being nine days since the last one.'[4]

The following day, he attacked five vessels escorted by a destroyer. He sank one, before being forced to dive to seventy feet to avoid the destroyer. It should be remembered that there were no depth charges until 1916, and no means of detecting a dived boat. Later that afternoon, he fired a torpedo at a steamer, but it missed underneath. He recovered the torpedo after the vessel had gone.

Two days later, he reported:

> Spent this day in clearing up the boat as much as possible, crew washing and bathing. We are beginning to have trouble with the state of the atmosphere whilst diving. The air soon becoming oppressively foul. This being probably due to the fact that there is so much dirty linen etc. about, and in consequence of the amount of sweat falling in the boat, most of the clothing in the boat is damp. These things, in addition, to the fact of the crew constantly eating and sleeping in the boat, and that only a minimum amount of cleanliness is possible, tend to make the boat anything but sweet smelling.[5]

On 31 May, E11 torpedoed a German steamer; her crew managed to beach her, but she was too badly damaged to warrant expending another torpedo. Two days later E11 sank another store ship, and missed another underneath, but recovered the torpedo. On 6 June, after discovering a cracked intermediate shaft, Nasmith sent a signal asking permission to return, which was granted. Early on the morning of 7 June, E11 passed the town of Gallipoli dived at ninety feet, and came to periscope depth to examine all anchorages, hoping to find a battleship. Finding none, Nasmith retraced his course to attack and sink a large liner being used by the Turks as a trooper, before tackling the Narrows. He passed Chanak at 2 p.m. A little later he heard a noise like the keel scraping the bottom, but knowing that this could not be so at his present depth, he rose, and looked through his periscope to see about twenty feet ahead of him a large mine snagged in his port forward hydroplane and being towed along. He said nothing to his crew, and in his report wrote:

> 4.0 pm: Rose to the surface, and by going full speed astern, and rising to the surface stern first, managed to shake clear a large mine which had been hanging to the port foremost hydroplane since passing Chanak. Two hours earlier on rising to the surface we were met by the *Grampus* who escorted us to Port Mudros.[6]

Towing a mine for over an hour while dived and negotiating the passage through the Narrows and down the Straits would test the nerve of the coolest customer. Nasmith was promoted to commander immediately and awarded the VC.

At 11.07 p.m. on 30 June 1915, E7 (Lieutenant-Commander Archibald Cochrane) left Mudros for the Sea of Marmara. The first lieutenant, Oswald Hallifax, kept a diary of the patrol. The first night negotiating the Narrows began badly with the CO, whom Hallifax refers to as 'C', apparently in bad humour; 'I regret to say that I had felt properly mutinous, C had been most infernally offside to me the whole time', and

> while diving he sat with his eyes closed and mumbled. It was not until next day that he told me how frightfully ill he felt all that night, so bad in fact that when abreast of Nagara he decided to return – it would require C to be mighty bad for that – only we ran aground then and that made him forget to do so. He told me he could scarcely see thro' the periscope. When we started up the Dardanelles, C came up to periscope depth and took three bearings to check. Then went to 80 feet; Twyman (Sub Lieutenant navigator) was told to get away forrard and stay there. C nearly broke the ruler roughly over the chart without any pencil marks, then folded up the chart and sat down. He took two more similar 'fixes' with Twyman kept well away – I sat on beam tube also well away. It was only Friday morning he told us the bearings were all shams for he could not see anything clearly!
>
> Apparently he told Twyman to see he did nothing silly. It's this infernal diarrhoea or dysentery: Twyman had it too and was feeling pretty bad. I did feel such a swine when I knew about this.

7.20. Rounded Nagara at 7.25 hit the bottom at 80 feet at the head of the bend; got a bad list and had to go 1,000 [revs] on each motor, and the port motor 'blew up' [raced out of control?] so that we nearly drove up on to the beach. We were off Gallipoli at noon having broken surface when a mile or two west of it; we also broke surface before that.

12.35 Went to the bottom and all went to sleep, nobody worrying about food. A gunboat had been nosing about after us at the Narrows, and made rushes when we showed our periscope. C says that she came at full speed at right angles to us on the last occasion and we dived to 40 feet and she must have passed over our stern; he added that as we were then very close to the beach he thinks she must have run aground.

8.50 pm came up to 20 feet to look round and then to the surface and went on deck and got quite a shock to find the land on either side so close to us; had to dive for a TBD which was about 400 yards off. Came up again at 11.45 and got under way on the engine and charged [batteries].

The next day, E7 was well out in the Sea of Marmara, surfaced, and 'stopped and shipped the gun'. Following Nasmith's difficulty torpedo-ing vessels in shallow waters, and their ability to evade him, and to save torpedoes, E7 had been issued with a 6pdr in Malta on her way to the Dardanelles. Subsequently all boats were fitted with a gun, or guns, of varying calibres.

In the evening, E7 found E14 [Boyle], and Cochrane went on board in the folding [?] boat: Stanley [first lieutenant of E14] came to see me. They have seen practically nothing this time, but have sunk a few steamers and sailing vessels; their engine is apparently badly carbonised and Stanley hopes they may go to Malta. He said that Bruce [CO of E12] had told them that there had been a lot of hesitation as to giving more VCs when [E]11 went in, and that it was finally given to Nasmith for entering Constantinople like that. Now what is there for us to do?

The next day saw E7 off Rodosto looking for targets. They found two brigantines and a small steamer anchored close inshore:

I got an order to prepare a 16¼ lb charge, and while doing so was told to come up with a tin of petrol and two boxes of matches as C did not want to waste time. I told him the charge was nearly ready and he said he would use it on the brigantine and told me to jump on board the steamer with Matthews and set her on fire.

They poured the petrol over some old mattresses below in two small cabins, and forgetting how petrol vaporizes – 'I thought of it as paraffin' – Hallifax told Matthews to light inside the port cabin, and he would follow suit in the other:

The compartment we were in was quite small. He lit his match and I leant forward and there was a blinding flash and all the air round us seemed to burst into flame. I felt a horrible pain in my legs below the knees – I had sandals on, no socks, and my trousers rolled up to my knees – I thought I was alight and instinctively thought of the petrol in the starboard cabin and we tore up the hatchway; Matthews slipped halfway up so that we reached the door together and one half being closed, we jambed there for a second and burst thro' on deck. Thinking I was alight behind, I was going to jump in the 'ditch' [sea] but Cochrane who was waiting on the after end of the casing held out his hand and told me to jump and got hold of Matthews's hands and let him jump and we both hurried below.

Once down the pain got worse and worse; Matthews was burnt on the face, neck, forearms and hands, and the outer side of my right arm was burnt raw, and both feet and up as far as the thickest part of the calves blistered.

I could not think of the right thing to put on, but everyone said oil, so the large can of sperm oil was brought along and poured over us and lint soaked and laid on the burns. Then Sims appeared and said Picric was the stuff and put that on instead and constant wetting of the stuff had a soothing effect.

While being soused with oil I began to feel faint so got hold of the bottle of Sal Volatile and thinking there was not time to find if this had to be diluted – for no one there knew of that, I poured out about a third of a wine glass and tossed that off! It stopped me fainting but I am certain it nearly killed me for I couldn't breathe or do anything but glare at the bottle and sign for water. When that came I drank two big tumblers to drown it.

While this charade was taking place, the brigantine had been blown to pieces with the charge and the steamer was burning merrily. The other brigantine was sunk by gunfire, and at 12.25 a gunboat was seen approaching from the westward and we dived. At 2.20 she got fed up with it and proceeded West. We could see a small steamer going west through the Marmara channel, surfaced and made for her, which caused the gunboat to turn back after us and at 3.5 she opened fire; shot fell short but she was overhauling us so we dived but could not get near her.

On 4 July, another brigantine was burned, but using paraffin this time. While dived, Cochrane examined Hallifax's feet and legs:

They were a horrid sight with huge blisters like Portuguese men-of-war [jelly fish]; the arm which was raw, he washed with Boric lint [wrung out in water]; and then looking at my feet again, said he would send me back in E14 if we met her that evening. Thinking that the blisters would heal in about a week and I should be able to move about in a fortnight at the most, I objected and nothing more was said. They did not hurt much then, not enough to prevent me sleeping.

Sunday July 4 1915 Sea of Marmara

I lie on the upper bunk all day and climb on to the lower bunk for meals; yesterday I had my meals at the table, but this dysentery business has started again, so I only have soup, biscuit and tea now, and vegetables at lunch.

July 5 Sea of Marmara

5.50 surface.

I now suffer torture when I have to use my feet; I sort of climb along from pipe to pipe and beam to beam with [only] my heels touching the deck.

July 8th Sea of Marmara

I had a sleepless night; I could not keep my feet still for one moment for in every position the part in contact with the bunk got red hot pains; from 9 to 4 I felt like going mad; I did drop off about 3 for a quarter of an hour out of sheer exhaustion but the pain continued and took shape in a horrible dream in which one side of my leg would be blown out with high pressure air, and the air allowed to rush from that to the opposite side of the leg.

Lying on the blankets day after day and night after night, they seem to grow more like thistles every minute and the temperature of my skin seems enormous; after lying on one's back for a time the pillow feels positively hot where my neck has been. I simply long for a hospital or hospital ship where they would have means of keeping ones feet supported, and where one would lie on sheets with a cool pillow instead of hot service canvas things. It has done a lot of good to write down my unhappy feelings as I can not tell them to anyone.

When we came to the surface we saw three lots of thick smoke along the western coast towards Gallipoli. Dived to intercept and found the first smoke to be from a hospital ship; the other being caused by two tugs each towing two dhows escorted by four destroyers. Attacked the convoy at long range, and fired the port beam tube at one line of barges. A destroyer was nearly on top of us so we had to dive to 60 feet; about three minutes later we heard the explosion and the torpedo must have hit the beach we supposed. Later. – the explosion was rather prolonged as the lighter was close inshore, we have great hopes of one.

After sighting more hospital ships and another steamer, and a brush with a gunboat then with a destroyer, E7 remained dived until dark, when she surfaced and attempted to make wireless contact with base to no avail.

Friday July 9th Sea of Marmara

Another sleepless night, not so much pain, but my head is the trouble. There seems to be a noise going on inside it the whole time and I can not think of anything; if I try to say my prayers I drift off into a hundred other subjects before I have got through six words and yet I don't know what these subjects are.

The generator of the gyro compass gives a loud hum and also a high note that eats into every corner of one's brain. If I get into a fairly comfortable position – last night they all were [comfortable], for my feet from the knees down were numb – I turn my head over on the pillow, but there is the gyro drumming thro' it, and I sob and curse the thing from 9 or 10 at night till 8 in the morning.

At 3.0 pm sighted a large Xebec and altered course to intercept her. At same time we sighted a TBD. Put four shells into Xebec and dived hastily as TBD had seen us by this time and was making for us at full speed.

TBD hung round for a couple of hours so we stayed down till 9.45, came to the surface for quarter of an hour and dived for the night. I took some Phenacitin before 9.0 and stuffed my ears with cotton wool and that seemed to soothe me for although I did not sleep, I was able to lie still – my feet again being numb – and tell myself a long yarn I am now engaged on, since my eyes get so tired from reading. But from 3 am onwards the gyro got hold of my head again and I seemed to have 20 voices telling 20 different yarns in my head at once. It was just hell.

Saturday July 10th

To our great joy we sighted a 3–4,000 ton steamer alongside the pier. Dived at 9 and this time she did not shove off; she had thought to protect herself by having two sailing ships lashed outside her, but from her mainmast aft she was exposed. We fired a torpedo at about 1,500 yards and hit her abreast the mainmast. Our first torpedo hit of the war. This was a TNT head with a very sharp explosion. The effect was terrific, C said a column of water was thrown 300 feet into the air and the ship just broke in two by the main mast.

Hallifax was taken on deck when at 12.30 hands went to bathe.

I did envy the men washing and bathing. Twyman does not bathe lest his stomach takes offence again.

3.20 that infernal gunboat came meandering in its foolish way along the coast and seeing us started towards us, so I had to go below, both hatches were closed and we dived soon after. C very angry as he was just going to bathe.

On 13 July E7 found the old Turkish battleship *Muin-i-Zaffer*:

At about 11.30 we got the bow tube ready, at the critical moment just as the sights were coming on, Kelly who was steering, who by the way seems unable to grasp the idea of working the helm, got 1° to port of his course and put starboard helm on to bring her back and before C realised what he was doing had 20° of helm on and the boat could not be brought back in time and the attack was lost.

C went after her again and ordered the stern tube ready; the fools aft must have been spinning a yarn when we dived, I suppose, and forgot to crack the stern cap, result being that it took them nearly 10 minutes to open it – the pressure had stuck it on the rubber of course – by which time we were out of range.

To have got a battleship would have been splendid. But to have the chance twice and lose it each time thro' the stupidity of fools filled me with horror for it will make him [Cochrane] as mouldy as can be – just as he was bucking up a bit too.

Got both torpedoes back and ready again, then I heard the order to stand by bow tube and hoped it was the ship again. Fired and heard no explosion but they did amidships, a very slight noise; he had fired at a cluster of steamers alongside the quay.

Poor old thing it is rather hard luck on him, and he does deserve some luck.

In a note added in the margin later, Hallifax wrote:

on our return to Mudros C was officially informed that the torpedo hit a gunboat and blew her bows off. Hurrah.

and later: 'C getting over his unhappiness, I am glad to say'. The following day E7 saw a destroyer towing a submarine, which later turned out to be a German boat:

We dived and sped up to cut them off; they must have seen us just before we dived and the tow having been slipped the TBD started zig-zagging about.

We could not quite do it [cut them off], so we came to the surface at 3.30 and saw them steering past Marmara Island. We went ahead on the engines and dashed along the European coast close inshore in the hope of being able to get ahead of them unseen against the land for they were only making about 6 knots.

When off [indecipherable] the inhabitants opened a very accurate rifle fire, which caused Twyman and Cochrane to get inside the conning tower. There was one good shot who watched for C to shove his head up and every time a bullet whistled overhead or hit the bridge, which worried C as his coat was hanging on the fore periscope standard and he wanted to bring it down before diving. He got it safely in the end.

6.15, by this time we were slightly ahead of the enemy who were about 4,000 yards off and had evidently been steering over towards more than we thought, so we dived and went 700 [revs] on each [motor] for some time, but just couldn't do it.

On 15 July, Cochrane took E7 into Constantinople:

12.10 dived in towards Constantinople. There is a devil of a tide on the entrance of the Bosphorus and we were first carried across on to Seraglio Point where we grounded at 80 feet and then along the bottom for some time. When we got clear of that we ran aground several times at 30 feet off Skutari. Once to my horror we touched and ran along the bottom at 22 feet.

Cochrane said the water there is so thick and greasy that after the periscope had been up a few seconds, a film dried over the glass, so he had to be constantly dipping it to clear it. He fired the bow tube close to Leander's Tower at 3.30 pm, being that moment aground at 23 feet. He fired at the Arsenal, there was no steamer alongside, but plenty of dhows and lighters.

On our way in we passed two tugs with two strings of lighters escorted by four TBDs on their way west.

1 minute 35 seconds after firing, while we were turning ourselves on the shingle, the explosion took place. It was a mighty big one. We got off the bottom and retired at 40 feet.

Cochrane awfully bucked up and can't stop smiling. We dived to San Stephano and at 6.50 went to the bottom there, and are coming up at 10.00 to bombard the powder mills. How many rounds we shall be able to get off, I wonder, as since the day E11 chased a steamer ashore there 18 guns are reported to have been mounted round the mills.

At 10.15 came to the surface and just got the top of the casing out of the water. A very dark night, but clear and bright stars; C and Hooper (the gunlayer) sat up there and watched for a long time and after about an hour they saw the Powder Mills against a train which passed close behind them, so they opened fire and got 10 rounds off. There was no reply, but we dived as a patrol boat had been knocking about all the time.

From Constantinople, Cochrane headed for the Gulf of Ismid (present-day Izmit). The railway, from the eastern part of Turkey and eventually Baghdad, ran along the northern shore of the Gulf from Ismid to Skutari on the eastern shore of the Bosphorus. Here E7 engaged the trains with her gun. Twyman described it in a letter, written the day after returning from the patrol:

We shelled a railway and destroyed two troop trains. We shelled the embankment and blocked the line, and then caught the trains as they came along. It was the funniest thing you can imagine to see the trains try to hide behind trees. But we caught them and smashed them to blazes. The ammunition blew up with a tremendous explosion. The soldiers of course got out and took cover and fired at us, but we were out of range.

E7 headed west towards Rodosto, on the north-west shore of the Sea of Marmara, and carried out more shore bombardments of likely targets, destroying two more dhows on the way. By 22 July, E7 was back in the Gulf of Ismid, and had been away for over three weeks. Cochrane had spotted a short tunnel on his last visit and was determined to have a 'go at it'. Although, as Hallifax remarked in his diary, 'it is very doubtful what effect a 6-pdr shell would have'.

We were closing in to the tunnel at 7.45 when C saw a train coming along – quite a short train – so we dashed to the surface and opened fire. They had just got the range, one shot just missed the funnel of the engine, when the train nipped into the tunnel. There are so many cuttings along here that when ranging they could only take the occasional shot.

We retired to the westward to the accompaniment of a furious rattle of rifle fire; apparently as a result of our last visit, the line is now well guarded.

The next day, E7 rendezvoused with E14:

Boyle and Stanley came on board, and the latter gave me all the news. The Turks have announced that in view of the attacks by British submarines on harmless people etc. they will send French and Englishmen now in their hands into the war zone; Gray [British Foreign Secretary] has replied that he will hold Enver Bey and others (named) personally responsible for them and they have piped down. He also warned them that they are suspected of sending troops down in steamers and sending wounded back in those ships and not announcing and painting those ships according to Hague Convention; and warning them that they render themselves liable to attack.

It is good to know that our doings here are noticed by the Turks.

E2 has arrived in Malta with a broken shaft, what on earth do they want to send that crock out here for?

E14 was sent up for two reasons; one to warn us that nets have been laid across the Dardanelles from Nagara (an aeroplane saw them) and secondly that a French boat might be expected here and to warn us lest we should shoot at her. E14 saw the buoys of the nets; they extended two thirds of the way across. She fouled something off Kilid Bahr; felt a heavy bump and then something like a mooring rumbled all along her side.

E7 left the Sea of Marmara and made the passage of the Dardanelles on 24 July 1915, encountering the effect of the freshwater layers, which when going with the current made steering and maintaining a constant trim even more difficult than when heading into it:

> 9.40 passed the nets off Nagara Point by keeping close to the point. We are going grouped down [i.e. at slow speed] past here as the periscope is continually being used and we don't want it to splash; there is a nice fresh NE breeze which makes it better for us [it ruffled the surface of the water and made periscope wake more difficult to see].

> 10.50 we went on 'passing' those [indecipherable] nets for half an hour and the bearing of Nagara Point still remained on the port bow. At last we did get past the Point and altered course to southward (heaven knows what had got hold of us all that time). When C suddenly saw a fresh line of buoys right across our track and not more than 1,100 yards away, we dived to 90 feet, but must have gone through the bally thing for we started to come up instead of going down, and had to let in a lot of water into Y [ballast tank].

> 11.0 Nearly down to Kilid Bahr

> 11.5 rounded it and shaped course S 50 W at 40 feet, and next minute helmsman reported the helm hard a'starboard, and the boat still swinging to starboard and then the boat started to come up.*

> Filled Y then Z and she would only stay down with the motors stopped. Reversed the helm, ahead port, astern starboard, and she turned right round, but we had to stop port for that brought her up. Flooded number 3 compartment for a bit and also number 3 fuel tank and after 20 minutes (anxious ones) we were suddenly able to steer and keep our depth.

> C says it was a mine which must have caught up forward tho' we heard nothing [when they made no headway past Nagara Point]. He said he began to fear we should have to wait till dark and then come up and clear it.

> 11.50 he ordered 'Watch diving stations' [standing down men not on watch], and passed the word to the people right aft that 'we are now clear' and having given the Coxswain a bottle of beer, he opened one for himself. He got half a glass poured at which 'Helm hard a'port, still swinging to port, Sir', and then 'She's coming up, Sir'. So there was another blooming wire caught up on us, and we were now twisting and turning, and backing and filling trying to clear the brute.

> It took about 25 minutes to drop him, but we dropped him somehow

---

* Astounding as it may seem, helm orders in the Royal Navy throughout the First World War and well after it were given as though steering wheels had not been fitted in ships for the past several hundred years. Instead the orders were given as if in a sailing ship with a tiller, in which putting the helm to starboard turns the ship to port. (The helm is the name for the tiller, which governs the rudder directly.) So to turn a ship to port (left) a helmsman in the Royal Navy would be ordered: 'Starboard your helm.' He would respond by turning the wheel to the left (to port).

and freed her again. Later we just caught another, aft this time, but dropped it almost at once. The battery could not have been nearly up [fully charged] last night for before we rounded Nagara we only had 85 volts on the lights with all resistance out; we switched off all but 3 groups, but even then there was not enough light to see the chart by and we had to have emergency lights to see the gauges by. When we got clear of the two mines, we went along on one motor grouped up. By 2 pm the two lights in the fore compartment were just red and the compartment in darkness.

At 3.5 came to the surface near Morto Bay [near Sedd el Bahr]; tried to start the engines on air but they didn't like it much so the motors gave them a hand. The lights went clean out in that load. I reckoned there weren't any amps left in the box! Closed a TBD at 3.20 got underway and got a charge on en route for Mudros.

Among Hallifax's papers is the original signal from De Robeck announcing her arrival to his fleet which states that she had torpedoed a destroyer at the Arsenal, against which Hallifax has annotated 'No!'

E7 was cheered all the way into Mudros harbour. But her welcome was still no more than she deserved, she had sunk a gunboat, five steamers, and seventeen large sailing ships, and destroyed two trains. Hallifax spent some time in hospital, thereby missing being taken prisoner along with Cochrane and the whole crew when E7 was caught in nets off the Dardanelles on her next patrol.

Nasmith's second patrol in E11 was even more remarkable than his first. Nasmith was either lucky or was better at making his own luck than Cochrane in E7, or perhaps just a natural submarine CO. Before he passed Gallipoli on the first day, he had torpedoed a steamer. The next day, having met E14, he torpedoed a gunboat, and shelled Turkish troops marching down to Gallipoli. On 8 August he sighted the Turkish battleship *Heireddin Barbarossa* escorted by one destroyer:

5.0 am: Torpedoed battleship starboard side amidships. She immediately took up a list of about 10° to starboard, altered course towards shore and opened a heavy fire on the periscope

5.20 am: A large flash was observed forward after which she rolled over and sank

5.20 am: A second destroyer was observed to approach from Gallipoli. Attacked and fired torpedo at her which passed immediately underneath.

12.45 am: Observed two-masted, one funnelled steamer to north eastward. She was attacked by E14 and ran ashore, where she was subsequently torpedoed by E14 and set on fire by gunfire from both boats. The last round fired caused the upper half of E11's gun mounting to fracture – the gunlayer being thrown overboard and the gun nearly following him. Upper portion of pedestal removed and gun replaced in lower position. Gun ready for action in 24 hours.[7]

Four days later, having burned eight small sailing vessels, bombarded a shore gun, and shelled a steamer in a small harbour, Nasmith revisited Constantinople. Here he torpedoed a steamer alongside the Haidar Pasha Railway Pier. On his way out he burned two more sailing vessels. The following day he shelled a viaduct on the Baghdad railway.

On 21 August, having had no further encounters with enemy shipping, Nasmith decided to raid the railway and blow up a portion of line or the viaduct. His first lieutenant, D'Oyly-Hughes, volunteered for the task, using a raft specially made for the purpose. This was the first occasion in history that such a raid had been launched from a submarine – the precursor of hundreds of similar ventures, especially in the Second World War and subsequently. Without in any way wishing to denigrate D'Oyly-Hughes and his bravery, a charge of 16¼ lb of guncotton would have hardly scratched the viaduct, and only caused minor damage to the line. Nasmith's report tells the story.

The boat to approach the shore half a mile to the Eastward of Eski Hissar a village. Lieutenant D'Oyly-Hughes to swim ashore with raft carrying charge (16¼ pounds Guncotton) and proceed to railway line, there to place charge in a convenient position for breaking the line. If however the watch kept on the line appears to be inefficient he should proceed to Viaduct and place charge in the best position for demolishing same. In the event of meeting a vigilant watch en route to return to a position on the line if possible adjacent to the boat and there explode the charge making as rapid a return as circumstances permit. The boat will remain as close to the shore as possible.

The following signals to be made on landing:
1 flash – About to start Boat invisible
2 flashes – About to start Boat visible
3 flashes – Returning at once

On returning when two or three hundred yards from the shore blow one blast on the whistle or show one flash. Boat to reply with one red flash. This to be repeated as necessary.

Trimmed boat down till conning tower only was above water. Proceeded slowly towards shore until the nose just grounded three yards from the rocks, the cliffs on either hand being sufficiently high to prevent the conning tower being observed. In order to prevent boat being swept broadside on to the rocks it was necessary to keep her going ahead Port and astern Starboard with the helm hard to Port. Lieutenant D'Oyly-Hughes dropped into the water abreast of the conning tower and pushed the raft carrying the charge, his accoutrements and clothes to a spot some

60 yards on the Port bow of the boat. His weapons consisted of an automatic service revolver and a bayonet sharpened in order to silence detached sentries without noise. He also carried an electric torch and a whistle.

The Cliffs proved unscaleable [sic] at the first point of landing, he therefore re-launched the raft and swam along the coast until a less precipitous spot was reached. Here after a stiff climb the top was arrived at, no coast watchers apparently being in the vicinity. Half an hour later after a considerable advance he reached the railway line. He then proceeded very slowly with the charge towards the Viaduct, keeping a little above the line on the Northern side. Having advanced some five or six hundred yards voices were heard ahead and shortly afterwards three men were observed sitting by the side of the line talking quite loudly. After watching them for some time he decided to leave the charge which was very heavy and cumbersome and go forward making a wide detour inland to inspect the Viaduct. This detour was successfully carried out the only incident being an unfortunate fall into a small farm yard, disturbing the poultry but not rousing the household.

From a distance of about 300 yards the Viaduct could easily be seen as there was a fire burning at the near end of it. A stationary engine could be heard on or just beyond the viaduct and men were moving about incessantly. He decided that it was impossible to destroy viaduct so he returned to the demolition charge and looked for a convenient spot to blow up the line. He found a low brickwork support over a small hollow and placed it underneath. Unfortunately it was not more than 150 yards from the three men sitting by the line, but there was no other spot where so much damage could be done. He muffled the fuse pistol as tightly as possible with a piece of rag but the noise was very loud on such a still night and the men heard it and instantly stood up. They then came running down the line so a hasty retreat was made. After running a short distance he turned and fired two shots to try and check the pursuit but these proved ineffectual. Soon after, two or three ineffectual shots were fired from behind.

In view of the fact that speed was necessary Lieutenant D'Oyly-Hughes decided that to return down the cliffs at the place of ascent was impossible so he followed the railway line to the Eastward for about a mile till it came out close to the shore. He plunged into the water about three quarters of a mile to the Eastward of the small bay in which the boat was lying. The Charge exploded as he entered the water fragments falling into the sea near the boat although the distance between the boat and the charge was between a quarter and half a mile. After swimming some four or five hundred yards straight out to sea he blew a long blast on his whistle but the boat being in a small bay behind the cliffs did not hear it. Day was breaking very rapidly, so after swimming back to the shore and resting for a short time on the rocks, he commenced swimming towards bay in which boat was lying. At this point he discarded his pistol, bayonet and electric torch, their weight making his progress very slow. It was not until he had rounded the last point that the whistle was heard and at the same time he heard shouts from the cliffs overhead and rifle fire was opened on the boat. As the boat came astern out of the bay the early morning mist made her appear to him to be three small moving boats, the bow, the gun and the conning tower being the objects actually seen. He swam ashore and tried to hide under the cliffs but on climbing a few feet out of the water realised his mistake and shouted again before entering the water. I picked him up in an extremely exhausted condition about 40 yards from the rocks he having swam the best part of a mile in his clothes.[8]

Nasmith remained on patrol in the Sea of Marmara, harassing and destroying Turkish shipping, for almost two months: he sank 35,000 tons. He took food and water from captured vessels, and carefully maintained his diesels, which were liable to carbon up. Before transiting the Narrows on 3 September 1915, he fitted an extra jumping wire running from the bow up over the periscope standards and back aft, to avoid snagging nets and other obstructions with his conning tower or periscope standards. His report:

> 6.25 am: Ran through the Nagara net at depth of 80 feet. Increased speed to 8 knots on touching the net and broke through. Boat was pulled up to 60 feet before net parted. The course was only deflected a few degrees. Lieutenant D'Oyly-Hughes who was placed in the conning tower with the deadlights open to observe described the net as follows: A number of 2½in wires crossed and securely joined together forming about a ten foot mesh. He also observed a dark object hanging down the Port side which might well be a sinker. It is anticipated from this that the net might safely be passed without encountering obstruction if taken between two buoys and at a depth of 120 feet or more, observing that on the passage up a very stout horizontal wire was met at a depth of 110 feet. It is supposed that this wire was the lower jackstay supporting the sinkers.
>
> 9.15 am: Came to surface off Cape Helles and was escorted to Kephalo by *Bulldog*.[9]

D'Oyly-Hughes was strongly recommended for the VC by De Robeck, but received the DSO instead to add to the DSC awarded for the first patrol in the Sea of Marmara. He was to earn a second DSO as a CO later in the war. By the Second World War he had become the captain of the carrier *Glorious* with a dislike of aviators that amounted to a phobia. Thanks to a series of unwise decisions on his part, *Glorious* and her two escorting destroyers were needlessly caught and sunk by the German battle cruisers *Scharnhorst* and *Gneisenau* off Norway in 1940 with the loss of 1,519 lives.[10]

Nasmith went on a third patrol in November 1915, but was recalled in December, when it was decided to evacuate the Gallipoli peninsula. Lieutenant-Commander Stocks's E2 was the last British submarine to return through the Dardanelles, in early January 1916. Some boats were sent home, and others remained to take part in the blockade of the Adriatic.

Although the operations of British submarines in the Sea of Marmara were the most stunning and noteworthy in the First World War, they never achieved the aim of cutting the Turkish sea lines of communication to their front on the Gallipoli peninsula, despite the undoubted daring and initiative of their COs. The Turks quickly abandoned the movement of supplies and troops by large vessels and transported them in shallow-draught barges towed by tugs, able to creep along the coastline often out of reach of submarines. These operations were however an inspiration to the Royal Navy as a whole and the fledgeling submarine service in particular. They established a tradition that almost a century later endures.

9

Jutland

The lesson of this long and weary wait is that you MUST leave things
to individual initiative, there is no time to make signals.

– Commodore Le Mesurier, 4th Light Cruiser Squadron

The Long Wait

It is a misconception that in the eighteen months between the Battle of
Dogger Bank and the Battle of Jutland there was no activity in the North
Sea. There was plenty, but none of it led to contact between the Grand
Fleet and High Seas Fleet, the meeting for which all ship's companies
yearned. The British battle squadrons took part in frequent sweeps of
the North Sea, but had not fired a shot in anger. Sub-Lieutenant Bowyer-
Smyth in the *Superb*, based at Scapa, wrote in his diary:

> We live for two things and two things only, our scrap on the Day, and the
> trip south and our little bit of leave and a sight of some of the gentler sex.
> They don't even give us the illustrated papers now – they're full of this
> infernal war which we hear such a lot about and see so little of. Upon my
> soul it is a bit hard – we are supposed to be England's first line of defence
> and senior service, haven't so much as seen a German, or anyone who has
> been in action themselves.

Not only had Beatty's battle cruisers been the only capital ships of
the Grand Fleet to see any action, but his Battle Cruiser Fleet (BCF),
consisting of the 1st, 2nd, and 3rd Battle Cruiser Squadrons, three light
cruiser squadrons, and four destroyer flotillas, was based at Rosyth. Not
for their officers and sailors the dreary windswept vistas of Scapa, or the
slightly better amenities afforded by a run ashore at Invergordon, where
one battle squadron was based.

The BCF's ship's companies were able to go ashore to Rosyth and
Edinburgh (the latter strictly 'officers' country'). For the officers
especially, with trips to Edinburgh and hospitality bestowed by local
landowners, life could be pleasant, and it is little wonder that the rest of
the Grand Fleet were envious of the BCF. For Midshipman Alexander

Scrimgeour, appointed to the *Invincible* in July 1915 from the 10th Cruiser Squadron, it was a welcome change, as he related to his parents:

> This ship has already been in three actions this war – the Heligoland Bight, the Falkland Islands and the Dardanelles.
>
> Yesterday I went to tea with Mrs Hood [wife of Rear Admiral the Hon. Horace Hood, commanding 3rd Battle Cruiser Squadron] and family; they have a house on shore near our base, with a tennis court and some excellent strawberry beds. As there are two A1 daughters of seventeen and nineteen, you can bet their hospitality is fully appreciated.
>
> Most of the married officers have imported their wives and families up here, as we are by no means constantly at sea. It is a pleasant change after the weary four or five weeks at sea on end in the *Alsatian*.
>
> The Beattys are very much in evidence here; they have taken a huge place on shore in the vicinity, and the anchorage simply stinks of Lady Beatty's hospital ships, yachts, motor boats, etc.
>
> The battle cruisers correspond in most ways to, and are usually known as the 'cavalry' of the Navy. Not an unmixed blessing, as living in this ship, even in war-time, is twice or three times as expensive as the *Alsatian*. Still in peace we have a reputation for setting the pace, so if we are still afloat then we shall no doubt have a good time.

Scrimgeour's diary entries reveal no let up in the social round between spells of watch-keeping in harbour, coaling ship, and battle practice at sea: the BCF undeniably worked hard, but played likewise.

> Thursday, 11th [November 1915] – Landed at 11 a.m. and went to Edinburgh; saw Mrs Hood and Sammy, Mrs Alexander-Sinclair, and Stroma [a female acquaintance] (who have returned from Dunbeath Castle) shopping in Prince's Street. I had a spot with Morse at the Waverley, and then went off to lunch with Aunt Jessie at Merchiston Park. De Lisle and 'Young Yonnie' shot with Lord Linlithgow at Hopetoun.

> Thursday, 18th – Landed at eleven [AM] and went up to Edinburgh in 'Recky' Portal's sidecar. Portal, Hutchinson, Reid and I had a stupendous mixed grill gorge, which developed into a vile debauch at the Waverley. Then life having a pleasant aspect, we lurched along to the skating rink at Haymarket. Great fun. Lots of naval and military officers and fair young things there. A large party went over with the Admiral to skate with the Beattys at Aberdour; others went to Dundas Castle.

A 'vile debauch' by midshipmen in 1915 should not be confused with an early twenty-first-century teenage alcohol-and-Ecstasy-fuelled thrash. Some entertainment was laid on for the sailors:

went to show at YMCA house in Rosyth Dockyard, entertainment by
Ellaline Terriss and Seymour Hicks and some others. A jolly good show.
She is very nice. One hundred men from each ship, parties from the
smaller ships attended, and heaps of officers. All the admirals and their
families attended, also the old Duke of Leeds, an RNR Commander, whose
patrol yacht was sunk the other day, and he is now living in the *Australia*
with Rear-Admiral Pakenham. Sir David Beatty made a speech after the
show; he speaks very well. All went up to a birthday party at Northcliffe
House afterwards; quite amusing. Stroma was there, and we had a long
chat; she is back off to the Highlands again till April, which is rather sad.

The maids of all work, the destroyers, worked harder than anybody,
as Douglas King-Harman, now First Lieutenant of the *Midge*, based at
Inverness, wrote to his mother:

We have just come in off patrol after a perfectly unspeakable night.
Between wind, snow, sleet and a continual succession of green seas over
the bridge, I could hardly keep my eyes open, an oilskin is as much good
as brown paper in a packet like this punching into it at 25 knots.

The skipper is a simply undefeatable person, always cheery, mad as a
hatter, and grins stolidly at you through the whistling biting smother of
spray as if he enjoyed it. We went out of harbour past some big ships the
other morning at 6 am with the gramophone on the bridge playing, 'It's
nice to get up in the morning'.

Drink and boredom sometimes led to trouble. King-Harman wrote to
his mother describing the aftermath of a visit in July 1915 to Rosyth
Dockyard to change a propeller:

We ended up with a jolly good row on board. It all started with a fracas
the evening we arrived, with some of our men fired with beer, and rum
and whisky laid into about half a battalion of Gordon Highlanders, and
defied the efforts of the police and an enormous crowd to eject them from
a tram car over an hour.

Three of them, ABs, seem to have terrorised the town for an considerable period. They were hauled off to jug and fined the next day. On their
return to the ship started a lot of trouble on board. When I went on board,
there was pretty well a state of mutiny, with half the men threatening to
break out of the ship, and two of them under arrest.

Things were looking uncommonly nasty, so I picked half a dozen
reliable men, and stationed them along the jetty with orders to shoot
anyone attempting to break out. I fell the hands in and promised I'd let
daylight into [i.e., shoot] the first man I saw making trouble, that quiet-
ened them a bit, but then the two prisoners broke loose somehow. Their
escort was clearly afraid of them, and no wonder, they were absolutely

mad with drink. The two of them nearly laid out the coxswain, and then made for me. However I held them up with a shooting iron, and they eventually went below.

The two troublemakers were given lenient sentences by a court martial. A witch-hunt ensued, attempting to lay blame on King-Harman or the captain. When King-Harman was told that he would receive a severe reprimand, he demanded to be court-martialled, which took the wind out of the sails of the authorities. The captain was relieved of command, but King-Harman was left to serve on.

While the Grand Fleet whiled away the months of boredom speculating on when the High Seas Fleet would come out, a change of command led to a series of sorties by the Germans. On 23 February 1916, Vice-Admiral Reinhard Scheer became C-in-C of the High Seas Fleet. He was determined to adopt a much more aggressive concept of operations than his predecessors. He had no intention of taking on the whole Grand Fleet, but hoped to lure part of it onto the whole of his fleet and destroy it. Thus he would whittle away at the Grand Fleet until the two fleets reached parity, at which point he might dare to engage in a full fleet action. Scheer's arrival in the High Seas Fleet after a frustrating year of inactivity was greeted with enthusiasm.

On 5 March 1916, Scheer took his whole fleet, less one battle squadron, to a position off Texel – the furthest south the High Seas Fleet ventured in the entire war. He sent Zeppelins ahead to bomb Hull, in the hope that he could snap up any force sent out to chase them away. The operation achieved nothing.

The counter-move by the British, ten days later, nearly played into Scheer's hands. Plans were made for a seaplane attack on the Zeppelin base from which raids had been launched on several east-coast towns, and London in particular. Five seaplanes from the seaplane carrier *Vindex* took off at dawn on 25 March headed for the Zeppelin hangars thought to be at Hoyer on the coast of Schleswig. Tyrwhitt's Harwich Force was in close support, and the BCF stood off about forty-five miles west of the Horns Reef, ready to take a hand if need be. The only result was the loss of three seaplanes and the realization that there were no hangars at Hoyer (they were actually at Tondern a few miles away). The Germans struck back with a seaplane raid on the Harwich Force. They scored no hits, but the destroyer *Laverock* rammed the *Medusa* while taking evasive action.

Tyrwhitt towed *Medusa*, while Beatty stood off in case the German battle cruisers put in an appearance. When the weather deteriorated, Tyrwhitt abandoned the tow, but in gathering darkness he ran into

German torpedo boats. In a winter night of gales and snow flurries, the light cruiser *Cleopatra* rammed a German torpedo boat. As she was stopped with her bows embedded in the sinking German boat, the light cruiser *Undaunted* crashed into her. *Undaunted*'s bows were stove in and her speed reduced to 6 knots.

With part of the Harwich Force damaged, and aware from wireless direction-finding reports that Beatty was in the offing, Scheer ordered the whole High Seas Fleet to sea. As the Germans sortied, Hipper – commanding the battle cruisers and in the lead – reported that action was impossible in the colossal seas and poor visibility. Scheer ordered the High Seas Fleet home. Beatty and Tyrwhitt were only sixty miles away. Had Scheer pressed on, he would have found what he sought: an isolated detachment of major units of the British Fleet, without any hope of support from the battle squadrons of the Grand Fleet.

Scheer's next effort, planned to coincide with the German-supported rising by Irish nationalists on Easter Sunday in Dublin, was a raid on Lowestoft. He hoped the British government, responding to public demand, would be forced to order the Grand Fleet to disperse to protect the east coast. As usual the German battle cruisers steamed ahead of the High Seas Fleet with the battle squadrons some seventy miles astern. Hipper was on sick leave, so Rear Admiral Friedrich Bödicker, in the *Seydlitz*, was in command of the battle cruisers.

The Admiralty, alerted by Room 40 decrypts of German wireless traffic to the sortie by the High Seas Fleet, ordered the Grand Fleet to sea, without knowing the German objective. By midnight on 24 April 1915, Jellicoe and Beatty were punching south into a heavy head sea, and the Harwich Force (three light cruisers and eighteen destroyers) headed up the coast towards Lowestoft.

The previous afternoon, *Seydlitz* struck a mine, part of a minefield laid by the British in 1915. She suffered considerable damage, and headed home; Bödicker shifted his flag to the battle cruiser *Lützow* before pressing on. The next morning the German battle cruisers were nearing Lowestoft, when two light cruisers screening Bödicker's southern flank reported the approach of the Harwich Force. Bödicker refused to be diverted, and at 5.11 a.m., his four battle cruisers (*Lützow*, *Derfflinger*, *Moltke*, and *Von der Tann*) began bombarding the town. Having destroyed two hundred houses and killed a few civilians, the battle cruisers turned north towards Yarmouth. Here the visibility was so poor that the Germans were unable to shoot with any accuracy. Meanwhile Tyrwhitt ran into six enemy light cruisers, all positioned south of Bödicker. No sooner had the engagement begun than the German battle cruisers joined in, forcing Tyrwhitt to withdraw. Two of his ships were hit, his flagship the light cruiser *Conquest* was badly damaged with forty men killed and her speed reduced to 20 knots, and the destroyer *Laertes* had one boiler disabled. Bödicker, worried about mines and submarines, failed to follow Tyrwhitt and destroy, or at least severely maul, the Harwich Force; instead he turned and steamed east to rendezvous with Scheer. As he approached, Scheer, warned by wireless intercept that the British were at sea in strength, ordered everyone home. The Admiralty discerned from Room 40 decrypts that the High Seas Fleet was too far ahead to be intercepted by the Grand Fleet, whose progress south had been hampered by heavy seas, so Jellicoe and Beatty were ordered to reverse course and head for their bases.

The British did not react by dispersing major units to protect the east coast, as Scheer had hoped, so he now hatched a more ingenious scheme for mid-May. While Hipper, now back in command of the battle cruisers, bombarded Sunderland, to tempt the Grand Fleet out, two battle squadrons were to lie in wait between the east coast and Dogger Bank. U-boats were to patrol off Scapa, the Moray Firth, the Firth of Forth, and the Humber. All available Zeppelins were to reconnoitre the likely tracks that would be taken by the Grand Fleet as it sortied from its bases.

For a number of reasons, including repairs to the *Seydlitz* taking longer than forecast, Scheer was forced to postpone the operation. If he did not mount the operation by 1 June, most of the U-boats lying in ambush off the British bases would have run out of fuel, and would have to withdraw. By 28 May, the north-easterly wind was so strong that the Zeppelin reconnaissance on which Scheer relied to give him warning of the approach of the Grand Fleet was impossible. He therefore discarded the Sunderland plan, and instead ordered Hipper to trail his coat towards the Skagerrak, as if threatening the British cruisers and merchant ships in the area south-west of the southern tip of Norway. This had the advantage over the Sunderland plan that if the British came out in strength, Scheer could more easily run for home.

The High Seas Fleet Comes Out

At 2.0 am on 31 May, Hipper left the Jade Roads and steamed north. His force consisted of: I Scouting Group – five battle cruisers, *Lützow* (flag), *Derfflinger*, *Seydlitz*, *Moltke*, and *Von der Tann*; II Scouting Group – four light cruisers, *Frankfurt* (Rear Admiral Bödicker), *Wiesbaden*, *Pillau*, and *Elbing*; and thirty torpedo boats of II, VI, and IX Flotillas led by the light cruiser *Regensburg* (Commodore Heinrich). An hour and a half later Scheer's sixteen dreadnought battleships of I and III Battle Squadrons weighed and proceeded, accompanied by five light cruisers of the IV Scouting Group, and thirty-one torpedo boats. Astern came the six pre-dreadnought battleships of the II Battle Squadron, whose commander, Rear Admiral Franz Mauve, had begged Scheer to be allowed to come along. These old ships of the *Deutschland* class were unkindly called the *Fünf-Minuten Schiffe* ('five-minute ships') by the rest of the High Seas Fleet, that being the length of time they were expected to survive if engaged by dreadnoughts. What induced Scheer to agree to Mauve's request is uncertain; it was his old squadron, so perhaps it was sentimentality.[1] By bringing them, he reduced his battlefleet speed to 17 knots, three less than Jellicoe's dreadnoughts. This, as Andrew Gordon points out, was the first of four incompetent decisions made by Scheer, any one of which could have lost him his fleet.[2] Fortunately for him, the Grand Fleet was not sufficiently 'quick on the draw' to take full advantage of his errors; and the Admiralty's contribution to the battle worked to the enemy's further benefit.

Room 40 warned that the High Seas Fleet was about to put to sea, although not Scheer's intentions; the Admiralty told Jellicoe to take the Grand Fleet to sea and concentrate about a hundred miles east of Aberdeen. Assessing that U-boats would be lying in wait, Jellicoe ordered the Grand Fleet and BCF to sail after dark.

Between 10.00 and 11.00 p.m., the BCF slid under the Forth Bridge: 1st Battle Cruiser Squadron, *Lion* (Vice-Admiral Sir David Beatty), *Princess Royal*, *Tiger*, *Queen Mary*; 2nd Battle Cruiser Squadron, *New Zealand* (Rear Admiral William Pakenham) and *Indefatigable*; 5th Battle Squadron, *Barham* (flagship of Rear Admiral Evan-Thomas), *Valiant*, *Warspite*, and *Malaya*; nine light cruisers of the 1st, 2nd, and 3rd Light Cruiser Squadrons; and twenty-six destroyers and two light cruisers of four destroyer flotillas, plus the seaplane carrier *Engadine*.

The magnificent *Queen Elizabeth*-class fast 15-inch gun battleships of the 5th Battle Squadron were a temporary replacement for Rear Admiral the Hon. Horace Hood's 3rd Battle Cruiser Squadron (*Invincible* (flag), *Inflexible*, and *Indomitable*), temporarily detached to Scapa for live firing practice. Unfortunately, Beatty had not seen fit to use the eight days that the 5th Battle Squadron had been part of the BCF to discuss his operational concepts with Evan-Thomas, and ensure that the latter was in 'his mind'. In this respect, as in others, Beatty failed to measure up to Nelson, on whom he modelled himself, and with whom he was so often compared. It has to be said, however, that Evan-Thomas did not use his initiative to call on Beatty to ask how he wished the 5th Battle Squadron to fit into Beatty's design for battle.

By 10.30 p.m. Jellicoe's Grand Fleet was at sea, heading for the next afternoon's rendezvous with Beatty. Jellicoe left Scapa with the 1st and 4th Battle Squadrons, the 3rd Battle Cruiser Squadron, the 2nd Cruiser Squadron, the 4th Light Cruiser Squadron, and forty-two destroyers. From Cromarty, Vice-Admiral Sir Martyn Jerram took the 2nd Battle Squadron, the 1st Cruiser Squadron, and ten destroyers. Thanks to Room 40's information, twenty-eight battleships, nine battle cruisers, eight armoured cruisers, twenty-six light cruisers, seventy-eight destroyers, a minelayer, and a seaplane carrier, 151 ships in all, sailed two and a half hours *before* the first German warship weighed anchor and put to sea. Not one U-boat attack was made.

Although it was clear from Room 40 decrypts that the High Seas Fleet, including the pre-dreadnoughts of II Battle Squadron, was going to steam up the Danish coast, Rear Admiral Oliver, the Chief of War Staff at the Admiralty, feared an attempt to 'rush the Dover Straits' with these ships. He therefore refused to allow the Harwich Force to join Jellicoe, as he had been promised. When, the next day, Tyrwhitt intercepted reports that the enemy had been sighted, he used his initiative and put to sea. Oliver recalled him, so this battle-experienced and well-trained force under a great leader took no part in the battle; a considerable loss to Jellicoe.[3]

Petty Officer Francis, the captain of X Turret, remembered there was not much excitement in the *Queen Mary* as she steamed with her sisters out into the darkness of the North Sea:

> Of course the usual 'buzzes' were started, but I now know that no one had any idea we were on a big errand. The night went off very quietly, with no spasms of any description, except that an order was passed round the Gunners Mates that a very special watch was to be kept in the [4-inch secondary armament] batteries during the night.

The next morning, 31 May, Francis and the other three gunner's mates (petty officer turret captains) were ordered by the gunnery commander to carry out a check of their turrets. On reporting his turret in good order, the gunnery commander told Francis that he thought the enemy was out, to which Francis replied:

> 'I sincerely hope they are sir, as it is uphill work keeping the men up to the idea of meeting them again, and if we can only manage to get a few salvoes into our old opponents, the German battle cruisers, it will put new life into the crowd'
> The conversation then drifted back to the Heligoland scrap, and he said 'If we do have a "smash", I hope it will be your luck to repeat your previous performance'. He was referring to my third round in turret control which smashed up the *Köln*, and of course I agreed with him; I did hope

for such luck again. The remaining gunner's mates made a joke about 'old guns' trying to make us think 'they' were really out.

Just before midday, Captain Jackson, the Director of Operations, visited Room 40, and asked where the direction-finding stations located call sign DK. He was told the call sign was in Wilhelmshaven. This was a case of a little knowledge being dangerous. Jackson knew that Scheer's *harbour* call sign was DK. What he did not know, presumably because he never asked, was that whenever Scheer put to sea he always adopted a different call sign, transferring DK to a harbour ship, which continued to transmit in the hope that anyone listening would think that the C-in-C was still in Wilhelmshaven. The Room 40 staff knew this, but Jackson had visited them only twice since the war began, on both occasions to complain. He was a rigid naval officer of the type who does not welcome advice, and made it plain that he regarded the 'amateur' officers in Room 40 with suspicion; they were naturally very wary of him. He left the room without saying why he wanted to know the whereabouts of call sign DK. Had he asked where Scheer was, they would have told him 'at sea'.

Jackson reported to his boss, Vice-Admiral Oliver, another naval officer with a pathological dislike of delegating, who drafted a signal in his own hand, which was transmitted to Jellicoe and Beatty. It read:

No definite news of enemy. They made all preparations for sailing early this morning. It was thought that fleet had sailed but Directionals place flagship in Jade at 11.10 am GMT. Apparently they have been unable to carry out air reconnaissance which has delayed them.

Jellicoe received this signal at 12.48 p.m.[4] It had two serious consequences. First, he was steaming at economical speed to conserve fuel, and the signal convinced him that there was now no urgency. Time was wasted searching neutral ships, and destroyers detached for this duty did not rejoin at full speed, again to conserve fuel. Consequently he was late arriving at the rendezvous with Beatty, and was further away than he need have been when Beatty sighted Hipper. The hour or so of daylight lost was critical in the coming battle. Second, when German capital ships were encountered less than three hours after Jellicoe and Beatty had been told they were still in harbour, their trust in intelligence supplied by the Admiralty suffered a rude shock. This was to have grave repercussions later in the battle. The immediate effect of Oliver's signal was to deflate expectations in the Grand Fleet, and generate an atmosphere of it being yet another sweep with no prospect of meeting the enemy. Men not on watch relaxed, some went to sleep, or looked forward to being piped to tea.

Beatty had been ordered to turn north at 2 p.m. GMT, or when he reached a 'waypoint' 260 miles east of the Forth, and steer for the Grand Fleet which by then should be about 70 miles north-north-east of Beatty's position. At 1.30 p.m. he made a number of re-stationing signals to his screening destroyers and cruisers to bring them into a forma-tion to cover his rear during his passage to meet Jellicoe. He followed this with a signal at 2 p.m. ordering a turn on to the new course at 2.15 p.m., the time he would reach his turning point.

At that moment, a small Danish tramp steamer was sighted by the light cruiser *Elbing*, the westerly ship of Hipper's screen, and two torpedo boats were detached to investigate. Simultaneously, the light cruisers *Galatea* and *Phaeton*, on Beatty's eastern wing, sighted the Dane. Fol-lowed by the light cruisers *Inconstant* and *Cordelia*, the British ships raced to investigate. As *Galatea* closed the Danish tramp, she sighted the two enemy torpedo boats, and at 2.20 p.m. hoisted the signal 'enemy in sight', and broadcast by wireless, 'Urgent. Two cruisers [sic], probably hostile, in sight bearing ESE, course unknown'. A few minutes later, *Galatea* and *Phaeton* fired the opening shots of the Battle of Jutland, with their 6-inch guns, on the German torpedo boats.

By this time the BCF had completed its 'waypoint' turn and was steaming north, with the 5th Battle Squadron in the lead. At 2.32, on receipt of *Galatea*'s signal, Beatty turned the BCF about, to steer south-south-east towards the enemy. In the *Queen Mary*, Petty Officer Francis had been napping in the diving store, and having been woken by an able seaman, as arranged, he had just finished washing in a bucket when he heard

> a bugle sounding off 'Action'. I was so surprised I could not believe my ears, but the rush of feet by the door forced it upon me. I called Harrison, Chief Gunner's Mate, and Petty Officer Clark, and told them. Harrison said, 'What's the matter with you? Can't you sleep?'. Before I could answer, another bugle sounded off and no more words were necessary. It was a scramble to get away. I took the first hatchway up as doors were closing, and raced for X turret. When I got inside, everyone was there.

Clerk Lloyd Owen, also in X Turret: 'We were not expecting any-thing to happen, and thought it an ordinary "stunt" like we have often done before. We had all our cages loaded with armour-piercing lyddite.'

The signalmen in the *Barham*, Evan-Thomas's flagship, could not read Beatty's flag hoist, and the 5th Battle Squadron continued north at 20

knots, away from the rest of the BCF. Evan-Thomas, even though urged
by his flag captain to turn to follow Beatty, did not do so until *Lion*
flashed him by searchlight. His squadron, consisting of the fastest and
most powerful battleships in the world, armed with huge 15-inch guns,
would have been invaluable in the early stages of the forthcoming
battle, but now, thanks to Evan-Thomas's lack of initiative, they would
be late on the scene.

Midshipman Frampton was on watch on the bridge in the *Barham*
when action stations were sounded on the bugle. He rushed to his
action station, where he joined Lieutenant Ryan RMA in the 'silent
cabinet' in X Turret (the after superimposed one), the Marines' turret
commanded by Captain Clutterbuck RMA.

> I longed to stay up on the bridge to see something of the enemy. The
> Captain of Marines realising we were for it, hurriedly jumped out of
> the turret and threw overboard several tins of petrol which he kept in his
> small motor boat on deck which he used for his shooting expeditions at
> Scapa.
> All the mechanisms in the turret were tested and found in good order,
> and we sat still waiting for the order to load – never thinking it would
> really come.

In the *Warspite*, third in line in the 5th Battle Squadron, Commander
Walwyn, the executive officer, went to his action station in B Turret,
but had forgotten to bring any cotton wool with him to block his ears.
'[Midshipman] Grenfell produced a handful of [cotton] waste enough to
stuff the ears of a donkey. I handed it back to him, and almost at once
got the order to load and stand by'.

Hipper meanwhile played into Beatty's hands by pressing on so that
he and the BCF were on converging courses, until at 3.22 the Germans
sighted the British battle cruisers, followed at 3.25 by the British sighting
the German battle cruisers. As Beatty raced to intercept, Hipper turned
on to a south-easterly course to draw Beatty on to Scheer's battle fleet.
Beatty, still under the impression that the battle squadrons of the High
Seas Fleet were in harbour, hoped to cut off Hipper and annihilate him.

When Jellicoe received *Galatea*'s message, he thought that all the
heavy units of the High Seas Fleet were still in harbour, and only some
light cruisers were out. Therefore he did not increase speed. The picture
changed when *Lion* signalled by wireless that five enemy battle cruisers
and several torpedo boats had been sighted. A further message told him
that a running fight to the south-east was in the offing, but again thanks
to the Admiralty signal, Jellicoe thought that the action would merely
be a repetition of the battle-cruiser chase at Dogger Bank over a year

earlier. But he increased to 20 knots at 4 p.m., and ordered Hood's 3rd Battle Cruiser Squadron to join Beatty at full speed. Hood, on his own initiative, had already increased to 22 knots and steered east to cut off the route to the Skagerrak. On hearing that the enemy had turned south, Hood with *Invincible*, *Inflexible*, and *Indomitable*, the light cruisers *Chester* and *Canterbury*, and the destroyers *Christopher*, *Ophelia*, *Shark*, and *Acasta* altered course to the south-east and increased speed to 25 knots.

Bowyer-Smyth, now a lieutenant in charge of Y Turret in the *Marlborough*, thought that this sortie by the Grand Fleet was one of the 'usual stunts', and was surprised to hear General Quarters (GQs) sounded, it having already been practised that morning.

> It was a mistake, and the bugle should have sounded 'Action' not 'GQs' which is an exercise action. Having reported Y Turret cleared away, I looked out and saw that *Iron Duke* was flying the signal to prepare for action in every respect. Shortly after came the order to 'load all cages'. None of this of course created any stir at all, as we have done and undone it so often, that it has ceased to be a disappointment when nothing comes of it.
>
> The first hint we had that something might materialise this time, was a message to the effect that a squadron of enemy light cruisers had been sighted some 40 miles ahead. A smile stole round the guns' crews as I passed this on, a smile of mingled sympathy and grim satisfaction for a squadron of light cruisers running up against the Grand Fleet will probably not remain long afloat. Soon another message came that 'our battle cruisers are engaging the enemy's battle cruisers about fifty miles ahead'. This really began to look like business. The next message said 'the High Seas Fleet is 30 miles ahead of us'.
>
> The men were laughing and joking, but one could see that mixed with the relief of at last getting a rap at someone, there was a certain amount of nervousness and wondering what it would be like. I went round the Gun House, Working Chamber, Magazine and Shell Room now to have a last look and word here and there with the men, to tell them to load carefully rather than hurriedly, as from doing loading competitions we have got into the way of loading faster than is really necessary for firing.

The acting executive officer of the *Collingwood*, Commander Buckle, managed to 'get some tea into the men' by falling them out of action stations for a few moments. Midshipman Hext, hoping to rustle up some tea in the gunroom, found 'the chairs and tables in two piles'.

Scheer's battle squadrons were about sixty miles to the south-west of Hipper, and on receiving the report that enemy battle cruisers were in sight Scheer increased speed to 17 knots (the maximum the old *Deutsch-land* class could achieve) and went to action stations. To Scheer, unaware that Jellicoe was out with all his battle squadrons, the prospect of cutting off and destroying part of the Grand Fleet looked promising.

The Battle Cruisers Engage

The westering sun silhouetting Beatty's ships gave the advantage to Hipper, as he closed to come within range of the British, whose heavier guns outranged his. The misty horizon and dull grey sky, and the inferior range-taking equipment, made spotting much more difficult for Beatty's ships, and they held their fire as the range steadily decreased. Hipper's ships opened fire first, followed half a minute later by Beatty's. The first British salvoes landed a mile behind the German line. With rangefinders, which magnified the target twenty-three times, and being to leeward so their own gun smoke cleared quicker, the Germans found their targets far more quickly. Soon great columns of water from burst-ing shells sprang over 200 feet into the air as German salvoes straddled Beatty's ships. Despite Beatty having one more battle cruiser than Hipper, bad fire distribution by his ships resulted in *Derfflinger* being left unmolested for at least ten minutes.[5] Soon *Lion* and *Princess Royal* had been hit twice, and *Tiger* four times, putting two of her turrets out of action for a long time.

Leading Torpedoman Thorne, in the destroyer *Nicator* of Beatty's 13th Destroyer Flotilla, found the

> noise deafening, and being between the two fleets, we soon felt the heavy shells passing uncomfortably close overhead, even seeing some turning lengthwise over and over. Expecting every moment to be hit and blown to bits, I perched on the foremost torpedo tube, taking a very dim view of events.

The next shell to hit *Lion* exploded in her midships turret (Q), blowing off most of the roof so that it fell on the upper deck with a resounding crash. The explosion killed or wounded everyone in the gunhouse, and ignited cordite charges in the loading cages which were about to be rammed into the guns. Major Harvey RMLI, who was dying with both legs blown off, gave the order to flood the magazine, saving the ship. But some smouldering fragments of charges must have remained in the turret or supply hoist, because around twenty or so minutes later *Lion* altered course, which caused a draught to ignite eight charges in the supply hoist. Flames shot as high as the masthead and flashed down the main trunk (the big tube up which shells and charges passed into the turret from magazine and shell room). The turret magazine and shell-room crews, some seventy men, were killed instantly.

By this time the range had closed sufficiently for the German secondary armament to join in. Three minutes after *Lion*'s Q Turret had been hit, *Indefatigable* was hit simultaneously by two or three shells of one salvo near the after turret. At least one shell penetrated deep inside the ship, and a tremendous cloud of black smoke rose twice the height of her masts. She staggered and started to go down by the stern. This was followed by two more hits, one on the forecastle and the other on the forward turret. Thirty seconds later flame and smoke burst from the hull, hurling fragments 200 feet into the air. She rolled to port and sank, taking 1,017 of her ship's company with her. Two men were picked up later by a German torpedo boat.

Viewed from the German ships, *Indefatigable*'s loss seemed to cause the British to lose tactical cohesion. In fact, unknown to the Germans, a rash of 'submarinitis' in several of Beatty's ships caused spurious reports of torpedo tracks from U-boats. The result was frequent alterations of course, and a consequent slackening of the rate of fire as deflection changed too fast for the inadequate Dreyer gunnery-control systems to cope. There were no U-boats in the area.

Beatty kept opening the range, causing Hipper to alter course, which brought him within range of the 15-inch guns of the 5th Battle Squadron. The latter had at last managed to catch up, and opened fire at 19,000 yards (10¾ miles). Evan-Thomas's great ships concentrated their fire in pairs on *Moltke* and *Von der Tann*, soon obtaining hits on both, which caused considerable damage. Their fire would have been even more effective had it not been for the great range and the clouds of smoke enveloping the German line.

Walwyn in the *Warspite*:

Sighted four columns of smoke in the mist and gave orders to load, Commenced firing on four light cruisers [sic]. Could not see well from B [turret] lookout hood, blast from A [turret] struck me as worse than usual. Number two light cruiser suddenly obscured by mass of smoke and flame. Turned to starboard and engaged battle cruisers on Port bow. Could hardly see anything to lay on. Spotting very bad. Time of flight watch keeper was first rate and could nearly always identify splashes where they came down. Saw several salvoes splash just short of us. Tried to see next ahead [*Valiant*] but could not see her through the slit, only just caught her wake through the corner of my eye.

Aware that the 5th Battle Squadron had now joined him, Beatty closed the range. Hipper held on, and the battle raged ever more fiercely. Frampton in *Barham*'s X Turret:

> Now and again during lulls in the firing, one of our gunlayers would have a squint through his periscope. He was fat, cheerful little man and obviously a wag. He spun us all sorts of yarns which we believed – several German ships on fire and sinking etc. But unfortunately in most cases they turned out to be our own.

Petty Officer Francis in the *Queen Mary*:

> I had been anxious to have a look, but could not spare the time, but as soon as my gun had fired, and while loading was being completed, I had a quick look through the periscope, and it seemed that there were hundreds of masts and funnels. I dropped back into my seat, laying my gun by pointer, being in director firing. I told the turret crew that there were a few battle cruisers out, not wishing to put a damper on them in any way.

Because of bad fire distribution in Beatty's squadrons, *Queen Mary* found herself under fire from *Derfflinger* and *Seydlitz*. She managed to score one hit on *Seydlitz*, but was herself hit in the after 4-inch battery; the flying debris blocked the turret trainer's periscope in Francis's turret. Someone dashed out of the turret and must have been hit as he was clearing it, because he fell in front of the periscope. Francis felt the turret training round, when *Queen Mary* was hit by three shells out of a salvo of four. An explosion shook the gunhouse, and he noticed the hydraulic pressure gauges winding down. This was followed by a massive explosion which threw two men under one of the guns, just as it fell off its trunnions and smashed them to pulp. The gunhouse floor bulged up, and in the silence one of the gun's crews asked what had happened.

Francis and Lieutenant Ewart, the officer in charge of the turret, agreed that as the guns were useless, the crews should be sent to man the 4-inch guns. Francis stuck his head out of the turret and nearly fell back at the sight which greeted him. The after 4-inch battery was destroyed, and the ship had a big list to port. Ewart, on hearing this, told Francis to clear the turret. As the crew tumbled out of the hatch on the top, and clambered down the ladder at the back of the turret, Ewart stopped and went back, possibly because he thought there was still someone left inside, as indeed there were in the working chamber, magazines and shell room, about forty men in all.

The ship was listing so badly that many who had cleared the turret slid down the deck to port, smashing themselves against projections.

Francis managed to make the starboard rail with the help of two able seamen. Here he found what he describes as 'quite a crowd', reluctant to take to the water, saying that the ship would float for a while yet. Francis, not knowing what impelled him, clambered up over the slimy bilge keel, and fell off into the water followed by a handful of men.

Midshipman Lloyd Owen was one of the last out of X Turret, and found the ship lying on her side, broken amidships, bows in the air, and stern protruding from the water at an angle of forty-five degrees. He stood on the back of the turret, which was trained to port, guns down towards the sea. The stern was red hot, plates blown away, exposing the frames like a skeleton. All around him, men fell into the water as the bows disintegrated in a colossal explosion. The stern lurched, throwing him into the sea.

Q Turret, superimposed and forward of X, had taken a direct hit, putting one gun out of action, but killing nobody. A big explosion followed that smashed up the turret, breaking the left gun in half, collapsing it into the working chamber, and hurling the right gun backwards. Cordite in the gunhouse caught fire, and many of the crew were killed. Midshipman Storey:

> Those of us who were left got into the silent cabinet. All the lights were out, both main and secondary. I managed to get my pad over my face, and those still alive got on the top of the turret, to find the foremost part of the ship blown off, and after part sinking rapidly. I had got my coat off and one shoe, when the after magazine went up and blew us into the water.

For a few minutes, her stern remained afloat with its four propellers still revolving. *Tiger* nearly ran into her at 24 knots, but swerved, passing so close that a glowing shower of debris fell on her decks, and her ventilating fans sucked in clouds of poisonous smoke.

Francis had swum about fifty yards off when in his words there was a 'big smash'. After further shattering explosions, *Queen Mary*'s stern rolled and sank. 1,266 of her crew went with her. Francis dipped under water to avoid the flying debris, and on surfacing was overtaken by a rush of water like surf breaking on a beach. He was sucked under, but, resisting the urge to give up, he struggled to the surface and found a hammock, to which he clung, until a wooden target floated near, onto which he climbed. Here he clung, shivering with shock and cold, covered in oil, and nauseous with some he had swallowed, until rescued by the destroyer *Petard*.

There were eight survivors, including Midshipman Storey, who was picked up by the destroyer *Laurel*. Clerk Lloyd Owen was in the water when

> The 5th Battle Squadron steamed past in perfect order firing continuously. The enemy's shells were falling a good deal short of the squadron, but one of them must have exploded in the water close to me, causing me to lose consciousness. I have no more recollection of what happened until I found myself on the forecastle of the *Laurel*.

The range had now decreased sufficiently for the destroyers on each side to take a hand. Between the two battle lines, the flotillas hurled themselves at the opposition. Thorne in the *Nicator*, in the 4th Division of the 13th Destroyer Flotilla:

> about half way across, we saw ahead the German destroyers coming to attack our battle cruisers. Commander Bingham [*Nestor*] never deviated but led us straight at the enemy destroyers who broke away as we charged through. Their formations were so dislocated that their attack on our battle cruisers never materialised. Some reversed course to pursue us, but our speed put us ahead. *Nomad* was hit in the engine room by a large shell which brought her to a dead stop. Both *Nestor* and *Nicator* fired two 21-inch torpedoes each, but before anyone could see if they hit, we had swung round to rejoin the battle cruisers now some 10 miles distant.

The British destroyers, superior in armament and speed, held off the German torpedo boats at about 9,000 yards from Beatty's battle cruisers. The British got closer but their torpedo attack on Hipper's battle cruisers also failed to sink any ships. They damaged the *Seydlitz*, but not sufficiently to reduce her speed or fighting efficiency.

Despite his success in sinking two of Beatty's battle cruisers, Hipper was in a critical situation with five battle cruisers against Beatty's four battle cruisers and four 15-inch-gun battleships. *Von der Tann* was hard hit with two of her turrets out of action, and she and the *Moltke* each had a thousand tons of water on board. *Lützow* had a large hole in her foredeck, and *Seydlitz*'s after superimposed turret was out of action. At that moment the message was passed through the voicepipes in Hipper's ships, 'own battlefleet in sight'.

Beatty with greater numbers and superior gunpower had failed to defeat Hipper, who had made no effort to avoid action. The Germans hit more often (forty-four hits to seventeen), and many British hits failed to cause damage due to faulty shells. After the war Ordnance Board research established that between 30 and 70 per cent of heavy shells issued to the Grand Fleet were duds. Indifferent armour on the battle cruisers made nonsense of Fisher's dictum that speed is armour; not helped by poor anti-flash precautions in most British ships.

High Seas Fleet in Sight

At 4.30 p.m., Commodore Goodenough in the light cruiser *Southampton*, two miles ahead of *Lion*, saw to his astonishment lines of battleships and myriad torpedo boats. A few minutes later he signalled Beatty and Jellicoe by wireless: 'Have sighted enemy battlefleet SE. Enemy's course north. My position is 56° 34' N 6° 20' E'. Beatty, thinking the German battlefleet was still in harbour, was exceedingly surprised. Goodenough's report was soon confirmed by the light cruiser *Champion*. The reports from both *Southampton* and *Champion* of their own dead reckoning positions were out by thirteen and twelve miles respectively. This did not affect Beatty, as he could see both light cruisers, but these errors were to cause Jellicoe considerable concern later.

Beatty turned to close the *Southampton*, and seeing sixteen dreadnoughts approaching, immediately ordered a turn to the north-west to close Jellicoe. He reported the enemy sighting and his own position by wireless to Jellicoe. Goodenough in the *Southampton* with the rest of the 2nd Light Cruiser Squadron pressed on towards the High Seas Fleet in order to confirm the speed, course, and strength of the enemy, and having done so turned away, his ships zigzagging like snipe under the fire of ten German battleships.

As Beatty's battle cruisers were wheeling round, the 12-inch shells of the leading German battle squadron (*König, Grosser Kurfürst, Kronprinz Wilhelm*, and *Markgraf*) splashed all around, but without hitting. Evan-Thomas was still some eight miles to the north of Beatty when the turn was ordered. Poor procedures in the *Barham* resulted in Evan-Thomas being unaware of Goodenough's signal. Neither did *Barham*'s signalmen see Beatty's flag signal, and Evan-Thomas pressed on, although he could plainly see Beatty on a new course. Walwyn in the *Warspite*:

> Suddenly saw our battle cruisers coming the opposite way, and felt rather anxious to know what was up. Saw *Queen Mary* was adrift [late], but never thought she had gone up. Before this passed close by a destroyer in a mass of black water and wreckage apparently picking up survivors and wondered what it was. But it never occurred to me that it was one of ours.

Only as the squadrons approached on opposing courses at high speed, and after Beatty made another signal, did Evan-Thomas understand that his squadron was to steer north. As his squadron turned, *Barham* was hit, not as thought at the time because the enemy concentrated on the turning point, but from good shooting by *Kronprinz* and *Kaiserin*. The captain of the *Malaya*, the last in the line, avoided going through the area where the salvoes were falling by turning early. Most of the damage to the 5th Battle Squadron was suffered during the run to the north. Evan-Thomas increased speed and opened the range, which caused the Germans to concentrate on *Malaya*. Lieutenant Brind in charge of *Malaya*'s B Turret:

> The enemy continued to fire rapidly at us during and after the turn, but did not really get near us until about 5.15 pm, when their salvoes began to arrive thick and fast. From my position in the turret I could see them falling just short, and just over several times, and a great column of black water fall on top of the turret.
>
> I was trying to make out our target, but expected at any moment we would get a nasty knock, and that if any of these shells falling all round us should hit us in the right place, our speed would be sadly reduced, and we should not stand a very good chance. The salvoes were coming in at a rate of about six to nine per minute.
>
> At 5.20 pm I saw a large column of water rise between my guns and felt the turret shake heavily. We had been hit abreast the turret, below the water line. So heavy was the shock that I feared that our fighting efficiency had been gravely impaired; not so much that a shell had pierced any part of the turret, but that the shock of the impact had seriously damaged our loading arrangements. I went into the gunhouse to enquire whether all was well below and received the report that they had been somewhat shaken by the blow, but that everything seemed all right.
>
> This proved too optimistic, because when the main cage arrived in the working chamber, it was found that shell could not be withdrawn and there was a proper jam-up. I dashed down and we had to work like anything to clear it. After what seemed an age, but could not have been very long, we succeeded, and managed to get the cage back into working order.
>
> During this time the secondary method of loading was in use for the right gun, and although five rounds had been loaded in this way, the turret never missed the chance to fire.
>
> I found everyone very cheery and full of go. They had no thought that we should come off worse than the enemy, but wanted to know how many German ships were left afloat requiring to be finished off.
>
> Until about 5.40 the enemy's fire continued to be very brisk and fell all around us. The visibility had been getting steadily worse, and we had very rarely been able to see anything but the flashes of the German guns. During this time we were several times hit, to what extent I could not tell, but we had a bad list to starboard.

In fact a shell struck the roof of *Malaya*'s after turret, destroying the rangefinder. This was followed by two shells hitting the starboard battery starting cordite fires which killed or burned 102 officers and men. A few minutes later two shells struck just under the armoured belt, ten feet below the waterline, flooding her wing compartments and giving her a four-degree list. It says much for her construction that she was able to steam at full speed, with salvoes falling all round her for about half an hour. Had she fallen back, she would have been at the mercy of the whole enemy battlefleet.

Warspite also came under heavy fire from the German dreadnoughts. Walwyn:

Very soon after the turn, could see leading ships of High Seas Fleet, hardly discernible but counted six or eight. Long lines of orange flame seemed to ripple along continuously, and realised they were firing at us. Felt heavy shakes, but didn't think much of it. Blast of A blew water into my eyes and it was very uncomfortable in the hood.

In fact *Warspite* had been hit aft, and soon Walwyn got a

message from the Captain to leave turret and go aft at once to see what the matter was as we had been badly hit. Called Coates and told him to take charge, that all was well and we were in primary control. Thought for half a minute should I go out over [i.e. on upper deck] or down through shell room, and decided I ought to go over. Grenfell [midshipman] that moment opened the door and bowed to me, which decided me, and I jumped out telling Walken to go down through the trunk the other way and meet me on the messdeck. Out of the turret in a bit of a funk, and ran. A [turret] fired as I was half down ladder at side of turret, but I was on the lee side. Ran aft and down port superstructure ladder, tried to get into door, but all clips were on, so I climbed over second cutter. Shell came through after funnel and spattered everywhere. Put my collar up and ran like a stag down through door to battery deck. Marines in the compartment were all right, but they had the door half open luckily for me. Told them to shut it at once.

All peace below, went right aft along mess deck port side, aft down by spirit room door, through lobbies saw nothing. Number 6 fire brigade patrols reported everything all right. Went forward again and met Walken grinning all over. Sent him to Captain to say all was well below and nothing the matter as far as I could see.

As a matter of fact we had been holed in side by direct hit below the water line, which flooded Capstan engine flat, but of this could see nothing. Crossed Cook's lobby to port side and was just going forward to the Fo'c'sle deck, when 12 inch came in through the starboard side and burst with terrific sheet of flame, impenetrable dust, smoke, stink, and everything, seemed to fall from everywhere at once.

Called for number 2 fire brigade and several rushed out and we got fire out fairly easily, but place was full of smoke, and several men were sick – awful stench.

Went aft to port side again, and right aft to lobbies – found water pouring through Admiral's doorway and was told we had been badly hit aft, and water was then 12 inches deep.

Much of the ingress of water into the *Warspite* aft was caused by her stern being dug deep into the water as she steamed at utmost speed. Walwyn and his damage-control teams slowly won control of the fires, and stemmed the gush of water into her compartments.

As both British and Germans pelted north at high speed, the gunnery duel continued, until Beatty had hauled out of range. The engineer lieutenant-commander in the *Falmouth*, to the north-east of Beatty with her sisters of the 3rd Light Cruiser Squadron, came on deck for a moment to see

the Huns astern of us, and I began to be a bit anxious about the engines, as I knew that if we broke down, we should very shortly have been in the centre of the High Seas Fleet, where we would have been in a similar position to the proverbial cotton wool rabbit being chased through Hades by an asbestos terrier.

Two of Beatty's destroyers, *Nestor* and *Nicator*, returning from their attack on Hipper, disobeyed the recall signal flying from *Lion*'s yardarm, and turned to attack the High Seas Fleet. Thorne in *Nicator*:

It was an amazing sight, five battle cruisers followed by twelve battle ships [sic: actually sixteen, not counting the six pre-dreadnoughts] firing every possible gun. Commander Bingham suddenly changed course followed by the *Nicator*, and made for the German battleships to 'attack with remaining torpedoes', both having two each. Only a miracle could save us from the intense fire of the German ships, but we came through unharmed, until at 5,000 yards approximately the order came 'fire torpedoes'. *Nestor* fired at a battle cruiser and *Nicator* at a battleship [actually they engaged the *König* and *Grosser Kurfürst*, both battleships, neither scoring a hit].

Within moments of turning for our hectic race back, *Nestor* was struck by a large shell stopping her in her tracks. The *Nicator* by brilliant helmsmanship on the part of her coxswain, CPO Gates, just avoided colliding with her. Turning to render assistance, the *Nicator* was ordered away by Commander Bingham. We raced away from *Nestor* with sad hearts, and got clear. Knowing we were the survivors of the 4th Division of the 13th Flotilla.

Nomad, crippled earlier, and *Nestor* lay in the path of the High Seas Fleet. Both destroyers fired their last torpedo at the oncoming giants, before being smashed to smithereens. The survivors were rescued by enemy torpedo boats. Bingham was awarded the VC, and *Nomad's* captain Lieutenant-Commander Whitfield the DSO.

The 5th Battle Squadron continued to draw fire from Hipper's battle cruisers and the leading German battleships, but the 15-inch guns scored hits in return on *Grosser Kurfürst, Markgraf, Lützow, Derfflinger,* and *Seydlitz*. The British ships were now in line with the sun, and it blinded the German spotters. Taking advantage of the slackening fire, Beatty altered course to the north-north-east to cross ahead of the German battle cruisers, to mask the approach of Jellicoe's squadrons from German view. The Germans also altered course as they were being outflanked by the 5th Battle Squadron.

Scheer apparently did not ask himself why the fleeing Beatty had diverted from the direct course home, bending round on to one which took him well to the east, putting himself at greater risk. It never seems to have occurred to him that Beatty might be leading him into the arms of Jellicoe. This was the second of what Andrew Gordon calls Scheer's 'death wishes'. Jellicoe was twenty-three miles north of Beatty, steaming at 20 knots in a south-easterly direction in columns of divisions, thus:

Agincourt	St Vincent	Vanguard	Canada	Thunderer	Erin
Hercules	Neptune	Temeraire	Superb	Conqueror	Centurion
Revenge	Collingwood	Bellerophon	Royal Oak	Monarch	Ajax
Marlborough	Colossus	Benbow	**Iron Duke**	Orion	King George V
			Fleet Flagship		
			Adm Sir John Jellicoe		
6th Division	**5th Division**	**4th Division**	**3rd Division**	**2nd Division**	**1st Division**
(V/Adm Sir Cecil Burney)	(R/Adm Gaunt)	(V/Adm Sir Doveton Sturdee)	(R/Adm Duff)	(R/Adm Leveson)	(V/Adm Sir Martyn Jerram)

Jellicoe was still unaware of the exact position of the High Seas Fleet, partly thanks to poor visibility, but mainly because Beatty failed to keep him in the picture by wireless. Jellicoe made the situation more difficult for himself, by keeping Commodore Le Mesurier's 4th Light Cruiser Squadron on a tight rein just ahead of the Grand Fleet as a protection against U-boats, instead of in their proper role, scouting well forward.

As he approached Jellicoe, the visibility favoured Beatty, and he was able to close the range and increase the rate and accuracy of fire, while the German battle cruisers could fire only intermittently. All but one of the hits on the Germans were by 15-inch shells from the 5th Battle Squadron.

Meanwhile Hood, who had gone ahead to join Beatty, could not find him in the murk. At 5.30 one of Hood's light cruisers, the *Chester*, steered towards the sound of firing to the south. She ran into three light cruisers and some destroyers, coming under hot and accurate fire. Hood steered towards *Chester*. His battle cruisers hammered the enemy light cruisers, and sent them running back to their own battle cruisers, except for the *Wiesbaden*, which was badly damaged and remained in the area.

At 5.50 p.m., the *Marlborough*, leading the battlefleet starboard wing column, sighted *Lion* pelting up through the murk and surrounded by shell splashes. Bowyer-Smyth: 'As our battle cruisers passed close ahead of us, we could see they had been pretty severely handled. *Lion* was heavily on fire and several of the others showed spasmodic bursts of flame.'

Jellicoe still did not know exactly where the German battlefleet was, and the few signals he was receiving from his subordinates were not at all helpful. He had to decide his deployment plan very quickly if he was not to run onto the enemy still in cruising formation. In a few seconds, in one of the most critical moments of the war, Jellicoe ordered his fleet to deploy into line of battle, by forming single line ahead on the port wing column, with *King George V* leading, The course set was south-east by east (125°).

The next fifteen minutes as the Grand Fleet was deploying were hectic. Commodore Le Mesurier, commanding the 4th Light Cruiser Squadron, flying his broad pennant in the *Calliope*, wrote to his wife later: 'we were mixed up at the head of our battle fleet line in a first class scrimmage as the battle cruiser action passed across our front; we then got sorted out a bit, and got our five little ships in correct station.'

Lieutenant Brind in the *Malaya*:

> We in the 5th Battle Squadron took station in rear of the 1st Battle Squadron. In doing so we must have been going too fast, for we ran up on to the last ship of the line and were actually overlapping each other, thus presenting an excellent target to the Huns, who were extremely quick in taking advantage of it.
>
> At the rear of our line was a regular bunch of ships; the 5th Battle Squadron, a light cruiser squadron, and a destroyer flotilla, gathered together in a remarkably small area, into which concentrating fire. Amidst this perfect deluge of shells, the light cruisers and destroyers were twisting and turning, endeavouring to avoid each other and the big ships, who were themselves manoeuvring violently. There were no collisions, and few ships hit; a wonderful display of seamanship and clear-headedness.

The leading German battleships were only seven miles away from the long line of wheeling British dreadnoughts, but in the murk were invisible to many of the Grand Fleet, only the occasional stabbing muzzle flame through the battle smoke marking their approximate position. But Bowyer-Smyth in *Marlborough*, leading the rear division, saw

enemy battle cruisers showing up through the mist away on our beam, their leading ship, probably *Seydlitz* [actually *Lützow*] was very heavily afire and several others burning at intervals. We tried to engage them, but owing to the mist failed to get the guns off. Following their battle cruisers came battleships with one of the Kaiser class [the *König*] leading. We engaged her immediately, opening fire without being able to get the range due to mist, and hit her with our fourth and fifth salvoes. All rear ships of our battle line were now engaged, but I could not see their splashes as it required ones whole attention riveted on the spot and a careful warning [that rounds were on the way] to enable one to see our own [splashes] though the range was only 10,000 yards, as it was so hazy and misty.

Beatty cut the corner to take up position between the head of the battleship line and the approaching Germans in order to mask their view of the deploying Grand Fleet. Rear Admiral Sir Robert Arbuthnot elected to take up his allotted station with his 1st Cruiser Squadron, the old armoured cruisers *Defence* (flag), *Warrior*, *Black Prince*, and *Duke of Edinburgh*, by going down the enemy side of the BCF. On his way, he decided to finish off the *Wiesbaden*. In doing so he nearly collided with *Lion*, and put himself in the most dangerous position, right between the two fleets. As he moved in for the kill, the huge outlines of German capital ships loomed up through the smoke. Arbuthnot's two leading cruisers were engaged by two battle cruisers and four battleships. *Defence* was blown apart in a monumental explosion, and lost with all hands. *Warrior* staggered away with enormous damage. The *Duke of Edinburgh* and *Black Prince*, astern of station, avoided being embroiled in this fiasco.

At the same time the *Warspite*'s rudder jammed while carrying out violent manoeuvres at top speed to avoid a collision with the *Valiant*. She went round in a full circle twice, once round *Warrior*, a 31,000-ton monster careering around out of control, while her engine-room staff frantically disengaged the faulty steering engine and engaged the back-up motor. Her guns were switched to local control and continued firing when they would bear. Although repeatedly hit during this impromptu performance, she managed to pull out of range. Her antics drew most of the fire, and probably saved *Warrior* from destruction.

A few minutes later, while the Grand Fleet was still deploying, Hood saw Hipper's battle cruisers to the south, and immediately engaged. Approaching the action in the *Midge*, King-Harman was at his action station at the forward 4-inch gun, where the crew had already chalked messages on the shells, such as 'a present for Fritz', and 'two years at Scapa Flow'.

Invincible shot magnificently, hitting *Lützow* and *Derfflinger* several times. But in exchange she drew the fire of four enemy battle cruisers and one battleship. She appeared to be able to take this punishment, until a shell penetrated Q Turret and exploded inside, hurling the roof into the air, and igniting the charges below. Thanks to inadequate anti-flash precautions, the sheets of flame ignited the charges in the tube and on down to the magazine. She blew exactly in half. The two inner ends settled on the bottom upright, bow and stern protruding from the surface of the sea like a pair of goalposts. She took 1,026 of her crew with her, including young Scrimgeour, and the forty-five-year-old Rear Admiral Horace Hood, one of the brightest young flag officers in the Royal Navy. Six survivors were rescued by the destroyer *Badger*, including Commander Dannreuther, her gunnery officer.

By now the German battle cruisers were in a poor state, with only the *Moltke* being fully fit for action. As the Grand Fleet completed its deployment, it lay right across Scheer's path. Jellicoe had achieved the tactical masterpiece of crossing the enemy's 'T'. Scheer was horrified. His first intimation that he was facing the whole Grand Fleet was the long line of flashes curving across his line of advance. King-Harman remembered, 'the flames of their broadsides was staggering and the scene was like a regular picture battle.'

The head of the German line was brought under devastating fire from a six-mile-long line of twenty-four heavy ships in an arc from north-west to north-east. Only part of Scheer's line could reply; it did so. Midshipman Hext in the *Collingwood*:

> Shots fell around us and we were straddled more than once. One short shot ricocheted, [missing and eventually] swerving to starboard. The shell was plainly visible, a reddish brown, probably an armour-piercing. When I saw the shell flying towards us I remarked to Midshipman Stoneham, 'That shell is going to hit A Turret'. It did not. It passed over the forecastle and fell into the sea close on our port side.

A Turret of the *Collingwood* was the action station of Prince Albert, later George VI and the present Queen's father.

Lieutenant-Commander Palmer in the destroyer *Defender* in 1st Destroyer Flotilla with the 5th Battle Squadron:

A 12-inch projectile hit us on the foremost boiler room causing a fire, loss of steam, and putting it out of action, reducing our speed to 15 knots. By the mercy of Providence the shell did not explode, and it is on board now. It wrecked the place a bit, but if it had exploded we should have been blown to pieces. With my speed reduced, I could not keep my station in the line, so turned round and steamed between the British and German Fleets on fire and belching steam.

Here I saw a destroyer in worse state than myself, and offered assistance. She proved to be the *Onslow* [Lieutenant-Commander Tovey]. *Onslow* could not steam, so I offered to tow him as with my speed reduced it was impossible to continue the action.

While getting him under tow, four light cruisers came straight at us with shells falling around them. I thought they were Huns and our number was up. But found they were British.

Tovey in the *Onslow* had intended to finish off the *Wiesbaden*, but on his approaching to torpedo range had spotted Hipper's battle cruisers and turned his attention to them. No sooner had Tovey's first torpedo, aimed at the *Seydlitz*, left the tube than *Onslow* was hit by *Lützow*'s secondary armament. Immediately afterwards, *Lützow*, threatened by the sudden appearance of the destroyer *Acasta*, turned away. Tovey turned back towards *Wiesbaden* and fired a torpedo which hit but did not sink her. At that moment, bigger game in the form of the German III Battle Squadron appeared through the smoke. *Onslow* could make only 10 knots, but Tovey charged in, fired his last two torpedoes, and escaped in the confusion. It was his last confrontation with German capital ships until as C-in-C he led the Home Fleet to hunt down the *Bismarck* twenty-five years later.

Scheer was 150 miles from Wilhelmshaven, and severely limited in speed by the 'five-minute ships' of his II Battle Squadron. Running south for home was not an option. He had to play for time, for the onset of darkness, for he knew that the British were poorly trained at night fighting. He ordered a manoeuvre practised assiduously by the German navy, the *Gefechtskehrtwendung* (battle turn-about): every ship put its helm over and turned sixteen points (180°), while his III Destroyer Flotilla attacked and laid a smokescreen. It was as if a curtain had fallen on stage, and the actors had crept away behind it.

Jellicoe declined to follow through the curtain and risk a mass torpedo attack. The light was bad, and he decided to place the Grand Fleet across the German line of withdrawal. He knew that they could not maintain their westward course for long, for this would have taken them further from home than ever. As Jellicoe turned the Grand Fleet to a south-easterly course in columns of divisions, *Marlborough* in the rear division

was hit by a torpedo, the only one to hit a British capital ship throughout the battle. Bowyer-Smyth:

> The ship gave a heavy heave and shook up and down violently for a
> minute or two. I was sitting at the chair at the [turret] periscope, I was
> thrown off the chair, and at first thought thank goodness now we know
> what a shell on the outside of the turret is like, and it is not so bad after
> all. Then I got to the slit and saw a swirl and bubbles round the ship's side,
> I saw at once it was a torpedo or a mine. By this time we had got a fairly
> heavy list especially where the helm went over as we were doing 19 knots.

Who fired the torpedo is a mystery which remains unsolved to this
day. One theory is that it was the disabled *Wiesbaden*, which *Marlborough* was passing about 9,000 yards away. Bowyer-Smith saw what
he describes as a four-funnelled cruiser which was heavily engaged by
the *Marlborough*, but later in his account of the battle he is not so sure
and thinks it was a three-funnelled ship, which could have been the
Wiesbaden.

Scheer now made his third 'death wish' decision. He turned and had
another try at barging his way through the Grand Fleet, being forced
into yet another 'battle turn-about'. He then tried yet again, and was
taking so much damage that he told his battle cruisers to charge the
enemy, while he executed his third about turn. Hipper closed to within
7,000 yards of Jellicoe's battle line, before turning and scampering back
to join Scheer, covered by a mass torpedo-boat attack and smokescreen.

Le Mesurier, leading the 4th Light Cruiser Squadron in the *Calliope*:

> Our first chance came about 7.30 o/c, when they slipped some destroyers
> at our leading battle squadron; got two of the German TBDs on that
> occasion. Luckily all their torpedoes missed us (Four close to *Calliope*). Our
> second little excursion came soon after 8 o/c: another German destroyer
> attack: this time I only took out three ships; we pushed the German
> destroyers back, when suddenly out of the haze, loomed large the High
> Seas Fleet about four miles off. We held on a bit and fired torpedoes at
> 'em – *Calliope* has good ground for thinking hers got home [they did not],
> and then ran like billy-oh for shelter with at least three big battle ships
> plunking at us. A most uncomfortable five or ten minutes, as their shooting
> was 100 percent A1. We were hit, in *Calliope* three times, and lost, I am
> sorry to say, close on a dozen killed, with many wounded.

Jellicoe had ordered a turn away to avoid the torpedoes, something
he said he would always do in this situation. It was perhaps the key
moment of the battle. As one historian writing from the German point
of view has remarked: 'The Germans were tactically beaten and in

headlong flight'.[6] Jellicoe has been criticized for not pressing on and turning to 'comb' the torpedo tracks, a standard Second World War procedure that meant steering to position your ships to head between and parallel to the tracks of the oncoming torpedoes. Had he done so he might have been able to continue to pursue the enemy and inflict a major defeat on him. But this is possibly asking too much; commanders in the Second World War were able to profit from mistakes made in the First. No one at the outbreak of the First World War had experienced torpedo attacks by massed destroyers, and the mayhem of the first (and only) fleet action of the whole war was probably not the time to try a tactic that had not been practised. Only a Nelson might have done so, and there were no Nelsons at Jutland on either side.

In the opinion of the captain of the *Collingwood*, expressed in his after-action report, the German destroyer attacks were 'very weak' considering the poor visibility that favoured such attacks. Notwithstanding this, he admits that a large number of torpedoes passed through the line of battle ships, adding, 'the smooth water helped my fore top lookouts to distinguish the tracks of the torpedoes'. So perhaps the German destroyers did not do too badly.

Notwithstanding the post-battle judgements based on hindsight, Jellicoe was still well positioned between Scheer and home. Unless Scheer could escape before daylight, he stood a good chance of being caught and destroyed come the morning. Bowyer-Smyth in the *Marlborough*:

> Everything seemed splendid, we were doing a good 17 knots, list and all, with A Boiler Room on the point of flooding outright, at present there was six feet of water in it. We were keeping our place in the line and the Grand Fleet was still between them and home, and with a whole day before us this time, make a job of it one way or the other.

Before night fell there was one more clash between the battle cruisers. The general direction of the two fleets, allowing for changes of formation, and manoeuvring, took them down opposite sides of a V, the Germans south-south-east down the left, and the British south-south-west down the right. Beatty was at the point of the British formation with light cruisers, and Hipper was on the eastern flank of the High Seas Fleet. Beatty, hearing sounds of gunfire of an engagement between British and German light cruisers, closed to find enemy battle cruisers to the north-west. Soon *Inflexible*, *Princess Royal*, *Tiger*, *New Zealand*, *Lion*, and *Indomitable* were firing. Hipper was astonished to find Beatty so far to the south of him, and so difficult to discern in the gloom. The British fire was the more effective, and two leading battle cruisers, *Seydlitz* and *Derfflinger*, took heavy punishment. The German battle cruisers fled west. At this point Admiral Mauve with his old battleships unwisely intervened, but was quickly seen off by Beatty. He did not follow, perhaps because the light was failing, and passing ahead of the German van, turned to steam on the same course as the enemy. This scrap between Beatty and Mauve was the last engagement between capital ships in the war, which still had two and a half years to run.

Jellicoe steered towards the sound of Beatty's guns, and from Beatty's signal was aware of the enemy course and position. Indeed his van battleships could discern the dim shapes of the enemy dreadnoughts through the murk, silhouetted against the last glimmers of light in the west. The Germans saw nothing. However, night was falling, and the visibility was further hampered by drifting veils of funnel and cordite smoke, and by fog. Had Jellicoe pressed on there was no doubt that he would have encountered the German fleet, but he was determined to avoid night action at all costs – he was wary of the known German expertise in night fighting, especially their control of their vastly superior searchlights. He altered course, slightly diverging from the enemy. His aim was to keep between Scheer and home, and engage him in the morning.

A few minutes later, Scheer turned the High Seas Fleet on to a course of south-south-east a quarter south at sixteen knots, ordering this course to be maintained at all costs. He was heading for the Horns Reef 105 miles away, come hell or high water ('death wish' number four). There were about six hours of darkness ahead. Jellicoe now had to decide whether the Germans would head for the Horns Reef entrance to Wilhelmshaven, taking them north of British minefields, or the southern Ems entrance (180 miles away). He discounted the long haul home through the Skagerrak. Jellicoe surmised that Scheer would head for the Ems as the Grand Fleet lay squarely between him and the Horns Reef. If he was wrong and Scheer did try to break through the tail of the Grand Fleet to head for the Horns Reef, he relied on his destroyer flotillas positioned astern of his battle ships to drive the Germans off with massed torpedo attacks. He was confident that he had barred Scheer's escape routes. Ordering the minelayer *Abdiel* to lay mines in the Horns Reef channel just in case (there were also three British submarines lying in wait there), he shaped course for the Ems channel. It would have been of enormous help to him if Tyrwhitt had been available to watch the Horns route, but thanks to the malign influence of Oliver, the Harwich force was in its base.

Night

Jellicoe was unaware that his speed of 17 knots would cause him to draw steadily ahead of the enemy. The last battle between Beatty and Mauve may have given both Jellicoe and Scheer the impression that the other's main body was further south than they actually were. Jellicoe ordered his destroyers to cover his rear from a position five miles astern. The British heavy units went to defence stations (main armament partially manned, and secondary armament fully closed up). It was time for a meal, sorting out the damage, collecting the dead, and tending the wounded.

Midshipman Frampton in the *Barham*:

We were allowed to take it in turns to leave the turret and find what we could [to eat]. My dismay can be imagined when I saw the Gunroom, which of course I expected to find as usual. It was a complete shambles both inside and out, and there was obviously no hope of getting anything to eat there. I remember among other things, the butter dish which had been blown with its contents out of the pantry and had stuck to the bulkhead. The Wardroom was intact, and we were invited to take part in the feast – such as it was. Some tongue, biscuits and a drink was about all, but it revived us.

In the *Marlborough*, Bowyer-Smyth:

Had a biscuit in the turret, and now it came in useful as we were hungry. Now the suspense was more or less over, I felt frightfully tired and my legs ached. During the scrap though one was a bit squeamish now and again it was ripping when we were hitting, and a fine sight. Now I felt I wanted to get right away out of it and inland away from the sea and bed.

Lieutenant Brind in the *Malaya*:

I was very glad of a sandwich of bread and tinned salmon, which was served out. Nothing warm could be obtained as the galley was out of action. The men managed to get some sleep during the night, but I was not so fortunate, as my perch was not very comfortable, and I hardly dared sleep, for it seemed so necessary to be absolutely ready.

The two fleets were once again heading down two sides of a V, only a much more slender one this time. The Germans on the left side were slower, so as the night drew on, instead of meeting at the point of the V, the foremost German ships encountered the rearmost British ones. Scheer's 'bash on regardless' tactics could have 'cost him his fleet', as one distinguished Jutland historian has commented, adding 'had the British been on the ball'.[7]

Throughout the night there were a number of encounters between the destroyers and cruisers of both fleets. While the Germans kept Scheer in the picture by wireless, Jellicoe was badly served by his subordinates. It has to be said that nothing was done to keep the Grand Fleet in the picture either. At first the clashes took place towards the rear of the Grand Fleet, and later behind it. At one stage the courses of the fleets took the shape of a lop-sided X, as Scheer's battleships snaked their way through avoiding contact.

In a letter to his father written immediately after the battle, and based on conversations with his fellow flotilla officers, King-Harman of the *Midge* conveys some of the confusion of a night battle at sea:

How the big ships were steering in the night I don't know. The 4th and 11th Destroyer Flotillas both got into the Germans, and the adventures of individual ships are more like fiction than fact. To start with the Fourth, our Flotilla. At the start of the action it consisted of:

Tipperary Flotilla Leader Captain Wintour.

*Shark**	*Achates*	*Broke* (half flotilla leader)
*Acasta**	*Ambuscade*	*Porpoise*
Spitfire	*Ardent*	*Unity*
Sparrowhawk	*Fortune*	*Garland*
Contest	*Christopher*	*Ophelia*
Owl	*Midge*	*Hardy*

[**Shark* was sunk, and *Acasta* badly damaged during the first clash of the battlefleets well before nightfall]

Owing to the extreme darkness of the night, the flotilla seems to have been rather scattered, *Owl*, *Midge* and *Hardy* never picked up the flotilla attack though we were all somewhere about the same position.

We legged it to the westward at full speed, the darkness occasionally lit by isolated gunfire, while about 10.30 a large ship (German we think) could be seen burning furiously a long way off [possibly the light cruiser *Frauenlob*]. About 11.30 several searchlights switched on on our beam, between two and three miles off, or perhaps more. As the searchlights switched on, an unseen line of ships let loose a perfect tempest of fire. Lit up in the glare of the lights was the *Tipperary*, heeling over, flames bursting from her hull. She seemed red hot. In less than 15 seconds she was foundering, still being plastered.

Almost simultaneously the *Ardent* and *Fortune* were lit up and literally blown into the air in less time than it takes to write it, most terrible to see. Another destroyer we could see twisting and turning going full bore, and disappeared. The searchlights were switched off, and the whole thing was over.

Achates and *Ambuscade* were the only ones who escaped from this effort. It appears that *Tipperary* saw some ships, which for some reason she thought were the 11th Flotilla making a signal to that effect to the four destroyers astern of her. Then on went the searchlights – *Tipperary*, *Ardent* and *Fortune* were blown to bits. *Ambuscade* and *Achates* both fired torpedoes, *Ambuscade* hitting a cruiser, and crashed off untouched, though pursued by a torrent of shells.

We made at full speed towards the place where this happened, *Owl* signalling 'I am going to attack with torpedoes'. We couldn't see a sign of anything, and after some time altered course again. At about 12.30 am, we suddenly seemed to be surrounded by ships. Two German destroyers plainly recognisable by their silhouettes slid by us a couple of hundred yards off, exchanging shots with us as they went. Immediately the place seemed full of guns, all going off. Shots were dropping and exploding all over and round us, the red flashes stabbing out all over the place. *Owl* fired a torpedo, ditto *Hardy* – we didn't – couldn't see anything to aim at.

We zig-zagged about, turned round in circles, crashing about, passed a British destroyer and then lost everything again – not a sound, nothing to be seen. Still later there was intense firing some miles off – and glares on the horizon as if ships were burning. Early daylight – about 2.45 am we ran into the same cruiser squadron we had left the evening before, and were ordered to take up screening stations. We now turned north. *Broke*, *Sparrowhawk*, *Unity*, and *Christopher* nearly had the same fate as the *Tipperary* – surprised by a sudden burst of firing. *Broke* was badly damaged, her upper deck covered with dead and wounded. The *Sparrowhawk* rammed her in the confusion, and *Contest* ran into *Sparrowhawk* who sank at once. *Broke* somehow managed to get away – none of them fired a torpedo.

Garland had an extraordinary night. She was all alone – three times she fell in with the enemy, and each time she made a successful attack under concentrated fire – once on battleships, twice on cruisers – and claims three hits. At dawn she engaged four German destroyers, hit one with her first salvo, whereupon all four ran like hares. Later she was chased by a whole flotilla but got away, and finally being very short of oil, made her way to the Tyne at slow speed. She was untouched except for one hit which destroyed her whaler at the davits.

Spitfire, also alone, collided with a German cruiser [actually the battleship *Nassau*] – crumpling up her own bows of course. The captain was thrown down by the bump, which saved his life, for the Germans fired a gun point-blank at *Spitfire*'s bridge, killing everyone else there. It is a mystery how *Spitfire* got clear. *Ophelia* saw nothing all night. *Contest* says she sank a destroyer by gunfire.

Only four of us eventually returned with the fleet – *Owl, Midge, Hardy* and *Ambuscade* the remainder being accounted for as follows:

Tipperary, Ardent, Fortune, Sparrowhawk, Shark – sunk in action.

Broke, Spitfire, Acasta, Contest, Porpoise – damaged, the first three maimed severely.

Achates, Christopher, Garland, Unity, Ophelia – chased by enemy at daylight, short of oil, put into various east coast ports for fuel. Arrived at base two days later.

The 12th Flotilla had much the same kind of show. *Faulknor* [light cruiser flotilla leader], *Onslaught*, and *Obedient*, and one other attacked and torpedoed a battle ship or battle cruiser [the pre-dreadnought *Pommern*]. *Onslaught* being hit and suffering many casualties, including all officers except the sub-lieutenants.

Of the destroyers sunk, *Marksman* picked up a few of their crews next morning. Captain of *Ardent* and engineer of *Fortune* were the only ones saved off their ships – both wounded and in the water for five hours. A few survivors of *Tipperary* were also found by *Marksman*. *Broke* saved nearly all the *Sparrowhawk*'s crew. *Shark* was lost with all hands.

There was no overall control of the British destroyer attacks. They were handicapped by lack of night training; and whereas all German ships were a light grey they were easily visible because painted black. It is a measure of the unimaginative nature of night-fighting training in the Royal Navy at the time that no one appears to have learned how an all-black shape is often the most easily discernible colour at night, sometimes more so than an all-white one, especially if there is any ambient light, or the enemy is using star shell, which the British did not have, but the Germans did. The Grand Fleet was further disadvantaged by the Germans' discovering the British night-recognition signal and flashing it when challenged, whereas the German night-recognition signal was a pattern of coloured lights, flicked on then off, and impossible to copy. One should also remember there was no radar – it had not yet been invented.

Although the Germans were subsequently full of praise for their torpedo boats and critical of the destroyers of the Grand Fleet, in fact the German boats were even more ill-coordinated than the British flotillas, sinking no one and achieving nothing. The ten best torpedo boats in the German navy opted out of the battle by going home via the Skagerrak and Denmark, the only part of the High Seas Fleet to do so. The British destroyers, not all brilliantly handled by any stretch of the imagination, were responsible for the loss of one pre-dreadnought battleship, three light cruisers, and a destroyer.

British ships failed to report engagements and sightings of enemy. Officers on the compass platforms of the 1st and 5th Battle Squadrons watched the 'fireworks' in rear, seeing enemy battleships and cruisers loom past as Scheer forced his way through. Frampton in Evan-Thomas's flagship, the *Barham*:

> About 10.30 pm, or perhaps a little after, we stood on the roof of the turret, we were able to witness a magnificent but terrible spectacle not far off our starboard bow. A truly terrific bombardment was taking place and lasted about quarter of an hour. Although we were so close, it was not advisable to show ourselves by turning on a searchlight and joining in the melee. We did not want to give away our position to the enemy. Some silly fellow did turn on a searchlight, but it was soon switched off, and we hoped the enemy was too busy to notice.

Admiral Evan-Thomas, thinking it no more than an encounter between destroyers, ignored it. The *Malaya*, last ship in the 5th Battle Squadron line, thought she saw an enemy battleship lit by a searchlight, but did not report it. Lieutenant Brind in the *Malaya*:

> We heard and saw several destroyer attacks on the Germans. One especially we had an extremely close view of. Some German shells fired at our destroyers actually fell around us.
>
> I have a very vivid impression of those destroyers dashing into the blinding searchlights and light [star] shells and into perfectly furious fire. The leading boat was hit badly and was ablaze from stem to stern. Two others seemed to make good their escape after firing their torpedoes. On this occasion as during other attacks, we heard and felt heavy explosions as though a torpedo had hit, and one ship was seen to sink. One of these explosions lit up the whole sky.

Midshipman Hext in the *Collingwood* also saw the battle at about 10.30 p.m., adding, 'there were intermittent cannonades during the night, but we were not attacked.'

Nothing was reported. No attacks were made, except by the destroyers in the rear. Even from ships near *Iron Duke* flashes of the engagements could be seen. The capital ships of the Grand Fleet steamed on, watchkeepers on their bridges drinking cocoa. Jellicoe, thanks to the supine behaviour of his battleship admirals and captains, had no idea what was happening. But a small group of people knew exactly what Scheer was up to.

From the onset of darkness, a stream of German signals was decrypted and passed by Room 40 to Admiral Oliver's staff. Some of the information was transmitted to Jellicoe, some of it late, much of it not at all. After the ridiculous signal at noon stating that the German Fleet was still in harbour, Jellicoe was inclined to disbelieve any intelligence emanating from the Admiralty. At 10.23 p.m. he received a signal based on a Room 40 intercept which gave the position of the rear battleship in the German Fleet. Jellicoe thought the position was wrong, and this merely reinforced his view that any information sent to him by Oliver was specious.

For the same reason Jellicoe ignored the information sent to him by Oliver at 10.41 p.m. that the High Seas Fleet had been ordered home on a course of south-south-east three-quarters east at 16 knots (this was a decryption or transcription error by Room 40). It was firm information that Scheer was heading for the Horns Reef.

A few minutes later Room 40 told Oliver's staff that Scheer had ordered a Zeppelin reconnaissance of the Horns Reef swept channel. But this news was never passed to Jellicoe. Between 9.55 p.m. on 31 May and 3.00 a.m. on 1 June, no less than sixteen decodes, all of which were pertinent to the situation, were passed by Room 40 to Oliver's incompetent staff in the Operations Division. Only three were sent to Jellicoe.[8]

Anticlimax

At 2.30 a.m., as the first glimmers of daylight appeared, Jellicoe ordered his fleet round to a northerly course. A few minutes later a signal from the Admiralty informed him that Scheer was nearly home. Throughout the Grand Fleet, as sixty thousand men fell out from action stations, there was a sense of being cheated, of depression, and bitterness. Le Mesurier wrote to his wife a month after the battle:

> Yep [sic]; 1 June was a day of many emotions. I fully thought and expected to have another smack at 'em early daylight, for to be quite frank, the opportunities missed on that Wednesday evening were a-many. Here had come <u>the</u> opportunity of all. What one had seen, once the main fleets got into touch gave no cause for anything but absolute confidence. Their great asset, destroyer attacks in large numbers had not been developed to anything like the extent we had anticipated, and once hit their gunnery went to pieces. All the omens were good, and yet, as the day wore on, and we swept back and forth on our track of the day before, one realised bitterly they had given us the slip. My little push [4th Light Cruiser Squadron] passed thro' a whole heap of debris about 8 am: oil, life-buoys, dead bodies, relics of one of our many destroyer attacks.

In the damaged ships heading for home, men had to stay at their action stations as they ran the gauntlet of U-boats waiting to pick up stragglers, not helped by uncertainty and incorrect information about the whereabouts of the High Seas Fleet. Bowyer-Smyth in the *Marlborough*:

We closed up in the turrets, eat some more biscuit and told each other that we would get a fine drop of leave out of it to try and hide the fact that we were feeling a bit squeamish. This was at about 3.30 am. We steered NW over the track we had come during the night and in an hour sighted a Zeppelin astern. X and Y turrets fired eight or nine rounds at it more with the idea of frightening it away than hitting, though we made him dip, the anti-aircraft gun also fired. As soon as it was out of sight we altered to SW hoping to avoid the submarines or destroyers he would be sure to put on our track. We now had twenty-four hours in the turrets and ships company was sent away by watches to get cocoa. Later the same was done for breakfast.

Soon after breakfast a report came through by telephone, 'a torpedo has just missed astern', they had judged by our list and not given us credit for twelve knots.

By this time *Fearless* had joined with us again to act as a submarine screen, but of course this was quite inadequate. Evidently signals had been received giving approximate whereabouts of High Seas Fleet for we were now warned to be absolutely prepared for eventualities as we 'may meet High Seas Fleet any minute'. This was not reassuring and one of my precautions was to make sure my swimming waistcoat was all right. Quite unnecessary as had we met them, it would have been no use.

I was so sleepy and tired continually training on ships or supposed ships that turned out to be friends or phantoms. At some time a submarine was sighted on the surface some 12,000 yards on our starboard bow. We trained guns on him but did not fire, holding our course and watching. As soon as he dipped [dived] we put our helm over and altered course to port. The commander plotted our relative positions, giving him 10 knots submerged [too much] with a range of 10,000 yards, shaped a course to gradually bring us back on our original track, while keeping outside his range. Shortly he came up and had a look at us, and in desperation fired at us from astern, and missed, though we swung our stern further to make sure.

Now the trouble was we had an incensed submarine astern who could quite possibly go as fast submerged as we could on the surface [unlikely if the *Marlborough* could maintain 12 knots]. We installed a good lookout aft. He fired once more in desperation, missed and was seen no more, though we kept a good lookout on till nightfall. We had passed the supposed rendezvous with the High Seas Fleet and were feeling a little better despite the submarine, only hoping they had by now been caught by J[ohn] J[ellicoe], it being a nice clear day.

Towards noon a flotilla of destroyers hove in sight to the southward. Taking no risks we trained on them and started ranging, but on being challenged they turned out to be our own Harwich Flotilla under Commodore Tyrwhitt going presumably into the bight to sweep up the crumbs. They detached four destroyers to screen us, which was a tremendous relief. We really felt we had more than a sporting chance of getting in now, and a little later when four more, our proper screen, turned up, we felt we could snap our fingers at Fritz.

Our course was shaped for a northern port, where if all went well we would arrive about five pm the next day, 2 June. Towards evening the glass started to fall, a breeze coming from westward. By dark it was blowing fairly fresh, and at twelve [midnight] there was a fair sea running, washing in heavily on the upper deck starboard side, the side our list was. The wind had chopped round to Northward and was blowing a stiff breeze. On taking over [the watch] I found some sheers had slipped and a pump choked, so we were making water faster than the pumps were throwing it out. Also the bulkhead in the damaged compartments, although sheered, were ominously springing, so we altered away to port and shaped course for the nearest land – Flamborough Head – and made an urgent signal for tugs, warned destroyers to stand by to take off the ships company if necessary and reduced to ten knots. The list was by now eight degrees, and the ship very much down by the head.

About 2 am the situation began to improve, we got the upper hand of the water and weather moderated, while four oil tracks to windward made a great difference to the break in the sea. *Fearless* was close up against our forebridge directly to windward and gave us a good lee. We sighted Flamborough at 3.30. By 4.0 we had made a signal cancelling the tugs, and by 7.0 we were secured to a buoy in the Humber.

On many ships the journey home was occupied with clearing up as much of the damage as possible, and with the sad business of collecting the dead. Midshipman Frampton in the *Barham*:

Throughout the ship there was a most unpleasant smell. I have no doubt it was the smell of gas from exploded shells, but many people believed that it was from burnt human flesh. Of course, it might have been as the cordite fire in the 6 inch battery had caused many terrible deaths. It stayed in the ship for months and sometimes I can smell it now. Twenty-six men and four officers lost their lives, and of our wounded, 37 in all, some had received very bad burns.

One of our first duties was to prepare the dead for burial. This proved a gruesome task. The horrors which some of our men had to go through

Right. Commander Evans of HMS *Broke* wearing his Polar Medal ribbon. He was a member of Scott's 1911 Antarctic expedition. [Q 19611]

Centre. Leading Seaman Ingleson of the *Broke* on the forecastle, where he fought German boarders hand-to-hand. [Q 18207]

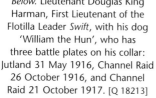

Below. Lieutenant Douglas King Harman, First Lieutenant of the Flotilla Leader *Swift*, with his dog 'William the Hun', who has three battle plates on his collar: Jutland 31 May 1916, Channel Raid 26 October 1916, and Channel Raid 21 October 1917. [Q 18213]

British submarines alongside a depot ship, showing the bridge and two periscope standards of the inboard boat, whose bows are towards the top of the picture. The outboard boat has a gun abaft the bridge. [Q 18630]

An F2A flying boat of the RNAS of the type flown by Captain Leckie. [Q 27501]

Bombing from the rear cockpit of the gondola of an SSZ-class airship. [Q 67695]

Zeppelin aces of the RNAS. Left to right: Flight Lieutenants J. S. Mills, A. W. Bigsworth DSO, Wilson and Warneford VC. Mills and Warneford destroyed Zeppelin LZ38, the first Zeppelin to attack London, in the shed at St Evre. [Q 69479]

Gondola of an SSZ-class airship. [Q 89185]

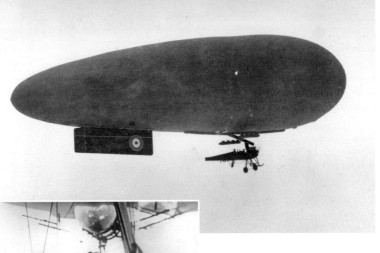

Above. An SS-class airship in flight, showing the modified BE2 fuselage suspended beneath the balloon. [Q 89162]

Left. Crew of an SSZ airship in flight. [Q 27431]

Below. An SS-class airship being prepared for a flight. [Q 89165]

A North Sea type airship about to launch. [Q 27433]

A North Sea type airship, showing the enclosed cabin. Two crews could be carried for long patrols. In flight, access to the engines is by a rope walkway. [Q 89057]

Above. A Curtiss H12 flying boat, showing its gun positions. [HU 67888]

Right. A Curtiss Large America flying boat. [Q 67581]

Lieutenant Culley takes off in a Sopwith Camel from a lighter towed by a destroyer. [Q 27511]

HMS *Furious* after conversion in early 1918, but still with her central bridge and funnel, which created too much turbulence over the landing deck aft to recover aircraft. Aircraft could still be launched from the flying-off deck forward. She launched a successful raid on the Zeppelin sheds at Tondern in Schleswig-Holstein on 19 July 1918. *Furious* was later converted to a proper flush-deck carrier, served in the Second World War and was broken up in 1948. [Q 19557]

Furious with Camels ranged on her foredeck. [Q 20627]

Commander Dunning goes over the side and is killed on his second attempt at a deck landing on *Furious*'s foredeck. [Q 80597]

HMS *Vindictive*, with some of the crews of the 5.7-inch howitzers
and Stokes guns (mortars). [Q 55568]

A Sopwith Strutter taking off from the flying platform mounted on the
gun turret of the battle cruiser *Australia*, with her sister ship the *New Zealand*
in the background. [Q 18729]

extricating the bodies from the debris, especially from one of the hydraulic engine rooms which had been flooded are best left out.

In 1916, anti-flash clothing was not worn, and many men suffered from cordite flash burns. This clothing was soon manufactured and issued, and is worn in action in the Royal Navy to this day. The medical techniques for dealing with burns in the First World War were rudimentary by present-day standards. To the surprise of the doctors, an unexpectedly large proportion of those burned soon died of shock. Lieutenant Brind in the *Malaya*:

> At noon I was not sorry to get out of the turret for lunch, for I had had no rest and no food [sic] for the last twenty-four hours, and I was quite ready for both, especially the latter. The next and most trying duty was to discover the casualties of my division [stationed in the starboard battery] which had suffered heavily. The majority of the wounded were unconscious for they had been dreadfully burnt, but those to whom I spoke, only wanted me to write to their people saying that all was going well, and to know about the action. Several of these afterwards died.

The bitterness felt in the fleet was exacerbated by the reports in the British press, based on a totally inadequate statement issued by the Admiralty. The German press crowed triumphantly about the British losses, concealing their own damage, and saying nothing about having run away. King-Harman wrote to his father:

> The papers have probably given you all the describing you will want for some time to come. Most of the accounts are moderately accurate as to facts, but the hopeless 'journalese' in which they are written makes it rather ridiculous to one who was actually there [nothing changes]. They're funny people these journalists – they've been howling half the war to be told the 'truth', and when the unfortunate Admiralty tells it, or as much as they knew at the time, there was a bigger howl than ever. The solid fact is that the Germans had a thundering good hammering, while our battle fleet is practically untouched.

Le Mesurier wrote to his wife on 6 June 1916:

> Really our press give me the fantals [sic]. The all-Tory papers, *Times*, *Globe*, *Morning Post*, went off at half cock with 'Jeremiahs' of the deepest purple. Damned if I don't turn Radical. I am more than inclined to and have been for some years. The *Westminster Gazette* was quite sound, *Daily Chronicle* stupidly rabid.
>   Sunday rags absolutely beneath contempt – yelling for Jacky [Fisher] to come back and for every VA's head, in command at sea, to be cut off. Makes me sick. The truth is that we missed the chance of annihilating

Germany at sea. On the other hand, they got as much as they had stomach for, and were badly rattled. Let us keep our heads – NOT despise our enemy – as we were rather prone to do, and make up our minds to let 'em have it properly next time.

The British public, brought up to believe in the absolute invincibility of their navy, reacted hysterically to the press reports. Some ships, such as the *Marlborough*, were hissed by dockyard workers and spectators as they came in to dock. Midshipman Frampton recorded: 'Fortunately, we were spared the unpleasantness of being hissed by our countrymen as we went to Scapa Flow where there were only heather-covered islands to greet us'.

The British public's faith in the navy may have been dented, but the sailors certainly did not share their countrymen's view. On 6 June 1916, a young rating, James Gavan, wrote to his parents from the Royal Naval Barracks Portsmouth where he was awaiting a draft to sea:

I have seen many survivors from the big Naval fight off various ships, all of them assert that what is now left of the German Navy is not worth much more than scrap iron. The fresh report issued in the press re this fight was to say the least of it pessimistic and as everybody here and almost throughout the service are confirmed optimists, absolutely hopeless and unreasoning optimists it is no wonder that the report was taken with a grain of salt. Nobody would accept the fact that the Germans could sink so many of our ships, without getting something for their money – and bit over in return; and now the facts have come to light [reports of German losses and damage] the Germans really have got full value for the damage they did.

Who won? Unquestionably the Grand Fleet. The battle had no effect whatever on the Royal Navy's ability to carry out its task. Two days after the battle Jellicoe was able to report twenty-four battleships coaled, restocked with ammunition, and in all respects ready for sea, against ten German capital ships. The damaged British ships were also repaired more quickly. Scheer did not achieve his aim of cutting off and destroying part of the Grand Fleet, and he nearly ended up being destroyed several times himself. Just as wars are not won by evacuations, battles are not won by running away. Authors who argue that the Germans achieved a moral victory by dint of having inflicted more casualties on the Grand Fleet than they suffered themselves (true) are adopting an academic bean-counting approach to battle and war. To use a land-fighting analogy, the army in possession of the field of battle after an engagement is the winner, however heavily it has suffered. Not only was the Grand Fleet in possession of the field, it was in a better state, in terms of having more serviceable ships than the High Seas Fleet, ready to fight immediately. Hipper's observation in his memoirs, 'my only thoughts were that we should have the whole English Fleet before us at the Horns Reef the next morning and there decide the issue', is bluster worthy of a 'spin doctor'.[9]

The thought uppermost in the High Seas Fleet from the minute they encountered Jellicoe was to high-tail it for home as fast as they could. From then on the Germans were on the defensive. They used their priceless night-fighting superiority defensively – never offensively. They were reactive, not proactive. They lost.

10

Unrestricted U-boat Warfare:
the Royal Navy nearly loses the War

April 1917 saw 869,000 tons of Allied shipping sunk, 90 per cent of it by U-boats. The odds on a ship safely completing a round trip from Britain to a port beyond Gibraltar was one in four.[1] This was a higher rate of loss than in any single month in the Second World War, when at its height there were considerably more U-boats at sea in all areas than there were in the First World War. The most successful U-boat in the First World War, U-35, sank 224 ships in twenty-five sorties, compared with the record holder in the Second, U-48, which sank 51. In spring 1917 the German Naval Staff's promise to bring Britain to her knees by unrestricted U-boat warfare was well on the way to being fulfilled, and the Admiralty's efforts to stem the losses were frustrated at every turn. Defeat stared Britain in the face. It was the gravest crisis faced by the Royal Navy in the entire war.

In October 1916, the Germans had returned to waging restricted submarine warfare, officially under prize rules. Despite this, there were a number of sinkings of passenger ships without warning, especially in the Mediterranean where there were likely to be fewer American passengers. This final burst of 'restricted' submarine warfare resulted in a mounting toll of Allied losses, mainly thanks to the introduction of newer and faster U-boats, which had a greater radius of action, were able to dive deeper and quicker, and were equipped with heavier guns and better torpedoes. U-boats preyed on Allied commerce in the Western Atlantic approaches to the British Isles, the Irish Sea, the Channel, the east coast of Britain, the Mediterranean, and the approaches to Gibraltar from Cape Finisterre off the coast of Spain and Portugal. Nevertheless, by the end of 1916 the German High Command realized that it would not be possible to defeat the British by restricted submarine warfare before Germany was exhausted. But if Britain could be brought to her knees by autumn 1917, France and Italy would collapse, and Germany would be victorious.

On 1 February 1917, the Germans declared unrestricted submarine warfare again, having abandoned it on 30 August 1915. They took this step knowing that it might overcome American reluctance to come into the war on the Allied side. In fact arrogance and obtuseness on the part of the German foreign office was to do that. The German foreign minister, Zimmermann, suggested in a coded telegram to his Ambassador in Washington that in the event of war between Germany and the United States, Mexico should be encouraged to declare war on the USA and, specifically, invade Texas and New Mexico, which she had lost in 1836 and 1848. Room 40 at the Admiralty decoded the telegram and ensured that its contents were revealed to the Americans. This combined with the subsequent loss of American lives on two liners sunk by U-boats led to the United States' declaration of war on 6 April 1917.[2]

America's decision to join the Allied cause would be meaningless unless supplies and troops could be shipped across the Atlantic. It would be well over a year before America, totally unprepared for war, would even begin to make a significant contribution to the fighting on the Western Front, the key theatre for defeating Germany. In the meantime, unless the rate of Allied shipping losses was drastically cut, Britain would be out for the count well before America's efforts could begin to take effect.

Meanwhile the Admiralty had been toiling away trying to bring the shipping losses under control, with about the same success as if it had attempted to put out a forest fire with a garden hose. In November 1916, Jellicoe was made First Sea Lord, handing over the Grand Fleet to Beatty. Jellicoe created an Anti-Submarine Division of the Naval Staff under Rear Admiral Alexander Duff, which cast around for weapons to defeat the U-boat. Some of its ideas, such as improvements to hydrophones and depth charges and copying the excellent German mines, yielded some results. Others, such as training circus sealions to detect U-boats, or disguising a trawler to look like a disabled Zeppelin in the water to entice submarines to its assistance, were not so successful. Fantastic though both these schemes were, they seem models of tactical common sense compared with the earlier suggestion that the North Sea be filled with barrels of Eno's Fruit Salts, so that the resulting stream of bubbles would force the submarines to the surface.[3]

Accurate detection of dived submarines and maintaining contact with them were problems that remained unsolved for the whole war.[4] This lack of a means to do so made nonsense of the tactic so strongly supported by the Admiralty, and the great majority of senior naval commanders, of 'hunter' groups of destroyers roaming the sea after U-boats, which sporting naval officers likened to hounds scenting and killing a fox. Thanks to Room 40 intercepts, it was sometimes possible to discern the *general* area in which enemy submarines were operating, but the hounds could not scent the fox when it was out of sight (when the U-boat had dived).

As part of the 'hunting' tactic, the Auxiliary Patrol, consisting of large numbers of small, slow craft such as armed yachts, trawlers, and drifters, hunted for U-boats in areas near the coast where shipping was concentrated and funnelled. By the end of the war there were more than 3,700 such vessels in the patrol. They worked hard but were generally ineffective. Even when they encountered a U-boat, it had a fourteen to one chance of escaping.[5] How many submarines they failed to detect we shall never know.

Hydrophones proved ineffectual unless the vessel operating them stopped to lower them into the water. Very occasionally fixes on submarines were obtained when three stationary ships used their hydrophones to obtain a triangulation on the sound of the U-boat's propeller. However, even this produced only marginally better solutions, and sitting stopped for protracted periods in the vicinity of a U-boat was unwise. Random dipping of hydrophones in the hope of hearing a U-boat without some indication of its whereabouts was almost invariably a waste of time. Post-war analysis shows that the total number of U-boat losses credited to detection by hydrophones was three.[6] U-boats were very difficult to see on the surface at night, and their periscopes could be difficult to detect even in daytime.

The answer to the U-boat, the convoy, stared the Admiralty in the face, but it took an inordinate amount of time and persuasion for realization to sink in to the Royal Navy's collective brain, despite there being plenty of evidence for it. As noted earlier, troopships had been convoyed from the outset of the war, without one being lost to a U-boat. Trade on the Hook of Holland route had been convoyed since 26 July 1916, to protect vessels against forays by enemy destroyers and submarines from Heligoland or Zeebrugge. Despite the proximity of these German destroyer and submarine bases on either flank of this convoy route, there were only six losses out of a total of 1,861 sailings (0.32 per cent), and all these were before June 1917, when stricter control of stragglers was instituted.[7] Tyrwhitt was responsible for protecting these convoys, and dubbed them the 'Beef Trip', because some of the cargoes consisted of Dutch food that an Anglo-Dutch agreement diverted to Britain from Germany. A further example was provided by vessels carrying coal from Britain to France: the loss in convoys on the four cross-Channel coal trade routes throughout the war was 53 out of 39,352 sailings (0.13 per cent).

When it was suggested to Jellicoe's predecessor, and his chief of war staff, Oliver, who still exercised his baleful influence in the Admiralty, that convoys should be extended to all trade routes, they came up with a number of objections; all of them appear to have been conjured up from thin air, and to be without basis in fact. Convoys, they argued, were only successful when it was possible to allocate a separate escort for each vessel, and it was impracticable to supply the enormous number of escorts needed. It would be difficult for convoys to find the rendezvous, and they would be in danger while assembling. Large convoys would be unable to zigzag. It would be difficult to form convoys of equal speed. Congestion in ports would be caused by ships all arriving at once, and there would be an increased risk from mines. Convoys would present too big a target. Masters would be incapable of maintaining station. In the words of the Naval Historical Branch study after the war, 'Not one of these objections was valid'.[8]

The merchant navy, instead of rebutting the Royal Navy's lack of confidence in its seamanship, tamely agreed, adding that only two ships could sail in company, thus ignoring the success of the large convoys that had successfully transported Dominion troops over great distances in the early months of the war.

The statistics on which the number of ships requiring convoying were based were found by Commander Henderson, who contacted the Ministry of Shipping, to be wildly exaggerated, as was the number of escorts required, once it was accepted that one per merchant ship was too many.

Finally, on 26 April 1917, Rear Admiral Duff proposed to Jellicoe that a trial convoy be sailed, and it was approved on the following day. This was three days before Lloyd-George, then Prime Minister, made a visit to the Admiralty and, according to his mendacious memoirs, forced the decision on a reluctant First Sea Lord.

The first trial convoy, consisting of sixteen merchant ships escorted by the Q-ships *Mavis* and *Rule*, sailed from Gibraltar on 10 May. It was a complete success, laying to rest anxieties about the inability of merchant skippers to keep station and zigzag. There were no submarine attacks, possibly a very early indication that U-boat commanders preferred to attack undefended convoys.

The first trial convoy from the USA was escorted by the British armoured cruiser *Roxburgh*. Ten ships that remained in the convoy reached port safely, but two, unable to maintain convoy speed, straggled; one was torpedoed, an important object lesson learned the hard way. The captain of the *Roxburgh* reported that the ships' masters had kept good station, coped with zigzagging, and reacted promptly to signals, adding that he would be happy to escort as many as thirty ships in future.

All was not immediately sweetness and light, however. Despite these encouraging results, Jellicoe, Duff, and especially Oliver, were still not fully converted, and the adoption of the convoy system was unduly slow. To begin with only homeward-bound vessels were convoyed; outward-bound and ocean-going ships moving around British waters still proceeded independently. By the end of 1917, only just over half of Britain's overseas trade was convoyed, despite the system having already been shown to be almost fool-proof. By the end of the war 90 per cent of trade was convoyed.

By this time dissatisfaction with the way the Admiralty was running the war at sea had led to Jellicoe's supersession as First Sea Lord, on 24 December 1917, by Admiral Sir Roslyn Wemyss. (Jellicoe was retired.) Other changes included sending Oliver to command the 1st Battle Squadron in the Grand Fleet, his job as Deputy Chief of the Naval Staff being taken over by Admiral Freemantle; and replacing Bacon with Keyes as Flag Officer Commanding the Dover Patrol. Despite these 'new brooms', the Admiralty continued to be obsessed with the problems of finding enough escorts, having created the difficulty in the first place by keeping destroyers for totally unproductive 'offensive operations' on the grounds that escorting convoys was too passive. They appeared to fail to understand that convoying was not a defensive strategy, it presented the opportunity to act *offensively* against U-boats attacking the convoy. (Although this was in fact a bonus, because *the safe arrival of merchant ships* with their precious cargoes, not sinking enemy sub-marines, was what ultimately counted in the U-boat war and was *the aim* of the game.) Using escorts and aircraft to hunt U-boats in waters where there was no convoy was a waste of time and precious resources. As one officer is alleged to have remarked in the Second World War, the presence of a U-boat in such areas was irrelevant; there was nothing there except fish.

'Sweeping' for U-boats in a zone several hours ahead of a convoy was usually a waste of time and effort in the First World War, because as already been noted, no means existed of detecting a dived submarine from a moving vessel. Even hydrophones lowered from stationary ships were almost useless.

Room 40 played a key part. Thanks to wireless intercepts, the approx-imate location of U-boats could be established. On security grounds, independent merchant ships could not be sent signals giving them the whereabouts of U-boats. Anyway many of them had no wireless and their locations were not known. But every convoy commodore had a wireless in his ship, and his convoy could be diverted. It is impossible to tell how many ships were saved by convoy diversions.

Why were convoys so successful? The perception among senior officers in the Admiralty that a bunch of twenty to thirty ships was easier to find than the same number strung out across the ocean was proved wrong. The ocean is vast, and even a large number of ships steaming in formation could easily be missed by a submarine which, even when surfaced, was low in the water, and had a limited range of vision. A single ship could probably be seen by a U-boat lurking within ten miles of its track. A convoy of ships two miles wide would be seen by a U-boat lying within eleven miles of the centre of its track. When a convoy was sighted, a submarine might not be well positioned to attack, and especially if dived, lacked the speed to catch up, particularly when a convoy was zigzagging, whereas a submarine that was unable to catch an independent ship, or that had fired and missed, merely had to wait for the next one to come along. The CO had time to reload before the next target appeared, and take good aim when it did. Furthermore, since a U-boat could fire only a single spread of torpedoes, it was unable to damage a larger convoy any more than a small one, and convoy speed and swift retaliation by escorts would prevent it overtaking the convoy and setting up another attack.

Once a U-boat attacked a convoy, rather than dealing with a lone merchantman equipped with a gun, it found itself being aggressively counter-attacked by escorts with depth charges. Although once the U-boat dived and lowered its periscope it could not be located, it could be kept down and therefore blind. Every time it popped up and showed its periscope it would be 'charged' by an escort, risking being depth-charged, or rammed, or at least having its periscope damaged.

Dönitz was convinced that the convoy was the key to the Allied success in defeating the U-boat.

The oceans at once became bare and empty; for long periods at a time the U-boats, operating individually, would see nothing at all; and then suddenly up would loom a huge concourse of ships, thirty or fifty or more of them surrounded by a strong escort of warships of all types. The solitary U-boat, which had probably sighted the convoy by chance, would then attack, thrusting again and again and persisting, if the commander had strong nerves, for perhaps several days and nights, until the physical exhaustion of both commander and crew called a halt. The lone U-boat might well sink one or two of the ships, or even several; but that was but a poor percentage of the whole. The convoy would steam on. In most cases no other German U-boat would catch sight of it, and it would reach Britain, bringing a rich cargo of foodstuffs and raw material safely to port.[9]

In the First World War the Germans did not use 'wolf pack' tactics, so although a successful lone U-boat might sink a couple of ships in a convoy over a period of hours, this represented a small percentage of the whole. This was noted by Karl Dönitz, who was taken prisoner in 1918 when his UB-68 was sunk in the Mediterranean by British escorts; and his experience put to good use twenty-two years later.

Successful U-boat commanders were in the minority: of 400 U-boat COs, a mere 20 were responsible for 60 per cent of Allied sinkings.[10] But the risks they took to notch up a high score meant that a substantial proportion of the best submarine skippers were themselves lost with their crews. Soon Room 40 was decoding messages to the High Seas Fleet requesting transfers to replace U-boat crews lost attacking convoys.

Another fact that escaped the Admiralty was that the *bigger* the convoy the more economical it was in the use of escorts. (Analysis after the war found that an increase in the average size of convoys from 32 to 54 ships was associated with a reduction in losses of 56 per cent.) The doubling of the number of ships in convoy would double its area, but would increase its circumference by a smaller factor, and the circumference determined the escort required. A convoy of twenty ships, for example, would ideally have five escorts, so three such convoys would need fifteen escorts. But by combining the three convoys into one sixty-ship convoy, the escort requirement would be only nine. Larger convoys would clearly effect economies in escort numbers while reducing the number of convoys to be protected at any one time.[11] It was to take until the Second World War for this simple mathematical fact to sink in.

Despite the obvious success of convoys, the Admiralty continued to resort to panaceas throughout the war in their efforts to defeat the submarine. It was a good example of failing to follow the first principle of war: *select and maintain the aim*. They consistently failed to make a correct selection of the *aim* (get the ships to port safely), and when they hit on it, mainly by accident, they failed to *maintain* it, instead being diverted by schemes, some little better than 'stunts', many of which were hugely expensive in resources and effort.

One of the biggest of these was the Northern Barrage, aimed at barring the exit from the North Sea to submarines. It was similar to the minefield and net barrage in the Dover straits (see Chapter 13), but on a prodigious scale. The Northern Barrage, initially an American idea, eventually stretched from the Orkneys to the approaches to Hardanger Fjord south of Bergen in Norwegian territorial waters. By the end of the war some 70,263 mines were laid – in places the field was thirty-five miles deep. The barrage was covered by 'hunting groups'. On one occasion, reacting to Room 40 intelligence that a large U-boat was heading home, one of these groups, consisting of three destroyers, three sloops, and five divisions of trawlers, swept the area between the Shetlands and the Faroes and achieved nothing. Post-war analysis shows that probably six U-boats were sunk by the Northern Barrage, and possibly a seventh. At best the Northern and Dover Barrages deterred, discouraged, and delayed U-boats, the latter resulting in reducing the amount of time they could spend on patrol.

Convoy work was boring and unglamorous. Some escorts spent months, or indeed the whole war, at sea and never saw, let alone engaged, a U-boat. The most successful convoys were those on whose voyages nothing happened. Accounts of action and excitement are rare; most speak of boredom and bad weather.

The North Sea

As in all other areas, before the introduction of convoys, U-boats were caught and sunk more by good luck than anything else. The experience of the old destroyer *Thrasher* is typical. She was small (355 tons and 200 feet long), 1890s vintage, coal-fired, with a turtle-back bow, one 12pdr forward in a 'bandstand', and five 6pdrs. She belonged to the 7th Destroyer Flotilla based at Immingham on the Humber. On Friday 9 February 1917, *Thrasher* was escorting a British submarine, D4, out to the start of its patrol. Signalman Baker recorded in his diary:

As my watch was the first dog, after dinner I turned in expecting to get a good sleep. At 1.30 the action station bell sounded. We all jumped up and ran on deck. Passing through the conning tower, I heard gun fire and on arrival on the bridge, saw a big merchant [ship] being shelled. A lookout shouted 'there she is', and looking ahead I saw a German submarine. Orders were given for full speed ahead and open fire. The first two shots were well over, but the third was very near her as she was diving. We were fairly close to her at the time, and as we passed over the spot, a depth charge was dropped. There was a tremendous explosion and we were severely shaken.

A few seconds later the submarine appeared with a decided list to port. The moment she appeared, all our guns that would bear opened fire, four of them. Our crew went mad, all of them shouting, swearing, and cheering. The language was the worst I have ever heard, all were at it. At the call for ammunition, I joined up with the supply party and helped to supply ammunition to the foremost gun. In the usual way I can just manage to lift one of those boxes, but now I found I had extra strength. I was holding them with one hand and running up the steps to the bridge.

In less than a minute one of the members of the submarine's crew appeared, he ran about wildly holding up his hands. One was not sufficient, so the firing continued until the submarine stopped. One by one the others came up and joined the first, holding up their hands. It was quite evident they were in a state of panic. At last a white flag was hoisted and we ceased fire, keeping all our guns trained on her. Rifles and revolvers were served out, and armed guard was told off, and the whaler lowered and sent over to take possession.

As soon as the boat was alongside, two men shouted out 'we are English prisoners'. They were taken on board first, and then as many wounded as possible and rowed back to us. As they arrived I was by the gangway helping them in. The whaler made three trips, and besides the prisoners, brought over two officers and 14 men, three of whom were very badly wounded. They were a rough old lot, but when I looked at our men, I was bound to admit there was not much difference. Besides prisoners, we took their log, charts, binoculars, and nautical instruments.

Before they were all aboard, the *Itchen* arrived followed by the *Quail*, and *P 52*. It was decided for us to take back the prisoners, and the other boats to endeavour to take in the submarine. On the way we received a W/T message telling us to go alongside the *Albion* and put captives in her. While we were there, Captain Nasmith VC who is in charge of submarines in this region, came on board and we started to take him out to see the prize. However we intercepted a W/T signal saying she had sunk, so we returned to Immingham. The German sub was the U 39, almost new, this being her second trip. She carried a 4-inch gun, larger and better than any gun we carry. Her bows were fitted with a saw-like arrangement for cutting nets. At no time did her crew make any attempt to use the gun, although they were using it fast enough on an unarmed merchant [ship].

My own feelings were of intense excitement. At first I felt I could have blown them all to pieces with pleasure, but when I was helping the wounded aboard, I felt nothing but sorrow for them. At first they were put into the after bandstand (gun platform), and later taken down to the stokers' mess and given cocoa and cigarettes, some of them had brandy.

We received many signals of congratulation from *Quail*, *Itchen*, *Kale* and Captain D [Destroyers]. They consisted of such terms as 'Well done old *Thrasher*', and 'Good boy'. The greatest surprise I got when it was all over, I looked at my watch, and found that from first to last it had lasted only nine minutes. Of course we are all very proud, one of the oldest boats on the East Coast and catching a new sub in a few minutes. A special word of praise was given to the engine room staff, who increased speed from ten to twenty-eight knots in two minutes.

Sorties were usually tedious, unsuccessful, and often unpleasant. Baker:

Mon. Mar 19th [1916]. As we were coaling, a signal was received reporting a German submarine sighted off Croquet Island, and telling us to go and investigate. Joined up with *Ness*, *Albatross*, and *Bonetta*. Made sweeps all day long, but found no trace of submarine. Wind had been blowing up all day, and by four it was a gale. We were a very wet and sad ship by the time we got in.

Thurs. Mar 27th. At 7.30 a signal was made to the *Kale* from the SNO ordering him to send out a destroyer to patrol off the mouth of the Tyne. As we were the only boat without any defect, out we went. It was blowing hard with blizzards of snow and sleet every few minutes and a very heavy swell was running. We were unable to go more than 6 knots, and every time we turned all hands were ordered off the upper deck and all hatches were battened down. In view of the weather and the fact that no submarine could operate in such conditions, we requested permission to return to harbour, but our application was refused. We stuck it all day until dark and weren't we pleased to get in. It was just boring and uncomfortable.

Mon. Apr 2nd. We slipped at 4.35 with *Kale* and *Itchen*, having been warned that the weather forecast was bad. When I took over the watch, we were off Whitby doing 19 knots. The ships were in line abreast with *Thrasher* on the outside, both wind and sea were rising, and before 9.0 AM it began to get very uncomfortable. At 9.30 it was blowing a gale from the south-east, and we were compelled to reduce speed. First we went down to 14 knots, then 12, then 8 and finally to 125 revolutions. From 10 to 1.30 we were shipping water by the ton. The ejector got choked up and [water from] the chain locker ran over into the mess deck which was soon 18 inches deep. The lockers were floating around, and everything loose was sculling about the deck. The ejector was soon cleared, but the water was coming in so fast, the pump could not keep pace with it. Almost all moveables were washed off the deck, and she was rolling so heavily that the whaler and dinghy dipped with each roll. Seas over a foot [high] were sweeping across the deck, with the consequence our sea boots got full of water. We almost forgot we had feet. There were continuous heavy snow blizzards during which it was impossible to see more than a few yards. In the midst of one of these blizzards, a trawler almost rammed us, missing us by a few feet. All we could do was to hang on to the stays to keep ourselves on board. Shortly before 12 we sighted a buoy and got our bearings. Shortly after 1.30 we rounded Spurn greatly to the relief of all. Men who had been years in the RN said it had been one of the worst days they could remember.

In June, the *Thrasher* took part in her first convoy, up to Lerwick in the Shetlands, the first leg of the Scandinavian Convoy route to Norway. Baker:

> We left the Tyne at ten on Tuesday night. The convoy consisted of seven merchant vessels, Danish, Norwegian, and Swedish escorted by a whale boat, four trawlers, and two destroyers, the *Seal* and ourselves. Roughly the method is this: the merchant ships keep in a double line. The whale boat is the guide of the fleet, and carries the navigating officer, always she leads. The trawlers are disposed on either side about 700 yards distant from the merchants, and the destroyers hop about all over the place, but keeping handy.

Thrasher's next trip was a White Sea convoy bound from Lerwick for Archangel. Baker:

> <u>Fri. June 29th</u>. The *Seal* and ourselves got under way at 4 pm, and were soon outside with five trawlers and eight merchants, all of them large. We were to escort them to a latitude fifty miles north of Muckle Flugga, the most northerly point of the Shetland Isles, approximately 100 miles north of Lerwick. At that point the destroyers and two trawlers were to return independently, while the remainder proceeded to Archangel. The weather was bad, it had been blowing up steadily and by midnight it was a gale, and we were almost helpless in a very rough sea. I had the middle watch [midnight to 4 a.m.], and for over a half an hour was trying to get a signal through to the *Seal*. Two strips of glass across the front of the cruiser arc lamp got broken, and the wind was so strong it blew the lamp out. As it is a 2,000 candlepower electric lamp, this gives some idea of the force of the wind. It was almost impossible to keep one's feet and work the lamp at the same time. At one time the Captain sent out a man to hold me while I made the signal. In the end I could get no reply, and later found that on the *Seal*, conditions were the same, and in one roll their lamp had gone over the side. Eventually the signal was passed by buzzer [W/T]. We left the convoy at 5.30 and returned to Lerwick at 1.30.

A selection of the next diary entries give a feel for convoy duties in the North Sea in a small destroyer.

> <u>Mon. July 2nd</u>. Down south once more. We left Lerwick at 8 am Saturday with the *Seal* and a convoy of six. The weather had improved very much and at first all went quietly. At 4.28 Sunday morning one of the convoy, the *Germania*, was torpedoed. We went to Action Stations and scouted around for a while, but found no trace. She sank in 53 minutes, all the crew being taken off by one of the trawlers. All were saved, but several were hurt.

<u>Mon. July 9th</u>. We are all getting a bit tired of running day and night and being in two watches [four hours on and four hours off]. We left yesterday at 6 am, and with orders to pick up a coastal convoy. Leaving the Tyne we turned north and found the convoy off St Mary's. It was a slow convoy and could do only five knots, as a result we were not off Scarborough until 6 pm. For an hour we lay and rolled while waiting for orders. The trawlers left and the convoy went on its way alone. It was a rotten day with a heavy swell, and we washed over all the time. Finally we received orders to proceed as far as possible with the convoy, but to arrive off the Humber before dark. We reached Immingham at 10 pm, and were told to tie up for the night, slip at 4, and coal, and proceed north with a convoy tomorrow.

<u>Thurs. July 12th</u>. At Lerwick once more and it looks as if we shall have a couple of days rest. We left Immingham at 4 am on Tuesday and were clear of the Humber at 6 with a convoy of seven. The weather at first was rotten, but after 24 hours it eased quite a lot, and by the third day it was lovely. We picked up two ships at Hartlepool, and six at the Tyne, we dropped five at the Tyne, two off Croquet Island. Nothing happened until this morning. I had done the first watch [8 a.m. to midday], and turned in at 12.15. Woke to find the mess in darkness and everything in a state of confusion. The ship was going at speed, and everyone turning out, someone shouted 'Action Stations'.

I slipped out, grabbed my boots and clothes, and rushed up on deck. One of our convoy, a Norwegian, the *Balzac*, had been torpedoed in the bows, and went under in less than 10 minutes. She stood up nearly perpendicular, bows under and then dived. All her crew were saved. We did the usual drill, rushing to the spot, releasing a depth charge, and generally kicking up a 'dust', but no sign of Fritz. Turned in again about 5 pm. She was torpedoed at 4.15 pm and sank very near where the *Germania* was sunk.

I noticed that a Danish ship, *Elsborg*, lowered her boats and started to abandon ship as soon as Fritz made himself felt. Arrived in harbour at 4.30 this afternoon.

During the last month we have lost two destroyers, the *Cheerful* mined off Lerwick with the loss of 40 men, and the poor old *Itchen*, torpedoed off the Orkneys with a loss of nine. Both ships were on convoy duties at the time.

<u>Fri. July 13th</u>. This morning was spent cleaning up and during the afternoon had a bath and shave. On all convoy trips we were short of water and were rationed. The cause of this shortage is that we can carry only 110 tons of coal, and if we have several spasms and are compelled to go at full speed, this supply will scarcely be enough. To economise, the evaporator is not worked. Our ration for washing is four buckets twice a

day, and this for twenty-four men. If you are lucky and get there early it is
all right, but after the first dozen it gets a bit thick, and it is as well to wait
for the next issue. We had one humorist, Cook by name, who rejoiced in
the name of Doctor. Before we left Immingham, he would have a thorough
wash, fold up his towel, and say, 'next wash Lerwick'.

In August, *Thrasher*, with her sister old destroyers, was sent down to
the Nore Defence Flotilla.

The Royal Naval Air Service

Operations in the primitive and unreliable aircraft of the day were
hazardous enough, especially over the North Sea, without any interference from the enemy. Engine failures would end in the aircraft landing
on water that even in summer was bitterly cold. In May 1917, Flight
Sub-Lieutenant Morris and his wireless operator set off in a Short
Seaplane to find Flight Sub-Lieutenant Maxton, who had ditched his
Sopwith Baby seaplane. They suffered engine failure and force-landed in
a British minefield. Their aircraft broke up in the swell, and they clung
to a float for five days and nights. They managed to release two pigeons,
which carried a message back to base, but their eventual rescue was a
matter of luck, as searchers could not find them. Only because a flying
boat returning from patrol spotted them were they picked up. Even then
their troubles were not over. They were dragged into the flying boat
with waves washing over them, but the extra weight and sea conditions
damaged the aircraft on take-off and it failed to get airborne. Eventually
it taxied on the surface the twenty-two miles to Felixstowe. Such
incidents were by no means the exception, and long taxis were carried
out on a number of occasions.

The earlier patrols, looking for submarines before the introduction of
coastal convoys, were almost invariably fruitless and extremely boring.
In the pea-soup conditions of the North Sea a fully dived boat was
invisible. Only the wake from its periscope would betray its presence, or
a swirl of water would sometimes show where it had dived when taken
by surprise. Flight Sub-Lieutenant Gordon Hyams was on patrol in a
Sopwith Schneider seaplane when he saw his first and only U-boat

off Scarborough, it was a very rough day, there was no shipping about,
and there he was on the surface, about half a mile away, probably
recharging batteries. I made for him immediately, but he crash-dived. The
sea was so rough and full of foam, he didn't leave an trace of a swirl. I
judged where he was and dropped a 65lb bomb. Nothing happened.

As the war progressed, the Royal Naval Air Service played an increasing role in anti-submarine operations. In 1915 and 1916, most maritime air patrols were carried out by non-rigid airships. Unlike the German navy, the British had not built, or even experimented with airships before the war, and had certainly not considered how they would use them. The RNAS non-rigids were sausage-shaped gas-filled balloons with at first an aircraft fuselage, and later a motorized gondola, suspended underneath – not as efficient as the rigid airship, such as the Zeppelin, built round a metal frame. Nevertheless the RNAS's Submarine Scouts (SS-class) and Coastal (C-class) non-rigid airships gave valuable service on long-range patrols over the North Sea, the Channel, and the Irish Sea.

Sub-Lieutenant Thomas Williams was one of the earlier airship pilots, and joined when they were still at the experimental stage. He and the others were trained on ballooning techniques at the Hurlingham Club, a pre-war recreational ballooning centre. Here, in unpowered balloons, they learned how to adjust gas and ballast to climb and descend, and to land safely, techniques that were to prove useful in the days ahead when, as frequently happened, the engines on the rudimentary airships broke down. He and another pilot, Taylor, carried out trials on SS14, powered by a BE2C fuselage:

> We went up at crack of dawn, I always tried to go up at dawn, so I had the whole day to get out of trouble. We went up to 7 or 8,000 feet to give ourselves a bit of elbow room. Suddenly the engine overheated and seized solid. We took it in turns to climb out and stand on the skids to try to spin the propeller, which wasn't very funny, considering you'd a drop of 7,000 feet if your foot slipped. We were unsuccessful, so we ballooned down to the ground, and as luck would have it it was dead calm.
>
> When we reached the ground, we tied the aircraft to a tree. We went to the village shop and bought chewing gum to stop up the holes in the radiator, and filled it up with water from the village pump. We got the engine started again, but as we had lost gas coming down, the airship wouldn't carry both of us, so Taylor flew home and I walked.

Williams was posted to Anglesey to cover the Irish Sea right across to Ireland, south halfway to Pembroke, and north to the Isle of Man, with responsibility for escorting convoys in the whole area and especially the entrance to Liverpool, and the Mersey estuary.

> I was allocated SS25, a BE2C airship, with uncomfortable open cockpits, so the rain poured down your neck, and a continual draft. Some people carried cans and some bottles into which to pee. I found this, after long patrols, rather unpleasant. I evolved my own system which became

standard. I bored a hole in the floor, to which I attached some rubber hosing, with a petrol funnel at the other end. It was stowed on a cup hook on the side of the fuselage.

We wanted to be out at sea by dawn, as that was the time the German submarines would come to the surface [or still be on the surface]. We would pick up convoys as far south as the Fastnet, taking over from airships from Pembroke, or in the north channel, where airships from Stranraer operated.

On one of his early convoys, Williams was escorting a troop convoy to Ireland. The senior escort officer was Captain Campbell, in the elderly light cruiser *Patrol*. Williams:

Halfway across the Irish Sea, I was ahead scouting, and saw something in the water, I came low, but couldn't make it out. I immediately flashed to the Patrol by Aldis lamp, 'suspicious object in your track, right ahead'. The message was hardly sent, when the *Patrol* ordered every ship to scatter. I was most flattered at what I'd done.

A destroyer was sent to investigate, and eventually discovered that the object was a fisherman's float. When Williams apologized for causing unnecessary alarm, Campbell told him that he was very grateful for his sharp eyes, adding, 'it could have been something very different'. One wonders why Campbell scattered the convoy, instead of ordering a change of course, but these were early days.

Williams had a more alarming experience later, when on a wet blustery day, on coming in from an all-day patrol at dusk, he was given a signal from the senior naval officer at Holyhead, telling him that a straggler from a convoy was being attacked by a U-boat off Holyhead. Williams was senior flying officer and decided he must go rather than detailing someone else. By now he was flying SSZ35, a considerable improvement on the SS. It had a purpose-designed gondola, a crew of three, and a 'pusher' engine. 'A real airship', remembered Williams, 'instead of a botched up job of half an aeroplane and half an airship'. In the bow sat the wireless operator/gunner. Behind him sat the pilot, and behind him the engineer.

It was a moonless night, no stars, just blackness. I turned on my course for Holyhead, realising how ridiculous it was, I could see nothing. The Holyhead lighthouse had been turned on to give me help. I turned south realising I was going down-wind. After a long time of futile looking, I got a message that the straggler had crawled into Holyhead, and thanks for the assistance.

I turned back to make the Holyhead light once more, now against the wind. I was well south of the Welsh coast in very heavy, unpleasant conditions, driving rain and a vicious wind. I could just see the Holyhead light in the distance, and pointed my bow in that direction. We seemed to sit there for hours. I'd no means of telling whether I was making progress or not, and kept on looking at the light; was it getting bigger or not. I had a feeling of dread that I'd never reach the light, and be driven out to sea, fatal.

I sat there saying nothing to my crew, who sat quietly doing their jobs. After what appeared to be hours, I turned the lights off, to see better in the dark. At last I thought the Holyhead light was getting brighter, when the engine started to cough. Eventually the lighthouse came up under me, and I turned on my course for the aerodrome, and they had big oil flares to guide me in. I was very glad to be hauled into the shed and quietness once more. The engineers found two faulty valves the next day.

Williams, along with everybody else, saw few U-boats. No submarine would stay on the surface if an airship was about, and dived long before it could be spotted. 'We never saw a submarine', remembered Lieutenant Goddard; 'we were animated scare-crows who were doing a useful job keeping the submarines under the surface. When I or any of the others was about, no ship was ever attacked by a submarine.'

An attempt was made to design binoculars that would allow airship crews to see dived submarines just below the surface, or surfaced submarines in the glare caused by sunlight on the water. Goddard: 'a young boffin called Lindemann came down from Farnborough with the idea of using polarised lenses.[12] It was difficult to use binoculars without getting a great deal of joggle, so that you couldn't get a steady image, so an interesting experiment but a waste of time.'

By 1917, wireless intercepts identified that the main route used by U-boats passed close to the Hinder Light Vessel, halfway between Felixstowe and the Hook of Holland. Furthermore, especially on the outward leg, U-boats travelled on the surface as much as possible to conserve battery power. To counter this a 'spider-web' patrol was mounted by flying boats from Felixstowe. At first these were Curtiss Large American biplanes, with boat-shaped fuselages and twin engines, but as the war progressed more sophisticated types were introduced. The 'spider web' consisted of an octagonal grid centred on the Hinder Light Vessel, sixty miles wide and divided into eight sections, covering 4,000 miles of sea. A U-boat would take about ten hours to transit the 'web'. Flying-boat crews were briefed on the latest submarine locations fixed by wireless intercept.[13] The aim was to force the boat to submerge and stay under for at least ten hours, which would exhaust its batteries.

In the first three weeks eight submarines were found, and three attacked. In addition, three enemy destroyers were intercepted on their way to Zeebrugge after a sortie across the North Sea. The destroyers fired on the flying boats, forcing them to evade and eventually flee. On 20 May a flying boat attacked what was thought to be UC-36 just as she dived, and on their return to Felixstowe, the crew reported seeing oil in the water, claiming a kill. It is possible that the incident was what we now call a 'blue on blue', because the British E33 reported being attacked at the same time in the same way.

By early 1918, the North Sea class airships were coming into service, marking another leap forward in design. Their 250hp Rolls Royce engines, with twin propellers, gave them an endurance of twenty hours, and a maximum speed of 57 m.p.h. They were still non-rigid, but with two cars. The forward one was the bigger, and consisted of several compartments in an enclosed cabin. One coxswain was responsible for steering, the other for maintaining height. The first officer was responsible for maintaining trim by using water ballast, and for navigation. The captain did not fly the airship, but commanded it in the manner of a seagoing vessel, and their crews referred to her as a 'ship'. A wireless operator completed the complement of the control car. Between the two engines two engineers manned the engine-control car. The two cars communicated with each other by voicepipe. Despite these improvements, airships were still underpowered, unwieldy gas sausages, driven by unreliable engines, and dangerous in bad weather. After taking delivery of the new NS5, Goddard was the first officer for the trip from Howden to East Fortune, which should have taken three to four hours. Goddard:

> We began to encounter head winds soon after take off. These became stronger, the clouds came lower, and we began to encounter heavy rain, and adverse conditions from the time we crossed the border north of Newcastle. Soon we sighted a sister ship, the NS3, on the ground tethered. We were not in touch by wireless, and just waved to them. They were obviously having difficulties. We learned later that she was buffeted so much she broke up.
>
> Although we were battling against increasingly strong winds, we thought we would get to East Fortune all right. We were unaware that the engines were overheating and boiling away the cooling water. On the stretch from Dunbar to East Fortune, we followed a road flying at about 60 feet to minimise the effect of the wind, and were overtaken by a pony and trap.
>
> Within half a mile of the boundary of East Fortune, we could see the landing party waiting for us in the dusk. Our engines had been going at full speed for about an hour and a half, and just as we were about to cross

the boundary, one engine stopped. We began to drift astern, and the other engine cut. We became a free balloon, drifting rapidly backwards in a south-easterly direction, over St Abbs Head, and out to sea.

The only way to cool the engine was by taking cups of water from the water ballast in the forward car, up a rope ladder walkway to the engine-control car, completely in the open and in darkness and a howling gale. The engineer tipped the water into the radiator cap in the wind. 'An unrehearsed operation in a very precarious manner in the night', remembered Goddard. Even getting the cup of water from the water ballast in the front of the forward car to the rope walkway at the after end of the car was an obstacle course in itself:

it wasn't possible to walk from one end of the control car to the after end, because of the braced girder construction. You had to get on all fours, or lie down and ooze yourself to get underneath the bracing wires. The deck of the control car, beyond the area being used for control, was only partly covered with a narrow walk-way [for lightness], the rest was fabric. If you put your foot through, you'd fall through.

While we were slowly passing cups of water from our water ballast, we hit the sea. We were heavy because the ship had cooled down in the night making it heavier. We got one engine started by then, and it wasn't long before we had the other going. By that time the speed of the wind had abated a little and we began to creep back over the coast. We could see the breakers, but not the land. We were relieved to see those craggy cliffs of St Abbs disappear, and to feel sure that we had land underneath us although we couldn't see it in the pitch darkness and there were no lights in the countryside.

I knew that in the area there was an airfield under construction, at midday I had seen a great number of men working. I thought we had a ready-made landing party, and if I could find the area, we could flash a signal for assistance.

When they arrived over the airfield, which they located by its proximity to the lights in the village of Haddington, they flashed with their signal lamp to no avail. The only response was that the lights in the village started going out. Their engines were providing just enough power to keep them over the airfield, and fuel was running out. They decided to land, and dropped the trail rope and grapnel, and with engines still running brought the airship down towards the ground although they still could not see it. Suddenly the car lurched. They had landed on the only two oak trees that had not been felled on the airfield. Branches pierced the car and envelope. They pulled the rip cord to release the gas:

we were enveloped, we stopped the engines. Mercifully nothing caught fire, but we were suddenly in a very dark tent smelling of gas, smothered by our own envelope, with the car at an angle of 45° and in a bit of a mess. The front of the car was on the ground, and we clambered out. Wrapping ourselves in the fabric of the airship, by now fully deflated, we thankfully slept until morning. Daylight revealed the sad sight of an airship envelope draped over some oak trees. We found out that the villagers and troops had all seen us and thinking we were a Zeppelin, decided we should be allowed to wreck ourselves.

To the average twenty-first-century person the First World War RNAS airships have a 'Heath Robinson' appearance. One wonders how they survived the harsh environment of maritime operations, and just who would be crazy enough to fly in them. Yet in many ways they were more successful in the anti-submarine war than other types of aircraft. For example, airships sometimes picked up convoys just before sunset and accompanied them until morning, a feat well beyond the capability of any heavier-than-air aircraft of the time and for many years to come. Lieutenant Verry, an airship captain, was ordered to carry out such an escort down-Channel at the end of June 1918:

The most dangerous time was thought to be dusk and in first early light, when a submarine might attack and get away quickly in the darkness. I picked up the convoy before dark, and remained with it throughout the night. There was nothing much one could see except the pale blue lights on the sterns of the escorting destroyers. I eventually left the convoy and returned to base having flown for thirteen hours.

To begin with there was no air combat over the North Sea. The RNAS based in Flanders was almost wholly committed to support of land operations, but flew some sorties in support of the Felixstowe-based spider-web patrols. The German naval aircraft were almost passive, limiting themselves to combating British incursions. They did however mount a couple of raids on Felixstowe in July 1917, destroying one flying boat and damaging another.

The picture changed in September 1917 with the delivery of the Hansa-Brandenburg W 12 seaplane fighter. It was designed as a fighter from the outset, with a rear gunner, and an airspeed of 100 m.p.h. RNAS aircraft on patrol were attacked by W 12s, and dogfights ensued – such as the battle in June 1918, when four F2A large flying boats and a Curtiss flying boat were on patrol under Captain Leckie. One aircraft had mechanical problems and headed for the Dutch coast; it was set upon by twelve German seaplanes. Leckie turned to help and opened fire, while three of the flying boats circled the crippled aircraft as it taxied to

Dutch waters. At this point another sixteen German seaplane fighters put in an appearance. Leckie led his flying boats in a V-shaped wedge formation straight at the attackers, firing their twin nose-mounted machine guns as they passed. Leckie then led another pass in line astern, and fired another broadside. The dogfight lasted forty minutes, with two British flying boats and two German seaplanes downed.

Bad weather conditions imposed severe limitations on the use of aircraft in anti-submarine operations. This, and the fact that aircraft in service in the First World War did not have the weaponry to 'kill' submarines, explains why so few U-boats were destroyed by the RNAS, or the US Naval Air Service, which was playing an increasing role in the anti-submarine war by mid-1918. A post-war study showed that the Germans were surprised by the large Felixstowe flying boats in 1917, and this led to the RNAS' initial successes. However, the Germans quickly took the lead in equipment and tactics to counter air attack, including fitting all U-boats with 'altiscopes' enabling them to look upwards through the periscope to sweep the sky for aircraft before surfacing.

The value of aircraft lay in their keeping the submarine down and thwarting its attempts to achieve a favourable torpedo-firing position. When convoys had air cover, they were hardly ever attacked. It is of course impossible to say how many ships would have been sunk if aircraft had not been present. One outcome was that U-boats increasingly attacked at night on the surface, and by the end of the war about two-thirds of all attacks were made in this way. German submarines were also driven out of coastal waters, and towards the end of the war most attacks were carried out more than fifty miles from land. All the RN and USN aircraft engaged in the U-boat campaign were land-based with a short radius of action and limited endurance on task. The era of carrier-based anti-submarine aircraft operating far out into the open ocean had not yet arrived, although it was just round the corner.

By January 1918, the RNAS had a total of 291 seaplanes (flying boats and float planes), 23 aircraft, and 100 airships on anti-submarine operations. In the last six months of the war there was a daily average of 310 aircraft available for these tasks. This was still well below the Admiralty requirement. The target was not met because in April 1918 the Royal Air Force (RAF) had been formed from the RFC and RNAS, and Trenchard's newly formed Independent Air Force took aircraft from anti-submarine work. From then on the Air Ministry decided how many aircraft to allocate to the anti-submarine war. Trenchard's Independent Air Force was engaged in strategic bombing of Germany – a waste of effort with the aircraft, technology, and weapons available at the time.[14] This was the first, but by no means last, occasion that the RAF's insistence on fighting the war in its own way, regardless of any other service's needs, was to have a baleful effect on the maritime war in general and the navy's Air Arm in particular.[15]

11

The Mediterranean and the Western Patrol: U-boats, aircraft, and battle cruisers

The U-Boat War in the Mediterranean and the Western Patrol

The submarine campaign in the Mediterranean began when the Germans sent U-boats to attack the British and French ships involved in the Dardanelles campaign in April 1915. Based in the Adriatic at Pola and Cattaro (present-day Boka Catorska, twenty-seven miles south-east of Dubrovnik), the early U-boats lacked the range to operate successfully in the Dardanelles area, and also had difficulties mastering the currents. However, between the Suez Canal and the Straits of Gibraltar there were a number of choke points through which traffic had to pass when transiting the Mediterranean, either to Italian and French ports or to Britain, and these offered fruitful hunting grounds. Few US ships used the Mediterranean, which reduced the possibilities of offending American sensibilities.

The Germans pioneered the technique of refuelling their submarines at sea. The *Acacia* captured a large oil tanker with a German crew used by U-boats for refuelling. The armed yacht *Jeanette* found a long string of oil drums over a mile in length moored off the Spanish coast used as a refuelling station by U-boats. These afloat points saved the U-boats the long haul back to Austrian ports in the Adriatic to refuel. The first U-boat kill was on 25 May, when U-21 sank the *Triumph*, and the U-boat campaign in the Mediterranean gathered momentum from October, a month when three times as many ships were sunk there as in all the other theatres.

On 3 December 1915, the Allies divided the areas up into patrol zones, British, French, and Italian. But here, as elsewhere, hunting tactics, patrolling the choke points, and escorting individual ships through them were largely a waste of time, because submarines avoided attacking in these areas when 'hunters' or escorts were about, and pitifully few losses were inflicted on the U-boats. Throughout 1916 the losses mounted, and nearly half the ships sunk by U-boats were lost in the Mediterranean.

The experience of Sub-Lieutenant Eady, the first lieutenant of the *Hollyhock*, based at Gibraltar, is typical of those engaged in the anti-submarine war in all areas before the introduction of convoys. The *Hollyhock* was an *Acacia*-class coal-fired single-screw sloop of 1,200 tons, with a maximum speed of 16½ knots, armed with two 12pdrs and two 3pdr anti-aircraft guns, originally ordered in August 1914 for mine-sweeping. She was initially assigned to the Western Patrol, which

operated on the trade routes leading to the Straits [of Gibraltar] from the Atlantic. These routes were constantly being altered to deceive enemy submarines. The duty of the ships on patrol was to meet and escort all ships along the particular route in force at that time, and also to hunt any submarines that might be in the danger zone.

On our first day out, we received several signals reporting submarines sighted in our vicinity. Probably these all referred to the same submarine, but sighted in different positions by various ships. About mid-day we 'spoke to' a French armed trawler who had just seen 'Fritz' shelling two merchant vessels. He had dived as soon as the trawler opened fire, and got away. We immediately altered course for the position where 'Fritz' had last been seen, and increased to full speed. At 6 pm we came across a large amount of wreckage which covered the glassy surface of the sea as far as the eye could reach. It was quite clear that a large ship had been sunk here a few hours previously. We lowered boats that cruised about among the debris for some time in search of survivors, but there were none to be found. While our boats were away examining the wreckage, the ship was stopped, a sitting target for 'Fritz' who can not have been far off. We succeeded in salving a large number of sides of bacon, and we fed in first class style during the remainder of the trip. The only other thing we picked up was a soldier's puttee.

The next day, *Hollyhock* continued her patrol, until she

received an SOS signal from an unknown ship. Her position was some way off, and even at full speed it took us some hours to get there. On our arrival we found nothing but a mass of wreckage. Later in the day we went to investigate the reported position of a periscope of another submarine in our area. In due course the crow's nest lookout sighted a periscope, to which we altered course with the intention of ramming. On approaching, we saw that it was a ship's mast floating upright with just a few inches showing above the water. The sea at this period was so strewn with debris of torpedoed ships that any floating object was regarded with suspicion as either a submarine or mine. A merchant ship on sighting such an object would report it by wireless and give it as wide a berth as possible.

The thankless task of investigating the truth of these numerous reports fell to the patrol craft.

These fruitless excursions placed additional distractions on patrol craft, which were already engaged patrolling to no good effect, as Eady records:

we shifted our patrol to a line between Cape St Vincent and Cape St Mary. A submarine was sighted off the latter two hours before we arrived there. At 4 am next morning, we received a wireless message from a merchant [ship] six miles away saying that she had just passed a submarine in the dark. There was no more sleep for anyone on board that night, all hands were turned out and went to Action Stations while we steamed at full speed for the position.

We were on the spot in a very short time and cruised in the vicinity until daylight, when we sighted an abandoned Norwegian steamer. She had been shelled by 'Fritz' during the night, and the crew had escaped in their boats. The ship was not badly damaged, so we ordered her crew back on board again and sent her back to Gib, escorted by a Motor Launch [ML]. While we were doing this 'Fritz' came up and began coolly shelling a large American schooner which was lying becalmed some five miles away and in full sight of us. We charged off to the rescue, arriving just after an ML. She had come up on the opposite side of the schooner to the submarine, taking him off his guard, and managing to fire several rounds at him before he submerged.

Some days later, on the Western Patrol:

We received an SOS signal and made for the position indicated only to find the sea strewn with wreckage, but no signs of any survivors. Shortly after this we met and spoke to a British steamer which had been unsuccessfully attacked by a 'Fritz' earlier in the day, so we knew that he was still on the war path. Wireless messages came pouring in all day long from ships who had sighted him, and we chased him about, hot on his trail from one position to another, but he always managed to escape us.

Next morning, another submarine joined in the game, and while we were hustling about after them we came across the dead body of a soldier in ASC [Army Service Corps] uniform. The *Celandine* [*Arabis*-class and more heavily armed] joined us later and we continued hunting Fritzs in company for the rest of the day [fruitlessly].

Finally, in May 1917, a convoy system was introduced in the Mediterranean, but only along certain legs of the route between Port Said and Gibraltar. After a refit, the *Hollyhock* took part in one of the first of these. The concept of 'sweeping' the area clear of U-boats was still being followed, although as has been seen, this was a nugatory exercise. Eady:

We put to sea with the *Acacia* to sweep a clear route to the westward for a convoy. This was the very beginning of the convoy system, and we were Danger Zone escort of the first convoy homeward bound from Gib. The ships some forty in number left harbour the day after us, and we met them off Cape Spartel [North Africa, west of Tangier] on the conclusion of our sweep. They were strung out in four long lines and it was our job to keep them together and whip in stragglers, rather like a sheepdog barking round his flock.

No U-boats attacked, but the *Hollyhock* was hit by a French merchant-man on the first night. One of the depth charges on the *Hollyhock*'s stern was detonated by the collision, which started a fire. Only quick reaction by her crew under Eady's direction saved the other depth charges from exploding, but there was a large hole in the *Hollyhock*'s stern. The Frenchman had a large hole in the bows, and could only steam astern. The *Hollyhock* stood by the Frenchman all day, until a torpedo boat from Gibraltar took over. After the *Hollyhock* left, the Frenchman sank despite the efforts of tugs sent out to save her.

Not every convoy got through unscathed, especially when inade-quately escorted, or, as happened on occasions, had no escort at all on a particular leg of the voyage. One such convoy, outward-bound from England to Gibraltar, ran into several U-boats off Cape St Vincent who were themselves heading for the Straits of Gibraltar from the Atlantic. Patrolling still went on, diminishing the number of vessels to escort convoys. While on patrol, *Hollyhock* sighted some red flares:

We put on full speed and steered towards them. On the way we passed a raft which was barely sufficient to support the crowd of poor lascars who were on it. They were completely exhausted and huddled up together not daring to move for fear of capsizing. Dawn was just breaking and we could see a TB coming to their assistance, as we went on to investigate the flares. The lascars thought we were leaving them to their fate, because they could not see the TB, and as we passed they set up a most pitiful howl of terror. We afterwards discovered they were part of the crew of the SS *Clan Ferguson*, which had been torpedoed and sunk within three minutes. The crew had been in the water all night. Another ship had been sunk at the same time and gone down with all hands. The weather was perfectly atrocious for open boats, making it almost impossible to get away. Both these ships had belonged to this luckless convoy from England.

We found that the flares were coming from the only surviving boat of a third ship, which was also torpedoed that night. The boat contained the mate, chief engineer, two apprentices (mere boys of about seventeen), and a few of the crew. We took them below and gave them food and clothing.

They told us that their ship was the *Broadmead*, and that two submarines had attacked her at about 2 am [probably on the surface – a favourite tactic, especially at night]. The explosion of the torpedo sent up a great column of water high above the bridge, and flooded all the cabins in the vicinity. The *Broadmead* altered course to bring her stern gun to bear, but 'Fritz' altered round too, keeping on the *Broadmead*'s bow where she could not be hit. From this position she opened fire with her gun, the first shot carrying away the wireless aerial before the operator had time to send out an SOS. The Chinese crew now panicked and attempted to lower a boat while the ship was going full ahead. It was swept away, and the occupants drowned. 'Fritz' continued to shell them for about twenty minutes, peppering everything on the upper deck. One apprentice was shot through the ankle, three crewmen were killed, and about twenty badly wounded. The submarine hung around until the crew abandoned ship, she then took the captain prisoner and departed.

A few hours later we found the *Broadmead* still afloat. So we put her crew back on board, with some of our stokers to assist in raising steam. We found two more badly wounded Chinese crewmen who had been left aboard when the ship had been abandoned. They had given up all hope of being rescued, and were too weak to speak or move.

Escorts from Gibraltar came to *Hollyhock*'s assistance, and though it was touch and go whether the *Broadmead* would make port, she eventually limped in, commendable work by the *Hollyhock* since she was carrying a valuable cargo.

Two days later, while escorting a convoy, two ships were torpedoed twenty miles to the south of the *Hollyhock*. One managed to stay afloat, and *Hollyhock*'s captain detached an American ship from his group to go to her assistance; both crews were rescued. Eady noted that, 'although Fritz was so close on our track, our convoy passed through the Danger Zone unmolested, and we left them early on the 13th to return to our patrol line in the submarine area'.

It was a measure of the failure at the time to really comprehend the tactics being employed by U-boats that some convoys in the Mediterranean travelled only by night, creeping along the North African coast. Eady in the *Hollyhock* escorted one of these, a small four-ship group heading for Palermo and Port Said. 'The first night we followed up the Spanish coast keeping inside territorial waters as far as Cape de Gata, where we cut across to Oran on the African side. The night was inky black, our best protection against submarines, but making it hard to keep the convoy in sight, and a great strain on the watchkeepers'.

In fact, however dark the night, a surfaced U-boat being low in the water could often see a convoy silhouetted against the sky, and was itself invisible against the sea background to lookouts higher up. The U-boats in service by 1917 could make between 15 and 16 knots on the surface, and were thus able to match sloops like the *Hollyhock* for speed, and hence all but the fastest convoys (16 knots and above – a rarity). This was not the case for a dived boat in daylight. For this reason the night was the *most* dangerous time for even an escorted convoy.

Not until October 1917 were 'through convoys' run from Britain to Port Said. The Allies' troubles were not over, however, mainly because many convoys were still inadequately escorted. Once again the number of escorts was reduced by allocating them to hunting groups, which achieved very little.

Escorts were also employed patrolling the Otranto Barrage, a combination of minefields, mine-net barriers, kite-balloons, patrolling trawlers, drifters, sloops, motor launches, and destroyers, which eventually stretched from the heel of Italy across the Adriatic to Corfu and the Dalmatian coast. The Otranto Barrage, yet another 'white elephant' scheme, accounted for the grand total of two U-boats in the entire war.

The French had a string of flying-boat and airship stations along the coast of their North African colonies. Eady comments on a convoy leaving Bizerta for Oran:

> French flying boats went ahead of us over the swept channel searching for stray mines. On our way we passed a French convoy escorted by an airship, a seaplane and two trawlers. The French appeared to make far more use of aircraft in the Mediterranean than we did. We found flying boat stations at every large French port we visited. They carried out systematic patrols twice daily, besides escort work. Our attempts seemed rather feeble in comparison.

In fact, to be fair to the RNAS, air cover was provided from Malta, and Alexandria. But as elsewhere, aircraft were most effective when in the vicinity of a convoy. In 1917, in all theatres, only one U-boat was accounted for by an aircraft (a probable), and in 1918, none. The bombs carried by aircraft were too small and patrolling was a waste of time. Contacts were a matter of luck. The logbook of Sergeant Hosken, an RNAS observer, records the results of a mine patrol starting at 4 a.m. on 28 August 1917, in which he and Lieutenant Mayer flew forty miles out from Malta to meet a convoy: 'No convoy. Return via Valetta. Enemy submarine 1½ miles off Grand Harbour. Bombed same. TBD (destroyer) French drops 5 depth charges.' And later that same day with Second Lieutenant Nunn: 'Submarine chase. Following W/T instructions. NTR (nothing to report).'

Hosken also kept a private diary, and on 8 February 1918 he wrote:

Patrol with Lt Nunn. Sight submarine attacking French super dreadnought. Sub bombed and hit about 30 feet behind tail [sic]. No photograph so no credit. Saved French battleship *Provence* from torpedo. Mr Nunn got Croix de Guerre.

One of the most successful forms of air cover in the Mediterranean was a kite balloon, a sausage-shaped gas-filled balloon with a basket underneath for the observer. It had no form of propulsion, and was tethered to a destroyer or sloop and towed by it. One objection to kite balloons was that they advertised the approach of a convoy from miles away. But in the Mediterranean the air was so clear that the funnel smoke of the convoy could be seen when it was over the horizon anyway, whether a kite balloon was being flown or not. Although air cover did not succeed in destroying U-boats, it deprived them of their chief advantage, surprise attack. A U-boat could approach unseen, but had to put up its periscope to attack. Aircraft preceding a convoy also forced the U-boat to stay dived and this reduced its ability to manoeuvre into a favourable attacking position ahead of the convoy. Even if the U-boat was bold enough to attack, the shadowing aircraft could locate its position by following the torpedo track back to its source.

But to begin with no air cover was available from anybody at night, another reason why U-boats preferred night surface attacks on convoys. On one trip, escorting just two ships, Eady records:

The night was oily calm, with a bright moon shining through a clammy mist which hung low over everything making visibility very bad. At about 11 pm, I was roused by the alarm ringing frantically outside my cabin. I was at my post, the after 12-pdr gun in a few seconds, clad in pyjamas and a greatcoat. One of our convoy, the *Mensalah*, had been fired at, but she had eluded the torpedo by skilful use of the helm. Fritz had not seen us, and came to the surface on the far side of the *Mensalah*, which opened fire on him. She dived at the second round just as I reached the deck. We buzzed round at top speed for some time to keep him under, but had no more trouble with him that night. He evidently thought that these two ships were unescorted, as he hopped it directly we made our presence known to him.

This occurred off Cape Sigli, near Algiers, quite close to the coast in the full glare of the lighthouse, which probably gave away our position to Fritz. It was a nasty spooky feeling to know that cruising somewhere near beneath that peaceful looking surface was a boat with some sixty odd men striving their utmost to attack and destroy us.

Escorts gradually became better at shepherding their charges. Convoy commodores, mainly senior naval officers brought out of retirement, travelled in one of the merchant ships. Eady:

We proceeded to sea with a convoy of eleven large ships bound for Port Said or beyond, chiefly war material for Palestine and Mesopotamia. We could see several carriages of a Red Cross train lashed on the deck of one of them. The *Hollyhock* was senior escort vessel, the remaining escorts consisting of the sloops *Narcissus* and *Snapdragon*, and the destroyer *Acorn* [27-knot, oil-fired 1910 vintage].*

A convoy bound for Genoa with an Italian escort left harbour at the same time, as another was arriving from England. The Straits were full of shipping and we had a very busy time sorting out our little fleet.

The next afternoon, a submarine was reported to be in our track fifty miles ahead. The Commodore held his course, and we never met Fritz; he could not have been aware of our approach. The commodore of this convoy was a very loquacious retired naval officer. Being senior officer of the escort, we got the full benefit of his talkativeness, he kept us busy from daylight to dusk with innumerable unecessarily long-winded signals.

The last three days we had very bad weather, and in spite of being in the danger area off Pantaleria Island, the convoy was forced to reduce speed from twelve knots to nine. Zig-zagging was almost impossible, but extra lookouts were posted, and guns kept loaded. We were relieved by an escort off Malta, which took the convoy on to Port Said. Soon after we left them, we heard that three ships had been torpedoed just east of Malta.

The policy of hunting U-boats, and sailing small, uneconomical, under-escorted convoys still persisted. Eady: 'on leaving the convoy we were sent in company with Narcissus to hunt for Fritz off Pantaleria which was a favourite cruising ground of his'. On leaving Malta, where the *Hollyhock* had a two-day rest,

Pentstemon arrived from Suda Bay after a very lively trip. She had started out with a four ship convoy. Two were sunk, and Fritz had fired a torpedo at her, but it went underneath. She returned the compliment with a couple of depth charges, and Fritz worried them no more.

We proceeded back to Gib, passing along the north African coast as far as Algiers, then cutting across to Cape de Gata and running down to Gib along the Spanish coast. Fritz had been very active in this region as we could see from the amount of wreckage we passed. We found Gib in high spirits, as everybody had been sinking submarines. The *Rule*, a Q boat had rammed and sunk one; *TB 90* [1890s vintage,140-foot torpedo boats] had destroyed another with depth charges, and the *Parthian* [35-knot, oil-fired modern destroyer] had rammed one and attacked another with depth charges. The former U-boat was seen next day with all her upper works

---

* Just enough escorts.

ripped off, and *Parthian*'s propellers were chewed to pieces and a large chunk of submarine was found wound round them when she was docked for repairs.

U-boats attacking a lone armed merchantman did not always have it their own way. The *City of Belfast* with one 12pdr gun fought for two hours with a submarine armed with two 4-inch guns: it eventually dived, having killed three men.

The routine for convoys is described by Eady of the *Hollyhock*.

We left harbour on the morning of Oct 26th [1917] and proceeded round to the west side of the Rock [of Gibraltar] and anchored in Catalan Bay until our convoy was ready. We eventually got under weigh at about three o'clock that afternoon, and spent the rest of the daylight hours hustling our division of ships into their proper stations. I had the last dog watch and had a most unpleasant time keeping touch with the convoy as it was very dark and stormy. The ships scattered during the night and we had a lively time chasing them into position as soon as daylight broke.

When clear of the danger zone, we left them to carry on to England in charge of their 'Ocean Escort', our job being that of 'Danger Zone Escort' only. The 'Ocean Escort' accompanied them the whole way home, as a protection against raiders such as the *Moewe* [surface raider]. On entering submarine-infested waters again off Ireland they would be met by another 'Danger Zone Escort'.

Until the convoy system became effective, U-boats sank merchant ships well out into the Atlantic. By the period November 1917 to January 1918, Queenstown had been given up as an assembly port, and replaced by Milford Haven, and the sinkings were concentrated around the western approaches to the English Channel, in the Channel itself, in the approaches to Hull, and some in the Irish Sea. This last was contained by instituting local convoys to Ireland and Anglesey.

Eady continues, and his account reveals the unremitting nature of convoy work in all weathers, a totally different life to the one he led in the battle cruiser *New Zealand*, and still being experienced by shipmates left behind, months spent swinging round a buoy in Scapa:

At 7 am on Oct 28th we rendezvoused with the outward bound convoy of eleven large ships from England, with the seaplane carrier *Manxman* as Ocean Escort.* Our job was to escort them through our danger area to

---

* *Manxman* was a railway ferry converted by the Admiralty in late 1915 with a flying-off deck and two hangars, but no facility to recover (land on) wheeled aircraft. In the period mentioned by Eady she would have been operating Sopwith Pups (wheeled) and Sopwith Baby floatplanes. The latter had to be lowered over the side for take-off, and hoisted back

the Straits and on into the Mediterranean as far as Malta, where we would be be relieved by a fresh escort to take them on to Port Said. A submarine armed with four guns had been doing a great deal of damage off Cape Spartel, and became known as 'Spartel Jack'.* He was still very busy off the entrance to the Straits, but by means of a detour we slipped past him in the dark. He torpedoed a ship [unescorted?] two hours after we passed.

We reached Gib at daylight on the 29th, when two more ships joined our convoy, and a trawler brought us out our mails. Shortly after going on watch at 8 am, I received an SOS from the P&O SS *Namur* torpedoed twenty miles ahead of us, and fully in sight of the look-out station on the top of the Rock. We had all hands at gun and depth-charges and extra lookouts posted all day as it seemed likely that Fritz would have a smack at our very fine convoy. It was strongly escorted and no attack was made. We passed through the sinking of the *Namur* an hour later. The sea was a mass of wreckage, deserted lifeboats, grain and merchandise of all sorts. The destroyer *Larne* passed us on her way back to Gib with the survivors. The conditions were ideal for Fritz, very calm, clear weather with a full moon at night; we could see mountain tops in Spain and Africa over eighty miles away on either side of us.

A submarine was sighted ahead of us on the 31st, so we went to action stations at daylight, but passed the position without anything happening. One always felt on these occasions as if one was waiting for a gun to go off. If Fritz had come along and torpedoed somebody, the strain would have been far less, and in one way, we would have felt almost relieved.

French seaplanes escorted us through the danger area off Cape Bon, and on Nov 2nd we were relieved by another escort and proceeded to Malta. It was blowing a hurricane with a fifty-mile an hour wind, and enormously heavy seas. We were rolling gunwales under and nearly lost all our boats. None of us had any sleep that night, and I in my short experience of the sea [a mere three years of continuous war service!], never imagined a ship could roll so far without capsizing. We reached Malta after sunset when Grand Harbour closes, so we had to anchor in Marsa Scirocco for the night. Even here it was very rough, and I had to sleep on the bridge all night so as to be on the spot in case we began to drag. We weighed anchor the next morning in a rain storm, and made our way by the swept channel to Grand Harbour where we went alongside the Canteen Wharf in Dockyard Creek, and coaled ship all day. I managed to get ashore for a breather just before dinner, but was almighty glad to turn in for a long unbroken night's rest when the time came.

---

after landing on the sea. There is no evidence that she flew off aircraft in support of the convoy.

*   This was unusual as no U-boats were built at this time with four guns fitted.

The *Hollyhock* left Malta on 9 November 1917, alone, laden with stores and confidential mail. Eady:

It was pretty rough outside, and the first meeting of the 'Guzzle Club' [dinner] was in consequence, not a success. We passed Cape Bon in safety although floating mines had been reported there. On the 11th we went to the help of a ship which had been in collision and mined off Cape Bougaroni. We escorted her to Philippeville, and resumed our passage to Gib. The weather grew steadily stormier, and eventually developed into the worst gale anybody in this ship had ever experienced. Waves were breaking right over the ship, green seas came pounding down on the boat deck and water found its way everywhere. I had the most delightful watch that night, with terrific seas, a continuous downpour of rain, enormous gusts of wind blowing the rain and sea spray into ones face with stinging force, and pitchy blackness that could almost be cut with a knife. We also passed through a violent thunderstorm, which was almost a relief, as the lightning enabled me to keep a better lookout for shipping. Sleep was out of the question, and one night I was rolled clean out of my bunk with mattress and all on top of me. Luckily I did not fall far, as the long drawers under my bunk had been shot out by the same roll, and I fell clean into one of them.

The task for the escorts was unremitting. The sloops *Hollyhock*, *Acacia*, *Marguerite*, *Sweetbriar*, and *Spiraea* and the 32-knot destroyer *Attack* left Gibraltar on 18 December to pick up a fifteen-ship convoy off Europa Point. It was a well-escorted convoy, especially with the addition of the *Attack* to add a touch of punch and speed. The convoy was capable of steaming at 12 knots and was on a non-stop trip from Falmouth to Port Said. Eady:

These fast, non-stop convoys were run out and home about once a fortnight, and we usually escorted them between Gib and Malta. Each convoy was numbered, the outward bound being Outward Eastern (OE) and HE for the Homeward Eastern. This was OE 6. Several of them were ships on their maiden voyages. We rigged up our disguise [camouflage] on the first day out, and asked them what they thought of it. The general opinion was that it was impossible to tell which way we were going, and the *Acacia* said we had the appearance of two ships on different courses.

A vast variety of camouflage schemes were tried throughout the anti-submarine war, in an attempt to make it difficult for a submarine, especially in poor light, to obtain an accurate picture through the periscope of the range, speed, overall length, and course of the target, to obtain a firing solution. The camouflage concepts included painting patterns on the side of the ship, or a false bow wave, in an effort to confuse an attacking U-boat CO when he was trying to calculate the speed and course of his target by observing it through his periscope. (Readers may wish to refer to note 3 on pp. 435–6 on estimating target speed.) Eady continues, and his account shows how effective the convoy system had become,

> We encountered very bad weather for the first three days, tremendous winds and violent rainstorms. Submarines were working off Algiers, but we passed them in safety. Conditions improved on the 21st. At 12.30, just as I was leaving the bridge after my forenoon watch, one of the convoy was torpedoed and dropped astern. She was the *City of Lucknow*; the *Acacia* and two other escorts were ordered to stand by her, leaving us to protect the rest of the convoy.
>
> We at once crammed on full speed and headed them away from the vicinity of the submarine. The hands were at action stations ready to loose off guns and depth charges should we meet Fritz anywhere during our frantic efforts to guard all sides of the convoy at once. We kept this up for half an hour or so and then as Fritz did not attack, we resumed our normal condition again. At five o'clock we intercepted a message from the *Acacia* saying that the *City of Lucknow* had gone down, and that she was bringing the crew with her to Malta. This occurred off Cape Bon, a favourite hunting ground of Fritz's. It was the first ship lost in a convoy escorted by the *Hollyhock*, and spoilt our record that we had never lost a ship while we were in charge of her. During 1917, the *Hollyhock* escorted eleven convoys comprising 175 ships in all, with the loss of only one ship.

While escorting an eleven-ship convoy from Malta to Gibraltar, with the *Acorn*-class destroyers *Cameleon* and *Sheldrake* and the sloops *Marguerite* and *Petunia*, *Hollyhock*'s crow's nest lookout sighted an object 'low in the water some seven miles away on the port bow'. Eady:

> informed the Captain, and immediately signalled by flags to the convoy 'suspicious object in sight bearing WSW'. The senior officer of the escort in *Cameleon* ordered, '*Hollyhock* investigate on that bearing at full speed'. We did so with hands at action stations. The next thing we saw about thirty minutes later was a torpedo passing under our stern in the direction of the convoy. We at once ran up the flag for 'torpedo in sight' to warn the convoy, but nobody was hit. The *Cameleon* chased at full speed in the direction from which the torpedo came but saw no sign of Fritz [not surprisingly since the boat was dived]. We returned and zig-zagged at high speed across the front of the convoy, but no further attack was made that day.
>
> On our arrival at Gib, the Senior Officer Escorts complimented us on our smart signalling and good lookout which undoubtedly saved the convoy from further attack. Our action had forced Fritz to submerge earlier

than he intended and he had to fire a 'browning' shot in consequence [a shot fired into the convoy into the 'brown' of it without selecting any particular ship].

After some appalling weather, including encountering grape-sized hail, and buffeting into a head sea with her screw racing as her stern lifted, the *Hollyhock* arrived at Gib with her convoy and escorts on 1 January 1918.

Our new Mark IX 4-in gun had come out from England during our absence [replacing the forward 12pdr, and about an inch bigger in bore], and we went alongside the gunwharf where it was hoisted in and mounted by midday. The rest of the day was occupied coaling ship, as we were expecting a convoy out from England the next day. It rained solidly during our whole forty-eight hours in harbour. It did not worry us much as we were at one hours notice for steam and no leave allowed ashore.

The convoy commodore was in overall charge of the convoy, whereas the senior officer of the escort was only responsible for the tactical handling of the escort vessels. *Hollyhock* and her sisters were off Cape Bon with a nine-ship convoy bound for Malta, when

a submarine was sighted on the starboard beam. We turned and went at full speed for the position where Fritz was last seen, while *Cameleon* and *Sheldrake* put up a fine smoke screen round the exposed side of the convoy. We made one ahead of them, and the convoy dropped smoke boxes astern. It was the first time we had seen these smoke boxes in use. Each ship was vomiting great clouds of smoke over her stern. The wind was very strong and blew the smoke clear almost as soon as it was made. The Commodore made the general signal, 'make as much smoke as possible', and for a while the convoy was completely hidden. We saw no more of the submarine and no attack was made.

Malta was informed by wireless of the position in which the submarine was sighted and that the convoy was safe. Signals were sent out as a matter of course whenever a submarine was sighted to warn everyone where to expect her. It was not uncommon for us to get a dozen separate submarine reports in as many hours.

On a subsequent convoy:

a lascar in the crow's nest of the SS *Leicestershire*, the Commodore's ship, sighted a submarine ten miles off. The convoy turned away from the submarine, and the destroyer *Acorn* was ordered to attack. Fritz calmly remained on the surface in full view for about twenty minutes, only submerging when *Acorn* got within gun range. *Acorn* swept in the vicinity with explosive paravanes for two hours, thus keeping Fritz down and enabling the convoy to escape.

Sometimes whales and porpoises were reported as submarines. But in March 1918, the *Hollyhock* was involved in a protracted action with a succession of U-boats. The narrative demonstrates just how difficult it was to sink a submarine in the First World War, even if it was known to be in the vicinity. Eady:

After lunch I was just settling down to a much longed-for siesta when the alarm bell rang. I tore up to my gun in waistcoat, trousers, socks and a revolver. Each officer was provided with a revolver on the off chance of us ever getting close enough to a Fritz for boarding; rifles and lance bombs were stowed on the upper deck for the same purpose.

A submarine had been sighted on our side of the convoy. She had tried a long range shot and torpedoed a ship right on the far side of the convoy. This gave the impression that Fritz was over on that side and the convoy altered course accordingly. The *Demorocus* had her engine room flooded, and was left behind with the *Bryony* and *Nereide* standing by. We heard later she got back to Malta under tow from tugs sent out to her. We remained at action stations for half an hour, guns loaded and everything on a 'split yarn' for immediate action, but nothing happened so we packed up and I went below to sleep again.

My eyes were scarcely shut when the alarm sounded again. Another Fritz had been sighted by one of the convoy, which was blowing a succession of six short blasts on her siren for all she was worth. She was determined to let us know, and kept up her tooting long after there was any need for it. We put up a smoke screen, and *Campanula* dropped a depth charge which exploded beautifully, sending up a fine great snowy mound of water and spray. The convoy contributed by burning smoke boxes. It was a great show, and foiled Fritz in his attack. Perhaps *Campanula*'s brick had been too much for him. We had no further alarms after this, and I continued my nap uninterrupted until tea-time.

At four o'clock, when I had just set foot on the bridge again and was taking over the watch from the navigator, the fun began again. I spotted the track of a torpedo passing astern of us in the direction of the SS *Morvada*, who was only about three hundred yards away on our port beam. I rang the alarm; simultaneously the *Morvada* opened fire with her stern 4.7-inch gun and depth-charge howitzers, at the same time altering course and sounding six blasts on her siren. We next saw a large wake splashing alongside the *Morvada*. It looked at first like a periscope, and thinking Fritz had got into difficulties we prepared to attack with depth charges. We could not make use of our guns as some ships of the convoy were in the line of fire.

However, on getting nearer we found that this wake was produced by a torpedo running with about a foot of its head above the surface. It must have been a trying time for the crew of the *Morvada* to see this thing running along beside them, expecting every moment it would strike the ship's side and explode. Its energy expended, the torpedo dropped astern coming into full view of the rest of the convoy, who so far had been rather confused as to what was going on. The torpedo came to rest in a vertical position with about one foot projecting above the surface, bobbing up and down in the swell.

The sun shining on the highly polished steel gave it the appearance of a periscope. The war head was missing; every ship that could bring a gun to bear, opened fire on this harmless torpedo. How the war head came to be knocked off we never discovered. But it was conjectured that a shell from *Morvada*'s gun must have hit it and severed it from the torpedo without exploding it. This was the view taken by the Admiralty and they shortly issued an order to all ships which was a direct outcome of this incident: gun's crews were to fire at approaching torpedoes on the off chance of hitting and exploding them before they reached the ship.

Four months later the gunners of the *Justicia*, a 32,000-ton White Star liner, were able to deflect torpedoes in this way during a fight which this great vessel maintained for twenty-four hours against several U-boats. Eight torpedoes were fired at her during that time, three hit, and two of the remaining five were warded off by gunfire. Eady continues:

We approached the torpedo to pick it up, while the convoy was all blazing away enjoying itself. The shooting was very wild and we had several close shaves. We hoisted the signal to 'cease fire', but this was too good an opportunity to miss, and they would not stop. Shells were pitching all round us, several ricocheted over us, and one exploded just short of our fo'c'sle sending a few splinters on board. We could see the shells approaching quite plainly, turning somersaults in the air, hitting the water and bouncing off in another direction. Eventually the ships stopped firing, and we remained behind to deal with the torpedo. It took us the best part of an hour, during which time we were stopped and alone, a perfect target for Fritz, whom we knew must be somewhere close by. Why he never attacked us, goodness knows, as it must have been galling for him to see us recover his torpedo. We decided it was worth the risk if we could get the torpedo which might be of great value to the authorities at home. After getting it on board we proceeded at full speed to catch up the convoy.

Next morning at 7 o'clock, a submarine was sighted on the convoy's port side, several ships opened fire. *Campanula* and *Valerian* attacked with depth charges, dropping four altogether. We were miles away on the convoy's starboard side, and distinctly felt the under water concussion. We saw a large amount of black stuff thrown up by the explosion, and *Valerian* signalled that a lot of wreckage had come to the surface.

It was a perfect day, the sea like a mill pond, with a cloudless sky. It must have been really too smooth for a submarine as periscopes could be spotted very easily under these conditions. However, they seemed to be determined to have one of us, and at noon we were attacked again. The convoy turned away and opened fire. As far as we could judge, no damage was inflicted on either side. It was all over in ten minutes. Truly this region off Cape Bon was a very hot place, submarines seemed to swarm there. They were sighted in twenty-four different places in this area during two days.

At 5 pm that day we had another alarm, but as before we managed to thwart Fritz and nothing exciting occurred. These numerous attacks tended to make the convoy rather jumpy, and the next morning one of them reported a submarine which turned out to be a barrel. The convoy blazed away at it.

We passed through a great deal of wreckage one morning and *Campan-ula* picked up a ship's life boat. Needless to say the convoy had previously reported this as a conning tower.

Convoys got larger as the war progressed. The *Hollyhock* took one of twenty-nine ships and another of forty through the Straits of Gibraltar in April 1918. After handing over the latter, the *Hollyhock* was ordered to take part in a hunt in the Straits for two U-boats expected to pass through. 'A welcome change after much convoy work', says Eady. Only one U-boat was sunk, by 'sheer luck', according to Eady. ML 413 was patrolling at slow speed in the Straits.

It was a very dark night, suddenly a merchant ship's port and starboard and masthead lights were seen approaching. Her hull was scarcely visible, but appeared to be almost on top of ML 413, who switched on her lights and put on full speed to avoid being run down. The merchant ship turned away, but started to dive as well. Of course this gave the show away and when two hundred yards off ML 413 saw that it was an enormous submarine. She rammed, just missed the conning tower and dropped four depth charges on her. To prove that Fritz had been sunk, 413 brought back pieces of chests of drawers and a fragment of a mahogany table picked up in the wreckage which came to the surface.

The second submarine did not attempt to pass us, but kept just outside the limits of our beat. She was sighted on the surface on the evening of the 24th by *Chrysanthemum* who was escorting an outward bound convoy to Gibraltar. She dropped depth charges and claimed to have sunk her. It seems more likely that Fritz got away and was responsible for what followed that night.

We left our beat after dark for Gibraltar. It was a filthy night, a howling gale and a solid downpour of rain which made it impossible to see a yard ahead of the ship. This weather was probably the only thing that stood between us and a watery grave that night.

The weather cleared soon after we had passed Tangiers, and two hours later the *Cowslip* was torpedoed in the very position through which we had steamed. She was hit aft in the wardroom killing all the officers except the captain and sub-lieutenant who were on the bridge. All the men were saved. Later that night TB 90 capsized in the Straits off Terifa Point in a very heavy swell rolling in from the Atlantic. There were only eight survivors. It had been a truly disastrous night for us, and cast a gloom over all on the Rock, as both ships had been based on Gibraltar.

We arrived in harbour at 4 am on the 25th, and I was able to snatch a short rest then until we began coaling two hours later. Coaling went on all day, and I was working at official correspondence until late at night. We were off to sea again next morning, escorting a convoy through the danger zone. There were twenty-two ships, and we had to keep a sharp lookout as we knew the *Cowslip*'s assailant was somewhere about.

We left our convoy at noon on April 27th and picked up an outward bound one of seventeen ships which we escorted to Gibraltar. After seeing our convoy safely to the commercial anchorage, we were preparing to enter harbour ourselves when we were ordered to go out to meet and bring in another convoy. We caught them up after dark a fast convoy of eight fine ships.

Escorts were sometimes switched from one convoy to another as reinforcements. Eady:

Just as we were parting company from our convoy at dusk, we received an SOS call from another convoy outward bound from Falmouth to Gibraltar. They were being attacked off Cape Finnesterre and one ship had been torpedoed and sunk. All the crew had been rescued by the USS *Sacramento*, the Ocean Escort. It was thought that Fritz would keep in touch with the convoy through the night and make a second attack at dawn. We raced to meet them at full speed. We came up with them at daylight followed within an hour by *Northesk*, *Grangemouth*, *Woodnut*, and the Q-Ship *Privet*. We took up our escorting stations all round the convoy and Fritz was baulked of his second victim.

We arrived at Gib on July 30th, and were in harbour only long enough to fill up with coal and provisions, and left next day with another large homeward bound convoy of twenty-three ships. We left our convoy at the western end of our patrol line and picked up another which we brought back to Gib. A submarine was tracking us most of the time [he had been given this information by the Admiralty; though he did not know it, its source was probably Room 40], but we were not molested. She was probably working off the Straits waiting for a chance to slip through into the Mediterranean. She [or another] was sunk by a destroyer on 5 August. It was pitch dark night, and Fritz suddenly broke surface not more than ten yards off the destroyer's port bow, too close even for ramming. Six depth charges were dropped on her and shouts were heard in the water as the destroyer swept by. It was all over in a few seconds. When the searchlight was switched on there was nothing to be seen.

The submarine war continued in the Mediterranean right to the last. Gordon Hyams, by now an RAF lieutenant based at Alexandria, was involved in escorting convoys bound from Egypt to Salonika. On 31 October 1918, he was ordered to take his two-seater 260 Short seaplane (with air gunner/observer Second Lieutenant Standish) to reconnoitre the swept channel out of Alexandria and on to the limit of his radius of action to ensure the area was clear, before joining the convoy:

About 30 to 40 miles out my engine conked out. I made a reasonably good landing in a fairly good sea, and tried to start the engine, but couldn't. We both got out and stood on the floats, normal practice to keep the tail out of the water, or she would flip backwards and turn upside down. After a bit, we climbed back and I managed to get the engine started. I didn't trust the engine at flying revs, so taxied at slow speed back towards Alex, until the engine got too hot and I had to stop it. After a while I tried to start it again, but the second compressed air bottle used to fire the engine was a dud. We only had two. That was that. We could do nothing except climb back on the floats and wait.

Eventually, the machine sank by its tail, and turned on its back, so we climbed on to the top of the half-submerged floats. A Short seaplane appeared, perhaps looking for us, but came nowhere near. I had stored the cartridges for my Verey pistol in my cap, and during the night fired some of these to no avail.

We had given up all hope of coming out of this alive, when we saw a lot of ships coming up from Port Said – the convoy we were supposed to have escorted the day before, but delayed. As luck would have it one of their zig-zags brought them so that we were in the centre of the convoy. We were picked up by the Australian destroyer Swan, and taken to Salonika. It was my 20th birthday.

The Second Escape of the *Goeben* and *Breslau*

In January 1918, the RNAS also played a key role in the second incident involving the Royal Navy with the battle cruiser *Goeben* and the light cruiser *Breslau*, when the dramatic escape of these two ships in the very first days of the war was replayed in the Aegean. Despite the fuss it engendered at the time, it was, thanks to the RNAS, not nearly so humiliating as in 1914. After the two ships had 'joined' the Turkish navy, their crews sporting fezzes, they operated in the Black Sea against the Russians, under the command of Vice-Admiral Souchon. A few months before the Russian Bolshevik Government signed a separate peace with Germany in December 1917, Souchon was posted to a battle squadron in the High Seas Fleet, and handed command to Vice-Admiral Hubert Rebeur-Paschwitz. With no Russian navy to fight, Rebeur-Paschwitz looked elsewhere for action.

He decided to sortie and destroy British naval patrol craft off the Dardanelles, then bombard Mudros harbour. A submarine would lay mines off Mudros and wait to snap up any targets that presented themselves. This he hoped would draw Allied ships from the Palestine coast, where they were supporting Allenby. Thus Turkish morale would be boosted, after the recent loss of Jerusalem, and he would show them that warships were an asset to be used.

The British had foreseen that such a sortie was likely and taken precautions. These included establishing lookout stations on the islands of Tenedos and Mavro, and on Cape Kephalo on Imbros. The RNAS base on Imbros launched daily reconnaissance sorties over the Dardanelles. Lieutenant Graham Donald RNAS was in charge of two Sopwith Camel flights based there whose function was

> to carry out dawn and evening patrols over the Straits keeping an eye out for the *Goeben* or *Breslau*. One of our regular jobs was to send a two seater (with observer) on a minefield reconnaissance from a low height, escorted by two Camels. Flying around in the sunshine only six feet above the blue waters of the Aegean may sound like an idyllic pastime, but it is not. For one thing if your engine splutters twice you're in the ditch, and the middle of a minefield is the loneliest place on earth (or water). For another if an enemy wishes to impede your progress, all he has to do is drop a heavyish bomb in front of you, from a nice safe height, and you ram the waterspout which at 90 knots is as hard as granite.
>
> On 17th January, the reconnaissance two-seater was a DH9, and the two escorting Camel pilots were myself and Geoff Wincott. Our practice was to send one Camel over low-down with the DH9, and the other

watching from 6,000 to 7,000 feet. Everybody preferred the upper berth with a much better chance of intercepting a marauding Hun, so Wincott and I tossed for it, and I won.

Just off Suvla and Anzac Cove, I could see our two planes zig-zagging across the minefield. Also watching with keen interest were the two occupants of a biggish German Friederichshafen two seater. The observer staring at them so eagerly with his binoculars, that he never noticed a Sopwith Camel sitting some 35 yards behind him. Which was an error. Absurd as it may sound, I simply hadn't the heart to obey the advice of Wyatt Earp, 'shoot 'em in the back, when they ain't looking'. So I just let go about 15 or 20 rounds in the air, well below them. Never in my life have I seen such a rapid reaction.

The binoculars flew out of their owner's hands, obviously breaking the strap, and disappeared in the direction of the Aegean, while the pilot must have rammed his control hard forward, as the plane practically folded into a 80° dive. This was another error. A straight dive with a Camel behind you is *always* an error.

It then became a matter of following the enemy down from about 6,000 feet, keeping right behind his fin and rudder, thereby laying a dead 'stymie' for his rear gunner, as he can't hit the Camel pilot without shooting his own tail off. In the meantime the Friederichshafen was collecting 750 rounds per minute from each of the Camel's boosted twin Vickers guns, through and around its fuselage. Halfway down it was over. It went into a vertical dive, and then slowly on its back, with bits and pieces falling off. As 180 knots was regarded as the top safe speed, and we must have been doing about 200 by then, I was too busy gently levelling out to see the Friederichshafen strike the water. However from about 1,000 feet I could see wreckage floating. The only mystery was numerous splashes in the water, which turned out to be infuriated shore batteries at Suvla hurling salvo after salvo at me.

Four to six destroyers patrolled the waters off the Dardanelles. The pre-dreadnoughts *Agamemnon* and *Lord Nelson* were kept at one hour's notice at Mudros, and an old French battleship was similarly deployed at Lemnos. Although these ships were too slow to catch the *Goeben* or *Breslau*, the two British battleships had four 12-inch and ten 9.2-inch guns each, and could act as cut-offs and protect the naval base. In addition a comprehensive series of minefields had been laid from Suvla round to Mavro Island, barring the exit from the Dardanelles. Any effort at sweeping the mines would, the British believed, provide warning of an impending sortie.

Rebeur-Paschwitz had no plans to sweep the minefields, however, believing that air reconnaissance would show him exactly where the gaps were, and that their effectiveness would have been diminished with the passing of time (the earlier ones had been laid in mid-1916). On 20 January 1918, the day he broke out, the recently arrived rear admiral commanding the British Aegean Squadron, Arthur Hayes-Sadler, was away in Salonika in the *Lord Nelson*. The French battleship was in dock, leaving the *Agamemnon* at Mudros. The Germans, thanks to air reconnaissance, were aware that there was only one battleship in the area. They were also aware that the Aegean Squadron was widely spread. In Mudros harbour, in addition to the *Agamemnon* there were three light cruisers, a sloop, two monitors, *Raglan* (two 14-inch guns) and the M28 (one 9.2-inch gun), and four destroyers (only two fit for action). There were twenty-four other warships spread from Suda Bay in Crete to Salonika. The British plan, designed by Hayes-Sadler's predecessor, Rear Admiral Sydney Freemantle, was to draw the German ships into a trap, where they could be destroyed by superior forces.

In thick mist the *Goeben* and *Breslau* passed the exit to the Dardanelles, at 6 a.m., accompanied by four Turkish destroyers, passing through two minefields without incident. At this point the Turkish destroyers turned back as planned. The mist hid the ships from the lookout on Mavro Island some six miles off. The patrolling destroyers, *Tigress* and *Lizard*, were at the time off Mudros.

The day before, Donald

had to go to Mudros, our HQ, to collect a new Sopwith Camel. Quite a number of chaps were going home on leave and we had a terrific party which lasted until about 2 am. To everybody's horror we were wakened by shouts of 'The *Goeben*'s out! The *Goeben*'s out!' Here was I about twenty-five miles away from the *Goeben*, with no plane, neither my new nor old one were serviceable. The planes at Imbros were all bombed up, and the nearest fighter I could grab as an escort was a Sopwith Pup. I took her off, and after about five minutes I had a hunch that all was not well. We didn't have a petrol gauge, and I thought, I've no check that she's been filled up, so I returned hastily, and found the tank verging on empty.

By that time 'Dad' Hicks had landed with his Camel, having been out and had a look, which gave me a rough idea of where *Goeben* and *Breslau* now were. The dawn patrol had been out and reported the straits clear, not knowing that the two ships were already out. By this time I had got a Camel, filled up, and went in to escort the bombers against German fighters from the mainland and help in the attack on the *Goeben* and *Breslau*.

At 6.10 the *Goeben* struck a mine, but suffered only slight damage. She turned north by now beyond the minefield, although Rebeur-

Paschwitz did not know its extent, and headed for Imbros. In the destroyer *Tigress*, which had just parted company with her sister ship, the *Lizard*, Signalman Archer was just coming off watch at 7.30 a.m. As he passed the W/T office, the operator sang out:

> The *Goeben*'s out. I thought he was joking, but when he showed me the signal, I reported it to the Captain who was in the chart house asleep. It was not long before we were going at full speed and ready for immediate action. We joined *Lizard* at about 8 am and at 8.30 we saw the *Goeben* and *Breslau*. They began firing salvo after salvo at us

The *Breslau*, sent ahead, chased off the *Tigress* and *Lizard*, and was soon joined by *Goeben*. Together they sank the two monitors at anchor. There being no more targets, Rebeur-Paschwitz decided to retrace his course, which he believed to be mine-free, and shape course for Mudros forty miles away, where he hoped for rich pickings.

As the Germans were off Cape Kephalo, RNAS aircraft appeared and attacked the *Breslau*. As she steered to port to clear the field of fire for *Goeben*'s anti-aircraft guns, she struck a mine. Her steering was badly damaged and she was soon out of control. As *Goeben* came to her assistance, she too struck a mine. The Germans could see mines all round them in the clear water, and the aircraft kept attacking; *Breslau* took a direct hit. Donald's view was that:

> Although we hit both ships, the bombs were not very heavy, and couldn't have done the armoured ships much harm. But the crews of both ships lost their nerve, and started zig-zagging, which in a minefield is fatal. We pelted them with everything we had, machine guns the lot. It was funny to see machine-gun bullets bouncing off their conning towers.

The *Tigress* and *Lizard* now joined the attack on the *Breslau*, like hyenas nipping at a wounded lion. Signalman Archer:

> We ordered *Lizard* to take station astern of us, and although we were being heavily shelled, we still shadowed the enemy. We were tearing about all over a very thickly laid minefield, never knowing at any minute that we might hit one ourselves. At 9.5 there was a big explosion and we saw that the *Breslau* had struck about four or five mines. We saw her bows raised high in the air, and she sank stern first in three or four minutes. There were loud cheers from us, and we had the pleasure of making a last signal to her by searchlight *Fahre Mohle* which means farewell.

Donald: 'It wasn't the bombs that sank her, but we'd bombed her on to the minefield, the mines sunk her so we claimed that as an RNAS victory'.

Rebeur-Paschwitz decided to head for the Dardanelles. In fact he was in no danger from British warships because Hayes-Sadler, at Salonika, although alerted to the sortie by a wireless message from the *Raglan*, took an inordinate amount of time to react, and then incorrectly.

Meanwhile the *Goeben*, retracing her course exactly, hit another mine in the same position in which she had been struck on the way out. But damage was slight, although she now had a 15° list to port. As she steamed up the Dardanelles she was under almost continuous attack from RNAS aircraft. Donald: 'Machines were going back to Mudros and Imbros, loaded with bombs, back again and pelting away. The *Goeben* was going slower and slower.'

The *Tigress* and *Lizard* were picking up survivors from the *Breslau* when

four or five Turkish destroyers appeared, which we raced after at full speed, and commenced to engage the eastern destroyer at 7,000 yards. Looking through telescopes we saw two hits, one underneath her bridge, the other tore her funnel out. Clouds of steam escaped, and after continuing firing in the hope of destroying the Turk, we saw that she was nearly done for, and making off back to the Dardanelles followed by the others. We could not follow too closely or we would have received a lovely lot from the forts.

We went back and carried on picking up survivors. The forts did not fire on us, but if they had, we were going to shove off and leave them. We could not help but pity them as they struggled in the water shouting '*kamerad*', and 'save me'. We lowered all boats, picking up anyone who was alive. As they came aboard they fell down with exhaustion and cold. We had 110 survivors and the *Lizard* had about 60.

Having negotiated the German minefields at the entrance to the narrows, Rebeur-Paschwitz must have thought that he was almost home, when *Goeben* ran aground off Nagara Point. For six days she was under air attack by RNAS from Mudros and Imbros and some RFC aircraft sent specially over from Palestine to bases in the Aegean. They were joined by aircraft from the seaplane carriers *Ark Royal* and *Empress*.*

A mix of aircraft joined in, the bombers consisted of Sopwith 1½ Strutters, Sopwith Bombers, DH4s, DH9s, RFC BE2Cs and BE2Ds, and Henri Farmans. Fifteen tons of bombs were dropped in 270 sorties but to no good effect. The aircraft were driven to attack at height by accurate anti-aircraft fire, and the small bombs available at the time were

---

* Both carriers had to lower the seaplanes over the side by crane before take-off, and recover them in the same way as described in Chapter 7. They should not be confused with their successors of the same name.

incapable of doing serious damage to a ship as powerful as the *Goeben*.
Donald:

> There was a German seaplane station at Nagara Point, and they had a very
> fine battery of anti-aircraft guns there. It was an awful place to fly through
> in normal times, let alone when the *Goeben* was sitting there. We were
> getting quite a lot of hits, but we knew we were only making things
> difficult for the people repairing her. She was being bombed at least once
> every hour during daylight, and every two hours by night. The lighters
> carrying workmen and materials were forced to cast off and keep clear
> during every attack.
>
> One of our RNAS pilots got a biggish bomb down the *Goeben*'s funnel,
> and was sure he'd blown up her boilers. He had never heard of shell
> gratings which would laugh at bombs. *C'est la guerre mes enfants!*
>
> German fighters tried to butt in quite often. I never saw any of ours
> brought down by them, but we did lose three to anti-aircraft fire. I reckon
> we shot down about six German fighters (Albatross D IVs and Halber-
> stadts). On one occasion, I saw a small Halberstadt fighter climbing at an
> unbelievably steep angle to attack Ralph Sorley and Smithy in their DH4.
> He was right below me, so I put my old Camel into a vertical dive and
> practically fell on top of him, with both Vickers going. He went down in a
> queer sort of tumbling spin, but nobody saw him crash. You can't leave
> escorted bombers to go down and confirm kills.

The only British submarine in the locality was unserviceable because
of a fractured propeller shaft. When the E14 arrived, she was sent in to
deal with the *Goeben*, but arrived to find she had been towed off. The
anti-submarine defences in the Dardanelles were by now far stronger
than they had been in 1915, and the E14 was detected by shore-
mounted hydrophones, depth-charged, blown to the surface and sunk
off Kum Kale by shore batteries.

The *Goeben* was too badly damaged to be repaired at Constantinople
and took no further part in the war. She eventually became genuinely
part of the Turkish navy, remaining in commission until 1970.

12

Patrolling and fighting in the North Atlantic and North Sea

Contrary to the popular belief that the High Seas Fleet never came out after Jutland except to surrender, Scheer made a sortie on the night of 18/19 August 1916. He had eight Zeppelins on patrol ahead, and twenty-four submarines off the east coast of England and in the southern North Sea. Thanks to Room 40 picking up his wireless traffic, Jellicoe and Beatty were once more at sea some hours before the High Seas Fleet. This time the Harwich Force, five light cruisers and twenty destroyers, was ordered to be in position fifty miles east of Yarmouth at dawn on 19 August.

Despite the efforts of Room 40, there was no fleet encounter that day. Early in the morning the British submarine E23 torpedoed the German battleship *Westfalen* about sixty miles north of Terschelling. The battleship was not badly damaged, but in returning to port she transmitted by wireless, revealing the position of the High Seas Fleet to the listening British direction-finding stations. Jellicoe was informed, but had been delayed by the sinking of the light cruiser *Nottingham*. At first he was unsure whether she had been struck by a torpedo or a mine. Fearful of the latter, he turned north for a while, losing four hours. He might still have encountered Scheer, but for a German error. The commander of Zeppelin L13 shadowing the Harwich Force reported that a strong force of British warships was advancing on Scheer from the south. Scheer, hoping to catch a detached portion of the Grand Fleet, headed in that direction. The Zeppelin commander, not a professional naval man, but the chief of the Magdeburg Fire Department, had mistaken Tyrwhitt's Harwich Force for heavy units of the Grand Fleet. Tyrwhitt had headed north after hearing E23's signal about the *Westfalen*, but having seen nothing, reversed course to proceed to his station, unknowingly missing Scheer.

Scheer meanwhile had turned from a southerly course to head for base, at which stage he learned from one of his U-boats that the Grand Fleet was heading south towards him. Jellicoe was soon told by the

371

Admiralty that Scheer was too far ahead to catch, and turned north. The British now encountered the U-boat line, and the light cruiser *Falmouth* was torpedoed by U-66, and finished off by U-63 the following day while under tow.

Tyrwhitt, alerted to Scheer's course, increased speed and chased him, catching sight of him at 6.00 p.m. He briefly toyed with attacking him after dark, but realized that he would not be able to reach a good attack position ahead of the enemy before moonrise, after which he would be blown out of the water by Scheer's heavy units. He rightly decided to abandon the chase.

The major outcome of this disappointing day was the decision by Jellicoe and Beatty that because of the submarine and mine threat the Grand Fleet should not go south of latitude 55° 30′N and east of 4° E unless circumstances were exceptional. Meanwhile, work on improving Rosyth so that the whole of the Grand Fleet could move there from Scapa, and be based further south, was put in hand.

Scheer's plans for further sorties were now scrapped because his U-boats, which he needed to give him advance warning that Jellicoe was at sea, were required for restricted submarine warfare, begun in October, and later for unrestricted warfare (covered in the previous chapter). He was not to sortie until April 1918. His destroyers were sent to Zeebrugge to engage the Harwich Force and Dover Patrol.

The Grand Fleet may have spent most of the remainder of the war swinging round their buoys in Scapa and Rosyth, but most of the other players in the North Sea and North Atlantic approaches were busy, some to the point of exhaustion. A few minutes after Cook Evans joined the *Tribal*-class destroyer *Amazon*, part of the 6th Destroyer Flotilla based at Dover, he met the first lieutenant. On being asked if he knew where his action station was, Evans replied that he did not, adding that he had only just arrived on board. To which the first lieutenant replied:

> You have been on board this ship for nearly ten minutes, that is sufficient time for you to have found out where your action station is. Where have you come from? The Grand Fleet I suppose. Well, let me inform you this is the 6th Flotilla, and we may be in action tonight. Go back to the Coxswain, find out where your action station is and come back and report to me.

The key sea lines of communication supplying the BEF in France and Flanders ran through the Straits of Dover. The Royal Navy was conscious that not only were U-boats transiting to their patrol areas via the Straits, but that the line of communication was vulnerable to periodic attacks by destroyers, detached from the High Seas Fleet for the purpose. In April 1916, Vice-Admiral Sir Reginald Bacon, commanding the Dover

Patrol, had laid the Belgian coast barrage, a mixture of moored mines and mine nets. Shortly afterwards, the Admiralty ordered the construction of a similar barrage, called the Cross-Channel Barrage, stretching from the Goodwin Sands to the Snouw Bank off the Belgian coast. Neither barrage was successful in totally stopping the passage of submarines. Finally, in 1917, a field of deep mines was laid between Folkestone and Cap Gris Nez.

Before the Cross-Channel Barrage was complete, the German destroyers attacked. Twenty-four destroyers of the III and IX Flotillas under Captain Michelsen were detached from the High Seas Fleet and, with half a flotilla of Zeebrugge-based destroyers, attacked the line of communication under the cover of darkness. The *Amazon* was in harbour that night, her crew enjoying a rare stand-down. Cook Evans was in his hammock looking forward to a full night's sleep:

I heard the Bosun's mate of the watch call out, 'Signalman what do you make of that? I think it's gun flashes'. The signalman replied that it was lightning. I heard him clattering forward on deck to report to the duty officer, when the signalman shouted that he had a signal telling us that an enemy raid on Dover units was in progress, and ordering all units to sea.

In seconds the alarm buzzers were sounding and men were running to their stations. Running to mine in the after magazine, I could see that we had slipped from our buoy, and were heading for the harbour exit. The *Viking* sped past, with the senior officer, and signalled 'Follow me'.

I was the last to arrive, and the shell room and magazine were ready for action. We were at sea travelling fast. The First Lieutenant rushed down the gangway, cracking his head on the deckhead, and said 'listen to this signal from HQ; "Eleven enemy destroyers raided Dover Straits, sunk the destroyer *Flirt* and transport *Queen*. They have been plotted off Folkestone". That happens to be our position, and we have lost contact with other units, so we are on our own, and may encounter them at any moment. That is all. Good luck'. With that he ran on to the deck above.

There were five of us at this action station: 1st Class Stokers Lewis, Kavanagh, and Wheatley, one ordinary seaman, Hugget, and me. We cracked jokes waiting for something to happen. It was not long in coming. I heard the gunlayer of the after gun on deck above call out, 'train right, steady, stand bye'. The gun fired, and everything started happening. I could hear the enemy replying and we were passing ammunition swiftly by hand to the deck above. Suddenly there was an explosion, as the enemy got a direct hit on the gun platform above, hitting a case of cartridge which had just been passed up, setting fire to the gun platform, killing or wounding the gun crew, and scattering blazing cordite into the magazine flat below. I leapt up into the flat, jumping and stamping on the burning cordite. In the smoke and light from the dim blue bulb, I could see two bodies motionless on deck. I shouted 'magazine flat on fire', and heard a lone voice from one of the gun's crew above say, 'put it out you silly bugger'. At that moment the stoker's fire party arrived playing out a hose, and extinguished the blaze. I could hear gunfire but the gun overhead was silent.

Two of our party was dead, and one mortally wounded. The 'Jimmy the One' [first lieutenant] appeared ordering me to check that I was not wounded, not realising he was himself. That was the last I saw of him, he was sent to hospital when we got in.

I heard that the destroyer *Nubian* had switched on her bridge search-light, and the enemy had promptly blown her bows off with a torpedo. The *Viking* had her forrard 6-inch gun jam and rendered useless after the first round. The *Mohawk* had suffered casualties and damage. One torpedo had just missed our stern, and another our bows. A shell had passed through our boiler room just skimming the top of one boiler, had it exploded everyone there would have been killed. We had been engaged with five enemy destroyers, which had closed up around us, three off the starboard side, two off the port side, and engaged at 30 yards range. Considering all things, our casualties were light: five killed and eleven wounded. We were very lucky, several star shells had been fired in the distance, and the enemy made off, [possibly] fearing that reinforcements were arriving and anxious to get back.

The leading torpedoman had been about to launch a torpedo on the enemy leader of three destroyers in single line ahead on the starboard beam, but the torpedo officer clapped his hand on his shoulder and shouted, 'For God's sake don't fire, the Captain says they are our own ships'. The torpedoman later said his sights were on and he could not have missed. The following two were so close behind they would have collided in a bunch with the leader. But the opportunity was lost. Battles are won or lost in split seconds

The Germans sank the destroyer *Flirt*, six escorting drifters, and the empty transport *Queen*. Fortunately they did not find any of the fifty-seven other vessels plodding back and forth that night. The Admiralty was appalled, and the British press howled. The Admiralty's fears were not calmed by Bacon remarking that 'It is as easy to stop a raid of express engines with all lights out at night, at Clapham Junction, as to stop a raid of 33-knot destroyers on a night as black as Erebus, in waters as wide as the Channel'.[1]

The diary kept by Able Seaman Phipp of the destroyer *Lance*, which did not take part in the action, expresses the view of the affair as seen by the lower deck:

It is generally agreed by service men around here and by people ashore in Dover that [heavily crossed out and illegible] was to blame entirely for [heavily crossed out and illegible] in not sending boats to attack the Germans also in not sending light cruisers out. It also appears that there were at least two divisions of destroyers, one at Dunkirk and our division standing by doing nothing [heavily crossed out] which took 1½ hours to come after the known approach of the enemy.

The Admiralty's confidence in the Cross-Channel Barrage took a knock when fourteen British destroyers crossed over it by mistake without suffering a scratch. The Admiralty decided to reinforce Bacon with more destroyers from Tyrwhitt's Harwich Force and the Humber, and sent more destroyers down from the Grand Fleet to replace the Humber flotillas. There were now not sufficient destroyers to screen the entire Grand Fleet, and part of the 4th Battle Squadron would have to remain behind. Destroyers were now more important than dreadnoughts, a turnaround from the situation at the outbreak of war.

The Germans found that large numbers of destroyers at Zeebrugge created problems. Because of the danger of air attack, they could not lie alongside the mole, and had to be sent up the canal to Bruges. Negotiating the locks was a time-consuming business: it could take four destroyers two and a half hours to make the trip. The British air reconnaissance of the canal, which usually revealed destroyer movement, was stepped up after Michelsen's attack on the Dover Straits line of communication. The Germans sent one flotilla back to Wilhelmshaven, but mounted another attack on the northern entrance to the Downs on the night of 23/24 November 1916, achieving little except a desultory bombardment of Margate, and stirring up the British press, which harassed the Admiralty.

The High Seas Fleet continued to send destroyers to reinforce the Flanders flotillas from time to time. On the night of 22/23 January 1917, Room 40 intercepts spotted the move of eleven enemy destroyers of VI Flotilla to Zeebrugge, and warned Tyrwhitt, who tried to cut off the enemy between the Schouwen Bank and the Maas. Tyrwhitt took six light cruisers and eighteen destroyers, including six destroyers from the Dover Patrol.

Phipp, now in the *Surprise*, a super-fast Yarrow special destroyer (39 knots):

Jan 22nd At 5 pm all the Flotilla put to sea to intercept a German Destroyer flotilla which had left Borkum [at the mouth of the Ems] to join forces with the Zeebrugge Flotilla.

Lieutenant Bowen, a watch-keeping officer in the light cruiser *Aurora* (two 6-inch and six 4-inch guns), was napping below after coming off watch:

At 2.38 AM, the harsh rattle of the alarm hooter on the aft deck brought me instantly to full wakefulness, and I raced on deck. Everything was pitchy black, and hearing someone say 'port beam', I ran up to the port battery, to find that someone had sighted something on the other side. I crossed to S1, the foremost 4-inch gun and at once saw, about 1,500 to 2,000 yards distant, three low, dark shapes, easily recognisable as destroyers, I could not with certainty say that they were hostile. The Captain had no doubt, for just as I had my glasses focussed on the leading one, the tinkle of the fire-gongs sounded, immediately followed by the crash and blinding glare of our starboard broadside. I could see nothing for about half a minute, very nearly walking overboard as a result.

Having opened fire and betrayed our presence, we loosed off as hard as we could, in rapid controlled salvoes; the enemy destroyers, of whom the flagship sighted six, loosed off torpedoes at us and turned away in flight. They opened fire with their after guns. In their haste to be gone, they heaped on fuel not too wisely but too well, and four out of the six flamed at the funnels, giving our gunlayers a reasonable point of aim. About the sixth or seventh salvo, they were about four to five thousand yards distant, a hit was observed. A moment later one of them was lit up in a clear silhouette against a dull red glare, emanating from somewhere near her engine room. The glow died down to a mere spark of light, but not before the outline of masts, funnels, and bridge could be seen as a modern destroyer of the [blank] class.

The flagship, and next astern had opened fire soon after us, but a moment or two, after the second hit, we all ceased firing. The action had taken place about 17 miles north of the Schouen Bank [sic] light vessel, at about the centre of the triangle formed by the Schouen, North Hinder, and Maas lights. It was evident that the alarm having been given, all twelve German boats known to be in the vicinity, would either dive for Zeebrugge, or, if still to the north of us, make tracks for the Ems. We remained full closed up and ready for action, but without much hope of meeting them again, since we could not follow them down.

At about half past three, a ship was spotted some way off on the port side, apparently motionless without lights; we did not open fire, as it was difficult to say, owing to the darkness and uncertainty of outline what she might be. A little before four o'clock, however, the [blank: possibly *Cleopatra*] and her division, following behind us, also passed her, but this time close enough to see that she was a German destroyer; the [blank] opened fire and hit her several times, and on turning 16 points and passing over the same spot, found she had sunk, leaving some wreckage and men struggling in the water. The probability was she was the one hit in the engine room by us, and stopped, thus falling easy prey to the [blank] when she came along.

A few minutes after four, flashes of guns were observed to the south'ard, and at 4.12 a huge flare over the southern horizon lit up the whole scene with an astonishing brilliance. We hurried in that direction, and soon intercepted signals from N—— [sic] who was in command of the Dunkerque lot, to the effect that they had been in action with several enemy destroyers near the Schouen Bank light, where our people had been lying in wait, and that the S—— [Simoom] had been torpedoed.

The division we had fired on, had fled straight past the the Schouen, their quickest way to Zeebrugge, and on encountering the N—— and her crowd, a general melee had ensued. The Simoom closed to a couple of hundred yards of one of the enemy boats, and for a few minutes let her have it at point blank range with all three guns, scoring hit after hit (this was probably V69 whom she engaged); meanwhile a second Hun crept up on the blind side, and planked in a torpedo, which caught the Simoom under the foremost magazine, blowing fo'c'sle and bridge sky-high. Under cover of the pause consequent on the explosion, the Germans disengaged, and pursued their homeward way through the elaborately mined channels, where it would have been hopeless for our boats to have followed.

Thereafter, and indeed throughout, the predominant feature of the entertainment was the cold, which was quite the most intense any of us had experienced in the North Sea. Travelling at high speeds, clouds and sheets of spray continually swept the upper deck, and as it fell it froze forming a crust of thin ice. It was positively dangerous to be on the fo'c'sle or quarterdeck when the ship heeled to the helm, and I am convinced that if they had put the helm hard over, half the 6-inch guns crews would have gone in the 'ditch'.

At 7.30 we passed the remains of the Simoom, who presented a pitiable sight; her bows and fo'c'sle were gone, cut off sheer under the mast, while the foremost part of the upper deck had been blown backwards up against the foremost funnel; the rest of her was intact and floating with her stern high out of the water. Having heard and seen her condition, N—— was ordered to sink her by gun-fire.

Phipp in the *Surprise*: 'we arrived in Harwich at 12.30 pm, oiled, and are at one hour's notice'.

Despite the action being hotly refought in the British and German press, in fact no German boats were lost. The German *V69* was rammed by S50, but survived, whereas the *Simoom* was torpedoed by S50. *V69* was spotted limping home and engaged by the light cruisers *Penelope*, *Cleopatra*, and *Undaunted*, but they switched off their searchlights too early, thinking that the German was sinking, and *V69* eventually made

Zeebrugge. It was a poor effort by Tyrwhitt, given that the element of surprise was on his side thanks to Room 40. In his defence, the reinforcing destroyers lent by the Grand Fleet were used to being kept on such a tight rein that they were unaccustomed to the freedom of action that Tyrwhitt allowed, and did not use their initiative. The battle also highlighted the problems of command and control in the fast-moving destroyer and light cruiser night actions so typical of the engagements in the Straits and southern North Sea. So perhaps Jellicoe was right not to fight at night at Jutland.

The next attack by the German flotillas was on the night of 25/26 February. Room 40 did not detect the impending sortie, but the Germans inflicted no damage, other than hitting the destroyer *Laverock* with a torpedo that failed to explode. A much more serious attack took place a month later when sixteen destroyers attacked shipping in the Downs. Room 40 provided warning, but the Germans managed to torpedo two British destroyers (*Paragon* blew up and sank, but *Llewellyn*, hit in the bow, was able to steam stern first), sank a steamer, and shelled Ramsgate and Broadstairs. No enemy destroyers were hit.

As 'maids of all work', destroyers escorted convoys, which had been established on the cross-Channel routes well before they were brought in on other routes. On 19 April 1917, the *Surprise* dropped a convoy safely in harbour, then received a W/T message from a merchant ship proceeding down-Channel, and not under escort. Phipp:

> 'Submarine sighted, assistance'. We turned WSW and steamed for the spot, arrived there to find the ship hadn't been sunk. Evidently our friends had seen us coming up. We cruised around a bit, and suddenly spotted a streak of oil some distance away, and made full speed for it, dropping our paravanes as we went. When we were halfway through the patch of oil, our starboard paravane struck something and up went a great column of water 30 to 40 feet high. We at once slewed right round and dropped depth charges to make sure of our tiresome friend. Our skipper lowered the whaler and gave orders to pick up anything that might belong to a submarine. But we were doomed to failure, as nothing was picked up so we had no sure evidence.

This was an all too typical example of the frustrations experienced when trying to find and kill a dived submarine in this war. In stopping to lower and recover a boat, the captain of the *Surprise* risked being on the receiving end of a torpedo.

The German destroyers and torpedo boats in Flanders, forty in all, were well placed to interdict the British line of communication in the Straits of Dover, but got a bloody nose on the night of 20/21 April when twelve of their big new destroyers attempted an attack on the barrage patrol and bombardments of Calais and Dover, six to each side. Room 40 failed to provide any warning, and so there were only the flotilla leaders *Broke* (Commander Evans) and *Swift* (Commander Peck) on the Dover side and four other destroyers on the Calais side. *Swift*, a big 35-knot destroyer, had recently been refitted with a 6-inch gun replacing her two forward 4-inch. Her first lieutenant was Douglas King-Harman. After bombarding Calais then Dover, the Germans withdrew at full speed.

The *Amazon* had been ordered to proceed to Calais with two escorts to bring back a very important passenger leaving Calais at midnight. Cook Evans:

> We waited with gangway in position, speculating on the identity of our passenger who was to have an escort of two destroyers. Suddenly a burst of gunfire was heard from seaward. The trip was cancelled, Calais was under bombardment, the gangway was quickly pushed back on to the jetty. As we gathered speed out of the harbour, 'action stations' was shouted. There was no sign of our escort. Suddenly one of our lookouts spotted a row of fiery glows away in the distance, the enemy boats being coal-burners, the tops of their funnels were emitting a glow at high speed, we being oil-burners did not. The enemy position was reported to HQ.

This led to *Broke* and *Swift* intercepting. Peck ordered King-Harman, who was navigating, to ram the leading German destroyer. With only gun flashes to steer by, the *Swift* shot past the leading enemy destroyer, the *G42*, but the *Broke* following on *Swift*'s quarter slammed into the German. The enemy crew boarded, and a hand-to-hand fight ensued on *Broke*'s deck, until the Germans realized their ship was sinking. The *Swift* had turned back, torpedoed another destroyer, the *G85*, and engaged the *G42* with her 6-inch gun. The *Swift* picked up most of the surviving hundred Germans and took the crippled *Broke* in tow.

Although the British were damaged, with the *Broke* having to be towed to port, two German destroyers were sunk. The captain of the *Broke*, Commander Edgar Evans, was instantly dubbed 'Evans of the *Broke*' by the British press, eager to publicize success.[2] King-Harman was awarded the DSC. He wrote to his mother: 'It was a splendid show, a terrific melee and quite indescribable. We were very pleased. We made a dramatic entry into harbour listing somewhat and cheered frantically by all the ships in harbour.'

The *Amazon*, whose report had led to the engagement, remained on patrol until daylight and was not engaged. On her return to Dover, Cook Evans remembered:

We were tied up quite close to the *Broke* on the jetty, and I saw a staff car from HQ arrive with a commander from HQ, who called out, 'Well done Evans'. He shouted back, 'Thanks, I could not get my towing gear out in time, or we would have brought her in as a prize'. He was of course referring to the ship he had put out of action.

Douglas King-Harman wrote to his grandfather:

It is very satisfying to catch the Germans at last; it is heartbreaking work patrolling night after night, and then to miss the enemy when he does come. However we have got something to keep us going to next time and the experience will be useful. No one is more sensible of the extraordinary escape we had. It is perfectly miraculous that we were not considerably damaged. The Germans have had it all their own way for some time, it has always been their torpedoes which hit and ours which missed. It was a great advantage to be only two against six, although we hadn't the faintest idea what the *Broke* was doing, yet we felt every ship we saw was the enemy and blazed off all round quite happily. The guns did very well indeed especially the 6-inch which got off 18 rounds – pretty good work considering we were never on a steady course and it is a heavy gun to train by hand. Unless you get a lucky hit in the engines or boilers, there is not enough time to do serious damage by gunfire in these night actions.

The Germans were sufficiently shaken by the loss of two destroyers to call a halt to any further raids on the Cross-Channel Barrage for ten months.

The effort and resources expended by the British in patrolling the Cross-Channel Barrage was largely nugatory, and at times the mines proved more hazardous to the Royal Navy than the U-boats they were intended to sink. The U-boats took to floating over the net barrage in darkness and at high water. It was later established that from January to November 1917, only one U-boat in six was sunk by a mine in the Dover Strait out of the 253 transits of the barrage.

It was about this time that the British began hatching plans to attack the Flanders submarine bases, and indeed their capture was a key objective in Haig's offensive in the Third Battle of Ypres from July to November 1917 (popularly, but incorrectly, known as Passchendaele after one of the engagements in the campaign). Haig's troops got nowhere near the bases, but amphibious attacks were mounted on Zeebrugge and Ostend, as will become apparent in the next chapter.

Meanwhile the daily round for the Dover Patrol and Harwich Force continued relentlessly. Accounts of their activities are vivid proof of the meaning of the expression 'sea power'. The Germans darted out, sometimes inflicted damage, and scampered home. But the Royal Navy carried on with its daily tasks uninterrupted, and despite losses and set-backs spread a wide tapestry of maritime operations across the sea. Able Seaman Snelling in the destroyer *Tempest*:

Saturday 23rd June 1917 Slipped at 8 pm and proceeded to sea in company with three light cruisers and two divisions TBDs back up 'beef-trippers'.

Sunday 24th June 1917 At sea, explode a mine starboard forward which made a pepper box out of ship's side, funnels etc. One man seriously wounded and one officer slightly wounded. Returned to harbour 10.30 am oiled and discharged wounded, after which went alongside *Dido* to have defects made good.

Work on the defects took only two days, and *Tempest* was back at sea. A typical week in July 1917 shows no let-up:

Saturday 21st Usual Saturday routine until 9.20 am when we slipped and proceeded to sea backing up beef-trip.

Sunday 22nd At sea – 8.20 am picked up survivors of SS *Utrecht* (Dutch) which was shelled and finally sunk by three U-boats. Dropped survivors at Nord Hinder Light and proceeded to base.

Monday 23rd Escorting Dutch lighters.

Tuesday 24th At sea, dropped consort 3 pm, back to base, arriving 7.30 pm, oiled and proceeded to sea 10 pm.

Wednesday 25th At sea (Zeebrugge) and in action with enemy destroyers, Taubes etc, with shore batteries occasionally livening things up with 'coal boxes',* 'Jack Johnsons', and other lumps of frightfulness. Anchored Dunkerque Roads 9.15 pm. This was the end of a perfect day.

Thursday 26th HMS *Terror* (monitor) collided with *Tempest* and *Sceptre* while the latter two were at anchor, with result both bows badly damaged. Weighed and proceeded to Dover arriving 10.30.

Friday 27th Left for Portsmouth 1.30 pm, arriving and going alongside jetty at 7.30 pm.

Phipp's diary of life in the *Surprise* gives a similar picture:

15 July Put to sea a force of eight light cruisers and four divisions of destroyers [around twenty-four ships in all]. We went out to intercept a convoy of German food steamers leaving Rotterdam for Germany.

---

* 'Coal boxes': the name for a low-velocity German shell emitting black smoke.

16 July At 6 am we were waiting outside Rotterdam about 10 miles off. At 6.30 am they came out and made a dash north to meet their escort at Terschelling. We soon cut them off, and sunk two who put up resistance, chased two aground and badly holed them, and captured four more. Two crews abandoned their ships and made for the coast a mile and a half away. We put prize crews aboard each ship. There were two more just leaving harbour when the panic began, and they promptly turned back.

We carried on back to Harwich escorting the prizes, there was no hindrance whatsoever except when we passed North Hinder Light Ship, two torpedoes were fired at our boats, but happily missed.

21st July 'Butter trip' [beef trip to most] – we fully expected an attack from the enemy over the steamers' capture the other day, but all went well.

22nd July Brought back 17 ships from Rotterdam all heavily laden. We are getting large supplies from Holland just now to save [stop] Germany having it.

9th Aug 'Butter Trip', when we were passing North Hinder Light Ship, at 10.45 PM, the *Recruit*, the last boat of our Division in line struck a mine amidships and went down in three minutes. The next carried on, and we turned and picked up the survivors: 47 officers and men out of 100. It was rather loppy at the time and great difficulty was experienced getting the survivors on board. We couldn't use a light in case of submarines in the vicinity. The men were all covered in oil fuel, and their stomachs were full of it. One man has since died from the effect of it. There are a large number of mines, British and German which have broken away from their moorings and are a constant source of danger at night.

Destroyers also escorted minelayers, and a number were converted to minelaying either before or after completion. Control of neutral shipping was also a general task. Phipp, in the *Surprise*:

16th August Minelaying [off Heligoland Bight] successfully completed, minelayers returned to base. We carried on steaming NE, at 10.45 am we sighted four German minelayers or sweepers and escorting destroyers. We opened fire and two minelayers caught fire. They hastily made for harbour. We could not chase them further inshore as there was a minefield between and we were a mere 15 miles from Heligoland, so we turned SW steaming towards Rotterdam. We received news at 4 pm that a large Swedish steamer had left Rotterdam with contraband for Germany. We met her at 6 pm, twenty miles off Rotterdam, and asked her to accompany us back to base. She readily complied.

Action off the Belgian coast and 'beef trips' kept ships like the *Tempest* busy. For example, in the last ten days of September 1917 she was off the coast in company with bombarding monitors and carrying out other duties, and snippets from Snelling's diary give a taste:

Thursday 20 September Patrolling Belgian coast, passing Ostend. Fritz generously presented us with three or four salvoes of 15-inch, luckily no hits. On reaching end of patrol spotted two Hun minelayers, which we sent home rejoicing with a few 4-inch shells under their tails.

Saturday 22 September Mine laying stunt and bombing operation. *Erebus* fired 36 rounds of 15-inch at the harbour. Air pilot attached to *Erebus* brought down German plane.

Sunday 23 September Mine-laying. Joined forces with *Erebus*.

Tuesday 25 September Proceeded to Dunkerque, *Falconer* and *Nugent* mined. Hostile planes raided Dunkerque. Harbour and town bombarded from Ostend by 15-inch guns

Thursday 27 September Weighed at 3.40 am, joined up with bombarding section. Monitors shelled enemy anti-aircraft positions, while our airmen dropping bombs Ostend. Anchored Dunkerque, usual air raid.

Friday 28 September In action with enemy destroyers 1.40 am, but with no apparent result, they having run back under cover of shore batteries. Sighted enemy again at 6.30 am, and opened fire. Commander of enemy forces politely wished us The Morning's Greetings, we answered with a salvo of 4-inch. 10 am fired at Taube and just missed. 3.20 again exchanged shots with Fritz. 4.30 sighted German submarine, and 18 depth charges were dropped. Bet it made her happy life miserable. Anchored Dunkerque 8 pm, and left for Dover 10 pm, anchoring in Downs 11.15 pm. Some night, some stunt, some sport.

Saturday 29 September Weighed at 5.30 am, proceeded in to harbour for oil and provisions, leaving for Dunkerque at 10 am. Enemy planes raiding Dunkerque, while shells fired from Ostend.

Sunday 30 September Weighed at 10.30 am, entered harbour, enemy aircraft bombing town. Left harbour and anchored in roads. Anxiously waiting for our reliefs, *Satyr* and *Sybille* arrived at 8 pm, *Tempest* and *Starfish* leave for Dover 10 pm.

Room 40's intercepts initiated many operations, and involved almost everyone at one time or another. From Phipp's comment overleaf, the security surrounding Room 40's intercepts in the First World War appears to have been looser than that of Ultra in the Second. Nevertheless, the enemy never found out that Room 40 was decrypting their wireless traffic. Phipp in the *Surprise*:

2nd Oct *Surprise*, *Torrent*, and *Tetrarch* put to sea for patrol off entrance to Scheldt to watch for German submarines returning to base, and to make them enter the channels submerged. [We knew] All German submarines were recalled to their base by 16 Oct per intercepted wireless. We had laid nets in their channels to catch them.

3 Oct We sighted German submarine off our port bow, 23 miles NE Terschelling, and compelled her to dive.

And there were always bombardment tasks, and escorting monitors on the other side of the English Channel. Phipp:

Oct 14 All ships got under way 6 am patrolled same course as before. At 5 pm three German destroyers came out of Ostend harbour. Our monitor fired a few 15-inch long range, 14 mile, rounds at them, and they immediately retired. Their shore batteries opened fire at us, but fell short. We turned and anchored in the roads 6.30 pm.

Oct 19 At 1.15 am German destroyers attacked this place, fired 200 rounds into the town [Dunkirk], or thereabouts, and torpedoed the monitor *Terror*. It was all over in four minutes, and they were making all speed for Ostend 14 miles away. The monitor was safely got to dry dock. [She survived to be sunk off Derna, Libya, by JU 87 dive-bombers in 1941.]

Surprise's luck ran out on 23 December 1917, by which time Phipp had left her, with his journal, and was in the Royal Naval Barracks Chatham awaiting a draft to the destroyer *Victor*:

At 10.10 pm, *Surprise*, *Torrent* and *Tornado* were sunk by torpedo from a flotilla of German submarines off Rotterdam. [Phipp is incorrect, all were mined.]

Forty-nine saved and 54 lost from *Surprise*; 18 saved and 88 lost from *Tornado*; and 7 men saved and 98 lost from *Torrent*. The *Torrent* was hit first, the men got the boats out and climbed in, but the captain ordered them back aboard, and another torpedo hit her [= she ran on to another mine].

The *Surprise* who had come close to rescue survivors was hit forrard, and the men took to the Carley float and dinghy. The whaler being away rescuing – there was another explosion amidships, and the *Surprise* went down within three minutes. The people who had filled the Carley float were all thrown out by the force of the explosion, some being lost. The dinghy had 13 men in her and a lot hanging on round the sides, but it was so terribly cold that the poor fellows had to let go and drown. The rest were picked up 2½ hours later by the surviving boat of the division, HMS *Radiant*.

Convoys continued. Snelling:

Proceeded to sea 2.30 am – Beef Trip – all going merry and bright until 11.32 am. *Ulleswater* strikes a mine [actually torpedoed] and sinks. *Scott* torpedoed while standing by and sinks. Five hands killed and missing in *Ulleswater*. Twenty killed and missing in *Scott*. 9 pm took in tow a disabled British seaplane and thus closed a day of eventualities.

Submarines v. U-boats

British submarines accounted for some eighteen U-boats. This involved catching the enemy on the surface, for although as time went on British submarines were fitted with hydrophones, they were incapable of giving an accurate enough range and bearing for a submerged boat to 'kill' another submerged boat. The danger in using submarines to hunt U-boats was that all ships and aircraft were prone to regard any submerged craft as hostile and attack on sight. Consequently there were several British submarines lost in 'blue-on-blue' encounters. Lieutenant-Commander Hallifax, first lieutenant of E7 in the Sea of Marmara in 1915, was CO of D7 in a flotilla commanded by Captain Nasmith VC in the submarine depot ship *Vulcan*. The D boats were older and smaller than the E-class, and could make 14 knots on the surface and a theoretical speed of 9 knots submerged, which depended on the state of the hull and motors. Except for D4 none of the class was fitted with a gun. The flotilla was having a rather idle and frustrating time on the east coast of England, when Nasmith arrived, and

things began to hum. Forty-eight hours later *Vulcan* and half the flotilla sailed for Queenstown [now Cobh, in southern Ireland]. *Vulcan*'s armament consisted of two Maxims; repeated attempts to make them fire a burst en route failed ever to produce more than a single shot followed by a jamb [sic]. They drew a couple of depth charges and secured these to the ends of two planks which were nailed and clamped down on the quarter deck with the ends over the quarter. As SSO (Senior Submarine Officer) I had the doubtful pleasure of being stationed one cable [200 yards] astern of *Vulcan*; in the steep following sea in the Channel, these depth charges could be seen trembling on the ends of their vibrating planks and just clearing each wave as it tried to poop *Vulcan*.

The submarines had a bad time – except D 3. We were continually pooped and on several occasions the water was up to my armpits (no part of the boat except the tops of the periscope standards being above water) while I stood on the conning Tower hatch which was closed on top of one clip [to allow some air to be drawn in for the diesel engine]. The switchboards of course, were on each side of the lower conning tower hatch so got the full benefit of every following wave and the inside of the boat was a mixture of tons of water sparking and burning switchboards and chlorine gas. After rounding Lands End matters improved.

I said except D 3 which had at some time previously been fitted with a breathing trunk for use on such occasions [the predecessor of the Second World War Schnorkel]. This consisted of a circular disc of 2 inch teak, cut to fit exactly into the hatch and to sit on the rubber joint. A 9 inch hole was cut in the centre of this disc and a metal tube was fitted in this hole. The length of the tube was about 4 feet. When placed on the hatch the suction of the engine held it firmly on the rubber. I was shown this fitting on arrival at Queenstown and I immediately had one made. Many a time later did I stand on the teak disc, clasping the tube tightly to me (the top came just below the chin and one could shout orders down it) while a following sea boiled over the whole boat and bridge within a foot of the top of the tube not a drop of water going below. Stowage for diving or when not in use was upside down on the bridge deck, the tube passing down through a hole in the deck, a couple of clamps holding it down.

Hallifax commented in Chapter 1 on the lack of any training courses for submarine COs before the war; by 1917 there were still none:

Owing to my total inexperience in attacking, I spent some uncomfortable moments at conferences in Capt. Nasmith's cabin when methods of attack were discussed and our opinions asked for.

However, Nasmith was about to take the training of his COs in hand. Soon after arrival at Queenstown, the flotilla sailed with Nasmith in the light cruiser *Adventure* for a patrol off the west coast of Ireland:

Found us rollers outside when we got clear of the land and I shall never forget my sensations as we topped over the edge of the first one and rushed down into a deep valley. It seemed inevitable that we must go through the oncoming wall. *Adventure* on my starboard beam showed her keel as far as the foremast and then plunged down and through the next wave. To my intense surprise we, being so short, never shipped a drop of water on board. Newcomers to the Atlantic, coming from the North Sea, experienced the same dread on first encountering these big seas, but soon realised that they merely gave one the same sensation as a Scenic Railway (without the shouting). Running before them, however was not so pleasant as one got badly pooped, but with the breathing trunk this did not matter to me.

On this patrol submarines were spread North and South 15 miles apart; *Adventure* patrolled well out of sight to the Westward ready to inform us of the approach of any Huns reported by the Directional W/T station. On bthe morning after our arrival *Adventure* wirelessed to say she would pass through all positions during the forenoon and submarines were to make dummy attacks on her. D7 being to the Southward was to have first go. I lay and rolled on the surface and eventually sighted her masts over the Northern horizon. Dashed off at full speed on the engines to cut her off. To stop to dive when getting near would have meant missing the attack so I had to continue on the surface if I was to get the practice I needed – and explain later! I got in to about 2–3000 yards on the beam and then got my mast up – and that was the first they had seen of me in the rough sea owing to the low bridge of the D7 and 8 class, only about 5 feet above water in a wartime surface trim though the periscope standards were about 7 ft above the bridge. These bridges were extremely wet and uncomfortable in bad weather (especially before the days of fixed bridge screens – we had canvas screens which had to be brailed down before diving and a most unpleasant task it was lying on ones belly a few feet above water spilling the water out of the screen when rigging it again after surfacing) but they certainly did make for invisibility on the surface.

By Captain (S)'s orders our upper works were painted a very light grey and in a breaking sea they merged with the white of the waves. Keeping station four miles astern of a 'Q' ship on one patrol, in a choppy sea they could not locate me. I always painted with a flatting so that there was no shine. Our oilskins and sou'westers were painted the same colour and we always wore cap covers in the daytime. My periscopes were painted a dirty white (just enough black to turn the colour) with a very dark grey spiral. This again was flatting and was put on at such a time that it would be slightly tacky on going to sea; as soon as I was clear of the swept channel I dived for trim and the weather gave a convenient dirtiness to the periscope paint and deadened any shine there might be in it.

Hallifax:

My next five attacks were made on Hun submarines. On every occasion but one I sighted the enemy a long way off and broad on his beam. Staggering along at full speed submerged (about 7 knots) never brought me within decent firing range and always on the quarter. And on two occasions only I fired a couple of long range bow heaters at about 5000 yards. The Hun I sighted in a good position, (before the beam), I tried to cut off at full speed submerged. When I eased down and came to periscope depth I swung the periscope round and when I got to the port beam saw a bridge and faces filling the eyepiece; she had altered course about 9 points and was passing me on opposite courses. I saw the Officer of the Watch jerk up his binoculars in my direction and they went off at full speed. Our patrols, from April to September were made from Killybegs in Donegal Bay. We left harbour at 1800 on the first day and returned to harbour at 0700 on the 13th day; sailing again at 1800 on the 6th day in harbour. i.e. twelve and a half days out, five and a half days in. D 7 never missed a patrol though she always returned from patrol with a long defect list. As we traversed the last leg of the swept channel leading in to Killybegs I always 'cleared lower deck' and read out to the hands the list of defects, which was invariably received with a cheer. They were a magnificent crowd and never failed to have all defects made good – or good enough to go to sea on the 6th day, though this meant working day and night, by the engine room staff. Each watch got 48 hours leave every time in harbour. There is no doubt that the lower deck appreciates being told what work has to be done; if they are told and know the worst they will never let you down.

Good leadership accounts for this high morale, as extracts from a report by Commodore (S) Sydney Hall in October 1917 show:

The diving patrols are most arduous. In summer they are submerged for 19–20 hours, after 12 hours of which the air is bound to be oppressive in spite of purifiers; certainly not even the head of a match will burn. In winter the North Sea weather and cold, and at all times the anxieties from mines and our own patrols are a great trial of patience and endurance, the worst part of which is that there has been little hope during the last year of a target beyond the extremely difficult one of a submarine.

What is required and given by these officers and men is 2 o'clock in the morning courage for the whole time they are at sea.

Two American officers who have recently been on a week's patrol in our submarines owned that they were in their own language all out and fit for nothing at the end of it, though they both had an encounter with the enemy to cheer them up, in one case sinking a German ship, and the cruises were not what our officers call trying ones.[3]

D7 went on her last patrol of 1917 on 2 September. On completion she was due to go to Belfast for a three month refit. Two days before going out, Captain Nasmith came over to show Hallifax

his ISWAS. He took me out in an E boat the next forenoon to see an attack made using this instrument. On return to harbour he gave me one which lacked only the celluloid disc for the track angles. For the first time I felt really confident of being able to do any kind of attack.

The IS-WAS had been invented by Nasmith to assist COs compute a torpedo-hitting solution for small, distant targets. It was in use in all navies until torpedo-data computers, known as 'fruit machines', were introduced in the late 1930s. Hallifax:

We spent seven days in one of the patrol areas about 200 miles west of Ireland and the weather was mostly bad. The aerial feeder frequently carried away and we were without news until the weather moderated sufficiently to allow the telegraphist to be lowered down the fore jumping wire to refit the feeder. On 10 September such a lull occurred and the feeder was refitted. Soon afterwards we received a signal ordering D7 and D8 to take up position between the Hebrides and the north Irish coast. Patrol lines were 50 miles along course 100° and 280°. D8's line was 30 miles north of us. The object of this was to intercept a Hun submarine concentration in the North Channel.

The weather got worse and by the morning of 12 September there were big rollers and a heavy sea on top of them. At 0600 it was found impossible to keep the trim at periscope depth (22 ft in smooth water) and we retired to 60 feet. At 0905 we surfaced for a [battery] charge and plugged along steering 280. I was sitting on the top of the foremost periscope standard and the signalman on the after standard. At 1030 we climbed up a big roller and as we surmounted the crest the signalman yelled out 'Conning tower 2 points on the port bow' (He had noticed something black in the middle of a breaking wave on the top of a roller a few rollers ahead – fortunate that we topped our 'mountain' simultaneously, for once one got down the slope the view was limited to the broad valley).

As we tumbled down and brailed down the bridge screen I ordered course to be altered 2 points to port. We managed to get under. Both mufflers were jambed wide open – they had been for the last few days – and water was rushing fore and aft over the battery boards as we dipped and rose, making depth keeping a most difficult job. I left that to my first lieutenant (Lt V Donne) who by flooding and blowing managed – heavens knows how – to keep the boat under control. I did not come up above 18 feet for fear of getting out of control in that sea and so I saw nothing through the periscope.

17 minutes after sighting 'Fritz' from the surface I decided to let the boat break surface and to use the high power periscope – an Italian Gallileo only 14 feet long. We broke surface on the top of a roller and there right ahead on top of another roller was 'Fritz', bow cocked up at a steep angle as she climbed the top. I was dead ahead of her. As we plunged down the far slope we got the boat under again, got the stern tube ready (18-inch Mark V* cold torpedo) and altered course to the northward for a 90 degree TA shot [TA = track angle, i.e. the angle between the attacking submarine's course and the target track]. There would not have been time to turn 270 degrees for a shot with the twin bow tubes; in any case the Mark VII heaters were bad depth keepers and would never have kept their depth in such a sea.

Terrified of running out of range and missing my last chance of a 'bag' I searched wildly for Fritz with the low power periscope. We were then running beam on to the sea and rolling terribly and had to go at high speed to keep control. I sighted her stem and a gun and the bridge – and that was all – and the latter looked like D 8. The next view again showed only one gun (before the bridge) and again she looked like D8 who might for all I knew be out of position. The sights would soon be on and at that moment we sank to 30 feet. Then Captain Nasmith's teaching and his 'Iswas' came in to play and I altered course for a 100 degree TA after what seemed ages we got up to 20 feet. The periscope was set to the D A [director angle] for 100 [degree] T A. As the periscope broke clear of the water I saw the complete submarine for the first time, for she was coming down the slope of the valley that I was in. There was the 2 gun [two guns] so it really <u>was</u> a Fritz, and the foremost gun was in my cross-wire.

I fired [the stern tube], ordered 30 ft, hard a port [i.e. swing to starboard], full speed port [engine] with the idea of getting round to fire the bow fish. I estimated her speed 8 knots as that was the speed they generally patrolled at.

When we got stern on to the sea we were lifted right up and I knew the standard would be out of the water. We tried to force her down before being seen, but as we were doing so there came to us the sound of an explosion. The time takers gave a range of 1200 yards. Everyone cheered and the Chief ERA nearly knocked me out with a clap on the back. We could see nothing so came up and astern of us was a big patch of oil and in it some objects. Surfaced and saw three men in the oil. Two were swimming strongly, one was floating on his back and frequently disappearing below the surface. He was in a leather suit and I made for him first. It took quarter of an hour to get hold of him as the rollers kept sweeping us on top of him, necessitating going full speed astern to avoid crushing him. We hauled him up on the bridge from where he discharged several gallons of oil fuel while we tried to get hold of the second man who had been on the lee quarter. A third further out but the strongest swimmer – would persist in holding both arms up and shouting something (probably '*Kamarad*'), and each time he did so he went under and finally drowned.

Having been swept down to within heaving line range he would sweep again out of range. We had just got a heaving line to the 2nd man when the 2nd Coxswain drew my attention to the fellow on the bridge. he kept saying Five Fritz – between his oil discharging acts. When I repeated 'Five Fritz?', he said 'Ja, Five Fritz' and held up 5 fingers.

As we always thought of Hun submarines as 'Fritz' I thought he meant there were five submarines diving round us and did not want to be torpedoed. Again sharing his feelings just as strongly I ordered the bridge to be cleared. Every time the Hun was shoved down the conning tower he popped up again to be sick so I finally jumped on his shoulder and he disappeared into the boat. By this time his pal had at last made contact with a heaving line and was on the bridge so he was hustled down and we dived to 60 feet and did not breathe freely till we got there. Later I discovered that the [German] telegraphist had been trying to tell me that 5 survivors were in the water.

These two swimmers, (a telegraphist and a stoker) had just come off watch and had been sitting by the conning tower hatch smoking. They were going below again – the stoker half way down, the telegraphist just bending over the hatch when our torpedo hit. The stoker was blown up the hatch into the water. The torpedo hit abreast the foremost gun – the point of aim, which speaks well for the old Mark V torpedo. It exploded in a fuel tank and also in the captains cabin – a fact which seemed to upset the survivors especially as the captain was lying in his bunk, so one said. Their speed was 8 knots. They said they never expected a torpedo attack in such a sea and in consequence were not zigzagging. The telegraphist said that as he was about to go below he heard an exclamation from the Officer of the Watch and saw him grab his binoculars and look at something on the port beam. That must have been the moment when we were forced up by the following sea. At that moment the explosion occurred.

The fact that they were not zigzagging is an illustration of the danger of trusting too much to books and omitting 'security' measures; also of thinking that what we believe is also believed, and acted upon, by the enemy. The German book on submarine attack stated that it was useless to fire torpedoes in a sea of (I think) over 4.* The sea was certainly well over 4 that day as will be realised when I say that during the forenoon while diving beam on to the sea at a depth of 60 feet we rolled 16 degrees, 8 each way. The victim was U 45, five officers and 49 ratings.[4]

The wireless in the D-class boats was poor. Reception was adequate, but transmission was weak. As a consequence signals from D boats to the base at Killybegs would only be received when the submarine was actually in sight of the depot ship's wireless mast. Hallifax and his crew's sole anxiety was to let the commodore know that his flotilla had at last met with success. This was its first, and as it turned out only, 'bag' during the war. Hallifax knew that the base was shifting to Lough Swilly while they were away on patrol, and hoped for better reception there, but wireless transmissions were made to no avail.

We were terrified of 'being done in', and the Commodore (S) being left in ignorance of our success. We suffered from effects of re-action. We had been doing regularly twelve and a half days out and five and a half in since April, and were all tired out. We were all buoyed up on every trip by our passionate desire to bag a Fritz. Directly the explosion occurred and

---

* See Glossary, 'Sea and wind states'.

our ambition was realised, I know I myself felt about 100 and intensely weary.

After dinner we surfaced and patrolled our line, charging. The weather and sea were worse than before and it was very wet and uncomfortable on the surface. Suddenly, 1455, came another report of a conning tower, right ahead (310) steering to southward. We dived and swung round to 220.

We wondered what our prisoners thought of a British submarine as they were led aft from the bow tubes to the Engine Room for the attack. The High Power periscope was being hoisted with a greasy tackle. (There was only one lifting motor in that class and it was usually kept connected to the Low Power periscope. To use it on the other meant unshackling the block of one set of wires and snatching on the other, so it was preferable to use a tackle on the High Power). The starboard engine, behind which the prisoners were placed, was in such a bad way that the supports were lashed to the hull with wires and ropes wherever possible, and every pipe-joint had tomato and tobacco tins hanging under them to catch the leaks. The Hun stoker looked up at the Chief ERA with a smile and said: 'All same us'

Our glimpses of the horizon were very infrequent as we were running into the swell and it was not until 1518 that I sighted Fritz bearing 292°; only a fleeting glimpse of her and impossible to make out her course; she was about 2000 yards off. The next time I saw her was at 1529, when she was crossing my stern – I was then steering 305°. At 1530 I took a chance and fired our one remaining stern torpedo (MkV*) at her (estimated range 1500 yards) but with no luck. I did not see her again. Our prisoners were obviously pleased with our lack of success. They eventually admitted that their submarine (U45) had been ordered to rendezvous that day with U.54 and our friend's silhouette fitted U.54.

That evening the wind fell and it rained very heavily, smoothing down the waves but making no difference to the rollers. I went on watch about 2030 and saw two Scotch and one Irish light flashing away. We had just turned at the Eastern end of our line to our course of 280. Looking aft a few minutes later, I saw a light appear about 2 points on the port quarter. It showed for about a minute and then went out. The Navigator, whom I had relieved knew nothing of this light and it did not fit in with any shore light. Twenty minutes later it again appeared about 1 point on the quarter; another twenty minutes and it was astern. On each occasion it showed for about 1 minute.

I came to the conclusion that this was probably U54 looking for U45 for no fishing vessel would be likely to show a light at regular intervals. It was unlikely to be a Q ship for our surface warships were always kept out of areas occupied by our submarines.

It was one of the darkest nights I have ever struck [sic] and the sea and sky were pitch black. As the strange vessel was gradually drawing across my track on to the starboard quarter I hauled out 10 degrees to port (course 270) so as to keep clear for the time being and in the hopes that visibility might improve later. I continued at 8 knots to the western end of my patrol line without again sighting the light and then turned back to course 100.

Soon after I had turned a light was sighted astern; it showed for a minute.

It seemed fairly close. Hauled out to port. Later the light showed to the southward and this time it remained burning. Got both bow tubes ready and turned to the southward on what I judged to be a right angle course. The light came closer and closer but nothing was visible underneath it. I had the impression of a light shade top and bottom. I thought it must be about 1000 yards away but still no hull or outline of a ship was visible the night being as dark as before. Stopped engines and listened on hydrophones but water noises were too great.

Turned away again and then on a parallel course and by keeping station got her speed. (8 knots). After a time I drew ahead and again turned on to the firing course but again could see nothing though I went in closer. Turned away and then resumed parallel course. It was maddening. I felt certain this must be U 54. She had been due to rendezvous with U 45 the previous day and who else would go about showing a light? I could not challenge, for if it was Fritz he would turn and run. If I took the risk and fired and hit – what language would I have spoken to any survivors?

Finally I ran in on the firing course as close as I dared. It seemed as if we were almost on top of the light but owing to the fact that no light was thrown up or down from it, it was impossible to gauge the distance. When I thought I was about 600 yards off I was terribly tempted to fire but resisted the temptation and turned away again.

By this time I was nearly dead with fatigue. We had been out 10 days on this last trip of ours and I had been on the bridge since 2030 after a very tiring day made the more tiring by the reaction following on our long awaited success. The visibility showed no signs of improving so I decided to dive and hope to find the mystery vessel still on my patrol line at daybreak. Dived at 0300.

No sign of any vessel at daybreak 0500, and dived again. Came up to charge at 1320. Wind was rising rapidly and a bad sea getting up. The Chief ERA reported that the starboard engine was so loose on its bed that if the sea got up much more he could not guarantee its remaining where it should be. It certainly was waving about in the oddest manner. Early in the afternoon it was blowing about force 8. We were due in Loch Swilly at 0700 the next day and if we kept to our programme it meant another useless night in the sea that was running. So, as the starboard engine was becoming more unsteady every minute, I decided to make for Loch Swilly. At 1520 (routine time for passing signals) we got the mast up to make our

ETA signal and also, the report of the sinking of U45 – in case we hit a mine on the way in! We had just started to call up when right ahead of us appeared a large Fritz. We let the mast go with a run and dived madly but nothing could be seen through the periscope except a welter of waves. Eventually we surfaced and there far away to the eastward was Fritz running for the North channel. I imagine she must have seen my mast and gone off at full speed.

We entered Lough Swilly unchallenged by anyone. Our navigation light circuits were led from uncovered terminals in the (low) bridge casing and every part was earthed. We brought up wandering leads, putting a green woollen glove on one lamp and a bit of red bunting on the other but each one earthed the moment it was brought up, for the bridge was continually being swept by heavy seas and bursts of smoke and flames were continually coming up the conning tower. The boom vessel seemed surprised at our unreported arrival and we lay close to her, convincing the skipper of our British nationality before he would open the boom – a situation not without its humorous side.

Got alongside *Platypus* [submarine depot ship] at 2315 where my request for an escort was received with hearty laughter by the First Lieutenant and other submarine officers on board and it was only after I had lost my temper and cursed everyone in sight that I was believed. I reported U.54 as approaching North Channel. Two days later D.7 proceeded to Belfast for a refit.

Naval Aviation

As the war drew on, naval aviation played an increasingly important part in maritime operations. The first recorded use of an aircraft to scout for the Grand Fleet took place on 11 June 1915. Wheeled aircraft gradually replaced seaplanes for ship use in the Grand Fleet in 1917 and 1918. There was a problem, however, for whereas wheeled aircraft could and regularly did take off from catapults and short platforms in the bows of ships, the turbulent air behind a ship caused by its superstructure and funnels made landing on the stern very hazardous.

On 2 August 1917, Squadron Commander Dunning tried landing a Sopwith Pup on the flying-off deck of the *Furious*, a battle cruiser with forward turret removed. By flying up alongside the ship as she steamed into wind, producing a wind over the deck of 30–35 knots, above the stalling speed of the Pup, he was able to match the speed of his aircraft to that of the ship, and in effect hover to the side of the *Furious*. Once in position, he side-slipped in, landed on the deck, and his aircraft was grabbed by the deck-handling party. It worked the first time. The second time he groundlooped on the deck, went over the side, and was killed. The *Furious* was sent to the dockyard in November 1917 to have her after turret removed and replaced with a 284-foot-long landing deck, complete with arrester wires to catch a hook on the aircraft's tail. But her superstructure was left in place.

The RNAS also became involved countering Zeppelin raids on Britain. By the end of 1916, a number of Zeppelins had been shot down, and in November two were despatched out of a raid of ten. Lieutenant Cadbury RNAS accounted for the second:

> Early one morning I was on duty at Yarmouth Air Station, and we were warned that the Zeppelin had dropped its bombs in the Midlands and was making its way to the coast. I with two other pilots immediately got into the air to wait for it. At 5,000 feet I saw the Zeppelin approaching the coast, and chased after it, climbing to 8,000 feet. I approached from astern, about 300 feet below it, and fired four drums of explosive ammunition into its stern setting it alight.
>
> Another of our aircraft flew over the top of the Zeppelin, and to his horror saw the man in the machine-gun position on top of the airship jump over the side. Having watched the Zeppelin circle down to the sea in a blazing mass, a horrible sight, I landed back at Yarmouth. I was not very elated or pleased, somehow I was overawed by the spectacle of the Zeppelin with all the people on board going down into the sea.

This was the last Zeppelin raid on Britain until much later in the war, and these pinprick raids were highly exaggerated, despite the hysteria they generated. But until the end of the war, Zeppelins were still a threat at sea: bombing Britain had not been on the agenda when they were designed and constructed, whereas reporting British ship movements, acting as lookouts, and carrying out reconnaissance for the High Seas Fleet and enemy flotillas certainly was.

Attacks on Zeppelin bases, starting with the Cuxhaven raid in 1914, had so far proved fruitless. More successful were intercepts of Zeppelins by flying boats, set up by wireless intercept. Although even then there was an element of luck involved, such as the Zeppelin found mine-spotting near the Terschelling Light Vessel in May 1917, by Captain Leckie in a flying boat from fifteen miles away. He was above the Zeppelin, and put his aircraft into a shallow dive to pass under the enemy's tail. A burst of incendiary rounds fired up into the Zeppelin's hull did the trick, and she crashed tail-first into the sea, destroyed in a mere forty-five seconds.

In June, Flight Sub-Lieutenants Hobbs and Dickey spotted the Zeppelin L43 at 1,500 feet, and climbing above her, they dived and fired incendiary at her. Two bursts were sufficient, and the Zeppelin burst into flames. Later, Leckie found the L46, but she dumped ballast and rocketed up to 18,000 feet far faster than the flying boat could climb, and got away. Leckie found L46 and L44 a few days later, and was approaching from astern when he was seen, and the Zeppelins shot skywards again escaping.

In April 1918, Chief Mechanical Engineer Henry Stubbington had a similar experience in a Curtiss H12 flying boat. The 'boat', as Stubbington refers to her, had taken off from Killingholme in response to a report of a Zeppelin off Flamborough Head in low cloud and overcast. The Curtiss H12 had a crew of four, the captain, observer, WT operator, and engineer. Stubbington:

It was a horrible day with rolling banks of fog, heavy rain, squalls and a choppy sea. We got very wet in the open cockpits. We could see nothing but on our wireless could hear the Zeppelin transmitting morse. We didn't know what he was saying, but got some idea of his position, so flew in smaller and smaller circles until we saw him on our port side, at 9,000 feet. We opened fire with our machine-guns, and after we had fired about 200 rounds, he put his nose up at about a 30 degree angle, ditched ballast, and shot up into cloud. We climbed at full throttle, but lost him. Then we were in trouble.

The starboard engine was losing oil fast, the tailplane was covered in oil. We carried four gallons of oil in each engine cooling tank. We were 300 miles from base. I told the captain to throttle down both engines and make a landing. I got some tools, and as soon as we touched down, climbed out on to the upper plane and on top of the engine. I found the trouble, a split oil pipe, and wound tape round it. This seemed to work as with the engine ticking over to keep us head to wind, no oil spurted out any more.

After climbing back I found the crew in a dejected state. When they had looked back to ask what I proposed doing, and I was nowhere to be seen they thought I had fallen overboard or jumped, and all was lost.

I told them I had been on the upper plane, and we were ready to take off. To which they replied that it was impossible in this sea state. I said; 'It's Hobson's choice, we either take off or drown. Everything is in our favour. We are half a ton light, having used this amount of petrol. We have a wind of 40 or so knots, we only have to do 20 knots over the sea to get airborne.' I lied slightly, saying, 'I've taken off in worse weather than this at Scapa', which I hadn't.

When they objected that we would get smashed up by the waves, I said, 'No we won't. Keep the tail up, don't try to pull her up or you'll break her back, keep her low, she can take the waves on her bow. There will be a few bangs at first, but as speed increases, the wings will start taking some of the weight, she will rise on her step like a speed boat, and come off on her own. The alternative is certain death.'

I had to rave and scream before they would try it. The first waves hit hard, but it was soon obvious we would make it, and in no time at all she was riding the step, and airborne a few seconds later with no damage.

We arrived over Killingholme at 10 pm. We flew in low to wake everybody up. The motor launch switched on her searchlight, we landed, and she towed us in.

Stubbington was awarded a well-deserved Distinguished Flying Medal, a new decoration, since the RNAS had by now formed the RAF.

The lumbering flying boats climbed so slowly that catching a Zeppelin rocketing up was impossible. The solution was wheeled fighters. The Grand Fleet Aircraft Committee, established by Beatty in January 1917, came up with a plan to fit a platform over the forward gun of the light cruiser *Yarmouth*. In June 1917, a Sopwith Pup from the *Yarmouth* shot down a Zeppelin while the 1st Light Cruiser Squadron was supporting a minelaying operation off the Jutland coast. The Pup had to ditch alongside the cruiser on its return. Soon a number of other light cruisers were fitted with platforms. In October 1917, a revolving platform was fitted on the forward gun turret of the battle cruiser *Repulse*, allowing the ship to maintain its course, while pointing the platform into wind for launch. This satisfied the gunnery fraternity, who feared that altera- tions of course to turn into wind to launch aircraft would seriously interfere with the ship maintaining its place in the line of battle when action was imminent. Eventually every major ship in the Grand Fleet carried an anti-Zeppelin fighter on the after turret platform, and a two- seater for reconnaissance on the forward turret platform. These measures drastically reduced the ability of Zeppelins to shadow the Grand Fleet, which hitherto they had been able to do with impunity.

Towards the end of the war, the intrepid Samson, now commanding the air station at Great Yarmouth, experimented successfully with launching wheeled fighters from lighters towed by a ship. On 11 August 1918, Lieutenant Culley took off in a Sopwith Camel from a lighter being towed behind the *R*-class destroyer *Redoubt* to attack the Zeppelin L53, which had been shadowing light cruisers and destroyers of the Harwich Force. Culley took an hour to reach the Zeppelin at 19,000 feet, at which height he was almost stalling, but he got in a long head-on burst from his wing-mounted Lewis guns, before his aircraft fell off in a stall. The Zeppelin fell in flames three and a half miles to the sea. Culley had to ditch in the sea, and was rescued by a destroyer.

Leading Seaman Snelling in the destroyer *Tempest*, part of Tyrwhitt's Harwich Force covering the operation, saw the signal that Tyrwhitt sent:

'Attention is called to Hymn 224 verse 7', which on being looked up was found to be the following:
> Oh happy band of pilgrims
> Look upwards to the skies
> Where such a small affliction
> Shall win so great a prize.

However, the British did not have it all their own way. Snelling:

Coastal Motor Boats three hours adrift – presumed lost. Enemy aircraft attacks squadron, all bombs falling wide of the mark. Opened fire with all anti-aircraft guns and made the pace a trifle too warm for them, they made off with all possible speed. Again attacked by aircraft at 5.10 pm, 6.20 pm and 7.10 pm, no hits, splendid shooting by our anti-aircraft guns.

British airships played an important part scouting and spotting, but they were never used by the RNAS in the offensive role, mainly because the British types were even more vulnerable than Zeppelins against attack from the air and to gunfire from ships and the ground. SS- and C-class airships accompanied convoys in coastal waters providing warning of U-boats and mines. The C-class had an endurance of up to twelve hours, and to provide extended coverage of approaches to the British Isles and work with the flying boats, the North Sea (NS) class was brought into service in early 1918. These had a covered cabin, a considerable improvement on the open cockpits of earlier models, and Rolls Royce engines which gave an endurance of twenty hours. The NS class could carry two crews for long patrols. Even these later airships have a ramshackle appearance to the modern eye: access to the engines in flight was by a rope ladder.

The task of the airship was to fix the position of enemy submarines or surface vessels. As soon as an enemy was sighted, the airship reported to the local naval commander. By obtaining fixes from her wireless transmissions, an accurate plot of the airship's position could be maintained throughout her patrol, and back-up surface forces could be sent to assist. The drawback was that the enemy could use this same system to find the airship and attack it using seaplanes from Belgium.

Towards the end of the war, Beatty planned to mount offensive operations bombing North Sea Zeppelin and naval bases, including ships in harbour. He hoped to use the Sopwith Cuckoo torpedo-carrying aircraft, and other types armed with bombs, but the Admiralty looked coolly on such ideas. In hindsight the Admiralty were probably right;

given the bomb loads that could be carried at the time, the damage done would have been insignificant. Torpedo-carrying aircraft attacking ships in harbour was a much more promising prospect, but was only practicable if the operation could be carried out by wheeled aircraft launched from and recovered by a flush-decked carrier in the North Sea. The war ended too soon for that.

The *Argus*, the first flush-deck carrier (the converted liner *Conte Rosso*), was tried out in the Firth of Forth in October 1918 with eighteen Sopwith Cuckoos. The *Furious*, having come out of dockyard conversion, had actually preceded her into service in March 1918, as the flag ship of Rear Admiral Sir Richard Phillimore, Admiral Commanding Aircraft, but she was not a true aircraft carrier as she still had a centre-mounted funnel and bridge. Landings were therefore hazardous: all but three of the trials ended in crashes, and were suspended pending further reconstruction. She could launch aircraft, however, and on 19 July 1918 sent seven Sopwith Camels in for a successful attack on the Zeppelin sheds at Tondern. One Camel came down with engine trouble before reaching the target, three had to divert to Denmark (where they were interned), one pilot was drowned, and two got back to the ships, but had to ditch because they could not land on, and were recovered by a destroyer. One of the sheds was destroyed, as were Zeppelins L54 and L60. It was the first raid by wheeled aircraft from a carrier, and the most successful carrier operation of the war.

Two carriers were being built when the war ended, and might have been in service in 1919 had production not slowed down at the outbreak of peace. The *Eagle*, built from the half-finished Chilean battleship *Almirante Cochrane*, was launched in June 1918, but not completed until 1920. The *Hermes*, the first carrier in the world to be designed and built from the keel, was not completed until February 1924. Had the First World War lasted well into 1919, as was being forecast in the autumn of 1918, the world would have seen the first successful use of the naval air arm from true aircraft carriers. The *Argus*, *Furious*, *Eagle*, and *Hermes* all served in the Second World War.

13

The Zeebrugge and Ostend Raids and the last sortie of the High Seas Fleet

By the end of 1917, an estimated thirty U-boats were passing each month through the Straits of Dover to attack shipping in the English Channel, and their continuing success led to Sir Reginald Bacon's replacement as commander of the Dover Patrol by the forty-five-year-old acting Vice-Admiral Roger Keyes. He immediately put in hand improvements to the Channel Barrage that Bacon had opposed. Deep minefields were laid. Seventy drifters were stationed on the barrage, keeping station on lit buoys. They were backed up by numerous old vessels (destroyers, paddle minesweepers, and the like) with searchlights, lighting flares at distance intervals. The aim was to turn the whole area into a sea of light, forcing the submarines to dive into the minefield.

It seemed to work. Between 19 December 1917 and 22 April 1918, minefields claimed seven U-boats, and one further boat was sunk by depth charges from the destroyer *Leven*. Before this only two U-boats had been sunk by mines in the Dover Straits in the entire war. It forced the Germans to route the larger High Seas Fleet submarines north round Cape Wrath. The smaller Flanders-based boats continued to use the Straits of Dover, although less frequently than before.

The Germans counter-attacked the ships on barrage patrol with destroyers. Bigger and more potent destroyers were now coming into service in the German navy armed with 88mm and 105mm guns and capable of speeds up to 36 knots. On the night of 14/15 February 1918, seven large destroyers achieved complete surprise in the darkness, the first such attack since April 1917. British patrols, warned that a German submarine might attempt to break through the barrier on its homeward passage, thought that the firing was drifters engaging this boat, and the Germans were allowed to escape unscathed, having sunk a trawler and seven drifters, and damaged a trawler, a paddle minesweeper, and five drifters. The Germans crowed in triumph, and claimed that the barrage was now undefended.

Keyes was furious and the captains of the *Termagant* and *Amazon*, who had sighted the enemy ships but taken no action because they thought them to be friendly, were court-martialled and relieved of command. In fact the barrage continued to be maintained and operational, and this was the last destroyer raid on it. Keyes was not to know this and planned to block Zeebrugge and Ostend to prevent further sorties.

The submarine pens at Bruges were connected to Zeebrugge by an eight-mile-long canal, and smaller canals connected Bruges with Ostend. The submarine pens were protected by concrete shelters, far too thick to be penetrated by the bombs available at the time. The mole at Zeebrugge provided a sheltered base for the powerful W12 seaplanes, and the even more deadly W29 monoplane seaplane. Since the beginning of the war the British had bombarded Zeebrugge and Ostend from time to time, but had achieved very little. Destroying the canal locks by bombardment was beyond the capabilities of contemporary gunnery techniques: it involved hitting a target ninety feet long and thirty wide, out of sight to the bombarding ships, at a range of thirteen miles.

The plan submitted to the Admiralty by Keyes was to simultaneously sink as blockships the minelayers *Iphigenia*, *Intrepid*, and *Thetis* in the entrance to the Zeebrugge–Bruges canal, and the *Sirius* and *Brilliant* in the entrance to Ostend harbour.*

The first intimation that officers and ratings had that something was afoot came in February 1918, when according to Engineer Lieutenant Boddie, then serving in the battleship *Hercules* in the 4th Battle Squadron of the Grand Fleet,

> The Admiralty called for a limited number of volunteers from the Grand Fleet for a 'dangerous venture'. The volunteers were to be unmarried and of VG character. The engine room quota for the 4th Battle Squadron was six stokers from each ship and one Lieut Commander. No other particulars were given.
>
> To my astonishment, the secret nature of the venture discouraged the men from volunteering, and I had great difficulty in persuading and cajoling six eligible but rather indifferent men to accompany me. To the officers the mystery was attractive, but it left the men cold.

On 1 March, Boddie joined the *Hindustan* in the Nore

> with 40 officers, 200 seamen, and 250 stokers all from the Grand Fleet. The *Hindustan* was an elderly battleship and was to be our home until the expedition was ready to sail.

---

* The three minelayers were originally 1890/91-vintage *Apollo*-class cruisers, converted to minelaying in 1907. *Sirius* and *Brilliant*, although Apollo-class, were not converted.

Boddie was allocated as engineering officer to the *Thetis*, selected as one of the blockships, and commanded by Commander Ralph Sneyd RN:

On 2 March, Rear Admiral Keyes gave the assembled officers a full explanation of the intended operation.

The general scheme was for the *Vindictive* to go alongside the Mole [at Zeebrugge], on the seaward side and land storming parties on it, to create a noisy and flashy diversionary demonstration to enable the blockships to sneak undetected into the harbour and up the channel.

Three blockships were to be sunk at the Zeebrugge end of the Bruges to Zeebrugge canal, and simultaneously two blockships were to be sunk at Ostend, to block the Bruges to Ostend canal. If successful, this operation would put the U-boat base at Bruges out of action for some considerable time. Five mines were fitted in the double bottoms of each blockship, which would blow the bottoms out of the ships when they arrived at their destinations. One mine was fixed under the engine rooms, although I could have found a happier place for it. A motor launch was to accompany each blockship into the harbour and rescue the crew.

An elaborate smoke screen was to be laid by numerous motor launches and Coastal Motor Boats (CMBs) in such a manner that we should pass through one belt of smoke, and then get a brief clear view before entering another belt. Bombardment of the Belgian forts in the vicinity of the Mole by monitors would take place, and would cease before our arrival.

Two C class submarines, each with five tons of high explosive, would ram the bracing of the viaduct that connected the Mole to the shore, and blow themselves up to prevent reinforcements from reaching the Mole.

Fine weather was essential for the preliminary bombardment on the Mole and adjoining batteries. Several hours of darkness were required for the approach, and withdrawal. The blockships must arrive about high water. There should be a light breeze from seaward to carry our smoke screen on to the defences. Few of us felt confident that all these conditions would be met on any one night.

After giving us some further particulars, Keyes said that in his opinion, the *Vindictive*'s storming parties of Marines and Seamen should give the Germans on the Mole a good hammering, but he was less sanguine about the rescue of crews of the blockships. He ended by saying that any officer who wished could withdraw from the enterprise without further prejudice. There were no takers.

Boddie discovered that:

The fitting out of the blockships had been in the hands of Chatham dockyard a month or two before our arrival. This continued until 4 April. About 1,000 tons of rubble and cement were evenly distributed on board each blockship on the protective and upper decks, in lumps of about 50 tons. These concreted lumps would be just about awash at low water when the vessels were sunk. To facilitate rapid sinking on an even keel, all important water tight bulkheads were punctured. The five mines fitted in the double bottoms could be exploded collectively from positions on the fore bridge, or [as a precaution in case the forebridge was knocked out] on the poop and individually from positions on deck. If necessary a group of the latter would be my responsibility. At the last moment before firing, certain seacocks and condenser doors had to be opened. In the event I ordered the seacocks to be opened, but not the condenser doors, because of the general uncertainty at the time. This was fortunate, as we had to return later and shut the seacocks.

All unnecessary stores, equipment and machinery were landed, including fire and bilge pumps, all evaporators, fresh water pumps, and worst of all the Capstan Engine. The ship's masts were removed, the fresh water tanks, and most of the coal bunkers were made inaccessible by the concrete. The officers cabins were demolished, and fresh water had to be stored in the hammock nettings. It can not have been foreseen that crews would ever have to live on board the blockships again, that bunkers would have to be replenished, or that the anchor would have to be weighed by hand; but all these became necessary.

Protective mattresses were plastered thickly about the two bridges, and the armoured gratings over the hatches to the engine and boiler rooms were reinforced by torpedo matting. Smoke fittings of the burning tyre and Chlorine-Ammonia type were fitted round the forecastle and poop.

The stokers from the Grand Fleet were at first disappointed when they were drafted to the lousy looking blockships to handle coal, raise steam and clean up unwanted rubble and cement. They could be told nothing of the objective, or purpose of the expedition until we moved to the Swin, near the Maplin light off Sheerness, a month later. No leave was granted to them at Chatham. Their messes in the *Hindustan* were overcrowded and uncomfortable. They had gathered the impression that they would be going to France, and would see some fighting. It was necessary to eliminate a few of the more troublesome, after which a sort of restless peace reigned.

Bury [Engineer Lieutenant-Commander in *Vindictive*] and I became great friends.

Apparently officers were allowed to go ashore, which cannot have helped the morale of the ratings, as Boddie comments that Bury was 'serious at work and frivolous at play', adding: 'while at Chatham, Bury and I indulged in a few weekend jaunts together to London and Eastbourne.'

At Zeebrugge the three blockships, *Thetis, Intrepid,* and *Iphigenia,* had to enter the harbour protected by the curved mole (breakwater), 1,840 yards long, 80 yards wide, and connected to the shore by a wooden viaduct. They were to arrive at slow speed off the Mole thirty minutes after the storming parties assaulted:

> and then increase to full speed, round the lighthouse at the end of the Mole, and enter the channel about a mile long leading to the pier heads at the entrance to the Bruges canal. If the *Thetis* managed to reach these pier heads, she was to proceed up the canal half a mile, and ram the dock gates there. If the *Thetis* ran into any obstruction she was to show a red or green light to indicate to the other two ships astern, which side of her they should pass, and they were to be sunk at the pier heads. If one ship only seemed likely to reach the pier heads, it was to make an attempt on the lock gates.
>
> At Ostend, *Brilliant* and *Sirius* were to be sunk inside the pier heads.
>
> Bury made a very fine scale model with Plasticene, of the Mole, the harbour and docks, and showing all the known defences. Aerial photographs provided much of the information for the defences. Everyone, including Keyes, took a lively interest in the model.

On the seaward side the mole rose about thirty feet above the sea at high water. On the top there was a raised pathway about ten feet wide, with a railing on the outmost side. There was a drop of about sixteen to twenty feet from the raised pathway to the mole itself. At the seaward end of the mole there were three 105mm and two 88mm guns. There were five batteries sited on the land, covering the approaches to the mole, and the entrance to the canal. There were three large sheds on the mole: No. 1, the seaplane base at the shoreward end, and Nos. 2 and 3, about two-thirds along. There were submarine shelters on the harbour side, and sheds and concrete shelters for personnel on the seaward side.

Aerial attacks and bombardment by monitors on both ports, under the cover of smoke, would be carried out for weeks before the raid to lull the enemy into believing that these were routine, so that a similar softening-up programme on the night of the raid would not warn them that something was up. Keyes flew his flag in the destroyer *Warwick*, commanding a force of 165 vessels of many types, as well as some 1,800 officers, sailors, and marines in the assault parties and other special teams.

The mole was to be assaulted by some 700 men of the specially formed composite 4th Battalion Royal Marines (RMA and RMLI), landed from the old cruiser *Vindictive*, and the Mersey ferries *Daffodil* and *Iris*.[1] In addition to the 4th Battalion RM, there was a seaman storming party of 8 officers and 200 men under Captain H. C. Halahan RN, divided into four groups of 50. There was also a demolition party of 50 seamen under

Lieutenant Dickinson RN in *Daffodil*, to which was attached 22 NCOs and 4 men of 4RM.

The duties of the seamen storming parties can be summarized thus:

1 Work the additional Stokes guns (trench mortars) in the ships, landing them on the Mole if ordered.
2 Place the gangways in *Vindictive* and scaling ladders in *Iris*, and help secure these two ships alongside the Mole.
3 Form the first flight (sic) on the Mole, attack the batteries at the end, and fight their way to the light house on the end, and there light flares to guide the blockships.
4 Finally cover the withdrawal of the large ships with the Stokes guns.

In the *Vindictive* there were four Stokes guns on the forecastle and four astern, manned by seamen and Royal Marines, and eight on the boat deck manned by seamen until they joined the storming party. After getting ashore, three sections of seamen were to form for the attack on a 4.1-inch battery near the end of the mole.

The seamen demolition party were also divided into three sections; one was to destroy the guns in the 4.1-inch battery when captured, and the others were to work under command of the CO 4th Battalion in creating damage on the Mole.

The *Vindictive* was specially adapted for the task. Boddie:

The *Vindictive* looked more like a Christmas tree than a cruiser. Special fenders were fitted to the Port side of the ship, and a huge spar protruded from the Port side of the quarterdeck to help fend off the stern when leaving. A steel hut was erected on the Port side of the fore bridge and another on the Port after end of the boat deck, and contained *Flammenwerfer* [flame thrower] apparatus under the control of Commander Brock (of Brock's Fireworks Limited). Many underwater compartments were stuffed full of drums and casks to preserve buoyancy, and dozens of grapnels were lying about on deck.

In addition to the modifications noted by Boddie, her boat deck had been planked over, and broad ramps led up from the main deck below. On the port side of the boat deck fourteen narrow brows, or gangplanks, had been fitted, designed to be lowered so that the outer end rested on the top of the mole. The stormers would run up these, and drop four feet off the end onto the raised pathway. *Vindictive*'s foretop had been strengthened and raised to enable machine guns to fire over the mole.

The *Vindictive* was to tow *Iris* and *Daffodil* across the Channel, and after casting them loose to proceed under their own power she was to secure alongside the mole about two hundred yards from the seaward end. The *Iris* was to secure alongside the mole ahead of the *Vindictive*, while the *Daffodil* pushed against *Vindictive*'s starboard side to keep her pinned hard against the mole. The *Vindictive* was to engage the guns at the seaward end of the mole with her 6-inch guns, while howitzers, pom-poms, Lewis guns, and Stokes mortars manned mainly by Royal Marine Artillerymen of the 4th Battalion RM, and sited at various places on *Vindictive*'s deck, engaged the mole itself. Stokes mortarmen and Vickers machine-gunners carried in the *Iris* were also to engage targets on the mole, until ordered to land, which they would do up ladders carried for the purpose.

The 4th Battalion RM had originally been formed to help restore law and order in Ireland, still simmering in the aftermath of the 1916 Easter Rising. It never served there, and was used to provide drafts for the RMLI battalions in France. In late 1917, on being reassigned to the Zeebrugge operation, it was reorganized and brought up to strength with volunteers. Private Calverley RMLI was serving in the old battleship *Hibernia* when

> there was a rumour that volunteers were needed to take part in a hazardous enterprise. The *Hibernia* was not a happy ship. I saw the chance of having a change and submitted my name, hoping to be withdrawn from the ship and trained for whatever lay ahead.

He eventually found himself with 200 others, forming A Company under Major Eagles RMLI, carrying out intensive training near Rochester, and was surprised to find himself promoted to lance corporal over the heads of a number of old soldiers:

> The training was different to the usual. We were firing at targets by the light of Verey lights, giving a glimmer of light for a few seconds. We advanced down the range firing at targets through smoke, and there was more than the usual amount of bayonet practice. In January 1918, we went to Deal where we joined the other companies.

During the training period, the Adjutant General Royal Marines visited the battalion, and without disclosing the objective said that any man who did not wish to go could pull out. Nobody accepted the offer, so in effect every man in the battalion was a volunteer.

The main assault force was provided by the 4th Battalion RM, and objectives included clearing the mole up to and including No. 3 Shed, and clearing and occupying the sheds, shelters, and the seaplane base. The seamen were ordered to confine their movements to the raised pathway on the outer side of the mole, and endeavour to destroy or at least enfilade the guns at the north end. The 4th Battalion RM operation order implies that the success or failure of the seamen to silence these guns would affect the 'actions' of the battalion.[2]

The assault plan was complicated and ambitious; so often the hallmark of beginners when devising an operation, especially a joint one – the more complicated it is the better it looks, whereas anyone who knows anything about such matters will tell you, 'keep it simple'. It should be borne in mind that in 1918 the Royal Navy had had little experience of amphibious raiding since the end of the Napoleonic Wars. It neither possessed the specialized equipment nor had it studied the necessary techniques. Within living memory the Royal Navy had never seriously trained in the art of raiding (or indeed any kind of amphibious operation, and apparently learned nothing from its sole amphibious experience in this war: Gallipoli). For example, no rehearsals were ever carried out to test such elementary matters as putting the vessels alongside a mole similar to that at Zeebrugge, in a swell, to see if the various contraptions would actually work. So those involved in the raid were striking out in the dark and had to make as good a fist of it as they could.

Mixing professional soldiers (marines) with seamen volunteers from the Grand Fleet hardly made for simplicity. By clinging to centuries-old naval habits, the planners disregarded the high standards of training and skills required by a raiding force, most of which would have been a closed book to the self-regarding naval officers of the period. The tactics employed by the assault parties once ashore appear to ignore what had been learned about close-quarter battle in the previous three and a half years of fighting on the Western Front and elsewhere.

Each man in the 4th RM carried around 60lb of kit, consisting of sixty rounds of ammunition, personal weapon (SMLE rifle) or a Lewis gun, and two grenades. Each wore a steel helmet, belt and ammunition pouches, bayonet, gas mask, a swimming belt under his tunic, and rubber-soled gym shoes. Some had weighted clubs or coshes for close-quarter fighting. Each platoon had a Lewis gun, a flamethrower, and two ladders and four ropes to enable them to descend from the raised pathway to the mole. In addition one platoon of B Company was to position heavy ladders for the same purpose. No grenade launchers were carried nor were there enough grenades. The seamen wore 'blue clothing with white patches 10 inches square, on back and chest'[3] – a handy aiming mark for the enemy; they were equipped similarly to the 4th RM, except that the Stokes gun party carried pistols and cutlasses.

Boddie:

On 4 April the whole ragtime Fleet sailed to the Swin. For much of the time at the Swin, a desolate waste of water, the weather was wet and stormy. My bunk was the desk in my office; the Captain lay huddled in a wash-deck locker under the bridge; while Lieut Lambert (the First Lieut), and S/Lt Belben found even less comfortable quarters.

Our supplies of fresh water and food, and in particular bread depended on the state of the weather. When this permitted we could go to the *Vindictive* for a bath, and a meal. The blockships crews were allowed 'hard lying' money from the date of arrival in the Swin, and the officers were granted a rum ration. These concessions were appreciated and made everyone contented.

In the fashion characteristic of naval officers of the period, Boddie makes no mention of where the ratings slept, ate, or bathed. He was allowed ashore to Sheerness, where his friend Nops, an officer in the *Dominion*, and his wife Cicily had taken rooms. 'They pressed me to stay to supper, but with the severe rationing which prevailed in 1918, and Cicily's indifferent cooking at this stage in her married life we fared poorly.'

Boddie also had to make a final selection for the final watch of men for his engine and boiler rooms:

The intention was to have the smallest possible crew on board each blockship when the Belgian coast was approached. The journey across the North Sea would take eight hours, and additional time would have to be added to raise steam, and standing by. So it was necessary to have two watches of Engine and Boiler room ratings on board when we sailed from the Swin, one of which would be disembarked when we reached the Belgian coast.

From the six ERAs I chose Chief ERA Gale, and he was keen to come. The other five I told to make their own choice, as I should be happy to have any two of them. They refused, saying they preferred to be detailed, as none liked the responsibility of volunteering. I chose the two youngest. The stokers I selected were all Grand Fleet men who had volunteered.

The day the force arrived in the Swin, Keyes wrote to Beatty about the forthcoming operation:

The preparation has been pretty thorough particularly that of the Marines and Grand Fleet force – also the Blockship crews. I have decided to go in one of the offshore covering destroyers as if the *Vindictive* fails to get alongside the business must still be shoved through and *will* be. Your people are simply magnificent – so is the Marine Battalion – the latter have practised on ground laid out to represent the Mole, night and day. They, the Marines, are told that it is a portion of the line [in France] the RND

[Royal Naval Division] is to attack.* Of course that has rather exploded in these last few days [with the German March offensive in France]. The Camouflage story at Chatham has gone very well – i.e. clinging to Dunkirk and Calais and blocking them at the last possible moment [in the event of the German offensive getting that far, presumably]. They [the assault force] have been trained by Army instructors in bayonet fighting, bombing etc. by night and day. One unit is exclusively demolition 1st BS' [1st Battle Squadron's seamen]. The task of the other 3 units [of seamen] is to capture the guns at the end of the mole and lighthouse, supported by the Marines. When that is done, the latter will fight their way down the mole, destroying all they can.

Keyes's letter raises the question, expressed earlier, about the wisdom of having a mixed marine/seamen force. The seamen were to cover the landing for the marines' storming party, but the marines were to cover the seaman demolition party. Keyes' orders attached to his report say: 'It must be clearly understood that the Marines are the main fighting force. No forward movement along the Mole ahead of our ships will be possible until the marines [sic] have disembarked and filled the gaps in the seamen storming party.'[4] The complicated nature of the plan has already been noted, and the orders are actually far from clear, for example the caveat about movement 'ahead of our ships' when the direction is actually astern of them.

Keyes continued:

I only hope we get light northerly weather next week – otherwise we will have to do it in moonlight, I can't afford to wait until May. The hour is 'written' and I feel sure that when it comes it will be the best possible for the operation – anyhow, I am happy and confident.

The force sailed at 4 p.m. on 11 April 1918. Boddie in the *Thetis*:

to the accompaniment of hearty cheers from the *Hindustan* and *Dominion*. *Vindictive* towing the two ferry boats, *Daffodil* and *Iris* at 10 knots led the way, closely followed by the *Thetis* leading the five blockships. Each blockship had a CMB in tow. As evening advanced a number of destroyers and MLs from the Dover and Harwich flotillas joined to escort us across the North Sea. Keyes in the destroyer *Warwick* fluttered about here and

---

* A poor substitute for a proper rehearsal. The fact that the scenario posed was a raid on the Western Front, and rehearsed on a taped-out flat piece of land at Deal, would not have exposed the troops to the realities they would have encountered had they practised the complete raid from a ship or craft. For example, in a rehearsal carried out in realistic conditions, just getting ashore in the right place may turn out to be the major problem, as transpired at Zeebrugge.

there. Sneyd had provided a special dinner of grouse and other luxuries from Fortnum & Mason for this occasion.

In Keyes's flagship, the W-class destroyer *Warwick*, Stoker Charles Minter wrote afterwards (in the historic present tense):

Night comes on and all hands are waiting for the 'action station' gongs to sound. Everything is darkened and the accompanying ships can only be discerned by the phosphorescent glow of their wash. It is an anxious time and everyone is ready, some sitting around the funnels, others around the guns and torpedo tubes. While last but not least the engine room ratings are below with steam for full speed at immediate notice, and entirely in ignorance of their position as regards enemy etc. and practically as indifferent as their work in boiler and engine room requires their undivided attention.

Boddie in the *Thetis*:

When we approached the Belgian coast minefields at about 10 pm, the surplus steaming watches of the blockships were disembarked into the MLs, and the fleet passed through the gap in the minefields, marked by two TBDs. From the gap onwards, the *Vindictive* and two ferry boats pushed on at 10 knots, the *Brilliant* and *Sirius* parted company and pushed on for Ostend, the *Thetis*, *Intrepid* and *Iphigenia* reduced speed to 7 knots in order to arrive 30 minutes after *Vindictive* reached the Mole. No sooner had these manoeuvres been carried out, than the wind veered round to a southerly direction, making our elaborate smoke arrangements ineffective, and Keyes had the courage and mortification of having to order the fleet to make a 16 point turn, and retrace our steps. Meanwhile Keyes had lost touch with the *Brilliant* and *Sirius*, but after an anxious search found them near Ostend and brought them back to the Swin.

In the *Thetis* we were faced with a long journey home, with only one steaming watch, which had already been on duty for several hours. As is usual in such circumstances, I obtained the services of a party of seamen to trim coal in the bunkers, but was surprised to find them the worse for drink. It turned out that at about the hour we had seemed definitely committed to the operation, the Coxswain, a Chief Petty Officer with an excellent war record, had with some of his seamen cronies, raided the spirit room, broached the rum cask, and issued to his friends a supply of rum sufficient for the entire ship for two days.

The Coxswain was immediately discharged, and his successor was one of those killed at Zeebrugge ten days later. The stokers felt indignant about the rum incident, mainly because they had not been invited to participate in the orgy, and partly because the seamen were unfit to assist them in the stokeholds.

As soon as we arrived in the Swin, the *Hindustan* sent over volunteer parties to replenish the coal bunkers. As a second expedition was likely the next night, Keyes decided to call it a day, and to let us have a much-needed night's rest.

The force was sailed on the night of 13/14 April, but after steaming for an hour, the weather deteriorated, and the operation was post-poned again. The next night with the right combination of tides was 22/23 April, and despite there being a full moon, Keyes decided to go ahead, although the tidal conditions meant that *Vindictive* would have to retract from the mole much earlier than originally planned, leaving a mere fifty-five minutes for the assault parties to carry out their tasks. Unknown to Keyes, during the cancelled attempt on 11 April a CMB had run aground with a copy of the operation order. Amazingly, the enemy reaction to this priceless information was lacka-daisical, and only some of the coastal defences were placed on a higher state of alert.

Despite criticism levelled above about flaws in the plan, the composi-tion of the force, and lack of raiding experience in the Royal Navy, no one should be in any doubt that everyone who took part in the raid displayed sublime courage and resource in its execution. There is no record of anyone flinching from sacrificing themselves in the effort to make the raid a success in the face of devastating point-blank shell and machine-gun fire. Now, nearly ninety years on, one can only wonder at the spirit of those men.

By 5 p.m. on 22 April 1918, most of the force was at sea. Naval Mechanic William Gough was attached to the 4th Battalion RM as a flamethrower operator, and recorded that in the *Vindictive*:

Contrary to what might be expected, there was no undue show of expectancy or excitement. This was partly due to the fact that twice before – on the 11th and 13th – an attempt had been made and abandoned owing to unfavourable weather conditions, and partly because everyone felt that, assuming the stunt came off, there was about a thousand to one chance of the *Vindictive* ever getting home again. We felt, somewhat 'windy'. This was not the case on the first occasion. Then everyone was worked up to the highest pitch of excitement and was eager to have an opportunity of fighting. On the second attempt, the general feeling was a great desire to get the job over and done with. But between these two abortive attempts there had been time to think things over and when we finally set out, we felt anything but ready for heroics.

The time dragged heavily and without incident as the *Vindictive* ploughed her way forward through the darkness until 11 pm when we fell in on the decks at 'action stations'. Our destroyer escort had disappeared and we felt very lonely indeed.

Boddie in the *Thetis*:

12.10 am. Robed myself in duffel suitings, knapsack containing First Aid outfit, iron ration, and brandy flask, Boddy [pattern] life jacket, pistol, water bottle, whistle and a shillelagh. Just as I was wondering whether it would be possible to get through the hatch leading to the engine room wearing all this paraphernalia, I saw my first star shell, followed by many others. It was a stirring sight, the dark night had been converted into daylight and the three blockships and surrounding sea seemed brilliantly illuminated.

My first reaction was a sensation of nakedness, and a feeling of certainty that we would be immediately fired on from the shore batteries. All that happened was that my teeth started chattering. I got below without difficulty, saw the armoured gratings closed behind me, got the secondary batteries started in the engine and boiler room, through which I waddled, and found everyone merry and bright. The stokers were having an easy hour at 7 knots, and building up fires for the expected full speed burst when we reached the mole. Finally I took up my station in the Starboard Engine Room.

The Captain who had promised to keep me acquainted with the progress of events, now phoned to tell me that we had been spotted by a star shell which I knew, but that we had been shielded by a smoke screen laid by the CMBs and that all was well at present. It was interesting to observe the men; they showed similar symptoms of nervousness to those I had felt, and which I hoped I had not shown. They smoked cigarettes hard, almost violently. They stoked fires far more vigourously than was necessary for 7 knots. It was very important to maintain this speed accurately as the hour's run from the gap to the end of the mole was done on dead reckoning.

As the *Vindictive* approached Zeebrugge, the destroyers and CMBs passed ahead of her to make smoke. The air attack drove the enemy gunners to their shelters, but unfortunately the wind blew the smoke away, and *Vindictive* and the other ships were silhouetted by the light of star shells slowly drifting down. Gough in the *Vindictive*:

Suddenly, all around appeared light from hundreds of searchlights and flares, and we could see our that destroyers and motor launches had been carrying out their part of the programme. All around lying close to the water was a solid bank of artificial fog illuminated from the shore by the searchlights with which the Germans were trying vainly to locate us.

Still we went on giving no sign. Then the Germans tried other means of penetrating our protective fog. One after another, star shells burst into flame so near us that for some time we thought they had actually found us, and every moment we expected a comparatively harmless star shell to be followed by others of a more deadly kind.

On the port side we could see a dark mass looming large through the fog and knew we were nearing the mole. Minutes seemed like eternity. Then came the order to load our weapons. It was a welcome relief to have something to divert ones thoughts. Excitement was at fever heat, and our nerves strained. Suddenly there was a sharp crack, and everyone must have jumped in unison. Someone loading a revolver, had accidentally discharged a shot. We were so near land, we thought the chance explosion must have been heard and given away our position.

They must have suspected something because the guns on the mole began firing, but the shells were a long way wide of the mark. Still we gave no sign. The suspense and uncanny silence of the ship were terrible. The explosions of the shells caused rifts to appear in the fog through which we could see momentarily the outline of the mole.

Just as it seemed to me that our nerves were about to give out, there came a short blast on a Boatswain's whistle; the signal we anxiously awaited.

Still 250 yards from the mole, the guns in *Vindictive*'s foretop opened fire, the signal for all guns to start firing. Gough:

With one terrific crash every gun on board spoke, and pandemonium reigned. Six inch naval guns, howitzers, pom-poms, machine guns and trench mortars added their quota to the general noise. The Germans located us quite easily and shell of every description and calibre was rained on us. The situation for the landing party was terrible, lying on the deck unable to defend ourselves.

Illuminated by searchlights from the shore, *Vindictive*'s upperworks were swept by fire, causing heavy casualties among the crews of the specially fitted howitzers and the troops packed like sardines waiting to climb the brows. Gough:

The few minutes between the first shell and when we landed were the worst of the whole business. We lay there hardly daring to move, or even help the wounded down below, because we did not know when we were due to start our part in the affair. Our casualties were fearful. Out of the platoon to which I was attached – over 40 men – not more than eight or ten got up to land when the signal was given.

During the run-in to the mole, the adjutant of the 4th RM, twenty-two-year-old Captain Chater, on going to his action station on the bridge with the commanding officer of the battalion, found the second-in-command there also. Unlike them, Chater had a wealth of battle experience fighting at Gallipoli; they not only ignored his advice that they should not all be together in the same place, but failed to take cover when incoming fire started hitting the bridge. Both were killed. Chater sought out Major Weller, commanding C Company, to tell him he was now CO, but Weller had his own tasks to perform, and Chater effectively commanded the battalion during the rest of the operation.

William Gough:

> We ran alongside, or to be correct, charged the mole with a crash that sent a shiver from stem to stern of the *Vindictive*, and for a moment we believed that we had struck a mine or had been torpedoed. We quickly discovered what had happened, and our landing gangways (or what was left of them) were run out and we started to land. Our part in the game had begun.

Captain Alfred Carpenter, commanding the *Vindictive*, had increased speed to close the mole, but this had the effect of laying her alongside 300 yards further south than planned. This meant that the landing parties were much further from the guns at the end of the mole, and *Vindictive's* guns could not be brought to bear to give them support. The batteries on the northern end of the mole were left free to flay the *Vindictive* at point-blank range from behind the cover of the concrete walls. Of the fourteen brows only two could be dropped initially, although another two were dropped later. The special grapnels designed to keep the *Vindictive* secured to the mole proved useless, and the *Daffodil*, having shoved her against the wall, as planned, had to keep her pinned there for the whole fifty-five minutes the landing parties were ashore. The 11-inch howitzer engaged the shore batteries, but of the two 7.5-inch howitzers, one was damaged and only came into action as the *Vindictive* was retracting from the Mole, and the crew of the other was killed or wounded. Some seamen from one of the ship's 6-inch guns rushed to replace them, but they too were all killed or wounded.

Gough:

> It was a nerve-trying experience – walking along narrow gangways with a handrail one side only, encumbered by heavy equipment, being shelled by guns at close range, some not more than 100 yards. Shells were actually sweeping the deck, and clearing the wall of the Mole and gangways by a few inches only.

The *Iris* was to have gone alongside the Mole ahead of the *Vindictive*, while *Daffodil* pinned her to the wall. Lance Corporal Calverley with A Company 4th RM in the *Iris* saw as they swept past that

> The *Vindictive* took the brunt of the fire from the guns on the Mole at point-blank range as she went alongside and the *Daffodil* took up her position. As we passed them to take up our position ahead of her, flames were coming out of her funnel. All hell was let loose, troops were climbing the wooden scaling ladders onto the Mole as flame-throwers shot flames across it.
>
> The wall was very high and loomed above the *Iris* so blocking us from the guns on the Mole as we approached, but machine-guns on the coast caused casualties among us. Our troubles started when we got alongside. Although the sea was calm, there was a large swell, which lifted us, scraping against the wall, and as it receded pulled us away from it. We had a large grappling iron six feet long to hook onto the wall. Lieutenant Bradford managed to get it on under fire, but while doing so was hit and fell between the wall and the ship. (He was awarded the VC posthumously). We tried to get the scaling ladders into position, but because of the swell the grappling iron could not stand the strain and came off, this proved impossible.

Another naval officer was killed scrambling up onto the mole in an effort to secure her, but still the landing ladders could not be positioned. All the while the *Iris* was under heavy fire, and one shell hit a group of fifty-six men, killing forty-nine and wounding the remainder. Commander Valentine Gibbs was mortally wounded with both legs blown off. Eventually Lieutenant Spencer RNVR took command and took the *Iris* to lay her alongside the *Vindictive*, intending to land Major Eagles's A Company across her.

Meanwhile the heavily laden *Vindictive* assault parties lurched up the steeply inclined see-sawing ladders as she rolled in the swell, and shuddered with the explosions of shells on her upperworks, and jumped down on the wall to find that the plan was unravelling. The seamen assault parties never made the position at the end of the mole, from which to enfilade the batteries, which remained in action throughout. The two platoons of C Company detailed to lead the 4th RM assault suffered so many casualties before reaching the foot of the brows that they had virtually ceased to exist as formed bodies of troops. Chater ordered Lieutenant Cooke of B Company to take over the lead. On reaching the mole, Captain Bamford, OC B Company, took Cooke's platoon and killed the enemy riflemen who from No. 2 Shed had been firing on troops as they jumped onto the pathway.

Chater also landed early and found that the pathway above the mole where the ship had berthed was higher than expected, and withdrawal back up it on completion of the operation would be impossibly slow up the ropes taken to descend it. He ordered the RSM, Thatcher, to put ladders in place and keep them there for the withdrawal. Without these few men would have succeeded in getting back.

He then slid down onto the mole using one of the hook ropes carried by the assaulting parties and joined Bamford by No. 3 Shed. Only the funnels and foretop of *Vindictive* were visible above the mole from where he stood.

Meanwhile the follow-up platoons of C Company, coming up from below deck, passed dead and wounded lying everywhere on the boat deck, before climbing the brows, which were just hanging together. Sergeant Wright's officer was killed, and he took over Number 10 Platoon. Of the platoon, which numbered forty-five all ranks, only twelve made it up the brow. Lieutenant Lamplough's Number 9 Platoon took similar casualties. Lamplough arrived at No. 3 Shed in time to see a terrific explosion under the viaduct. Submarine C1 parted her tow on the run-in and never arrived. C3 was run in to jam between two piers. Her crew lit the fuses and escaped in a small boat. The explosion cut the viaduct.

Gough's landing party was divided into three sections. The task of the first, of which he was a part, was to 'smash any resistance'. This would be followed by a demolition party, whose task was destroy by explosives 'anything that might be of use to the enemy'. Last came the 'Red Cross Party', and as each man completed his allotted task, he transferred to this party and helped evacuate the wounded. Gough, with his flamethrower, had been told to 'reach some sheds on the inner side of the Mole and attend to any opposition from their occupants by means of liquid fire.'

The flame-thrower was a heavy, unwieldy cylinder containing a mixture of fuel oil and petrol, squirted from a nozzle, and ignited by a electrically fired flare in front of the nozzle. The jet of flame extended for about 30 yards. Because of the awkwardness of this weapon, I lost much time reaching the sheds, having to negotiate several obstacles including a 15–20 foot wall, using ropes and ladders to scramble down it. As a result I lost touch with my little party of marines.

On reaching my objective, and entering the shed, I realised I was not needed there. The building had been blown up leaving four wrecked walls, shattered rifles, and two dead Germans. Pressing on, I found myself up against an iron handrail at the water's edge, and in front of me a German destroyer, with her guns firing and most of her crew on deck.

I turned my *flammenwerfer* on them, sweeping the deck with flames. I must have killed a whole lot of them. I tried to reach the bridge, from which someone was potting at me with a revolver, but the range was too great, and my flame-thrower ran out of fuel. As the bullets from a machine-gun further up the Mole got too close for comfort, I left my now useless weapon and took cover behind a low wall. From here I watched my weapon smashed to bits by machine-gun fire. I then began to work my way back towards the *Vindictive*.

Chater and Bamford, by No. 3 Shed, assessed the situation. The attack on the batteries at the north end of the mole by C Company and the seamen, the principal objective of the assault parties, had failed. They made a plan to gather the remnants of the battalion, who had gathered at No. 3 Shed, and attack along the mole, an advance of some 200 yards over ground devoid of any cover. Just as Bamford was deploying his three platoons and starting to skirmish forward, *Vindictive*'s siren sounded. The signal for emergency recall was the Morse letter 'K', but the ship was not sounding this. In any case, Chater had not been told of the fifty-five-minute time limit and was under the impression that the assault parties were to be ashore for an hour and a quarter; only forty-five minutes had elapsed. He dashed back to the *Vindictive*, and up into the conning tower to ask Carpenter what the signal was, to be told 'the recall'. He rushed back up the brow and onto the pathway, and passed the order to all he could reach by voice and whistle signal.

Gough, withdrawing to the *Vindictive*:

While crossing the open part of the Mole, I became aware that I was being fired at, and turning saw three men break from the cover of a wrecked locomotive, and run towards our scaling ladders. Two fell almost immediately, but the third kept running, firing a pistol. I returned his fire with my revolver, and he seemed to single me out. A revolver duel followed at decreasing range – we had started at 30 yards – until we were up very close and he went down shot in the throat.

Lamplough and Wright and their platoons had been clearing German sandbagged positions, and were harassing a destroyer alongside the mole, when they heard the recall. Lamplough covered the withdrawal, by which time one scaling ladder was left propped up against the wall, and one of the brows to the ship. He thought he was the last to leave, and reported to this effect to Carpenter. He learned later that his company commander and thirteen NCOs and privates had failed to make the wall, and were taken prisoner.

Wright, having started to withdraw, was told that the siren sounding was not making the retire signal, and he and his platoon returned to their posts. Soon afterwards the little band of men had the terrible sight of their only means of escape slowly move away. They too were taken prisoner.

Chater was actually the last member of the 4th RM to make it back on board the *Vindictive*. As he stood on the wall by the *Vindictive*, several men asked if he needed help getting back on board, which he refused. As the ship withdrew, expecting to be heavily shelled, clouds of smoke were released from canister aft, and under this cover the ship was not hit again. As the fire died down and the adrenalin ceased to flow, Chater found his knee hurting, and realized he had been wounded quite badly, which was the reason for the offers of help he had received.

The *Iris* never landed her assault party. Before she could be made fast alongside the *Vindictive*, the recall was sounded. Calverley:

Major Eagles shouted 'all Marines below', to leave the deck clear for the sailors to work the ship. Being a ferry boat, there was a wide staircase to the deck below, which we descended, and standing with my back to the ship's side I said to one of my section about three feet away, 'Well Cornforth, the worst is over, now it's a matter of getting home – where are the others?'. As he opened his mouth to answer, he gave a gasp and fell at my feet. At the same time something came through the ship's side near my left shoulder. I bent down to him and woke up five yards from where we had been standing.

I don't know how long I was 'out', but gradually moved my limbs, and stood up, as my hearing came back, hearing moaning and cries of pain. Someone yelled 'put that light out', we were in darkness except for the occasional glimmer of a blue bulb. Finding I could walk, I made my way to where I had been standing, stepping over the wounded, and at the bottom of the staircase a heap of dead and dying in a terrible state. On deck I found similar conditions there.

We were moving very slowly, and on looking back I couldn't see the Mole or *Vindictive*, or *Daffodil*. We did our best for the wounded, which was very little because of the darkness and the severity of wounds caused by shrapnel. We were entirely on our own, and partly disabled. There appeared to be no officers around except the Naval Lieutenant who was navigating the ship. It was decided to get the ship into as good a defensive position as possible, and out of the eight Lewis Guns we found two which were serviceable, and rigged up a machine-gun on each side of the bridge. While we were doing this we found the body of Commander Gibbs with both his legs shot away.

Dawn came slowly, and we were able to search around for bodies on the deck. We had obviously been hit by two heavy shells as we left *Vindictive*. Out of the six Marine officers, Major Eagles and numbers 1 and

2 Platoon Commanders were dead, the Second-in-Command and my platoon commander were wounded and out of action, as was number 4 platoon commander who was shell-shocked. Wounded were dying every minute in spite of the little we could do for them. I came across Gunner White [RMA] and his mortar crew, all of whom were dead.

Our next task was to sort out the dead by laying them alongside each other in lines along the deck and bring up those from below to add to them. It was now full daylight, and someone called out that there was a ship in the offing. It had seen us and was turning towards us, we manned our machine guns and riflemen lined the rails. It was a destroyer, but was it enemy or ours – we couldn't see its ensign. To our relief it was one of ours'.

It had been sent from Dover to search for us. It came alongside and put a medical party on board (eleven hours too late), and took us in tow towards Dover and the time was noon. Two and a half hours later, the destroyer cast us off, and we steamed slowly towards the quay. As we approached I saw the long, lean figure of Commander Sneyd, captain of one of the blockships, with a bloodstained bandage round his head, watching us.

In the *Vindictive*, Chater discussed the operation with Bamford as they started back for Dover, and both agreed that it had been a total failure, as they had gained none of their objectives. A great many men had been lost for no result, and both were extremely despondent. In fact not all had been total disaster, as Boddie in the blockship *Thetis* relates:

When we got near the *Vindictive*, which had then been secured to the Mole for 20 minutes, we came under heavy fire, and the telegraphs went to 'Full Speed'. I passed the order to the boiler rooms, and as the engines gathered speed with a crashing and banging noise, the general anxiety that had prevailed gave way to a thrill of excitement. The sudden increase of speed caused the boilers to prime, and the water coming over with the steam, made the engines pound louder, and the piston glands gush bubbling water. While this inferno of noise lasted it was impossible to distinguish between the noise of our own guns being fired and hits on our own vessel. Chief ERA Gale and I had an engine room apiece, each with a young ERA to assist.

After pressing on like this for about six minutes, and at an estimated speed of 16 knots, the starboard engine suddenly came to a grinding stop, with steam and hot water gushing out. A moment later the port engine did the same. My first thought was that the steam pipe had been severed by gunfire, but a glance at the pressure gauge reassured me. I telephoned the bridge, to report the debacle and suggest that we had run aground.

Meanwhile Gale and I subjected those engines to the most violent treatment they can ever have experienced, but nothing would persuade them to budge an inch. After ten minutes I felt utterly defeated, and to complicate matters we were being continually plastered by, as we learned later, a heavy battery on the sea end of the Mole, which *Vindictive*'s storming parties had been unable to destroy, or even reach.

I tried to phone the bridge to report the position, and seek instructions about getting the men below away to the boats. There was no response; perhaps the bridge had been demolished. I instructed a stoker to make his way towards the bridge along the port side of the ship, find Sneyd, if he was still alive, make my report and get instructions. The messenger did not return. Ten minutes later I sent another along the starboard side. He did not return either. I decided to abandon ship on my own authority.

First I sent all the stokers up to their shelter stations, then with the ERAs opened the seacocks, adjusted boiler feed valves, and made my way to the quarterdeck. There I found a motley crowd of seamen and stokers, but no officers. From them I gathered the ship had fouled the boom at the entrance to the channel, and got the propellers entangled in the nets under the boom. We were stuck not more than 400 yards from the lighthouse and battery at the end of the Mole. When this battery had fired on us, our own smoke had been turned on, and we were now enveloped in a dense fog, but still getting some random plastering.

At last I came upon Belben, who told me that the Captain was wounded but alive. That Lambert had been gassed by a bursting shell, was bereft of speech, but otherwise uninjured. One of our two and only boats, a cutter had been shot to pieces, and one of the funnels had come down with a crash.

A few minutes later, a seaman found me with a message from Sneyd, saying he would like the engines to go ahead if possible. Futile as I felt this request to be, I nevertheless returned to the engine room, collecting the ERAs on the way, shut off the seacocks which were flooding the place, wrestled with both engines, and to my great surprise got both to move sluggishly ahead, causing the ship to move up the channel for half a mile, where we finally ran aground.

It transpired later that Sneyd had issued his order 15 minutes before I received it, and getting no response, had left the bridge. When he noticed the ship was moving, he went back, but arrived too late to prevent the grounding. It was a remarkable piece of luck that the ship should steam half a mile up a narrow channel with no one on the bridge to steer, and finally settle in an advantageous position.

Of the original crew of 50, there were 10 killed and five wounded; the survivors packed themselves into the remaining cutter. The Captain fired the charges, and then attempted to swarm down one of the falls, but was so weak from his wounds that he dropped into the sea. In helping to drag him into the cutter, I got the impression that he would have preferred to have been left to drown.

We shoved off from the ship under a falling shower of soot and ashes blown up by the exploded charges, in drifting clouds of smoke, with much desultory firing going on everywhere and the occasional machine gun bullet hitting the cutter. We rowed down channel towards the exit from the harbour. Our ML had disappeared, but after rowing for five to ten minutes, we came across another and boarded her, to find half the crew of *Intrepid* on board and taking up most of the space in the ML. The *Intrepid*s had no wounded, and put our five in the wardroom, where we dressed and bandaged them. It was ML 526, Lieutenant Hugh Littleton RNVR we boarded.

At 1.6 am on our way to the open sea we passed *Vindictive*. She was a magnificent sight, brightly illuminated by gunfire and star shell. Ten minutes later, the *Vindictive* sheered off from the mole and set course for Dover. Just before this, our engine conked out, and for five minutes we wallowed helplessly uncomfortably close to *Vindictive* which was taking a hammering. Our engine gave intermittent trouble all night.

The officers passed their brandy flasks to the men, most of whom had lost their duffel coats, as I had done. I had found a billet in the forecastle deck among a crowd of men, when the Captain sent for me. I found him sitting on a short bench in the wardroom pantry in a distressed state of mind. He had been shot in the legs and one heel, but refused to have his trousers or sea boots removed, and had been soaked to the skin when he fell into the sea. I sat down beside him, probably in less discomfort than the other 90 souls on board. The first thing Sneyd did was to pass me a saucepan in which he had been sick, saying that Lambert was still suffering from the shell fumes he had inhaled, and that everybody on board ought to vomit. I found no difficulty in complying with this order, as I was already feeling seasick, for every time the engine broke down, the ML pitched and rolled uncomfortably, and this happened all too frequently.

Sneyd was full of remorse and regret, and took full blame on himself for the *Thetis* not reaching her destination. He said that he had underestimated the speed at which we had rounded the Mole, that in consequence we had missed the entrance to the channel, and run into the nets supported by barges to the left of the entrance. Instead of concentrating on navigation at this vital moment, he had been preoccupied training the 6-inch gun on to the lighthouse at the end of the Mole. He expressed delight at my having succeeded in getting the engines restarted, but bitterly disappointed he had left the bridge at that crucial moment. But for this chapter of accidents, I firmly believe that the *Thetis* would have navigated the mile-long channel of the harbour, and entered the Bruges canal. These events have been omitted from the official despatch, but I have no doubt Sneyd related them in his report to Keyes.

Sneyd told me finally, that had Lambert or Belben been killed he would have shot himself. They had been with him in the Cameroons earlier during the war.

Two minor incidents occurred during the trip back to Dover; off the [Zeebrugge] Mole we collided with another ML and stove in her bows, and stood by her for some minutes to see if she would sink, but all was well. Some hours later we came across a floating mine, and tried to sink or explode it by rifle fire, but the rattle disturbed our wounded and we abandoned it.

On arrival at Dover at 8 a.m., Chater met Keyes who told him that air reconnaissance that morning showed that the operation had been a complete success: the canal entrance was now blocked. Out of a strength of 730 all ranks, the 4th RM suffered 360 casualties, including 17 officers of whom 10 were killed.

Gough in *Vindictive*:

We entered Dover harbour where we had a glorious reception. It was good to be alive. Then 'leave' and 'home'. It was a great adventure. One, which having emerged safely, I would not have missed for a fortune, but which I would not care to undergo again.

Lance-Corporal Calverley, 4th RM:

On arrival we went straight to the barrack room we had occupied before the raid. They had remained just as we had left them, with our kit bags still stacked at one end of the room. We discarded our equipment and took over the beds we had formerly used. Then the reaction set in, there were 24 men in the room originally, but now there were only 11. There were no jokes or quips in the room that night, and on looking around I began to realise how fortunate I was.

Boddie:

At 10.15 am we reached Dover, famished and filthy, and went alongside the depot ship *Arrogant*, where we got baths and breakfasts and a great welcome. Apparently we were the last ship to return, and had been given up for lost. The other blockship crews had been picked up by TBDs and had got home hours earlier. The *Intrepid*s on their way out had passed the *Thetis* stuck at the entrance and being heavily plastered, and reported there could be no survivors. Most of that day was spent hunting up survivors, and learning of casualties. The blockships had got off lightly, the others badly.

I found Bury [engineer lieutenant-commander of *Vindictive*], in the bar of the Burlington Hotel on the front, making an unnecessarily rude remark to the barmaid, for which she sent him off with a flea in his ear, to my amusement, and Bury's surprise. He told me he had already had an interview that morning with Keyes and had been accepted for a second attempt to blockade Ostend ten days hence. The *Vindictive* and *Sappho* were to be fitted out as blockships for this purpose. Bury promised me that if for any reason he had to fall out, he would nominate me.

The raid on Ostend failed because a shift in the wind blew away the smokescreen, and revealed the calcium light buoys laid by the British to mark the harbour entrance. These were immediately destroyed by German shell fire. The Germans had, unbeknown to Keyes, moved the harbour entrance light buoy, and so *Brilliant* and *Sirius* were scuttled a mile to the east of the entrance.

Keyes tried again at Ostend on the night of 10/11 May, using the *Vindictive* and *Sappho* as blockships. Stoker Minter in the *Warwick*, Keyes's flagship:

> On the evening of the 9th May, we are preparing for the night's work. We are taking on board extra stretchers and medical appliances besides extra sick-berth stewards, and additional doctor, and a chaplain. 'Looks like something is doing tonight', the lads remark.
>
> We are nearing Ostend when searchlights and starshells illuminate the scene, but we still carry on, and eventually the *Vindictive* goes in under cover of artificial fog, with a welcome of gunfire from the land batteries. The *Sappho* having developed engine trouble, was ordered back into Dunkirk.

Lieutenant-Commander Bury in the *Vindictive* wrote to Boddie on 12 May 1918:

> All went well till we left the Stroombank Buoy, the Huns say they saw three cruisers, as a matter of fact they saw us emerge from the fog three times to try for the entrance, third time we got it and crashed in. We got into a proper barrage of shrapnel which tore the funnels and superstructure to ribbons. Star shells made all as plain as day and the poor old 'bus' was peppered with everything from machine-guns to healthy 15-inch!
>
> They rang down 'abandon ship', stokeholds were cleared, and we lost several on the upper deck while making for the ship's side. We left the engines running to try to slew her across the entrance, but when I saw there was no movement on the ship, I fired the after mines which blew her bottom out in the engine rooms, with a hell of a crash. The ship sat down hard in the mud fairly upright. 'Little Willie', crouched in the corner of the upper deck watching for a Motor Launch to come, a thing none of us expected in the hail of bullets and shells.
>
> In a few minutes what were left of us got into a cutter, on which the Hun promptly turned a pom-pom, and then up came a faithful ML, which

had been struck by a shell, and we all scrambled on board her. Meanwhile the noise and frightfulness was terrific. They fired 'flaming onions', things chained together. I was lying flat across the bows of the ML, helping a chap out of the 'ditch', when I got a bullet through my right thigh, it grazed the other and passed into a bluejacket's leg. It bore a hole in my pocket and I lost three half-crowns. They raked the ML with machine-guns, and followed us out with 6 inch, all short. We sang hymns in the smoke.

The ML was badly hit, sinking, and on fire aft, when we closed the *Warwick*, where we jostled on board somehow, and blew up the ML. We had not gone far, when we struck a mine and once more 'abandoned ship' for the *Velox*, who took the *Warwick* in tow and got her in all right.

By this time I was a bit 'dithery' and didn't care what o'clock it was. They cut my clothes up in ribbons, gave me chloroform and put tubes through the hole in my thigh. I have heard unofficially that I'm to be promoted, but will believe it when I see it.

Keyes planned a third attempt using the *Sappho* and the old battleship *Swiftsure*, but the Admiralty called it off saying that the Germans appeared to have stopped using Ostend because of harassment from monitor bombardments and British heavy artillery based in Belgium. Ostend was never blocked.

Keyes was correct when he told Chater that air reconnaissance had seen blockships in the Zeebrugge canal mouth. Success seemed to have been achieved. The total casualties were 170 dead, 400 wounded, and 45 missing. The country's morale soared after Zeebrugge and Ostend. The years of waiting, seemingly only reacting to German sorties, and the dreadful losses exacted by U-boats had sapped the public's faith in the Royal Navy, and the German March offensive in France had dealt a blow to their confidence in the outcome of the war. The Zeebrugge raid provided a bright ray of hope among the gloom. Now the navy felt that at last they had done something which made up for what their country-men saw as apparent lack of action compared with the sacrifice and long years of fighting endured by the army. Boddie:

The newspaper headlines that morning [24 April 1918] were a startling sight, with enormous blaring headlines, and describing in glowing terms, and in great detail, the whole Zeebrugge exploit. The fact that the Army was having such a bad time in France, the government were glad to be able to seize an opportunity to put the Navy in the limelight.

Keyes was appointed KCB, and eight richly deserved Victoria Crosses were awarded.[5] A further three VCs were awarded for the second Ostend operation.[6]

However, despite air photographic reconnaissance showing enemy destroyers and submarines in the canal approaches to Bruges, apparently unable to get to sea, the Germans managed to dredge a channel round the blockships. Within two days of the operation the smaller torpedo boats and submarines were using the canal, and by mid-May bigger destroyers passed through the Zeebrugge locks. Furthermore, because Ostend was not blocked, submarines and destroyers could still access Bruges. Although the number of submarines using the Flanders bases did not decline until five weeks after the Zeebrugge Raid, this was outweighed by the effect on British morale.

The formation of the RAF had an adverse effect on Keyes's ability to strike submarines and destroyers in the canal system around Bruges. Until 1 April 1918, the date on which the RFC and RNAS combined to form the RAF, Keyes had under command ninety aircraft in five RNAS squadrons, based in the Dunkirk area, which he tasked. Although the RAF allocated some aircraft to respond to his requests, they never produced enough to have a real effect. Thus, from the earliest days of the RAF, we see how forming a third service with its own strategic priorities resulted in reduced support to the other two services, beginning with the Royal Navy. This would affect both the army and the navy well into the Second World War.

Despite this intransigence on the part of the RAF, the Flanders-based destroyer and submarines became progressively less effective as 1918 drew on. This was because of a number of factors: the increasing efficiency of the British east coast convoys; such air attacks as the RAF did mount; the Dover barrage, which the Germans declined to attack; and the British advance into Belgium in October.

The Last Sortie of the High Seas Fleet

In early 1918, the Admiralty was concerned that Scheer might sortie to raid the Dover Strait, break out into the Channel, disrupt the line of communication with France, and cause sufficient mayhem to draw the Grand Fleet south into a submarine and mine trap. Beatty resisted pressure to station a battle squadron in the Swin (in the Thames estuary), regarding this as a diversion of effort that would actually play into Scheer's hands by offering what he had always sought, a detached portion of the Grand Fleet which he might destroy by bringing overwhelming force against it. It would also dangerously weaken the main body of the Grand Fleet.

On 12 April, the Grand Fleet base was moved to Rosyth, thereby reducing the time it would take to intervene in the southern part of the North Sea. However, Scheer decided that the Scandinavian convoy was a more attractive target than the Dover Strait. This convoy was covered by a battleship force detached from the Grand Fleet. Scheer planned that Hipper, with the battle cruisers, the light cruisers of II Scouting Group, and II Destroyer Flotilla, would attack the Scandinavian convoy and its covering force on 23 April 1918. All available units of the High Seas Fleet would position to support him if necessary, and U-boats already at sea were ordered to seek opportunities to attack shipping off the Firth of Forth and report sightings of convoys. Although the Germans were still unaware that their wireless traffic was being read by Room 40, the sortie was to be carried out in strict wireless silence. The Germans could spend only one day off the Norwegian coast because it was at the extreme limit of the radius of action of their destroyers and some light cruisers without refuelling.

The Germans sailed early on the morning of 23 April, and by early the next day were positioned with Hipper sixty miles from the Norwegian coast north of Stavanger. The High Seas Fleet's battle squadrons were about eighty miles behind him. So far Scheer's sortie was undetected. Faulty intelligence had led him to believe that convoys sailed at the beginning and middle of each week, so he had chosen a Wednesday for his attack. He was wrong. The nearest convoy was miles away. The Germans could not carry out airship reconnaissance because of high winds. Hipper pushed north to the convoy track, before turning for base.

By this time the Germans were forced to break wireless silence, which revealed their position. The battle cruiser *Moltke* had serious engine-room damage after a turbine raced and flying metal cut pipes which led to flooding, boiler shut-down, and loss of power on three of her four screws. She took on 2,000 tons of water before a diver could be sent to close the necessary valves. To begin with the exchange of messages between Hipper and the cripple were by visual signals, as he pressed on looking for convoys. As the *Moltke*'s condition deteriorated, she had to break wireless silence to say that she could make only 4 knots, and then that she was out of control. Scheer closed, and the battleship *Oldenburg* took the *Moltke* in tow, as the High Seas Fleet turned for home. By that afternoon the *Moltke* was able to run at about half speed, and the High Seas Fleet headed south at around 10 knots.

Room 40, already on a high state of alertness because of the Zeebrugge Raid, was quick to detect this interesting wireless traffic. Beatty sailed the Grand Fleet from Rosyth, thirty-one battleships (including the four of the 6th US Battle Squadron), four battle cruisers, two cruisers, twenty-four light cruisers, and eighty-five destroyers. They cleared Rosyth in dense fog at top speed in three hours, no mean feat, and an indication of the high standard of seamanship in the Royal Navy. But they were too late to intercept the High Seas Fleet. As *Moltke*, now under her own power, was about forty miles north of Heligoland, the British submarine E42 hit her with a torpedo near the port engine room. E42 was attacked with depth charges, but managed to escape. The *Moltke* took on another 1,700 tons of water, but eventually docked safely.

This was the last sortie of the High Seas Fleet in the war. But for poor intelligence, it might have caused heavy damage to the Scandinavian convoy. Why Scheer did not have another try is something of a mystery. It may have been connected with the declining morale in the fleet, although action was the best antidote to the depression caused by inactivity.

The next time the High Seas Fleet came out was to surrender.

14

Finale

The German navy had already contributed to the collapse of Germany by the time the Armistice was signed in the railway carriage near Compiègne in France that suspended hostilities on 11 November 1918. Admiral Hipper's plan for a last sortie by the High Seas Fleet on 29 October, viewed by most of his ship's companies as a 'death ride', was scuppered by the crews refusing to sail. This was soon followed by a mutiny by the crews of most capital ships. By 9 November the navy could no longer be relied upon, and on the same day the Kaiser abdicated.

As a recognition of the part played by the Royal Navy in bringing Germany to the negotiating table, the First Sea Lord, Admiral Wemyss, represented the Allied navies, with Marshal Foch representing the Allied armies. The armistice terms demanded that ten German battleships, all six battle cruisers, eight light cruisers, and fifty of the most modern destroyers would be interned at a designated Allied port.* No neutral nation would accept the German fleet, and the Allies agreed with the British proposal that the place of internment should be Scapa.

On 15 November 1918, Rear Admiral Hugo Meurer of the Imperial German Navy arrived off the Firth of Forth in the *Königsberg*.† A boat bore him to the Grand Fleet flagship the *Queen Elizabeth* in the Firth. There, in the great cabin, he reported to Admiral Sir David Beatty to have the terms of the internment handed to him. The next day he returned to sign the documents, his attempts at demurring being curtly refused.

Beatty was determined that the internment should carry with it all the hallmarks of a surrender, which it was not. On 21 December, he took his entire fleet to sea: thirty-three battleships, nine battle cruisers,

---

* In the event, the actual number of ships interned initially was as listed by Rear Admiral Bruen in his letter (p. 429). One German destroyer had struck a mine in the Bight and sank; the battleship *König* and light cruiser *Dresden* (the second of that name) were in dock. Both came to Scapa early in December.

† The second of that name. The first had been sunk in the Rufiji River in 1915.

twenty-seven cruisers, and all the Grand Fleet destroyer flotillas, together with ships from Dover, Harwich, and the Channel ports – a total of three hundred and seventy ships and ninety thousand men.

As the High Seas Fleet was being escorted by the Grand Fleet into internment, Rear Admiral E. F. Bruen, in the *Minotaur*, flagship of the 2nd Cruiser Squadron, slipped down to his cabin, and wrote a hasty letter to his wife:

> Nov 21st   2.30 pm
> Well Pansy, we have met the High Seas Fleet at last. Not all of them, but the greater part and the best ships and the latest destroyers and nearly all his U-boats. It has been misty all day and that rather impaired the spectacle as we never could see more than about half a dozen big ships and a dozen or so of destroyers at a time. They have passed on to their anchorages in the outer Firth of Forth, 9 Battleships, 5 Battle Cruisers, 7 Light Cruisers, and 49 destroyers. Then they will be anchored with the 1st BS, the 2 BCS, & 2nd L Cruiser Squadron round them. Sir C Madden is arranging the necessary inspections & examinations & taking over the ships. That will probably take till Friday & on Saturday the 1st detachment is expected to sail for Scapa with their own care and maintenance parties on board & I think our navigating parties. The remainder of the crews being sent back to Hunland.
> We are now returning to harbour & on passing the *Queen Elizabeth* will give Sir David B very hearty cheers & then ring the curtain down on an extraordinarily interesting play. Interesting that is in the larger sense, but unutterably dull & monotonous in the particular for most of the actors. A play that has lasted 4¼ years in performance & which has been rehearsed and prepared for for 2 generations, or if you like to read it so for 1,000 years. A play in which the stage is the world wide sea, and the properties [props] everything from mens' souls to the finest production of their brains, & from millions of tons of coal to the ruin? of the 50 thousand ships that lie mouldering at the bottom of the sea.
> I must be off on deck as I think we are getting near the Fleet Flagship. But before I go Pansy I want to kiss you and tell you how I love you & how much I owe you for your love, your courage, your help & cheerfulness that have been my support under the good providence of God through these 4¼ eventful years. God bless you for it.

Sea-power exerted by the Royal Navy enabled Britain and her allies to win the war. Germany was finally humbled on the Western Front, and the lion's share of the humbling was the work of Field Marshal Sir Douglas Haig's five British Armies. But for the Royal Navy those armies would not have been transported to France, reinforced, built up, and supplied. France's armies alone were incapable of defeating the

Germans, and from 1916 on the burden was increasingly shouldered by the British, imperial, and dominion armies. Although by November 1918 the effect exerted by American formations on the Western Front was still of little account, its potential for the future was of huge significance. The safe passage of American troops owed everything to the Royal Navy. Although the Americans played a full part in escorting their own troop convoys across the Atlantic, without the Grand Fleet the convoys would have been subjected to massive attacks by units of the High Seas Fleet. Germany's efforts to starve the United Kingdom into submission, even at the expense of bringing America into the war, are proof that the United Kingdom was the linchpin of the Entente Alliance; a pin that could be kept in place only by sea-power, and hence must be knocked away by an attack at sea. All of which makes nonsense of Marshal Foch's assertion to Lloyd George, that the manpower allotted to the Royal Navy would have been better employed in the armies fighting in France.[1]

As is so often the way at the end of wars, by the end of this one, the British army was, through bloody experience, in every respect more fitted to fight the war than it had been at the beginning. So it was with the Royal Navy, and as the war was drawing to a close, possibly from late 1917, or early 1918 onwards, the remark made by Captain Richmond quoted at the head of Chapter 1, 'The fact is that in 1914 the Royal Navy was almost totally unprepared for war and remained in that condition for most of the period 1914–18', no longer applied. The work of Room 40 put the Royal Navy miles ahead of Germany in the field of intelligence. The fact that the priceless information garnered there was not always put to best use was the fault of poor staffwork and command and control at high level. The eight deficiencies quoted at the end of that chapter had all been corrected. In addition, the Royal Navy's expertise in conducting warfare in two extra dimensions, under water and in the air, by submarines and naval aviation, had developed beyond the imaginings of most naval officers four and a quarter years before. The latter especially was to have great significance in the next war, when the aircraft carrier superseded the battleship as the main striking weapon of the fleet. The Royal Navy was the first to build a true carrier. That its lead in naval aviation was lost between the First and Second World Wars by political decisions, and especially by having its air arm provided by the RAF, is not part of our story.

For many naval officers and for the British public the war at sea had been frustrating. Many expectations did not materialize, the biggest being the failure of the Grand Fleet to annihilate the High Seas Fleet in a replay of Trafalgar. Public disappointment in the navy, and indeed a sense of failure within the service itself, was misplaced. The Royal Navy was the sure shield that allowed the Allies to win. The U-boats nearly overcame the shield, but convoys were introduced in the nick of time. It bears repeating that without the Royal Navy the Allies would have lost the war.

Notes

Glossary

1. Marder, Arthur J., *From the Dreadnought to Scapa Flow*: vol. V, *Victory and Aftermath. January 1918–June 1919* (Oxford University Press, 1970), p. 302.
2. The introduction of lieutenant-commander as a rank in 1914 threw the rank equivalent with the army out of balance. Originally a commander was equivalent to a major, and both wear gold oak leaves on the brims of their caps to this day.
3. Chief and petty officers did not enjoy the status of non-commissioned officers in the army (colour sergeants and sergeants). They were senior ratings, and could be disrated on the whim of the captain of a ship.

1. The Royal Navy in 1914: 'the best navy in the world'

1. Marder, Arthur J., *From the Dreadnought to Scapa Flow*: vol. I, *The Road to War 1904–1914* (Oxford University Press, 1961), p. 405.
2. Gordon, Andrew, *The Rules of the Game: Jutland and British Naval Command* (John Murray, 1996), p. 340.
3. Gordon, pp. 155–92.
4. Gordon, p. 169.
5. Spector, Ronald, *At War at Sea: Sailors and Naval Warfare in the Twentieth Century* (Allen Lane, The Penguin Press, 2001), p. 60.
6. Marder, vol. I, p. 406.
7. Churchill, Winston S., *The World Crisis 1911–1918* (Odhams Press, 1938 edition), vol. 1, p. 69.
8. King-Hall, Stephen, *My Naval Life, 1906–1927* (Faber & Faber, 1952), pp. 97–8.
9. Gordon, p. 299. In 2003, a commander's pay amounted to £60,557 per year.
10. Marder, *From the Dreadnought to Scapa Flow*: vol. II, *The War Years: to the Eve of Jutland* (Oxford University Press, 1965), p. 7.
11. Spector, p. 35.
12. Roskill, Stephen, *Earl Beatty* (Collins, 1981), pp. 21–2.

13. Roskill, p. 22.
14. Lowis, Geoffrey L., *Fabulous Admirals* (Putnam, 1957), pp. 140–41.
15. Lowis, p. 125.
16. See for example *King's Regulations and Admiralty Instructions*, 1913, vol. I, ¶1422.
17. Carew, Anthony, *The Lower Deck of the Royal Navy 1900–1939* (Manchester University Press, 1981), p. 143.
18. Carew, pp. 70–71. See also Appendix at pp. 207–14.
19. Carew, p. 40.
20. Carew, p. 23.
21. Lambert, Nicholas, *The Submarine Service 1900–1918* (Navy Records Society, 2001), pp. x–xi.
22. King, Brad, *Royal Naval Air Service 1912–1918* (Hikoki Publications, 1997), p. 10.
23. Roskill, p. 129. Not in the First World War, but the Pollen system was adopted in the 1920s for all ships built or modernized thereafter.
24. Marder, vol. I, p. 432.
25. Marder, vol. I, p. 432.
26. Marder, vol. I, p. 430.
27. Marder, vol. I, p. 435.

2. Commence hostilities against Germany

1. Strachan, Hew, *The First World War*: vol. I, *To Arms* (Oxford University Press, 2001), p. 94, quoting May, Arthur J., *The Passing of the Hapsburg Monarchy: 1914–1918* (Philadelphia, 1966), p. 52.
2. The rank of lieutenant-commander was introduced to the Royal Navy on 9 March 1914 for all lieutenants of eight years' seniority. Up to that date, lieutenants 'shipped' a half stripe when they had been in that rank for eight years, but were addressed as lieutenant.
3. *Naval Review*, vol. V, 1917, p. 134. Quoted in Goldrick, James, *The King's Ships Were at Sea: The War in the North Sea August 1914–February 1915* (Naval Institute Press, Annapolis, Maryland, USA, 1984).
4. Churchill, Winston S., *The World Crisis 1911–1918*, vol. I (Odhams Press Limited, 1938 revised edition), p. 359.
5. See King, Brad, *The Royal Naval Air Service 1912–1918* (Hikoki Publications, 1997), pp. 18–25 for an account of the RNAS in Belgium and France in the early months of the war.
6. Roskill, Stephen, *Earl Beatty* (Collins, 1981), pp. 111–12.
7. Marder, Arthur J., *From the Dreadnought to Scapa Flow*: vol. II, *The War Years: to the eve of Jutland* (Oxford University Press, 1965), p. 159.
8. Marder, vol. II, p. 170. According to Professor Marder, *Tiger* had not had time to train in gunnery and before the Dogger action had never fired at a moving target. She also had a very mixed ship's company with a large

number of recovered deserters. She was, however, fitted with director firing, and perhaps this accounts for the fact that she scored two hits: one each on *Seydlitz* and *Derfflinger*.

9. Roskill, p. 116.

3. Hunting the Raiders: Coronel, the Falklands and the Rufiji River

1. This ship should not be confused with the *Königsberg* (ii) class *Emden* completed on 16 December 1916, with eight 5.9-inch guns.
2. Churchill, Winston S., *The World Crisis 1911–1918*, vol. I (Odhams Press Limited, 1938 revised edition), p. 371. For yardarm clearing, see Jolly, Rick, *Jackspeak: Naval Slang* (FoSAMA Books 2000): 'clear your yardarm', the process of taking steps to ensure that no blame will attach if something goes wrong.
3. Churchill, vol. I, p. 365.
4. Churchill, vol. I, p. 370.
5. Ross, Stewart, *Admiral Sir Francis Bridgeman: The Life and Times of an Officer and Gentleman* (Baily's, 1998), p. 255.
6. From German Semi-Official Account entitled *Graf von Spee's Squadron*, translated by British Naval Staff Intelligence (in Phillimore papers IWM Docs 96/33/1 RFP 5).
7. Strachan, Hew, *The First World War*: vol. I, *To Arms* (Oxford University Press, 2001), p. 478.
8. So named because Alexander Selkirk, the model for Defoe's Robinson Crusoe, had been marooned there.
9. Strachan, vol. I, pp. 588–9.

4. Northern Waters: the Northern Patrol

1. Barnett, Correlli, *The Collapse of British Power*, and *The Audit of War*. In both world wars, dockers, munition workers, shipbuilders, and miners frequently went on strike.
2. See Grainger, John D. (ed.), *The Maritime Blockade of Germany in the Great War: The Northern Patrol, 1914–1918* (Navy Records Society, 2003), pp. 16–22.

5. Northern Waters, 1914–1916: submarines and Q-ships

1. Halpern, Paul G., *A Naval History of World War I* (UCL Press, 1994), p. 180.
2. Halpern, p. 199.
3. I am indebted to Rear Admiral Jeremy Larken DSO, a distinguished submariner and captain of the assault ship *Fearless* in the Falklands War of 1982, for the following information on calculating speed from an attacking submarine.

'I know of five ways of estimating target speed during visual attacks, of which four will have been used by the pioneers.

1. Estimating speed by second bow wave. COs observed that the position of the second bow wave relative to target length gave a rough speed estimate. You would need to be past an AOB [angle on the bow] of about 50°, and therefore within quite a short time of the firing position, so it was most useful as a late check.

2. Estimating speed just by the look of the ship and its bow wave & wash/ wake. Very useful to the experienced CO, and easier of course with the high-quality periscopes of my day rather than WWI.

3. Timing the target crossing the periscope cross-wire, assuming a good estimate of its length of proportion thereof. It has the mathematical advantage of being independent of AOB, but range would need to be pretty short (say less than 2,500 yds). It depends (especially in those days when all attacks were conducted on relative bearings, with the CO relating target bearing to submarine course and therefore true bearing in his head) on the submarine steering dead steady during the observation. It is clearly most accurate at close range, nearing the firing moment and involving an unwelcome amount of periscope exposure (although it could be done in two or three looks possibly). This sounds to me like the "Periscope method" referred to. Not much used in my day, if at all, but I can envisage its attractions in 1915.

4. Determining speed by a cumulative plot of ranges and bearings as submarine and target close. A crude cut can be determined by timing the target by stopwatch between two consecutive ranges, taking due allowance for the attack geometry. This just could be the 'Periscope method', but I opt for 3 above.

5. Estimating speed by rev-count – not available pre-sonar.

The principle has always been to deduce speed by a combination of indicators, with the CO finally going for a speed solution, as in your case.'

4. Lambert, Nicholas, *The Submarine Service 1900–1918* (Navy Records Society, 2001), p. 336.

5. Cromie, by now Senior Officer Baltic Submarine Flotilla and under command of the Russian Naval C-in-C, to Commodore Sydney Hall (Commodore (S)), 10 October 1917: Lambert, pp. 335–7.

6. Marder, Arthur J., *From the Dreadnought to Scapa Flow*: vol. II, *The War Years: to the eve of Jutland* (Oxford University Press, 1965), pp. 346–7.

7. The figures for U-boat losses in the war are given by Marder, vol. V, *Victory and Aftermath. January 1918–June 1919* (Oxford University Press, 1970), p. 120 as follows:

Ramming	18
Gunfire	22
Sweep	3
Depth Charge	29
Torpedo (incl German)	20
Mine (incl German)	61

8. Marder, vol. II, p. 355.
9. NMM: DFF/2–16, quoted in Peter Hore, *The Habit of Victory* (Sidgwick & Jackson, 2005), pp. 319–20.
10. Coles, Alan, *Slaughter at Sea: The Truth Behind a Naval War Crime* (Robert Hale, 1986), p. 164.
11. Coles, p. 125.

6. War against Turkey, 1914–1915

1. Peacetime manning ended on mobilization (28 July for the Royal Navy, and thus before the outbreak of war). But wartime manning on foreign stations could only be effected as soon as drafts could be sent out or the ship returned to a home port to embark extra men.
2. Thompson, Julian, *The Imperial War Museum Book of the War at Sea: The Royal Navy in the Second World War* (Sidgwick & Jackson, 1996), pp. 24–9.
3. Thomas Troubridge provides a good example of the flexible system of promotion from the lower deck in the eighteenth- and early nineteenth-century navy, compared with the rigid Victorian practice mentioned in Chapter 1. Thomas Troubridge joined the navy as a seaman in 1773, was commissioned by Sir Edward Hughes in 1781, and by 1785 had become his flag captain.
4. Marder, Arthur J., *From the Dreadnought to Scapa Flow*: vol. II, *The War Years: to the Eve of Jutland* (Oxford University Press, 1965), p. 41.
5. Denham, H. M., *Dardanelles: A Midshipman's Diary* (John Murray, 1981), p. 34.

7. Dardanelles – the landings

1. For a critique of this subject see Thompson, Julian, *The Royal Marines: From Sea Soldiers to a Special Force* (Sidgwick & Jackson, 2000), pp. 90–106.
2. See for example: Thompson, Julian, *The Imperial War Museum Book of War Behind Enemy Lines* (Sidgwick & Jackson, 1998).
3. Coates, John, *An Atlas of Australia's Wars* (Oxford University Press, Melbourne, 2001), p. 38.
4. Coates, p. 42.
5. Thompson, *The Royal Marines*, p. 100.
6. Thompson, *The Royal Marines*, p. 343. For example, at Walcheren in November 1944, as at Normandy in June, the air and sea bombardment was largely ineffective. Of the twenty-five heavy guns at Walcheren only three were put out of action. This was after air bombardment by 167 heavy bombers, and shelling by *Warspite*, *Roberts* and *Erebus* (a total of ten 15-inch, and two 14-inch guns), plus artillery support from the south bank of the Scheldt (three heavy regiments and one super-heavy regiment), and intimate support from

twenty-five gun-armed landing craft firing direct. *Warspite* fired over three hundred 15-inch shells at Battery W17, sited in open emplacements, without putting any of its guns out of action.

7. Thompson, *The Royal Marines*, p. 119.
8. King, Brad, *The Royal Naval Air Service 1912–1918* (Hikoki Publications, 1997), pp. 41–2.
9. Speech to House of Commons 4 June 1940.

8. Dardanelles – submarine operations

1. Lambert, Nicholas ed.), *The Submarine Service, 1900–1918* (Navy Records Society, 2001), pp. 300–301.
2. Lambert, p. 302.
3. Lambert, p. 307.
4. Lambert, p. 308. Nasmith means washing themselves, not their clothes.
5. Lambert, pp. 309–10.
6. Lambert, p. 313.
7. Lambert, p. 316.
8. Lambert, pp. 320–22.
9. Lambert, pp. 326.
10. Slessor, Tim, *Ministries of Deception: Cover-ups in Whitehall* (Aurum Press, 2002), pp. 174–227.

9. Jutland

1. Halpern, Paul G., *A Naval History of World War I* (UCL Press, 1994), p. 315.
2. Gordon, Andrew, *The Rules of the Game: Jutland and British Naval Command* (John Murray, 1996), p. 122.
3. Beesly, Patrick, *Room 40: British Naval Intelligence 1914–18* (Hamish Hamilton, 1982), p. 153.
4. Beesly, p. 155.
5. Although the British enjoyed a 6:5 advantage, they did not all follow Beatty's distribution of fire signal. *Queen Mary* apparently did not receive it, and *Tiger* failed to read it. *Lion* and *Princess Royal* engaged *Lützow*, in accordance with Beatty's orders; *Queen Mary* should have engaged *Derfflinger*, but engaged *Seydlitz*, while *New Zealand* and *Tiger* engaged *Moltke*, and *Indefatigable* engaged *Von der Tann*.
6. Tarrant, V. E., *Jutland: The German Perspective* (Arms and Armour Press, 1995), p. 177.
7. Gordon, p. 479.
8. Beesly, pp. 161–2.
9. Quoted in Philbin, Tobias R., *Admiral von Hipper: the Inconvenient Hero* (B. R. Grüner, Amsterdam, 1982), p. 137.

10. Unrestricted U-boat Warfare: the Royal Navy nearly loses the War

1. Halpern, Paul G., *A Naval History of World War I* (UCL Press, 1994), p. 341.
2. America declared war against the German government only, in order to remain an 'associated power' rather than an 'allied power'.
3. Marder, Arthur J., *From the Dreadnought to Scapa Flow*: vol. IV, *1917: Year of Crisis* (Oxford, 1969), p. 79.
4. The British invention, ASDIC, named after the Allied Submarine Detection Investigation Committee, did not enter service in the Royal Navy until just before the Second World War. The first experiments were carried out at Harwich on 5 June 1917, but it was still under trial throughout the 1920s. ASDIC, or sonar (sound navigation and ranging) as it is now known, is based on the principle that if a sound wave being transmitted through the water hits an object, such as a submarine, an echo is heard, and the direction from which the echo comes and the time it takes to return indicate the bearing and range of that object.
5. Marder, vol. IV, pp. 79–80.
6. Marder, vol. IV, p. 77 n18.
7. Halpern, p. 351.
8. Halpern, p. 354.
9. Dönitz, Karl, *Memoirs: Ten Years and Twenty Days*, quoted in Marder, vol. V, *Victory and Aftermath. January 1918–June 1919* (Oxford University Press, 1970), p. 89.
10. Marder, vol. V, p. 83.
11. I am indebted to Tony Wilshire, whose review in the *Naval Review* on the subject of convoys in the Second World War caught my eye. As he explains: 'The Admiralty rule-of-thumb for the required number of escorts was a minimum of 3 plus (N/10), where N was the number of ships being convoyed. A twenty-ship convoy thus needed (3+20/10), or five, escorts. It followed that three twenty-ship convoys would require fifteen escorts yet, if combined into one sixty-ship convoy, it would need only (3+60/10), or nine, escorts.' Thus saving escorts overall, and the bigger convoy would be no easier for a U-boat to find and attack, as discussed in the text above.
12. Lindemann became Lord Cherwell, and Churchill's scientific adviser in the Second World War.
13. King, Brad, *Royal Naval Air Service 1912–1918* (Hikoki Publications, 1997), p. 105.
14. See Budiansky, Stephen, *Air Power from Kitty Hawk to Gulf War II: a History of the People, Ideas and Machines that Transformed War in the Century of Flight* (Viking, 2003), pp. 99–104 for an analysis of the abysmal record of Trenchard's strategic bombing offensive of 1918. The formation of the RAF was, in Budianksy's words, 'a radical, indeed almost a mad step', made in a mood of panic caused by the pin-prick raids on Britain by German bombers and

Zeppelins, whose total effort throughout the war caused fewer casualties than one would find on a typical 'quiet day' on the Western Front. The total property damage was less than half what the First World War cost the British each day (Budiansky, pp. 97–9).

It is arguable that strategic bombing in the Second World War, with aircraft, navigation systems, and bombloads beyond the most extravagant fantasies of airmen in 1918, also fell far short of meeting the expectations so fervently promised by the 'bomber barons' of the RAF and USAAF.

15. It persists to this day (2004), the latest stratagem to emasculate the Fleet Air Arm fixed-wing force being to withdraw the Sea Harrier Mk II from service and replace it with the inadequate RAF GR Mk IX, as a stopgap, rendering the fleet vulnerable to air attack until the Joint Strike Fighter comes into service with the Fleet (if indeed it ever does).

12. Patrolling and fighting in the North Atlantic and North Sea

1. Halpern, Paul G., *A Naval History of World War I* (UCL Press, 1994), p. 346.
2. Sub-Lieutenant Edgar Evans, as he was then, had been a key member of Scott's 1911 expedition to the Antarctic. Cape Evans is named after him.
3. Lambert, Nicholas (ed.), *The Submarine Service, 1900–1918* (Navy Records Society, 2001), p. 361.
4. I am again indebted to Rear Admiral Larken DSO, for his analysis of what he calls Hallifax's 'brilliant attack'. He took great trouble to explain the terminology and drew track diagrams for me. It should be remembered that when Hallifax talks about hard a port, he is using the old pre-1931 helm orders and wants to go to starboard.

13. The Zeebrugge and Ostend Raids and the last sortie of the High Seas Fleet

1. The Royal Navy already had an *Iris*, so *Iris* was renamed *Iris II* for the operation, and appears as such in some contemporary accounts, but *Iris* is the name by which she is generally known.
2. Thompson, Julian, *The Royal Marines: From Sea Soldiers to a Special Force* (Sidgwick & Jackson, 2000), pp. 168–9.
3. The National Archives (PRO copy), ADM 137/3894 (Keyes' report to the Admiralty on the Zeebrugge and Ostend operations), p. 69.
4. Ibid., p. 70.
5. Acting Captain Carpenter RN (*Vindictive*), Lieutenant-Commander Bradford RN* (*Iris*), Lieutenant-Commander Harrison RN* (*Vindictive*), Lieutenant Sandford RN (*C3*), Lieutenant Dean RNVR (*ML 282*), Captain Bamford RMLI and Sergeant Finch RMA (4th Battalion RM), Able Seaman McKenzie* (*Vindictive*). * posthumous

6. Lieutenant Crutchley RN (*Vindictive*), Lieutenant Bourke RNVR (*ML 276*), Lieutenant Drummond RNVR (*ML 254*).

14. Finale

1. See Marder, Arthur J., *From the Dreadnought to Scapa Flow*: vol. V, *Victory and Aftermath. January 1918–June 1919* (Oxford University Press, 1970), p. 297.

Bibliography

Many works were consulted during research for this book, but the following were particularly valuable:

Beesly, Patrick, *Room 40: British Naval Intelligence 1914–18* (Hamish Hamilton, 1982).

Budiansky, Stephen, *Air Power from Kitty Hawk to Gulf War II: a History of the People, Ideas and Machines that Transformed War in the Century of Flight* (Viking, 2003).

Carew, Anthony, *The Lower Deck of the Royal Navy 1900–1939* (Manchester University Press, 1981)

Conway's All the World's Fighting Ships, 1906–1921 (Conway Maritime Press, 1985)

Goldrick, James, *The King's Ships Were at Sea: The War in the North Sea August 1914–February 1915* (Naval Institute Press, Annapolis, Maryland, 1984)

Gordon, Andrew, *The Rules of the Game: Jutland and British Naval Command* (John Murray,1996)

Grainger, John, (ed.), *The Maritime Blockade of Germany in the Great War: The Northern Patrol, 1914–1918* (Navy Records Society, 2003)

Halpern, Paul G., *A Naval History of World War I* (UCL Press, 1994)

Hawkins, Nigel, *The Starvation Blockades: Naval Blockades of WWI* (Leo Cooper, 2002)

Jane's Fighting Ships of World War I (Jane's Publishing Company, 2001 edition)

King, Brad, *Royal Naval Air Service 1912–1918* (Hikoki Publications, 1997)

Lambert, Nicholas (ed.), *The Submarine Service, 1900–1918* (Navy Records Society, 2001)

Lowis, Geoffrey L., *Fabulous Admirals* (Putnam, 1957)

Marder, Arthur J., *From the Dreadnought to Scapa Flow, The Royal Navy in the Fisher Era, 1904–1919*

— Vol. I, *The Road to War, 1904–1914* (Oxford University Press, 1961)

— Vol. II, *The War Years: to the eve of Jutland* (Oxford University Press, 1965)

— Vol. III, *Jutland and After (May 1916–December 1916)* (Oxford University Press, 1966)

— Vol. IV, *1917: Year of Crisis* (Oxford University Press, 1969)

— Vol. V, *Victory and Aftermath. January 1918–June 1919* (Oxford University Press, 1970)

Philbin, Tobias R., *Admiral von Hipper: the Inconvenient Hero* (B. R. Grüner, Amsterdam, 1982)

Roskill, Stephen, *Earl Beatty* (Collins, 1981)

Ross, Stewart, *Admiral Sir Francis Bridgeman: The Life and Times of an Officer and a Gentleman* (Baily's, 1998)

Spector, Ronald, *At War at Sea: Sailors and Naval Warfare in the Twentieth Century* (Allen Lane, The Penguin Press, 2001)

Strachan, Hew, *The First World War: Vol. I, To Arms* (Oxford University Press, 2001)

Tarrant, V. E., *Jutland: The German Perspective: A New View of the Great Battle, 31 May 1916* (Brockhampton Press, 1995)

Index of Contributors

This index serves two purposes: it lists those whose writings or recordings are here quoted, and it gives due acknowledgement to the copyright holders who have kindly allowed the publication of material held in the Museum's collections. Where the papers quoted are not contained in a collection under the contributor's name, but form part of another collection, they are listed under the relevant collection. Every effort has been made to trace copyright owners; the Museum would be grateful for any information which might help trace those whose identities or addresses are not known. The number in square brackets is the accession number for the collection.

Ranks are as they were at the time of the experiences described. Decorations are not shown.

Department of Documents

Commander the Hon P. G. E. C. **Acheson** [P160].
— Captain A. E. M. **Chatfield** (Acheson papers).
— Commander H. T. **Walwyn** (Acheson papers).*
— Commander R. A. **Wilson** (Acheson papers).
Midshipman G. C. **Adams** [P389].
Midshipman F. H. **Alderson** [90/41/1].
Signalman C. J. **Archer** [91/11/1].
Signalman E. R. **Baker** [68/6/1].
Midshipman P. N. StJ. **Baldwin** [78/47/1].
Barrie papers [67/117/1–2]
— Vice-Admiral Sir Lewis **Bayly**.
— Corporal F. **Collins** RMLI (Barrie papers).
— Commander G. **Herbert** (Barrie papers).
— Sub-Lieutenant G. C. **Steele** (Barrie papers).
Boy Telegraphist W. J. H. **Blamey** [86/53/1].
Engineer Lieutenant R. C. **Boddie** [96/47/1].
— Engineer Lieutenant-Commander W. A. **Bury** (Boddie papers).

---

* Handwritten on signal pad. A different copy is with the Phillpotts papers [86/31/1].

Lieutenant J. H. **Bowen** [76/114/2].

Midshipman (later Lieutenant) C. W. **Bower** [91/28/1A].

Sub-Lieutenant (later Lieutenant) P. W. **Bowyer-Smyth** [65/42/1].

Cadet (later Midshipman) J. E. P. **Brass** [76/116/1].

Commander H. C. R. **Brocklebank** [PP/MCR/63].

Rear Admiral E. F. **Bruen** [04/31/1].

Buckle papers [66/36/1]

— Captain of HMS *Collingwood*, after action report.

Midshipman T. A. **Burnett** [90/39/1].

Private (later Lance Corporal) G. **Calverley** RMLI [02/30/1].

Lieutenant-Commander (later Commander) Gordon **Campbell** [66/2/1–3].

Surgeon Lieutenant R. S. **Carey** [96/20/1].

Cadet F. J. **Chambers** [82/30/1].

Lieutenant D. J. **Claris** [P477].

Lieutenant V. H. **Danckwerts** [90/41/1].

Rear Admiral D. R. S. **de Chair** [P 38–41].

Cadet B. **Dean** [97/31/1].

HMS *Defence* Wireless Signal Log [Misc 1009].

Midshipman H. M. **Denham** [77/61/1].

Commander C. C. **Dix** [96/20/1].

Midshipman G. L. **Drewry** [P216].

Assistant Paymaster A. D. **Duckworth** [76/207/3 & 76/207/3a].

— Exchange of signals Vice-Admiral Sir Doveton **Sturdee** and Admiralty
   (Duckworth papers).

Lieutenant-Commander J. J. **Dusting** [92/47/1].

— Flight Commander H. A. **Busk** RNAS (Dusting papers).

Sub-Lieutenant G. M. **Eady** [86/58/2].

Cook W. G. **Evans** [84/34/1].

Midshipman D. T. C. **Field** [90/41/1].

— Engineer Lieutenant-Commander HMS *Falmouth* name unknown (Field
   papers).

— Petty Officer E. **Francis** (Field papers).

— Clerk R. C. **Lloyd Owen** (Field papers).

— Midshipman J. D. **Storey** (Field papers).

Admiral of the Fleet Lord **Fisher** [Special Miscellaneous W9].

Midshipman R. H. C. F. **Frampton** [65/27/1].

Ordinary Seaman J. S. **Gavan** [65/105/1].

Goodenough papers [65/104/1]

— Vice-Admiral Sir David **Beatty** (Goodenough papers).

Lieutenant-Commander F. H. H. **Goodhart** [92/53/1].

Naval Mechanic W. H. **Gough** [91/11/1].

Commander F. H. **Grenfell** [P 43].

Lieutenant (later Lieutenant-Commander] O. E. **Hallifax** [85/41/1].

Lieutenant J. S. **Hammill** [92/18/1].

Able Seaman W. T. C. **Hawkes** [85/25/1].

P. **Rooke** [76/235/1].
Lieutenant (later Commander) C. R. **Samson** [72/113/5].
Engineer Lieutenant-Commander J. F. **Shaw** [P 400].
Engineer Lieutenant-Commander P. J. **Shrubsole** [P400].
Able Seaman A. G. **Snelling** [P117].
Chief Yeoman of Signals H. W. G. **Spencer** [P464].
Sub-Lieutenant (later Lieutenant) H. E. **Spragge** [76/110/1].
Sub-Lieutenant (later Commander) C. P. **Talbot** [81/42/4].
Leading Torpedoman P. R. **Thorne** [82/26/1].
Commander C. F. **Walker** [65/104/1].
Lieutenant B. C. **Watson** [P192].
Signalman H. S. **Welch** [Con Shelf].
Cadet (later Midshipman) W. B. C. **Weld-Forester** [P261].
Cadet (later Midshipman) H. W. **Williams** [04/1/1].
Cadet W. H. **Wykeham-Musgrave** [P327].
Cadet R. T. **Young** [P103].

Sound Archive

Gilbert **Adshead** [660/24].
Cadet H. W. **Barry** [9932].
Franz **Becker** [4015].
Sub-Lieutenant D. **Bremner** [4/9].
William **Broadway** [9009].
Lieutenant E. **Cadbury** [4048].
James **Cox** [728/21].
Lieutenant G. **Donald** [18].
William **Ford** [719/23].
Lieutenant V. **Goddard** [303/16].
Telegraphist William **Halter** [721/21].
George **Hempenstall** [9534/8].
Flight Sub-Lieutenant Gordon **Hyams** [10409].
Chief Mechanical Engineer H. R. **Stubbington** [298].
Lieutenant F. **Verry** [311/7].
Sub-Lieutenant T. B. **Williams** [313/2].

Department of Printed Books

Midshipman A. L. **Scrimgeour** diary and letters 1914–1916 [23(=41)/3–2].

Index

Serbia 52, 54, 55, 58, 60, 172
Seymour, Ralph, Flt Cdr RN 97, 100
Shaw, J. F., Engr Lt-Cdr RN 116
Sheerness (Nore) 48, 401, 408
Shetland Islands *see* Busta Voe; Lerwick; Muckle
    Flugga
Short, Horace 43
Short seaplanes 43
    Number 10 44
    Number 260 364
Shrubsole, P. J., Engr Lt-Cdr 108–9, 110, 111,
    128, 132, 133
Shuter, J. A., Lt RN 158
Sinai 220, 222
Sinclair-McLagan, Ewen, Col. 241–2
Sippe, S. V., F/Lt RN 88–9
Skagerrak 73, 175, 291, 297, 314, 318
Skutari 278
Smith, J. E., Sub-Lt RNR 207, 209
Smith, Wilmot, Lt-Cdr RN 204
Smith, Wilbur 134
Smith's Knoll 71–2
Snelling, A. G., AB 381, 383, 384–5, 398
Sneyd, Ralph, Cdr RN 402, 410, 419, 420, 421–2
Soerakarta (Dutch steamer) 210
Somaliland 37–8
Sopwith aircraft
    Babies 338
    Camels 365–6, 367, 370
    Cuckoos 398–9
    Pups 367, 394, 397
    Schneiders 338
    Tabloids 88
Souchon, Wilhelm, R/Adm. (later V/Adm.) 213,
    214, 215, 216, 217–18, 219, 365
Spee, Graf von, Adm. 7, 84, 103, 104, 105, 106,
    107, 109–15, 117, 118, 120, 132, 134
Spencer, H. W. G., CPO 108, 109, 110, 111
spies 80
Spragge, H. E., Sub-Lt (later Lt) RN 79, 95–6,
    266–7
Stalin, Joseph 219
Stamboul (Turkish steamer) 271
Stavely, Cecil M., Capt. RN 265
Steele, G. C., Lt RN 199, 200–1, 202, 203–4
Stocks, D., Lt-Cdr RN 285
Stoddart, Archibald, R/Adm. 113–14, 131
Stopford, Sir Frederick, Lt Gen. 256, 260, 262
Storey, J. D., Mid. 301–2
Strachan, Professor Hew 132
Straits of Denmark 142
Straits of Dover 48, 55, 56, 160, 293, 372, 373,
    375, 378, 380, 399, 425, 426
Straits of Gibraltar 347, 348, 354, 359, 362–3
Straits of Magellan 106, 108, 115
Straits of Messina 213, 214, 215, 223, 224, 231
Stubbington, Henry R., CME 396–7
Sturdee, Sir Frederick Doveton, V/Adm. 76, 88,
    113, 114, 118, 120, 130, 131, 132

submarines *see* German navy, U-boats; Royal
    Navy, Submarines
submarinitis 96, 175, 299
Suez Canal 220–2, 347
Sunderland 291
Sussex (French steamer) 196
Suvla 245, 249, 256, 257–9, 260, 262, 263–4, 265,
    266, 366
Swan Hunter (ship builder) 153
Swarbacks Minn 146, 150, 160
Sweden/Swedish 163, 172
Swin 407–8, 410–11, 425

Talbot, Cecil 39, 40–1, 53–4, 56, 65–7, 70–2,
    176–81
Talbot, Dilli 179
Taube 264
Tenedos 226, 229, 234, 235, 268, 269, 365
Terriss, Ellaline 288
Terschelling Light Vessel 395
Texel 289
Thames, River 26
Thomson, G. L., RN 236
Thomson, A. J., Capt. RA 249–50
Thorne, P. R., Torpedoman 298, 302, 306
Thorp, C. F., Capt. RN 151
Thursby, Cecil, R/Adm. 237, 239
Times, The (newspaper) 323
Tirpitz, Alfred 50
Titan (Dutch trawler) 74
Titanic (liner) 192
Tondern 399
Tor 222
Torbay 41
torpedo-data computers ('fruit machines') 388
Tovey, John C., Lt-Cdr RN 311
Trenchard, H. M., Maj-Gen. 345
Triple Alliance (Austria-Hungary, Italy, Germany)
    213
Trondhjemsfjord (Norwegian steamer) 163, 164
Troubridge, Ernest, R/Adm. 112, 212, 213–17,
    218
Troubridge, Thomas, Capt. RN 218
Tryon, Sir George, V/Adm. 4
Tsingtau 103, 104
Tupper, R. G. O., V/Adm. 170
Turkey 172
    anti-naval defences 223
    British war against, 1914–1915 212–32
    Dardanelles landings 233–67
Turkish army 212, 220
Turkish navy 220, 269–70, 365, 367, 369, 370
    Heireddin Barbarossa (battleship) 254, 269,
        281–2
    Messudieh (battleship) 268–9
    Muavenet-i-Millet (destroyer) 252
    Muin-i-Zaffer (battleship) 276–7
    Torgud Reis (battleship) 269